PENGUIN CLASSICS

METAMORPHOSES

PUBLIUS OVIDIUS NASO was born in 43 BC at Sulmo (Sulmona) in central Italy. Coming from a wealthy Roman family and seemingly destined for a career in politics, he held some minor official posts before leaving public service to write, becoming the most distinguished poet of his time. His published works include *Amores*, a collection of short love poems; *Heroides*, verse-letters written by mythological heroines to their lovers; *Ars Amatoria*, a satirical handbook on love; *Remedia Amoris*, a sequel to the *Ars*; and *Metamorphoses*, his epic work on change. He was working on *Fasti*, a poem on the Roman calendar, when, in AD 8, the emperor Augustus exiled him to Tomis on the Black Sea, far from Rome and the literary life he loved. The reason for this is unclear; the pretext was the immorality of *Ars Amatoria*, but there was probably a political aspect to the affair. He continued to write, notably *Tristia* and *Epistulae ex Ponto*, and revised *Fasti*. He never returned to Rome and died, in exile, in AD 17 or 18.

DAVID RAEBURN was educated at Charterhouse and Christ Church, Oxford. He followed a career as a Classics Teacher and as the headmaster of two schools. On retiring from the headship of Whitgift School in 1991, he returned to Oxford where he taught Greek and Latin to undergraduates for the Classics faculty and later for individual colleges. He is particularly interested in the performance aspects of classical poetry and is known for his productions of Greek tragedy with school and university students, mostly in the original, but also in his own translations. Another special love is Roman poetry of the Augustan period.

DENIS FEENEY was born and received his first education in New Zealand, and went to Oxford for his D.Phil. He is now the Giger Professor of Latin at Princeton University, having held posts in Wisconsin, Bristol and Oxford. He is the author of *The Gods in Epic: Poets and Critics of the Classical Tradition* (Oxford, 1991) and *Literature and Religion at Rome: Cultures, Contexts and Beliefs* (Cambridge, 1998).

RICHARD ASHDOWNE was born in 1977 and educated at the Judd School, Tonbridge, and New College, Oxford, from where he graduated in Classics in 2000. He has since continued his studies at Oxford and gone on to do further research in the field of linguistics, where he has specialized in the history of Latin and the Romance languages. As well as being a linguist and classicist, he is also a keen musician and composer, whose published works include his *Missa S. Michaelis* (Oriana, 2002).

OVID

Metamorphoses
A New Verse Translation

Translated by DAVID RAEBURN
with an Introduction by DENIS FEENEY

PENGUIN BOOKS

PENGUIN BOOKS

Published by the Penguin Group
Penguin Books Ltd, 80 Strand, London WC2R ORL, England
Penguin Putnam Inc., 375 Hudson Street, New York, New York 10014, USA
Penguin Books Australia Ltd, 250 Camberwell Road, Camberwell, Victoria 3124, Australia
Penguin Books Canada Ltd, 10 Alcorn Avenue, Toronto, Ontario, Canada M4V 3B2
Penguin Books India (P) Ltd, 11, Community Centre, Panchsheel Park, New Delhi – 110 017, India
Penguin Books (NZ) Ltd, Cnr Rosedale and Airborne Roads, Albany, Auckland, New Zealand
Penguin Books (South Africa) (Pty) Ltd, 24 Sturdee Avenue, Rosebank 2196, South Africa

Penguin Books Ltd, Registered Offices: 80 Strand, London WC2R ORL, England

www.penguin.com

First published 2004
14

Text copyright © David Raeburn, 2004
Introduction copyright © Denis Feeney, 2004
All rights reserved

The moral right of the translator has been asserted

Set in 10.25/12.25 pt PostScript Adobe Sabon
Typeset by Rowland Phototypesetting Ltd, Bury St Edmunds, Suffolk
Printed in England by Clays Ltd, St Ives plc

ISBN-13: 978-0-140-44789-7

www.greenpenguin.co.uk

Contents

Metamorphoses

Preface

This translation would have been impossible without the help of a number of commentaries, in particular those of William S. Anderson (Books 1–10: 2 vols., 1972, 1997), A. A. R. Henderson (Book 3: 1979), A. S. Hollis (Book 8: 1970), Neil Hopkinson (Book 13: 2000), A. G. Lee (Book 1: 1953) and G. M. H. Murphy (Book 11: 1972). D. E. Hill's four-volume edition of *Metamorphoses* (Aris and Phillips: 1985–2000) is invaluable on Ovid's sources and on many points of mythological and historical background. When in difficulty, I have often consulted the formidable commentary on the whole work in German by Franz Bömer (7 vols., 1969–86). In addition, Professor Philip Hardie most kindly allowed me to read Books 14 and 15 with the aid of his own material, which will form part of the full commentary on the *Metamorphoses* eventually to be published by the Fondazione Lorenzo Valla.

I have much appreciated the interest shown in the venture by colleagues and undergraduates at New College, Oxford, where much of the work was done. My very special thanks are due to Pat Dawson-Taylor and Andrew Johnson who between them typed out my manuscripts and subsequently processed a long series of revisions. Also to Denis Feeney for writing the Introduction and checking my summaries and notes in draft; to Richard Ashdowne for his painstaking work in compiling the Glossary Index and the map; and to my editor, Peter Carson, for his steady encouragement and detailed comments on the work in progress. Finally, to my wife, Mary Faith, who carefully read my early drafts as I produced them and made notes

which resulted in countless improvements. This project owes
more than I can say to her moral and practical support; so the
translation is dedicated to her.

DAR

Chronology

(Many of the dates, especially the publication dates for Ovid's works, are approximate and controversial.)

BC

43 *20 March*: Ovid born at Sulmo.

31 *2 September*: Battle of Actium; Octavian defeats Antony and Cleopatra.

28 Propertius 1.

27 Octavian becomes Princeps and Augustus.

25 Tibullus 1.

23 Horace *Odes* 1–3.

22 Propertius 2–3.

20 Ovid publishes the first edition of the *Amores*.

19 *21 September*: Virgil dies; his virtually finished *Aeneid* is published soon after.

    Death of Tibullus; his second book is probably published posthumously.

16 Propertius 4. Propertius publishes no more, and the date of his death is unknown.

15 Ovid publishes the first collection of the *Heroides*, letters from heroines.

10 Ovid publishes the second edition of the *Amores* sometime around here. He then probably goes on to write a first version of the *Ars Amatoria*, in two books.

8 *27 November*: Horace dies.

2 By now Ovid has almost certainly written his (now lost) tragedy, *Medea*; he embarks on a process of revising his elegiac works, adding a third book to a revised *Ars Amatoria*,

publishing the *Remedia Amoris*, and adding the double epistles to the *Heroides*. After this process is complete (by ?AD 2), he is embarked on the *Fasti* and *Metamorphoses*.

AD

8 Ovid is relegated (in effect, exiled) to the Black Sea town of Tomis. His *Metamorphoses* is virtually complete and the *Fasti* half finished. He continues to work on the *Fasti* intermittently in exile, but never completes it.

9–12 Ovid composes the *Tristia* and the *Ibis*.

13 *Ex Ponto* 1–3 published.

14 9 *August*: Augustus dies. His adopted stepson, Tiberius, becomes emperor.

17 Ovid dies in exile. *Ex Ponto* 4 is published posthumously.

Introduction

Funny, devastating, flip, throat-catching – the moods of the *Metamorphoses* are as various as the hundreds of stories that form the poem's subject-matter. The title of the poem, *Metamorphoses*, is the Greek word for 'transformations', and the myths that provide the source material for Ovid's torrent of stories are all linked together by this theme of transformation, which Ovid, with an insight of characteristic genius, had at some moment realized to be the single potential unifying thread that ran through the chaotically diverse bundles of stories in the Greek and Roman traditions. A classical text with impeccable formal credentials and an encyclopaedic stock of Greek and Latin literary history, the *Metamorphoses* has nonetheless always appealed to iconoclastic readers, who have responded to its energy, verbal wit and subversive intelligence. Just as its author prophesied in the last lines of the poem, the *Metamorphoses* has been a success with a popular reading public ever since it left his study: 'The people shall read and recite my words. Throughout all ages, / If poets have vision to prophesy truth, I shall live in my fame.' The poem's fingerprints are everywhere in the European tradition, from the 'Pyramus and Thisbe' of Shakespeare's 'rude mechanicals' and the Adonis of Spenser's *Faerie Queene* to the 'Diana and Actaeon' of Titian and the *Tales from Ovid* of Ted Hughes. No one with an interest in European literature and art can afford not to know this poem.

It is a totally unexpected masterpiece. The ancient world had never produced anything like it before and would never see anything like it again. When the *Metamorphoses* appeared, its author was the most famous poet in the world, but his earlier career could not have led anyone to expect that he would one day write a monstrous epic of myth, longer than Virgil's *Aeneid*, as long as Homer's *Odyssey*. From his adolescence the poet Ovid had appeared set for a completely different kind of fame.

Early Career

Publius Ovidius Naso was born on 20 March 43 BC, in the mountain town of Sulmo, some 90 miles east of Rome. Ovid is therefore one of the very first generation of Romans to be born on a date we can accurately plot, since only just over two years previously Julius Caesar had abolished the ramshackle lunar priestly calendar of the Roman Republic and replaced it (on 1 January 45 BC) with his new solar calendar, the product of the finest Greek science and, in effect, the calendar we still use. This new Julian calendar was to be the unlikely subject of one of Ovid's poems, the *Fasti*.[1] Ovid's birthplace, the modern town of Sulmona, still proudly claims the poet as its most famous son, adorning municipal insignia with his words *Sulmo mihi patria est* ('Sulmo is my homeland', *Tristia* 4.10.3). The local people, the Paeligni, had been at the centre of the fierce revolt of the Italian allies against Rome between 91 and 89 BC, and the capital of the rebels, 'Italica', had been located in Corfinium, just ten miles up the road from Sulmo. By Ovid's time that sense of anti-Roman local identity was only a memory (*Amores* 3.15.8–10), and Ovid grew to adolescence in a linguistic and educational environment that was thoroughly Roman.

His talent and his family's ambition took him to further education in the metropolis itself, where his precocious brilliance in the schools of rhetoric was still being talked about years after his death. He appeared to be on track for a career in the imperial service or the courts and senate, but he found – as he put it in an autobiographical poem towards the end of his life – that everything he tried to say kept coming out as verse (*Tristia* 4.10.25–6). After putting his foot on the lowest rung of the ladder of a political career and serving as a member of a lowly bureaucratic board called the 'Committee of Three', he abandoned public life, against the protests of his father, and devoted himself completely to poetry. He claims that he was known for his recitations of poetry when he was still a teenager. In any event, by the time he was thirty he was famous all over the Empire for his *Amores* ('Loves'), poems in elegiac metre that still crackle with intelligence, ambition and panache. Virgil and Tibullus had died in 19 BC, when Ovid was not yet twenty-five; after that, Horace and Propertius were his only possible rivals for fame, and following their deaths, in Ovid's mid-thirties, he stood alone as the undisputed leading poet of Rome.

Inventive energy and driving self-reliance marked his writing from the start. Poetry about passionate love and the conflicts forced upon a well-born Roman by a life of love had been at the heart of Roman literature since Catullus, who died some ten years before Ovid was born. Following Catullus, a string of diverse and talented elegiac poets had in sequence collaborated on this tradition so as to produce a novel genre, known nowadays as Latin love elegy. The greatest of these poets, Propertius, was still actively writing when Ovid audaciously took it upon himself to make this well-acknowledged field uniquely his own, by cutting back on the expanding options of the genre and concentrating on its most essential elements. His major triumph was to make the tradition look as if it had always been destined to find its fulfilment in its Ovidian form. Although we now call this tradition 'Latin love elegy', it is virtually certain that we would be calling it something else, or not even regarding it as a tradition in the first place, if Ovid had never written. Each new phase of his career was to demonstrate the same phenomenal ability to put his own distinctive mark of ownership on a long-standing inheritance.

Ovid's poetic career carried him on to explore the theme of love in a variety of genres and contexts. He followed the *Amores* with another elegiac collection, the *Epistulae Heroidum* ('Letters from Heroines'). In these letters glamorous figures such as Helen, Penelope or Dido, often from the lofty genres of epic and tragedy, write to treacherous or inaccessible lovers and husbands. Here he shows the zestful relish for dissonance that marks so much of his work, not least the *Metamorphoses*. Characters and scenarios that the audience knows well from other contexts are transmuted into a different genre and metre, with discordant effects that transform the way we think about both the old and the new contexts. He next took on the pose of the scientist of love, writing a series of didactic works that purport to do for sex what Lucretius had done for atomism and what Virgil had done for agriculture: *Ars Amatoria* ('Art of Love' / 'Handbook of Sex Technique'); *Remedia Amoris* ('Cures for Love' / 'How to Fall out of Love Now I've Taught You How to Fall In'); *Medicamina Faciei Femineae* ('Compounds for the Lady's Face'). These stunningly inventive and accomplished works show Ovid at the top of his comic form, and they open up a profoundly interesting theme, as they reveal how sex and love, the most apparently natural of all human processes, are experienced through societal conventions that are so deep we cannot recognize them as conventions.

Ovid and Augustus

In his early to mid forties, somewhere around 2 BC, Ovid appears to have drawn a formal line under his career as a love poet in the elegiac mode. It is at this stage of his career that we should probably place his only major work that does not survive, the tragedy *Medea*. It is at this stage, also, presumably after the *Medea*, that he began the simultaneous composition of two works far different in scale and style from anything he had written before, the *Fasti* ('Calendar') and the *Metamorphoses* ('Transformations'). The *Fasti* was still to be in elegiac metre, conventionally a metre used for comparatively short works, but it was planned to be in twelve books, one for each month of the Roman year. The *Metamorphoses* was to be even longer, fifteen books, three longer than the total of Virgil's *Aeneid*; and it was not going to be in the elegiac metre of Catullus or Propertius, but in Virgil's own metre, the dactylic hexameter of Homeric epic, with a mighty scope to match – the whole of human experience from the beginning of the world down to Ovid's own day.

The thematic range of these two poems was also very different from anything in his earlier work. In particular, Ovid displays a keen interest in the nature of his contemporary society's rituals and power-structures, for he had been observing the new political order for the whole of his adult life. Unlike the poets of the generation before him, who had been personally affected by the chaos attending the disintegration of the Senatorial government of the Republic, Ovid had grown up in a political environment of comparative stability and calm. It is certainly true that his boyhood was lived against a background of civil strife and the growing threat of a new round of civil war between Mark Antony and Caesar Octavian, the adopted son of Julius Caesar, but he was still only twelve when Caesar Octavian won his definitive victory over Antony and Cleopatra at Actium on 2 September 31 BC. We should, likewise, bear in mind that it is a mistake to regard the years of Ovid's maturity as ones of an unruffled *status quo* in which everyone happily foresaw decades of relaxed peace to come. Octavian, who took the name Augustus and the informal title of 'Princeps', 'First Citizen', in 27 BC, never stopped experimenting as he consolidated his control over the Roman world, and people well knew that any chance event could mean a return to chaos: Augustus almost died of illness, for example, in 23 BC, at the age of only thirty-nine, and anxiety over the succession marked the new political dispensation, the Principate, from its earliest days. Still, in comparison with Virgil, who saw his family's estate confiscated to pay off veterans, or with Horace, who fought against Caesar Octavian at Philippi and had to rebuild his life from scratch, or with Propertius, who lost relatives in the fighting in central Italy, Ovid did not experience personal disaster in civil war as part of his adult life, and lived under conditions of civil tranquility that the Roman world had not known for a century.

We do not find in his poetry, then, the pendulum swings of intense anxiety and equally intense relief that may be found in Virgil, Horace or Propertius. The insouciance that so many readers detect in Ovid has something to do with the way in which he had the luxury of being able to take a lot for granted. What we do find in Ovid, however, is a highly intelligent contemporary's prolonged observation of the Principate as a gradually evolving institution, together with all the consequences of that evolution for Roman politics, religion and society in general. These themes are of particular importance for the *Fasti*, which treats the Roman year as the backbone of a study of Roman religious and political institutions, but Ovid's interest in the power-structures of his society comes through very clearly in the *Metamorphoses* as well, especially in the last book, where we see the sweep of Roman and world history apparently culminating in the deification of Julius Caesar and the reign of his adopted son, Augustus. The problem of succession is a major theme of the last book, reflecting the obsessive interest contemporaries were compelled to take in the possible future destinies that awaited them after Augustus' inevitable departure. The last two books also show an astute comparison between the revived monarchy of Augustus and the first monarchy of Romulus, together with an intelligent appraisal of how the new monarchy diverges from the corporate and anti-individualistic ideals of the Roman Republic. When readers get to Book 15, they may contrast for themselves the attitude to personal power of Augustus and the Republican hero Cipus, or the self-aggrandizing religious policies of the Augustan monarchy as opposed to the religious solidarity displayed by the Senate and People of the Republic when they import the god Aesculapius from Greece to save the whole state from plague.

After some six or seven years' work, it seems that the *Fasti* was half-finished, at six books, and the *Metamorphoses* virtually finished, when in AD 8 catastrophe struck the poet. We will never know the details, but he was somehow involved in a scandal that touched the imperial family, although it is clear that he committed no actual crime. An outraged Augustus banished him into an informal state of exile, throwing into the charge for good measure the *Ars Amatoria*, which even some years after publication apparently still rankled the ageing and increasingly authoritarian Princeps. Augustus had poured a good deal of his prestige and credibility into legislation re-forming the supposedly degenerate morals of his people; many modern readers see Ovid's response in the *Ars Amatoria* as a flippant puncturing of a hypocritical charade, and it looks as if Augustus read it more or less the same way. Ovid's place of banishment was practically as far from Rome as could be found on the map – Tomis, modern Costanza on the Black Sea, on the very fringe of the Empire. Here Ovid lived for another nine or ten years, cut off from everything that had meant anything to him: his wife and daughter, his circle of friends, the whole metropolitan cultural experience. His courage and self-belief did not fail him, for he continued to write, trying to win pardon and justifying himself through the medium of his 'exile poetry', *Tristia* ('Sorrows') and *Epistulae Ex Ponto* ('Correspondence from the Black Sea'). The death of Augustus in AD 14 led only to the accession of his grim stepson, Tiberius, who also turned his face against the poet, and Ovid died some three years later, in his late fifties.

Structure and Scope

In one of his finest poems from exile, *Tristia* 1.7, Ovid says that the *Metamorphoses* was not quite finished when he was banished, and that he tried to burn it, so that existing copies of the poem were still rough and unpolished. There is no doubt, however, that his masterpiece is indeed complete. His claim in *Tristia* 1.7 is intended to establish a parallel between himself and Virgil, for when Virgil had died almost thirty years earlier his *Aeneid* had been genuinely unfinished, and there was a persistent story that the dying poet had ordered the poem to be burnt, only for his wishes to be overruled by Augustus. Ovid's tactic simultaneously establishes his similarities to Virgil as a classic of Latin literature, and reproaches Augustus for under-valuing him so drastically by contrast: the same Augustus who was now wantonly destroying Ovid had personally intervened to save the *Aeneid* and have it properly edited and preserved for posterity.

There is, as usual, a good deal of irony in this claim, not least because it was central to Ovid's self-definition that he could never occupy the same ideological niche as Virgil. Still, Ovid knew what he was doing when he made this oblique claim to be ranked with Virgil, who had been acknowledged for decades as the greatest Roman poet who had ever lived. It is only comparatively recently that professional scholars have taken seriously the idea that the *Metamorphoses* is, in its own way, as great a poem as the *Aeneid* – although, as we shall see below, other poets and artists have always known this to be the case. The kaleidoscopic variety of the poem, its baffling shifts in register and mood, its manifold layers of irony and self-consciousness, its capacity to move readers deeply despite appearing to be all surface, its intensely intelligent and teasingly elusive wit – these are some of the factors that have made the poem central to the European tradition ever since it first appeared, and they are also the factors that have made the poem difficult for scholars to work on with the critical techniques they have used for more 'classical' works of literature.

The sheer scale and diversity of the poem make it hard to grapple with. The *Metamorphoses* spans the whole of time 'from the world's beginning / down to my own lifetime', as Ovid puts it in the Prologue to Book 1. Typically, he even includes more than this apparently total coverage, since he begins before time, before earth and sea and heaven (the first word of the narrative after the Prologue is 'Before'); and at the end he continues the momentum of his poem into the future, predicting his own immortal progress in reception ('I shall live in my fame'). Practically every major story of Greco-Roman myth, and many a previously minor one, finds a place in the poem: the household names of Hercules and Achilles and Romulus are there, together with creatures such as Salmacis, Clytië and Leucothoë, who would have been unfamiliar to all but the most learned members of his audience.

The scope of the poem is universal and comprehensive, and Ovid toys with his readers' expectation that such a massive narrative should have cohesion and structure, in the same way as 'proper' epics like the *Iliad* and *Aeneid*. The poem certainly does have patterns of order and arrangement, and one of the many pleasures of reading it lies in following the inexhaustible cunning Ovid displays in knitting together his diverse stories and in juggling his basic compositional unit, the book. The singing competition in Book 5, of which Minerva hears an account, is immediately followed by the weaving competition in Book 6, where Minerva is a contestant against Arachne; the stories of human presumption that Minerva depicts on her tapestry are followed next by the tragic story of Niobe's appalling punishment for her presumption against the goddess Latona; Niobe's story is in turn followed by a comically down-market story of another punishment inflicted on presumptuous people by this same goddess, Latona; the next story is the grotesquerie of the flaying of Marsyas, which is motivated by mention of, again, Minerva and of Apollo, the son of, again, Latona . . . and so on. The haphazard chain of association is entertaining, but it also reinforces the Ovidian theme of the very contingency of connectedness.

Still, any overarching scheme that attempts to impose too rigid an order invariably fails. There is, for example, a broad division into three parts of five books each, corresponding to the epochs of the gods, the heroes and of history. The epoch of the heroes begins with the introduction of the city of Athens in Book 6, and the epoch of history begins with the introduction of the city of Troy in Book 11. But these divisions are blurred by the poet, for the introduction of Athens should come at the beginning of Book 6, not 400 lines into the book, if the main lines of division are to be tidy, and when we get to Troy in Book 11, expecting to hear of its fall, we find that the city has already fallen – not once but twice – to mythical heroes.

Ovid's toying with such structural lines of division is symptomatic of his attitude to all kinds of divisions and categories. He mistrusts and dislikes anything that resembles a straitjacket, but he does not simply deny the importance of perceiving limits and divisions between different categories. If distinctions were meaningless there would be nothing but chaos, and Ovid is very careful in the first lines of his narrative in Book 1 to show how the world has moved away from its original state of Chaos precisely by a process of acquiring distinctions. Ovid's Chaos is not, as one might think, a tussle or jumble, but a great blandness without distinction and differentiation: 'the whole of nature displayed but a single / face' (1.6–7). And in this state of undifferentiation 'None of the elements kept its shape' (18), so that Ovid's poem could never have begun. What was needed was distinction, and this is what divine nature provided: god 'severed', 'parted', 'separated', 'disentangled', 'gave ... separate places', 'divided the substance / of Chaos and ordered it ... in its different constituent members' (22–33). The final order of nature is one where it has 'its separate compartments' (69). Of course these compartments are not rigidly separate, since all through the poem we see individuals crossing between them as they change form, but without these compartments having identity and separateness in the first place, the changes of form would be impossible.

Transformation is the title of the poem and the single linking thread that unites the hugely various stories. As we repeatedly see, however, transformation is not just part of the way the stories work, and not just a human and philosophical theme of inexhaustible richness, but a dynamic that permeates every level and facet of the poem. In fact, Ovid's very first example of a transformation involves a part of the poem that is not strictly a part of the poem – the title. *Metamorphoses* (for Ovid, something more like *Metamorfoseis*) is a Greek word, like *Aeneid*, Virgil's title. In anticipation of the way in which the Greek inheritance will be Romanized in the course of the poem, this Greek word for transformation is transformed into Latin in Ovid's first line: *meta-morfoseis*, 'trans-formations', becomes *mutatas formas*, literally, 'changed forms'. At first one only notices that the sound of the Latin words for 'changed forms' is very like the sound of the Greek word, so as to reinforce the idea of similarity in translation; but then one realizes that in fact the Latin word for 'form', *forma*, has the same letters as the Greek word for 'form', except with the 'm' and 'f' transposed – *morfe*.[2] It is a disconcerting moment, as we see the very word for 'form' undergoing a metamorphosis as it moves across the linguistic divide, while still retaining all of its essential individual elements.

Ovid immediately shows us how important the question of form and identity is for him when he opens the poem with a brilliant play on the question of what kind of formal identity the very poem itself will have. For a poet in a literary tradition as formalized and self-conscious as the Greek and Roman one, it is perhaps not surprising that one of the most important categories to put under pressure will be the formal and generic, but in the opening of the *Metamorphoses* Ovid manages to turn his whole previous poetic career into the set-up for a dazzling punchline about the generic category of his poem.

As we have seen, with the exception of his tragedy, *Medea*, everything Ovid had written before the *Metamorphoses* had been in the same metre, the elegiac couplet. This metre was composed of a line of six feet, a dactylic hexameter, the same line used for continuous narration by Homer and Virgil, followed by a slightly shorter line, really of two and a half feet times two, but conventionally called a pentameter ('five-footer').[3] This was a very versatile metre, used for all sorts of purposes by Greek authors, but by Ovid's time it had come to be strongly marked in the Roman tradition as a metre for poetry from the 'lighter' or 'lower' genres, such as love poetry, and it had therefore increasingly been identified by opposition to the 'grander' and 'higher' genre of epic poetry, composed in the parent metre of Homeric dactylic hexameters. The Roman poets in the elegiac tradition had constructed a genealogy for their unpompous and deft style in which the third-century BC Greek Hellenistic poet Callimachus was the founding father. They alluded repeatedly to Callimachus' polemical introduction to his elegiac collection of origin stories, *Aetia*. Here Callimachus defends his small-scale and highly wrought art against the long-winded and traditional stuff favoured by his competitors, claiming that he has been taught by Apollo that his 'slight' and 'fine' poetry is superior to their preferred long, single, continuous poems about kings and heroes. Callimachus' Prologue made a profound impact on the Roman poets of the generation before Ovid. Virgil, for example, in his first collection of poetry, the *Eclogues*, represents himself as wanting originally to write epic but receiving Callimachean advice from Callimachus' god, Apollo (*Eclogue* 6.3–5): what the modern poet should write is not epic but a *deductum carmen*, a poem that has been drawn out the way a thread is drawn out in spinning, so that it becomes a fine strand out of the original glob of raw wool.

Now, in the second line of the *Metamorphoses*, at the very

point where his audience might have expected to hear the metrical marker in the pentameter of Ovid's characteristic elegiac couplet, Ovid transforms the line into the hexameter of grand epic as he invokes the gods and tells them 'it is *you* who have even / transformed my art' – that is, from elegiac to hexameter. It must have been even more of a shock for his first readers to carry on and find Ovid in the next lines describing the new poem as a *perpetuum carmen*, a 'continuous poem', for this phrase is a translation of the sardonic Greek phrase which Callimachus had used to describe his despised adversaries' preferred kind of poem. Yet Ovid introduces an extra twist, for the verb he uses to describe what he wants the gods to do to this 'continuous poem' is *deducite*, 'spin . . . a thread', the same verb that Virgil's Apollo had used to describe the 'spinning out' process characteristic of the best modern poetry. The new poem will be an oxymoronic compound, both Callimachean in its finely spun aesthetics and continuous as well, epic in its sweep and ambition.

Literary Heritage

The poem, then, makes itself generically uncategorizable. Again, this is not to say that distinctions of genre are unimportant in the poem. Because the *Metamorphoses* is always refusing to be one thing, it is not the case that the differences between the various individual things it is refusing to be do not matter. Throughout the poem Ovid continues to exploit the imaginative and moral possibilities of hybridism. The weaving competition between Arachne and Minerva in Book 6 is, in part, an example of a competition between two inherently opposed views of the world, as expressed in two different generic modes. Minerva's tapestry shows majestic and dignified gods in an ordered pattern, punishing presumption and acting in comprehensible ways. Arachne's tapestry shows a wilfully unepic view of the world and its divine governing forces, with a pell-mell series of images of randomly topsy-turvy mutation and seduction. Some readers think it is Arachne's vision that is more true to the poem's overall vision of human experience, and some think it is Minerva's, but in Ovid's universe each view of the world needs the other as its double, and inevitably exaggerates by polarization.

As in the case of Arachne and Minerva, epic is the genre that Ovid usually entertains as his foil. It is remarkable just how much of Homer, Apollonius and Virgil the *Metamorphoses* manages to encompass somehow or other. Great tracts of those epic plots and their accompanying characteristics find their way into the poem. The gods of the epic tradition, for example, are mercilessly exposed. Juno's hellish vindictiveness is re-enacted again and again, and Ovid gives us a series of hilarious set-pieces on Jupiter's bluff and pompous smugness, a smugness that masks an unfathomable capacity for violence. Ovid's treatments of such epic set-pieces as the battle, catalogue or hunt can provide some of his finest moments of comedy and of literary criticism. Once you have read his burlesque version of epic battle narrative in Book 12, for example, with the battle of the Lapiths and centaurs, it is very hard to read Homer or Virgil in quite the same way again, for he has made you actually think about what is involved in the elaborate versification of disgusting brutality and agony, instead of just taking it for granted, as so many readers of Homer and Virgil do. In both of these examples, as is usually the case, Ovid is not inventing an issue but responding to something already there in his models. Homer and Virgil are, in their own way, just as aware as Ovid is of the problem of aestheticized violence or divine unaccountability, but Ovid knows that the inertia of the tradition keeps desensitizing us to the issues.

As we have already seen, epic for Ovid is not just a narrative genre, but a way of viewing the world. The whole epic idea that human actions and history make sense and are part of a meaningful pattern is ultimately called into question by Ovid's poem. The enormous speech of Pythagoras at the beginning of the final book is notoriously hard to assess, but it certainly presents a compelling view of a world of flux in which even the Roman empire is merely one passing feature of the world like any other. In the end, this vision of mutability is inconsistent with the sense of durability and direction that Augustus was trying to impose on the Roman empire, a sense that was, for Ovid, represented emblematically by the quintessential Augustan epic, Virgil's *Aeneid*. This Ovidian perspective has been memorably expressed by E. J. Kenney: 'For him the Augustan settlement was not, as it had been for Virgil, the start of a new world, *nouus saeclorum ordo*, but another sandbank in the shifting stream of eternity.'[4]

In addition to epic, virtually every significant ancient genre is somehow made part of the poem. We can detect what looks suspiciously like the later novel lurking beneath the stories of the exotic East at the beginning of Book 4: among these, the story of Pyramus and Thisbe was to have the most potent afterlife. Tragedy's agonized soliloquies and moral dilemmas figure prominently, as in the story of the competing claims upon Althaea, mother of Meleäger, in Book 8. Individual tragedies with their plots can regularly be discerned behind the lines of the *Metamorphoses*. Sophocles' now lost *Tereus* is the template for the excruciating tragedy of Procne and Philomela in Book 6, and his still extant *Trachiniae* provides the backbone for the narrative of the river-god Acheloüs in Book 9. By far the most popular Greek tragedian in Ovid's day was Euripides, and Euripides recurs constantly in the poem: we glimpse his *Bacchae* in the Theban stories of Books 3 and 4, his *Trojan Women* and *Hecuba* in the fall of Troy of Book 13, and his *Hippolytus* revived in an Italian landscape in Book 15 – although only Ovid could have thought of rewriting the messenger-speech of Euripides' *Hippolytus* in the first person, so that instead of a messenger telling of the hero's grisly death, the hero gets a chance to tell us all the horrific details himself. The fashionable genre of pastoral poetry receives devastating attention in Book 1, when Mercury lulls the monster Argus to sleep by singing him an origin story of pastoral. Mercury is only halfway through the story of Pan and Syrinx when Argus nods off; although Mercury proceeds immediately to chop off his head, Ovid with mock earnestness fills out the rest of the story for his readers so that we do not miss it. Ovid is not the only person to feel bored to death by the affectations of pastoral, but as we see his character Argus undergoing the fate of being actually bored to death we see that no one has expressed this disgust more memorably.

A vital part of Ovid's poetic education was the 'new poetry' of Catullus and his generation, and the *Metamorphoses* shows a fascination with their favoured form of the epyllion, or mini-epic. Taking as their model Callimachus' *Hecale*, in which the great hero Theseus is shown not engaged in derring-do but eating scraps for dinner with an old peasant woman, Catullus and his friends produced hexameter poems of a few hundred lines that looked at the heroic age from unexpected and freakish angles. These poems homed in on bizarre amatory passions, cultivated a precious style, and revelled in the elaborate description of artistic objects from other media (the so-called 'ecphrasis'); they also explored narrative eccentricities as they looped back on themselves, confused time-frames, covered their narrative tracks and generally did their best to make it hard to keep a grip on what was the 'real' story and what was the digression. All of these features find their way into Ovid's poem. The descriptive ecphrasis appeals to Ovid's highly developed visual sense, and the palace of the Sun in Book 2 or the tapestries of Minerva and Arachne in Book 6 are masterpieces of the genre. Ovid's interest in narrative technique is alive on every page, and his approach has its roots in the mazes of the epyllion. Orpheus takes over the song, for example, in Book 10, and gives us a series of bizarre love stories, so absorbing that it is easy to forget that he and not Ovid is the narrator. At the end of Book 10 we see a set of 'Russian dolls', as Ovid shows us Orpheus telling his audience of trees and beasts about how Venus tells Adonis the story of Atalanta and Hippomenes.

The schools of rhetoric in which Ovid first cut his teeth and made his name have left their mark everywhere in his poetry. His heroes and, especially, his heroines will regularly launch into lengthy internal dialectic, arguing the rights and wrongs of potential courses of action, just as the students of rhetoric did in their set-piece training exercises known as 'declamations'.

Where the student would argue whether a rapist should be executed or made to marry his victim, or whether Agamemnon should sacrifice his daughter, Ovid's characters will debate whether to sacrifice their father for a potential lover (Scylla in Book 8), or whether to have sex with their brother or father (Byblis in Book 9, Myrrha in Book 10). People have often criticized Ovid's declamations for their unreality and artificiality, but they forget that every ancient author who talks about declamation also criticizes it for its unreality and artificiality. Ovid is ahead of his critics, in other words. He is not simply reproducing declamatory style because that is what people expected and what he was good at, he is making the adequacy of the form part of his subject. And he is capitalizing on the hysterical and manic view of the world that the hothouse environment of the declamation schools had refined over the years. If you glance at the index of the standard modern edition of the Elder Seneca's declamations, from the early first century AD, you get a hair-raising vision of a universe of vice, paranoia and excess: under 'A' we find 'abortion', 'accomplices', 'accusation, motives for', 'actors', 'adoption', 'adultery' (many entries here), 'adversity, triumphs over' . . .; under 'B', 'banquets', 'barrenness', 'bastards', 'beggars' . . . 'blindness', 'boats, disabled', 'brothels, see prostitutes', 'buildings', 'burial', 'burning of books'.[5] This is a universe that readers of the *Metamorphoses* will instantly recognize.

Ovid had read voraciously since childhood and had thought hard about the whole Greek and Roman literary tradition. In a sense, the entirety of ancient literature and myth is the background for his poem, although the particular poetic sources for the theme of transformation itself are some distinctly out-of-the-way pieces of Hellenistic learning, the *Heteroeumena* ('Metamorphoses') of Nicander, and the *Ornithogonia* ('Generation of Birds') of Boios (or Boio). In this medley of styles, there is no one genre that dominates, but the most consistent pose is that of the knowing, learned and ironic Hellenistic master, best embodied in the figure of Callimachus. Like Callimachus, Ovid knows and loves the traditions of his literary past, but refuses to be intimidated or enslaved by them. Everything is

to be invigorated by unexpected perspectives, everything is to
be made new.

Themes

We have already noted that the theme of transformation allows
Ovid to bring together into one frame any myth he wants to
include. In addition to whatever else it might be, the *Meta-
morphoses* is an encyclopaedia of myth: Ovid's insight that
transformation could be the unifying factor in such an encyclo-
paedia is comparable in its power to the insight he displays in
the *Fasti*, where he saw that the Roman calendar could provide
the thread for an encyclopaedic enquiry into Roman religion.
In aiming at constructing a compendium of myth, he succeeded
beyond any expectation he could conceivably have had, because
Graeco-Roman myth in Europe since the fall of the Roman
empire has been Ovidian myth – even the *category* of Graeco-
Roman myth is dependent on Ovid. Apart from Homer's Troy
and Odysseus, Sophocles' Oedipus and Virgil's Dido, it is hard
to think of a Graeco-Roman myth which is common coin in
contemporary culture that is not an Ovidian myth.

Ovid's myths cover an extraordinary range of experience, and
he displays a penetrating psychological knowledge of the variety
of human motivations and delusions. In the face of this variety
and range, readers have regularly tried to isolate what the unify-
ing theme of metamorphosis might be. This is not easy. Meta-
morphosis can be a liberation in this poem, or a claustrophobic
nightmare; it can be banal, or sublime, a realization of a person's
possibilities or 'a savage reduction',[6] sometimes an apparent
appendage with no evident link or motive. The main connecting
thread is an interest in identity: what is it about a person that
makes them that person, and what is it about humans that
makes them human? As one human character after another
transgresses into different categories of the animate and inani-
mate, the poet charts the bizarre mixture of convention and
nature that cumulatively works to establish what we take to be
normal for humans. Books 9 and 10 take this interest to the
limit, as Ovid and then Orpheus give us successive stories of

aberrant sexual desire, with successive heroines battering on the glass walls of convention that divide them from other worlds – human, animal or divine – where their desires are normal.

Ovid works throughout to animate the question of who we think we are, and how we think about who we think we are. The stories in which people are alienated from themselves are the most disturbing vehicles for exploring this question. In particular, the metamorphoses in the appalling stories of rape often capture the sensation of being forced to conceive of yourself in terms totally different from the ones you had taken for granted, as you realize that who *you* thought you were no longer means anything. In Book 2, for example, an Arcadian nymph becomes one of Jupiter's many rape victims. Ovid does not tell us her name, Callisto. Ovid's audience, familiar with the tale, would have known the name anyway, but its omission is significant. In Greek, Callisto means 'most beautiful', but the very beauty that attracted Jupiter and caused her ruin is obliterated by the experience, as Juno turns her rage upon the nymph, and 'Most Beautiful' sees her familiar body, no longer her or hers, changing into the unrecognizable fur and snout of a bear.

In the *Metamorphoses* Ovid continues to be Rome's great expert on love, and virtually all of the most memorable stories explore the realms of love and sexuality. Ovid unforgettably evokes the sensation of sexual obsession (Tereus in Book 6, Scylla in Book 8, Byblis in Book 9, Myrrha in Book 10), and his ability to take us into the mind of aberrant compulsion is profoundly disturbing. He is particularly fascinated by the question of the right degree of distance and identification between lover and beloved. His most famous story, of Narcissus and Echo, probes this conundrum. The two stories had originally been separate, but when Ovid brings them together for the first time he creates an image of two opposite and complementary aberrations from a healthy sexuality, for Narcissus is too fixated upon himself, and Echo is too fixated on someone else. Ovid's fascination with love does not stop with aberration. His interest in marriage stands out, in particular. After Homer, who could do anything, portraits of a marriage are vanishingly rare in ancient literature, but Ovid gives us Deucalion and Pyrrha in

Book 1, Baucis and Philemon in Book 8 and Ceÿx and Alcyone in Book 11. Most striking of all is the story of Cephalus and Procris in Book 7. Their tale could form the plot of a Victorian novel, with its initial fidelity, lapse into adultery, forgiveness and eventual destruction by morbid obsessive jealousy.

Such snapshot summaries of different plots can make Ovid look rather pompous, or earnest, when in fact it is his consistent refusal to be earnest that most typifies his style. The wit is everywhere and can destabilize any subject. When Julius Caesar is becoming a god, for example, at the end of the poem, it is very hard to keep a straight face as Ovid exploits etymological play on the two current explanations of the name 'Caesar'. The first etymological explanation was from the verb 'cut', *caedo*, so that the family was named from an ancestor who was delivered by what we still call 'Caesarian section'. Ovid reminds us of this etymology when Jupiter tells Venus to snatch Caesar's soul 'from his *cut*-ridden body' (*caeso de corpore*, 15.840). The alternative explanation for the family's name was from *caesaries*, the Latin word for a full head of hair; no surprise, then, to see the soul of the famously bald Caesar turning into a 'comet', which is Greek for a 'hairy' star. The moments of wit can occur in contexts of horror that call the very word 'wit' into question. What do we make of Marsyas' cry in Book 6, as he is being flayed alive? – ' "Don't rip me away from myself!" ' (385).

More shocking yet are the four lines Ovid devotes to a description of Philomela's tongue jerking on the ground after it has been cut out by Tereus, in Book 6: the amputated tip quivers and murmurs, it is like the severed tail of a snake as it tries to reach its mistress's feet (557–60). Such moments are an affront to usual canons of taste, and those who have seen Shakespeare's highly Ovidian *Titus Andronicus* will recognize the composite thrill of aesthetic and moral disgust that accompanies these grotesque violations of form.

At such moments, Ovid can resemble the type of 'decadent' artist to which Vladimir Nabokov has been compared, 'an artist who, while not necessarily corrupt or cruel, sensational or over-ingenious, is liable to make such an impression, in his evident wish to secure certain sorts of novel or striking effect'.[7]

The extreme difficulty of doing simultaneous justice to Ovid's aesthetic and moral dimensions is in general reminiscent of the problems facing critics of Nabokov, who is in many ways the closest modern parallel to Ovid as far as the dialectic between style and content is concerned. Nabokov exhibits an Ovidian obsession with formalism, wit and parody, resolutely proclaiming his realm to be a pure art of aesthetic bliss, forswearing messages, values and social or moral relevance; like Ovid, he maintains ambiguities of atmosphere and intention, and has an authorial voice that is abstracted, intangible, yet somehow relentlessly present. Despite these heartfelt artistic stances, readers of Ovid and Nabokov respond to the intuition of an intense moral dimension, which resists the kind of elucidation we might expect to win from other authors: 'He is an unsettling writer as well as a funny one because he is deep where he looks shallow, moving when he seems flippant.'[8] Nabokov refers (with irony, naturally) to this moral dimension in the following quotation, which could be seen as a description of the fate that befell Ovid around the end of the twentieth century: 'I believe that one day a reappraiser will come and declare that, far from having been a frivolous firebird, I was a rigid moralist kicking sin, cuffing stupidity, ridiculing the vulgar and cruel – and assigning sovereign power to tenderness, talent, and pride.'[9]

Impact

Analogies only take one so far, and Ovid differs from Nabokov above all in the range of his ambition. He meant to construct a repository of myth that would accommodate every dimension of human experience, and that would make the Greek store of myth available for a completely different culture to work on as it saw fit. The staggering extent of his success is most evident in the impact that the *Metamorphoses* has had on other creative artists ever since it first appeared, an impact that shows no sign of abating even in the contemporary world, where so few people know Latin. Indeed, Ovid's poem is having a new lease of life as it approaches its two thousandth birthday in 2008, with highly popular dramatizations on both sides of the Atlantic, and adaptations by some of the modern world's most distinguished poets, most notably Ted Hughes (1997). This is only the latest chapter in a story that begins in the generation immediately after Ovid's death. The *Metamorphoses* bulks as large as the *Aeneid* in the imagination of the first-century AD poets Lucan, Seneca and Statius, while it is the main repository of antiquity for the poets of the Middle Ages and Renaissance. The poem's impact on the visual arts is likewise so pervasive as to be incalculable, with the names of Titian, Bernini and Rubens only the most obvious ones that first come to mind. There is no space here to do more than refer the reader to the numerous recent excellent treatments of Ovid's influence on European art and literature (see Further Reading). For me, the point was summed up by a Princeton undergraduate who had never read the *Metamorphoses* before. Halfway through our course she visited the Metropolitan Museum of Art in New York and returned after the weekend intoxicated by her rediscovery of the familiar collections: 'It's all Ovid!'

Notes

1   This poem can be read in the Penguin Classics edition, ed. and trans. A. J. Boyle and R. D. Woodard (Harmondsworth, 2000).
2   F. Ahl, *Metaformations: Soundplay and Wordplay in Ovid and Other Classical Poets* (Ithaca, NY, 1985), p. 59.
3   Tennyson's parody gives some idea of the feel of the elegiac couplet: 'These lame hexameters the strong-winged music of Homer! / No – but a most burlesque barbarous experiment', 'On Translations of Homer' (1863), lines 1–2.
4   E. J. Kenney, *The Cambridge History of Classical Literature II: Latin Literature*, ed. E. J. Kenney and W. V. Clausen (Cambridge, 1982), p. 441.
5   M. Winterbottom, *The Elder Seneca*, Loeb Classical Library (Cambridge, Mass., 1974).
6   Leonard Barkan, *The Gods Made Flesh: Metamorphosis and the Pursuit of Paganism* (New Haven and London, 1986), p. 66, on Lycaön in Book 1. On the theme of metamorphosis, see also Andrew Feldherr in *The Cambridge Companion to Ovid*, ed. Philip Hardie (Cambridge, 2002), pp. 163–79.

7   John Bayley, in Peter Quennell (ed.), *Vladimir Nabokov: A Trib-
     ute* (London, 1979), p. 42.
8   Michael Wood, writing of Nabokov, *not* Ovid, in *The Magician's
     Doubts: Nabokov and the Risks of Fiction* (Princeton, 1994),
     p. 8.
9   Vladimir Nabokov, *Strong Opinions* (New York, 1973), p. 193.

Further Reading

Ahl, F., *Metaformations: Soundplay and Wordplay in Ovid and Other Classical Poets* (Ithaca, NY, 1985)

Barkan, L., *The Gods Made Flesh: Metamorphosis and the Pursuit of Paganism* (New Haven and London, 1986)

Bate, J., *Shakespeare and Ovid* (Oxford, 1993)

Brown, S. A., *The Metamorphoses of Ovid: Chaucer to Ted Hughes* (London, 1999)

Due, O. S., *Changing Forms: Studies in the Metamorphoses of Ovid* (Copenhagen, 1974)

Forbes-Irving, P. M. C., *Metamorphosis in Greek Myths* (Oxford, 1990)

Fränkel, H., *Ovid: A Poet Between Two Worlds* (Berkeley and Los Angeles, 1945)

Galinsky, K., *Ovid's Metamorphoses: An Introduction to the Basic Aspects* (Oxford and Berkeley, 1975)

Hardie, P., *Ovid's Poetics of Illusion* (Cambridge, 2002)

Hardie, P. (ed.), *The Cambridge Companion to Ovid* (Cambridge, 2002)

Hardie, P., Barchiesi, A. and Hinds, S. E. (eds.), *Ovidian Transformations: Essays on Ovid's Metamorphoses and its Reception* (Cambridge, 1999)

Hinds, S. E., *The Metamorphosis of Persephone: Ovid and the Self-conscious Muse* (Cambridge, 1987)

Hinds, S. E., 'Ovid', in S. Hornblower and A. Spawforth (eds.), *The Oxford Classical Dictionary* (Oxford, 1996), pp. 1084–7

Kenney, E. J., 'Ovid', in E. J. Kenney and W. V. Clausen (eds.), *The Cambridge History of Classical Literature* II: *Latin Literature* (Cambridge, 1982), 420–57

Martindale, C. (ed.), *Ovid Renewed: Ovidian Influences on Literature and Art from the Middle Ages to the Twentieth Century* (Cambridge, 1988)

Myers, S., *Ovid's Causes: Cosmogony and Aetiology in the Metamorphoses* (Ann Arbor, 1994)

Otis, B., *Ovid as an Epic Poet* (Cambridge, 1970)

Skulsky, H., *Metamorphosis: The Mind in Exile* (Cambridge, Mass., and London, 1981)

Solodow, J., *The World of Ovid's Metamorphoses* (Chapel Hill, 1988)

Tissol, G., *The Face of Nature: Wit, Narrative, and Cosmic Origins in Ovid's Metamorphoses* (Princeton, 1997)

Wheeler, S., *A Discourse of Wonders: Audience and Performance in Ovid's Metamorphoses* (Philadelphia, 1999)

Wieden Boyd, B. (ed.), *Brill's Companion to Ovid* (Leiden, 2002)

Wilkinson, L. P., *Ovid Recalled* (Cambridge, 1955)

Translator's Note

Of all the major literary works which we have inherited from ancient Rome, Ovid's *Metamorphoses* is arguably the most enjoyable to read for pleasure. Scholars have shown how its author originally composed this monumental series of stories for a sophisticated audience well familiar with the various Greek and Latin models on which they are based. At the same time, the poet evidently reckoned that this achievement would survive 'throughout all ages' (Epilogue, 15.878). He has been proved right, and that can only be because successive generations have found him instantly accessible and entertaining. Ovid is, quite simply, a brilliant story-teller, whose powers of human observation and vivid description transcend the taste, conventions and erudition of his own period. That also must explain why the *Metamorphoses* inspired so much new literature in the second millennium, from Chaucer through Shakespeare down to Ted Hughes in our own day, not to speak of the poem's immense influence on medieval and Renaissance painting and sculpture.

This translation, therefore, aims primarily to appeal to a new readership which knows little or no Latin and may not necessarily be familiar with the classical world generally. I have not been concerned, though, to revamp Ovid for the twenty-first century, but rather to reflect his detailed meaning as faithfully and clearly as I could, in a style which captured the flowing movement of his verse and the lively spirit of his story-telling for a modern audience.

I have also started from the assumption that Ovid designed his long poem to be delivered aloud in acceptable lengths. In all classical poetry (and a great deal of prose for that matter) the sound of the unfolding language was an inseparable part of its sense. We know that poets in ancient Rome gave public recitations of their work and that Ovid himself did so at an early age. We can be sure too that Ovid's books were circulated for private consumption and doubtless were available for reading in the public libraries which existed in Augustan Rome. If people read silently in those days, it is still self-evident that Roman poetry and artistic prose, even when studied in private, were meant to be listened to with the mind's ear as well as perused with the eye. We should not lose sight either of Ovid's dramatic quality, seen especially in the long speeches of appeal or internal debate which he puts in his characters' mouths. These bear witness not only to the poet's rhetorical training but also to the influence of the Greek tragedians, Sophocles and Euripides, no less than the epic traditions of Homer, Apollonius and Virgil.

It is helpful, I suggest, to think of each of the fifteen books as a skilfully constructed 'unit of performance', lasting an average of about seventy minutes – a reasonable length of time for a reciter to hold an audience's attention. Of course, the design of the whole poem is an extraordinary achievement in itself; the work is certainly not a hotch-potch, even if its scheme cannot be too precisely pinned down. The end of each book, as in any ongoing serial, is carefully planned to anticipate the next 'instalment'. But each book also has its own internal design, to be seen sometimes in thematic links but chiefly in the variety and contrasts it displays. Less obviously, a book's ending will always be found to be linked with its beginning by what is known as 'ring composition', in the form of some verbal or thematic echo.

My general aim, then, was to be entertaining in serial form and also readable aloud. How was I to put this into practice? One question was that of idiom. Ovid's own vocabulary is not, for the most part, elaborately poetic; most of the words that he uses were current in normal Latin parlance. I therefore decided that the idiom of my translation should, as far as possible, be natural and spontaneous, avoiding archaism but without being over-colloquial. It was also important to respond to the varying tone of the different stories.

As I had decided to compose this new translation in verse, another crucial question was the one of verse form. Ovid wrote his *Metamorphoses* in dactylic hexameters, the standard line adopted by Greek and Roman poets composing in the epic or didactic genres. The repeated hexameter (only used by Ovid in this one work), coupled with skilful variation in the placing of sense-pauses, is an essential aspect of the poem's style. So also is the elegant convention which allowed Roman poets to exploit the inflexions of the Latin language to abandon normal word-order and create artificial, but beautifully significant, sentence structures within the framework of their chosen metre. The translator who is tied by the regular patterns of English word order can only aspire to that kind of elegance in a very limited way; but a standard repeated form of line can still serve extremely well.

In English the traditional metre for narrative poetry, as for poetic drama, has been the iambic pentameter; and translators of the *Metamorphoses* have commonly used this, whether in rhyming couplets or blank verse, with economical and stylish results. I have preferred a metre which was closer to Ovid's dactylic hexameter; that is, in technical terms, a verse with a rhythmical pulse of six stressed syllables, which may each be separated by two unstressed syllables rather than just one, as in an iambic line. This, I felt, would best reflect the relaxed flow and tone of Ovid's narrative as I perceived it, and allow me more space to communicate his meaning on a line-for-line basis. An exact assimilation to Ovid's hexameter is, of course, impossible, as Latin metre is based not on stress but on syllabic 'quantity', long or short. However, an English line of six main 'beats', each separated by one or two unstressed syllables, with the flexibility (not in the Latin hexameter) to use either stressed or unstressed syllables at its beginning and end, seemed to offer the kind of approximation I was looking for.

In consequence of the decision over metre, the number of lines in the translation is very close to that in the original. I have occasionally compressed five lines of Ovid into four and, more rarely, expanded five to six. Lines treated as interpolations have been omitted, so that in the end the translation totals about

11,870 lines as compared with 11,995 in the original. For purposes of reference, the line-numbering follows that of the Latin text, and correspondence with that should be accurate within one or, at the most, two lines.

The translation has not been based on any one edition of the Latin text. Where a reading is obviously corrupt or in dispute, I have made my own decision after consulting various authorities. How close is my version to the original? As close as I could make it, within the limits of clarity, idiomatic English and my chosen metre; but students who need help with translating the original Latin will probably be better served by one of the more literal versions available. In the interests of a flowing narrative, I have felt free to recast the structure of Ovid's sentences; I have sometimes amplified his meaning to help a modern reader where, for example, a brief allusion would have been immediately intelligible to his own audience. Similarly, I have been inclined to compress where Ovid elegantly says the same thing twice in different ways, if I found that this sounded simply redundant in English. Where Ovid uses a variety of proper names to refer to the same character, I have generally stuck to one, except with well-known equivalents like Jupiter/Jove, Apollo/Phoebus and Minerva/Pallas/Athena. It has seemed sensible too to disregard the poetic convention whereby Ovid, for metrical reasons, sometimes apostrophizes characters and uses the second person to make a plain statement about them. In such cases, the third person has been used to avoid artificiality.

The summaries which precede the fifteen books are designed to give an overview of each one in turn, to suggest what may be specially worth looking out for, and also to aid the reader's appreciation of the whole poem's continuity as well as its constant variety. The notes (signalled by an asterisk) offer more background material on points of detail and supply cross-references where appropriate. Further information about characters and places may be found in the Glossary Index. Both summaries and notes refer selectively to Ovid's sources for those who are interested; but the reader may well prefer simply to enjoy the stories themselves as Ovid tells them.

Since the translation is intended to be read aloud or heard

with the mind's ear, guidance is also offered on the assumed
stressing and pronunciation of the Latin proper names. Modern
practice varies widely, even among professional classicists. The
Glossary Index is therefore prefaced by a statement of the rules
I have adopted for the purposes of my rhythmical design (with
very rare exceptions for the sake of euphony). The stressing of
individual names is given both there and also, unless it is obvious
or very well known, where each one occurs for the first time in
any book. I have thought this important since the flow of the
verse will be interrupted if, for example, Ulysses is pronounced,
as often today, with an accent on the first syllable rather than
on the second, as in the Greek Odysseus.

Incidentally, is the poem's title to be pronounced *Meta-
morphóses* or *Metamórphoses*? Strictly speaking, the former is
more correct, as the second *o* in the original Greek word is long.
Those, however, who prefer the second may quote the example
of Shakespeare.

In conclusion, it has been a strange challenge to try to bring
Ovid alive in present-day English nearly 2000 years after his
colossal work was in composition. At the end of the task, I am
conscious that the hardest element in the *Metamorphoses* to do
justice to is its verbal wit, which can only be properly appreci-
ated in the original Latin. I hope, however, that my readers will
be able to share my enjoyment of the poet's humour, particularly
in the characterization of Jupiter and Juno, and the subtle deli-
cacy of his human observation. Those things apart, if I have
succeeded in communicating a little of Ovid's extraordinary
power and versatility as a story-teller to another generation or
two, the labour will be well rewarded.

Metamorphoses

BOOK 1

In a short *Prologue* (1–4) Ovid announces his theme of meta-
morphosis: his stories of change will form one continuous poem,
ranging in time from the beginning of the universe to Ovid's
own lifetime.

The first great change is *The Creation* of the Universe (5–88)
out of Chaos, culminating in the appearance of Man. Ovid's
grand description draws on a variety of poetic and philosophical
sources, including the earlier Roman poet Lucretius (first cen-
tury BC). We will naturally compare it with the biblical account
in Genesis, chapters 1 and 2. The process of change continues
through *The Four Ages* (89–150) of early human existence,
viewed as a degeneration from natural innocence and abund-
ance to a world governed by selfishness and aggression. At this
stage *The Giants* (151–62) attempt to oust the gods from their
home on Olympus but are struck down by Jupiter's lightning.
The Earth transforms their blood into new men whose brutality
is true to their origin.

Human depravity is exemplified by *Lycaön* (163–252), the
savage king of Arcadia. Jupiter calls an assembly to indicate his
intention to destroy mankind; but in response to objections
from the other gods, he promises to breed a new and better race.
Mankind's destruction follows in Ovid's description of *The
Flood* (253–312) and its transforming effects. (The story of a
world-wide flood recurs in the Greek and Near Eastern tra-
ditions, particularly in Genesis, chapters 6–9.) *Deucalion and
Pyrrha* (313–415) are the Greek Mr and Mrs Noah, two god-
fearing and mutually devoted survivors. After the flood's effects
are reversed, they miraculously produce a new race of hardy

men. The after-effects of the flood lead to the birth of strange
new creatures, including the terrifying *Python* (416–50), who
is killed by the god Apollo.

Apollo is the link with the first in a series of metamorphoses
involving the amours of gods. The next story concerns the
virginal nymph *Daphne* (451–567), who is relentlessly pursued
by Apollo but finally eludes capture by being transformed into
a laurel tree. The lighter tone and pace of this contrast vividly
with the earlier part of the book.

A noble description of the Vale of Tempe provides an ingeni-
ous transition to the parallel story of Jupiter's successful pursuit
of *Io* (568–686, 713–47), whom the god transforms to a cow
to protect her from Juno's jealousy. Here we can see an element
of comedy in the relationship between the gods, as well as of
touching pathos in Ovid's account of Io's unhappy predicament.
Here too we have the first inserted story, told by Mercury to
Io's hundred-eyed sentinel, Argus, of *Pan and Syrinx* (687–
712), another instance of a nymph pursued by a god and meta-
morphosed at the last minute.

The book concludes with an introduction to the story of
Phaëthon (748–79), which is to occupy a large part of Book 2.
When the young man's claim to be the child of the sun god is
questioned, he is determined to establish the truth and sets
out to find his father. The closing lines ring with excited
anticipation.

PROLOGUE*

Changes of shape, new forms, are the theme which my
        spirit impels me
now to recite. Inspire me, O gods (it is you who have even
transformed my art*), and spin me a thread from the
        world's beginning
down to my own lifetime, in one continuous poem.

THE CREATION

Before the earth and the sea and the all-encompassing
        heaven   5
came into being, the whole of nature displayed but a
        single
face, which men have called Chaos: a crude,
        unstructured mass,
nothing but weight without motion, a general
        conglomeration
of matter composed of disparate, incompatible elements.
No Titan the sun god was present to cast his rays on the
        universe,   10
nor Phoebe the moon to replenish her horns and grow to
        her fullness;
no earth suspended in equilibrium, wrapped in its folding
mantle of air; nor Amphitríte, the goddess of ocean,
to stretch her sinuous arms all round the earth's long
        coastline.
Although the land and the sea and the sky were involved
        in the great mass,   15
no one could stand on the land or swim in the waves of
        the sea,
and the sky had no light. None of the elements kept its
        shape,
and all were in conflict inside one body: the cold with the
        hot,

the wet with the dry, the soft with the hard, and weight
20   with the weightless.
    The god who is nature* was kinder and brought this
          dispute to a settlement.
He severed the earth from the sky and he parted the sea
          from the land;
he separated translucent space from the cloudier
          atmosphere.
He disentangled the elements,* so as to set them free
from the heap of darkness, then gave them their
25   separate places and tied them
down in a peaceful concordat: fire flashed out as a
          weightless
force in the vaulted heaven and found its rightful place
at the height of the firmament; air came next in position
          and lightness;
earth was denser than these, attracted the larger
          particles
and sank through the downward thrust of its weight; in
30   the nether region
came water, confining the solid disc in its liquid
          embrace.
    When the god, whichever one of the gods, had
          divided the substance
of Chaos and ordered it thus in its different constituent
          members,
first, in order that earth should hang suspended in
          perfect
symmetrical balance, he moulded it into the shape of a
35   great sphere.
Next he commanded the seas to scatter and swell as
          they fronted
the blast of the winds, surrounding the earth with its
          circle of shore.
To the ocean he added the springs, huge standing pools
          and the lakes,
and rivers to wind downstream as their sloping banks
          confined them.

These in their various places may be absorbed by the earth
            itself,   40
or travel as far as the sea, where they enter the broad
            expanse
of more open water and beat on the shore instead of their
            banks.
Then he commanded the plains to extend and the valleys to
            sink,
the woods to be decked in their leaves and the rock-faced
            mountains to soar.
And just as the sky is cut into zones, with two to
            northward,   45
two to the south and a fifth which burns with more heat
            than the others,
so with the earth which the sky encloses: the god in his
            wisdom
ordained five separate zones* or tracts to be traced on its
            surface.
The central zone is too hot for men to inhabit the region;
two are buried in snow; but two he placed in between,   50
and thus he blended the heat with the cold in a temperate
            climate.
    Hanging over the lands is the air, whose weight exceeds
that of fire by as much as the weight of earth exceeds that of
            water.
It was here that the god commanded the mists and the
            clouds to settle,
here that he posted the thunder to trouble the hearts of
            men,   55
with the winds which cause the lightning that burns and the
            lightning that flashes.*
Still the creator did not allow the winds dominion
over the whole wide range of air. As it is, they can scarcely
be stopped from tearing the world to pieces, though each of
            them governs
his blasts in a distant quarter; so angrily brothers can
            quarrel.   60

Eurus' retreat is the home of the dawn, from the realms of
          Arabia
and Persia through to the mountains* that gleam in the
          morning sunlight;
Zephyr is close to the evening and fans the shores that are
          warmed
by the setting sun. Bóreas, lord of the blizzard, sweeps
into Scýthia, land of the frozen north; while Auster,
65   opposite,
drenches the soil of the south with his clouds of
          incessant rain.
Above the turbulent lower air the creator imposed
the weightless translucent ether, untainted by earthly
          pollution.
     Nature had hardly been settled within its separate
          compartments
when stars, which had long been hidden inside the
70   welter of Chaos,
began to explode with light all over the vault of the
          heavens.
And lest any part of the world should be wanting its
          own living creatures,
the floor of heaven was richly inlaid with the stars and
          the planets,
the waves of the sea were assigned as the realm of the
          glinting fishes,
the earth was the home of the beasts, and the yielding
75   air of the birds.
     Yet a holier living creature, more able to think high
          thoughts,
which could hold dominion over the rest, was still to be
          found.
So Man came into the world. Maybe the great artificer
made him of seed divine in a plan for a better universe.
Maybe the earth that was freshly formed and newly
80   divorced
from the heavenly ether retained some seeds of its
          kindred element –

earth, which Prométheus, the son of Iápetus, sprinkled with
    raindrops
and moulded into the likeness of gods who govern the
    universe.
Where other animals walk on all fours and look to the
    ground,
man was given a towering head and commanded to stand   85
erect, with his face uplifted to gaze on the stars of heaven.
Thus clay, so lately no more than a crude and formless
    substance,
was metamorphosed to assume the strange new figure of
    Man.

THE FOUR AGES

First to be born was the Golden Age. Of its own free
    will,
without laws or enforcement, it did what was right and
    trust prevailed.   90
Punishment held no terrors; no threatening edicts were
    published
in tablets of bronze; secure with none to defend them, the
    crowd
never pleaded or cowered in fear in front of their
    stern-faced judges.
No pine tree had yet been felled from its home on the
    mountains and come down
into the flowing waves for journeys to lands afar;   95
mortals were careful and never forsook the shores of their
    homeland.
No cities were yet ringed round with deep, precipitous
    earthworks;
long straight trumpets and curved bronze horns never
    summoned to battle;
swords were not carried nor helmets worn; no need for
    armies,
but nations were free to practise the gentle arts of peace.   100

The earth was equally free and at rest, untouched by the
          hoe,
unscathed by the ploughshare, supplying all needs from
          its natural resources.
Content to enjoy the food that required no painful
          producing,
men simply gathered arbutus fruit and mountain
          strawberries,
cornel cherries and blackberries plucked from the prickly
105   bramble,
acorns too which they found at the foot of the
          spreading oak tree.
Spring was the only season. Flowers which had never
          been planted
were kissed into life by the warming breath of the
          gentle zephyrs;
and soon the earth, untilled by the plough, was
          yielding her fruits,
and without renewal the fields grew white with the
110   swelling corn blades.
Rivers of milk and rivers of nectar flowed in
          abundance,
and yellow honey, distilled like dew from the leaves of
          the ilex.
     When Saturn* was cast into murky Tártarus, Jupiter
          seized
the throne of the universe. Now there followed the age
          of silver,
meaner than gold but higher in value than tawny
115   bronze.
Gentle spring was no longer allowed to continue
          unbroken;
the king of the gods divided the year into four new
          seasons:
summer, changeable autumn, winter and only a short
          spring.
The sky for the first time burned and glowed with a dry
          white heat,

and the blasts of the wild winds froze the rain into hanging
      icicles.   120
People now took shelter in houses; their homes hitherto
had been caves, dense thickets or brushwood fastened
      together with bark.
For the first time also the corn was sown in long ploughed
      furrows,
and oxen groaned beneath the weight of the heavy yoke.
   A third age followed the Silver Age, the bronze
      generation,   125
crueller by nature, more ready to take up menacing
      weapons,
but still not vile to the core. The final age was of iron;
the floodgates opened and all the forces of evil invaded
a breed of inferior mettle. Loyalty, truth and conscience
went into exile, their throne usurped by guile and
      deception,   130
treacherous plots, brute force and a criminal lust for
      possession.
Sailors spread their sails to the winds they had tempted so
      rarely
before, and the keels of pine that had formerly stood stock
      still
on the mountain slopes presumptuously bobbed in the alien
      ocean.
The land which had been as common to all as the air or the
      sunlight   135
was now marked out with the boundary lines of the wary
      surveyor.
The affluent earth was not only pressed for the crops and
      the food
that it owed; men also found their way to its very bowels,
and the wealth which the god had hidden away in the home
      of the ghosts
by the Styx was mined and dug out, as a further incitement
      to wickedness.   140
Now dangerous iron, and gold – more dangerous even than
      iron –

had emerged. Grim War appeared, who uses both in his
          battles,
and brandished his clashing weapons in hands
          bespattered with slaughter.
Men throve on their thefts: no guest was safe from his
          host, no father
secure with his daughter's husband; love between
145   brothers was found
but seldom. Men and their wives would long for each
          other's demise;
wicked stepmothers brewed their potions of deadly
          wolfsbane;
sons would cast their fathers' horoscopes prematurely.
All duty to gods and to men lay vanquished; and
          Justice the Maiden*
was last of the heavenly throng to abandon the
150   blood-drenched earth.

THE GIANTS

The upper air was not to be left in greater peace
than the earth below. The story goes that the giants*
          aspired
to the throne of heaven and built a path to the stars on
          high,
by piling mountain on mountain. Then it was that
          almighty
Jupiter launched his lightning bolts to shatter Olympus,
and shook Mount Pélion down from its base on the
155   ridges of Ossa.
When, crushed by the mass they had raised, those
          fearsome bodies lay prostrate,
Mother Earth, as the story continues, now steeped and
          drenched
in the blood of her offspring, gave fresh life to the
          seething liquid.

Unwilling that all the fruits of her womb should be lost and
    forgotten,
she turned their blood into human form; but the new race
    also   160
looked on the gods with contempt. Their passionate lust for
    ferocious
violence and slaughter prevailed. You'd have known they
    were born of blood.

LYCAÖN

When Jupiter, son of Saturn, looked down from the heights
    of heaven,
he sighed, and remembered the gruesome banquet* served
    at Lycäön's
table, a recent event and not yet publicly rumoured.   165
Mightily angry, as only Jove can be angry, he called
a general assembly and all responded at once to his
    summons.
  In cloudless skies you can clearly see a path in the
    heavens;
men call it the Milky Way, well known for its brilliant
    whiteness.
This is the road which the gods must take to the mighty
    Thunderer's   170
royal palace. The well-thronged halls to the right and the
    left,
with their doors flung open, belong to the gods of the
    highest rank.
The common divinities live outside; right here the élite
and heavenly powers that be have established their hearths
    and homes.
And this is the place which, if I could muster the boldness to
    say it,   175
I'd not be afraid to describe as the Pálatine Hill* of the
    firmament.

After the gods had taken their seats in the marble
    chamber,
Jove, enthroned on a dais and clutching his ivory sceptre,
shook the awesome locks of his head three times and
    again,
so causing the earth and the sea and the constellations to
180   tremble,
then opened his lips to give vent to his wrath in the
    following manner:
'The fear that I feel today for the sovereign power of
    the universe
equals my fear when each of the snake-footed giants
    was striving
to lay his hundred hands on the sky and make it his
    own.
Fierce as that enemy was, its impetus sprang from a
185   single
body and source. But now I am forced to commit the
    whole race
of mankind to destruction wherever the ocean roars on
    the shore.
By the streams of the Stygian river below I swear I shall
    do it!
Let other cures be attempted first, but what is past
190   remedy
calls for the surgeon's knife, lest the parts that are
    sound be infected.
I have my demigods, all those powers of the
    countryside: nymphs,
and fauns and satyrs, my woodland spirits who dwell
    on the mountains.
These we have not yet chosen to welcome to heavenly
    honours,
but let us allow them at least to dwell on the earth we
195   have given them.
Or do your honours believe their safety is firmly
    assured,

when I, who am lord of the lightning and master of all you
      gods,
am the object of plots hatched up by that infamous savage,
      Lycaön?'
   The house was in uproar; passions blazed as they called
      for the blood
of the reckless traitor; as, when that band of disloyal
      malcontents   200
raged to extinguish the name of Rome by murdering
      Caesar,*
all mankind was suddenly struck by a terrible fear
of grievous disaster to come and the whole world shuddered
      in horror.
And just as your people's loyal devotion is welcome to you,
Augustus,* so was his subjects' to Jove. A word and a
      gesture   205
sufficed to control the murmuring hubbub and all were
      silent.
Then Jupiter broke the silence again to make his
      pronouncement:
'Lycaön has paid for his crimes, so far you may rest
      assured;
but let me describe his offence and the punishment meted
      out.   210
An evil report of the times had come to my ears. Desirous
of proving it false, I made my descent from the heights of
      Olympus
and wandered over the earth, a god disguised as a mortal.
It would take too long to recount the story of all the
      wickedness
I discovered. The truth was worse than rumour reported.   215
Crossing over the high Arcadian mountains (Maénalus,
home of wild beasts, Cyllénc, and cold pine-covered
      Lycaéus),
I entered the palace of King Lycaön and ventured beneath
his inhospitable roof in the twilight hour of the nightfall.
I gave a sign that a god had come, and the common people   220

turned to their prayers. Lycaön began by mocking their
          piety;
then he said, "Is it a god or a mortal? I'll settle the matter
by using a simple test. There will be no doubt where the
          truth lies."
His plan was to make a sudden attack in the night on my
          sleeping
body and kill me. This was his chosen method of
225   proving
the truth. Not content with that, he applied his sword
          to the throat
of a hostage sent from Epírus and under my own
          protection;
and while the man's flesh still held some warmth, he
          roasted part of it
over the fire and poached the remainder in boiling
          water,
then set this repast on the table. My moment now had
230   arrived.
My lightning of vengeance struck, and the palace
          collapsed in ruins
on top of the household gods* who shared the guilt of
          the master.
Frightened out of his wits, Lycaön fled to the country
where all was quiet. He tried to speak, but his voice
          broke into
an echoing howl. His ravening soul infected his jaws;
his murderous longings were turned on the cattle; he
235   still was possessed
by bloodlust. His garments were changed to a shaggy
          coat and his arms
into legs. He was now transformed to a wolf. But he
          kept some signs
of his former self: the grizzled hair and the wild
          expression,
the blazing eyes and the bestial image remained
          unaltered.

One house has fallen, but more than one has deserved to
      perish.   240
The demon of madness is holding dominion the wide world
      over;
you'd think that the human race had joined in an evil
      conspiracy.
This is my sentence: let all of them speedily pay for their
      crimes!'
  Jove had spoken. Some fuelled his anger further by
      cheering
loudly, while others simply expressed their approval by
      clapping.   245
But still a murmur went round: 'The loss of the human race
will be widely deplored! And what will a world bereft of
      mortals
be like in the future? Who will bring to our altars the
      offerings
of incense? Is earth to be left to the mercies of ravaging wild
      beasts?'
Such were their questions; but Jupiter told them not to be
      anxious.   250
He would take care of the future, he said; and he promised
      to breed
a new race of miraculous birth, unlike the people before it.

THE FLOOD

The god was now on the point of launching his bolts on the
      whole wide
earth, but he feared that the conflagration might cause the
      holy
ether* to catch fire too in a blaze from pole to pole.   255
He also remembered the Fates' decree, that a time would
      arrive*
when the sea and the land and the royal palace of heaven
      would burst

into flames and the complex mass of the universe come
        to grief.
So he put the lightning, forged in the Cyclops' workshop,
        aside
and chose a different method of punishing mortals, by
260   massing
his storm-clouds over the sky and destroying the race
        in a great flood.
    All of the gales which scatter the gathering clouds,
        and among them
the north wind Áquilo, Jupiter promptly imprisoned
        inside
the caverns of Aéolus. Notus, the wind of the south, he
        released.
265 Notus flew out on his soaking wings, his terrible visage
covered in pitchy gloom; his beard was a bundle of
        rain-storms;
water streamed from his hoary locks; his forehead a
        cushion
for mists; his wings and the folds of his garments were
        sodden and dripping.
He squeezed the bank of menacing clouds like a
        sponge, and a thunderclap
followed. Instantly rain poured down from the sky in
        torrents.
Juno's messenger, decked in her mantle of many
270   colours,
Iris the rainbow, sucked up moisture to thicken the
        clouds.
The corn was flattened; the farmer wept for his wasted
        prayers;
and all the fruits of a long year's labour were gone to
        no purpose.
    Jupiter's anger did not stop short in the sky, his own
        kingdom;
Neptune the sea god deployed his waters to aid his
275   brother.

He summoned the rivers and, when they'd arrived at their
    master's palace,
he spoke to the meeting: 'No need for a lengthy harangue,'
    he said;
'Pour forth in the strength that is yours – it is needed! Open
    the floodgates,
down with the barriers, give full rein to the steeds of your
    streams!'   280
He had spoken. The rivers returned to relax the curbs on
    their sources,
and then rolled down to the ocean flats in unbridled
    career.
Neptune himself now struck the earth with his trident. It
    trembled
under the blow, and a raging torrent gushed from the
    chasm.
Bursting their confines, the rivers engulfed the plains and
    the valleys.   285
The orchards along with the crops, and the cattle along
    with the people,
houses and shrines with their sacred possessions were swept
    to oblivion.
Dwellings, which stood their ground and were able to face
    such an onslaught
untoppled, were still submerged from above by an
    overwhelming,
mountainous wave, which levelled their pinnacles deep in
    the floodtide.   290
    And now no more could the land and the sea be clearly
    distinguished.
The world was reduced to an ocean, an ocean without any
    coastline.
Look at the man on that hill, or sitting alone in his
    fishing-boat,
rowing across the fields where he recently guided his
    ploughshare.
Another is sailing above his cornfields or over the roof   295

of his vanished farmhouse, or casting his line in the top
    of an elm tree.
He might have dropped anchor to catch in the soil of a
    grassy meadow,
or else his dinghy is scraping the vineyard trellis below
    him.
There in the field where the slender goats were lately
    browsing
300   on tufts of grass, the seals are resting their clumsy bodies.
Under water the Néreïds gaze in utter amazement
at coppices, cities and buildings. The woods are
    invaded by dolphins,
blundering into the branches and bumping the trunks
    till they shake them.
Wolves are swimming among the sheep; tawny lions
and tigers are swept along in the flood; no use to the
305   boar
is his lightning strength, nor the speed of his legs to the
    floundering stag.
At the end of a tedious search for land and a resting
    place,
with wings exhausted the wandering bird flutters down
    to the waves.
Small hills are completely submerged by the sea in its
    limitless freedom,
and billows are strangely beating against the peaks of
310   the mountains.
All but a few have been drowned in the flood, and any
    survivors
for shortage of food are destroyed by long-drawn-out
    starvation.

DEUCALION AND PYRRHA

Phocis lies in the country between Boeótia and Thessaly,
fertile land, when still it was land. At the time of the flood
it was part of the sea and a plain of suddenly spreading
    water.   315
Here you can visit a twin-peaked mountain, called
    Parnássus,
towering up to the stars and hiding its head in the clouds.
This was the only feature the ocean had left uncovered;
and here Deucálion, sailing a tiny boat with his wife,
ran aground. On landing they paid the homage due to the
    nymphs   320
of the great Corýcian cave, to the mountain spirits and
    Themis,
goddess of prophecy, then in control of the Delphic oracle.
You'd never find a better or more right-minded man
than Deucalion, neither a more god-fearing woman than
    Pyrrha.
When Jupiter saw that the world was a pool of swirling
    water,
that only one was left of so many thousand men,   325
and only one was left of so many thousand women,
both of them guiltless of sin and both devout in their
    worship,
he scattered the mists; with the north wind's help he
    banished the storm-clouds,
Exposing the earth once more to the sky and the sky to the
    earth.
Neptune's anger subsided as well. Laying his trident   330
aside, he calmed the turbulent waters and called upon
    Triton,
the sea-green merman, who heaved his shoulders, encrusted
    by nature
with shells of the murex,* above the surface, with orders to
    blow

on his resonant conch and signal the rivers and waves to
    withdraw.
Triton lifted his hollow horn, which wreathes in a
335   spiral
up from its mouthpiece to broaden out to a bell, the
    horn
whose notes, when once he has filled it with breath in
    the midst of the deep,
rebound on the echoing shoreline from east to west. So
    then,
when the god had raised his instrument up to his lips,
    with the salt drops
streaming down from his beard, and the blast had
340   sounded the bidden
retreat, it was heard by all the water of land and ocean;
and all the waters by which it was heard were held in
    check.
The sea recovered its shores; the rivers, though full,
    were confined
to their channels; the flooding receded; the hills were
    seen to emerge.
The earth rose up; as the waves died down, dry land
345   expanded.
At the end of a long, long day the tops of the trees in
    the forest
began to appear, their leaves still thick with a coating
    of slime.

The world was restored; but when Deucalion saw it
    was empty
and felt the silence brooding over the desolate earth,
he burst into tears and said to Pyrrha, his dear
350   companion:
'My cousin, my wife, the only woman who still
    survives,
first we were tied by our kindred blood, and then by
    our marriage;

now our very danger unites us. Here is the world
with its glorious lands from east to west; and here are we,
an inglorious crowd of two. All else belongs to the sea.   355
As yet, indeed, we can hardly be certain the life that we
    have
is safely assured. These clouds still fill me with fear and
    foreboding.
How would you now be feeling, my poor dear love, if I
had been lost and you had been snatched from death? How
    could you have suffered
fear on your own, with no one there to comfort your
    sorrow?   360
Believe me, if you were lying beneath the waves, my
    beloved,
I should follow you there to be drowned in the waves beside
    you.
I wish I could use my father Prometheus' skill to create
mankind once again and breathe new life into moulded
    clay!
Today we two are all that is left of the human race.   365
That is the will of the gods. We survive as nothing but
    relicts.'
  He spoke and they wept. They then decided to pray to the
    heavenly
power of Themis and crave her help in a sacred oracle.
Speedily, side by side, they made their way to Cephísus;*
the river was still disturbed but cutting its usual channel.   370
Drawing some water, they sprinkled it over their heads and
    their garments,
and bent their footsteps towards the shrine of the holy
    goddess.
Its gable was pale with unsightly moss, and the fires on the
    altar
were dead. When they reached the temple steps, they both
    prostrated
                                                         375
themselves and fearfully pressed their lips on the cold, hard
    pavement,

saying aloud: 'If the prayers of the righteous can soften
         the hearts
of the gods and win them over, transforming their anger
         to kindness,
gentle Themis, declare to us how to repair the loss
of our wretched race, and come to the aid of our deluged
380   world.'
The heart of the goddess was moved and she gave her
         response to them, saying:
'Leave this sanctuary, cover your heads and ungirdle
         your garments,
then cast the bones of your mighty mother behind your
         backs.'
They were long dumbfounded. Pyrrha was first to
         break the silence
and voice her protest aloud. She refused to obey the
385   goddess'
commands. With trembling lips she begged for pardon,
         too frightened
to give such offence to her mother's ghost by casting
         her dead bones.
Meanwhile they silently pondered the words of the
         puzzling reply
which had come from the oracle's dark recess, and
         discussed them together.
Prometheus' son then gently suggested, to calm
390   Epimétheus'*
daughter: 'Unless my wits are awry and sorely
         deceiving me,
oracles must be holy and never command what is
         sinful.
Our mighty mother is Earth. I believe what is meant by
         her bones
are stones on her body, and these we are bidden to cast
         behind us.'
    Though Pyrrha was much impressed by her
395   husband's interpretation,

her hopes still wavered. They both distrusted the oracle's
        bidding,
but saw little harm in trying. Proceeding down from the
        temple,
they covered their heads, ungirdled their robes and,
        stepping out boldly,
scattered some stones behind their backs, as the oracle
        ordered.
Who would believe what ensued, if it wasn't confirmed by
        tradition?   400
The stones started to lose their essential hardness, slowly
to soften, and then to assume a new shape. They soon
        grew larger
and gathered a nature more gentle than stone. An outline
        of human
form could be seen, not perfectly clear, like a
        rough-hewn statue   405
partially carved from the marble and not yet properly
        finished.
But still, the part of the stones which consisted of earth
        and contained
some moisture was turned into flesh; the solid, inflexible
        matter
was changed into bones; and the veins of the rock into
        veins of blood.   410
In a moment of time, by the will of the gods, the stones
        that were thrown
from the hands of a man were transformed to take on the
        appearance of men,
and women were fashioned anew from those that were
        thrown by a woman.
And so our race is a hard one; we work by the sweat of
        our brow,
and bear the unmistakable marks of our stony origin.   415

PYTHON

Other creatures after their various kinds came forth
from the earth by spontaneous self-generation. The
            lingering moisture
was warmed by the rays of the sun, and the heat made
            the mud in the water-logged
marshes swell and expand. The seeds of animal life
were fed in the mother's womb of life-giving soil which
420   engendered them,
growing in course of time to the shapes of the different
            species.
Such we can see when the seven-mouthed Nile has
            withdrawn from the flood-drenched
fields and brought its waters back to their normal
            channels.
After the freshly deposited mud grows hot in the
            sunshine,
the farmers turning the clods with their ploughs
425   discover a horde
of new creatures. Some have arrived on the threshold
            of life and can even
be watched at the moment of birth, while others are
            still half-formed
and without their limbs; it will sometimes appear in a
            single body
that one of its parts is alive and the rest is composed of
            mere earth.
When heat and moisture are blended, we know that
430   they lead to conception;
everything owes its first beginning to these two
            elements.
Though fire is at war with water, their combination
            produces
the whole of nature – procreation from friendly
            enmity.*

So at the time straight after the flood, when the earth was
    muddy
and heated again from above by the rays of the sun, it
    produced   435
an infinite number of species. Some of the forms which
    emerged
were familiar before, but others were new and amazing
    creations.
   Amongst these forms was an unknown serpent, the
    monstrous Python,
also brought forth by Earth at the time, though she cannot
    have wished for it.
Sprawling over Parnassus, it horribly frightened the
    new-born   440
peoples, until it was killed by the deadly shafts of Apollo,
whose only targets before were the timid gazelles and the
    roe deer.
The snake was transfixed by a thousand arrows (the quiver
    was almost
emptied) and out of its wounds there spewed black gushes
    of venom.
In order that time should never destroy the fame of this
    exploit,   445
Apollo established the sacred games, attended by huge
    crowds,
the Pythian Games,* called after the serpent he vanquished,
    Python.
Here the athletes who won their events on track or on field,
or the chariot-race, would receive the glorious crown of an
    oak-wreath.
The laurel had not yet appeared, and Phoebus would
    garland the flowing
locks of his comely head with any available foliage.   450

DAPHNE

Apollo's first love was Daphne, the child of the river
      Penéüs.
Blind chance was not to be blamed but Cupid's spiteful
      resentment.
Phoebus, still in the flush of his victory over the
      serpent,
had noticed the love-god bending his bow and drawing
455   the string
to his shoulder, and asked him: 'What are you doing
      with grown-up weapons,
you mischievous boy? That bow would better be
      carried by me.
When I fire my shafts at my foes or beasts, they're
      unfailingly wounded.
My numberless arrows have just destroyed the
      venomous Python,
which filled whole acres of mountainside with its
460   belly's infections.
You be content with your torch and use it to kindle
      some passion
or other; but don't usurp any honours belonging to
      me!'
The son of Venus replied: 'Your arrows, Apollo, can
      shoot
whatever you choose, but I'll shoot you. As mortal
      creatures
must yield to a god, your glory will likewise prove to
465   be subject
to mine.' Then he beat his wings and cut a path
      through the atmosphere,
nimbly alighting upon the heights of shady Parnassus.
Once there he drew from his quiver two arrows of
      contrary purpose:
one is for rousing passion, the other is meant to repel it.

The former is made of gold, and its head has a sharp, bright
        point,   470
while the latter is blunt and weighted with lead one side of
        the reed shaft.
That was the arrow which Cupid implanted in Daphne's
        bosom;
the other was aimed at Apollo and smote to the core of his
        being.
Phoebus at once was filled with desire, but Daphne fled
from the very thought of a lover. She joyed in the forest
        lairs   475
and in spoils of captive beasts, like the virgin goddess
        Diana,
binding her carelessly flowing locks in a simple headband.
Courted by suitors in droves, Peneüs' daughter rejected
        them.
Stubbornly single, she'd roam through the woodland
        thickets, without
concern for the meaning of marriage or love or physical
        union.   480
Often her father remarked, 'You owe me a son, my
        daughter,'
or else he would say, 'Now when, my child, will you give
        me a grandson?'
Marriage torches to Daphne were nothing less than
        anathema.
Blushes of shame would spread all over her beautiful
        cheeks,
she would lovingly cling to her father's neck in a coaxing
        appeal   485
and say to him, 'Darling Father, I want to remain a virgin
for ever. Please let me. Diana's father allowed her that.'
Peneüs granted her wish; but Daphne's peculiar beauty
and personal charm were powerful bars to her prayer's
        fulfilment.
Phoebus caught sight of her, fell in love and longed to
        possess her.   490

Wishes were hopes, for even his powers of prophecy
          failed him.
Think of the flimsy stubble which burns in a harvested
          cornfield;
and think of a blazing hedgerow fired by a torch which a
          traveller
has carelessly brought too close or dropped behind him
          at daybreak.
So was the god as his heart caught fire and the flames
          spread through
495
to the depths of his soul, and passion was fuelled with
          empty hope.
He eyes the hair hanging loosely over her neck, and
          murmurs,
'What if that hair were neatly arranged!' He looks at
          her bright eyes
burning and twinkling like stars; he studies her lips, so
          teasingly
tempting; he fondly admires her hands with their
500   delicate fingers;
he dotes on the shapely arms, so nearly bare to the
          shoulder;
what's hidden he thinks must be even better. But swift
          as the light breeze,
Daphne is gone, with never a pause as he calls out after
          her:
'Stop, dear Daphne, I beg you to stop! This isn't an
          enemy
chasing you. Stop! You would think I'm a wolf
505   pursuing a lamb,
a lion hunting a deer or an eagle pouncing on fluttering
doves in mid-air, but I'm not! It is love that impels me
          to follow you.
Have pity! How frightened I am that you'll fall and
          scratch those innocent
legs in the brambles. You mustn't be hurt on account
          of me!

The ground where you're rushing away is so rough. Slow
    down, my beloved,   510
I beg you. Don't run so fast and I promise to slow down
    too.
Now ask who it is that desires you. I'm not a wild
    mountain-dweller;
this isn't an uncouth shepherd, minding the flocks and the
    herds
round here. Impetuous girl, you have no idea who you're
    running from.
That's why you're running so fast. Listen! I am the master
    of Delphi,   515
Claros and Ténedos, Pátara's temple too. My father
is Jupiter. I can reveal the past, the present and future
to all who seek them. I am the lord of the lyre and song.
My arrows are deadly, but one is even more deadly than
    they are,
the shaft which has smitten a heart that has never been
    wounded before.   520
Healing is my invention, the world invokes me as Helper,
and I am the one who dispenses the herbs with the power to
    cure.
Alas! No herbs have the power to cure the disease of my
    love.
Those arts which comfort the whole of mankind cannot
    comfort their master!'
    Apollo wanted to say much more, but the terrified
    Daphne   525
ran all the faster; she left him behind with his speech
    unfinished.
Her beauty was visible still, as her limbs were exposed by
    the wind;
the breezes which blew in her face managed also to flutter
    her dress;
and the currents of air succeeded in blowing her tresses
    behind her.
Flight made her all the more lovely; but now the god in his
    youthful   530

ardour was ready no longer to squander his breath on
        wheedling
pleas. Spurred on by desire, he followed the trail with
        new vigour.
Imagine a greyhound, imagine a hare it has sighted in
        open
country: one running to capture his prey, the other for
        safety.
The hound is about to close in with his jaws; he believes
535   he is almost
there; he is grazing the back of her heels with the tip of
        his muzzle.
The hare isn't sure if her hunter has caught her, but
        leaps into freedom,
clear of the menacing jaws and the mouth which keeps
        brushing against her.
So with Apollo and Daphne, the one of them racing in
        hope
and the other in fear. But the god had the pinions of
540   love to encourage him.
Faster than she, he allowed her no rest; his hands were
        now close
to the fugitive's shoulders; his breath was ruffling the
        hair on her neck.
Her strength exhausted, the girl grew pale; then
        overcome
by the effort of running, she saw Peneüs' waters before
        her:
'Help me, Father!' she pleaded. 'If rivers have power
545   over nature,
mar the beauty which made me admired too well, by
        changing
my form!' She had hardly ended her prayer when a
        heavy numbness
came over her body; her soft white bosom was ringed
        in a layer
of bark, her hair was turned into foliage, her arms into
550   branches.

The feet that had run so nimbly were sunk into sluggish
    roots;
her head was confined in a treetop; and all that remained
    was her beauty.
  Tree though she was, Apollo still loved her. Caressing the
    trunk
with his hand, he could feel the heart still fluttering under
    the new bark.
Seizing the branches, as though they were limbs, in his arms'
    embrace,   555
he pressed his lips to the wood; but the wood still shrank
    from his kisses.
Phoebus then said to her: 'Since you cannot be mine in
    wedlock,
you must at least be Apollo's tree. It is you who will always
be twined in my hair, on my tuneful lyre and my quiver of
    arrows.
The generals of Rome shall be wreathed with you, when the
    jubilant paean   560
of triumph is raised and the long procession ascends the
    Capitol.
On either side of Augustus' gates your trees shall stand
    sentry,
faithfully guarding the crown of oak-leaves* hanging
    between them.
As I, with my hair that is never cut, am eternally youthful,
so you with your evergreen leaves are for glory and praise
    everlasting.'   565
Apollo the Healer had done. With a wave of her
    new-formed branches
the laurel agreed, and seemed to be nodding her head in the
    treetop.

IO (1)

Théssaly boasts a ravine called Tempe, enclosed on
    each side
by a rock face covered with trees; and down it the river
    Peneüs
pours and rolls on his foaming way from the foot of
570   Mount Pindus.
Powerfully tumbling, the cataract leaps into clouds of a
    wandering,
wispy vapour; the spray besprinkles the trees on the
    clifftops
like showers of rain; and a constant roar is returned
    from the distance.
This is the dwelling, the mansion, the innermost shrine
    of the mighty
575 river-god; here he dispenses justice, enthroned in a cave
carved out of the rock, to all of his waters and nymphs
    of the waters.
This was the gathering point of firstly the local rivers,
uncertain whether they ought to congratulate
    Daphne's father
or offer condolence: Sperchéüs whose banks are
    bordered with poplars,
580 restless Enípeus, ancient Apídanus, gentle Amphrýsus
and Aéas. These were shortly followed by other
    streams,
who wander lazily down to the sea as their currents
    impel them.
Only Ínachus* failed to appear; he was buried away
in the depths of his cavern, adding tears to his waters,
    in pitiful
grief for the loss of his daughter Io. He didn't know
585   whether
she still was alive or had gone to the shades; but as she
    was nowhere

at all to be found, he feared the worst and believed she had
    vanished.
  What happened? As Io was one day coming away from
    her father's
river, Jupiter saw her and cried, 'You beautiful maiden,
worthy of Jove, how happy the husband who makes you his
    own!   590
You should rest in the depths of these shady woods,' and he
    pointed them out,
'while the sun is so high in the sky, at its zenith, and
    burning so fiercely.
If you are afraid to enter the wild beasts' lairs on your own,
you'll be safe with a god to guide you into the forest's
    secret
recesses – no ordinary god, but I who wield in my mighty   595
hand the sceptre of heaven and hurl the volatile lightning.'
She started to flee. 'Don't run from me now!' Already she'd
    left
the pastures of Lerna and woody Lyrcéan country behind
    her,
when Jupiter, throwing a mantle of darkness over the wide
    earth,
halted the flight of the runaway nymph and stealthily raped
    her.   600

Meanwhile Queen Juno directed her gaze on the middle of
    Argos.
The day had been bright and sunny, but now to her great
    surprise
the clouds had suddenly turned it to night. The mist didn't
    come
from the river, she saw; and it couldn't be due to the earth's
    own moisture.
Where was her husband? She looked all round. She was
    quite familiar   605
with Jupiter's amorous tricks, as she'd caught him straying
    so often.

As soon as she failed to find him in heaven, her instant
      reaction was,
'Either I'm wrong, or I'm wronged!' and, gliding down
      through the air,
she alighted on earth and commanded the mists to
      remove themselves.
610 The god, however, anticipating his consort's arrival,
had changed the daughter of Inachus into a
      snow-white heifer.
Even so she was perfectly lovely; Saturnian Juno,
much as it galled her, was forced to admire the
      beautiful creature.
'Whose is it? Whence does it come? What herd?' she
      enquired in pretended
ignorance. 'Born of the earth,' lied Jupiter, hoping to
615   silence
her searching questions. Juno then asked him, 'Please
      will you give her
to me as a present?' What was he to do? To surrender
      his love
would be cruelly painful, but not to give her would
      look suspicious.
Conscience would argue for her surrender; his love was
      against it.
Love indeed would have won the battle; but if he
      refused
the paltry gift of a cow to the wife who was also his
620   sister,
it could have appeared that the creature was not
      exactly a heifer.
   Juno's rival was now in her power, but her fears
      continued
to haunt her. She still suspected Jove and his
      treacherous wiles,
until she put Argus, the son of Aréstor, in charge of Io.
625 Argus' head had a hundred eyes, which rested in relays,
two at a time, while the others kept watch and
      remained on duty.

Whichever way he was standing, his eyes were always on Io;
even behind his back, she could never escape from his
        watchful
stare. She could graze in the daytime, but after sundown
        he'd pen her   630
inside an enclosure and tie her innocent neck with a halter.
Her food was tree leaves and bitter herbs; her bedding was
        earth,
not always too grassy; her water came from the muddy
        streams.
When Io wanted to supplicate Argus with outstretched
        arms,   635
no arms were there to outstretch. When she opened her
        mouth to complain,
her own voice startled her; all that emerged was a hideous
        lowing.
She came to the banks where so often she'd played, the
        banks of her father
Inachus. Here when she looked in the water and saw her
        reflected
head with its strange new horns, she recoiled from herself in
        a panic.   640
The naiads had no idea who she was, and even Inachus
failed to know her; but still she followed her father and
        sisters
quickly along, and allowed them to pat her back and
        admire her.
Inachus plucked some grass and tenderly held it out to her.   645
Licking and kissing her father's hands, she couldn't help
        weeping.
If only words could have followed her tears, she'd have
        begged him for help;
she'd have told him her name and described her plight. Two
        letters* were all
that could serve for words, two letters traced by a hoof in
        the dust,
which revealed her name and the sorry tale of her
        transformation.   650

'Woe and alas!' old Inachus cried, as he tenderly fondled
the horns and clung to the snowy neck of the moaning
          heifer.
'Woe and alas!' he repeated. 'Are you the daughter I
          searched for
over the whole wide world? My sorrow was not so heavy
when I was unable to find you. You're silent and cannot
655   reply
to my questions. You only respond with a deep, deep
          sigh from your heart.
When I speak to you, all you can offer me back is a
          melancholy low.
Blind to the future, I busied myself with plans for your
          wedding,
in hope to gain a new son and soon to become a
          grandfather.
Now your husband and children must come from a
          herd of cattle.
660 If only death could allow me to end this terrible
          sorrow!
Sadly I have to remain a god and the gates of Hades
are barred to me. Grief must be my companion for ever
          and ever.'
So the father lamented, but star-eyed Argus discreetly
eased him aside and led the daughter away to more
665   distant
pastures. There he transferred himself to the heights of
          a mountain
summit, from where he could sit and keep watch in
          every direction.

The king of the gods could no longer endure his
          beloved Io's
pain and distress. He summoned his son, whom Maia
          the radiant
Pleiad had borne, and gave him his orders to murder
670   Argus.
Mercury only paused to don his winged sandals, cover

his head, and seize the sleep-giving wand which empowers
    his hand.
Thus attired, the offspring of Jupiter leapt from his father's
    citadel
down to the earth; once there he discarded his
    wide-brimmed hat,
took off his sandals and simply clung to his snake-twined
    staff,   675
which he used in herdsman's fashion to drive the goats he
    had rustled
along his way through the scrubland, playing the while on
    his reed pipe.
Juno's guard was entranced by the unfamiliar music.
'You there, whoever you are,' said Argus, 'do come over
and sit with me here on this rock. You'll find no richer
    abundance   680
of grass for your goats, and you see there's plenty of shade
    for a herdsman.'
Mercury then sat down and filled the lingering hours
with desultory chat. He attempted to conquer those
    watchful eyes
with the drone of his panpipes; but Argus fought to resist
    sleep's soft   685
seduction. While some of his hundred eyes were allowed to
    surrender,
others were kept awake. The pipe had been newly invented,
so Argus drowsily asked his companion about its invention.

INTERLUDE: PAN AND SYRINX

The god then told him a tale: 'In the cold Arcadian
    mountains,
among the Nonácrian wood-nymphs, there lived a
690   remarkable naiad
(Syrinx her sisters called her), whom all admired for her
    beauty.

More than once she'd eluded pursuit by lascivious
        satyrs
and all the various gods who dwell in the shadowy
        forests
and fertile fields. She modelled herself on the goddess
        Diana
in daily life and by staying chaste. When she dressed as a
695   huntress,
you might have been taken in and supposed she was
        Leto's daughter,
but for her bow, which was made of horn, where
        Diana's is gold.
Despite it, she passed for Diana. One day she was
        spotted returning
from Mount Lycaeus by Pan. Bedecked with a garland
        of sharp
pine needles, he spoke to her, saying –' but Mercury
700   broke off there,
and didn't describe how the nymph rejected the god's
        advances
and fled through the fields, until she arrived at the river
        Ladon
peacefully flowing between its sandy banks. Since the
        waters
were barring her way, she called on the nymphs of the
        stream to transform her.
So just at the moment when Pan believed that his
705   Syrinx was caught,
instead of a fair nymph's body, he found himself
        clutching some marsh reeds.
But while he was sighing in disappointment, the
        movement of air
in the rustling reeds awakened a thin, low, plaintive
        sound.
Enthralled by the strange new music and sweetness of
        tone, Pan exclaimed,
'This sylvan pipe will enable us always to talk
710   together!'

And so, when he'd bound some reeds of unequal length with
    a coating
of wax, a syrinx – the name of his loved one – stayed in his
    hands.

IO (2)

That was the story the god of Cyllene was going to tell,
when he saw that his enemy's drowsy eyes had all
    succumbed
and were shrouded in sleep. At once he stopped talking and
    stroked the sentry's   715
drooping lids with his magic wand to make sure he was out.
Then he rapidly struck with his sickle-shaped sword at his
    nodding victim
just where the head comes close to the neck, and hurled him
    bleeding
down from the rock to bespatter the cliff in a shower of
    gore.
Argus was finished. The light that had glittered in all those
    stars   720
was extinguished; a hundred eyes were eclipsed in a single
    darkness.
   Juno extracted those eyes and gave them a setting like
    sparkling
jewels in the feathers displayed on the tail of the peacock,
    her own bird.
Blazing with anger, she wasted no time in venting her
    fury
by sending a horrible demon to frighten the eyes of Io   725
by day, and her mind at night. A goading terror was
    planted
deep in her heart, which hounded her over the world in
    flight.
At the end of the road was the Nile, where the tale of her
    toils was concluded.

As soon as she reached it, she sank to her knees by the
      bank of the river,
looked up with her neck thrown back and, lacking the
730   arms to lift up
in prayer, uplifted her face to the stars. The groans that
      she uttered,
the tears that she shed and her piteous lowings, seemed
      to be challenging
Jupiter, pleading with him to grant her an end to her
      sufferings.
Jupiter then drew Juno gently into his arms
and asked her to punish Io no more: 'You may banish
735   your fears
for the future,' he said; 'she will never provide you
      with cause for vexation
again,' and he called on the Stygian marshes to witness
      his promise.
Once the goddess had been placated, Io recovered
her human face and her body, the horns shrank down,
740   the cow eyes narrowed,
the gaping mouth grew smaller, the shoulders and
      hands came back,
the hooves dissolved and faded away into five smooth
      toenails.
All that survived of the snow-white cow was its
      glowing beauty.
Happy once more to be standing on two feet only, the
      fair nymph
rose from the ground; but frightened to speak, in case
745   she still lowed
like a heifer, she nervously tried a few words in her
      long-lost language.
Attended by linen-clad priests, she is worshipped today
      as a goddess.*

PHAËTHON (1)

Finally, Io gave birth to a son, called Épaphus, thought
to be sprung from mighty Jupiter's seed; and throughout the
    cities
his temple is linked with his mother's. One of his peers and
    rivals   750
was Pháëthon, child of the sun god. On one occasion,
    Epaphus
took exception to Phaëthon's boastful talking, his failure
to show him respect and his arrogant pride in his father,
    Phoebus.
'Ridiculous booby,' he sneered, 'to believe every word that
    your mother
tells you. The picture you have of your father is false and
    inflated!'
Phaëthon's face grew red, but shame put a brake on his
    anger;   755
he went and reported Epaphus' gibes to his mother,
    Clýmene.
'To distress you further, dear mother,' he added, 'I,
    Phaëthon, known
as so open and savage-tempered, said nothing. I'm deeply
    ashamed
that these scandalous taunts should be thrown at our heads
    and I couldn't refute them.
Mother, if I am truly the son of a god, please give me   760
a sign of my glorious birth and establish my title in heaven!'
After he'd spoken, he threw his arms round his mother's
    neck,
imploring her, if she valued the life of himself and her
    husband
Mérops, and if she hoped that his sisters would happily
    marry,
to offer him positive proof that his father was really the sun
    god.

We cannot be sure whether Phaëthon's prayers or
765   Clymene's anger
at what was imputed against herself affected her more;
but she raised both arms to the sky and her eyes to the
              sun's bright beams,
to protest: 'By yonder resplendent orb with his
              glistening rays,
who hears and surveys us all, my child, I swear to you
              now
that the sun you gaze on in wonder, the sun which
770   governs the whole world,
is truly your father. If I speak false, may he ever refuse
              me
his light, and may this day be the last when my eyes
              shall behold him!
Small effort is needed to find your way to your father's
              hearth.
The domain from where he arises begins where our
              own land ends.
If your spirit impels you,* be off on your way and
775   question the sun god
himself!' As soon as his mother had finished speaking,
              Phaëthon
darted out in excitement. The sky was already his own!
Crossing his native Ethiopia and India, nearing
the land of the sun, he hastened east to discover his
              father.

BOOK 2

The story of *Phaëthon* (1–400) is continued in the grand opening description of the Sun's palace, which sets the tone for the tale of the young man's request to drive his father's chariot for a day, followed by its disastrous consequences. This is the longest single story in the whole poem, a mini-epic in its own right, with much to be admired for its dramatic quality and descriptive detail. The account of the burning earth balances the flood narrative in Book 1. We may also enjoy Ovid's descriptions of the various constellations and signs of the zodiac, together with his resonant 'catalogues' of mountains, springs and rivers. The actual metamorphosis, when it comes, is not of Phaëthon himself but of his sisters the Heliades, who change into poplars dropping amber tears, and of his friend Cycnus, who is transformed into a swan – the first of many metamorphoses into birds. Here we can note a marked change of tone which gradually leads Ovid's audience on to the more frivolous character of the stories in the rest of the book. The concluding section in which the sun god threatens to go on strike is undoubtedly comic.

We return to Jupiter inspecting the earth after the fire caused by Phaëthon. This leads the god into another amorous adventure with *Callisto* (401–530), and to his impersonating the virgin goddess Diana. Juno's inevitable jealousy results in the nymph's metamorphosis into a bear; but Callisto and her son Arcas, much to the goddess's indignation, are later transformed into a constellation.

An artificial transition leads to a group of stories about tell-tales who all get their come-uppance in various ways. In *The Raven and the Crow* (531–632) we have two interwoven stories, with a third about the Daughters of Cecrops inserted inside the second. The thread of the gods' amours continues in Apollo's love for Coronis and in the rape by Neptune of the Phocian princess who was changed by Minerva to the crow.

Less amusingly, Chiron the Centaur's daughter, *Ocyrhoë* (633–75), apparently incurs the wrath of the gods in her prophetic revelations about the infant Aesculapius and is metamorphosed into a mare. In lighter vein again, *Battus* (676–707) is an old self-serving chatterer who reports Mercury to the god himself in disguise and is punished by transformation to the 'informing' rock which supplies the touchstone.

Mercury is the link with the next story, in which we re-encounter the daughters of Cecrops who briefly featured earlier on (552–61). To gain the love of Herse, Mercury tries to engage the help of her avaricious sister *Aglauros* (708–832). The goddess Minerva punishes Aglauros' greed by infecting her with the demon Envy, whose sombre description is another great passage to be looked out for and enjoyed. The outcome is another metamorphosis into a rock.

We return to Jupiter on a more light-hearted note for the concluding tale of his transformation to a bull for the purpose of abducting the Tyrian princess *Europa* (833–75). The book ends in a memorably erotic sequence, with an entrancing image of the frightened girl in the last three lines.

PHAËTHON (2)

Picture the Sun's royal seat, an imposing building with
    towering
columns, resplendent in glittering gold and blazing bronze;
its pediment proudly surmounted by figures in burnished
    ivory;
the double doors at the entrance a sheen of shimmering
    silver.
More wonderful yet is the workmanship which Vulcan
    displayed   5
on the portals' reliefs: the ocean encircling the central earth
on a detailed map of the world, with the Sun's great canopy
    over it.
There in the waves are the sea-gods:* Triton holding his
    conch-horn,
Próteus who constantly changes his shape, and the giant
    Aegaéon,
gripping the monstrous backs of the whales with his
    hundred arms;   10
Doris along with her daughters, some of them shown to be
    swimming,
while others are resting upon the rocks and drying their
    green hair
or riding along on a fish. The nymphs have different
    features,
but show the family likeness that might be expected in
    sisters.
Embossed on earth are the men in their cities and beasts in
    their forests;   15
the water-nymphs next to their streams and the other rural
    divinities.
Crowning these pictures the heavens, brightly portrayed,
    with the signs
of the zodiac, six on the right-hand door and six on the left.
  Pháëthon quickly mounted the steep approach to the
    palace,

and entered the house of the god whom he wished to be
20   sure was his father.
Marching boldly towards the face of his sire, he halted
a little way off, as it hurt his eyes to come any closer.
Garbed in a robe of royal purple, radiant Phoebus*
was sitting there on a throne which was glowing with
        brilliant emeralds.
Standing close on his right and his left were the Spirits
25   of Day,
of Month and of Year, the Centuries and Hours at their
        equal intervals.
Also in waiting were youthful Spring with her wreath of
        flowers,
Summer naked but for her garland of ripening corn
        ears,
Autumn stained with the juice of trodden clusters of
        grapes,
And icy Winter, whose aged locks were hoary and
30   tangled.
   Then from his place in the centre the Sun, with his
        all-seeing eyes,
caught sight of the young man trembling in awe of his
        strange surroundings.
'Why have you come?' he enquired. 'And what do you
        seek in this stronghold,
Phaëthon, offspring of mine, whom his father could
        never disown?'
'O Phoebus, my father, light that illumines the infinite
35   universe,'
answered the youth, 'if you will allow me to call you my
        father,
if Clýmene is not trying to cloak some guilty secret,
grant me a sign, my father, whereby all men must
        believe
that I am truly your son, and banish this doubt from my
        own mind.'
Then, in response, his father removed the circlet of
40   sparkling

rays which adorned his head, commanded the youth to come
        nearer,
and folded him close in his arms. 'You are truly mine,' he
        assured him.
'Denial would do you injustice, and Clymene did not deceive
        you.
Away with your doubts! Now ask me whatever favour you
        will,
and I shall bestow it. To witness my promise, I call on the
        Stygian   45
marsh which the gods must swear by, though I have never
        set eyes on it.'
Phaëthon answered at once. He asked for his father's
        chariot,
with leave to control the wing-footed horses, for just one
        day.
   His father at once regretted his oath. Repeatedly shaking
his lustrous head, he exclaimed: 'Your request has proved
        my promise   50
too rash. How I wish I could break it! Dear son, I confess to
        you freely,
this is the only wish I could ever be moved to refuse you.
Still, I can argue against it. Believe me, you're looking for
        danger!
The favour you ask is great, my Phaëthon, far too great
for the strength that you have. You are only a boy, too
        young to attempt it.   55
Your destiny's mortal; your wishes transcend your mortal
        limits.
Indeed your ignorant heart is pursuing what even
        immortals
can never attain. We all may flatter ourselves as we will,
yet none save I has the strength to stand in the fiery chariot
and hold his footing. Even the ruler of vast Olympus,   60
who hurls the deadly thunderbolts forth from his awesome
        hand,
shall never control this car; and what have we greater than
        Jove?

The start of the journey is steep; though the horses are
     fresh in the morning,
the climb is a mighty haul. The highest stretch is
     mid-heaven,
65 where even I am often afraid to look down on the lands
and the sea below, and my heart is aflutter with
     quivering terror.
The end is a downward path and calls for impeccable
     steering;
then even Tethys, the goddess who welcomes me into
     the waves
as I set, can tremble with fear that my fall will be
     over-precipitous.
Recognize too that the sky spins round in a constant
70   vortex,
drawing the stars on high as they whirl in their swift
     revolutions.
My impetus thrusts against it, unswayed by the forces
     which master
all else, and in driving my steeds I oppose the sphere's
     swift motion.
Suppose that I lend you my car, what then? Can you
     really encounter
the poles without being swept away by their rapid
75   rotation?
Perhaps you imagine you'll find the groves of the gods
     up there,
with their beautiful cities and sanctuaries richly laden
     with offerings.
No! Your path is beset with beasts* that are lying in
     ambush.
Even supposing you hold your course and are not
     diverted,
your journey will take you straight to the horns of the
80   charging Bull,
straight to the centaur Archer and straight to the jaws of
     the raging

Lion; then on to the Scorpion, whose menacing arms are
      bent
in a long wide sweep, and the Crab with his claws of a
      smaller range.
Moreover, it's far from easy to govern those spirited horses,
strong with the fire in their breasts which they breathe from
      their mouths and nostrils,   85
and little inclined to obey even my firm hands when their
      mettle
is hotly aroused and their necks are resisting the pull of the
      reins.
Oh listen, my son! Don't force me to make you a gift that
      can only
prove fatal. Be warned and amend your prayer before it's
      too late.
I can understand that you need some indisputable proof   90
that my own blood runs in your veins. So here you have it:
      my fatherly
fears and misgivings prove me to be your father. Look, boy,
look at my face. How I wish your eyes were able to pierce
deep down to my heart and catch a glimpse of your father's
      anxiety.
Finally, look all round you: survey whatever the wealthy   95
cosmos contains, and make your choice of the bountiful
      riches
of earth and sea and sky. Be sure I'll refuse you nothing.
This one thing only I beg you not to demand. It's a
      sentence,
not honour you're asking for; punishment, Phaëthon, never
      a present.
Why are your fingers caressing my neck, you ignorant boy? 100
Never fear, I have sworn by the Stygian marsh, and I'll
      surely give you
whatever you choose to ask for. But choose more wisely, I
      beg you!'
   His warnings were finished, but Phaëthon still resisted the
      sun god's

pleas and pressed his request in his burning desire for the
          chariot.
And so, delaying as long as he could, his father
105   conducted
the young man down to the lofty conveyance which
          Vulcan had made him.
The axle and pole were constructed of gold, and
          golden too
was the rim encircling the wheels, which were fitted
          with spokes of silver.
Chrysolites, jewels arranged in a pattern along the
          yoke,
reflected their brilliant splendour on shining Phoebus
110   himself.
And while self-confident Phaëthon studied the car in
          amazement
at such fine workmanship, Dawn was awake to open
          her purple
gates in the glimmering east and bathe her forecourt in
          roseate
glory; the stars were routed, and Lucifer brought up
          the rear,
as last of all he abandoned his watch in the brightening
115   sky.
     When Titan saw that the morning star was inclining
          earthward,
the sky growing pink and the horns of the waning
          moon disappearing,
he gave the command to the fleet-footed Hours to
          harness his steeds.
The goddesses quickly performed his bidding. Forth
          from the lofty
stables they led the fire-breathing stallions, fully
120   refreshed
with ambrosia juice, and carefully fastened the jingling
          bridles.
Next the father anointed the face of his son with a holy

balsam, to offer protection against the scorching flames,
and placed his radiant crown on the young man's head.
            Then heaving
sighs from his troubled heart in gloomy foreboding, he
            said: 125
'If you are still able to take one piece of advice from your
            father,
spare the goad, my son, and put more strength in the reins.
My horses will speed unencouraged; the task is to curb their
            impatience.
Don't follow a route directly across the sky's five zones:
the path is cut at a slanting angle and runs in a wide arc,   130
well inside the three middle zones and carefully avoiding
the southern pole and the zone to the north with its biting
            winds.
You must keep to that road – the ruts from my wheels will
            be clearly visible;
then, to give earth and sky an equal share of your warmth,
don't drive the chariot down or scale the top of the ether.   135
Venture to climb too high, and you'll burn the ceiling of
            heaven,
the earth if you sink too low; for safety remain in the
            middle.
Swerving too far to the right, you'll be caught in the coils of
            the Serpent;
too far to the left, you'll collide with the Altar* near the
            horizon.
Hold to a course in between. The rest I resign to Fortune;   140
I pray her to help and take care of you better than you take
            care
of yourself. As I speak, the dewy night has reached its
            appointed
goal on the shores of the west. The time for delaying is over.
The summons has come, for the darkness has fled and
            Auróra is glowing.
Now grasp the reins in your hands – or if your ambitious
            purpose   145
can yet be altered, take my advice and not my chariot.

Allow me to give my light to the earth, and watch me in
        safety
While still you can, while still you are standing on solid
        earth,
Before you have blindly mounted the car you so foolishly
        asked for.'

Phaëthon nimbly jumped into place on the light-framed
150   chariot.
Standing aloft, he excitedly seized the featherweight
        reins
and shouted his thanks from the car to his worried and
        anxious father.
Meanwhile the sun god's team of winged horses –
        Fiery, Dawnsteed,
Scorcher and Blaze – were impatiently filling the air
        with their whinnies,
snorting out flames and kicking the bolted gates with
155   their hooves.
As soon as Tethys,* blind to the fate which awaited
        her grandson,
had shot the bolts back and the limitless sky was open
        before them,
at once they were off; and galloping forward into the
        air,
they cut through the mists which stood in their way;
        then rose on their wings
and quickly outdistanced the winds which had sprung
160   up too in the east.
But the load that they carried was light, not one that
        the Sun's strong horses
could easily feel, and the yoke seemed far less heavy
        than usual.
As ships with inadequate ballast will toss and roll on
        the billows,
swept along through the ocean, too light to be firmly
        stable,

so Phoebus' chariot, robbed of its normal weight, leapt
    high   165
in the air, tossed up from below, as though it were empty.
  As soon as they sensed this, the four-horse team ran wild,
    and leaving
the well-worn track, they continued galloping helter-
    skelter.
Phaëthon panicked. He lacked both the skill to manage the
    reins
entrusted to him and all idea of the line of his route;
and if he had known it, the horses would still have been out
    of control.   170
It was then that the stars of the Northern Plough, which are
    known as the Oxen,
lost their chill in the rays and, growing too hot, for the first
    time
vainly attempted to bathe in the sea which had always been
    barred to them.*
Likewise the Serpent, whose home is close to the polar
    icecaps,
sluggishly cold before and dangerous to none, for the first
    time
started to swelter and sweat and seethed with a new-found
    fury.   175
Even Boötes who guards the Bear is said to have fled
in confusion, slow though he was and heavily tied to his
    wain.
  But when the unhappy Phaëthon looked from the top of
    the firmament
down on the earth and saw it lying so far, far deep beneath
    him,
terror suddenly struck him: his face turned pale and his
    knees shook;   180
his vision grew darkly blurred in the dazzling, glaring
    brightness.
He dearly wished that he'd never set hands on his father's
    steeds;

he regretted the quest for his birthright and winning the
          favour he'd asked for.
Longing now to be known as Merops' son, he was swept
along like a ship at the north wind's mercy, whose pilot
185   abandons
the tiller as useless and trusts the craft to the gods and
          to prayers.
But what could he do? Long miles of sky lay behind
          him, more
were ahead. He measured his route both ways, as he
          first looked forward
out to the west, which fate never meant him to reach,
          and then
looked back to the east. Bewildered and dazed, he
190   could neither let go
of the reins nor cling on; and he couldn't remember the
          names of the horses.
To add to his terror, dispersed all over the patterned
          sky,
he spied some phenomenal shapes in the likeness of
          huge wild beasts.
Right there, a creature was curving its pincers out into
195   two great
arcs – the Scorpion, with menacing tail and its claws
          flexed round
each way to encompass the space of two whole signs*
          of the zodiac.
When youthful Phaëthon sighted it, soaked in a sweat
          of black venom,
curving its spear-point tail towards him and
          threatening to sting,
he was frozen with fear and, completely unnerved, let
200   go of the reins.
     When the steeds were aware of the reins lying
          loosely over their backs,
they broke from their course and, with no one to check
          them, they wildly bolted

through unknown regions of air, wherever their instinct led
    them.
They galloped at random, charging the stars in their fixed
    positions
high in the heavenly vault, and forcing the chariot along   205
through the trackless sky, now scaling the topmost heights,
    now hurtling
down in a headlong dive through space more close to the
    earth.
The moon was astonished to see her brother's horses
    careering
below her own; and smoke rose up from the smouldering
    clouds.

The earth now burst into flames on all of the hills and the
    mountains,   210
split into huge wide cracks, and dried as it lost its moisture.
The corn turned white and the trees were charred into
    leafless skeletons;
parched grain offered the perfect fuel for self-ruination.
These losses were trifling. Destruction fell upon great
    walled cities;
mighty nations with all their peoples the conflagration   215
turned into ashes. Fire swept over the forest-clad
    mountains:
Athos, Cilícian Taurus, Tmolus and Oeta were blazing;
Ida, once the home of innumerable springs, now waterless;
Hélicon, haunt of the Muses, and Haemus before it was
    known
to Órpheus; Etna ablaze to the heavens, its flames now
    doubled;   220
twin-summited Mount Parnássus with Eryx, Cynthus and
    Othrys;
Rhódope, forced at last to be free of its snows; then Mimas,
Díndyma, Mýcale, even the haven of worship, Cithaéron;
Scythia's frosts were of no avail; fire blazed on the
    Caúcasus,

225 Ossa with Pindus, and Mount Olympus, taller than both;
the Alps which soar to the sky and the cloud-capped
        Ápennine range.
    Phaëthon now looked down on a world in flames;
        not a region
remained unscorched. He couldn't endure the force of
        the heat;
the blasts of the air which he breathed seemed to come
        from the depths of a seething
230 furnace; his feet could feel his chariot growing red-hot.
The ashes and showers of flying sparks were more than
        the boy
was able to stand, while all around he was shrouded in
        hot smoke.
Wrapped in the pitchy darkness, he didn't know where
        he was going
nor where he might be, as the winged steeds swept him
        along at their mercy.
    It was then, as mortals believe, that the Ethiopian
235   peoples
acquired dark skins as their blood was drawn to the
        body's surface;
Libya then was turned to a desert when all of her
        moisture
was lost in the heat. And then the nymphs, with their
        hair spread loose,
wept over their fountains and pools. Boeótia lamented
        for Dirce,
Argos Amýmone, Éphyre sighed for the springs of
240   Piréne.
Even the waters whose rivers flow in commodious
        channels
suffered some evil effects: steam rose from the waves of
        the Tánais,
old Penéüs, Caïcus in Mýsia, swift Isménus,
Arcádia's broad Erymánthus, the yellow Lycórmas and
        Xanthus,

fated to burn again when it fought with Achílles;* the
    playfully   245
winding Maeánder, Mygdónian Melas and Spartan
    Eurótas.
Thc Babylonian Euphrátes was all aflame; likewise
Oróntes, rapid Thermódon, Ganges, Phasis and Hister.
The coursing Alphéüs boiled; Sperchéüs' banks were on
    fire;   250
and the gold in the sands of the Tagus was melted and
    flowed like its waters.
The Lydian swans, whose singing has made the banks of
    Caÿster
famous, succumbed to the sweltering heat as they floated
    mid-river.
Stricken with terror, the Nile took flight to the ends of the
    earth,
and covered its head where it still lies hidden;* its
    seven-mouthed delta   255
was emptied of water and filled with dust, seven riverless
    valleys.
A similar fate dried up the Thracian Hebrus and Strymon;
the western rivers as well, the Rhine and the Rhone and the
    Padus;
lastly the Tiber,* destined one day to be lord of the world.
   The whole of the carth-face split and the light penetrated
    the cracks   260
to the underworld, filling the King of the Shades and his
    consort with terror.
The sea contracted; a broad expanse of dry sand replaced
what had lately been ocean. Mountains hidden below the
    surface
emerged from the deep to increase the score of the scattered
    Cýclades.
Fish dived down to the seabed and dolphins dared no
    longer   265
to arch their bodies and jump the billows into the breezes.
Seals were lying with upturned bellies on top of the water,

lifelessly floating. They say that even Nereus and Doris
along with their daughters took refuge in caves which
      were far from cool;
and a grim-faced Neptune thrice attempted to heave his
270   shoulders
above the water, but could not endure the scorching
      air.
     The great Earth Mother, however, still girdled round
      by the ocean,
could sense its waters, although her springs were
      thinned to a trickle
and hidden away in the dark of her own bowels.
      Parched as she was,
she succeeded in raising her head and neck from the
275   smothering ashes,
and shielded her brow from the heat with her hand.
      With a violent tremor
she shook the world in a mighty quake, then subsided
      a little,
below the height of her normal level, and uttered in
      cracked tones:
'King of the Gods, if this is your wish and I have
      deserved it,
280 why is your lightning idle? If I must perish by fire,
let the fire be yours! The blow would be lighter if you
      had dealt it.
I hardly can open my lips to voice these very
      petitions –'
the smoke was choking her. 'Look at my singed hair,
      look at the ashes
coating my eyes and face! Is this the respect that you
      show me?
Is this the reward for the crops that I yield and the
285   service I render,
bearing the wounds of the plough and harrow, harshly
      exploited
and worked from one year's end to the next, supplying
      the grazing

cattle with wholesome verdure, the grain to nourish the
    human
race, and frankincense for you gods to receive on your
    altars?
Let's say that I have deserved my destruction; but what has
    your brother,   290
what have the waves done wrong? Why have the waters
    allotted
to Neptune by fate gone down and are farther away from
    the sky?
But if your brother's favours and mine to you count for
    nothing,
at least you can pity your own domain. Look round at the
    two poles:
smoke is pouring from each. If they suffer damage from
    fire,   295
the halls of the gods will collapse. See, Atlas himself is in
    trouble:
his shoulders can barely sustain the weight of the white-hot
    vault.
If the seas and the lands must perish and even the realms of
    the sky,
we are back to confusion and primal chaos. I beg you to
    rescue
whatever is left from the flames. Take thought for the good
    of the universe!'   300
    Earth had ended her speech; she couldn't endure the
    smoke
and the heat any longer or say any more. She lowered her
    head
back into herself and sank to the caves adjoining the
    underworld.
Now the Father omnipotent called on the gods to witness,
especially Phoebus who'd lent his chariot: failing his own
    help,   305
all of the world would be doomed, he said. Then he made
    for the heights
from where he normally veils the earth in a mantle of cloud

and also awakens the thunder and launches his lightning
      bolts.
But now the clouds that he needed to cover the whole
      wide earth
and the rain to pour from the sky were lacking. So what
310   was the answer?
A thunderclap! Next a bolt was carefully poised by his
      right ear.
Jupiter hurled it at Phaëthon, flinging both driver from
      chariot
and life from body at once. He quenched one fire with
      another.
The horses stampeded. Rearing up in different
      directions,
they slipped the yoke from their necks and tore the
315   reins as they broke loose.
Here the bridle was tossed, and there the pole with the
      ripped-off
axle, there the spokes of the shattered wheels and,
      scattered
all over the ether, the fragments of metal which once
      were a chariot.
   Phaëthon's corpse spun down head first, with the fire
      of the thunderbolt
scorching his flame-red hair. He fell through the sky in
320   a long trail,
blazing away like a comet which sometimes appears in
      a clear sky,
never to land upon earth, but looking as if it is falling.
Far from his home, in a distant part of the world, the
      Erídanus,
longest of rivers, received him and washed the smoke
      from his charred face.
The Hespérian naiads found his body, perceptibly
325   showing
the three-forked lightning's effects, and buried it there
      in a tomb.

They also inscribed the stone of his grave with the following
    epitaph:
      HERE LIES PHAËTHON, CHARIOTEER OF
      HIS FATHER'S HORSES.
      THEY BOLTED AND BROUGHT HIM LOW;
      BUT HIGH WERE HIS SPIRIT AND DARING.

What of his father? Wretchedly stricken and sick with grief,
he had covered his face with his robe. If we can believe what
    is said,   330
the Sun went into eclipse for a day. Such light as was there
was due to the fire – some good, at least, had come out of
    evil.
Clymene, for her part, gave voice to all the laments
which the terrible tragedy called for; and then, distraught in
    her sorrow,
she travelled the whole world, beating her breast and
    tearing her garments.   335
Her quest was firstly for Phaëthon's lifeless limbs, and later
his bones, which she found interred on the bank of an alien
    river.
Prostrating her body to read the name inscribed in the
    marble,
she steeped it in tears and warmed the words with her
    naked breasts.
   Phaëthon's sisters, the Héliades, mourned no less
    bitterly,   340
weeping in useless tribute to death and beating their
    bosoms.
Sprawled all over the grave, by night and by day they loudly
called on their brother, whose ears their wailing could never
    reach.
Four crescent moons had already waxed and come to their
    fullness;
the sisters had done their lamenting as usual (constant
    practice   345
had turned it into a habit), when Phaëthúsa, the eldest,

wishing to sink to the ground, complained that her feet
     had gone cold
and rigid. When lovely Lampátië tried to come and assist
     her,
her limbs were suddenly rooted fast to the place where
     she stood.
A third who was making ready to tear her innocent
350   tresses,
found she was plucking off leaves. Then one of her
     sisters moaned
that her legs were caught in the grip of a tree trunk,
     just as the other
woefully cried that her arms were changing to lengthy
     branches.
To crown their amazement, bark began to enclose their
     loins,
and gradually covered their bellies, their bosoms, their
     shoulders and arms,
till all that appeared was their pleading mouths calling
355   out for their mother.
   What was their mother to do but scurry about back
     and forth,
wherever her impulse led her, and kiss their lips while
     she could?
It wasn't enough. She attempted to strip the bark from
     their bodies
and break the young branches off with her hands, but
     all that emerged
was a trickle of human blood, like drops from an open
360   wound.
'Stop hurting me, mother, please!' whoever was
     bleeding entreated,
'I beg you to stop! It's *me* you are tearing inside the
     tree!
And now, farewell' – on these final words, the bark
     closed over.
However, the tears flowed on; as they dripped from the
     new-formed poplars,

the sun's rays set them to beads of amber, which fell in the
    gleaming   365
river, who sent them on to be worn by the brides of
    Látium.

There to witness this wondrous event was the son of
    Sthénelus,
Cycnus. He was related to Phaëthon through his mother,
but feelings of friendship between them were stronger than
    kinship. Distraught,
he abandoned his kingdom (he ruled the Ligúrian people
    and governed   370
their mighty cities) and chanted his sorrow along the
    Erídanus'
grassy banks and through the woods that the sisters had
    now joined.
Suddenly Cycnus' voice grew thin and his hair was
    disguised
in pure white feathers; his neck stretched out well away
    from his shoulders;
his toes grew red and were bound together in weblike feet;   375
his sides were covered with wings; and his face jutted out in
    a blunt bill.
Cycnus became a new bird, the swan; but he wouldn't
    entrust
himself to the sky and to Jove; he remembered the fire so
    unjustly
launched by the god. His haunts were the ponds and the
    open lakes;
abhorring all fire, he preferred to inhabit its opposite,
    water.   380

Meanwhile Phaëthon's father, unkempt in his mourning,
    had lost
his accustomed splendour, as though there had been a solar
    eclipse.
Detesting the daylight and so himself, he surrendered his
    spirit

to grief. He was angry into the bargain, and therefore
       refused
to work for the world any longer. 'Enough is enough!' he
385   protested.
'I've not been given a break since time began, and I'm
       tired
of endlessly toiling away without some small
       recognition.
Somebody else for a change can drive the chariot
       bringing
the light. If nobody volunteers and all of the gods
admit that the task is beyond them, let Jupiter have a
390   try.
If he takes over those reins of mine, at least he'll be
       forced
to dispense for a while with the lightning which steals
       young sons from their fathers.
Once he has tested the power of my fire-footed horses,
       he'll learn
that failure to keep them under control doesn't merit
       destruction!'
Such were the Sun's complaints till the rest of the gods
       stood round him,
humbly imploring him not to plunge the whole of the
395   world
into darkness. Jupiter also defended his hurling the
       thunderbolt,
dropping a regal threat or two to support the
       entreaties.
So Phoebus rounded his horses up, still out of their
       minds
and quaking with terror; then once they were
       harnessed, he vented his grief
by applying the goad and the lash with all of the rage
       that was boiling
inside him, cursing and blaming *them* for his son's
400   misfortune.

CALLISTO

Then the Almighty Father conducted a tour of inspection
around the walls of the sky, in case the great fire's impact
had caused them to weaken and crumble down. When he
    saw they were still
as strong and stable as ever, he turned his attention to
    earth
and the works of mankind. Arcadia, where he was born,
    engaged   405
his particular care. He revived the fountains and rivers
    which still
were reluctant to flow, put grass on the soil and leaves on
    the trees,
and ordered the blackened forests to burst once more into
    green.
As he busily came and went, an Arcadian virgin suddenly
caught his fancy and fired his heart with a deep-felt
    passion.   410
Callisto was not in the habit of spinning wool at the
    distaff
or stylishly dressing her hair; her garment was clasped by a
    simple
brooch, while a plain white band kept her loose-flowing
    tresses in order.
Armed with her smooth-polished javelin or bow, she served
    as a soldier
in Phoebe's troop; of the maidens who hunted on
    Maénalus' slopes   415
Diana cherished her best – but no one's favour is lasting.
  The sun had climbed to the height of the sky; it was soon
    after midday.
Callisto entered a forest whose trees no axe had deflowered,
and here she removed the quiver she wore on her shoulder
    and loosened
the string of her supple bow; then laid herself down on the
    greensward,   420

resting her pure white neck on her painted quiver for
        pillow.
When Jupiter spied her lying exhausted and unprotected,
he reckoned: 'My wife will never discover this tiny
        betrayal;
or else, if she does, oh yes, the joy will make up for the
        scolding!'
At once he assumed the features and dress of the goddess
425   Diana,
and said to the damsel, 'Young maiden, I see you are
        one of my dear
companions. Where on the slopes have you hunted
        today?' The young maiden
raised herself up from the grass and replied, 'Hail,
        goddess! I judge you
greater than Jove, though he hear it himself.' Jove
        chuckled to hear it,
delighted she judged him greater than Jove, and gave
430   her a passionate
kiss on the lips, not the kiss that a virgin goddess
        would give.
As she started to detail where in the forest she'd
        hunted, he gripped her
tight in his arms, and his subsequent felony gave him
        away.
Callisto herself, as far as a feeble woman was able
(if only Juno had seen it, she would have been more
435   understanding),
Callisto fought back; but indeed what man could a girl
        be a match for,
let alone Jupiter? He, in the flush of his victory, made
        for
the sky; while she could only detest the forests and
        woodlands
which knew her secret. Returning, she almost forgot to
        recover
her quiver and arrows and even the bow she had hung
440   on a tree.

    And now, the real Diana arrived with her train of
        attendants
along Mount Maenalus, flushed with pride in her hunting
        triumphs.
Sighting Callisto, she called to the girl, who responded by
        running
away, as she still was afraid that it might be Jupiter
        there
in the guise of Diana. But seeing her nymphs processing
        beside her,   445
she realized it wasn't a trick and attached herself to the
        others.
How difficult not to betray our guilt in our facial
        expression!
Her eyes were fixed on the ground, and she wouldn't
        resume her position
close to the side of the goddess in front of the whole
        procession.
Her silence and blushes were telling signs that she'd lost
        her virtue.   450
Diana, but for being a virgin, could well have detected
her guilt by a thousand tokens. The nymphs are said to have
        noticed.
    Eight moons had waned and the horns of the ninth had
        begun to appear
when, weary with hunting and overcome by the heat of her
        brother,*
the goddess entered the cool of a wood, where a babbling
        brook   455
was smoothly flowing along its familiar sandy bed.
'What a charming spot!' she exclaimed, as she dipped her
        toe in the water.
'The temperature's perfect, and nobody's here to spy on us
        bathing.
Let's take off our clothes and refresh ourselves with a nice,
        cool swim.'
Callisto's face turned crimson; while everyone else
        undressed,   460

she tried to wait; and while she dithered, they stripped
     off her tunic.
When this was removed, her naked body exposed her
     shame.
In utter confusion she moved her hands to cover her
     belly.
'Be gone!' cried the goddess. 'This sacred spring must not
     be polluted!'
And so her favourite was sternly commanded to leave her
465   presence.
    The mighty Thunderer's lady had long been aware
     of her husband's
liaison, but waited to wreak her revenge till a suitable
     moment.
That moment had now arrived: to aggravate Juno's
     resentment,
Jupiter's mistress had given birth to a boy called Arcas.
Swooping down on Callisto with eyes as mean as her
470   purpose,
'So this was the crowning insult, adulterous whore,'
     she exclaimed –
'becoming pregnant! You had to make your
     wickedness public
and testify to my Jove's disgrace by having a baby.
I'll make you pay, by destroying those lovely looks
     which allow you
to fancy yourself and attract my husband, you
475   shameless hussy!'
Saying these words, she grabbed Callisto's hair from
     the front
and tugged her down to the ground. As the girl
     stretched out her arms
in a plea for mercy, they started to grow black,
     bristling hairs;
her hands were turned into animal's feet, as they bent
     and extended
in long hooked claws; and the beautiful lips which Jove
480   had so lately

admired were broadened out and transformed to the ugliest
    jaws.
To prevent her appealing for pity by prayers or words of
    entreaty,
her powers of speech were wrested away, and her hoarse
    throat only
emitted an angry, menacing, terror-inspiring growl.
But though her body was now a bear's, her emotions were
    human.   485
Continual groaning testified to her inner anguish;
such hands as she had were lifted up to the sky and the
    stars;
if Jove's ingratitude couldn't be spoken, she still could
    feel it.
Poor creature! She never dared to rest in the shady forest,
but often wandered over the well-known fields or in front   490
of her former home. She often was driven over the rocks
by the yelping hounds, and the huntress would flee in terror
    from huntsmen.
Often she hid when she saw wild beasts and forgot her new
    nature;
the she-bear trembled at bears whom she spied on the
    mountains, and even
was horribly scared of the wolves, though one was her
    father, Lycáön.*   495

And now Lycaön's grandson, the baby Arcas, had grown
to a lad of fifteen, with no idea of his mother's plight.
He was hunting beasts and choosing suitable glades to
    entrap them,
ringing the green Erymánthian woods with his close-woven
    nets,
when quite by chance he encountered his mother. On seeing
    the boy,   500
she stopped in her tracks and looked as if she recognized
    Arcas.
He took to his heels. Those staring eyes unceasingly fixed
    on him

filled him with terror, he knew not why. As she lumbered
    closer
towards her son, he'd have pierced her breast with his
    pointed javelin.
But Jove the omnipotent countered the blow, and averted
505   an impious
crime by transporting them both through space. They
    were wafted together
and granted places in heaven as neighbouring
    constellations.*
    Juno was furious, seeing her rival brilliantly
    sparkling
among the stars. Going down to the sea, she visited
    white-haired
510 Tethys and ancient Ocean, deities well respected
by gods as a rule; and when they enquired what had
    prompted her journey,
she answered, 'You ask why I who am queen of the
    gods have descended
here from my heavenly throne? My place in the sky is
    usurped!
I am telling a lie if tonight, when the heavens are
    shrouded in darkness,
you fail to observe new stars, given honour to mortify
515   *me*,
at the top of the sky, in the place where the outermost
    ring
with the smallest circumference orbits the farthest
    point of the axis.*
Will anyone now be reluctant to slight great Juno, or
    tremble
when I am offended? Who else means harm but can
    only do good?
Look at my splendid achievements, the vast extent of
520   my influence!
The woman I changed to a beast is now transformed to
    a goddess;

that's how I punish the guilty and show my tremendous
        power!
Oh, let him restore her human appearance and kindly
        remove
her animal face, as he did in the case of the Argive Io!
Juno could be divorced, Callisto married and duly   525
installed in my bedroom. Lycaön could be Jove's
        father-in-law!
Why doesn't he do it? I turn to you both as my
        foster-parents.*
If you are perturbed by these insults, debar those Bears*
        from your blue waves.
Reject any star which has won its place in the sky as a
        prize
for the lewdest indulgence. Don't let that harlot pollute
        your waters!'   530

THE RAVEN AND THE CROW

The sea-gods nodded assent, and Juno's chariot was ready
to mount the translucent ether, drawn by her
        bright-coloured peacocks,
whose feathers had recently gained their eyes from the
        murdered Argus,
about the time when the chattering raven, who once had
        been white,
was suddenly altered and given his plumage of dusky
        black.   535
To explain, this bird had long in the past been silvered with
        snow-white
feathers as gleaming and pure as the spotless wings of a
        dove,
pure as the watchful geese whose squawking would one day
        rescue
the Roman Capitol,* pure as the swans whose home is the
        rivers.

His tongue was the cause of the raven's downfall; thanks
540   to his talkative
nature, his earlier whiteness of colour was changed to
     its opposite.
  No other girl in the whole of Thessaly rivalled
     Laríssan
Corónis in beauty. Phoebus adored her, at least for the
     time
she was faithful and undetected in other affairs. But
     Apollo's
raven caught her being unchaste, and the merciless
545   tell-tale
thought he should go to his master, to tell him the
     truth of this secret
liaison. En route he was closely pursued by the
     chattering crow,
who flapped up beside him, agog to know all the latest
     news.
When the raven explained what his business was, the
     crow then told him:
'Your journey's in vain. Let my own tongue serve as a
550   serious warning!
See what I was and what I am now, and ask me the
     reason.
You'll find that my loyalty did me no good. Some time
     ago
a child, Erichthónius, born of the soil* and not of a
     mother,
was hidden by Pallas inside an Athenian osier basket.
She handed this on to the three young daughters of
555   two-formed Cecrops,*
with strict instructions not to examine its secret
     contents.
Concealing myself in the rustling leaves of an aged elm
     tree,
I watched to see what they'd do. Two of them, Hérse
     and Pándrosos,

faithfully heeded the goddess' orders; the third, Aglaúros,
calling her sisters cowards, unravelled the knots; and
    inside   560
they discovered a baby boy with a snake extending beside
    him.
I reported this to the goddess. And what was the thanks I
    received
for my help? I was formally stripped of my place as
    Minerva's protector
and ranked underneath the owl!* My punishment serves as
    a warning
to other birds not to chatter too much: it is asking for
    trouble.   565
  'It wasn't as if I had asked to attend on her, or that she
    had not
chosen me freely. Check the facts with Minerva herself.
Despite her anger, she won't deny the truth of the matter.
The story's well known. I started life as a royal princess,
the daughter of famous Coróneus,* king of the Phocians.
    In time,   570
my hand was sought by the wealthiest suitors, I'd have you
    know;
but my beauty proved my undoing. Once I was gently
    strolling
as usual across the sand on the shore, when Neptune the sea
    god
saw me and instantly glowed with a burning passion. So
    after
he'd wasted time in useless entreaties and flattering
    speeches,   575
he started to chase me with violent intent. I fled and
    abandoned
the firm seashore but shortly collapsed in the softer sand.
Then I called upon gods and men to support me. My cries
    never reached
any mortal ears; but a virgin goddess was moved by a
    virgin's

prayers to come to my aid. When I raised my arms to the
580   heavens,
they started to blacken and sprout light feathers. I next
         attempted
to cast my mantle away from my shoulders, but even
         that
was already plumage, rooted deep in the folds of my
         skin.
I tried to rain blows on my naked breast with my
         sturdy hands,
but my sturdy hands were no more and my breast was
585   no longer naked.
I started to run. This time my feet were not clogged in
         the sand
and I rose from the surface of earth and soon was
         soaring in air.
So thus I was given my role as Minerva's blameless
         attendant.
And yet what good does that do, if I'm forced to
         surrender my place
to the owl, who became a bird by committing a
590   dreadful crime?
That owl was once Nyctímene. Haven't you heard the
         story,
known through the whole of Lesbos, of how she
         corrupted her father*
by incest with him? For sure, she's a bird; but her
         guilty conscience
drives her to shun the eyes of men and the glare of the
         daylight.
She hides her shame in the dark, excluded by all from
595   the clear sky.'
   The raven ignored this tale: 'May these ominous
         warnings of yours
rebound on your own head! I've no use for your
         foolish predictions!'
Postponing his visit to Phoebus no longer, he told his
         master

he'd caught Coronis with her Thessalian in bed together.
When he heard of his lover's defection, Apollo's
        laurel-wreath slipped,   600
his colour faded, his jaw then dropped, and his plectrum
        fell
to the ground. His wounded heart was seething and
        swelling with anger.
He seized his familiar weapons and, flexing his bow from its
        horn tips,
fired his arrow, which none can escape, to transfix the
        bosom,
the lovely bosom he'd pressed to his own in their many
        embraces.   605
Coronis, wounded, groaned with the pain; as she drew the
        arrow
out of her body, the crimson blood gushed over her white
        limbs.
'Phoebus,' she cried, 'I might have paid you the price I
        deserved,
yet given my child to you first; as it is, we shall leave you
        together,
mother and baby in one.' She spoke no further; her blood   610
flowed out, and the chill of death crept over her lifeless
        body.
    Apollo sorely regretted exacting a vengeance so cruel,
but all too late. He cursed himself for his listening ear
and his fiery anger. He cursed the bird who had forced him
        to know
the offence which had given him cause for resentment. He
        cursed his bow   615
and the hand that had drawn it, along with the arrow he'd
        fired so rashly.
He clasped her fallen limbs to his breast, belatedly
        struggling
to baffle fate, but his healing arts were deployed to no
        purpose.
Finding that all his attempts were vain, that the funeral
        pyre

was being prepared and those limbs would soon be on
620   fire in the flames,
at last he burst into pitiful groans from the depths of
           his being
(the cheeks of the gods are never allowed to be
           moistened by tears),
like the pitiful groans of a heifer who's there at a
           sacrifice, watching
the hammer poised by the slaughterer's ear come down
           and shatter
the hollow skull of her unweaned calf with a sounding
625   crack.
He poured on his loved one's breast his ungrateful
           offering of incense,
embraced her once more and performed the rites that
           should not have been due.
But Apollo could not allow the fruit of his loins to be
           lost
in Coronis' ashes; he snatched his son* from the womb
           of the burning
mother and carried him up to the cave of Chiron the
630   centaur.*
As for the raven, who'd hoped to be thanked for
           revealing the truth,
he was barred by the god from the white birds' ranks
           and condemned to be black.

OCYRHOË

Meanwhile the centaur was taking delight in his
           foster-child
whom the god had fathered, enjoying the task no less
           than the tribute.
A vision of red-gold locks spread over white shoulders
635   suddenly
came on the scene. It was Chiron's daughter, the child
           of the nymph

Caríclo who'd borne her upon the banks of a fast-flowing
      river
and called her Ocýrhoë.* Not content to have merely
      mastered
her father's skills, the maiden could utter the secrcts of
      fate.
And so, with the wind of prophetic madness inspiring her
      soul,   640
aglow with the fire of the godhead imprisoned within her
      breast,
she gazed at the infant and cried: 'Grow up, dear child, to
      become
the Healer of all the world. To you sick mortals shall often
acknowledge a debt for their lives; to you shall be granted
      the right
to revive dead spirits. To heaven's displeasure you'll dare
      this once,   645
but your grandfather's bolt shall prevent you from working
      a second miracle.
Thus you'll be turned from a god to a lifeless body, though
      later
again from body to god; your fate shall endure two
      changes.*
You too, my beloved father, are now immortal and
      destined
under the law of your birth to survive till the end of time;   650
and yet you shall long for the power to die, when the
      wound from an arrow
infects and tortures your limbs with the venomous blood of
      the Hydra.*
Then even you shall be freed by the gods from your
      deathless condition;
the Sisters Three* will consent and the thread of your life
      shall be broken.'
   More words of fate remained to be spoken; but breathing
      a sigh   655
from the depths of her heart, and bedewing her cheeks with
      a fountain of tears,

the maiden continued: 'My destiny's running too fast,
         and I may not
prophesy further. My powers of speech are being
         obstructed.
My arts were purchased too dearly if they have directed
         the anger
of heaven against me. I wish I had never foreknown the
660   future!
Now it appears that my human form is creeping away
         from me.
Grass is the food that I long for; I feel an impulse to
         gallop
across the wide plains. I am turning into a mare, akin
to my father. But why completely? My father is still
         half human.'
While she was speaking, the final part of her plaintive
665   lament
could hardly be understood as her words had become
         confused.
Soon they were not even words, nor yet the sounds of a
         horse,
but more of a person aping those sounds. In the
         briefest of moments
she clearly whinnied and dropped her arms to the
         ground as forelegs.
Her fingers then coalesced and her five nails formed an
670   unbroken
line in the shape of a light horn hoof; her mouth was
         extended
and so was her neck; the greater part of her long cloak
         turned
to a tail; and the red-gold hair which had loosely
         covered her shoulders
was changed to a mane on the right of her neck. Her
         voice and her body
were altered alike; and the miracle gave her a new
675   name, Hippe.*

BATTUS

Chiron wept for his daughter and called on Apollo to help
    him,
but all in vain. The god was in no position to cancel
Jupiter's edict and, even supposing he had been able,
he then was abroad and firmly engaged in the Péloponnese.
That was the time when the god of Delphi was playing the
    herdsman,   680
dressed in a cloak of hide, with a rustic crook in his left
    hand,
clutching his pipes of seven unequal reeds in his right.
While his thoughts were distracted by love and he mooned
    away on his panpipes,
the cattle he'd left unguarded are said to have wandered
    into
the fields near Pylos. These were sighted by Mercury,
    Atlas'   685
grandson, who craftily rustled and hid them away in the
    forest.
No one observed this theft except for an old man, known
in that part of the country – Battus,* as all of the
    neighbours called him.
Battus was watching over a herd of pedigree mares
in the grassy pastures and glades of his master, the wealthy
    Néleus.   690
Mercury stopped him and, using his charm as he took him
    aside,
he said, 'Whoever you are, my friend, if someone by any
chance asks after these cattle, do say that you haven't seen
    them.
I wouldn't wish your kindness to go unrewarded. Here
is a nice plump cow for you!' Battus accepted the present
    and answered,   695
'Go safely on! This stone will inform on you sooner
    than I' –
and he pointed one out. So Jupiter's son pretended to leave,

but he soon returned in another guise with a different
      voice.
'Hey, herdsman, I need your help. Have you seen any
      cattle passing
along this way? They are stolen. Out with the truth! If
700   you tell me,
I'll give you a cow for reward, with her bull thrown
      into the bargain.'
Old Battus couldn't resist this double offer. 'You'll find
      them
there, at the foot of those mountains,' he said – which
      was where they were.
Mercury gloatingly laughed: 'Would you show me up
      to myself,
you treacherous bastard? Me to myself?' And he
705   turned the liar
into a hard flint rock, still known as a kind of
      informer,
the ancient stigma attaching itself to the innocent
      touchstone.*

AGLAUROS

Mercury shortly was on the wing, with his wand in
      hand.
In the course of his flight over Athens, Minerva's
      favourite city,
he saw the Munýchian fields and the groves of the
710   learned Lycéüm.
It chanced that day that some pure young maidens,
      ritually chosen,
were moving in solemn procession towards the temple
      of Pallas,*
bearing upon their heads the flower-wreathed baskets
      containing
the knife and the grain and other holy things for the
      sacrifice.

The winged god spied them on their return, and directed his
    course
not straight towards them but round about in a gentle
    curve.   715
As a rapidly flying kite, on spying a sacrificed victim's
entrails, circles aloft in fear while the priests are clustering
round the altar; not venturing far away on his flapping
wings, he greedily hovers above the prey that he hopes for;
so Mercury followed a bending course in an easy
    movement,   720
circling round in the sky above the Acrópolis hill.
As the morning star with his radiant gleam outshines the
    rest
of the stellar orbs and himself is outshone by the golden
    moon,
so all the rest of the virgins were put in the shade by Herse,
the pride of the festal procession as well as her own
    companions.   725
Her beauty dumbfounded Jupiter's son. As he hovered
    suspended
in air, he burned with the flames of desire, like a bullet of
    lead shot,
launched by a Bálearic sling,* which glows increasingly
    bright
on its path through the clouds, acquiring a heat which it
    lacked before.
Mercury now changed course and abandoned the sky for
    the earth.   730
He assumed no disguise, as beauty is always so full of
    confidence.
Justly sure of his charms, he still took care to enhance
    them
by smoothing his hair and adjusting his cloak to make quite
    sure
it was hanging correctly, with all the gold on the border
    showing.
He checked that his staff, which raises and lowers the
    curtain of sleep,   735

had a polished look, that his feet were clean and his
      sandals gleaming.
   The women's apartments had three bedchambers,
      richly adorned
with ivory-work and tortoiseshell inlay. The room on the
      right
was Pandrosos', that on the left Aglauros', with Herse's
      between them.
740 Aglauros, the first of the girls to notice Mercury coming,
ventured to ask his name and why he had entered their
      quarters.
The grandson of Atlas and Pleíone answered: 'I am the
      runner
who carries my father's orders from heaven, and he is
      none other
than Jove himself. I won't conceal my reason for
      coming.
I merely hope you'll be loyal to your sister and duly
745   consent
to be known as the aunt of Mercury's child. I have
      come to make love
to beautiful Herse. Do a good turn for a lover, I beg
      you!'
Aglauros regarded the god with the same avaricious
      eyes
with which she had recently peeped at the hidden
      secrets of fair-haired
Pallas. She asked for a mass of gold in return for the
750   service
he craved, then forced him to leave the palace until he
      could bring it.
   The warrior goddess, Minerva, now turned her
      threatening gaze
on Aglauros. She heaved such a troubled sigh from the
      depths of her heart
that, in line with her powerful feelings, the goddess'
      breastplate, the aegis,

was heavily shaken. To think that this creature, with hands
    profane,   755
had uncovered her secrets and broken a solemn promise
    when taking
a furtive look at the motherless baby whom Vulcan had
    fathered!
A god as well as her sister would now be beholden to her,
and she herself would be rich with the gold she had greedily
    asked for!
    At once Minerva sank to the cavern of Envy, a filthy   760
dwelling infested by black corruption. Buried away
in the depths of a valley, it never is blessed by the warmth of
    the sun
or the draught of a wind – a gloomy, numbingly cold
    domain,
forever without any fire, forever enveloped in darkness.
When the awesome maiden goddess of war had arrived at
    this cavern,   765
she stood on the threshold (she couldn't have entered so
    foul an abode)
and beat on the doors with the point of her spear. They
    unfolded open,
and there inside she saw Envy, consuming the flesh of
    vipers,
the food for her natural venom. She averted her face in
    disgust,   770
but the spirit picked herself up from the freezing ground,
    and dropping
the rest of her half-eaten snakes, lethargically ambled
    forward.
Seeing the goddess' handsome looks and her splendid
    armour,
she uttered a groan and contorted her face with a
    deep-drawn sigh.
That face is constantly pallid; her body is totally shrivelled; 775
her eyes are both at a squint, while her teeth are decayed
    and discoloured;

her nipples are green with gall and the poison drips from
    her tongue.
She never smiles, except when excited by watching pain,
nor can she sleep, there are so many torments to keep her
    awake;
she loathes the sight of human success, which adds to her
780   constant
wasting away; she is gnawed herself, as she gnaws at
    her victims,
by torture that's self-inflicted. Although Minerva was
    filled
with the utmost revulsion towards this demon, she
    briefly addressed her:
'One of the daughters of Cecrops, Aglauros, must be
    infected
by you and your poison. See to it!' Saying no more, the
785   goddess
took flight and launched herself up from the earth with
    the thrust of her spear.
   Envy followed the goddess' flight with her squinting
    gaze
and, feebly muttering, contemplated Minerva's
    triumph
with angry resentment; then seized her stick, which
    was studded all over
with prickly thorns, and swathed herself in her black
790   cloud cloak.
Wherever she made her progress, she trampled the
    flowering meadows,
withered the grass and lopped the tops of the tallest
    trees.
With the taint of her breath she foully polluted whole
    peoples, cities
and family dwellings. At last, when she'd sighted the
    heights of Athens,
strong in the pride of its talents and wealth, in the joys
795   of peace,

she almost burst into tears; there was nothing there to be
     wept for!
But after she'd entered the room where the daughter of
     Cecrops was sleeping,
she did as the goddess had bidden and stroked Aglauros'
     breast
with her rust-stained hand, so packing the heart with her
     barb-hooked brambles.
Breathing her noxious poison, she infiltrated her victim's   800
bones and infused the lungs deep down with her pitch-
     black venom.
Next, to focus her target's mind on the cause of the malady,
Envy implanted an image of Herse, then of her sister's
fortunate marriage, then of the god with his beautiful
     body,
magnifying each picture, so that Aglauros was maddened   805
and eaten up by her secret jealousy. Fretting by day
and fretting by night, she would moan in her wretchedness,
     slowly dissolved
by the foul corruption, as ice is melted by fitful sunshine.
Herse's good fortune rankled; the fire consuming her rival
burned like a bonfire of thorny brambles that's kindled
     beneath   810
but never bursts into flames, just steadily smokes and
     smoulders.
She often wanted to die to escape the sight of her sister's
happiness, or to report the affair as a wicked sin
to her strait-laced father. At last she crouched by her sister's
     chamber
to bar the god's way. When he blithely arrived and
     attempted to coax her   815
with honeyed words of entreaty, she said, 'You can stop all
     that nonsense.
I shan't budge an inch from this place till *you've* been sent
     packing!'
'An excellent bargain!' the speedy Mercury answered. 'Let's
     keep it.'

One touch of his magic staff and the door flew open.
        Aglauros
tried to get up, but found that the limbs that are bent
820   when a person
is sitting down were paralysed, gripped by a sluggish
        inertia.
She struggled hard to straighten her body and land on
        her feet,
but the joints of her knees had stiffened, a creeping
        chill had invaded
her fingers' ends, and her veins turned white as the
        blood retreated.
And like the malignant spread of a sadly incurable
825   cancer,
creeping on to affect other perfectly healthy organs,
little by little the deadly chill crept into Aglauros'
breast and finally blocked the vital paths of her
        breathing.
She made no effort to speak, but if she had so
        attempted,
the passage for words had gone; her neck was encased
830   in rock,
and her mouth had gone hard. She simply sat there, a
        lifeless statue;
the stone was not even white, but stained by her own
        black envy.

EUROPA

After the son of Maia had punished Aglauros' impious
words and ungodly thoughts, he abandoned the land
        called after
Pallas Athene and soared to the sky on his beating
835   wings.
Here Jupiter took him aside and, without confessing
        his amorous

motives, said to him: 'Son, who always performs my bidding
so faithfully, wait no longer but rapidly follow your usual
flight path down to the earth and make for the land that
    looks up
to your mother's star* on its left and is known by the people
    as Sidon.   840
There you will notice the royal cattle grazing some distance
away in the mountain pastures. Drive them down to the
    seashore.'
His words were obeyed. At once the cattle were off the
    mountains
and on their way to the beach, where the daughter of King
    Agénor
was often accustomed to play with her Tyrian* girl
    companions.   845
Love and regal dignity, scarcely the best of friends,
are rarely discovered together. And so the father and ruler
of all the gods, whose right hand wields the three-forked
    lightning,
whose nod can sway the whole world, discarded his mighty
    sceptre
and clothed himself in the form of a bull. He lowed as he
    mingled   850
amongst the steers, parading his beauty along in the fresh,
    lush
grassland. His hide was the colour of snow before it is
    trodden
by clumsy feet or turned to slush by the southerly rains.
The muscles stood out on his neck, he flaunted magnificent
    dewlaps,
his horns were curved in an elegant twist – they might quite
    well   855
have been crafted by hand – and were more transparent
    than flawless gems.
There wasn't a threat in his brow or a fearsome glare in his
    eyes;
his face was a picture of perfect peace. The princess Európa

gazed in wonder upon this gentle and beautiful creature.
At first, despite his unthreatening looks, she was
860   frightened to touch him;
but soon she approached with a garland of flowers for
          his gleaming head.
Her lover was blissful and licked her hands as a
          prelude to other
and sweeter pleasures, pleasures he barely, barely
          could wait for.
Now he would gambol beside her, prancing around on
          the green grass;
now he would rest his snow-white flank in the golden
865   sand.
As little by little her fears were allayed, he would offer
          his front
to be stroked by her maidenly hand or his horns to be
          decked with fresh garlands.
The princess even ventured to sit with her legs astride
on the back of the bull, unaware whose sides she was
          resting her thighs on;
when Jupiter, gradually edging away from the land and
870   away
from the dry shore, placed his imposter's hooves in the
          shallowest waves,
then advanced out further, and soon he was bearing
          the spoils of his victory
out in mid-ocean. His frightened prize* looked back at
          the shore
she was leaving behind, with her right hand clutching
          one horn and her left
on his back for support, while her fluttering dress
875   swelled out in the sea-breeze.

BOOK 3

This book consists of six main stories, with a seventh inserted within the sixth. The formal connection between them is Thebes and the house of Cadmus. The first two and last two are all mini-epics of substantial length and overall seriousness; the middle two are considerably shorter and more light-hearted. The metamorphosis is sometimes central, sometimes only peripheral. Each story is distinct in its content and literary tone; but in all six we can detect an underlying theme in the idea of 'intrusion' or 'seeing the forbidden holy', followed by unhappy, even violent, consequences. In the four major tales note also the *ecphrases*, formal descriptions of natural surroundings which are more than purely decorative: they suggest that elemental forces in nature are at work.

Cadmus (1–137) is in fairly traditional epic mode and we can relish the hero's exciting fight with the dragon and the sowing of the monster's teeth to grow into armed men. In *Actaeon* (138–252) the approach is more subjective and subtle. When Actaeon suddenly catches sight of Diana and her nymphs bathing, it is purely accidental. He is not a voyeur, but Ovid has already presented the sight to his audience in a voyeuristic way. He then invites us to sympathize with the stag, who (like Io in Book 1) retains his human feelings but cannot communicate with his own huntsmen and the dogs who tear him to pieces.

The blasting of *Semele* (253–315) by Jupiter's lightning may not be a laughing matter, but there is plenty of comedy in its telling, particularly in the characterization of the jealous Juno and the disguise she adopts. The story of *Teiresias* (316–38) is

also told in a light-hearted context, even if the blindness inflicted
by the slighted Juno is grossly unfair.

In *Narcissus and Echo* (339–510) the atmosphere changes
again in a mixture of sophistication and pathos. Echo's encoun-
ter with Narcissus is relayed in an extremely entertaining way,
but her demise is surely very sad. We can even identify too with
the egocentric youth who, when he falls in love with his own
reflection, is in a sense intruding upon himself and so acquiring
the self-knowledge which Teiresias has warned will have fatal
consequences. Here Ovid is evidently fascinated by the paradox
of an identification between subject and object, active and pas-
sive. The monologues that he gives Narcissus are extraordinarily
clever in their word-play as well as pathetic in tone.

Pentheus and Bacchus (511–81, 692–733) owes a number of
details to Euripides' play *The Bacchae*, as does the inset story
of *Acoetes and the Lydian Sailors* (582–691) (which provides
the metamorphosis) to the Homeric *Hymn to Dionysus*. How-
ever, readers who know Euripides' great tragedy will find many
differences. The central part of the first section (511–81) is
Pentheus' harangue to the Thebans, which seems to be a rabid
parody of the Augustan propaganda which championed the
Roman values of martial valour and denounced alien effemin-
acy. The narration of Acoetes has its moments of magic and
excitement, but the overall tone is cooler and almost jolly when
the mutinous sailors take to the waves as dolphins. The frenetic
mood returns for the violent climax to the book when Pentheus
is torn to pieces by his mother, Agave, and her sisters. Order is
restored in the quiet coda of the closing two lines.

CADMUS

Now they had landed on Cretan soil, when Jupiter dropped
the disguise of a bull, to reveal himself as the god who he
     was.
Anxious for news, Európa's father commanded Cadmus
to search for his kidnapped sister. 'Find her, or go into
     exile,'
he said – an iniquitous action, if also inspired by devotion.*   5
But who can detect Jove's thievish amours? Young Cadmus
     wandered
the wide world over, staying away from his country,
     avoiding
his father Agénor's wrath. At last he visited Delphi,
and kneeling down he questioned the god: 'What land must
     I live in?'
Phoebus replied, 'If you make for the wilds, you will soon
     be met   10
by a cow that has never been yoked or harnessed to draw a
     ploughshare.
She is to guide your path, and where she settles for grazing,
found a city with walls and name the region Boeótia.'*
  Cadmus had scarcely made the descent from Castália's
     cave,*
when he spied a solitary heifer slowly moving forward   15
without any guard or halter for sign of service to man.
He stalked her closely, following step by step in her wake,
silently praising the god of Delphi who'd shown him the
     way.
Once she had crossed the river Cephísus and Pánopeus'
     fields,
the animal halted. Lifting her beautiful head with its
     spreading   20
horns to the sky, she filled the air with a lingering low,
and glancing round at the men who were following close
     behind her,

sank to the ground and rested her flanks in the fresh-green
        pasture.
Cadmus knelt to give thanks. He pressed his lips to the alien
earth and greeted the mountains and plains of his
25   new-found land.
    Sacrifice now to Jove, he thought. So he sent his
        companions
in search of water from running springs for ritual
        libations.
Nearby stood an ancient forest whose trees had never
        been felled,
a cave in its midst all overgrown with creepers and
        brushwood.
A structure of rocks created an arch low down, and out
30   of it
water was gushing in streams. Deep down in the heart
        of the cave
was a dragon sacred to Mars, which flaunted a golden
        crest,
fiery glinting eyes, a flickering three-forked tongue,
three marshalled ranks of teeth and a body swollen with
        venom.
35 Here the Tyrian strangers came on their fateful mission.
They entered the grove and lowered their pitchers to
        catch the water.
A mighty splash! At once, with a fearsome hissing,
        down from
the length of the cave there emerged the blue-black head
        of the dragon.
Stricken with horror, they dropped their vessels, their
        blood ran cold,
their limbs were suddenly seized with a spasm of violent
40   trembling.
The serpent twisted his scaly spirals along in their
        slithering
coils, then shot right up in a curve like a huge bow,
towering towards the sky with more than half of his
        body,

overlooking the wood in a span as extensive as all
the stars of the Snake* between the Great and the Little
     Bear.   45
The poor Phoenícians, whether they drew their swords or
     attempted
flight or stood stock still in terror, the monster was on
     them,
to crunch them up with his fangs or crush in his strangling
     coils,
or else to blast with the venomous filth of his noxious
     breath.
  By now the sun had reached its zenith and shortened the
     shadows.   50
Wondering what had delayed his companions, the hero
     Cadmus
decided to track them down. To shield his body, he
     donned
the skin of a lion.* For weapons he took his iron-tipped
     spear,
his javelin and, more important than all, the courage to
     wield them.
Striding into the wood, he encountered a welter of corpses,   55
above them the huge-backed monster gloating in grisly
     triumph,
tongue bedabbled with blood as he lapped at their pitiful
     wounds.
'My faithful comrades,' he cried, 'if I cannot avenge your
     death,
at least I can share it!' With that he lifted a massive boulder
up from the ground and hurled it with all the strength of his
     arm.   60
Its violent force would have shaken the walls of a lofty
     fortress,
towers and all. The dragon, however, remained unscathed.
His scales protected him well like a coat of mail, and his
     blue-black
skin was sufficiently hard to repel the powerful impact –
but not sufficiently hard to counter the pointed javelin,   65

which flew through the air to lodge in the suppler flesh
    that enfolded
the monster's sinuous spine, and pierced right down to his
    flank.
Maddened by pain, the dragon twisted his head behind
    him,
glared at the wound on his back and bit at the weapon
    embedded there.
70 This way and that he struggled to ease the shaft, until he
    awkwardly wrenched it out; but the point was trapped
        in his ribcage.
The monster's temper was violent enough by nature;
        this was
the final whiplash. The veins swelled full on his bloated
    throat,
his jaws with their poisonous fangs were dribbling with
    yellow-white foam,
his scales rasped as they scraped the soil, and his hellish
75   mouth,
panting with foul black breath, infected the air with
    pollution.
See him writhing his coils on the earth to form a
    voluminous
ring; he then reared up as erect as the tallest treetop;
now on the rampage, he swept along like a swollen
    river
in full spate, breasting and toppling the trees that
80   blocked his advance.
On his side Cadmus retreated a step, withstanding
    attack
with his stolen lion skin and holding the menacing jaws
    at bay
with the point of his outstretched spear. The dragon
    furiously snapped
at the metal and worried the spearhead between his
    teeth to no purpose.
By now the blood had started to trickle from out of that
85   venomous

throat; the rich green grass was bespattered with deep red
      gore.
But the wound was far from fatal; the snake could still move
      clear
and retract his injured neck. By giving ground he prevented
the point being driven home or piercing him any deeper.
At last our hero was able to thrust it into his gullet;   90
then moving in close, he pressed on it hard, until his
      retreating
prey backed into an oak and his neck was nailed to the trunk.
The tree bent under the dragon's weight and groaned as the
      monster
flogged and flailed at its stout old stock with the tip of his
      tail.

The victor feasted his eyes on the bulk of his vanquished
      foe.   95
Suddenly a sound, a voice rang out. Cadmus could not
tell whence it came, but he heard it clearly: 'Son of Agenor,
why do you gaze on a slaughtered snake? You also shall
      live
as a snake to be gazed on!' Cadmus waited in apprehension,
stunned, white-faced, his hair on end in the chill of terror.   100
Look now! Gliding down through the ether, his patron
      goddess
Pallas appeared, with orders for him to turn the soil
and sow the teeth of the dragon as seeds of a race to come.
He did as she bade and after pressing a rut in the earth
with a plough, he scattered the teeth that were destined to
      grow into men.   105
At once – amazing to tell – the clods started to crumble;
out of the furrow a line of bristling spear-tips sprouted,
next an array of helmets nodding with colourful plumes,
then manly shoulders and breasts and arms accoutred with
      weapons
rose from the earth, a burgeoning crop of shielded
      warriors.   110
Think of a tapestry frontcloth* rolling up in the theatre

at festival time. The embroidered figures slowly and
    smoothly
ascend, their faces first and then the rest of their bodies,
till all is revealed and their feet stand firm on the base of
    the curtain.
    Another foe to be feared! When Cadmus made ready
115   to seize
his weapons, 'Leave those arms!' cried one of the troop
    of earth-sprung
warriors. 'This is a family feud. You stand aside!'
As he spoke he engaged in combat with one of his
    soil-born brethren
and felled him down with his sword. Then he himself
    was struck
by a javelin hurled from a distance. His killer survived
120   no longer
and soon had breathed the last of the breath he had
    just been given.
So madness got hold of them all. Their death was as
    quick as their birth,
from the wounds they dealt and received in their own
    unnatural warfare.
Those youths, allotted so brief a span of life, were
    already
beating the breast of their mother earth, till it bled with
125   their fresh warm
blood. Five soldiers only remained, and one was
    Echíon.*
He, at Minerva's prompting, threw his arms to the
    ground
and sued for peace with his brothers, promising peace
    in return.
These were the men whom Cadmus of Sidon took as
    his aides
when he founded his city as Phoebus Apollo's oracle
130   bade him.

ACTAEON

Thebes had her walls, and Cadmus' exile might have been
     thought
to have brought him nothing but luck. He had married
     Harmónia, daughter
of Mars and Venus, a most prestigious match which had
     yielded
a brood of numerous sons and daughters and much-loved
     grandsons,
grown into fine young men. But never forget the ancient   135
saying: 'Wait for the final day. Call no man happy
until he is dead and his body is laid to rest in the grave.'
   Prosperous in so much, great Cadmus was struck by
     disaster.
First, Actaéon, his grandson, had antlers sprout from his
     brow
and his dogs were allowed to slake their thirst in their
     master's blood.   140
If you look at the facts, however, you'll find that chance
     was the culprit.
No crime was committed. Why punish a man for a pure
     mistake?*
   Picture a mountain stained with the carnage of hounded
     beasts.
It was now midday, the hour when the shadows draw to
     their shortest;
the sun god's chariot was halfway over from east to west.   145
A band of huntsmen was strolling along through the
     pathless glades,
when their leader, the young Actaeon, calmly made an
     announcement:
'Comrades, our nets are soaked, our spears are drenched in
     our quarry's
blood. Our luck is enough for today. When the goddess
     Aurora

appears tomorrow and shows the gleam of her rosy
150   wheels,
let us all return to the chase. Now Phoebus is halfway
        over
from east to west and cutting the fields with his
        burning rays.
Leave off what you're doing and stow your knotted
        nets for the moment.'
The men did just as he told them and took a break
        from their hunting.
   Now picture a valley, dense with pine and tapering
155   cypress,
called Gargáphië, sacred haunt of the huntress Diana;
there, in a secret corner, a cave surrounded by
        woodland,
owing nothing to human artifice. Nature had used
her talent to imitate art: she had moulded the living
        rock
160 of porous tufa to form the shape of a rugged arch.
To the right, a babbling spring with a thin translucent
        rivulet
widening into a pool ringed round by a grassy clearing.
Here the goddess who guards the woods, when weary
        with hunting,
would come to bathe her virginal limbs in the clear,
        clean water.
On this occasion she made her entrance and handed
165   her javelin,
quiver and slackened bow to the chosen nymph who
        carried
her weapons. Another put out her arms to receive her
        dress
as she stripped it off. Two more were removing her
        boots, while Crócale,
more of an expert, gathered the locks that were
        billowing over
her mistress' neck in a knot, though her own stayed
170   floating and free.

Néphele, Hýale, Rhamis, Psecas and Phíale charged
their capacious urns with water and stood all ready to
        pour it.
And while the virgin goddess was taking her bath in her
        usual
pool, as fate would have it, Actaeon, Cadmus' grandson,
wandered into the glade. His hunting could wait, he
        thought,   175
as he sauntered aimlessly through the unfamiliar woodland.
Imagine the scene as he entered: the grotto, the splashing
        fountains,
the group of nymphs in the nude. At once, at the sight of a
        man,
they struck their bosoms in horror, their sudden screams
        re-echoing
through the encircling woods. They clustered around
        Diana   180
to form a screen with their bodies, but sadly the goddess
        was taller;
her neck and shoulders were visible over the heads of her
        maidens.
Think of the crimson glow on the clouds when struck by the
        rays
of the setting sun; or think of the rosy-fingered dawn;
such was the blush on the face of Diana observed quite
        naked.   185
Although her companion nymphs had formed a barrier
        round her,
she stood with her front turned sideways and looked at the
        rash intruder
over her shoulder. She wished that her arrows were ready to
        hand,
but used what she could, caught up some water and threw it
        into
the face of the man. As she splashed his hair with revengeful
        drops,   190
she spoke the spine-chilling words which warned of
        impending disaster:

'Now you may tell the story of seeing Diana naked –
If story-telling is in your power!' No more was needed.
The head she had sprinkled sprouted the horns of a lusty
        stag;
the neck expanded, the ears were narrowed to pointed
195   tips;
she changed his hands into hooves and his arms into
        long and slender
forelegs; she covered his frame in a pelt of dappled
        buckskin;
last, she injected panic. The son of Autónoë* bolted,
surprising himself with his speed as he bounded away
        from the clearing.
But when he came to a pool and set eyes on his head
200   and antlers,
'Oh, dear god!' he was going to say; but no words
        followed.
All the sound he produced was a moan, as the tears
        streamed over
his strange new face. It was only his feelings that
        stayed unchanged.
What could he do? Make tracks for his home in the
        royal palace?
Or hide in the woodlands? Each was precluded by
205   shame or fear.
    He wavered in fearful doubt. And then his dogs
        caught sight of him.
First to sound on the trail were Blackfoot and
        sharp-nosed Tracker* –
Tracker of Cretan breed and Blackfoot a Spartan
        pointer.
Others came bounding behind them, fast as the gusts
        of the storm wind:
Ravenous, Mountain-Ranger, Gazelle, his Arcadian
210   deerhounds;
powerful Fawnkiller, Hunter the fierce, and violent
        Hurricane;

Wingdog, fleetest of foot, and Chaser, the keenest-scented;
savage Sylvan, lately gashed by the tusks of a wild boar;
Glen who was dropped from a wolf at birth, and the bitch
      who gathers
the flocks in, Shepherdess; Harpy, flanked by her two young
      puppies;   215
River, the dog from Sícyon, sides all taut and contracted;
Racer and Gnasher; Spot, with Tigress and muscular
      Valour;
Sheen with a snow-white coat and murky Soot with a
      pitch-black;
Spartan, wiry and tough; then Whirlwind, powerful
      pursuer;
Swift, and Wolfcub racing along with her Cypriot
      brother;   220
Grabber, who sported an ivory patch midway on his ebony
forehead; Sable, and Shag with a coat like a tangled thicket;
two mongrel hounds from a Cretan sire and Lacónian dam,
Rumpus and Whitefang; Yelper, whose howls could
      damage the eardrums –
and others too many to mention. Spoiling all for their
      quarry,   225
over crag, over cliff, over rocks which appeared to allow no
      approach,
where access was hard and where there was none, the
      whole pack followed.
   Actaeon fled where so many times he had been the
      pursuer.
He fled from the dogs who had served him so faithfully,
      longing to shout to them,
'Stop! It is I, Actaeon, your master. Do you not know me?'   230
But the words would not come. The air was filled with
      relentless baying.
Blacklock first inserted his teeth to tear at his back;
Beast-killer next; then Mountain-Boy latched on to his
      shoulder.
These had started out later but stolen a march by taking

a short cut over the ridge. As they pinned their master
235   down,
the rest of the pack rushed round and buried their
      fangs in his body,
until it was covered with crimson wounds. Actaeon
      groaned
in a sound that was scarcely human but one no stag
      could ever
have made, as he filled the familiar hills with his cries
      of anguish.
Then bending his legs like a cringing beggar, he gazed
240   all round
with his silently pleading eyes, as if they were
      outstretched arms.
   What of his friends? In ignorant zeal they
      encouraged the wild pack
on with the usual halloos. They scanned the woods for
      their leader,
shouting, 'Actaeon! Actaeon!', as if he were far away,
though he moved his head in response to his name.
245   'Why aren't you here,
you indolent man, to enjoy the sight of this heaven-sent
      prize?'
If only he'd not been there! But he was. He would
      dearly have loved
to watch, instead of enduring, his own dogs' vicious
      performance.
Crowding around him, they buried their noses inside
      his flesh
and mangled to pieces the counterfeit stag who
250   embodied their master.
Only after his life was destroyed in a welter of wounds
is Diana, the goddess of hunting, said to have cooled
      her anger.

SEMELE

Comments varied: some felt that the goddess had overdone
her violent revenge, while others commended it – worthy,
    they said
of her strict virginity. All were prepared to defend their
    opinion.   255
Juno alone was less concerned to publish her judgment,
whether in praise or blame, but quietly gloated over
the blow to Agenor's house. Her hatred for princess
    Europa,
the whore of Tyre, was now transferred to her kinsfolk.
    Suddenly,
further cause for resentment: Sémele, Cadmus' daughter,   260
was pregnant by mighty Jove! Queen Juno's tongue was
    already
sharpened, when 'What has my scolding ever achieved?' she
    thought.
'I must target the woman herself and destroy her, if I am to
    merit
the title of mighty Juno; if I may properly wield
my jewelled sceptre as Queen of the Gods; if I am Jupiter's 265
sister and consort – at least his sister! She might, I suppose,
be content with a secret liaison; the insult to *me* may be
    shortlived.
But no, she has got herself pregnant! Her guilt is betrayed
    by her bulging
belly. So sure of her beauty, she means to become a mother
by none but Jupiter. How many times have *I* been allowed   270
to bear him a child?* I'll make quite sure that he plays her
    false.
Her Jove will drown her in the Styx, or I'm not Saturn's
    daughter!'
  She rose from her throne, then, veiling herself in a
    yellowish cloud,

she came to Semele's house and only emerged from her
          cover
after assuming the form of a crone with whitened
275   temples,
wrinkles lining her skin, bent back and tottering legs.
Adopting an old cracked voice, she quickly appeared in
          the spitting
image of Beroë, Semele's old Epidaúrian nurse.
Well now, they started to gossip and during a lengthy
          discussion
280 Jupiter's name came up. Then 'Béroë' said with a sigh,
'I hope it is Jove for certain; but everything makes me
          uneasy.
Hundreds of men have claimed to be gods, in order to
          take
young virgins to bed. It isn't enough to *say* that he's
          Jove.
If his godhead is genuine, make him give you a pledge
          of his love.
Ask him to take you in all the majestic splendour he
285   shows
when he comes to the arms of Juno, dressed in his full
          regalia!'
    Semele's unsuspecting mind was already persuaded
by Juno's suggestion. She then asked Jupiter, 'Please
          will you give me
whatever I ask for?' 'Choose!' he replied. 'I'll refuse
          you nothing.
To back my promise, I call on the power of the River
290   Styx,
the god whom all the other gods fear, to witness my
          oath!'
Joyful in ruin, with too much power for her good, and
          destined
to die because of her lover's devotion, Semele said to
          him,
'Come to my bed as you come to your wife, when Juno
          embraces

your body divine in the pact of Venus!' Jupiter wanted   295
to gag her lips, but the fatal words had already been
      uttered.
Neither her wish nor his solemn oath could now be
      retracted.
And so, with a heavy sigh and a heavier heart, he ascended
the heights of the sky. As his face grew dark, the mists
      closed round him;
he gathered his threatening clouds, the gales with the
      flashing lightning,   300
the rumbling thunder and fearful bolts that none can
      escape.
But he did whatever he could to lessen his violent impact.
The flaming bolt with which he had hurtled the
      hundred-headed
Typhon to earth was left on the shelf, too deadly to use.
Instead he seized a less heavy weapon ('his everyday
      missile',   305
they call it in heaven), forged by the Cýclopes, giant smiths,
to be less fiery and fierce, less charged with the power of his
      anger.
Armed with this he entered the palace of Cadmus; but
      Semele's
mortal frame was unable to take the celestial onslaught.
His bridal gift was to set her ablaze. The baby,* still   310
in the foetal stage, was ripped from her womb, and, strange
      as it seems,
survived to complete his mother's term stitched up in his
      father's
thigh. At first the child was secretly reared by Semele's
sister Ino. She handed him on to the nymphs of Nysa,
who hid him away in their private cave and fed him on
      milk.   315

TEIRESIAS

While these events, in accordance with fate, were
      occurring on earth
and the infant Bacchus, now twice-born, was cradled in
      safety,
the story goes that Jupiter once, well-flushed with
      nectar,
laid his worries aside and, as Juno was none too busy,
320 he casually cracked a joke. 'Now listen,' he said, 'I bet
you women enjoy more pleasure in bed than ever we
      men do.'
When Juno disputed the point, they agreed to ask the
      opinion
of wise Teirésias, since he'd experienced love from
      both angles.
How so? When a pair of enormous snakes in the leafy
      forest
were coupling together, a blow from his staff disrupted
325   their congress.
Teiresias then was somewhat amazingly changed from
      a man
to a woman for seven years. In the eighth, however, he
      saw
the very same snakes again and said, 'If cudgelling you
has the power to alter the sex of the person who deals
      you the wallop,
here is a second one for you!' With that, he struck at
330   the snakes
and promptly recovered the figure and bodily parts he
      was born with.
That was why he was chosen to settle this playful
      argument.
Jupiter won his bet, but Juno unfairly resented
Teiresias' verdict. They say that in disproportionate
      fury,

she sentenced her judge and condemned his eyes to perpetual
     blindness.   335
What of almighty Jove? As the gods are never allowed
to undo each other's work, for the loss of Teiresias' sight
he awarded the gift of clairvoyance and high prestige to
     console him.

NARCISSUS AND ECHO

Soon the prophet's fame was rumoured throughout
     Boeotia.
Folk consulted, and none could fault, his oracular powers.   340
The first to put his trusted authority under test
was sea-green Líriope,* whom once Cephisus the river-god
caught in the folds of his sinuous stream and then
     proceeded
to rape. The nymph's womb swelled and, now at her very
     loveliest,
Liriope gave birth to a child, already adorable,   345
called Narcíssus. In course of time she consulted the seer;
'Tell me,' she asked, 'will my baby live to a ripe old age?'
'Yes,' he replied, 'so long as he never knows himself'* –
empty words, as they long appeared, but the prophet was
     proved right.
In the event, Narcissus died of a curious passion.   350
   Sixteen years went by and already the son of Cephisus
was changing each day from beautiful youth to comely
     manhood.
Legions of lusty men and bevies of girls desired him;
but the heart was so hard and proud in that soft and slender
     body,
that none of the lusty men or languishing girls could
     approach him.   355
One day he was sighted, blithely chasing the scampering
     roebuck
into the huntsman's nets, by a nymph whose babbling voice

would always answer a call but never speak first. It was
        Echo.
Echo still was a body, not a mere voice, but her
        chattering
360 tongue could only do what it does today, that is
to parrot the last few words of the many spoken by
        others.
Juno had done this to her. The goddess would be all
        ready
to catch her husband Jupiter making love to some
        nymph
in a mountain dell, when crafty Echo would keep her
        engaged
in a long conversation, until the nymph could scurry to
365   safety.
When Saturn's daughter perceived what Echo was
        doing, she said to her,
'I've been cheated enough by your prattling tongue.
        From now on
your words will be short and sweet!' Her curse took
        effect at once.
Echo could only repeat the words she heard at the end
of a sentence and never reply for herself. So when
370 she saw Narcissus wandering over the country fields,
she burned with desire and stealthily followed along
        his tracks.
The closer she followed, the flames of her passion grew
        nearer and nearer,
as sulphur smeared on the tip of a pine-torch quickly
        catches
fire when another flame is brought into close
        proximity.
Oh, how often she longed, poor creature, to say sweet
        nothings
375 and beg him softly to stay! But her nature imposed a
        block
and would not allow her to make a start. She was
        merely permitted

and ready to wait for the sounds which her voice could
   return to the speaker.
 Narcissus once took a different path from his trusty
   companions.
'Is anyone there?' he said. '. . . one there?' came Echo's
   answer.   380
Startled, he searched with his eyes all round the glade and
   loudly
shouted, 'Come here!' 'Come here!' the voice threw back to
   the caller.
He looks behind him and, once again, when no one emerges,
'Why are you running away?' he cries. His words come
   ringing
back. His body freezes. Deceived by his voice's reflection, 385
the youth calls out yet again, 'This way! We must come
   together.'
Echo with rapturous joy responds, 'We must come
   together!'
To prove her words, she burst in excitement out of the
   forest,
arms outstretched to fling them around the shoulders she
   yearned for.
Shrinking in horror, he yelled, 'Hands off! May I die
   before   390
you enjoy my body.' Her only reply was '. . . enjoy my
   body.'
Scorned and rejected, with burning cheeks, she fled to the
   forest
to hide her shame and live thenceforward in lonely caves.
But her love persisted and steadily grew with the pain of
   rejection.
Wretched and sleepless with anguish, she started to waste
   away.   395
Her skin grew dry and shrivelled, the lovely bloom of her
   flesh
lost all its moisture; nothing remained but voice and bones;
then only voice, for her bones (so they say) were
   transformed to stone.

Buried away in the forest, seen no more on the
400   mountains,
heard all over the world, she survives in the sound of
        the echo.

Not only Echo, the other nymphs of the waves and
        mountains
incurred Narcissus' mockery; so did his male
        companions.
Finally one of his scorned admirers lifted his hands
to the heavens: 'I pray Narcissus may fall in love and
405   never
obtain his desire!' His prayer was just and Némesis
        heard it.
    Picture a clear, unmuddied pool of silvery,
        shimmering
water. The shepherds have not been near it; the
        mountain-goats
and cattle have not come down to drink there; its
        surface has never
been ruffled by bird or beast or branch from a rotting
410   cypress.
Imagine a ring of grass, well-watered and lush, and a
        circle
of trees for cooling shade in the burning summer
        sunshine.
Here Narcissus arrived, all hot and exhausted from
        hunting,
and sank to the ground. The place looked pleasant,
        and here was a spring!
Thirsty for water, he started to drink, but soon grew
415   thirsty
for something else. His being was suddenly
        overwhelmed
by a vision of beauty. He fell in love with an empty
        hope,
a shadow mistaken for substance. He gazed at himself
        in amazement,

limbs and expression as still as a statue of Párian marble.
Stretched on the grass, he saw twin stars, his own two
        eyes,   420
rippling curls like the locks of a god, Apollo or Bacchus,
cheeks as smooth as silk, an ivory neck and a glorious
face with a mixture of blushing red and a creamy whiteness.
All that his lovers adored he worshipped in self-adoration.
Blindly rapt with desire for himself, he was votary and
        idol,   425
suitor and sweetheart, taper and fire – at one and the same
        time.
Those beautiful lips would implore a kiss, but as he bent
        forward
the pool would always betray him. He plunges his arms in
        the water
to clasp that ivory neck and finds himself clutching at no one.
He knows not what he is seeing; the sight still fires him with
        passion.   430
His eyes are deceived, but the strange illusion excites his
        senses.
Trusting fool, how futile to woo a fleeting phantom!
You'll never grasp it. Turn away and your love will have
        vanished.
The shape now haunting your sight is only a wraith, a
        reflection
consisting of nothing; there with you when you arrived,
        here now,   435
and there with you when you decide to go – if ever you can
        go!
    Nothing could drag him away from the place, not hunger
        for food
nor need for sleep. As he lay stretched out in the grassy
        shade,
he never could gaze his fill on that fraudulent image of
        beauty;
and gazing proved his demise. He raised his body a little,   440
then stretching his arms in grief to the witnessing trees all
        round him,

'Wise old trees,' he exclaimed, 'has anyone loved more
        cruelly?
Lovers have often kissed in secret under your branches.
Here you have stood for hundreds of years. In all that
        time
has anyone suffered for love like me? Whom can you
445   remember?
I've looked and have longed. But looking and longing
        is far from enough.
I still have to find!' (His lover's delusion was
        overpowering.)
'My pain is the more since we're not divided by
        stretches of ocean,
unending roads, by mountains or walls with
        impassable gates.
450 All that keeps us apart is a thin, thin line of water.
He wants to be held in my arms. Whenever I move to
        kiss
the clear bright surface, his upturned face strains closer
        to mine.
We all but touch! The paltriest barrier thwarts our
        pleasure.
Come out to me here, whoever you are! Why keep
        eluding me,
peerless boy? When I seek you, where do you steal
455   away?
It can't be my looks or my age which makes you want
        to avoid me;
even the nymphs have longed to possess me! . . . Your
        looks of affection
offer a grain of hope. When my arms reach out to
        embrace you,
you reach out too. I smile at you, and you smile at me
        back.
I weep and your tears flow fast. You nod when I show
460   my approval.
When I read those exquisite lips, I can watch them
        gently repeating

my words – but I never can *hear* you repeat them! . . . . .
I know you now and I know myself.* Yes, I am the cause
of the fire inside me, the fuel that burns and the flame that
     lights it.
What can I do? Must I woo or be wooed? What else can I
     plead for?   465
All I desire I have. My wealth has left me a pauper.
Oh, how I wish that I and my body could now be parted,
I wish my love were not here! – a curious prayer for a lover.
Now my sorrow is sapping my strength. My life is almost
over. Its candle is guttering out in the prime of my
     manhood.   470
Death will be easy to bear, since dying will cure my
     heartache.
Better indeed if the one I love could have lived for longer,
but now, two soulmates in one, we shall face our ending
     together.'
   With that he turned distractedly back to his own
     reflection;
his tears were troubling the limpid waters and blurring the
     picture   475
that showed in the ruffled pool. When he saw it fast
     disappearing,
'Don't hurry away, please stay! You cannot desert me so
     cruelly.
I love you!' he shouted. 'Please, if I'm not able to touch you,
I must be allowed to see you, to feed my unhappy passion!'
In wild distress he ripped the top of his tunic aside   480
and bared his breast to the blows he rained with his
     milk-white hand.
His fist brought up a crimson weal on his naked torso,
like apples tinted both white and red, or a multi-coloured
cluster of grapes just ripening into a blushing purple.   485
Once the water had cleared again and he saw what his
     hand
had done, the boy could bear it no longer. As yellow wax
melts in a gentle flame, or the frost on a winter morning
thaws in the rays of the sunshine, so Narcissus faded

away and melted, slowly consumed by the fire inside
490   him.
His face had lost that wonderful blend of red and
          whiteness,
gone was the physical vigour and all he had looked at
          and longed for,
broken the godlike frame which once poor Echo had
          worshipped.
     Echo had watched his decline, still filled with angry
          resentment
495 but moved to pity. Whenever the poor unhappy youth
uttered a pitiful sigh, her own voice uttered a pitiful
sigh in return. When he beat with his hand on his
          shoulders, she also
mimicked the sound of the blows. His final words, as
          he gazed
once more in the pool, rang back from the rocks: 'Oh
500   marvellous boy,
I loved you in vain!' Then he said, 'Farewell.'
          'Farewell,' said Echo.
He rested his weary head in the fresh green grass, till
          Death's hand
gently closed his eyes still rapt with their master's
          beauty.
Even then, as he crossed the Styx to ghostly Hades,
he gazed at himself in the river. At once his sister
505   naiads
beat their breasts and cut their tresses in mourning
          tribute;
the dryads wailed their lament; and Echo re-echoed
          their wailing.
A pyre was raised, the bier made ready, the funeral
          torches
brandished on high. The body, however, was not to be
          found –
only a flower with a trumpet of gold and pale white
510   petals.

PENTHEUS AND BACCHUS (1)

Once this story was bruited abroad, Teiresias' credit
spread through the townships of Greece, as a prophet of
      high reputation.
One single person, however, was found to reject him –
      Péntheus,*
son of Echion, who treated the gods with contempt and
      scoffed at
the seer's forewarnings. 'You blind old fool,' he cruelly
      taunted,   515
'Lost in the dark!' Then, shaking his frost-white locks,
      Teiresias
answered the king, 'How lucky you'd be if you were
      deprived
like me of your sight and could never set eyes on the
      mysteries of Bacchus!
The day will dawn, which I can foretell is not far off,
when a new god comes, the son of your kinswoman
      Semele, Liber.*   520
Unless you pay him his rightful tribute of shrine and temple,
your mangled corpse will be strewn in a thousand places,
      polluting
the woods with your blood, polluting your mother and her
      two sisters.
So it shall be. You will surely deny that godhead his
      worship
and surely complain that my darkened eyes saw only too
      well!'   525
The words were spoken and Pentheus rudely flung the man
      out.
  But the words proved true and Teiresias' prophecies came
      to fulfilment.
Bacchus arrived and the countryside rang with ecstatic
      cries.
The crowds poured in; there were mothers and wives with
      their sons and husbands,

nobles and ordinary folk, swept up in the strange new
530   rituals.
'Children of Mars, have you all gone crazy?' Pentheus
        harangued them.
'Blood of the dragon's teeth, you're possessed! Are you
        so spellbound
by curling pipes of animal horn and clashing cymbals
to fall for this juggler's tricks? You, who were never
        dismayed
by the threatening swords of the foe on the march or
535   his blaring trumpets,
are now being worsted by screaming women, bibulous
        frenzy,
lewd and lecherous hordes and the futile banging of
        drums!
Elders, how can I respect you? You ventured across the
        ocean
to found a new Tyre* and establish a home for your
        household gods.
Is Thebes to be captured without a fight? You younger
540   citizens,
sharper in spirit, my own peers, you should be bearing
        arms,
not a thyrsus.* Your heads should be covered by
        helmets, not wreaths of ivy.
Remember, I beg you, the dragon's teeth from which
        you were sprung.
On his own the dragon destroyed a throng. Now
        muster that dragon
spirit again! The serpent died for a pool and a
545   fountain –
you are defending your own good name. Defend it and
        conquer!
The dragon's part was to kill brave settlers. Yours is to
        banish
effeminate eunuchs and save your inherited honour. If
        Thebes

is destined to perish so soon, I pray that its walls may be
      toppled
by missiles and men in the clashing of swords and the
      crackle of flames.   550
Wretched but guiltless, we might be compelled to bemoan
      our lot
but not to conceal it. Tears would never be mingled with
      blushes.
Now, though, our city of Thebes will fall to a weaponless
      boy,
not in war or backed by a host of spearmen and charging
      cavalry.
His gleaming armour is perfumed locks and womanish
      garlands,   555
purple dresses richly woven with golden embroidery.
Leave him to me – you keep to the side – I'll force the truth
      out of him:
Jupiter isn't his father and all these rites are a fraud.
If King Acrísius* found the courage to spurn this spurious
deity and close the gates of Argos against him, can
      Pentheus   560
with all the city of Thebes be scared of a wandering
      stranger?
Off with you quickly, slaves, and bring this evil influence
here to me now in chains. No dawdling, this is an order!'
   Everyone remonstrated with Pentheus: his grandfather
      Cadmus,
Áthamas and the rest of his friends. But their efforts to calm
      him   565
were wasted. Warning merely sharpened his purpose;
      constraint
provoked him to wilder madness and aggravated his fury –
as swollen rivers that I have seen,* where nothing obtruded
to hinder their course, proceeded smoothly with little
      commotion;
but when they were blocked by uprooted trees or rocky
      boulders,   570

they foamed and they seethed and their rage gathered
    force in the face of obstruction.
  There! the slaves had returned, all covered in blood.
    'Where's Bacchus?'
their master asked. 'We never saw Bacchus,' the men
    replied,
'but we've captured one of his band who serves the cult
    as an acolyte.
This is the wretch.' And they handed over a prisoner
575   whose arms
were pinioned behind his back, a bacchic disciple of
    Lydian
origin. Pentheus fixed his awesomely furious gaze
on the man. He found it hard to postpone the demise
    of his victim,
but said, 'Your life is forfeit, my friend, and your death
    can teach others
a lesson. First, though, tell me your name and the
580   names of your parents.
Where is your home, and why do you practise this new
    religion?'

ACOETES AND THE LYDIAN SAILORS

Cool and fearless, the stranger replied, 'My name is
    Acoétes,
my country Maeónia. My parents were humble and
    simple folk.
My father left me no fields to be ploughed by sturdy
    oxen,
flocks of sheep to yield wool, or herds of cattle for
585   farming.
Poor like me, he would use his angler's line and hook
to entice the fish and land his catch as it danced on the
    rod.
My father's skill was his whole estate. As he lay on his
    deathbed,

"My boy," he said, "I bequeath you the art which is all I
    possess.
You are my heir and successor in that." So what was my
    legacy?   590
Nothing, except for a stretch of water, to call my
    inheritance.
As time went by, I tired of treading the same old rocks
and learned a new skill, to steer a ship by plying a tiller.
I practised observing the stars: the rainy constellation
they know as the Goat, the Pleíades, Hýades, Arctus the
    Great Bear.   595
I studied the changing winds and where I could find good
    harbours.
   'One day, on a voyage to Delos, my ship was brought by
    the wind
to the island of Chios. By skilful rowing we made the shore,
jumped out of the boat and planted our feet in the squelchy
    sand.
There we remained for the night. As soon as the red dawn
    started   600
to glow in the east, I rose and ordered my crew to take on
fresh water, indicating the path which led to a spring.
For myself I mounted a look-out point to check the
    direction
the wind was blowing, then called to my men as I made my
    way back
on board. "All present, cap'n!" responded the mate
    Ophéltes,   605
leading along the shore what he thought was a prize he had
    won
in a lonely meadow, a boy with a beautiful face like a girl's.
Their captive appeared to be staggering and struggling
    behind in a drowsy,
drunken stupor. I looked at his dress, his face and his
    movements.
Nothing I saw suggested the form of a mortal creature.   610
Sensing this, I said to my crew, "Some god inhabits this
    body,

I don't know who, but a holy presence is surely there.
O spirit divine, whoever you be, be gracious and prosper
our ventures! I pray you to pardon these men." "Don't
      bother to pray
For *us*!" said Dictys, the nimblest sailor in scaling the
615   topmost
yard and sliding down to the deck with his hands on a
      stay.
"Hear, hear!" barked Libys, "Hear, hear!" joined in
      Melánthus the lookout;
Alcímedon backed them; so did the master oarsman,
      Epópeus,
who called the time for the rowers and rallied their
      spirits as needed;
and so did the rest of the crew. How blind is the lust
620   for plunder!
"I'm in command of this ship," I said. "I cannot
      allow it
to come to harm because it is bearing a god on board."
Placing myself on the gangway, I faced the fury of
      Lýcabas,
the worst of my crew for reckless violence, a Lydian
      outlaw
625 reaping his just deserts for a brutal murder in exile.
As I stood my ground, he landed a powerful punch on
      my throat
and all but sent me reeling into the water, had I not
dazedly managed to cling to a rope which prevented
      my falling.
My impious crew cheered Lycabas on. Then at long
      last Bacchus
(for Bacchus it truly was), as though the uproar had
630   banished
his drowsy demeanour and fully restored his befuddled
      senses,
said, "What are you doing? What does this shouting
      mean? Please tell me,

sailors, how have I come here? Where are you plotting to
    take me?"
"No need to be scared," said Próreus. "Give us the name of
    the harbour
you want to make, and we'll put you ashore wherever you
    ask."   635
"Naxos," Liber replied. "Please set your course towards
    Naxos.
That's where my home is. Sure, they'll make you welcome
    in Naxos."
Those treacherous ruffians swore by the ocean and all its
    gods
that so it would be and told me to get the ship under way.
Now, Naxos lay to the right. I was setting the sails to
    starboard,   640
when each of them, one by one, came up and angrily
    whispered
(though most of them made their meaning apparent by nods
    and winks),
"Acoetes, you fool, what the hell are you up to? Steer to
    port, man!"
I was aghast and answered, "Somebody take the helm!
I refuse to use my skill to further a wicked crime."   645
And now the whole troop of them, mutinously growling,
    railed against me.
"I suppose our safety depends on no one but you!"
    Aethálion
quipped, as he boldly advanced to take my place at the tiller
and steer the ship in a different direction, away from
    Naxos.
  'Now the god had his turn to mock. As though he had
    just   650
seen through the deception, he looked out over the sea from
    the curving
stern and pretended to weep. "This is not where you
    promised to land me,
sailors," he whimpered. "I never asked you to bring me
    here!

What crime are you making me pay for? What credit
        does this do *you*,
a gang of grown men, to play such a trick on a solitary
655   boy?"
Meanwhile I had long been weeping myself; but my
        evil companions
laughed at my tears and quickened the stroke as they
        bent to their oars.
And now I swear to you, sir, by the god himself (no
        other
god is more present than he is), the story you hear from
        my lips
is as true as it beggars belief: the vessel then stood
660   stock still
in the surge and swell of the waves, as though it were
        resting in dry dock.
Puzzled, the sailors continued to lash the sea with their
        oars
and all the sails were unfurled as they struggled by
        these two means
to keep the ship moving. Their oars, however, were
        tangled with ivy,*
which spiralled upward in creeping tendrils until it
665   bedecked
the sails in luxuriant clusters. And there was Bacchus
        himself,
his forehead adorned with a garland of ripening
        bunches of grapelets,
waving a spear emblazoned with vine leaves; lying
        around him
a mirage of savage tigers, lynxes and spotted panthers.
    'The sailors leapt to their feet, impelled by madness
670   or terror –
it matters not which. Then fate struck Medon first: the
        whole
of his body began to go black and his spinal cord to
        bend

in the curve of a bow. "What incredible shape are you
    turning into?"
Lycabas asked him. Whilst he was speaking, his own mouth
    widened,
his nose protruded and all of his skin grew hard and
    scaly.*   675
Libys in turn was trying to ship his entangled oars,
when he saw that his hands were suddenly shrinking away,
    until
they couldn't be called his hands any longer, but only his
    fins.
Another tried to secure his arms on the twisted ropes,
but he had no arms; with a dolphin's limbless body and
    turned-up   680
snout he plunged down into the waves, and the end of his
    tail
was curved like a sickle or like the horns of a crescent
    moon.
Everywhere now they were jumping clear to be drenched in
    the salt spray;
up they would surface again, then dive back down to the
    depths,
frolicking gaily like dancers, wantonly tossing their bodies,   685
spreading their nostrils to shoot the seawater fountaining
    upwards.
Moments before, there were twenty sailors aboard that
    vessel;
I was the sole survivor, shivering and quivering with terror,
almost out of my mind. But the god's voice filled me with
    courage:
"Away with your fears, hold course for Naxos!" As soon
    as I landed,   690
I joined the rites of Bacchus and serve in his holy mysteries.'

PENTHEUS AND BACCHUS (2)

Pentheus broke in: 'I've listened for long enough to this
      rambling
saga. By playing for time he is hoping to soften my
      anger.
Guards, be off with him quickly! Straight to the
      torture-chamber!
Rack his body, then cast it down into Stygian
695   darkness!'
At once the Lydian Acoetes was violently dragged
      away
and immured in a thick-walled dungeon. And while the
      men were preparing
the cruel instruments, iron and fire, for his execution,
the story goes that, as if by magic, the doors flew open,
and the shackles dropped from the prisoner's arms of
700   their own accord.
    Pentheus remained unshaken. He gave no further
      instructions,
but went for himself to Mount Cithaéron, the
      bacchanals' chosen
haunt for their rites and a resonant bowl for their
      jubilant cries.
As a spirited war-horse snorts on the trumpeter's
      braying call
for the battle charge to begin and champs at the bit in
705   excitement,
so Pentheus was roused when the sky re-echoed the
      maenads' drawn-out
shrieks of joy, and the noise in his ears refuelled his
      anger.
    Halfway up the mountainside was a treeless plateau,
edged by a circle of woods and open to view all round.
710 Here, as Pentheus profanely spied on the sacred rituals,
who saw him first? Who rushed on him first in
      maniacal frenzy?

And who first launched her thyrsus to savage her own dear
     son?
His mother Agáve. 'Watch me, sisters,' she shouted, 'both of
     you!
Look at the huge wild boar there wandering over our
     meadow.
That boar must be mine to spear!' He was all alone, but the
     whole band   715
charged him in fury. Massing together and screaming, they
     chased
their quarry, frightened at last and using less threatening
     language,
at last condemning himself and admitting his impious
     wrongdoing.
Wounded, poor wretch, he could still appeal to his mother's
     sister:
'Autonoë, help me! Actaeon's ghost* is pleading for
     mercy!'   720
Actaeon's name meant nothing to her. She wrenched her
     suppliant's
right arm off, as Ino seized and pulled at the left.
Their luckless nephew had no more arms to extend to his
     mother.
All he could show was the wounded stumps of his sundered
     limbs
as he yelled out, 'Look at me, mother!' Agave stared at him,
     uttered   725
a wild shriek, violently shaking her neck and tossing her
     hair,
then twisted his head right off. Displaying it high* in her
     blood-drenched
fingers, she shouted, 'Joy, my companions! Victory is ours!'
As fast as the leaves in autumn are stripped by the wind off
     a tall tree
after the first frost, when they can scarcely cling to the
     branches,   730
so Pentheus' members were rent apart by those guilty
     hands.

Warned by these signs, the Theban women practised
    the new god's
Mysteries and worshipped before his altars with
    offerings of incense.

BOOK 4

The destruction of Pentheus has brought all Thebes under the sway of Bacchus, affirmed by the elaborate recitation of his names and attributes (11–30). The only remaining resistance comes from *The Daughters of Minyas* (1–54), who stick firmly with the normal women's tasks of spinning and weaving, associated with the goddess Minerva, which others have abandoned. To pass the time, the three daughters take it in turns to tell stories, all involving a metamorphosis and all with some kind of love interest:

1. Shakespeare's hilarious parody of *Pyramus and Thisbe* (55–166) in *A Midsummer Night's Dream* is so well known that it is hard to be sure that Ovid's original is to be taken seriously. It may perhaps be interpreted as a sad, even touching, story of two star-crossed lovers like Romeo and Juliet – though one has to disregard the grotesque waterpipe simile when Pyramus stabs himself.

2. The atmosphere is certainly more mirthful in the Homeric *Mars and Venus* (167–89). This quickly leads on to *Leucothoë and Clytië* (190–273), where the theme of the gods' spiteful revenge, already sounded in Book 3, is further developed and the amorous sun god emerges with little credit.

3. *Salmacis and Hermaphroditus* (274–388) is the most titillatingly erotic story in the poem, and the predator for once is female. Its entertainment value is high and might be enhanced in recitation if Alcithoë, the sister who tells it, is delicately characterized.

The 'frame' of the preceding stories is completed when *The Daughters of Minyas* (389–415) have their looms covered with ivy and vines (Bacchus prevailing over Minerva) and they themselves are transformed into bats. The mysterious atmosphere of this passage is particularly good.

Spiteful revenge is very much the theme of *Ino and Athamas* (416–562), with its distinctly grim and macabre tone. Juno, still angry with Thebes because of Jupiter's affair with Semele (3.253 ff.), decides to destroy Ino, the only one of Cadmus' daughters who has not been compelled to suffer. This motivates her descent to Hades, with Ovid's magnificent *ecphrasis* (432–46) and his account of the underworld's inhabitants (447–63), where he must be alluding to Book 6 of Virgil's *Aeneid*. The rest of this vividly told but gruesome story speaks for itself.

The myths connected with Thebes, which were started at the beginning of Book 3, are rounded off in *Cadmus and Harmonia* (563–603). The metamorphosis of old Cadmus into a snake picks up Minerva's prophecy at the end of the hero's fight as a young man with the dragon (3.97–9), and there is a consoling tenderness in the strange detail.

By a very contrived transition (see note on 607) Ovid takes us on from the Theban legend to the story of *Perseus* (604–803), the hero renowned above all for his decapitation of the snake-haired Gorgon, Medusa. The grander epic tone returns for Perseus' confrontation with Atlas (621–62), and then for the rescue of the princess Andromeda in his fight with the sea-monster (663–739). A quieter passage (740–52) follows on the origin of coral, leading on to the rites connected with the wedding of Perseus and Andromeda (753–64). This provides a setting for Perseus to narrate how he killed the Gorgon (765–86) and how Medusa had acquired the snakes in her hair (787–803). The book ends, interestingly, with a powerful image of Minerva in her Gorgon-adorned aegis. In the poetic scheme, the goddess has redeemed her defeat by Bacchus.

THE DAUGHTERS OF MINYAS (1)

Only a handful of women rejected the revels of Bacchus.
One was Alcíthoë, Mínyas' daughter, foolhardy enough
to deny that the god was Jupiter's son; and her impious
    sisters
shared this wicked belief. Now orders had come from the
    priest
for a solemn festival: ladies and serving-women were
    therefore   5
excused from their household duties; all were to wear the
    fawnskin,
take off their headbands, garland their hair and carry the
    leaf-tipped
thyrsus; the wrath of the god would be dire against any who
    slighted him.
So the seer proclaimed. Obediently mothers and young
    wives
left their looms and baskets of wool with their tasks
    unfinished.   10
Burning incense, they called on the god by his different
    titles:*
Bacchus, the Spirit of Thunder, Lightning-Born, the
    Releaser,
twice-begotten and only child of two mothers,* Mount
    Nysa's
Nursling, Thýone's* unshorn son; the God of the
    Winepress,
Planter of grapes which delight the heart, and the Lord of
    the Night-Dance;
Father of revels and cries ecstatic, Mystic Iácchus,*   15
and all the other numberless names which Liber is
    known by
throughout the cities of Greece. For yours indeed is
    unperishing
youth and eternal boyhood. You have the comeliest form

of all the gods on Olympus, a face in your hornless
    epiphany*
20 fair as a virgin girl's. The East is under your sway
as far as the end of the world where the Ganges waters
    the land
of the swarthy Indians. You, dread god, have punished
    Péntheus
for his impiety, punished Lycúrgus who wielded his
    two-edged
axe; and you cast the Lydian sailors* into the sea.
The car which you proudly drive is drawn by a pair of
    lynxes,
splendidly harnessed in gaudy straps. Your train is
25   composed
of bacchants and satyrs with old Silénus, drunk and
    supporting
his battered legs on a stick or uncertainly clutching the
    sides
of a crook-backed donkey. Wherever you go on your
    glorious progress,
the shouts of the young attend you, the screams of
    women, the banging
of tambourines, the skirling of pipes and the clashing of
30   cymbals.
    'Lord, in your gentle mercy be with us!' the Theban
    women
prayed as they duly worshipped; only the daughters of
    Minyas
stayed indoors and marred the feast with their
    untoward housecraft,
drawing the wool into thread and twisting the strands
    with their thumbs,
or moving close to the loom and keeping their servants
35   occupied.
One of the daughters, while deftly spinning, advanced a
    suggestion:
'While others are idle and fondly observing their
    so-called festival,

we are detained by Minerva,* who better deserves our
    attention.
But why don't we also relieve the toil of our hands by
    telling
stories of different kinds and take it in turns to speak,   40
while the rest of us quietly listen? The time will go by more
    quickly.'
Her sisters approved the idea and asked her to tell the first
    story.
Then she pondered which of the many tales* that she knew
was the best one to choose: perhaps the story of Babylonian
Dércetis, goddess whose body was changed to a
    scale-covered fish,   45
now swimming about in a lake, as the people of Palestine
    think?
Or ought she to tell how Dercetis' daughter* acquired her
    wings
and passed her declining years perched up in a
    white-painted dovecote?
Or how a naiad made use of her spells and exceedingly
    potent
herbs to turn the bodies of youths into voiceless fishes,   50
until she was changed to a fish herself? Or should she relate
the tale of the mulberry tree, which used to produce white
    fruit
but was stained with blood and came to burgeon with dark
    red berries?
This was the story she chose, because it was less familiar;
and thus she began, as the thread whirled round on the
    twisting spindle.

PYRAMUS AND THISBE

'The tale of Pýramus, known as a youth of exceptional
    beauty,   55
and Thisbe, by far the loveliest maiden in all the East.
They lived on adjoining estates in the lofty city of Babylon,

ringed, as they tell, with its walls of brick by Queen
      Semíramis.
Neighbourhood made for acquaintance and planted the
      seeds of friendship
which time matured into love. They'd have been united in
60   marriage,
had not their fathers opposed it. But feelings may not be
      forbidden;
their hearts belonged to each other and burned with an
      equal passion.
No one was in their confidence; nods and gestures the
      only
means of conversing; the closer their secret, the stronger
      the flame.
   'The walls that divided the two estates had a tiny
65   hole,
a cranny formed long ago at the time the partition was
      built.
In the course of the years, this imperfection had never
      been noticed;
but what is not sensed by love? The lovesick pair were
      the first
to find it, and used it to channel their whispered
70   endearments in safety.
Often, when both had taken their places, Pyramus this
      side,
Thisbe on that, and caught the sound of the other's
      breathing,
"You spiteful wall!" they would cry. "Why stand in the
      way of poor lovers?
You mustn't think we're ungrateful; we grant that we
76   owe it to you
that our words have been able to find their way to the
77   ears of our loved ones.
74 If you would only allow us to lie in each other's arms!
If that is too much, could you open your cranny enough
75   for a kiss?"

Exchanges like these were useless, with such an impassable
    barrier.
Night came on and they said goodbye, each printing a
    kiss
their side of the wall with lips that never could feel a
    response.   80
   'Dawn on the following day had extinguished the stars of
    night,
and the sun's bright rays had melted the frost and dried the
    fields
when the lovers came to their usual tryst. This time, after
    sighing
their tale of woe, they made a decision: when all was quiet
that night, they would try to elude their guards and steal
    out of doors;   85
then once they'd escaped from their homes, they'd abandon
    the city as well.
In case they got lost on their journey out in the open
    country,
their rendezvous would be Ninus' tomb,* where they'd hide
    in the shade
of a certain tree – a tree which was tall and heavily laden
with snow-white berries, a mulberry – close to a cooling
    fountain.   90
The plan was agreed. Though the day passed all too slowly,
    at last
the sun plunged into the waves and night invaded the
    heavens.
   'Craftily, using the darkness, Thisbe manoeuvred the
    doors
on their hinges and crept from the house unseen. With her
    face well covered,
she came to the tomb and sat down under the mulberry
    tree.   95
Love made her brave; when all of a sudden a lioness also
arrived to slake her thirst in the nearby fountain, her
    foaming

jaws besmeared with the blood of the cattle she'd newly
     slaughtered.
The moonlight allowed Babylonian Thisbe to sight this
     beast
100   some distance away and scuttle in fear to a murky cave.
In her flight the cloak she was wearing fell to the
     ground behind her.
When the savage creature had quenched her thirst with
     a long, cool drink
and was padding back to the woods, she chanced on
     the flimsy mantle
without its owner and mauled it inside her gory mouth.
Pyramus stole out later and came on the scene to
105   observe
the unmistakable tracks of a wild beast, there in the
     deep dust.
At once he grew deadly pale; but when he had also
     discovered
the blood-drenched cloak, he exclaimed: "One night
     shall ruin two lovers!
Thisbe deserved far better to live to a ripe old age.
Mine is the guilty soul. Poor girl, it is I who've
110   destroyed you
by making you find your way at night to this
     frightening place,
without being there to meet you. I call upon all of the
     lions
whose lairs are under this cliff to tear *my* body apart,
not my innocent love's, and devour *my* flesh in their
     merciless jaws!
Yet merely to pray for death is a coward's part." Then
115   he picked up
Thisbe's mantle and carried it into the shade of the
     mulberry.
Bitterly weeping, he kissed the garment he knew so
     well,
and cried to it: "Now be soaked in the blood of
     Pyramus too!"

As he spoke, he plunged the sword he was wearing into his
      side
and at once, in his death-throes, pulled it out of the seething
      wound.   120
As he lay stretched out on the earth, his blood leapt up in a
      long jet,
just as a spurt from a waterpipe,* bursting because of its
      faulty
leadwork, gushes out through a tiny crack to create
a hissing fountain of water and cuts the air with its impact.
Splashed by the blood, the fruit on the mulberry tree was
      dyed   125
to a red-black colour; the roots were likewise sodden
      below
and tinged the hanging berries above with a purplish hue.
  'Thisbe now returned to the scene, still afraid, but
      reluctant
to fail her lover, anxiously looking this way and that,
and longing to tell him what terrible danger she'd lately
      avoided.   130
The spot she could recognize, also the shape of the tree that
      she saw,
but the fruit's strange colour was puzzling. Could she have
      come to the wrong place?
While she wondered, she noticed some blood, then
      quivering limbs
pulsating upon the ground. She stepped back, paler than
      boxwood,
shivering like the sea when a light breeze ruffles the
      surface;   135
but after a little while she realized this was her lover,
and hammered resounding blows of grief on her innocent
      shoulders.
Tearing her hair and flinging her arms round Pyramus' body,
weeping over his wounds and mingling her tears with his
      blood,   140
she covered his death-cold face again and again with her
      kisses.

"Pyramus! What dread chance has taken you from me?"
     she wailed,
"Pyramus, answer! It's Thisbe, your dearest beloved,
     calling
your dear name. Listen, please, and raise your head from
     the ground!"
Pyramus' eyes were heavy with death, but they flickered
145   at Thisbe's
name. He looked once more at his love, then closed
     them for ever.
     'Recognizing her cloak and his ivory scabbard lying
empty, Thisbe exclaimed: "Poor Pyramus, killed by
     your own hand,
aided by love! I also can boast a hand with the courage
to brave such a deed, and my love will lend me the
150   strength to strike.
I'll follow you down to the shades and be known as the
     ill-starred maiden
who caused and shared in your fate. Though nothing
     but death, alas,
could tear you away, not even death shall be able to
     part us.
You sad, unhappy fathers of Thisbe and Pyramus, hear
     us!
We both implore you to grant this prayer: as our hearts
155   were truly
united in love, and death has at last united our bodies,
lay us to rest in a single tomb. Begrudge us not that!
And you, O tree, whose branches already are casting
     their shadows
on one poor body and soon will be overshadowing
     two,
preserve the marks of our death; let your fruit forever
160   be dark
as a token of mourning, a monument marking the
     blood of two lovers."
She spoke, then placing the tip of the sword close
     under her breast,

she fell on the steely weapon, still warm with her Pyramus'
    blood.
Those prayers, however, had touched the hearts of the gods
    and the parents:
the fruit of the mulberry tree, when it ripens, is now dark
    red;   165
and the ashes surviving the funeral pyres are at rest in the
    same urn.'

MARS AND VENUS

There the tale ended. The briefest of intervals followed.
    Leucónoë
then took her turn to speak, while her sisters listened in
    silence:
'Even the Sun who sways the world with his brilliant star
Has fallen in love. My story's title is "Loves of the Sun
    God".*   170
This god is supposed to have been the first to spy the affair
between Mars and Venus;* this god is the first, in fact, to
    spy everything.
Shocked, he reported Venus' betrayal to Vulcan, her
    husband,
and also disclosed where the son of Juno could catch the
    offenders.
Vulcan's feelings were shattered; the piece of work he was
    crafting   175
dropped from his hands. At once he designed an intricate
    netting
by way of a trap, consisting of brazen links so fine
that the eye couldn't see them. The thinnest of wool threads
    couldn't be finer,
nor even a spider's web slung down from the height of a
    roof-beam.
He made the contrivance react to the gentlest of touches
    and slightest   180
of movements, deftly arranging it all to encircle the bed.

So when his wife and her paramour entered the chamber
        together,
the husband's exquisite art and ingenious netting enabled
the pair to be caught, unable to move, in the midst of
        their love-making.
Instantly Vulcan threw open the ivory doors and
185   admitted
the other gods. There were the guilty ones lying
        together, entwined
in their shame! The gods were amused, and one of
        them murmured: "If only
I could be shamed like that!" Then all of them burst
        into laughter.
This story went the rounds of the sky for a long time
        afterwards.

LEUCOTHOË AND CLYTIË

'Venus took her revenge on the Sun for informing
190   against her;
he had frustrated her secret affair and would soon be
        frustrated
in turn by a passion as strong. What use to Hypérion's
        son
would his beauty, amazing complexion and radiant
        beams be now?
The truth was, the god who burns the whole of the
        world with his fires
was burning himself with a strange new flame. The eye
195   supposed
to see all was fixed on Leucóthoë; looks which he owed
        to the world
were on one pretty girl. He was rising too early and
        setting too late;
to prolong his gazing, he made the daylight in winter
        last longer.

Sometimes he'd fail altogether; his sickness of heart
    infected   200
his rays and the darkness drove the human race into panic.
His pallor was never due to the moon interposing itself
too low between him and the earth; it was love that had
    altered his colour.
None but Leucothoë drew him. Clýmene, Rhodos* and
    Perse,
Aeaéan Circe's beautiful mother, were all forgotten –   205
and Clýtië too; although he had scorned her, she still was
    eager
to lie in his arms, and this new turn of events had wounded
    her
deeply. Leucothoë made him forget many earlier passions.
She came from the land of incense.* The mother who bore
    her was called
Eurýnome – fairest of all, but after Leucothoë came   210
to her prime, the daughter's beauty exceeded the mother's
    no less
than the mother outshone the rest. Her father was
    Órchamus, ruler
of Persia's cities and seventh in line from ancient Belus.*
  'Under the skies of the west are the fields where the Sun's
    steeds rest
and graze, not on grass, but ambrosia. That is the food
    which sustains   215
their exhausted limbs and revives their strength for the
    next day's journey.
So while his horses were munching on this celestial
    fodder
and night was on duty, the sun god entered his loved one's
    chamber,
taking the form of her mother, Eurýnome. There by the
    lamplight
he saw Leucothoë busy among her dozen handmaidens,   220
chastely spinning the fine smooth wool on a twirling
    spindle.

So, kissing the girl as a mother might kiss her beloved
        daughter,
he said, "My business is confidential. Women, please
        leave us
alone. A mother must have the right to a private
        discussion."
The servants obeyed and soon the chamber was empty of
225   witnesses.
"I am the one," he announced, "who measures the
        course of the long years,
who sees all things that exist and empowers the earth
        to see them,
the eye of the universe! Trust me, I love you!"
        Leucothoë trembled,
her fingers went limp, her distaff and spindle fell to the
        ground.
But even in fear she was lovely. The sun god waited no
230   longer,
but quickly returned to his natural likeness and radiant
        splendour.
Shocked as she was by this sudden appearance, the girl
        was utterly
dazzled. Protest was vain and the Sun was allowed to
        possess her.
    'Clytië's jealousy now was awakened – the passion
        the Sun
had felt for her once had not been half-hearted. Stung
235   by anger
against her rival, she spread the scandal abroad and
        informed
Leucothoë's father. His action was savage and showed
        no mercy.
Unmoved by her prayers when she stretched her arms
        to the Sun's rays, pleading,
"He took me against my will!", he brutally buried his
        daughter
deep in the earth and piled a hillock of sand on her
240   grave.

Hyperion's son then cut through the mound with his rays
        and opened
a gap which could have allowed her smothered face to
        emerge.
But the girl was unable to raise her head; she was totally
        crushed
by the weight of the earth and merely a lifeless, prostrate
        body.
Nothing, they say, had distressed the winged steeds'
        charioteer   245
so bitterly since the fire which destroyed his own son,
        Pháëthon.
The sun god tried to deploy the power of his rays to
        restore
his love's cold limbs, if only he could, to the warmth of life;
but all his attempts were opposed by fate. He therefore
        decided
to sprinkle the body and ground nearby with perfumed
        nectar.   250
Then, after a long lament, he cried: "You still shall return
to the air above!" At once the corpse, now permeated
with heavenly nectar, melted and soaked the earth with its
        fragrance.
Then gradually, through the soil, disrupting the mound
        with its tip,
there emerged the sprig of a fully rooted frankincense
        shrub.   255
   'Clytië's love could well have excused her angry
        resentment
and so her turning informer; despite it, the lord of the
        daylight
abandoned his visits and brought his affair with her to a
        close.
Thenceforth she wasted away, for passion had turned to
        madness.
Rejecting her fellow-nymphs and passing her days and
        nights   260
in the open air, she sat on the hard bare soil, bareheaded,

with hair dishevelled. For nine whole days she refused all
    food
and drink; pure dew and her tears were enough in her
    starving condition.
She never stirred from the spot. She only gazed on the
    face
of the god in the sky and followed his course with her
265   turning head.
They say that her limbs caught fast in the ground, and
    a bloodless pallor
changed her complexion in part to leaves of a
    yellowish green;
but the red in her cheeks remained and a flower like a
    violet covered
her face – the heliotrope, which is firmly rooted but
    turns
on its stem to its lover the Sun, still keeping faith in its
270   new form.'*
Leuconoë finished. Her wonderful tale had entranced
    her audience.
Some said, 'It couldn't have happened'; but others
    declared, 'Real gods
can do anything!' – Bacchus, however, was not
    included among them.

SALMACIS AND HERMAPHRODITUS

Alcithoë's turn came next when her sisters again were
    silent.
Running her shuttle through the threads of her standing
275   loom,
she started: 'No more of the loves* – they are too well
    known – of the shepherd
of Ida, Daphnis, turned to a rock by a nymph's proud
    anger
against her rival – lovers can be so wickedly jealous!

Nor shall I tell how once, in breach of the laws of nature,
Sithon's gender could alternate between male and female.   280
How about Celmis, who once looked after the baby Jupiter,
now transformed into steel? The Curétes,* born of the
        rain-shower?
Or Crocus and Smilax, his loved one, changed into tiny
        flowers?
No, I shall charm your ears with a tale that's completely
        new.
    'I'm going to tell you about the notorious fountain of
        Sálmacis,   285
how it is so and why it softens and weakens the men
who bathe in its strength-sapping stream. Its effects are
        renowned, though the reason's
a mystery. Mercury once had a son by the goddess Venus,
nurtured and reared by the naiads who dwell in the caves
        on Mount Ida.
Father and mother could both be seen in his handsome
        features.   290
Between them they also gave him his name,
        Hermaphrodítus.*
Once he had reached the age of fifteen, he abandoned his
        native
mountains; Ida, his foster-mother, was left behind
as he ventured forth to explore the unknown; the sight of
        new places,
new rivers, enthralled him, excitement taking the pain out
        of travel.   295
He came as far as the cities of Lýcia and Lycia's neighbours
in Cária. Here he discovered a pool which was perfectly
        clear
right through to the bottom, entirely empty of marshy
        reeds,
unfertile sedge-grass and spiky rushes; the crystalline water
was lushly fringed by a circle of fresh and evergreen grass.   300
Now this was the home of a nymph, but one who didn't
        enjoy

the normal pursuits of archery, hunting and running
     races,
the only naiad not to belong to the train of Diana.
Often, the story goes, her anxious sisters would say to
305   her,
"Salmacis, why don't you take your javelin or painted
     quiver
and vary this indolent life of yours with some hard,
     rough hunting?"
But Salmacis wouldn't take hold of her javelin or
     painted quiver
and vary that indolent life of hers with some hard,
     rough hunting.
Instead you would find her washing her beautiful limbs
310   in her favourite
fountain, or lazily drawing her boxwood comb
     through her tresses,
using the pool as a mirror to find the most fetching
     hairstyle;
or else she'd put on an alluring dress which was fully
     transparent,
and softly recline on a cushion of leaves of luxurious
     grass.
Sometimes she'd gather flowers; and she chanced to be
315   gathering flowers
when she saw this glorious boy and wanted at once to
     possess him.
  'Keen as she was to approach him, she didn't move
     closer until
she had made herself pretty. She cast a careful eye on
     her dress
and arranged her expression. Nobody now could have
     questioned her beauty.
At last she spoke:* "Magnificent boy, one could easily
320   take you
to be a god! If you *are* a god, you must surely be
     Cupid.

If only a mortal, why then, your parents are wonderfully
    blessed!
How lucky your brother is, and so for sure are your sisters,
and also the woman who nursed you and gave you her
    breasts to suck!
But far and away the most happy of all, if you are
    betrothed,   325
is the maid whom torches escort to your house in the
    wedding procession.
If she is already chosen, allow me a stolen pleasure;
if not, let *me* be your bride and take me at once to your
    bed!"
So much from the nymph. The cheeks of the lad were
    covered in blushes –
he didn't know what love was; but even his blushes became
    him.   330
His skin was the colour of apples on trees in a sun-
    drenched orchard,
or ivory steeped in dye, or the moon in eclipse when its
    whiteness
is turned to red and cymbals are clashed* in vain to
    restore it.
The naiad continually begged him to kiss her, at least like a
    sister,
and started to put her hands on his ivory-coloured neck,   335
when he shouted, "Stop, or I'll run away and abandon you
    here!"
Salmacis quivered with fear. "The place is entirely yours,
young stranger," she said, as she turned on her heels and
    pretended to leave;
but even then she kept looking back and secreted herself
in the bushes nearby, crouched down on her knee.
    Hermaphroditus,   340
thinking he had the grass to himself and that no one was
    watching,
walked up and down by the pool, then dipped his toes in
    the lapping

play of the stream and immersed his feet as far as the
        ankles.
The water was lovely, deliciously cool! Without further
        ado,
he removed his tunic so soft and so smooth from his
345   body so slender.
Salmacis now was wildly excited. The sight of him
        naked
fired her desire to new heights. Her eyes were also on
        fire,
like the dazzling light of the sun's reflected rays, when
        a mirror
is raised to capture its shining disc at its brightest and
        clearest.
Any delay or postponement of joy was almost
350   impossible.
Out of control in her frenzy, she had to embrace him
        now.
   'The young man, cupping his palms and slapping his
        torso, swiftly
jumped down into the pool. As his arms flashed out in
        alternate
strokes, his body gleamed in the glassy water, like
        ivory
statues or pure white lilies encased in transparent
355   crystal.
"Victory! He's mine!" the naiad shouted. Then
        stripping off all
her clothes and tossing them wide, she dived in after
        her quarry,
grabbed hold of his limbs as he struggled against her,
        greedily kissing him,
sliding her hands underneath him to fondle his
        unresponsive
nipples and wrapping herself round each of his sides in
360   turn.
For all his valiant attempts to slip from her grasp, she
        finally

held him tight in her coils, like a huge snake* carried aloft
in an eagle's talons, forming knots round the head and the
    feet
of the royal bird and entangling the flapping wings in its
    tail;
or like the ivy which weaves its way round the length of a
    tree-trunk,   365
or else an octopus shooting all its tentacles out
to pounce on its prey and maintain its grip in the depths of
    the sea.
The boy held out like a hero, refusing the nymph the
    delights
that she craved for. Salmacis squeezed still harder, then
    pinning the whole
of her body against him, she clung there and cried: "You
    may fight as you will,   370
you wretch, but you shan't escape me. Gods, I pray you,
    decree
that the day never comes when the two of us here shall be
    riven asunder!"
Her prayer found gods to fulfil it. The bodies of boy and
    girl
were merged and melded in one. The two of them showed
    but a single
face. You know, when a twig is grafted on to a tree,   375
the stock and branch will join as they grow and mature
    together;
so, when those bodies united at last in that clinging
    embrace,
they were two no more but of double aspect, which
    couldn't be fairly
described as male or as female. They seemed to be neither
    and both.
  'And so, when he saw that the pool which his manhood
    had entered had left him   380
only half of a man and this was the place where his limbs
had softened, Hermaphroditus stretched out his hands and
    appealed,

no more with a masculine voice: "Dear father and
       mother, I pray you,
grant this boon to the son who bears the names of you
       both:
whoever enters this pool as a man, let him weaken as
385   soon
as he touches the water and always emerge with his
       manhood diminished!"
Venus and Mercury both were moved and fulfilled the
       prayer
of their androgyne son by infecting the pool with a
       neutering tincture.'

THE DAUGHTERS OF MINYAS (2)

Alcithoë's story was ended, and still the daughters of
       Minyas
kept at their weaving in scorn of Bacchus, profaning his
390   feast day.
Suddenly, out of nowhere, their ears were harshly
       assaulted
by clattering drums, the fearful skirling of Phrýgian
       pipes*
and the strident clashing of cymbals. The perfume of
       myrrh and of saffron
pervaded the air. Then, hard to believe, the looms
       began
to grow green and the weaving to change into leafy
395   curtains of ivy.*
Part of it turned into vines, with the threads
       transformed into tendrils.
Fronds shot out of the warp, and the purple dye in the
       tapestry
lent its brilliant hue to clusters of deep-coloured
       grapes.
By now the day had completed its course, and the time
       was approaching

which couldn't be firmly established as either darkness or
    light   400
but a kind of disputed no man's land between night and
    day,
when the building suddenly seemed to be shaken and flames
    to leap
from the oil-rich lamps; the room was aglow with flickers of
    fiery
red and filled with howling spectres of savage beasts.
The sisters already were hiding in different corners around   405
the smoky house, to escape from the flames and the
    flickering lights;
and while they were searching for darkness, their limbs
    shrivelled up and a membrane
stretched across them to trap their arms in gossamer
    bat-wings.
How they had come to lose their former appearance they
    could not
tell for the gloom. They lacked any feathers to lift them
    upwards,   410
but simply hovered in air, sustained by their filmy,
    transparent
wings. When they tried to speak, their minuscule bodies
    would only
allow them to sigh for their lot in the thinnest and shrillest
    of squeaks.
Their haunts are covered spaces, not trees; as they loathe
    the daylight,
they fly in the night and take their Latin name from the
    evening.*   415

INO AND ATHAMAS

From that time onward the godhead of Bacchus was fully
    acknowledged
throughout all Thebes, and the newcomer's strength was
    widely proclaimed

by Ino, his mother's sister. Alone of the daughters of
    Cadmus
she knew nothing of grief, except what she felt for her
    sisters.
Her children, her marriage to Áthamas, filled her heart
420   with exalted
pride, and so did the god she had nursed in his cradle.*
    When Juno
saw her, she said to herself in resentment: 'The son of
    that harlot,
Sémele, metamorphosed the Lydian sailors and
    plunged them
into the sea; he handed Agáve her own son's flesh
to be torn to pieces; and gave three daughters of
425   Minyas bats' wings.
All *I* can do is to weep for sores that are never avenged.
Is weeping enough? Must that be the limit to Juno's
    sovereignty?
No! I can learn from my foe and follow Bacchus'
    example.
The slaughter of Pentheus is more than enough to
    demonstrate amply
the mischief that madness can work. Then why
430   shouldn't Ino also
be goaded to madness and follow the way of her guilty
    sisters?'
    Picture a path which is overcast by funereal yew
        trees,
sloping down to the realms below through a deathly
    silence.
Along this path, as the mist curls up from the
    motionless Styx,
the incoming shades are descending, the ghosts of the
435   recently buried –
a rugged region, pervaded by pallor and cold, where
    the alien
spirits can find no sign to the road which leads to the
    Stygian

city and so to the dreadful palace of gloomy Dis.
The city has room for all, with its hundred approaches and
        gates
that are everywhere open. As all the rivers on earth flow
        into   440
the sea, so Hades admits every soul that arrives; it is never
too small for its new population and never begins to feel
        crowded.
Bloodless, bodiless, boneless, the spirits endlessly wander,
perhaps frequenting the forum or thronging King Pluto's
        palace;
they could be plying some trade they pursued in their
        former existence,   445
or else they are serving the punishment meted out to each
        one.
    Yielding so far to her spiteful anger, Saturnian Juno
brought herself to abandon her heavenly throne and
        descend
to Hades. As soon as she'd passed inside and the threshold
        had groaned
beneath the weight of her sacred presence, Cérberus lifted   450
his three heads, barking with all three mouths at once. The
        goddess
then called on the awesome, implacable power of the sister
        Furies,
daughters of Night, who were sitting in front of the prison
        of hell,
with its great iron gates, and combing the black snakes out
        of their hair.
As soon as they recognized Juno approaching through the
        shadowy   455
gloom, they rose to their feet. She had come to the House
        of the Damned:*
here was the giant Títyos, sprawling across nine acres,
guts exposed to the vultures. There was Tántalus, failing
to drink any water or seize the elusive fruit-tree above him;
Sísyphus, pushing or chasing the rock which keeps rolling
        downwards;   460

Ixíon, pursuing and running away from himself on his
      wheel;
and Dánaus' daughters, who dared to murder their
      cousin husbands,
always refilling their jars with water, but only to lose it.
   Grimly inspecting these tortured criminals, Juno
      specially
gazed at Ixion and, turning from him to contemplate
465   Sisyphus,
asked herself: 'Why, of the sons of Aéolus,* why
      should this one
suffer perpetual torment, when Athamas, Sisyphus'
      brother,
proudly lives in a royal palace and joins his wife
in displaying contempt for *me*?' She then explained to
      the Furies
the grounds of her hatred and why she had come and
470   what she wanted,
which was that Cadmus' kingdom should fall and
      Athamas also
be driven by madness to crime. As she pestered her
      audience to help her,
commands were mingled with prayers and pledges.
      Then after she'd finished,
Tisíphone* shook her hoary old locks, dishevelled as
      usual,
tossing the wriggling adders away from in front of her
475   face.
'No need for a rambling explanation,' she said to the
      goddess.
'Consider your orders done. Now quit this loathsome
      domain
and take yourself back to your home in the healthier
      air of the heavens.'
Juno was glad to return; and just as she walked into
      heaven,
480 Iris sprinkled her body with water for purification.

Tisiphone wasted no time. In ruthless pursuit of her
        object
she seized a torch she had steeped in gore, she dressed in a
        red robe
dyed in a stream of blood, and girdled this with a writhing
snake as she left the house. She was joined on her way by the
        spirits
of Sorrow, Panic and Fear, and the wild-faced demon of
        Madness.   485
As soon as they stood on the threshold of Aeolus' palace,
        the doorposts
quivered (they say) and a sickly pallor spread over the
        maplewood
panels; the sun disappeared. The omens inspired Queen Ino,
Athamas too, with alarm. They at once made ready to
        leave,
but the sinister Fury blocked their way in front of the
        entrance,   490
firmly extending her arms coiled round in the knots of her
        vipers,
and tossed the locks on her head. The adders responded by
        noisily
straying across her shoulders or slithering over her bosom,
hissing and spewing gore and flicking their tongues in and
        out.
        Tisiphone next wrenched two of the snakes from the
        midst of her hair   495
and flung them forth from her hand with lethal aim. The
        reptiles
landed and glided over the breasts of Ino and Athamas,
breathing their noxious breath on their victims without
        inflicting
a physical wound. The deadly effect was felt in the mind.
The Fury had also come with a marvellous liquid poison: 500
froth from Cerberus' mouth, the dreadful Echídna's venom,
derangement which causes the mind to wander, blinding
        forgetfulness,

crime and tears, with frenzy and bloodlust, all of them
        pounded
together and blended with fresh-spilt blood. This brew
        had been boiled
in a brazen cauldron and stirred with a stalk of evergreen
505   hemlock.
Ino and Athamas quaked as she poured this poison of
        madness
over the breasts of them both and infected their
        innermost being.
Then seizing a torch, Tisiphone brandished and waved
        it around
in a circle, creating a rapid succession of flame after
        flame.
So in triumph, her mission discharged, she returned to
510   the shadowy kingdom
of mighty Dis and untied the snake she had worn as a
        girdle.
   Immediately Athamas, raving but still in the hall of
        his palace,
shouted, 'Huntsmen, your nets! And spread them over
        these woods here!
Look! I've sighted a lioness, there with two of her
        cubs!'
The madman then followed his wife, as though he were
515   stalking a wild beast.
Snatching the baby Leärchus away from his mother's
        breast
(the infant was laughing and stretching his tiny hands
        out), Athamas
swung him around in the air like a sling, then savagely
        shattered
his own child's skull on the hard stone floor. The
        mother, at long last
kindled to fury by grief or the power of the sprinkled
520   poison,
screamed and, with hair flowing wild, she fled from the
        hall in distraction,

her naked arms still clutching her other child, Melicértes.
'Help me, Bacchus!' she cried. At the name of Bacchus,
      Juno
laughed and replied, 'Let this be the thanks that your
      nursling repays you!'
Picture a cliff hanging over the sea, its lower part hollowed   525
out by the surf and protecting the waves beneath from the
      rain,
and its rocky summit jutting over the open water.
Ino, strong in her madness, climbed to the top of this
      headland
and into the ocean below, undaunted by fear, still holding
her baby, she jumped. The waves turned white where she
      struck the surface.   530
    Venus, by contrast, was moved to pity by innocent Ino's
sufferings. Gently coaxing her uncle Neptune, she begged
      him
to help her granddaughter:* 'Lord of the Ocean, whose
      power is second
only to heaven's, I know I am asking the greatest of favours;
but please take pity upon my children whose bodies you
      see   535
are afloat in the vast Ionian Sea. Transform them to
      sea-gods.
Some credit is owed me in your domain, if I once was
      formed
out of foam in the midst of the sea, as the story survives in
      my Greek name.'*
Neptune gave his assent and, removing whatever was
      mortal
in Ino and Ino's child, he invested them both with an
      awesome   540
majesty. Changing their names along with their human
      appearance,
he called the new god Palaémon; the mother became
      Leucothoë.
    Ino's companions from Thebes had followed the trail of
      her footprints

as far as they could, till they came to a halt at the edge of
  the headland.
Certain she must be dead, they tore at their hair, ripped
545 open
their dresses and beat their breasts in grief for the
  house of Cadmus.
They tried to bring hatred on Juno by calling her vilely
  unjust
and excessively cruel to her rival (Sémele, Ino's sister).
Angry at their reproaches, the goddess cried, '*You* are
  the people
I'm going to make my excessive cruelty's principal
550 monuments!'
True to her word, she acted. The friend whose
  devotion to Ino
had been the strongest declared, 'I shall follow and join
  my queen
in the water below!' She started to jump, but found
  herself rooted
fast to the rock, unable to move. A second attempted
the ritual of beating her breast and discovered her arms
555 had suddenly
stiffened. Another by chance had extended her hands
  to the ocean,
and now a figure of stone portrayed the identical
  gesture.
One more was clutching her hair and trying to tear it
  out;
you could see her fingers had hardened around the hair
  she was tearing.
Whatever pose those women were caught in, they held
560 it forever.
Some of the ill-starred daughters of Thebes were
  turned into gulls,
which even today still brush the Ionian Sea with their
  wing-tips.

CADMUS AND HARMONIA

Cadmus was never aware that his daughter and baby
     grandson
had been transformed into sea-gods. His grief, a string of
     disasters,
the numberless portents he'd witnessed had overwhelmed
     him; he therefore   565
abandoned the city he once had founded, as though his
     undoing
were due to a curse on the place, not his own bad luck.
     When he'd wandered
far with his wife in their exile, they reached the Illyrian
     frontier.*
There, weighed down by their years and their troubles, they
     traced their family
fortunes back to the start and recalled the evils they'd
     suffered.   570
'That serpent I pierced with my spear, at the time when I
     came from Sidon,
and scattered its teeth on the ground to grow into strange
     new warriors –
could it by any chance have been sacred?', Cadmus
     wondered.
'Perhaps I provoked the wrath of the gods and this is their
     certain
revenge. If so, let me also be changed to a long-bellied
     serpent!'*   575
As soon as he'd spoken, his form was changed to a
     long-bellied serpent.
He felt his skin growing hard and gaining a layer of scales;
his body was turning black and speckled with bluish spots.
Then down he fell on his front. His two legs melded to one
and little by little thinned down to a sinuous, slithery tail.   580
He still had his arms and, while they remained, he stretched
     them out,

as the tears streamed down the cheeks which still were a
    man's. 'Come close to me,
please!' he appealed to his wife. 'Come close, poor
    darling, and touch me
while something of mine is left. Please take my hand
    while it's there
to be taken, before the snake has enveloped the whole of
585   my body.'
Cadmus wanted to say much more, but his tongue was
    suddenly
split into two like a fork. The words he wanted to utter
failed to come out. Whenever he tried to express his
    sorrow,
he hissed, for this was the only voice which nature had
    left him.
    Beating her naked breasts in her grief, his wife
590   protested:
'Stay with me, ill-starred Cadmus! Abandon this
    monstrous shape!
Oh, Cadmus, what does it mean? Your feet have
    vanished, your shoulders,
your hands, your colour, your face – yes, everything,
    while I was speaking!
Heavenly gods, why cannot you make me a serpent too?'
Cadmus' response was to flicker his tongue on his dear
595   wife's cheeks,
glide his way to her breasts, as though he knew he'd be
    safe there,
fold himself round her and up to the neck which he'd
    loved to caress.
The friends who were present were filled with terror.
    Harmónia merely
stroked and fondled the sleek, smooth neck of the
    crested serpent.
Then all at once there were two of them, gliding with
600   coils intertwined
till they entered the woods nearby and quietly slipped
    into hiding.

As in the past, they will neither avoid nor attack human
      beings;
these snakes are harmless because they remember their
      former existence.

PERSEUS (1)

Although they were now transformed into serpents, Bacchus
      had given
his grandparents much to console them: India had been
      subdued   605
to his cult and Greece was showing him honour in fine-built
      temples.
Acrísius,* son of Abas, descended like Cadmus from
      Neptune,
alone among all the rulers refused Dionýsus admission
into his city of Argos, opposed him with arms and denied
he was Jupiter's son. Moreover, he didn't accept that his
      grandson   610
Pérseus, conceived in the shower of gold by his daughter
      Dánaë,*
was Jupiter's son. But truth will out. Acrisius later
regretted his violence against the god as much as his
      failure
to know his grandson. Bacchus now was enthroned in the
      heavens,
while Perseus was flying on whirring wings* through the
      yielding air,   615
bearing his famous trophy, the head of the snake-headed
      Gorgon;*
and as he triumphantly hovered over the Libyan desert,
some drops of blood from the Gorgon's neck fell down to
      the sand,
where the earth received them and gave them life as a
      medley of serpents;
which explains why Libya now is infested with poisonous
      reptiles.   620

Driven from there by the warring winds through the
        vast empyrean,
Perseus was wafted this way and that, like a scudding
        raincloud.
Poised high up in the ether he looked right down to the
        earth
such a distance below, as he traversed the whole of the
        world in his flight.
Three times he sighted the Bears in the north and the
625   great-clawed Crab
in the south; he would often be swept to the west, then
        back to the east.
And now, as the day declined, mistrustful of flying at
        night,
he touched down on to the western world, in the
        kingdom of Atlas,
and asked for a few hours' rest, till the star of the
        morning summoned
the fires of the dawn and signalled release for the new
630   day's chariot.
This was the home of the son of Iápetus, Atlas, whose
        massive
frame exceeded all mortal men's. His kingdom
        embraced
earth's farthest coasts and the sea, whose waters are
        ready to welcome
the panting steeds and the weary wheels of the setting
        sun.
A thousand flocks and a thousand herds were
635   wandering over
his grassy domain; no troublesome neighbours
        encroached on his borders.
Here was a tree whose leaves were shining with
        brilliant gold,
whose branches were also of gold and laden with
        golden apples.
'Sir,' said Perseus to Atlas at once, 'if you have respect

for distinction of noble birth, then I am descended from
      Jove;   640
if deeds of prowess impress you, you must be impressed by
      mine.
I therefore ask you for shelter and rest.' Then Atlas
      remembered
an ancient oracle, spoken to him by Themis at Delphi:
'Atlas, a time will arrive when your tree will be robbed of
      its gleaming
Gold and a son of Jove will achieve the glory of
      winning it.'   645
Fearing marauders, Atlas had carefully ringed his orchard
with thick-built walls and set an enormous dragon to
      guard it;
he wanted to keep all strangers firmly away from his
      boundaries.
Perseus was no exception. 'Remove yourself,' he insisted.
'You're lying. The exploits you boast of and even descent
      from Jove   650
may work to your disadvantage!' Force was added to
      threats
when Atlas attempted to throw him out; but Perseus refused
to shift and answered in tones that were mild as well as
      courageous.
He couldn't compete in physical strength – that was out of
      the question;
he merely said to the giant, 'Well, since you value my
      friendship
so little, here is a gift!' Then turning his face, he produced   655
from a bag on his left-hand side the loathsome head of
      Medúsa.
The mighty Atlas was turned to a mighty mountain; his hair
and beard were transformed into trees, his massive
      shoulders and arms
to a line of ridges, his erstwhile head to a cloud-capped peak;
his bones became rocks. Then rising high in every
      direction   660

he grew and he grew and he grew (so the gods had
    decreed), till the whole
of the sky with all of its stars could now bed down on his
    ranges.

The winds had all been imprisoned by Aéolus, god of the
    tempests,
inside his cave. The morning star which summons to
    work
665   had risen, bright in the sky. So Perseus fastened the wings
of his sandals again on his feet and girded himself with
    his hooked sword.
Soon he was cutting a path through the air on his
    fluttering anklets,
passing an infinite number of countries around and
    below him.
He finally sighted the realm of Ethiopian Cépheus,*
where Ammon, the god of the land, had unjustly
670   ordered the princess
Andrómeda, innocent girl, to pay the price for her
    boastful
mother who claimed to surpass the daughters of
    Néreus in beauty.
When Perseus noticed the maiden tied by the arms to a
    jagged
rock-face (but for the light breeze stirring her hair and
    the warm tears
coursing over her cheeks, he would have supposed she
    was merely
a marble statue), unconscious desire was kindled
675   within him.
Dumbly amazed and entranced by the beautiful vision
    before him,
he almost omitted to move his wings as he hovered in
    air.
Then once he'd alighted, he said to the maiden, 'Shame
    on such fetters!

You shouldn't be bound by these but the ties of passionate
    lovers.
I ask you to tell me your name, sweet girl, and the name of
    your country.   680
Tell me why you are chained here.' At first she was silent,
    constrained
by maidenly shyness in front of a man; if her hands had
    been free
of their bonds, she'd have lifted them up to her face to cover
    her blushes.
Her eyes could speak, though, filled as they were with
    welling tears.
He continued to press her and therefore, not to appear to
    be hiding   685
a fault of her own, she told him her name and the name of
    her country,
and how her mother had wickedly boasted about her
    beauty.
Her story was still unfinished, when out of the sea there
    resounded
a sinister roar and, advancing across the expanse of ocean,
breasting the surge of the waves, there emerged a menacing
    monster.   690
    Andromeda screamed; her sorrowing father and with him
    her mother
arrived on the scene, both greatly distressed, though the
    mother more justly.
They brought no help but simply engaged in the usual
    rituals
of weeping and beating of breasts. As they clung to the girl's
    chained body,
the stranger protested: 'Your tears and laments can be
    safely indulged   695
later on and at length; a rescue is needed now and with all
    speed.
I am the Perseus fathered by Jove and mothered by Danaë,
impregnated by Jupiter's gold as she languished in prison,

the Perseus who killed the snake-headed Gorgon and
        ventured to fly
through the air on fluttering wings. If I were courting this
700   maiden,
I'd be the suitor you surely preferred for her
        husband-to-be.
To these most splendid endowments, if heaven is kind,
        I shall add
my valiant service. These are my terms: if I rescue your
        daughter,
she shall be mine.' Her parents agreed – they could
        hardly refuse –
and to crown their entreaties they promised Perseus the
705   kingdom as dowry.
    There comes the monster, parting the waves with the
        thrust of his huge breast,
just as a war-galley, strongly propelled by its sweating
        oarsmen,
speedily furrows a path with its sharp-beaked prow
        through the ocean.
Now it was steadily nearing the cliffs, as close as the
        range
of a spinning bullet discharged through the air from a
710   Bálearic sling;
when suddenly Perseus, pushing away from the earth
        with his sandals,
soared aloft to the clouds. When the hero's shadow
        appeared
on top of the water, the frightened monster fiercely
        attacked it.
Imagine an eagle sighting a serpent, sunning its dark
        blue
715 back in an empty field, and swooping down on its prey
from behind; to escape the poison discharged from the
        fangs, it greedily
grips the scaly neck in its talons. So valiant Perseus
swooped straight down through the air to stab the
        beast in the back,

and through its right shoulder he buried his sword-blade
    up to the curved hilt.   720
Roaring with pain and severely wounded, the monster
    reared itself
high in the air, then plunged down into the waves, then
    turned
like a savage but terrified boar when the dogs are baying
    around him.
Poised on his swift wings, Perseus eluded his ravening
    enemy's
jaws and went for his weak points, hacking away with his
    hooked sword,   725
now at its barnacled back and then at the ribs, then
    again
at the narrowest point of the tail where it tapered into a
    fish.
The monster spewed forth seawater mingled with crimson
    blood,
drenching Perseus' sandals in spray and weighing them
    down.
Not daring to trust his sodden wings any further, the man   730
caught sight of a rock whose summit projects from a calm
    sea's surface
but cannot be seen when the ocean is rough. So Perseus the
    valiant,
bracing himself against this, gripping its top with his left
    hand,
plunged his weapon again and again through the monster's
    vitals.
    The shouts of applause re-echoed along the shore and
    above   735
in the halls of Olympus. Andromeda's mother, Cassiopeía,
and Cepheus, her father, were both delighted; Perseus was
    hailed
as their daughter's betrothed and proclaimed as the saviour
    and stay of the house.
The princess, quickly released from her chains, came
    forward to greet him.

Her danger had prompted his feat; she was now the
        reward for his courage.

The victorious hero cleansed his hands in the water they
740   drew for him.
Fearing to bruise the Gorgon's snake-covered head on
        the hard sand,
he softened the ground with leaves and covered it over
        with seaweed,
to serve as a mat for the head of Medusa, the daughter
        of Phorcys.
The fronds which were fresh and still abundant in
        spongy pith
absorbed the force of the Gorgon and hardened under
745   her touch,
acquiring a strange new stiffness in all the stems and
        the foliage.
The sea-nymphs tested this miracle out on additional
        fronds
of seaweed. Excited to find this yielded the same result,
they repeated the marvel by tossing the plant's seeds
        over the waves.
750 Coral even today preserves this identical property:
contact with air induces its hardness and what was a
        flexible
shoot under water is turned to rock on the ocean's
        surface.

Next Perseus built three altars of turf to three of the
        gods:*
the one on the left to Mercury, that on the right to
        Minerva,
755 the central altar to Jupiter. Victims were duly offered:
a cow for the warlike maiden, a calf for the
        wing-footed guide
and a bull for the king of the gods. Without any further
        delay,

Perseus claimed the reward for his valiant deed,
      Andromeda,
seeking no further dowry. The wedding torches were
      flourished
by Hymen and Love; the fires were richly supplied with
      incense;
garlands hung from the palace roof; and everywhere
      singing   760
to music of lyre and pipe auspiciously signified joy.
And now the doors were flung open, the golden halls were
      revealed
with a sumptuous banquet prepared, and Cepheus' court
      was admitted.
  The feasting was over and hearts were relaxed with the
      flowing wine,   765
when the bridegroom asked a few questions about the land
      and its products,
social customs and attitudes held by the people who lived
      there.
The prince who replied went on: 'Now, Perseus, bravest of
      heroes,
please will you tell us the story of how your remarkable
      courage   770
and skill combined to remove the head of the snake-haired
      Gorgon?'
Their guest then mentioned a freezing glen at the foot of
      Mount Atlas,
tightly enclosed by a fortification of massive rocks.
Two sisters had lived by the valley's entrance, the daughters
      of Phorcys,*
who shared the use of a single eye, which Perseus had
      craftily   775
stolen as one was passing it on to the other, by slipping
his hand underneath, thus forcing the Graiae to give him
      directions.
He travelled through rocky regions remote and secluded,
      littered

with broken trees, and finally came to the home of the
    Gorgons.
Across the fields and along the tracks he had seen the
780   statues
of men and of beasts transformed to stone at the sight
    of Medusa.
He, however, had only looked on those terrible
    features
as they were reflected in bronze, on the shield which he
    held in his left hand;
and while Medusa as well as her adders lay buried in
    sleep,
he had lopped her head from its neck. In consequence,
785   swift-winged Pégasus*
sprang from his mother's blood, along with his brother
    Chrysáor.

   Perseus also narrated the dangers he'd faced on his
    long voyage,
naming the seas and the lands he had viewed from his
    flight through the air,
and all the stars which he'd lightly brushed with his
    beating wings,
but his audience wanted more. He was asked by one of
790   the court
why Medusa, alone of her sisters, had snakes entwined
    in her hair.
'That is an excellent question,' responded the guest; 'let
    me give you
the answer. Medusa was once an exceedingly beautiful
    maiden,
whose hand in marriage was jealously sought by an
795   army of suitors.
According to someone who told me he'd seen it, her
    marvellous hair
was her crowning glory. The story goes that Neptune
    the sea god
raped this glorious creature inside the shrine of
    Minerva.

Jove's daughter screened her virginal eyes with her aegis* in
    horror,   800
and punished the sin, by transforming the Gorgon's
    beautiful hair
into horrible snakes.' (That explains why, to startle her foes
    into terror,
the goddess always displays those snakes on the front of her
    bosom.*)

BOOK 5

The story of *Perseus* (1–249) continues with a great wedding-banquet fight, as the hero who won Andromeda is challenged by Phineus, to whom she was previously betrothed. The battle is narrated in epic style, in imitation of Odysseus' fight with the suitors at the feast in the palace of Ithaca (*Odyssey* 22). The gory details were probably more to the taste of Ovid's audience in ancient Rome than they will be to some modern readers; but there are moments of genuine pathos in the deaths of the Indian boy Athis and his lover Lycabas, of the elder Emathion and the minstrel Lampetides. The poet naturally makes great play with the transforming power of the Gorgon's head – which Perseus might quite easily have produced a great deal earlier!

Minerva and the Muses (250–340) takes us into a more tranquil world, though one still troubled by strife. We meet the Muses, who report an unpleasant encounter with the tyrant Pyreneus and also the singing contest to which they were challenged by the daughters of Pierus, now transformed into magpies. The leading Pierid's song had imagined the giants as (contrary to tradition) defeating the gods in battle, and so had portrayed the earth as a source of evil. The Muses had chosen Calliope to represent themselves and she had responded with three stories in her (much longer) song:

1. *The Rape of Proserpina* (341–571). This is modelled on the Homeric Hymn to Demeter and opens with an invocation of Ceres, the Earth Mother, as a source of good. Calliope narrates the familiar myth of the seasons: Pluto abducts Ceres' daughter, Proserpina the spring goddess, to the underworld,

and her mother eventually obtains her restoration to earth for six months of the year. The story is interspersed with four short, thematically unconnected, metamorphoses:

the nymph Cyane (409–37)
the offensive boy (438–61)
Ascalaphus (533–50)
the Sirens (551–63)

In this long section, there is much vivid detail to enjoy, not least the description of the countryside in Sicily from which Proserpina is abducted, but it is not difficult to lose the main framework. One certainly forgets Calliope fairly quickly.

2. The same applies even more in *Arethusa* (572–642), a nymph (like Cyane) transformed to a spring at Syracuse, whom Ceres has encountered in her search for Proserpina and so discovered her daughter's whereabouts (487–508). Arethusa's account of her own metamorphosis and presence in Sicily following her pursuit by the lustful river-god Alpheüs is another story in Ovid's best erotic manner. It reminds us of Apollo's pursuit of *Daphne* (1.451 ff.) and, in its saltier details, of *Salmacis and Hermaphroditus* (4.274 ff.).

3. In *Triptolemus and Lyncus* (643–61) the beneficent power of Ceres is reaffirmed in her gift of corn to the Athenian Triptolemus and the transformation of his would-be-murderer into a lynx.

A brief conclusion (662–78): Calliope's song is judged better than that of the Pierides, who are punished for their clamorous objections by their transformation to magpies.

PERSEUS (2)

While Pérseus, Dánaë's son, was telling his story before
the assembled Ethiopian chiefs, a noisy commotion
broke out in the royal halls; it was not the convivial
    cheering
that graces a wedding feast, but the clamour which
    augurs a riot.
A banquet that suddenly turns to a brawl might well be
5   compared
to a calm sea rudely disturbed by a violent, howling
    gale,
which has made it exceedingly rough and lashed the
    waves to a fury.
Leading the riot was Cépheus' brother, Phíneus, who
    rashly
started a fight as he brandished his bronze-tipped ashen
    spear.
'Look!' he shouted to Perseus. 'I've come to avenge the
10   theft
of my bride.* You won't be saved by your wings or by
    Jupiter changing
himself into counterfeit gold.'* As he aimed his weapon,
    Cepheus
cried to his brother, 'What are you doing? What crazy
    notion
is goading you into a crime? Is this the reward to be
    offered
for such great service, the dowry you pay for
15   Andrómeda's rescue?
To tell you the truth, it wasn't Perseus who took her
    away from you.
No, you must blame the Néreïds' anger, the horned god
    Ammon,
the monster who rose from the sea to sate its ravening
    jaws

on the fruit of my own loins. That was the time when you
      lost her, the time
when death was about to takc hcr away – unless, cruel
      brute,   20
her death is what you're demanding and only our grief can
      console you.
It wasn't enough, I suppose, that you saw her chained to the
      cliff
and offered no help, though you were her uncle and
      promised husband.
To make matters worse, when someone has freed her, you
      have to resent it
and venture to steal the reward! If it matters so much to you
      now,   25
why didn't you fetch her away from the rocks to which she
      was pinioned?
The prize has gone to a hero who saved an old father from
      losing
his daughter. Allow him to take what I promised and what
      he's deserved.
Do realize we didn't prefer him to you but to certain death.'
  Phineus said not a word, but glared at his brother and
      Perseus   30
in turn, uncertain which of the two he should aim to kill.
After a brief hesitation he hurled his spear with all
the power that his angcr could lend him at Perseus – but
      missed his target;
the weapon was caught in the cushions. Perseus at last
      leapt up
from his seat and savagely flung the spear back; indeed he'd
      have pierced   35
his opponent's heart, if the villainous Phineus hadn't
      escaped
to the back of the altar and shamefully taken sanctuary
      there.
But the spear wasn't thrown in vain; it lodged in the
      forehead of Rhoetus,

who fell to the ground. When the point was wrenched
        from his skull, his feet
jerked out, and the food on the banqueting table was
40   spattered with blood.
Now furious passions rose in the crowd and tempers
        were blazing.
Weapons began to fly. There were some who argued
        that Cepheus
deserved to die with his daughter's bridegroom, but
        Cepheus already
had left the palace, invoking the names of Justice, Faith
and the gods of the hearth to protest that the riot was
45   none of his making.
    Minerva, the warrior goddess, arrived to encourage
        Perseus
and give her brother protection behind her impregnable
        aegis.*
Among the throng was an Indian youth, called Athis.
        Limnaée,
the Ganges' daughter, is thought to have given him birth
        in the crystal
waves of the river. His wonderfully handsome looks
        were enhanced
by his elegant clothes; still a pure and innocent boy of
50   sixteen,
he was dressed in a cloak of Tyrian purple, trimmed
        with a golden
border; his neck was adorned with a delicate golden
        chain,
while his hair was scented with myrrh and held in place
        by a circlet.
Athis had mastered the skills of throwing the javelin at
        targets
however remote, but his gifts as an archer were even
55   greater.
On this occasion his hand was bending his pliant bow,
when Perseus, seizing a smoking brand from the altar,
        struck him

across the face, which was smashed to pulp as the bones
    were shattered.
Assyrian Lýcabas, Athis' most intimate friend, who had never
concealed the truth of the love that he felt for him, saw the
    features   60
he'd fondly worshipped emblazoned in blood. In a passion
    of grief
for the youth who had suffered such cruel hurt and was
    gasping his life out,
he snatched the bow which Athis had aimed and shouted to
    Perseus,
'Your fight must now be with me! You shan't be gloating
    for long   65
over killing a boy whose murder has won you more hatred
    than glory.'
Before he had finished, his sharp-tipped arrow was shot
    from the string,
but Perseus ducked and it merely caught in the folds of his
    tunic.
Quickly Acrísius' grandson drew his sickle-shaped sword,
well-tried in the blood of Medúsa, and slashed his
    challenger's chest.   70
As Lycabas' swimming eyes grew blurred in the darkness of
    death,
he looked all round for his Athis and fell at the poor youth's
    side.
They had died together, and that was the comfort he took
    to the underworld.
   There! Syénian Phórbas, the son of Metíon, rushing
forward with Libyan Amphímedon, eager to join in the
    fighting!   75
Both slipped and fell in the pool of blood still warm on the
    earth.
As they tried to pick themselves up, they encountered
    Perseus' sword:
Amphimedon in the ribs and Phorbas across his throat.
Érytus, son of Actor, however, was armed with a great,
    broad

double-edged axe. To stand against him, our hero
80   discarded
his hook-shaped sword and instead grabbed hold of a
          massive bowl,
embossed by its craftsman in high relief and enormously
          weighty.
Lifting it up in both hands, he dashed it down on his
          victim,
who vomited blood in a gush as he fell on his back and
          pounded
the earth with his head. Polydégmon, scion of Queen
85   Semíramis'
house, was next to be laid on the ground; then Ábaris,
          born
in the Caucasus mountains; Lycétus who lived by the
          river Spercheüs;
Hélices, always with hair unshorn; and Clytus with
          Phlégyas.
Perseus was trampling on piles of the dying mounting in
          front of him.
    Phineus lacked the courage to brave his foe at close
          quarters,
but hurled his javelin, which went astray and fell upon
90   Idas,
who'd tried in vain to keep out of the fray and had
          stayed impartial.
Gazing with angry eyes on his cruel assailant, Idas
said to him: 'Phineus, since I am forced to take sides,
          you must now
accept the foe you have made and pay for a blow with a
          blow!'
Then drawing the spear from his body, he struggled to
95   throw it back,
but his limbs were drained of their blood and he quickly
          collapsed on the ground.
    Then also Hodítes, next in rank to the king of the
          Céphenes,

fell to Clýmenus' sword. Prothoénor was slaughtered by
    Hýpseus,
whom Perseus slaughtered in turn. Among the crowd was
    an elder,
Emáthion, known for his love of justice and fear of the
    gods.   100
His years prevented him fighting, so words had to serve him
    for weapons.
Striding forward, he cursed and denounced the impious
    brawl,
then knelt by the altar. His trembling hands were clutching
    its sides,
when Chromis cut off his head. It toppled straight on the
    slab,
and there a half-living tongue continued to utter its curses   105
until all life was exhausted and finally lost in the flames.
  Next a pair of twin brothers, Ammon and Bróteas,
    boxers
and champions unbeaten, if swords could be beaten by
    boxing thongs,
were struck to the ground by the hand of Phineus; so was
    Ámpycus,
priest of Ceres, although he was wearing his white wool
    headband;   110
Lampétides also was killed, who wasn't there for the
    fighting
but merely the peaceful purpose of playing the lyre and
    performing
the joyful songs he'd been ordered to sing at the wedding
    feast.
He was standing apart, with only his harmless plectrum in
    hand,
when Péttalus mockingly cried, 'You can sing the rest of
    your songs   115
to the shades of the Styx!' and he plunged his sword in the
    bard's left temple.
Lampetides fell. His dying fingers fumbled back

to the strings and, in tune with his fall, struck up a
    dejected lament.
Lycórmas, furious, wouldn't allow the minstrel to die
unavenged. He wrenched the stout wood bar from the
120   right-hand doorpost,
crashed it down on the nape of Pettalus' neck, and laid
    him
flat on the ground like a sacrificed bullock. Cinýphian
    Pélates
tried to remove the other bar, from the left-hand post,
but before he could do it, his hand was pierced by the
    Carthaginian
Córythus' spear and pinned to the wood. As he
125   helplessly clung there,
Abas wounded him through the side; unable to fall,
he hung from the post where his hand was nailed, until
    he expired.
    Death came also to Mélaneus, one of Perseus'
    supporters,
and Dórylas, known as the wealthiest man in the
    whole of Libya –
Dorylas rich in land, whose estates of cornfields and
130   mounting
heaps of imported incense were larger than anyone
    else's.
Rich as he was, he was struck by a javelin thrown from
    the side
in the groin, that sensitive place. When Bactrian
    Hálcyoneus,
who had thrown the weapon, could see him rolling his
    eyes in pain
135 and gasping his last, he said, 'Of all your acres of land
you may keep the patch where you're lying!' and left
    the body to rot there.
But soon he was punished by Perseus, who wrested the
    spear from the still warm
wound and flung it towards him. Landing on top of the
    Bactrian's

nose, the shaft emerged through his neck and protruded on
    each side.
While fortune favoured the hand of Perseus, he murdered
    Clanis   140
and Clýtius, born of the selfsame mother but differently
    wounded.
Clytius' thighs were skewered by Perseus' powerfully
    brandished
spear of ash, while Clanis' teeth had to bite on a javelin.
Céladon also was killed (he was born by the Nile in
    Mendes),
and Ástreus, child of a Palestine whore by an unknown
    father.   145
Aethíon perished who once was deeply versed in
    clairvoyance
but then had badly mistaken the omens; Thoáctes, the
    royal
armour-bearer; and lastly Agýrtes, the infamous parricide.
   Perseus was weary, but more was to come since he was
    alone
and the rest were determined to crush him. The milling
    throng had united,   150
sworn to fight in a cause that opposed all merit and good
    faith.
His only backers were Cepheus, whose loyalty counted for
    little,
along with the bride and her mother, who filled the hall
    with their screaming,
drowned though it was by the clashing of arms and the
    groans of the dying.
Meanwhile, the goddess of war* polluted the household
    gods   155
and drenched them in rivers of blood, as she caused fresh
    strife and confusion.
   Now Phineus and all of a thousand supporters were there
    in a ring,
surrounding Perseus alone. Their arrows were flying past
    him

thicker than hailstones to either side, by his eyes and his
    ears.
He stood with his back to a great stone pillar to cover his
160   rear,
then faced the crowd as they pressed towards him, and
    held them off.
Chaónian Mólpeus was close to his left, to his right
    was Arabian
Echémmon. Think of a tigress, goaded to madness by
    hunger,
who hears two herds of cattle lowing in separate
165   valleys;
she cannot decide which herd to attack, but is longing
    to pounce on them
both. So Perseus: was he to strike to the right or the
    left?
In the end he disposed of Molpeus by wounding him
    through the shin
and letting him flee, since Echemmon allowed him no
    further time
and was frantically trying to drive his sword through
170   his enemy's throat.
But his powerful thrust was clumsily aimed; the blade
    of his weapon
struck the edge of the pillar and shattered. A flying
    splinter
of metal lodged in Echemmon's throat, but it wasn't
    sufficient
to cause his death. While he stood there trembling,
175   vainly outstretching
his weaponless hands, the hero dispatched him with
    Mercury's hooked sword.
   When Perseus saw that the crowd was more than his
    courage could handle,
he cried to them all, 'Since you yourselves are forcing
    me to it,
I'll now seek help from my foe. If I've any friends here,
    I advise them

to turn their faces away!' – and he brandished the head of
    the Gorgon.   180
'Find another to scare with your riddles!' Théscelus
    answered;
but just as he started to cast his deadly javelin, his body
froze, like a statue, in throwing position. The next to
    challenge
Perseus the lion-heart was Ampyx, who thrust his sword at
    the hero's   185
breast; as he did it, his right hand stiffened, unable to move
either forward or back. Then Nileus, who'd falsely claimed
    to be sprung
from the Nile with its seven mouths, and whose shield was
    embossed with seven
rivers in silver and gold, called out to him, 'Perseus, look
at my family's founder! To have such a hero as me for your
    killer   190
must surely console you amongst the voiceless shades.' But
    his final
words were cut off as he said them. To judge by his open
    lips,
you'd suppose that he wanted to speak, but the sounds
    couldn't find a way through.
These three were taunted by Eryx: 'It isn't the power of the
    Gorgon   195
that's making you numb but your feeble courage. Now join
    me in charging
this youth as he toys with his magic weapons, and laying
    him flat!'
The charge was about to begin, when his feet stuck fast to
    the earth
and he stayed, a motionless rock in the lasting form of an
    armed man.
   These deserved to be punished; but one called Acónteus,
    a soldier   200
on Perseus' side, set eyes on the Gorgon during the fight,
and his body grew firm and hard as the stone crept over his
    frame.

Astýages, thinking the fellow was still alive, struck out
with his sword's full length, but all it produced was an
        echoing clang.
As he stood where he was, dumbfounded, he turned into
205   stone himself,
with a face which preserved his expression of wonder
        in marble for ever.
You'd find it tedious to learn the names of the rank
        and file
involved in the fray. Two hundred bodies survived the
        battle;
another two hundred were turned to stone at the sight
        of the Gorgon.
    Phineus at last regretted the riot he'd caused so
210   unfairly;
but what could he do? As his eyes travelled round the
        different statues,
he recognized his own friends and cried to each one by
        his name,
appealing for help. In disbelief he fingered the forms
that were nearest, and all were marble! Turning away
        and admitting
defeat, he extended his arms sideways* in a plea for
215   mercy.
'You win, Perseus,' he said. 'Put away your monster,
        remove
your Medusa, whoever she is, with the stare which
        turns us to stone.
Please take it away! It wasn't personal hate or kingly
        ambition
which drove me to start the fighting. I simply wanted
        my bride.
You surely deserved to win her, but I was betrothed to
220   her first.
I yield to you gladly. Only allow me, most valiant of
        heroes,
to keep my miserable life, and all the rest can be yours.'

He spoke without daring to look at the man he was begging
          to spare him.
Then Perseus gave him his answer: 'Phineus, you spineless
          coward,
no need to be scared. I'll allow you all that I can – a
          handsome   225
gift for a weakling like you. You shan't be put to the sword,
          man.
No, I shall make you a lasting memorial for all posterity.
You'll be on permanent view in the house of my
          father-in-law,
that my wife may console herself with her former intended's
          likeness.'
With that he quickly carried Medusa across to display her   230
where Phineus had turned his quivering head. As the
          cowering villain
attempted to shift his eyes away once again, his neck
grew stiff and the tears running down his cheeks were
          hardened to stone.
But still a coward's face and the suppliant's look were
          preserved
in marble, along with the pleading hands and the cringing
          posture.   235

Perseus returned with his wife to his native city in
          triumph.
Once there, he avenged and championed his grandfather
          (not that the old man
greatly deserved it) by challenging Proetus* who'd ousted
          his brother
by force of arms and taken control of Acrisius' fortress.
This time not force of arms nor the fortress he'd seized
          could enable   240
Proetus to counter the terrible eyes of the snake-wreathed
          Gorgon.
   Polydéctes,* however, who ruled the tiny island of
          Sériphos,

failed to be moved by the dangers that Perseus had faced
    and the courage
he'd shown in so many exploits. He still held on to his
    stubborn,
245 relentless hatred and never ceased from his unjust anger.
He even belittled the hero's glory and claimed that
    Medusa's
death was a fiction. 'Here is the proof that my story is
    true,'
cried Perseus to all. 'Watch out for your eyes!' And the
    face of the king
was turned at once into bloodless stone by the face of
    Medusa.

MINERVA AND THE MUSES

Minerva supported her brother, born in the shower of
250   gold,
throughout these trials. But now she wrapped herself
    in a hollow
cloud and departed from Seriphos. Cythnos and
    Gýaros lay
to her right; then finding the shortest crossing over the
    sea,
she made for Thebes and the mountain of Hélicon,
    home of the Muses.
Here she landed and spoke to the sisters who govern
255   the arts:
'A rumour has come to my ears of a fountain that
    started to gush
when the earth was struck by the hoof of the winged
    horse* sprung from Medusa.
Hence my arrival. I wanted to see this amazing spring,
as I witnessed the horse's birth from the blood of his
    Gorgon mother.'
Uránia answered: 'Whatever your reason for coming to
260   visit us

here in our home, kind goddess, we feel great pleasure.
The story you heard is correct: the winged horse Pégasus
    started
our spring'; and she took Minerva down to the sacred
    fountain.
Slowly admiring the waters which Pegasus' hoof had
    created,
the goddess surveyed the clusters of grand, primeval trees, 265
mysterious caves and grass bejewelled with myriads of
    flowers.
She declared that Memory's daughters were truly blessed in
    their dwelling
as well as the arts they ruled. Then one of the sisters
    addressed her:
'Minerva, goddess who fitly could join our musical
    company,
had not your own fine qualities marked you out for yet
    greater   270
tasks, your praise of our arts and our home is truly
    deserved.
Ours is a happy lot, if we could but be sure of our safety.
Sadly, the hearts of the virgin Muses are constantly
    anxious;
crime these days has no bars. The image of wicked
    Pyréneus*
is always in front of my eyes and the shock has not left me
    completely.   275
That savage tyrant was occupying Daulis and Phocis,
lands he'd unjustly seized with the aid of his Thracian
    soldiers,
and we were travelling through to our temple on Mount
    Parnássus.
He saw us coming and, smiling as though he respected our
    godhead,
said to us, "Memory's daughters" (he knew who we were),
    "please rest here.   280
You mustn't refuse to shelter under my roof in this
    shocking

downpour" (the weather was dreadful); "the gods have
    often been seen
in humbler abodes* than mine." So, swayed by his words
    and the storm,
we accepted his invitation and entered the hall of his
    palace.
Later the rain subsided; the wind had changed to the
285   north,
and the murky clouds were scudding away in a clearing
    sky.
As we made a move to depart, Pyreneus bolted the
    doors
and tried to assault us, but we escaped him by taking
    wing.*
As though he intended to follow, the king climbed up
    to the battlements,
shouting, "Whichever pathway you take, I'll find it and
290   follow!"
Quite out of his wits, he cast himself from the top of
    the tower
and fell face forward down to the ground. He shattered
    his skull,
and stained the earth with his impious blood as he
    crashed to his death.'

The Muse was speaking, when suddenly through the
    air there resounded
a whirring of wings, and voices of greeting were heard
295   from the treetops.
Minerva looked up and asked whose tongues could
    have possibly spoken
so clearly, supposing the sounds proceeded from
    human lips.
But they came from birds. There were nine of them,
    roosting up in the branches,
all bemoaning their fates; they were magpies,
    wonderful mimics.

The Muse replied to the puzzled goddess, 'Those creatures
    up there   300
have recently joined the mass of the birds after losing a
    contest.
Píerus was their father, a rich landowner in Pella,
their mother Euíppe, who came from Paeónia; nine hard
    times
she'd gone into labour and called on Lucína, the goddess of
    childbirth.
Puffed in the pride of their numbers, this rabble of ignorant
    sisters   305
travelled through all the towns of Haemónia and all of
    Achaéa
here to Parnassus and then presented the following
    challenge:
"Cease to deceive the uncultured mob with your empty
    attractions.
If you believe in your musical gifts, Helicónian Muses,
you'll surely agree to compete with us. We say that our
    voices   310
are finer, our skill is more expert; what's more, we match
    you in number.
If we are the winners, you'll yield us your two Boeótian
    fountains;
if not, then we will surrender our home in Emáthia's plains
as far as Paeonia's snow hills. The nymphs can adjudge
    between us."
  'Shame as it was to compete with these girls, we thought
    it was even   315
more shaming to bow to their claim. The nymphs who
    were chosen as jury
swore by their streams to judge fairly and took their places
    on benches
formed from the natural rock. Without any casting of lots,
the Píerid maiden who'd first presented the challenge began.
Her song was about the war in the sky:* she ascribed to the
    giants

320   a glory undue and belittled the deeds of the mighty gods.
       The monstrous Typhon, sprung from the deepest
              bowels of the earth,
       had struck such fear in the heaven dwellers, that all in
              a body
       were put to flight, until in exhaustion they found a
              refuge
       in Egypt, close to the banks of the Nile with its seven
              mouths.
       She told how the earth-born giant had followed them
325   even there,
       so forcing the gods to conceal themselves under alien
              guises.
       "Jupiter," said the maiden, "became a ram,* which
              accounts
       for Libyan Ammon's representation in modern times
       with his curving horns; Apollo lurked in the shape of a
              crow,
330   Bacchus a goat, Diana a cat and Juno a snow-white
       cow, while Venus appeared as a fish and Mercury an
              ibis."
          'Such was the song which the Pierid sang as she
              played on her lyre.
       We Muses were called upon to respond – but perhaps
              you haven't
       the time or the leisure to lend an ear to our own
              performance.'
       'I've plenty of time,' Minerva replied, as she took her
335   seat
       in the shade of the forest. 'Now sing me your song
              from beginning to end.'
       The Muse continued: 'Our cause was entrusted to one
              of our band,
       Callíope.* She, with her flowing hair in an ivy wreath,
       rose up and strummed a few plangent chords to test
              her lyre strings,
       then firmly plucked them to launch at once on the
340   following lay.

CALLIOPE'S SONG:
THE RAPE OF PROSERPINA

'"My song is of Ceres, first to furrow the soil with the
      ploughshare,
first to give corn to the earth and nourishing food to
      mankind,
first to give laws; all things are the gift of bountiful Ceres.
She is my theme. I pray that my song may prove to be
      worthy
of this great goddess. Surely the goddess is worthy of song.   345
    '"The enormous island of Sicily lies heaped high on the
      limbs
of the giant Typhon,* who dared to aspire to a throne in
      the heavens.
Often the monster strains and struggles to rise from his
      prison;
but Cape Pelórus, closest to Italy, weighs on his right
      hand,   350
Pachýnus his left, while his legs are crushed beneath
      Lilybaéum.
Etna presses on Typhon's head; laid out on his back,
he belches lava and vomits flame from the angry volcano.
Often he fights to shift the earth which is forcing him down
and to roll the cities and massive mountains away from his
      body.   355
The earth then goes into tremor and even the king of the
      shades
is afraid that the crust of the earth will crack and a chasm
      be opened
to let in the daylight and frighten the quivering spirits
      below.
It was fear of such a disaster that prompted the monarch of
      Hades*
to rise from his gloomy realm. In his chariot drawn by black
      horses   360

he toured round Sicily, carefully inspecting the island's
            foundations.
Once he'd assured himself that nothing was giving way
and his fears were dispelled, he was sighted wandering
            hither and yon
by Venus enthroned on her mountain of Eryx. Fondly
            embracing
her winged son, Cupid, she said to him: 'You, dear child,
365   are my weapons,
my hands and the source of my power. Now take your
            invincible shafts
and shoot those swift-flying arrows to pierce the heart
            of the god
whom fortune allotted the final share in the world's
            three kingdoms.*
You can subdue the gods of the sky and even Jove;
it is you who vanquish the sea-gods, including their
370   sovereign Neptune.
Why should the underworld lag behind? And why not
            extend
the empire of Venus and Cupid? A third of the world is
            at stake.
As it is, we are losing respect in heaven because we
            have been
too soft. Your power and prestige are diminished along
            with my own.
You can see that Minerva and also the goddess of
375   hunting, Diana,
have firmly rejected me. So will the virgin daughter of
            Ceres,
if we allow it to happen; her hopes are the same as the
            others'.
Now, in the name of the power we share, if you take
            any pride in it,
make that goddess her uncle's wife!*' So Venus
            commanded.
Cupid opened his quiver. Next, at his mother's
380   bidding,

he chose from his thousand arrows a single one, but the
    sharpest
and surest he had, the shaft which responded best to his bow.
Then resting his pliant weapon against his knee, he bent it,
shot the barbed reed and wounded dusky Dis in the heart.

'"Not far from the walls of Sicilian Henna you'll come to a
    deep lake,   385
Pergus by name. It is haunted by swans; you won't hear
    more of them
singing along the gliding streams of the river Cayster.
The water is wreathed all round by a garland of forest,
    where foliage
offers an awning against the burning rays of the sun;
the branches provide a delightful coolness; the well-watered
    soil   390
is a flowery carpet of Tyrian purple; and spring is eternal.
One day, Prosérpina, Ceres' daughter, was there in the
    woodland,
happily plucking bunches of violets or pure white lilies,
filling the folds of her dress or her basket in girlish
    excitement,
vying to pick more flowers than her friends – when Pluto
    espied her,   395
no sooner espied than he loved her and swept her away, so
    impatient
is passion. In panic, Proserpina desperately cried for her
    mother
and friends, more often her mother. Her dress had been
    torn at the top,
and all the flowers she had picked fell out of her loosened
    tunic,
which only served to increase her distress, poor innocent
    girl!   400
Her abductor was off in his chariot, urging the horses
    forward,
each by his name, and shaking the rust-dyed reins of their
    long-maned

necks. They galloped across deep lakes and the pools of
    Palíca,
reeking with sulphur and boiling up through a crack in
405   the earth,
to Sýracuse, where the Bácchiadae* from the isthmus
    of Corinth
had built a new city between two harbours, the great
    and the smaller.
   ' "Syracuse boasts two springs, Arethúsa and Cýane,
    either
side of a bay that is almost enclosed by narrow
410   promontories.
This was the place where Cyane lived, most famous of
    all
the Sicilian nymphs, who also gave her name to the
    fountain.
She rose from the midst of her pool as far as her waist
    and recognized
whom the god was abducting. 'Halt where you are!'
    she cried.
'You cannot take Ceres' daughter without her mother's
415   permission.
You ought to have asked for her hand, not stolen her. I
    was loved,
if I may compare the small to the great, by the river
    Anápis;
but I was won not by terror like her but by prayer and
    entreaties.'
So speaking, Cyane stretched her arms to the right and
    the left
and barred the way forward. Containing his anger no
420   longer, Pluto
roared at his fearsome steeds, then brandished his
    royal sceptre
with all the strength of his arm and hurled it into the
    depths
of the pool. As it struck the bottom, it opened a tunnel
    to Hades.

'"Cyane, deeply distressed by the goddess' abduction
          and also   425
the trespass against her spring, felt inconsolably hurt.
She brooded in silence and wasted away in her tears to
          nothing,
dissolving into the water she'd lately ruled as its guardian
spirit. Her limbs grew sodden, her bones started to bend,
her nails let go of their firmness. First to melt were her
          slightest   430
features: the dark green hair, the fingers, the legs and the
          feet –
it doesn't take long for the slenderer members to change
          into waves
of chilly liquid. The next to go were her shoulders and
          back,
her sides and her breasts, as they vanished away into
          insubstantial   435
rivulets. Nothing solid remained, when lastly the lifeblood
coursing her weakened veins was taken over by water.

'"Meanwhile Proserpina's mother anxiously searched for
          her daughter
over the world, by land and by ocean, but all to no purpose.
Neither the dewy dawn nor the evening star ever found
          her   440
at rest. She lit two torches of pine in Etna's volcano
and bore them in either hand to illumine her sleepless way
through the darkness of frosty night. When the stars were
          dimmed by the kindly
day, she continued the quest for her child from west to east. 445
Tired by her journey, she wanted to drink and hadn't yet
          moistened
her lips at a spring, when she happened to notice a
          straw-roofed cottage
and knocked on its humble door. Out came an old woman,
          who looked
at the goddess and, when she had asked for some water,
          provided a sweet brew

sprinkled with toasted barley. As Ceres drank what she
gave her,

450

an insolent, coarse-looking boy strolled up in front of
the goddess,

burst into laughter and jeered, 'What a greedy female
you are!'

Deeply insulted, she rapidly threw what was left of her
drink

in the prattling idiot's face and drenched him in barley
mixture.

His soaking cheeks were instantly covered in spots,
and his arms

455

were transformed into legs. As his body changed, it
acquired a tail

and shrank to a tiny size which made it comparatively
harmless,

shorter in length than the smallest lizard. Bewildered
and weeping,

the poor old woman attempted to catch this
extraordinary thing,

but it scampered away into hiding. The name that we
give it derives

460

from the patterning found on its skin: we call it the
star-speckled newt.

    ' "Listing the lands and the seas where the goddess
went on her travels

would take too long. No countries were left for her to
explore.

At last she returned to Sicily; there, in the course of her
wanderings,

she came to Cyane's pool. If the nymph had not been
transformed,

465

she'd have told the whole story. But much as she
wanted to tell it,

her lips and her tongue were gone and she had no
means of expression.

Evidence, though, could be pointed out. Proserpina's
girdle,

well known to her mother, had accidentally dropped into
    Cyane's
sacred pool and still lay floating on top of the water.   470
Once she recognized this, as if the truth of her daughter's
abduction had dawned on the goddess at last, she wildly
    tore
at her unkempt hair and beat on her breasts again and
    again.
She still did not know where Proserpina was, but she cursed
    every region
on earth as ungrateful and ill deserving her gift of the
    crops –   475
Sicily most of all, where she'd finally found the traces
of what she had lost. And so she savagely wrecked the
    ploughs
that furrowed the soil in Sicily's fields. Her bitterness drove
    her
to slaughter the cattle and farmers alike. She instructed the
    fields
to default on the dues that they owed, and blighted the
    fruits of the earth.   480
Sicily's worldwide fame as a fertile country was ruined
and given the lie: as the first shoots sprang from the earth,
    they would perish
at once, destroyed by the scorching sunshine or torrents of
    rain;
stars and the winds had a baleful influence; birds would
    greedily
gobble the seed as it fell on the soil; while the harvest of
    wheat   485
was choked by the thistles and tares and the indestructible
    twitch grass.
  ' "Then the nymph whom the river Alphéüs had loved,
    Arethusa,
raised her head from her waters and, brushing her
    streaming locks
away from her forehead, she said: 'Earth mother, you've
    searched for your maiden

daughter throughout the world. Abandon the endless
490   struggle
and calm your anger against the land which has served
      you so faithfully.
Sicily's free from blame; she wasn't happy to witness
your child's abduction. It's not for my native country
      I'm pleading
as I am a foreigner here; I was born at Pisa in Elis.
495 But Sicily is the land that I cherish above all others,
the land that I look on as home. Kind goddess, have
      mercy and save it!
The story of why I left Elis and crossed such a large
      expanse
of ocean to Syracuse here, I shall tell in a timelier
      hour,*
when you are relieved of your troubles and able to
500   smile again.
This much must suffice for now: the earth opened up
      to afford me
a way and I was conveyed underneath its bottommost
      caverns,
until my head rose and I saw the stars I had missed for
      so long.
Then, while I was gliding under the earth in the flood
      of the Styx,
I chanced to set eyes down there on your own lost
505   daughter, Proserpina.
Sad she appeared, to be sure, and the fear still showed
      on her face;
but yet she's the queen, the most powerful lady in all
      the underworld,
consort supreme to the sovereign lord of the regions
      infernal!'
   '"Hearing these words, Proserpina's mother was
      long dumbfounded,
as though she were stone or struck by thunder; but
510   when the force

of her shock was dispelled by the strength of her grief, she
     drove her chariot
straight to the realms of the sky. With a countenance
     clouded with fury,
her hair let loose, exuding malice, she stood before Jupiter,
telling him firmly: 'I've come to plead for my flesh and
     blood,
great Jupiter, mine and your own. If her mother merits no
     favours,   515
at least be moved as a father; and don't think any the less
of your child, I beg you, because she was brought into being
     by me.
Now look, the daughter I searched for so long at last has
     been found,
if finding means more certainly losing or merely
     discovering
where she is. I'm willing to bear her abduction, so long as   520
he gives her back. A bandit husband is hardly a match
for a daughter of yours, if she is no longer a daughter of
     mine.'
  ' "Jupiter answered: 'Your child remains a pledge of our
     bond
and a charge that I share with you. But please use words
     which accord
with the facts of the case. Lord Pluto hasn't committed a
     crime   525
but an act of love. No need for us to feel shame at the
     marriage,
if only you will accept it, Ceres. Setting aside
all other advantages, Pluto is Jupiter's brother, no less!
And what of the rest? He and I were allotted different
     kingdoms,*
but otherwise we are equals. Still, if you're so concerned
to see them divorced, Proserpina shall be restored to the
     heavens –   530
on one condition: no morsel of food must have touched her
     lips

while she stayed in Hades. These are the terms decreed
    by the three Fates.'
  ' "Jupiter made his point, but Ceres was still
    determined
to have Proserpina back. The Fates, alas, were
    against it.
The girl had already broken her fast. While taking an
535   innocent
stroll in the orchard, she'd plucked a crimson fruit
    from a hanging
bough; then peeling off the yellowish rind, she had
    picked out
seven pomegranate seeds and crunched them between
    her teeth.
No one at all observed her eating, except for one,
Ascálaphus, son of Orphne, a well-known nymph in
540   Avérnus
(she's said to have borne him in hell's dark woods to
    her lover Ácheron*).
Seeing, he turned informer and cruelly prevented
    Proserpina's
homeward return. The queen of Érebus* wailed in
    distress
and transformed the tell-tale witness into a bird of ill
    omen.
Sprinkling his hateful face with a handful of
    Phlégethon* water,
she turned it into a beak with feathers and great round
545   eyes.
Removed from his former self, he was mantled in
    tawny wings.
His body grew into his head and his nails into long
    hooked talons.
Scarcely ruffling the plumage which lay on his
    motionless arms,
he was changed to an odious bird, the prophet of
    doom and sorrow,

the indolent screech-owl, a dreadful portent to all
        mankind.   550

' "Ascalaphus surely deserved the reward that he won for
        his tattling.
But strange to tell, Achelöüs' daughters, the Sirens,* were
        given
the feet and feathers of birds, though they kept the faces of
        girls.
How so? Perhaps these maidens, renowned for their
        prowess in singing,
were there with Proserpina while she was picking her
        springtime flowers.   555
After they'd searched in vain for their mistress throughout
        the world,
in order to show the sea how deeply they felt their
        bereavement,
they prayed for the power to cross the waves on wings for
        their oars.
The gods were kind, and the suppliants suddenly found that
        their limbs
were covered with golden plumage. But lest their
        beguilingly soothing   560
singing should die and so much musical talent be wasted,
the Sirens retained their maiden faces and human voices.

' "Jupiter settled the conflict between his brother and
        grieving
sister by splitting the rolling year into equal parts: 565
Proserpina now, as the only divinity common to both
        realms,
spends six months* on the earth with her mother and six
        with her husband.
Once she returns, her heart is so light and her face is so
        happy.
A moment ago, she'd have struck even Pluto as sad, but
        now

she is glowing with radiant smiles, like the sun which
570   was formerly hidden
behind a blanket of rain clouds and then emerges
          victorious.

CALLIOPE'S SONG: ARETHUSA

' "Now that her daughter was safely recovered,
          bountiful Ceres
was tranquil enough to ask Arethusa why she had fled
from her birthplace and how she'd been changed to a
          sacred fountain. The waves
fell still as the goddess rose from the depths of her pool;
575   then wiping
the water away from her dark green locks, she began
          the tale
of how she had once attracted Alpheüs, the river of
          Elis.
'I was one of the nymphs,' she said, 'whose home is
          Achaea.
None was more active than I in scouring the forest
          glades
or spreading the hunting nets; but although I never set
580   out
to be famed for my beauty, brave as I was, I was
          always known as
"that beautiful girl, Arethusa". The praises rained on
          my comely
person gave me no pleasure. Where others are proud of
          their bodies,
I blushed like a rustic and thought it a crime to be seen
          as attractive.
     ' " "One day, I recall, I was travelling back from
585   Stýmphalus'* forest.
The heat was doubly oppressive as hunting had made
          me exhausted.

I came on a stream which was perfectly still and perfectly
    silent,
transparent down to the bed (you could count each one of
    the pebbles),
you'd never believe it was flowing. Silvery willows and
    water-fed   590
poplars provided a natural shade for the sloping banks.
I approached the brink and, to start with, put my feet in the
    water,
then waded in up to my knees. It wasn't enough. Untying
my girdle and tossing my soft clothes on to the branch of a
    willow,
I plunged in totally naked. And while I was wildly
    thrashing   595
and flailing around with my outflung arms in the folds of
    the river,
I suddenly heard, deep down in the stream, a peculiar
    murmur.
Startled I made for the nearer bank and jumped out quickly.
"Where are you going so fast, Arethusa?" the voice of
    Alpheüs
came from his waters. "Where are you going?" he hoarsely
    repeated.   600
Just as I was, completely undressed, as my clothes had been
    left
on the farther bank, I fled. This made him more eager to
    chase me;
and since I was naked, I must have appeared more his for
    the taking.
The faster I ran, the hotter the river-god pressed on the trail,
as doves will flee from a menacing hawk on their fluttering
    wings   605
and the menacing hawk will fly on the tail of the fluttering
    dove.
  ' " 'I ran as far as Orchómenus, Psophis and on to
    Cyléne.
Across the valleys of Maénalus, cold Erymánthus and Elis*

I kept on running, so hard that Alpheüs could never
    catch up.
But I was less strong than he was and couldn't survive
610   such a lengthy
pursuit; his endurance was greater. Still, over the plains
    and the tree-covered
mountains, the rocks and the cliffs, and places without
    any tracks
I continued to run. The sun was behind me; I saw a
    long shadow
looming in front of my feet – unless it was terror that
615   saw it.
At least I could hear the frightening sound of his
    pounding footsteps
and feel the blasts of his panting breath on the ends of
    my hairbands.
Overcome by the effort of running, I cried to Diana,
"Help! I am caught – your own dear nymph, who
    carried your weapons,
to whom you so often entrusted your bow and quiver
620   of arrows!"
The heart of the goddess was stirred. She brought
    down one of the clouds
and threw it around me. No sooner had I been
    enshrouded in mist
than the river-god prowled and searched in bafflement
    round the cloud.
Twice he unknowingly circled the spot where the
    goddess had hidden me,
twice he called out, "Arethusa, my love! Arethusa,
625   where are you?"
How do you think I felt? Like a lamb on hearing the
    howling
of wolves by the fence of the fold? Or a cowering hare
    in a thorn-bush,
watching the dogs' fierce muzzles, not daring to make
    any movement?

Alpheüs remained where he was; there weren't any
    footprints leading   630
onwards and so he concentrated his eyes on the cloud.
Cold sweat poured down my beleaguered limbs, and the
    blue-tinged drops
streamed over my body. I moved my foot and a pool seeped
    out.
My hair was dripping with moisture and, faster than I can
    describe it,   635
I changed into water. But now the river-god saw that the
    stream
was the nymph that he loved. He dropped the human guise
    he'd assumed
and reverted to water in order to be united with me.
Diana quickly created a cleft in the earth, and I plunged
    down
through its murky recesses until I arrived at Ortýgia,*   640
isle that I love, called after my patron Diana and first
to welcome me back to the upper air in Syracuse harbour.'

CALLIOPE'S SONG:
TRIPTOLEMUS AND LYNCUS

'"Arethusa's story was ended. The goddess of all the crops
now harnessed her twin snakes on to her chariot, fastened
    their bridles
and launched herself through the air between the sky and
    the earth,
till she brought her flying car down in the city of Pállas
    Athéne.   645
Here she handed it over to young Triptólemus'* charge,
with orders to sow the seeds that she gave him, partly in soil
which had never been tilled and partly in fields which had
    long lain fallow.
Triptolemus then took off and soared over Europe and
    Asia,

until he landed on Scythian soil, where the ruler was
650   Lyncus,
whose palace he entered. Asked where he came from,
           his reason for coming,
his name and his country, he answered: 'My country is
           far-famed Athens.
My name is Triptolemus. As for my coming, it wasn't
           by ship
or on foot overland; I travelled instead through the
           open sky.
I am bringing you gifts from Ceres. Now scatter these
655   seeds all over
your fields to return you a fruitful harvest of
           nourishing food.'
The barbarian king was filled with envy; he wanted the
           credit
himself for this marvellous gift. So he welcomed
           Triptolemus under
his roof and, once his guest was asleep, he crept to his
           bedside,
dagger in hand. As he raised his weapon to stab him,
           Ceres
turned him into a lynx and commanded the youth from
660   Athens
to drive his sacred chariot-team once more through the
           air.'"

THE DAUGHTERS OF PIERUS

'Our leader Calliope here concluded her brilliant
           recital,'
went on the Muse who was telling Minerva about the
           contest.
'The nymphs were agreed on their verdict: the victory
           should go to Helicon's
Muses. The losers responded by raining abuse. "So it
           isn't

enough," I then interposed, "that your challenge has won
    you a trouncing.   665
No, it appears that you feel the need to add insult to injury.
Since, moreover, our patience has come to an end, we had
    better
follow the course which our anger dictates and proceed to
    punish you."
All that the nine Piérides did was to laugh and make light
of my threatening words. As they tried to continue their
    shouting and screaming   670
and brandished their fists, they suddenly noticed that
    feathers were sprouting
out of their nails and their arms were growing a cover of
    plumage.
Looking at one another, they saw hard beaks stiffen out
of their faces. A novel species of bird was joining the forest.
Wanting to beat their breasts, they flapped their arms and
    were lifted   675
into the air, where they hovered, the scolds of the
    woodlands, magpies.
Even today they preserve their original gift of the gab
as raucous, chattering birds* with a limitless passion for
    talking.'

BOOK 6

The theme of divine punishment for mortal presumption con-
tinues through the first four stories (1–400), though each is
distinctive in its character. In *Tereus* (412–674) the gods fade
into the background and Ovid embarks on his series of meta-
morphoses arising from relationships between human beings,
some of them of a very strange kind.

Minerva is the link with Book 5 and we begin with another
contest, this time between the goddess herself and the mortal
Arachne (1–145), who has challenged her skill in weaving. The
story is characterized more sharply than the dispute between
the Muses and the Pierides. There is an enjoyable scene in which
Minerva, disguised as a crone, tempts Arachne into further
arrogance. Other excellent features are Ovid's accounts of spin-
ning and weaving; the descriptions of the two competing tap-
estries (see Introduction, pp. xxiv–xxv); and, naturally, the
detail of Arachne's transformation into the spider.

Niobe (146–312), who boasted that she had more children
than the goddess Latona, was a famous tragic figure and proto-
type of perpetual mourning in Greek literature and art. Ovid
tells her story in fairly down-to-earth terms. Her gross arrogance
is amusingly satirized in her address to the Theban crowd; and
we may also admire Ovid's narrative skill as he disposes of her
seven sons, one by one, followed by the seven daughters. Rather
less is made of the queen's final metamorphosis into a weeping
mountain crag.

In *The Lycian Peasants* (313–81) Latona features less as
an avenging deity and more as an injured victim of Juno's
persecution, who is then treated very rudely and unkindly by a

group of uncouth peasants. Here we have another lively story, culminating delightfully in the peasants' transformation into frogs. Less delightful is the disgusting description of the flayed *Marsyas* (382–400), who has lost to Apollo in a piping contest.

The story of *Pelops* (401–11) seems to provide a thematic transition. His dismemberment by his father Tantalus had incurred the punishment of the gods; and it also prefigures the dismemberment of Itys in *Tereus*. Pelops' restoration with an ivory patch on his shoulder evidently counts as a metamorphosis.

A darker quality altogether pervades the long *Tereus, Procne and Philomela* story (412–674), and some may find it the most sinister and unpleasant tale in the whole poem. The lust of the barbaric Tereus for his innocent sister-in-law from Athens is very powerfully developed; and we cannot help being moved by the ironical pathos of Pandion's speech as he entrusts his daughter Philomela to the treacherous Thracian. Violence attends sex in the ensuing action. The detail of the brutally raped Philomela's excised tongue is almost ludicrously gruesome; but we can perhaps enter more fully into the spirit of Procne's rescue of her sister and the horrible revenge which she and Philomela take on the abominable Tereus. The metamorphosis of the three characters into birds, which formally justifies Ovid's inclusion of this story, has little emotive value when it comes.

The book ends in rather more agreeable mode. In *Boreas and Orithyia* (675–721), the Thracian north wind forcibly abducts another Athenian girl; but Boreas' aggression is more boisterous than sinister, and the outcome resulting in the birth of Zetes and Calaïs is presented as positive. A heroic note is sounded in the concluding image of the Argonauts' quest for the Golden Fleece – which takes us on to Book 7.

ARACHNE

Minerva, who'd lent an attentive ear to the Muses'
    narration,
Commended their song and their justified anger against
    the Piérides.
Then she said to herself: 'Is praising enough? I also
need to be praised in turn. No mortal shall scoff at my
    power
unpunished.' She therefore considered how best to
5   dispose of a Lydian*
girl, called Aráchne,* who claimed (so she'd heard) to
    equal herself
in working with wool. Arachne's distinction lay not in
    her birth
or the place that she hailed from but solely her art. Her
    father, Idmon
of Cólophon, practised the trade of dyeing wool in
    Phocaéan
purple;* her mother was dead but, like her husband,
10   had come
from the people. Their daughter, however, had gained
    a high reputation
throughout the Lydian towns for her work with wool,
    although
she'd been born in a humble home and lived in a
    village, Hypaépa.
The nymphs used often to leave their haunts, Mount
15   Tmolus' vines
or the banks of the river Pactólus, to gaze on Arachne's
    amazing
artistry, equally eager to watch her handwork in
    progress
(her skill was so graceful) as much as to look at the
    finished article.
Perhaps she was forming the first round clumps from
    the wool in its crude state,

shaping the stuff in her fingers and steadily teasing the
        cloud-like   20
fleece into long soft threads. She might have been deftly
        applying
her thumb to the polished spindle. Or else they would
        watch her embroider
a picture. Whatever she did, you would know Minerva had
        taught her.
Arachne herself, in indignant pride, denied such a debt.
'Let us hold a contest,' she said. 'If I'm beaten, I'll pay any
        forfeit.'   25
    Minerva disguised herself as a hag* with hoary locks
and hobbled along with a stick to support her tottering
        frame.
She spoke at once to Arachne. 'Not all old age's effects',
she said, 'are to be despised; experience comes with the
        years.
So take a little advice from me: you should aim to be
        known   30
as the best among humankind in the arts of working with
        wool;
but yield the palm to Minerva, and humbly crave her
        forgiveness
for boasting so rashly. The goddess will surely forgive if you
        ask her.'
Arachne looked at her sullenly, left the threads she was
        spinning
and almost hit her rebuker. With anger written all over   35
her face, she made her response to the goddess she'd failed
        to recognize:
'Leave me alone, you stupid old woman! The trouble with
        you
is you've lived too long. You can give your advice to what
        daughters you have
or the wives of your sons. I'm clever enough to advise
        myself.   40
Don't think your warnings have done any good. I'm set on
        my course.

Why doesn't Minerva arrive in person? She's shirking this
        contest!'
'She's here!' the goddess exclaimed, as she dropped her
        disguise as a crone
and appeared as Minerva. At once the nymphs and the
        Lydian women
45 paid suitable homage. Only Arachne remained unafraid,
but she did turn red and her cheeks were suffused with a
        sudden, involuntary
blush which soon disappeared, as the sky glows crimson
        at early
dawn and rapidly whitens again in the rays of the
        sunrise.
50 She still refused to withdraw. In her crass determination
to win, she fell to her ruin. Minerva accepted her
        challenge
and offered no further warnings; the contest could start
        at once.
    Straightaway they both set up their looms in different
        places.
Each loom was carefully strung with the slender threads
        of the warp.
The warp was attached to the crossbeam, a stick
55   separated the threads,
and the weft could then be inserted between them by
        pointed shuttles,
drawn over and under by hand, and tapped into place
        as the wooden
comb with its notches between the teeth was sharply
        lowered.
The two contestants made haste; with robes hitched up
        to the girdle,
they moved their experienced arms, the labour lightened
60   by pleasure.
Webs were woven in threads of Tyrian purple dye
and of lighter, more delicate, imperceptibly merging
        shades.

Think how a tract of the sky, when the sun breaks suddenly
      through
at the end of a rain shower, is steeped in the long, great
      curve of a rainbow;
the bow is agleam with a range of a thousand various hues, 65
but the eye cannot tell where one fades into another;
      adjacent
tones are so much the same, though the difference is clear at
      the edges.
Such were the colours the two contestants used in the
      fabric.
Their patterns were also shot with flexible threads of gold,
as they each spun out an old tale in the weft of their
      separate looms.
   Minerva depicted the rock of Mars* on the heights of
      Cecrops   70
and wove the ancient dispute concerning the name of the
      land.
The twelve Olympians, Jove in their midst, with august
      dignity
sat upon lofty thrones. Each of the gods was denoted
by typical features. The image of Jove was proud and
      majestic.
Neptune, the god of the ocean, was shown on his feet and
      striking   75
the rugged crag with his great long trident, while sea-water
      gushed forth
out of the cleft in the rock, to establish his claim to the city.
Minerva characterized herself by her helmeted head,
her sharp-pointed spear, her shield and the aegis guarding
      her breast.
The picture suggested the earth had been struck by the
      goddess's spear   80
to produce the olive tree covered with berries and
      grey-green foliage.
The gods looked on in amazement, and victory crowned her
      endeavour.

So that Minerva's rival could have some clear
        indication
of what reward to expect for such crazily reckless
        defiance,
four contests were added, one in each of the web's four
85   corners,
all in their own bright colours, with smaller designs for
        the detail.
One corner was filled by Thracian Haemus and
        Rhódope,* snow-clad
mountains today but formerly mortals, a brother and
        sister
who'd claimed the titles of Jove and Juno. The second
        corner
contained the pitiful fate of a mother, the queen of the
90   Pygmies,*
who'd fought against Juno and lost; the goddess
        transformed her into
a crane and made her declare perpetual war on her own
        tribe.
Antígone* featured third, one more who had dared to
        compete
with great Jove's consort but later been punished by
        queenly Juno
and changed to a kind of bird. It sadly counted for
95   nothing
that she was the Trojan king Laómedon's daughter.
        Instead
she applauds herself with the clattering bill of a
        white-feathered stork.
The fourth and remaining design showed Cínyras* in
        his bereavement,
embracing the temple steps which had once been the
        limbs of his beautiful
daughters, and seeming to weep as he lay prostrate on
100   the marble.
Minerva finally added a border of olive branches,

symbol of peace, so using her tree to complete the tapestry.
  Arachne's picture* presented Európa seduced by Jove
in the guise of a bull; the bull and the sea were convincingly
    real.
The girl appeared to be looking back to the shore behind
    her,   105
calling out to the friends she was leaving, afraid of the
    surging
waves which threatened to touch her and nervously lifting
    her feet.
Astérië also was shown, in the grip of a struggling eagle;
Leda, meekly reclining under the wings of the swan.
And there was Jove once again, but now in the form of a
    satyr,   110
taking the lovely Antíope, sowing the seeds of her twins.
You could see how he caught Alcména disguised as her
    husband Amphítryon,
then how he stole fair Dánaë's love in a shower of gold;
how he cheated Aegína as fire; Mnemósyne, dressed as a
    shepherd;
Prosérpina, Ceres' child and his own, as a speckled
    serpent.
  Neptune's affairs were also revealed in Arachne's
    tapestry.   115
He changed to a menacing bull to possess the daughter of
    Aéolus;*
taking the shape of the river Enípeus, he fathered the giant
son of Alóeus; he posed as a ram to confuse Theóphane.
Ceres, the bountiful mother of crops, with her golden
    tresses,
knew the god as a horse; snake-haired Medúsa, who bore
the winged horse Pégasus, knew a winged bird; and
    Melántho a dolphin.   120
All these scenes were given authentic settings, the persons
their natural likeness. There was Apollo, dressed as a
    farmer,
shown as wearing the wings of a hawk or the skin of a lion,

and fooling the daughter of Mácareus, Isse, disguised as
    a shepherd.
Bacchus, appearing as counterfeit grapes to deceive
125   Erígone;
Saturn, as one more horse who fathered Chiron the
    centaur.
The outer edge of the tapestry, fringed by a narrow
    border,
was filled with flowers all interwoven with tendrils of
    ivy.
  Not Pallas, not even the goddess of Envy could
    criticize weaving
like that. The fair-haired warrior goddess resented
130   Arachne's
success and ripped up the picture betraying the gods'
    misdemeanours.
She was still holding her shuttle of hard Cytórian
    boxwood
and used it to strike Arachne a number of times on the
    forehead.
The wretched girl was too proud to endure it, and
    fastened a halter
around her neck. She was hanging in air when the
135   goddess took pity
and lifted her up. 'You may live, you presumptuous
    creature,' she said,
'but you'll hang suspended forever. Don't count on a
    happier future:
my sentence applies to the whole of your kind, and to
    all your descendants!'
With that she departed, sprinkling the girl with the
    magical juice
of a baleful herb. As soon as the poison had touched
140   Arachne,
her hair fell away, and so did the ears and the nose.
    The head
now changed to a tiny ball and her whole frame
    shrunk in proportion.

Instead of her legs there are spindly fingers attached to her
    sides.
The rest is merely abdomen, from which she continues to
    spin
her thread and practise her former art in the web of a
    spider.   145

NIOBE

The whole of Lydia buzzed with the news. The story was
    spread
through Phrygia's towns and discussed in the wider regions
    beyond.
Now Níobe, queen of Thebes, before she was married, had
    known
Arachne; she'd lived as a girl in Maeónia near Mount
    Sípylus.
Still, her compatriot's ugly fate hadn't served as a warning   150
to show the gods that she knew her place and to speak of
    them humbly.
She'd many causes for pride: she was pleased with her
    husband Amphíon's
skill on the lyre, their shared high birth and the broad extent
of their regal power. But nothing gave her so much
    satisfaction
as all the children she had. Yes, Niobe would have been
    known   155
as the happiest mother on earth, if only she had not
    thought it
herself. One day, Teirésias' daughter, the prophetess
    Manto,
stormed through the streets of Thebes in a state of divine
    possession,
loudly proclaiming: 'Isménian women, flock together,
and hurry with wreaths of bay in your hair, to offer incense 160
and reverent prayers to the goddess Latóna and her two
    children.*

Latona speaks through my lips!' Her command was
        obeyed, and every
woman in Thebes adorned her forehead as Manto had
        bidden.
Incense was cast on the altar flames and prayers were
        uttered.
    Here on the scene comes Niobe, flanked by a throng of
165   attendants,
splendidly dressed in a gold-embroidered Phrygian
        costume,
lovely as far as her anger allowed. Majestically tossing
her handsome head with its unbound hair flowing over
        her shoulders,
she halted. Then, loftily gazing round with an arrogant
        air,
she exclaimed: 'What madness is this to prefer the gods
170   you have only
heard of to one you can see? And why should worship
        be paid
at Latona's altar, when I have never been honoured
        with incense?
I am the daughter of Tántalus, the only mortal ever
permitted to feast with the gods.* My mother's sisters
        are Pleiads,
her father was Atlas, the giant who carries the sky on
175   his shoulders.
My other grandsire is Jove, who is also my husband's
        father.
The tribes of Phrygia hold me in fear. The walls of this
        city
were built to the sound of Amphion's lyre, and I with
        my husband
govern the Theban people. I'm mistress in Cadmus'
        palace.
Wherever I turn my eyes in my house, a profusion of
180   riches
confronts my gaze. My beauty, moreover, is surely
        divine.

Now add to these glories my seven daughters and seven
      sons
and to them, very soon, their seven husbands and seven
      wives.
Then answer this question: haven't I every cause to be
      proud?
And yet you presume to rank me below Latona, the
      daughter   185
born to some Titan called Coéüs – Latona, who couldn't
      obtain
the meanest refuge on earth when about to give birth to her
      children.
Your goddess could find no home in the sky or the sea or on
      land.
Exiled from the world, she wandered, until she inspired
      some pity
in Delos, who said to her, "You are a homeless stranger on
      land,   190
as I am on sea," and sheltered her there in his shifting
      island.*
Latona then bore two children, one seventh the number of
      mine.
I am undeniably blessed; and blessed I'll continue to be,
without any doubt. My abundance assures me I'll always be
      safe.
I am far too important a person for fortune's changes to
      harm me.   195
However much I am robbed, far more will be left to enjoy.
My blessings are such that I've nothing to fear; supposing a
      fraction
of all this people, my children, could ever be taken away,
my losses could never reduce me to only two, the
      magnificent
crowd Latona can boast, so near to making her childless!   200
Away with you, women, abandon your sacrifice, off with
      your laurel-wreaths!'
All discarded their wreaths and left their worship
      unfinished,

but no one could stop them invoking Latona under their
         breath.

The goddess was deeply angry. High on the top of
         Mount Cynthus
she said to her twins, Apollo her son, and Diana her
205   daughter:
'Outrageous! I, your mother, so deeply proud to have
         borne you,
The goddess who yields to no other but Juno, am
         hardly a goddess
at all, it appears! My children, unless you help, I'm
         excluded
from all the altars where I have been worshipped since
         time began.
To fuel my fury, Tantalus' daughter has now
210   compounded
her impious conduct with insults. She dares to consider
         her children
superior to you and has called me childless – I hope
         that her insult
recoils on her head! Her unbridled tongue is as bad as
         her father's.'*
Latona was going to add her prayers to this furious
         indictment,
when 'Stop!' interrupted Apollo. 'Complaining merely
215   delays
her punishment.' Phoebe agreed. So they rapidly glided
         down
through the air and, veiled in a cloud, alighted on
         Cadmus' citadel.
    Close to the walls there extended a level and open
         plain,
which was constantly pounded by galloping horses; a
         host of clattering
chariots and hammering hooves had softened the clods
220   underneath them.
Here it happened that two of Amphion's seven sons

had mounted their sturdy steeds and, firmly seated on
          trappings
of Tyrian red, were curbing their coursers with golden
          bridles.
One of the pair, Isménus, the first whom his mother had
          carried
inside her womb long ago, was riding his racehorse round   225
the circular track and straining hard on the foaming bit,
when a flying arrow went through his breast and he
          suddenly uttered
a cry of pain. The reins were dropped from his dying hands,
and slowly he slipped sideways to the ground from his
          mount's right shoulder.
Close by, his brother Sípylus heard the sound of the
          rattling   230
quiver and gave full rein to his horse, like a terrified captain
running before a storm on sight of a cloud, and unfurling
all of his sails so as not to miss the lightest of breezes.
Sipylus gave full rein, but the inescapable arrow
caught up with the rider. The quivering shaft held fast in
          the nape   235
of his neck, while the naked point stuck out of the throat in
          front.
Already slumping forwards, the youth pitched over the
          mane
to be trampled by galloping hooves and to stain the earth
          with his warm blood.
    Phaédimus, luckless youth, and Tantalus, heir to his
          grandfather's
name, had followed their usual ride by going across   240
to join their peers in the wrestling school and had oiled their
          bodies.
Then while the brothers were tussling away and locked in a
          tight clinch,
breast against breast, Apollo's bowstring was drawn and a
          single
arrow was driven right through the pair of their grappling
          frames.

Together the poor lads groaned; together, bent double
245   by pain,
they heavily fell to the ground; together they turned
          their eyes
once more to the sun from the earth; and together
          they breathed their last.
Alphénor saw this calamity. Beating his breast till it
          bled,
he rushed to embrace the cold dead bodies and lift
          them up,
and died in performing this duty of love. The god of
250   Delos
impaled him too, with the deadly point deep down in
          his chest.
After the shaft was pulled out, a piece of his lungs was
          torn
away on the barbs and the blood gushed out of the
          wound as he died.
     But one wound wasn't enough for the handsome
          boy, Damasíchthon.
He had been struck on the lower leg, in the soft and
255   sinewy
patch at the back of the knee. As he tried to extract
          the weapon,
a second arrow transfixed his throat right up to the
          feathers.
This was expelled by the force of the blood, which
          spurted and darted
260   out, and a hole was bored in the air by the leaping jet.
Ílioneus died last. He had raised his arms in a useless
appeal and cried, 'You gods, I pray to you all
          conjointly'
(he wasn't aware that he needn't appeal to all of the
          gods),
'Spare me, I beg you!' The god of the bow was
          touched – but his shaft
was already beyond recall. Still, Ilioneus had the
265   gentlest

death. The point had entered his heart, but not very deeply.
  Rumour of trouble, the people's grief and the tears of her
     family
made the mother aware that disaster had suddenly struck.
The queen was appalled that it could have occurred, and
     incensed that the gods
had dared to do such a thing and taken their rights so far.   270
(The brothers' father, Amphion, already had driven a
     sword
through his heart; in death he was rid of his grief as he was
     of the daylight.)
This was a different Niobe, far from that arrogant woman
who'd lately driven the crowd away from Latona's altars
and proudly marched through the middle of Thebes with
     her head held high.   275
She was envied before by her friends, but now her foes
     would have pitied her.
Throwing herself on the cold dead bodies, she frantically
     covered
each of her sons with her final kisses; then turning away,
she lifted her poor bruised arms to the heavens and boldly
     exclaimed:
'Now feed on my pain, hard-hearted Latona, and feast your
     heart   280
to the full on my sorrow! The biers which carry my seven
     sons
are my own cortège. Rejoice and be glad in your cruel
     victory!
Victory? No! In my grief I have more than you in your joy.
Although you have murdered all of my sons, I can still
     outshine you!'   285
  She ended her speech, and a bowstring twanged. All
     quaked in terror,
except for one. It was Niobe, bold in her tragic misfortune.
Her daughters were standing in robes of black, with their
     hair let down,
before the biers of their brothers. One was removing the
     arrow   290

lodged in Alphenor's heart when she fainted on top of his
     body
and died. Another, while trying to comfort her grieving
     mother,
went suddenly silent, doubled up by a wound from an
     unseen
archer. A third collapsed as she vainly attempted to
295   flee,
and a fourth expired on her sister's body. One more
     was in hiding,
another was visibly trembling. Now six of the sisters
     had died
of their different wounds, and the last remained. Then
     Niobe, standing
in front of her daughter with robes outspread, called
     out to Latona,
'Leave me but one – and the smallest! Of my great
     number of children
I beg you to spare me the smallest, I beg you to spare
300   me *one*!'
But while she was praying, the girl she was praying for
     died. Then childless,
she sank to the earth by the corpses – her sons, her
     daughters, her husband –
and there, in her sorrow, her body grew rigid. No lock
     of her hair
could stir in the breeze, her complexion was bloodless,
     the eyes never moved
in that sad, sad face. There wasn't a sign of life in her
305   features.
The palate inside her mouth went hard, and even her
     tongue
was frozen and stiff. The blood could no longer course
     in her veins.
She had lost the power to incline her neck, or to raise
     an arm,
or to walk on her feet; and her inner organs were
     turned to stone.

Yet her weeping goes on. In the swirl of a mighty wind she
      was swept   310
away to her native land. There, set on a mountain
      summit,*
she pines to this day, and the tears trickle down the crag of
      her cheeks.

THE LYCIAN PEASANTS

Latona had made her anger plain to the whole of Thebes.
Everyone, man and woman, was filled with fear and
      worshipped
the mighty mother of twins with greater devotion than
      ever.   315
Recent events, as so often occurs, reawakened the telling
of earlier stories. One said: 'This also happened a while
ago in fertile Lycia's fields, where the peasants rejected
Latona, much to their cost. The story isn't well known
as the people were humble folk, but it's strange enough to
      be told.   320
I have been to the place in person and seen the pool which
      the wonder
made famous. My father had asked me to fetch some
      particular cattle
from there; he was now an old man, unable to travel far,
so he gave me a Lycian guide, with whom I was crossing the
      pastures,
when there, in the midst of a pool, an ancient altar was
      standing,,   325
blackened with sacrifice embers and ringed by quivering
      reeds.
My companion stopped in his tracks and said in a terrified
      whisper,
"Be gracious to me!" "Be gracious," I timidly whispered
      myself.
I ventured, however, to ask my guide whether this was an
      altar

to Faunus, the naiads or one of the local gods; and he
330   answered,
"Young man, this altar does not belong to a mountain
           deity.
No, it's the home of the goddess who once was
           excluded by Jupiter's
consort from all of the world, whose prayers were
           barely answered
by shifting Delos, still an aimlessly floating island.
335   In Delos, pressing against a palm and Minerva's olive,
Latona gave birth to her twins, despite their
           stepmother's malice.
From Delos also, the story goes, when her labour was
           over,
she fled from Juno, the pair of baby gods in her arms.
Quite soon she arrived in Lycia, home of the
           monstrous Chimaéra,
tired and exhausted. The heat of the sun which was
340   scorching the fields
had caused her to wilt, she was parched with thirst,
           and her hungry babes
had sucked all the milk from her breasts. Then,
           chancing to look ahead,
she saw a lake with a little water down in a valley.
Country folk were at work there, cropping the bushy
           osiers,
rushes and sedge that you find in a marsh. Latona went
345   up
and knelt on the ground to slake her thirst with a
           cooling drink.
The rabble of peasants told her to stop, so the goddess
           said to them:
'Why must you stop me drinking? Water belongs to
           everyone.
350   Nature never intended the sun or the air or the flowing
streams to be private. I'm simply here for my common
           right.

Yet I beg you upon my knees to allow it. I wasn't attempting
to wash my weary limbs in this pool, but merely to quench
my thirst. As I speak, my mouth is dry and my throat is
        parched;
my words can hardly be heard. A drink of water would be   355
pure nectar. Indeed, you'll have saved my life if you give me
        water.
Look at these babes in my arms! Have mercy, they're
        stretching their arms out!' –
so the children by chance were doing. Who could have been
so heartless as not to be touched by the moving pleas of the
        goddess?   360
The men still wouldn't allow her to drink. They shouted
        abuse,
and warned her with threats to retire from the pool and to
        keep her distance.
To add to their kindness, they even disturbed the water
        itself
with their hands and feet, and spitefully stirred the soft and
        swirling
mud right up from the bottom by jumping wildly about.   365
Latona's anger made her forget her thirst for the moment.
She refused to humble herself any longer before these louts
or to plead any more for kindness in such an ungoddesslike
        manner.
She raised her hands to the heavens and cried, 'May you live
        in your filthy
pool for ever!' Her prayer was answered. The peasants'
        delight   370
is to be under water, now plunging the whole of themselves
        to the bottom,
now popping their heads out, sometimes swimming close to
        the surface.
Often they'll stay on the bank in the sun and often jump
        back
to the cool of the water. But even today they continue to
        wag

their tongues in loud and unseemly arguments; shameless
375   as ever,
although they are under the water, they'll try to
          indulge in abuse.
Their voices too have gone hoarse; their throats are
          inflated and swollen;
their noisy quarrels have stretched their jaws to a
          hideous width.
Their shoulders rise to their heads as their necks
          appear to have vanished;
their backs are green, while their huge protruding
380   bellies are white.
They leap about in the muddy pool transmuted to
          frogs.'"

MARSYAS

After the Theban had told this story about the demise
of the Lycian peasants, another recalled the horrible
          punishment
dealt to the satyr who'd challenged Latona's son to a
          piping
contest and lost. 'Don't rip me away from myself!' he
385   entreated;
'I'm sorry!' he shouted between his shrieks, 'Don't flay
          me for piping!'
In spite of his cries, the skin was peeled from his flesh,
          and his body
was turned into one great wound; the blood was
          pouring all over him,
muscles were fully exposed, his uncovered veins
          convulsively
quivered; the palpitating intestines could well be
390   counted,
and so could the organs glistening through the wall of
          his chest.

The piper was mourned by the rustic fauns who watch over
    the woodlands,
his brother satyrs, the nymphs and Olympus, the pupil he
    loved,
by all who tended their flocks or herds on the Lycian
    mountains.   395
Their tears dropped down and saturated the fertile earth,
who absorbed them deep in her veins and discharged them
    back to the air
in the form of a spring. This found its way to the sea
    through a channel,
which took the name of the Mársyas, clearest of Phrygian
    rivers.   400

PELOPS

The people rapidly turned from these tales to talk of their
    present
misfortunes and mourned for Amphion, destroyed with all
    of his children.
The mother was generally hated and blamed; but still she
    was wept for
by one, it is said – by the grief-stricken Pelops, who tore his
    garments
away from his breast and exposed the ivory patch on his
    shoulder.   405
This shoulder, the left one, was normal flesh at the time of
    his birth
and a match with his right. But later his father dismembered
    the boy,*
and the gods (so they say) reassembled the limbs. The rest
    was recovered,
and only the part which unites the neck with the upper arm
had been lost. A piece of ivory set in the empty space*   410
could serve the purpose as well, and Pelops was fully
    restored.

TEREUS, PROCNE AND PHILOMELA

Princes in neighbouring towns rallied round, and kings
    were urged
by their cities to travel to Thebes and offer their deepest
    sympathy.
Argos and Sparta were represented; Mycénae,
    afterwards
415 ruled by the sons of Pelops; Cálydon, long before
it incurred the wrath of Diana;* fertile Orchómenus;
    Corinth,
known for its bronzework; warlike Messéne, Patrae,
    low-lying
Colónae, Pylos and Troézen, not yet governed by
    Píttheus;
with all the other towns to the north or south of the
420   Isthmus.
You mightn't believe it, but only the city of Athens
    defaulted.
Duty was thwarted by war, as barbarian hordes had
    crossed over
the seas and were striking fear inside the Mopsópian
    walls.
   These hordes were dispelled through the military aid
    supplied by Téreus,
the Thracian king, whose victory won tremendous
425   acclaim.
Since Tereus was wealthy, backed by a powerful army,
    and also
happened to trace his descent from mighty Mars,
    Pandíon,
the king of Athens, forged an alliance by giving his
    daughter,
Procne, to him in marriage. The wedding wasn't
    attended
by Juno as bridal matron, the Graces or jovial Hymen.

Furies provided the escort with torches snatched from a
    funeral;   430
Furies prepared the nuptial couch; and a sinister
    screech-owl
swooped on the palace and came to rest on the roof of the
    bedroom.
These were the omens that marked the union of Procne and
    Tereus,
the union which brought them a child. Congratulations
    were offered,
of course, by Thrace; and the couple themselves gave thanks
    to the gods.   435
They decreed a holiday marking the day of the year when
    Pandion's
daughter was married to noble Tereus and so gave rise
to the birth of Itys. How blind we are to our genuine
    blessings!

Five autumns had come and gone in the course of the sun's
    revolutions,
when Procne coaxingly said to her lord, 'If you love me
    at all,   440
please send me to visit my sister, or ask her to visit us
    here.
You can promise my father it won't be long before she
    returns.
To see my sister again would be such a wonderful present!'
Tereus ordered a ship to be launched. His sails and his
    oarsmen   445
carried him safely towards Piraéus, the harbour of Athens.
As soon as he entered the royal presence, the kings clasped
    hands,
and on that propitious note negotiations were opened.
Tereus had started to broach the request from his wife
    which had brought him
to Athens, and promise the sister's speedy return from her
    visit,   450

when fair Philoméla arrived on the scene, very richly
        attired,
but even richer in beauty, just like the naiads and dryads
we hear of pacing the forest glades in stately procession,
if one can imagine them dressed in the robes and jewels
        of a princess.
The sight of this pure young woman made Tereus hot
455   with desire,
like fire which a farmer sets to the yellow-white corn in
        a field
or the piles of leaves and the hay that are stored in a
        barn for the winter.
That beautiful face was enough to excite him; but
        Tereus was also
pricked on by his lustful nature, confirmed by his
        countrymen's proneness
to sexual indulgence – a Thracian as much as a
460   personal weakness.
His instincts inclined him to bribe his target's watchful
        companions,
to sweeten her faithful nurse to connivance and woo
        Philomela
herself with extravagant gifts, if it cost him the whole
        of his kingdom;
or else to abduct her and fight for his prize in a fierce
        campaign.
Ensnared in the toils of unbridled desire, he'd commit
465   any crime
in the world; he couldn't control the flames that were
        raging inside him.
Waiting was not to be borne any more. He repeated
        the message
from Procne with fervour and used her prayers to
        forward his own.
Passion enhanced his powers of persuasion. Whenever
        his arguments
went too far, he claimed to be urging the wishes of
470   Procne.

He even burst into tears, as though they were part of the
    message.
Heavens above, how blind some mortals can be to the
    darkness
of evil! As Tereus pursued his wicked designs, he passed
for a model husband; his infamous treachery stood to his
    credit.
What's more, Philomela supported his pleas. She tenderly
    fondled   475
her father's shoulders and begged him to sanction this
    voyage to her sister's,
a voyage for the good of her health, she said – for her ruin,
    more likely!
As Tereus watched, his hands strayed mentally over her
    body.
He eyed her kissing Pandion, her arms encircling his neck.
Her every action served to provoke, to inflame and to
    feed   480
his lust. Each time Philomela embraced her father, he
    wished
that she were *his* child – though his thoughts would not
    have been any less sinful.
Pandion was swayed by his daughters' prayers. Philomela
    delightedly
thanked him, believing, poor soul, that she'd won the day
    for herself
and her sister, when tears and disaster were lying ahead for
    them both.   485
  The sun god's labours were nearing an end, and his
    chariot steeds
were galloping down the western sky to the waves of the
    ocean.
A royal banquet was spread and the wine flowed freely in
    golden
goblets. Then all, feeling pleasantly full, retired to their
    beds.
But the king of Thrace couldn't sleep. The desire Philomela
    had kindled   490

continued to rage. As he thought of her face, her hands
          and her sensuous
movements, his fantasy pictured the parts of her body
          he'd not yet
gazed on, feeding the flames of the passion which kept
          him awake.
Dawn broke; and as Tereus was leaving, Pandion
          grasped his son-in-law's
hand and committed his precious charge with tears in his
495   eyes:
'I entrust Philomela to you, dear son. Her sisterly
          kindness
has won me over. The two of them wanted it, so did
          you.
Tereus, I trust you, you're one of the family. Please, in
          the name
of the gods I implore you, watch over my child with a
          father's love,
and return her soon – she's the comfort and balm of
500   my anxious old age –
as soon as you can, for to me one day will seem like a
          lifetime.
And you, my darling – your sister's absence is sadness
          enough –
if you care for your father at all, Philomela, come back
          to me soon.'
As he made this appeal, Pandion repeatedly kissed his
          child,
and his tears betrayed the tender emotion behind his
505   entreaties.
To confirm their promise, he took their hands and
          joined them together,
begging them not to forget to give his love to his absent
daughter and grandson. His voice was choked by his
          sobs as he stammered
his last farewells from a heart tormented by fear and
510   foreboding.

Once Philomela was safely on board the bright-coloured
     ship,
as the crew pushed off from the land and were rowing out of
     the harbour,
Tereus cried out, 'I have won! My prayers are answered,
     she's sailing
beside me!' Triumphant, the vile barbarian scarcely could
     wait
for his moment of bliss, and his greedy eyes never swerved
     from his prey,   515
like an eagle closely watching the hare it has caught in its
     crooked
talons and dropped in the nest high up where it cannot
     escape.
   The end of the journey at last! They had disembarked
     from the wave-worn
ship and landed in Thrace, when Tereus dragged Philomela 520
up to a stone hut hidden away in an ancient forest.
White and shaking in abject terror, she tearfully asked him,
'Where is my sister?' But now she was trapped. His ugly
     intentions
were all too clear. His virgin prize was alone, and he
     brutally
raped her. Helpless, she screamed in vain for her father, she
     screamed   525
for her sister, and called above all on the gods to come to
     her rescue.
She trembled and shook, poor girl, like a frightened lamb
     that's been mauled
in a grey wolf's jaws but let go and is not yet sure of her
     safety;
or like a white dove, escaped on her blood-drenched wings
     from a hawk,
still shuddering, still afraid of the greedy claws that have
     gripped her.   530
But soon Philomela's senses returned; she tore her
     dishevelled

hair, she scored her arms with her nails like a woman in
    grief
and cried with her hands outstretched: 'You cruel
    barbarian! How could you
do such a dreadful deed? Were you wholly unmoved by
    my father's
entreaties and tears of devotion, my sister's longing to see
535   me,
respect for my maiden virtue and what you owed to
    your wife?
Nature is overthrown! Now I am my sister's rival,
you are married twice over and Procne must be my
    enemy.
Why don't you take my life for good measure, you
    treacherous monster?
I dearly wish you had murdered me first, before you so
540   vilely
assaulted my body! At least my ghost would be pure
    and innocent.
Still, if the powers of heaven can see, if there's any
    authority
left in the skies, if everything else is not lost with my
    honour,
sooner or later I'll have my revenge. All shame
    forgotten,
I'll tell the world of your crime myself. If I'm given the
545   chance,
I'll cry it aloud in the marketplace; and if you still hold
    me
prisoner deep in the forest, my words will ring through
    the trees;
the rocks will know and be moved to pity by what I
    have suffered;
the sky will listen and so will the gods, if any exist
    there.'
    These threats excited the brutal tyrant to violent
    rage,

and his fear was just as extreme. Spurred on by his anger
    and terror,   550
he moved his hand to his belt and drew his sword from the
    sheath;
then grabbing the girl by the hair, he twisted her arms
    behind her
and fastened her wrists in a rope. At the sight of his sword
    Philomela
was praying to die, and freely presented her throat to be
    cut.
Her tongue was still voicing her sense of outrage and crying
    her father's   555
name, still struggling to speak, when Tereus gripped it in
    pincers
and hacked it out with his sword. As its roots in the throat
    gave a flicker,
the rest of it muttered and twitched where it dropped on the
    blood-black earth;
and like the quivering tail of an adder that's chopped in
    half,
it wriggled and writhed its way to the front of its mistress'
    feet.   560
Even after this crime, though the story is scarcely
    believable,
Tereus debauched that bleeding body again and again.
  To crown these atrocious acts, he coolly went home to
    Procne.
As soon as she saw her husband, she asked for her sister;
    but Tereus
groaned in pretended grief and invented a story to make
    her   565
believe Philomela was dead. His weeping succeeded, and
    Procne
ripped from her shoulders her shining robe with its golden
    border
and swathed her body in black. She erected an empty
    tomb,

presented funeral gifts to the shade of the sister she
          thought
was dead, and mourned for a fate which was actually
570   worse than death.

A year went by as the sun passed through the signs of
          the zodiac.
Poor Philomela was helpless: her guards precluded
          escape,
the walls of the hut were firmly constructed of solid
          stone,
and her speechless lips couldn't tell the truth of her
          barbarous treatment.
But suffering sharpens the wits and misfortune makes
575   one resourceful.
She craftily strung a warp on a primitive Thracian
          loom,
and into the pure white threads she wove a message in
          purple
letters revealing the crime. When the piece was
          completed, she handed it
over to one of her sister's women and gestured her
          orders
to put it at once in her mistress' hands. The woman
          then took it
580 to Procne as bidden, with no idea of what it contained.
The wife of the merciless tyrant unrolled the woven
          material,
only to read the pitiful story of what had befallen
her very own sister. Amazing to tell, she said not a
          word.
All speech was choked by her grief. The words that she
          needed weren't there
to express her outrage. Tears were forgone, as she
585   rushed to confound
all right and all wrong. Her heart was totally set on
          revenge.

Now to the time when the women of Thebes, every two
        years, join
in the worship of Bacchus. Their sacred rites are conducted
        at night,
and darkness reigns when the cymbals are clashed in the
        glens of Mount Rhodope.
Darkness attended the queen of Thrace as she stole from the
        palace,   590
dressed for the bacchic ritual and armed with the weapons
        of frenzy:
vine leaves crowning her hair, dappled fawnskin carefully
        arranged
to hang on the left side, thyrsus lightly at rest on her shoulder.
Storming up through the woods with a crowd of her
        women behind her,
Procne in terrible rage, inspired by the frenzy of anguish,   595
mimicked the frenzy of Bacchus. At last she arrived at the
        lonely
hut. With screams and ecstatic cries she broke the doors
        down
and seized her astonished sister; then dressing her up in a
        bacchanal's
costume and hiding her features under an ivy garland,
she dragged Philomela along till they came to the walls of
        the palace.   600
        As soon as she sensed that she'd entered the doors of that
                house of wickedness,
poor Philomela shuddered and turned as white as a sheet.
Procne then found a place to remove the bacchic disguise
and expose her miserable sister's face, still covered with
        shame.
As she tried to embrace her, the girl she had rescued was
        quite unable   605
to look her straight in the eyes, since she felt she had
        cheated her sister.
With head downcast, Philomela wanted to swear in the
        name

of the gods that nothing but force could have made her
    incur such appalling
disgrace, and showed by her hands what her speechless
    lips could not tell.
610 Then Procne, herself inflamed by an uncontainable fury,
rebuked her sister for weeping and said: 'This isn't the
    moment
for tears! It's a sword that we need or a still more
    powerful weapon,
if one is available. I, dear sister, will stop at nothing.
I for one am prepared to apply a torch to the royal
palace and throw the treacherous Tereus into the
615   flames;
or else I'll cut out his tongue and his eyes and lop the
    offending
organ which raped you. I'll deal his body a thousand
    wounds,
till his guilty life is expelled. I've a terrible vengeance
    prepared –
though I'm not yet sure what it is.' As Procne was
    weighing her choices,
Itys entered and gave his mother the clue she was
620   seeking.
Gazing with pitiless eyes on her son, 'How like your
    father
you are!' she said. That was all. She knew at once the
    terrible
thing that she had to do, as she seethed with the fury
    inside her.
The boy, however, ran up and delightedly greeted his
    mother,
holding his little hands out to throw his arms round
625   her neck.
While he kissed her and whispered, 'Oh darling
    mother, I love you so much!'
her natural feelings were stirred and her anger abated a
    moment;

her eyes were moist as she failed to control her unsettling
        emotions.
But once she saw that maternal claims were making her
        purpose
waver, she turned away from her child to the face of her
        sister,   630
then looking at each in turn, she reflected: 'Should Itys be
        able
to say that he loves me, when poor Philomela has lost her
        tongue?
He can call out to his mother, but she cannot call to her
        sister.
Oh Procne, think who you're married to, then remember
        your father!
Be true to your birth! It's a crime to be true to a husband
        like Tereus.'   635
   She waited no longer, but dragged off Itys, just like an
        Indian
tigress dragging a suckling fawn through the forest
        thickets,
till they all three came to a room far off in the echoing
        palace.
Itys saw they were going to kill him and stretched his arms
        out;
'Mother, mother!' he screamed, as he tried once more to
        embrace her.   640
But Procne picked up a sword and stabbed her son in the
        side
of his chest without turning away. Though the blow on its
        own was enough
to murder the child, Philomela then used the weapon to cut
his throat. While his limbs were warm and retained some
        vestige of life,
they tore him apart. The chamber was running with blood
        as the pieces   645
bobbed in a bubbling cauldron or loudly spluttered on
        skewers.

This was the feast to which Procne coolly invited her
      husband
(the man knew nothing of what had occurred or what
      was in store).
Pretending to follow a family custom, with only the
      master
attending the rite, she excluded the servants and other
      attendants.
650   So Tereus sat on the throne of his fathers high on a dais
      and started to gorge himself on a dish of the fruit of his
            own loins.
      Blind to the truth, he actually called out, 'Go and fetch
            Itys!'
      Procne couldn't conceal her malevolent joy any longer.
      Bursting to tell him herself of the crushing blow she'd
            inflicted,
      she said to him, 'Itys is with you already – inside.' So
655   Tereus
      looked round and asked where he was; when he called
            once again for his son,
      Philomela leapt forward, just as she was, her hair
            besprinkled
      with blood from the crazy carnage, and Itys's gory
            head
      was tossed in his father's face. She had never wanted so
            much
      to be able to speak and to voice her joy in a paean of
660   triumph.
      The Thracian king, with a terrible cry, kicked over the
            table
      and summoned the snake-haired Furies to come from
            the vale of the Styx.
      One moment he longed to open his breast, if only he
            could,
      and expel the gruesome banquet of flesh already half
            eaten;
      at another he wept and spoke of himself as his poor
665   son's tomb;

at the next he was chasing Pandion's daughters around with
　　his naked
sword. You could picture the fugitives' bodies suspended on
　　wings.
And they *were* suspended on wings. The one, transformed to
　　a nightingale,
made for the forest, the other flew up to the roof as a
　　swallow;*
but badges of murder remained on their breasts in the
　　blood-tinged plumage.   670
Tereus, swiftly impelled by his grief and thirsting for
　　vengeance,
also changed to a bird, with an upright crest for a
　　headpiece
and beak jutting out to a monstrous length in the place of
　　his long spear,
looking as if he were armed for battle. We call him the
　　hoopoe.

BOREAS AND ORITHYIA

Grief for his daughters despatched Pandion to Hades
　　before   675
his time. The throne of Athens was then assumed by
　　Eréchtheus,
a king renowned for his justice no less than his prowess in
　　warfare.
Erechtheus begot four princely sons and as many daughters,
including two who were equally beautiful. Procris* was
　　married   680
to Céphalus, Aéolus' grandson; and Orithýia* was loved
by the north wind, Bóreas. Hatred, however, for Tereus and
　　all
the Thracians, who live in the north, impeded his suit for a
　　long time,
while he preferred to press it with soft words rather than
　　brute force.

When gentle wooing proved unsuccessful, his temper was
685   ruffled;
the god reverted to anger, his all too characteristic
mood, and he said: 'My failure's deserved! Why
           haven't I used
my proper weapons of fury and strength or my
           menacing anger,
instead of these futile entreaties which only do me
           discredit?
Force is my natural way. How else are the gloomy
690   storm clouds
driven along, the waves churned up, or the knotty oaks
overturned, the snows packed hard or the earth's tracts
           pounded with hail?
I am the god who confronts my brother winds in the
           open
sky, where my battleground is. The thrust of my power
           in the fray
is such that our clashes are signalled by thunderclaps
695   high in the air,
and the lightning fires leap forth, forced out of the void
           in the clouds.
I am the god who forces my way through the vaulted
           passages
deep in the caverns of earth. When I violently heave
           with my shoulders,
I trouble the ghosts and the whole of the world with
           my rumbling tremors.
That was the proper way to have courted my bride.
700   Erechtheus
should not have been kindly asked but *made* to give me
           his daughter.'
   With boisterous words like these, or others of
           similar fury,
Boreas beat the air with his powerful wings, and a
           howling
blast swept over the earth and ruffled the breadth of
           the sea.

As he trailed his dusty mantle across the peaks of the
    mountains,   705
he scoured the land; then, shrouded in darkness, the lover
    enfolded
his Orithyia, all trembling with fear, in his tawny pinions.
During their flight, the flames of his passion grew yet more
    strong;
and the kidnapper's journey across the sky continued
    unchecked,
until he arrived at the walls where the Cícones tribes were
    settled.   710
There the Athenian girl and the king of the frost were
    united,
and Orithyia became the mother of twins, who resembled
herself in other respects but were furnished with wings like
    their father.
Yet these, we are told, weren't part of the twins at the time
    of their birth;
before the golden down could be seen on their youthful
    cheeks,   715
Zetes and Cálaïs still were unfledged; but later, along with
their beards, the feathers started to sprout on the sides of
    their bodies,
as though they were birds. So when they had grown from
    boys to men,
they joined the Mínyae, sailing across the unexplored main   720
in the Argo, first of all ships,* on the quest for the Golden
    Fleece.*

BOOK 7

Almost half of this book (1–403) is concerned with *Medea*, the princess of Colchis, who used her magic arts to help Jason and the Argonauts to win the Golden Fleece and was later rejected by her heroic lover for a socially more advantageous marriage. Ovid was clearly fascinated by Medea as a character and, like Euripides in Greek, wrote a tragedy in Latin about her which is sadly lost to us. He also owed a great deal to the *Argonautica* by Apollonius of Rhodes (third century BC).

In the *Metamorphoses* Ovid describes Medea falling in love with Jason and gives her a grand dramatic soliloquy (12–71) which shows her torn between her passion and her duty to her father. Once she and Jason are committed to each other (74–99), the poet focuses on the incidents in the story which involve transformations. When Jason has yoked the fire-breathing bulls, he sows the dragon's teeth, which (as in the Cadmus story 3.104–30) produce armed warriors when sown in the earth (120–58). Medea then uses her magical powers benevolently to rejuvenate Jason's father *Aeson* (159–296) and malevolently to destroy Jason's wicked uncle *Pelias* (297–349). In all these exciting episodes the figure of Medea as a powerful sorceress clearly fires Ovid's imagination, rhetoric and powers of detailed description. By contrast, *Medea's Flight* (350–403) is in a much lower key: it offered the poet scope for a display of geographical learning and for a long series of mini-metamorphoses, only one of which (Cycnus, 371–9) is at all interesting.

Medea's landing at Athens and marriage to Aegeus allows Ovid the chance to include the king's son *Theseus* and his heroic exploits in the narrative (404–52). Soon we are introduced to

Minos, king of Crete, who is planning to make war on Athens and approaches *Aeacus*, king of the island Aegina, for help (453–500). Aeacus, however, prefers to side with the Athenians, who also send him a delegation led by the old hero Cephalus. Although his own people have been recently depleted by the appalling *Plague at Aegina* (501–613b), they have subsequently been restocked by *The Birth of the Myrmidons* (614–60), a new generation achieved by the miraculous transformation of ants occupying a sacred oak tree into an army of young fighters. In his brilliant account of the plague, Ovid (like Lucretius and Virgil in similar passages before him) will have returned to the famous description of the great plague at Athens by the Greek historian Thucydides (late fifth century BC). Though the detail is derivative, the passage is one of the finest in the whole poem.

The book ends with a tale in a totally different vein and genre altogether, the tragic love story of *Cephalus and Procris* (661–862). Cephalus, the Athenian envoy at Aegina, is asked to explain the history of the spear he is carrying. He tells how it had been given to him in his youth as a present by his wife, Procris, but it had destroyed them both. The story which Ovid inherited from others is somewhat bizarre, but the poet makes it strangely convincing, and the relationship between the two devoted lovers is movingly explored. The main theme is the destructive power of jealousy, first on the man's side towards the woman and then on the woman's towards the man. The physical metamorphosis (of a dog and a giant vixen to rock) is incidental, but the idea of change runs deeper in its application to human feelings, mutual trust and even personality (note especially 720–22).

An abrupt coda (863–5) reminds us that the aged Cephalus is in Aegina to find allied troops for Athens's protection against Minos.

MEDEA AND JASON

Behold the Argonauts ploughing the sea on their voyage
    from Greece!
Behind them was Thrace, where they'd seen King
    Phíneus, blind and impoverished,
passing a bleak old age, and Bóreas' twins had routed
the Harpies who'd tortured that wretched old man by
    snatching his food.
5 After many adventures under their captain, Jason,
they finally came to the muddy stream of the
    swift-flowing Phasis.
On reaching Aeëtes' palace, they laid their claim to the
    Golden
Fleece,* and the king dictated his terms to the heroes, a
    series
of hard and dangerous tasks. Meanwhile, his daughter
    Medéa
fell deeply in love with the handsome Jason. Despite a
10   long struggle
against her feelings, her reason was powerless to master
    her passion.*
'It's useless to fight, Medea,' she said. 'Some god is
    against you.
This, or something akin to it surely, is what they call
    love.
How else should I find my father's conditions
    excessively harsh?
For certain they are too harsh. How else should I fear
15   for the life
of a man I have only just seen? – But *why* should I feel
    so afraid?
How wretched I am! I *must* extinguish the fire which is
    raging
inside my innocent heart. I should be more sane, if I
    could!

I am dragged along by a strange new force. Desire and
    reason
are pulling in different directions. I see the right way and
    approve it,   20
but follow the wrong. I am royal; so why should I sigh for a
    stranger,
or ever conceive of a marriage which takes me away from
    my home?
Love can be found here too. It rests in the lap of the gods
whether Jason survives or is killed. – But I want him to live!
    I don't
have to love him to pray for that. What crime has Jason
    committed?   25
Only a cruel and heartless person could fail to be struck
by his youthfulness, breeding and courage. And who could
    be blind to his handsome
looks, if he lacked all else? *My* heart, at least, has been
    stirred.
But unless I assist him, those fire-breathing bulls will blast
    him to ashes;
the warriors sprung from the seeds which he sows in the
    earth will fight   30
and destroy him; or else the greedy dragon will make him
    its prey.
If I can allow all this, I'll confess that I'm born of a tigress,
confess that my heart is composed of nothing but rock and
    steel. –
Oh, why don't I watch him dying and so infect my
    eyes
with the taint of the spectacle? Why don't I shout to the
    fire-breathing bulls   35
or the earth-born brutes or the sleepless dragon to charge
    and attack him? –
O heavens, grant me better than that! Yet better is not
to be idly prayed for but done! – By me? Is it truly better
that I should betray my king and my father, that some tall
    stranger

should owe his life to my kind assistance, only to thank
      me,
the woman who saved him, by spreading his sails to the
40   wind without me,
marrying somebody else and leaving Medea to be
      punished?
If he can do such a thing and prefer a rival to me,
the ungrateful traitor can die! – Yet when I think of that
      face,
of that noble, heroic soul, of that strong and beautiful
      body,
I cannot fear he'd be false or forget my help. To make
45   certain,
he'll give me his word in advance and I'll force him to
      swear to our pact
in the name of the gods. All's safe; there is nothing to
      fear. So be done
with delay, and to action! Jason will always be in my
      debt.
The rites of the wedding torch will unite us. In all the
      cities
of Greece great throngs of women will praise me for
50   saving their sons. –
What now? Shall I sail away on the wind and abandon
      my father,
my brother, my sister, the gods and soil of my native
      country? –
Why shouldn't I leave such a heartless father, a
      barbarous land
and a brother who's only a child? My sister's prayers go
      with me.
The greatest of gods is alive inside me! I'll not forsake
55   greatness
but rather pursue it: the glory of saving the sons of
      Greece,
the knowledge of better lands and of cities with arts and
      civilized

customs, whose fame is proclaimed in climes as distant as
    this;
and lastly my Jason, the man for whom I would gladly
    surrender
all the treasures of earth. When I am his wife, they will call   60
me happy, beloved of the gods, and I'll rise to the stars in
    my glory!
What of those mountainous rocks* that are rumoured to
    clash in the ocean?
What of Charýbdis, who threatens the ships by swallowing
    up
the waves, then spewing them forth? And what of the
    ravening Scylla,
whose girdle of savage dogs barks over the sea of Sicily?   65
Clinging to what I love, held tightly to Jason's breast,
I can brave any voyage, however long. With him in my arms
I'll be frightened of nothing, or else my fears will be all for
    my husband. –
Your husband? Be careful, Medea. Are you using
    respectable words
to cover your evil designs? No, no! Face up to the terrible   70
wrong you're about to commit and recoil from the guilt
    while you may!'
She ended. Now virtue, daughterly feeling and maidenly
    conscience
had come to the fore. Desire, now vanquished, was in
    retreat.

Medea then made her way to the ancient altar of Hécate,
goddess of spells, far off in the depths of a shadowy grove.   75
Her purpose was firmly set and the flame of her love had
    subsided,
when Jason appeared on the scene and the fire which had
    died was rekindled.
A blush came over her cheeks and the whole of her face
    glowed hot.
As a tiny spark that is hidden under a pile of ashes

is fanned and fed once again by the wind and grows to
80   recover
    its earlier strength, so the love you might have supposed
      was dwindling
    and dying away flared up when she saw young Jason
      before her.
    That shining morning it chanced that the son of Aéson
      was looking
    more handsome than ever. Medea could hardly be
85   blamed for her passion.
    Her gazing eyes were fixed on his face, as though she
      had never
    seen it before. 'It must be a god who is standing there,'
    she thought in her madness, unable to turn her body
      away.
    But when the stranger began to speak and, suddenly
      gripping
    her right hand, begged in the humblest of tones for her
90   help and promised
    to make her his wife, Medea burst into tears and
      replied:
    'I see what I'm doing; so if I am cheated, I cannot blame
      ignorance,
    only my love. You shall owe your life to the help that I
      give you.
    Be sure that you keep your promise!' He swore by the
      rites of the threefold
    goddess* and all the power which haunted that sacred
95   wood;
    he swore by his future father's father, the all-seeing sun
      god,*
    by all the successes he hoped for and all the dangers he
      feared.
    Medea believed him. At once she gave him some
      magical herbs,
    then explained how to use them; and Jason returned to
      his tents with a light heart.

The next day's dawn had driven the glittering stars from
    the sky.   100
By the sacred field of Mars the people of Colchis were
    gathered
and standing to watch on the hills; enthroned in their midst
    King Aeëtes,
garbed in his purple robe and wielding an ivory sceptre.
There were the bronze-hooved bulls! They were breathing
    fire from their steely
nostrils and scorching the grass on the plain with the force
    of their hot breath.   105
Loudly they roared like a blacksmith's furnace filled to the
    full,
or the sizzling sound of the molten stone from a builder's
    limekiln
igniting when sprinkled with running water. A noise as
    tremendous
came from the chests of the bulls, while the flames rolled
    round in the prison
inside them and then poured forth from their burning
    throats. But Jason   110
calmly went forward to face them. The great beasts angrily
    turned
their ferocious heads to meet his advance and levelled their
    iron-tipped
horns; they pounded the dusty earth with their cloven
    hooves
and vomited clouds of smoke as they filled the air with their
    bellowing.
The Argonaut sailors were rigid with terror; but Jason
    approached,   115
not feeling the fiery blasts, so potent the herbs that
    preserved him.
He daringly stroked the bulls with his hand on their
    pendulous dewlaps,
then placing a yoke on their necks, he forced them to draw
    the heavy

weight of a plough and cut a path through a virgin plain.
The Colchians watched in amazement, while all the
120   Argonauts cheered
and encouraged their captain, who took the teeth of
        the Theban dragon*
out of a golden helmet and scattered them into the
        furrow.
These seeds, being steeped in a virulent poison,
        softened the earth,
and the sown teeth started to grow and assume a new
        kind of body.
125 Just as a baby takes human shape in its mother's womb
and the different parts are arranged inside to compose
        one whole,
which doesn't emerge in the outside world till it's fully
        developed,
so when the ripened form of a man was complete in the
        womb
of the pregnant earth, he rose from the fertile soil to
        the surface
and, even more wonderful, clashed the weapons which
130   came up with him.
Seeing these warriors aiming to cast their
        sharp-pointed spears
at Jason's head, his companions lowered their eyes in
        dismay.
Even Medea, who'd made him safe, was quaking with
        fear.
As she watched that army advancing towards their
135   solitary target,
her face turned suddenly pale and she sat in a frozen
        trance.
In case the herbs she had given him proved too feeble,
        she chanted
a spell for his extra support and called on her secret
        devices.
Jason then hurled a gigantic rock right into the midst

of his foes, and repelled their attack by making them fight
    with each other.   140
The earth-born soldiers died of the wounds they received
    from their brothers,
as though they had fallen in civil war. With cheers of
    rejoicing
the Greeks swarmed round the victorious hero and hugged
    him tightly.
The princess of Colchis would also have liked to embrace
    the victor,
but modesty would not permit it. She merely exulted in
    silence,   145
and offered thanks for her spells to the gods of her magical
    powers.*
   Jason's remaining task was to use Medea's herbs
to drug the unsleeping dragon, who guarded the golden
    tree   150
in the pride of its towering crest, its three-forked tongue
    and its hooked fangs.
After he'd sprinkled the monster with juice of a herb from
    the Lethe,
repeating a spell three times to induce a motionless
    slumber,
a spell which could calm a troubled sea or a river in spate,
sleep finally settled on eyes which had never known it, and
    Jason   155
was able to capture the Golden Fleece. Then, proud in his
    spoil
and bearing a further prize in the woman who'd helped him
    to win it,
the hero returned with his bride to Iólcos' harbour in
    triumph.

THE REJUVENATION OF AESON

In Thessaly mothers and aged fathers brought gifts to
        the gods
in thanks for their sons' return; the altars were laden
160   with incense
which melted over the flames; the promised victim with
        gilded
horns fell under the axe. But Aeson, the father of
        Jason,
could play no part in the general rejoicing; the tired old
        man
was nearing the end of his life. His son then said to
        Medea:
'I grant, dear wife, that you've saved me from death;
165   you have given me all,
and the sum of your many kindnesses truly passes
        belief.
Yet I ask, if your magical powers can do it – and what
        can they not? –
Subtract a few of my years to add to the years of my
        father.'
He couldn't restrain his tears. Medea was moved by
        the loyal
devotion which prompted this plea, and remembered
170   the father she'd falsely
betrayed and abandoned. Without confessing these
        feelings, she answered,
'Dear husband, how could you suggest such a crime?
        Do you truly think
that I could ever transfer a part of your life to another?
Hecate wouldn't allow it and you should never have
        asked.
175 But still, my Jason, I'll try to do you an even greater
favour than what you are begging. I'll use my arts to
        prolong

your father's years without lessening yours, if only the
    three-formed
goddess will help and support this daring attempt with her
    presence.'
  Three nights had still to go by before the horns of the
    moon
could meet in a perfect orb. When it shone at last in its
    fullness,   180
and gazed on the earth below with all its glory restored,
Medea stole out of the palace. Her robes hung loosely
    about her,
her feet were unshod and her unbound hair flowed over her
    shoulders.*
All on her own, in the deadly stillness of deep midnight,
she followed her wandering path. Other people, the birds
    and the beasts   185
were softly buried in sleep. Not a sough could be heard in
    the hedgerows;
the leaves were silent and still; silent the dank air;
    motionless
all but the twinkling stars. Extending her arms to the
    spheres,
she turned full about three times; three times she sprinkled
    her head
with water drawn from the stream; three times she opened
    her lips   190
to utter a piercing cry; then, kneeling down on the hard
    earth,
prayed: 'O night, most faithful keeper of secrets; you golden
stars who companion the moon in succeeding the fires of
    the day;
Hecate, three-formed goddess, who knows of my deep
    designs
and comes when invoked to assist the spells of skilful
    magicians;   195
earth, who yields all enchanters the potent herbs for their
    witchcraft;

breezes and winds of the air, you mountains, rivers and
    lakes,
gods of the forest and gods of the night, be here with me
    all!
By your aid, whenever I will, to the banks' amazement,
    the rivers
return to their fountain-heads. By your aid, I can quieten
200   the troubled
seas or ruffle their calm with my spells. By your aid I
    can banish
the clouds or cause them to gather; I summon and
    scatter the winds.
With my incantations I force fanged serpents to split
    their skins;
I dislodge the rocks and uproot the trees, shift forests
    and order
the mountains to tremble, the earth to rumble and
205   spirits to rise
from their graves. I can draw the moon from the sky,
    no matter how loudly
the cymbals may clash* to avert it; the Sun, my
    grandfather's chariot,
pales at my song and my poisons can rob the Dawn of
    her colour.
At my request, you deities blunted the force of the
210   fire-breathing
bulls and bowed their heads underneath the weight of
    the hooked plough;
you forced the brood of the dragon's teeth to savage
    each other;
and after you closed the eyes of the sleeplessly vigilant
    serpent
who guarded the gold, you stole it away and restored it
    to Greece.
Now I have need of the juices to make an old man in
215   his weakness
recover his youthful strength and return to the bloom
    of his prime.

You will grant them, I know. The stars are not twinkling so
    brightly in vain,
and it must be at your command that my chariot, drawn by
    winged dragons,
is ready to take me' – and there stood her car, sent down
    from the sky.
As soon as she'd mounted and stroked the bridled necks of
    her serpents,   220
she gave a shake to the slender reins and was swept to the
    sky,
from where she looked down on Thessalian Tempe and
    steered her dragons
to places she knew would provide her with herbs. Mount
    Ossa and Pélion,
Othrys, Pindus, Olympus, the highest mountain of all,   225
were crossed and explored. When she found what she
    wanted, she either plucked it
up by the roots or cut it away with a curved bronze
    sickle.
Much that she needed could also be found on the banks of
    the river
Apídanus, or the Amphrýsus, or else by the streams of
    Enípeus;
Penéüs, the waves of Spercheüs, the reedy shores of Lake
    Boebe,   230
all contributed plants; and Medea discovered a special
grass for long life in Boeótian Anthédon, facing Euboéa,
a city later renowned for the transformation of Glaucus.*
   Nine days, nine nights went by as, drawn by her team of
    winged dragons,
she roamed the whole of the region to gather those herbs of
    renewal;   235
and then she returned. The dragons had only inhaled the
    scent
of the plants, but their skins were old with the years and
    they sloughed them off.
On reaching the palace, she halted outside the doors and
    the threshold,

with only the sky to cover her head; and avoiding her
    husband's
embraces to keep herself pure, she built two altars of
240   green turf,
one on the right to Hecate, one on the left to the
    goddess
of Youth. When she'd twined these round with
    branches and leaves from the woodland,
she dug two pits in the earth close by, and started her
    ritual
sacrifice. First she plunged her knife in the throat of a
    black-fleeced
victim, whose blood was allowed to flow in the open
245   trenches.
Then, as she tipped a bowl of honey to add to the
    liquid,
followed in turn by a chalice of milk still warm from
    the udder,
she chanted her incantation and called on the spirits of
    earth
together with Pluto, the king of the shades, and his
    stolen consort,
to wait before they purloined the life in the old man's
250   body.
    Now that she'd soothed these gods with her long,
    low-muttered petitions,
she ordered the servants to carry the feeble body of
    Aeson
outside; then intoning a spell till sleep had fully relaxed
    him,
she laid him out, as though he were dead, on a bed of
    herbs.
The old king's son and attendants were ordered to
255   stand far off
and not to look with unhallowed eyes on her secret
    mysteries.
All dispersed as she bade. With hair flowing loose, like
    a bacchant,

Medea circled the blazing altars; she dipped two split-wood
torches into the trench and, once they were steeped in the
     sheep's
black blood, she set them alight at her altars, and purified
     Aeson   260
thrice with the fire, thrice with water and thrice with
     sulphur.
   Meanwhile in the brazen pot on its stand the potent elixir
was boiling, bubbling and frothing white in the rising foam.
The brew consisted of roots which Mcdca had cut in
     Thessalian
valleys, with cornseed, flowers and juices as black as pitch;   265
strange stones she had fetched from the farthest east and
     sand that the ocean
had washed in an ebbing tide. She had added some
     hoarfrost gathered
by blazing moonlight, the wings and the flesh of an
     ominous screech-owl,
guts of a wolf with the power of changing its bestial
     features   270
to those of a man, the scaly skin of a water-snake caught
in a Libyan stream, the liver drawn from a long-lived stag,
with the eggs and head of a crow that had chattered for
     nine generations.
With these and a thousand nameless objects, the Colchian
     witch   275
was ready to work her spell transcending the powers of a
     mortal.
Dipping the branch of an olive, once fruitful but long since
     withered,
she stirred the ingredients up and mingled the top with the
     bottom.
And look! the dry stick, circling around in the boiling
     cauldron,
changed – to start with from grey to green, and then in a
     short while   280
sprouted with leaves and was suddenly laden with fat, ripe
     olives.

Whenever the foam on the fire spilt over the side of the
          vessel
and hot drops fell to the ground, the soil turned green
          and a cluster
of flowers arose on the soft, lush grass. As soon as she
          saw this,
Medea unsheathed her sword and drew a cut in the old
285   man's
throat, so letting the blood drain out of his body. She
          then
replaced it with juice from the pot. When Aeson had
          fully absorbed this,
either by mouth or by way of the wound, his hair and
          his beard
lost all of their whiteness and quickly returned to a
          lustrous black.
His leanness, pallor and withered features had all
290   disappeared;
those wrinkled and creased old cheeks filled out with
          their firm new flesh;
his limbs grew supple and strong. In utter amazement
          and wonder,
Aeson remembered himself in his young days forty
          years earlier.

From his home in the sky Dionýsus had watched
          Medea perform
this astonishing miracle. Seeing his nurses* could still
295   be restored
to the years of their youth, he obtained this boon from
          the woman of Colchis.

THE PUNISHMENT OF PELIAS

Black treachery next. Medea, pretending that she and Jason
were now estranged, took refuge in Pélias' house* to
      implore
protection. The king himself was enfeebled by age, but his
      daughters
welcomed her gladly. In no time at all, their Colchian
      guest   300
had cunningly won their hearts by a show of counterfeit
      friendship.
Among her signal achievements Medea was careful to cite
the rejuvenation of Aeson and dwelt at some length on the
      details,
so planting the hope in the gullible daughters' minds that
      their father
could also recover the bloom of his youth with similar
      treatment.   305
This they requested and told her to name any price that she
      chose.
Medea was quiet for a while, as though she were still
      undecided,
keeping them all in suspense while she seemed to be mulling
      it over.
Then, when she'd promised to help them, she said, 'To
      prove that I really
can do what I say, I shall use the power of my magic herbs   310
to change the oldest tup in your flocks to a new-born lamb.'
At once the daughters brought forward a sheep, a
      clapped-out creature
of years untold, with its horns all twisted around its
      forehead.
Medea then thrust her Thessalian knife in its scraggy old
      throat
(the metal was hardly stained, as the blood was so thin),
      and plunged   315

the carcass into the cauldron containing her potent
      mixture.
The ram's frame shrunk and its years burned up along
      with its horns;
then a feeble bleating was heard right down in the depths
      of the cauldron,
and while they were all still frozen in wonder, a lamb
320   jumped out
and friskily scampered away in search of an udder to
      suck.
    Pelias' daughters were quite dumbfounded, and now
      that Medea's
claims were confirmed, they pressed their demand with
      greater insistence.
Three times the sun god had plunged his steeds in the
      streams of the Ebro*
and lifted their yokes. The fourth night came and the
325   radiant stars
were glittering bright, when the treacherous visitor
      kindled a raging
fire underneath a cauldron she'd only filled with plain
      water
and herbs which had no effect. The king and his guards
      beside him
were all relaxed in a deathlike sleep, induced by the
      magical
power of the sorceress' tongue as she chanted her
330   incantations.
Medea had ordered the daughters to join her inside the
      palace;
when all were standing around the bed, she attacked
      them: 'Cowards!
Why are you shrinking now? Unsheathe those swords
      and empty
his aged veins, so that I may refill them with youthful
      blood.
Your father's life and his years are now dependent on
335   you.

If you have any daughterly love and your hopes are not
     wishful thinking,
then show your father the duty you owe him and use your
     weapons
to purge his old age. Release his blood with the points of
     your swords!'
Lashed on by these taunts, the child whose sense of duty was
     strongest
was first to betray it, avoiding guilt by committing a crime;   340
and so with the others. But none could look at the wounds
     they were dealing;
with eyes averted, they blindly, wildly stabbed at their
     father.
Dripping with blood, he still was able to lift himself up
on his elbow. Though covered with gashes, he tried to get
     up from his couch
and, braving the circle of sword-points round him,
     extended his pale arms.   345
'What are you doing, my children?' he cried. 'Who gave
     you these weapons
to murder your father?' Their courage failed, and they
     lowered their swords.
He would have said more, but his words were cut off by
     Medea, who knifed
his throat and plunged his butchered limbs in the boiling
     water.

MEDEA'S FLIGHT

If she hadn't been borne to the sky on the wings of her
     dragon chariot,   350
Medea would surely have paid for her crime. Her flight
     through the air*
took her over the woods of Mount Pelion, home of Chiron
     the centaur,
then over Othrys and pastures renowned for the tale of
     Cerámbus

(when Earth's huge mass was submerged beneath the tide
          of the ocean,
Cerambus was lifted on wings to the sky with the help of
355   the nymphs
and so escaped Deucálion's flood and was rescued
          from drowning).
Next, on her left, she passed the Aeólian city of Pítane,
facing the great long petrified snake* on the shore of
          Lesbos;
and Ida's forests, where Bacchus protected his thieving
          son
360 by hiding a stolen bullock within the form of a stag.
She passed where Paris was modestly buried in shallow
          sand;
where Maera, transformed to a dog, once startled the
          fields with her barking;
Eurýpylus' city in Cos, where the women were changed
          into cows
at the time when Hercules' army was journeying home
          from the Troad;
Phoebus' Rhodes and the town of Iálysos, where the
365   Telchínes,
magicians whose evil eye could destroy whatever they
          gazed on,
were drowned in the waves of the sea by Jupiter's
          powerful hatred.
She also traversed the walls of Carthaéa on ancient
          Ceos,
where old Alcídamas later in time would be greatly
          surprised
when a peaceful dove sprang out of the corpse of his
370   daughter, Ctesýlla.
Medea looked down on Hýrië's lake in the beautiful
          valley
renowned for a boy called Cycnus,* who suddenly
          changed to a swan.
This was the story: on Cycnus' orders, his lover
          Phýlius

captured some vultures and slaughtered a lion, which he
          brought to his friend;
when also commanded to tame a wild bull, he had done so,
          but angry   375
because his love had been spurned so often, he wouldn't
          hand over
this final prize. In a fury the boy cried out, 'You'll be sorry
for this!' and jumped off a cliff. While everyone thought he
          had fallen,
in fact he'd been changed to a swan and was gliding on
          snow-white wings.
His mother Hyrië, though, unaware that her son had been
          rescued,   380
dissolved in her tears and gave her name to the pool she
          created.
Close by is Aetólian Pleuron, where Óphius' daughter
          Combe
escaped on fluttering wings from a savage attack by her
          children.
Next Medea set eyes on Calaúrea, Leto's island,
which witnessed the change of the king and his wife to a
          pair of birds.   385
There to the right was Mount Cylléne, the place where
          Menéphron
was destined to sleep in shame with his mother, as though
          they were wild beasts.
Far in the distance behind was the river Cephísus
          bemoaning
the fate of his grandson, changed to a plump wet seal by
          Apollo;
and there the house of Eumélus, who grieved for his
          wing-borne son.   390
    At last Medea arrived in her dragon car at Pirénian
Corinth; here, in the earliest times, according to ancient
tradition, our human bodies grew from the rain-fed
          mushroom.*
But after Jason's new bride* had blazed in the poisoned
          robe,

and fire in the royal house had been watched each side of
395   the Isthmus,
the wicked Medea then steeped her sword in the blood
      of her children.
Proud in this evil revenge, the mother escaped from the
      father's
wrath. She was swept through the sky by her dragons,
      until she entered
the fortress of Pallas at Athens, where Phene, most
      righteous of women,
400 and aged Périphas soared together as vulture and eagle;
Alcýone too could be seen, borne up on her kingfisher
      wings.
King Aégeus welcomed Medea, itself enough to
      condemn him,
but more was offered than shelter; he also made her his
      wife.

THESEUS AND AEGEUS

Now Theseus, whose father Aegeus had never known
      him, arrived;
his heroic deeds* had established peace on the Isthmus
405   of Corinth.
Bent on his murder, Medea prepared him a potion of
      aconite,
brought by her earlier over the sea from the Scythian
      shores.
This poison is said to have come from the teeth of the
      monstrous dog
whom Echídna bore. Imagine a cave with a murky
      entrance,
410 inside it a sloping path up which the hero from Tíryns,
Hercules, dragged along Cérberus fastened in steel-link
      chains.
Persistently stopping, the dog kept blinking and
      turning his eyes

away from the dazzling light of the sun; in a frenzy of anger,
he filled the air with his barking from all three heads at the
          same time,
sprinkling the green of the fields with the white of the foam
          from his mouth.   415
This foam is supposed to have then congealed; it was
          fertilized
by the rich, rank soil and acquired the power of a deadly
          poison.
Seeing this new plant grows and thrives on a hard rock bed,
our peasant folk call it aconite, based on the Greek for a
          whetstone.
Such was the potion Medea had craftily given to Aegeus,   420
Theseus' father, to offer the son whom he thought was an
          enemy.
Theseus, suspecting nothing, had taken the cup in his hand,
when the old king spotted the family emblem engraved on
          the ivory
hilt of the young man's sword and dashed the brew from his
          lips.
   Though Theseus' father was filled with joy that his son
          was safe,   425
he was also filled with horror that such a terrible crime
had been so closely prevented. He kindled the fires on his
          altars
and lavishly plied the gods with his gifts: the ritual axes
struck on the muscular necks of the bulls with their
          ribboned horns.
No day of rejoicing, they say, ever dawned in the city of
          Athens   430
more hallowed than that one. Elders and humbler folk
          celebrated
at banquets together and sang their songs as the wine
          inspired them:
'All praise to you, Theseus, greatest of heroes! The people
          in Márathon's
Plain were amazed when you slaughtered the dangerous
          Cretan bull.*

It is thanks to you that the farmers of Crómyon plough
435   their fields,
unafraid of the monstrous boar; that fair Epidaúrus
             was rescued
when vile Periphétes who carried the club was struck
             to the earth;
that ruthless Procrústes* was also destroyed on the
             banks of Cephisus;
that Ceres' city, Eleúsis, was witness to Cércyon's*
             downfall.
You also disposed of the giant Sinis, that mighty
440   abuser
of strength, who would bend two pines and lower their
             tops to the ground,
then release them and scatter his victim's fragments*
             over the land.
No Sciron* to haunt it, the path to the Léleges' city of
             Mégara
now lies open and safe; the robber's bones have been
             scattered,
but neither on land nor on sea have they found any
445   resting place;
long tossed on the waves, and hardened by time, it is
             said, they were finally
changed into rocks, which will always be called the
             Scirónian rocks.
If we wished to count over your exploits and also
             declare your age,
your deeds would outnumber your years. For you,
             most valiant of heroes,
we offer the thanks of our people, and yours is the
450   health that we drink!'
The cheers of the crowd and the prayers of
             well-wishers resounded throughout
the palace. There wasn't a corner of gloom in the
             whole of the city.

MINOS AND AEACUS

And yet no pleasure is ever unmingled; anxiety always
intrudes upon joy. So Aegeus' delight in his son's return
was marred by disquiet. King Minos of Crete was preparing
    for war.   455
Though powerful on land and by sea, he was strong above
    all in the anger
he felt as a father in seeking a just revenge for Andrógeos'*
murder at Athens. Moreover, he'd mustered his allies
    beforehand
by scouring the sea* with the rapid fleet for which he was
    famous.   460
Ánaphe joined his cause and the kingdom of Astypalaéa,
the former induced by his pledges, the latter by force of
    arms;
low-lying Mýconos farther off; Cimólus renowned
for its chalk; then Syros, the thyme-growing island, with
    low-hilled Sériphos;
Paros, famed for its marble, and Siphnos, betrayed by the
    treacherous   465
Arne, who after receiving the gold she had greedily asked
    for
was changed to a bird and even today retains her incurable
passion for gold as the black-footed, black-winged,
    pilfering jackdaw.
  But several islands – Olíaros, Dídyme, Tenos and
    Andros,
Gýaros, and the producer of olive oil, Peparéthos* –   470
refused to support the navy from Crete. So Minos turned
    west
and sailed to the island ruled by the Aéacid clan, Oenópia
(so the kingdom was called in ancient times, but Aegina
was how King Aéacus liked to refer to it, after his mother).
A crowd flocked down to greet the arrival of Minos,
    longing
                                                    475

to see such a famous person. The welcome party
  consisted
of Aeacus' three sons, Télamon, Péleus and Phocus, the
  youngest.
Aeacus too, although he was slow with the weight of his
  years,
came out of the palace himself and enquired what Minos
  had come for.
Reminded at once of the son he was mourning, the king
480   of the hundred
cities in Crete sighed deeply before he declared what he
  wanted:
'I ask for your help in a war of revenge for my
  murdered son;
I beg you to join in my mission of duty to solace the
  buried.'
Aeacus answered: 'I have to refuse your request. Aegina
may not be involved in your plan. No city is closer to
485   Athens
than we are; we could not betray the treaties of
  friendship between us.'
Minos sadly departed. 'Those treaties will cost you
  dear,'
he said to them, thinking it wiser to threaten the
  Aeginétans
with war than to fight on the spot and waste his
  strength prematurely.
490 The Cretan galleys were still in sight of Aegina's walls,
when a ship from Athens approached full sail and
  entered their ally's
harbour; on board was Céphalus, bearing his country's
  commission.
Though many years had elapsed since Aeacus' sons
  had set eyes
on Cephalus' face, they knew him at once and, greeting
495   him warmly,

conducted him into their father's palace. The aged hero,
whose handsome features preserved some marks of his
        youthful appearance,
entered the royal palace, holding a branch of Athenian
olive and flanked to the right and the left by two of his
        younger
compatriots, Clytus and Butes, whose noble father was
        Pallas.   500

THE PLAGUE AT AEGINA

After the usual exchange of introductory greetings,
the envoy delivered the message he'd brought from Aegeus
        in Athens,
asking for help in the terms of the treaty between their two
        cities,
and adding that Minos was aiming to conquer the whole of
        Greece.
This appeal was made with persuasive eloquence. When it
        was ended,   505
Aeacus answered, his left hand resting upon his sceptre:
'Athens, you need not ask for our help; you have only to
        take it.
Treat the strength of this island as yours without
        hesitation.
Provided my present good fortune continues – and long
        may it do so –
the power is there, I have soldiers in plenty and, thanks to
        the gods,   510
the time is propitious. I cannot for any good reason refuse
        you.'
'I trust that is so,' said the envoy. 'I pray for the growth of
        your city
and people. Indeed, as I landed now, I was truly delighted
when such a procession of handsome youths, all equal in
        age,

came forward to meet me. However, I've noticed that
515   many are missing
from those whom I saw last time when I came as a
          guest to your city.'
Aeacus heaved a sigh and sadly explained what had
          happened:
'Earlier days of distress have been followed by happier
          times,
and I only wish I could tell you the end without the
          beginning.
But now I'll return to the start. No beating about the
520   bush:
the friends you remember and miss are nothing but
          bones and ashes,
and they were only a fraction of what I lost when they
          perished.
   'My people were struck by a terrible plague, through
          the anger of cruel
Juno, who hated the island that takes its name from
          her rival.*
So long as the illness seemed to be due to natural
525   causes,
and other reasons for such a disaster were not yet
          apparent,
the battle against it was fought by our doctors. But all
          their skills
were of no avail; the people died and they couldn't
          prevent it.
In the beginning the sky weighed down on the earth in
          a thick, black
fog which trapped the prostrating heat in a blanket of
          clouds;
and throughout the time that it took four moons to
530   wax and to wane,
the south winds blew with their sweltering currents of
          toxic air.
All are agreed that the springs and the lakes were also
          infected,

when thousands and thousands of slithering serpents
    infested the untilled
fields and polluted the rivers and streams with additional
    poison.   535
The dogs and the birds, the flocks and the herds, the beasts
    of the wild
were the first to reveal the destructive power of the sudden
    disease.
In blank amazement the wretched farmers looked on, as
    their sturdy
oxen collapsed at their ploughs and sank in the midst of the
    furrows.
The woolly sheep were bleating away in sickly tones,   540
when their fleeces fell off unshorn and their bodies wasted
    away.
Horses once highly mettled, renowned for their speed on
    the racecourse,
now brought shame on their former triumphs; old prizes
    forgotten,
they groaned in their stables, waiting to die in feeble inertia.
The boar forgot he could ever be angry; the hind could no
    longer   545
trust to her heels, and the bear was powerless to raid the
    cattle.
Lethargy overtook all. The putrid carcasses lay
in the forest, the fields and the roads, and the air grew foul
    with the stench;
but strange to tell, the dogs, the vultures and grizzly wolves
wouldn't touch those infected bodies, which decomposed
    into liquid,   550
noxiously reeking and spreading contagion throughout the
    country.
   'The plague grew stronger and next attacked the peasants
    and farmers;
it then proceeded to lord it inside the walls of the city.
First a burning sensation inside the intestines, then flushes
and short-drawn breathing were early symptoms of latent
    disorder.   555

The tongue became rough and swollen, the lips were
        parted and dry
from the winds, as the pestilent air was gulped in the
        gaping mouth.
No one could bear to be covered with even the lightest of
        blankets;
people would lie in the nude prostrate on the earth, and
        the soil
never cooled them down but was warmed instead by the
560   heat from their bodies.
The virulent sickness was out of control, and even the
        doctors
succumbed; their skills, indeed, proved fatal to those
        who possessed them.
The nearer a relative came to a patient, the more
        devoted
his care, the sooner he died himself. When hope of
        recovery
faded and death was perceived as the only end to their
565   illness,
the sick would indulge their desires regardless of what
        might be best for them;
nothing, they knew, could do any good. All shame
        forsaken,
they crowded the springs and the streams and clung to
        the sides of the wells;
but before they could slake their thirst, their lives were
        quenched by their drinking.
Some were too bloated to rise to their feet and were
570   drowned in the stream
that their tongues were lapping, though others still
        greedily went on drinking.
Many poor sufferers couldn't endure their beds any
        longer
and leapt to the floor or, if they hadn't the strength to
        stand,
they'd roll out of doors on the ground; and thus each
        person would flee

from the hearth and home which seemed to them now to be
   haunted by death;   575
not knowing the cause, they could only blame the house
   they had lived in.
Some could be seen to be roaming the streets in a dazed
   condition,
so long as their strength held up; if not, they'd be lying in
   tears
flat out on the ground, quite still but for rolling their
   sleepless eyes;
then, weakly extending their arms to the stars in the
   lowering heavens,   580
here or there, wherever death took them, they gave up the
   ghost.
   'How do you think I felt? What *ought* to have been my
   feelings
but loathing for life and a longing to join my people in death?
Whichever direction I turned my gaze, my eyes were
   confronted
by corpses, scattered like rotten apples fallen from shaken   585
branches, or else like acorns under a wind-tossed oak tree.
Look at that temple over there with its towering columns
and lines of steps. That's Jupiter's temple. But who did not
   offer
incense upon those altars in vain? How often the
   worshippers
saying their prayers, whether husbands for wives or fathers
   for children,   590
ended their lives in front of the shrine with their prayers
   unanswered
and some of the incense still unused, found clutched in their
   hands!
How often a bull was brought to the temple and, while the
   priest
was solemnly praying and pouring the wine libation
   between
its horns, it slumped to the ground, unfelled by the axe it
   awaited!   595

When I was sacrificing to Jove for myself, my country
and three sons, all of a sudden the victim moaned with a
        fearful
bellow and then collapsed of its own accord; when its
        throat
was cut, the knife was merely stained with a feeble
        trickle.
Entrails too were diseased and had lost the signs of the
600   truth
or divine admonition; the frightful plague had infected
        the vitals.
I saw that corpses were strewn at the foot of the temple
        portals;
people had hanged themselves outside in front of the
        altars,
to make their death more offensive. They'd banished
        the fear of death
by inflicting death and inviting the fate which they
605   knew was in store.
Dead bodies no longer received the customary funeral
        rites;
there wasn't room at the gates to take so many
        processions.
Corpses were either exposed on the ground unburied
        or heaped
on pyres without any honours; respect for the dead
        was forgotten.
The living fought over the pyres, and bodies were
610   burning in flames
intended for others. With no one left to weep for their
        loved ones,
the souls of the old and the young, the spirits of
        husbands and children,
restlessly wandered in limbo, unsped by the rituals of
        mourning.
No space was left for a tomb, no wood to allow a
        cremation.'

THE BIRTH OF THE MYRMIDONS

Aeacus next explained how sorrow had yielded to gladness:
'Overwhelmed by this powerful whirlwind of pain, I
      protested:
"Jupiter, hear me! Lord! If the story isn't a lie,   615
that you lay long ago in the arms of Asópus' daughter,
      Aegina,
if you, great father, are not ashamed to acknowledge your
      son,
then either restore me my people or send me too to my
      grave!"
The god gave a sign with a lightning flash and a peal of
      thunder.
"I welcome your omen!" I duly exclaimed, "and pray it
      betokens   620
your kind goodwill. I take your response as a pledge of
      your favour."
Nearby there happened to stand a magnificent spreading
      oak tree,
sacred to Jove and sprung from the seed of an oak in
      Dodóna.
Here we saw a long column of ants which were gathering
      grain,
all bearing their heavy loads in their tiny mouths and
      steadily   625
trudging along their familiar path on the wrinkled tree
      bark.
"How many there are!" I reflected in wonder and cried,
      "O Father,
of gods the most excellent, grant me as many subjects as
      these
to replenish my empty walls!" Then a noisy trembling came
      over
the oak, though there wasn't a breath of wind to disturb the
      branches.   630

My own limbs shuddered in quaking terror, my hair
    stood on end;
yet I kissed the earth and the tree, not confessing my
    hopes to myself,
though I dearly hoped and cherished my wish deep down
    in my heart.
Night followed, when bodies worn out with care are
    taken over
by sleep, and I dreamed a dream: before me was standing
635   the same oak,
with all of its many branches and all those thousands
    of creatures
crawling along them. I heard the noisy trembling
    again,
as the column of grain collectors was shaken down to
    the earth.
The ants then suddenly grew, appearing larger and
    larger,
until they rose from the ground and stood with bodies
640   erect.
Their thinness was gone, they had only two feet, and
    their colour no longer
was black; their limbs were completely changed into
    human form.
Then I woke from my sleep; now conscious again, I
    cursed my dream
and complained that the gods were no help. But a
    deafening hubbub was echoing
round the house, and I thought I could hear the
645   unfamiliar
sound of a human crowd. "This must be part of my
    dream,"
I supposed; when Telamon opened the doors of my
    chamber and burst in,
crying, "Father, come out, for a sight you would never
    have hoped for,
never believed!" I followed him out, and there were the
    men

who'd appeared to me in my dream, exactly the same as I'd
    seen them   650
down to their order of march, approaching to hail me as
    king.
So offering thanks to Jove for my new-found subjects, I
    gave them
homes in the city and fields to be ploughed where their
    previous owners
had left them vacant; I called them Mýrmidons after the
    ants*
they had come from. You've seen the bodies they now
    inhabit;   655
they also preserve their original nature – a thrifty,
    industrious
people, who cling to their gains and store them away for the
    future.
All of them young and brave, they'll follow you into the
    field,
as soon as the wind from the east which happily brought
    you here' –
he was right, it *was* the east wind* – 'is replaced by one
    from the south.'   660

CEPHALUS AND PROCRIS

Aeacus filled the length of the day in talking of these
and other affairs with the envoy from Athens. The evening
    was given
to feasting, the night to sleep. The following morning at
    sunrise
the wind was again in the east and staying the ships from
    their homeward
voyage. So Clytus and Butes collected their older
    companion,   665
Cephalus; then the three of them made their way to the
    palace
to find the king. But the king was in bed and not yet awake.

They were met at the entrance by Phocus, one of the
          royal princes;
his brothers, Peleus and Telamon, were choosing men for
          the army.
670   Phocus led the Athenian guests to the inner courtyard,
thence to a beautiful room, where they all sat down
          together.
While they were talking, he noticed Cephalus holding a
          spear
with a golden point and made of an unfamiliar wood;
so he interrupted the conversation to question the
          hero.
'I love the forests,' he told him, 'and have a passion for
675   hunting.
I keep on wondering where the shaft of the spear you
          are carrying
started its life. What wood was it cut from? It cannot
          be ash,
as it isn't a pale gold colour; and if it were cornel, it
          surely
would have to be knotted. I've no idea where your
          javelin came from,
but have to confess that I've never set eyes on a lovelier
680   weapon.'
Clytus or Butes answered, 'You may be surprised by its
          beauty;
but when you have learned how it's used, your surprise
          will be even greater.
This spear never misses its target, its flight isn't subject
          to luck,
and it comes back, covered with blood, with no one
          there to return it.'
This made young Phocus extremely eager to know the
685   full story:
why the spear had been given to Cephalus, where it
          had come from,
and who had presented this wonderful gift. Then
          Cephalus answered

the questions he put, though shame forbade him to mention
    the price
he had paid.* In tears of grief for the wife he had lost, he
    began:
'Prince Phocus, son of a goddess;* it's hard to believe, but
    this javelin   690
is causing these tears of mine and long will continue to
    cause them,
if heaven decrees that I live much longer. This weapon
    destroyed
my wife and destroyed me too. How I wish I had never
    possessed it!
   'You've probably heard of Orithýia, whom Bóreas loved
and abducted. Procris, my wife, was Orithyia's sister.   695
If you wished to compare the two for their beauty and
    disposition,
she was the one to abduct! Our love, no less than her father
Eréchtheus brought us together. They called me happy, and
    rightly.
But heaven was jealous, or else I might be as happy today.
A month had passed since our wedding-day, and I was
    spreading   700
my nets for the antlered deer, when over the top of
    Hyméttus,
the mountain always in flower, Auróra, the goddess of
    dawn,
caught sight of me there in the saffron light of the morning
    and forced me
away to the sky. Let me tell you the simple truth, without
offence to the goddess. For all the charm of her blushing
    face,   705
although she controls the frontiers of night and day,
    although
she quaffs her juices of nectar, Procris remained my adored
    one,
Procris was there in my heart and the name of Procris was
    always
upon my lips. I constantly spoke of our wedding rites,

of the joys of love when a man and his bride are first
          united,
our marriage so new and fresh, and now already
710   forsaken.
The goddess got angry and cried, "Stop moaning,
          ungrateful man!
You can keep your Procris. But I can foresee the future:
          you'll wish
you had never possessed her!" With that she
          indignantly sent me packing.
Journeying home, I pondered over Aurora's words
and started to doubt: had my wife been faithful during
715   my absence?
Her youth and her beauty suggested she might quite
          well have betrayed me;
her character told me she must be true. But
          nevertheless,
I had been away for some time, Aurora herself was
          scarcely
a model of chaste behaviour, and anything frightens a
          lover.
I therefore decided to look for a grievance and use
720   inducements
to shake my Procris' loyalty and virtue. Aurora
          encouraged
my doubts and altered my features – I seemed to feel I
          was changing.
   'And so I returned to the city of Athens without
          being recognized.
Passing into my house, I found not a trace of scandal
or misbehaviour, only concern for the kidnapped
725   master.
A thousand ruses could scarcely gain me access to
          Procris;
and seeing her stunned me again – I almost abandoned
          my plan
to test her fidelity, barely restraining myself from
          confessing

BOOK 7   285

the truth or kissing her on the lips as would have been
    proper.
Sadness sat on her brow, though sadness became no
    woman   730
better than her. She was pining in grief for the loss of her
    stolen
husband. Oh Phocus, imagine what glorious beauty she
    had,
when beauty shone out of her even in grief! I need not tell
    you
how often her modest nature repulsed my attempts to
    seduce her,
how often she said, "I am saving myself for one alone;   735
wherever he is, my joys are reserved entirely for him."
What sane man wouldn't have felt that he'd tested his wife's
    fidelity
far enough? But I couldn't be satisfied, only determined
to wound myself. In return for a night, I promised a
    fortune;
and then by more and more gifts I at last broke down her
    resistance.   740
In wicked triumph I cried, "It is I, disguised as a lover,
but truly your husband! I've caught you myself, you
    treacherous harlot!"
She said not a word. Just overcome by her unvoiced shame,
she fled from her evil husband and left that house of
    entrapment.
  'Resentment against me made her detest all men, and
    she wandered   745
over the mountains, engaged in the chaste pursuits of
    Diana.
I was alone and the flames of my love burned even more
    fiercely
inside my heart. I implored her forgiveness, confessed I had
    wronged her,
and said that I too could well have succumbed to a like
    temptation,
if I had ever been offered such hugely extravagant gifts.   750

When I'd made this confession, she felt she had punished
    the slight to her honour;
I won her back, and we passed the years in peace and
    delight.
As though the gift of herself were too little, she made me
    a further
present, a dog she'd received from her patron goddess
    Diana,
who'd spoken these words, "No dog will ever run faster
755   than this one."
My dear wife also gave me the javelin you see in my
    hands.
Would you like me to tell you about the fate of my
    earlier present?
Listen; the story's a strange one, you'll find it very
    surprising.

'Oédipus, son of Láïus, had solved the riddle* which
    baffled
the brains of others before him. The Sphinx was
760   defeated and lying
toppled beneath the cliff, her own dark secrets
    forgotten.
At once a second monster, a giant vixen, was sent
to ravage Boeótian Thebes; and many countryfolk
    feared
for their lives and the lives of their flocks and herds.
765   The men in the district
joined me in forming a cordon extending all round the
    plain,
but the great fox swiftly surmounted our nets with the
    lightest of leaps,
bounding over the line at the top of the trap we had
    laid.
Our hounds were at once unleashed; but the vixen
    evaded pursuit
and cheated the pack by running as fast as a bird can
770   fly.

Then all the hunters loudly appealed to me for my
      Whirlwind
(that was the name of my dog); he had long been struggling
      like fury
to slip his own leash and straining against his constricting
      collar.
The hound was released, and at once we had no idea where
      he was;
his footprints showed in the baking sand, but Whirlwind
      himself   775
had vanished, gone with the speed of a spear or of bullets
      hurled
from a whirling sling or an arrow shot from a Cretan bow.
I climbed to the peak of a hill overlooking the country all
      round,
and so obtained an excellent view of a new kind of chase,   780
in which the vixen one moment appeared to be caught, but
      the next
to escape from the hound's very jaws. The crafty creature
      refused
to run in a line straight ahead, but eluded the fangs at her
      tail
by circling around and denying her foe the use of his
      spring.
But the dog kept close on his quarry's heels; and yes, he
      had got her!   785
But no, he had not; he was only snapping at empty air.
I turned to my javelin for help, and while I was poising it
      over
my shoulder and trying to slip my fingers inside the thong,
I looked away for a moment and then looked back to the
      same place.
There, in the midst of the plain, I saw with surprise two
      figures   790
in marble; you'd guess that one was in flight, while the
      other was barking.
I suppose, if a god was there with the runners, he must have
      decided

that neither should win that astonishing race and neither
be beaten.'

Here Cephalus paused and was silent. Then Phocus said,
'Now for your javelin,
what was the crime it committed?' and Cephalus told
795   him the story:
'In my case, Phocus, joy was the first beginning of
sorrow.
I'll tell you at once of my joy. Oh Phocus, I love to
remember
that blessed time, those early years of our married life,
when I was so happy with Procris and she was happy
with me!
We were truly together; we loved and looked after each
800   other so fondly.
In her eyes Jove could never have made such a
wonderful lover,
and I could not have been drawn to a woman other
than Procris,
not Venus herself. Our hearts were on fire with the
passion we shared.
When the sun god's earliest rays were striking the
mountain peaks,
I'd venture outdoors to hunt in the woods, as a young
805   man will.
No attendants, horses or keen-nosed hounds would be
keeping me company;
I never bothered with knotted nets, but relied on my
spear.
When my arm was weary with slaughtering beasts, I'd
return to the cool shade,
wooing the breeze which rose from the chillier valleys
810   below.
The gentle breeze in the noonday heat was all that I
wanted,
all I was waiting for, all that I needed to ease my
tiredness.

"Come to me, beautiful breeze, steal into my breast, you're
    so lovely. This heat
is burning me up. Relieve me I beg you, as only you
    can!"   815
My fate was leading me on, and I might perhaps have
    continued
with further endearments. Perhaps I would say, "You give
    me such pleasure!
oh breeze, your refreshing caresses! It's for you that I
    worship the forest
and lonely places. Yours is the breath that I'm always
    longing
to catch in my lips." Some eavesdropper heard these
    equivocal words   820
and misunderstood what they meant. The breeze that I
    called to so often
he thought was the name of a nymph with whom I must be
    in love.
At once, without thinking, he went to my wife to report this
    imagined
affair and repeat in a whisper the words he had overheard.   825
Love is a credulous thing. As I learned later on, poor
    Procris
collapsed and fell to the ground in shock. When at last she
    revived,
she declared how wretched she was, how cruelly fate had
    treated her,
I had been so unfaithful. The charge against me was
    groundless,
her fears were inspired by nothing, only the ghost of a
    name;   830
but she suffered, poor woman, as though I were keeping a
    genuine mistress.
Yet often she felt uncertain and desperately hoped she'd be
    proved
mistaken. It couldn't be true, she said; unless she caught me
red-handed, she never would find her husband guilty of
    falsehood.

'The following morning, when saffron Aurora had
835   banished the night,
I left for the forest as usual and, after a fruitful hunt,
stretched out on the grass. "Now come to me, breeze,"
          I chanted,
"Soothe me and cure my weariness!" Suddenly, while I
          was speaking,
I thought that I heard a moan. "Come, beautiful
          breeze!" I continued.
Another disturbance, this time the rustle of fallen
840   leaves.
A beast on the prowl, I decided, and sent my javelin
          flying.
Procris was there under cover and, clutching her
          wounded breast,
cried out in her pain. When I recognized the voice of
          my faithful
wife, my own wife, I rushed like a madman towards
          the sound.
I found her dying, her clothes all stained and spattered
845   with blood;
she was trying to draw from her wound, alas, her own
          dear present
to me. I tenderly lifted her body towards me, the body
dearer to me than my own; then tearing her dress from
          her bosom,
I bound her wound and attempted to staunch the flow
          of her blood,
while I begged her not to desert me, defiled by the guilt
850   of her death.
Though her strength was failing, she forced herself to
          murmur this much
with her dying breath: "I implore you now, by the
          vows of our marriage,
by all the gods of the sky and the gods where soon I
          shall be,
by any kindness I've shown you and by our love which
          continues

even now when I'm dying, although it has caused my
    death,   855
please never allow your Breeze to take my place as your
    wife."
As she spoke, I at last understood that a name had caused
    this confusion,
and told her the truth. But what was the use of her learning
    the truth?
She sank in my arms and her last faint strength ebbed out
    with her blood;
and while she was able to see, her eyes were on mine, and
    mine   860
were the lips which caught her breath as the poor soul
    breathed her last.
But the look on her face was enough to show me she'd died
    in peace.'

The hero ended. His audience, like him, was in tears. Then
    Aeacus
came on the scene with a pair of his sons* and a party of
    fresh-raised
soldiers. Cephalus quickly took charge of the armed
    contingent.   865

BOOK 8

Structurally, this book contains a long epic centre-piece, *Meleäger and the Calydonian Boar*, framed on either side by what may be seen as two pairs of complementary stories. More important, however, is the variety of tone and originality of treatment which is to be found in the ingeniously knitted narrative. In two of the episodes, dramatic rhetoric is a crucial element.

Scylla and Minos (1–151) shows a daughter betraying her father for love and suffering rejection from the object of her passion. The heart of this section is Scylla's formal speeches, expressing first her personal conflict and later her fury in rejection. Ovid cleverly leaves us asking how far his heroine deserves the short shrift she receives from Minos. The much shorter and slighter companion piece, *The Minotaur and Ariadne* (152–82), also involves a daughter in a parallel situation; but the interest here lies in the labyrinth created by Daedalus, who provides the link with the next pair of stories.

More tenderness and compelling detail may be found in *Daedalus and Icarus* (183–235). There is a tragic poignancy in the boy Icarus' fall after refusing to fly as his father has told him to – we must be reminded of Phaëthon in Book 2. The complementary *Daedalus and Perdix* (236–59) is once again much slighter, but here there is a situational contrast: Daedalus tries to make Perdix fall, while metamorphosis allows his pupil to fly.

The story of *Meleäger and the Calydonian Boar* (260–546) was a very old favourite; it went back as far as Homer and was the subject of (lost) plays by Sophocles and Euripides. The first section, which concerns the boar-hunt itself (260–444), starts out in the grand epic manner with a brilliant description of the boar and the usual catalogue of participant heroes. But then Ovid's subversive originality takes over: famous figures, such as Theseus, Jason and the young Nestor, acquit themselves with conspicuous lack of distinction; and Meleäger's own success in killing the boar is immediately marred by his killing both of his uncles. The following section (445–525) is in contrasting tragic mode and we may be inclined to take it more seriously. Althaea's dramatic soliloquy, as the queen agonizes between her loyalty to her dead brothers and her living son, is in typical Euripidean vein, and we may empathize better with her than we did with Scylla. Even so, the climax of Meleäger's painful death and his mother's suicide is undermined in the final section (526–46) by the comic exaggeration of his sisters' grief, leading on to their metamorphosis to guinea-fowl.

Acheloüs, the Naiads and Perimele (547–610) is a relaxing interlude. An attractive scene in the river-god's grotto is followed by his account of the metamorphosis of five naiads, who had slighted him, into a group of islands. This contrasts with the transformation of Perimele, the nymph he had loved and rescued from drowning, into a separate island on her own.

The final pair of stories offers a contrast on a much larger scale. In both tales Ovid is almost certainly indebted to the Greek poet Callimachus (third century BC), the arch-exponent of the mini-epic. *Philemon and Baucis* (611–724) centres on the piety and reward of two needy old people who unwittingly offer hospitality to two gods in their humble home. The homely detail makes this, perhaps, the most charming piece in the whole poem, and the final metamorphosis is genuinely touching. The complementary story of *Erysichthon* (725–884), which portrays impiety and its awful punishment, is a great deal less pleasant. The detail is much more sinister and exaggerated, with the description of Hunger (personified like Envy in 2.760–832) as a superlative high-spot. The nastiness of Erysichthon's growing obsession with food is only mitigated towards the end, when the focus shifts more humorously to his daughter Mestra eluding pursuit from her slave-master on the seashore through repeated metamorphosis.

SCYLLA AND MINOS

The morning star was dispersing the night and drawing
    the curtain
for shining day, when the east wind fell and the clouds of
    moisture
lifted. A southerly breeze provided a smooth home
    passage
for Céphalus with the troops from Aegína, and after an
    easy
voyage they entered harbour sooner than they had
5   expected.
Meanwhile King Minos was laying waste to the coast of
    Mégara
and trying out his military strength on the city where
    Nisus
reigned, Alcáthoë. Nisus' dignified head with its
    snow-white
hair was marked on the crown by a magic lock of
    resplendent
crimson, and on this lock the power of his kingdom
10   depended.
   Five moons had waned and a sixth was newly
    displaying her horns.
The fortunes of war still hung in the scales, as the bird
    of victory
soared and wavered between the kings but never
    descended.
A tower rose up on the echoing walls of the royal
    palace,
the walls where Apollo, Latóna's son, is said to have
15   rested
his golden lyre, whose music lingered on in the
    masonry.
Scylla, the daughter of Nisus, would frequently make
    her way up,

to play on the musical wall by throwing the smallest of
      pebbles –
that was in peacetime. When war broke out, she would still
      quite often
ascend the tower to watch the battling hosts in contention.   20
As war dragged on, she had come to know the names of the
      chieftains,
their Cretan arms, their horses, their dress and magnificent
      quivers.
She had specially come to know the face of the leader,
      Európa's
offspring – more indeed than was proper. When Minos
      covered
his head in a casque bedecked with a crest of plumage, she
      thought,   25
'How handsome that helmeted warrior looks!' And now he
      was wielding
his gleaming bronze-plated shield. How well it became him
      to wield it!
Tensing his muscles, he launched his spear in a graceful
      curve;
such strength and such skill together excited the young girl's
      praise.
He had levelled his arrow and now was bending his pliant
      bow;   30
she swore that it might be Apollo there, standing to shoot
      his arrows.
At last he had lifted his visor to bare his face; in his glorious
purple cloak, he was mounted astride his milk-white,
      brightly
caparisoned steed and curbing his charger's foaming mouth.
Beside herself with excitement, the daughter of Nisus was
      almost   35
out of her mind. 'How happy the spear which *he* is
      grasping!'
she said to herself. 'How happy the reins that his hands are
      gripping!'

Girl though she was, she felt a strong impulse to find her
    way
through the enemy lines, if only she might; she was filled
    with the urge
to leap from the top of the tower right down to the Cretan
40   encampment,
or open the great bronze gates of the city to welcome
    the foe
or to do what else King Minos might wish. And while
    she sat there,
raptly watching the sunlit tents of the lord of Cnossos,
'This heart-breaking war!' she said. 'Should it fill me
    with grief or with joy?
45 I cannot be sure. I adore King Minos and he is my foe;
for that I must grieve. But without the war I should
    never have known him.
Perhaps we could put an end to the war, if he took me
    hostage,
as I should be there beside him; my presence could
    vouch for the peace.
Peerlessly beautiful prince, if your mother Europa was
    half
as lovely as you are, Jupiter's passion was richly
50   deserved!
Oh for the wings of a bird which could waft me down
    through the air
and ground me in Minos' camp! How utterly blessed I
    should be!
I should make myself known and confess my love and
    ask him what dowry
would buy him for me – so long as it wasn't my father's
    fortress.
Indeed I would rather forswear the bed of my dreams
55   than achieve
my desire by treason. Yet often a lenient conqueror's
    mercy
has turned a defeat from shameful loss to glorious gain.

The war he is fighting, at least, is just – to avenge the son
who was murdered.* His cause is strong and so are the
    arms that support it.
Defeat awaits us, no doubt. If the city is destined to fall, 60
then why should it be for his gallant warriors and not
    my love
to open the gates of my own walls up to him? Better the
    victory
won without carnage, tedious delay and expense of his
    own blood.
At least I should have no need to fear some soldier in
    ignorance
piercing your manly breast, dear Minos. (Who could
    be so   65
hard-hearted, to aim his merciless javelin against you
    on purpose?)
   'Excellent plan! I am fully resolved to surrender
    myself
with my country as dowry and bring the war to a
    speedy conclusion.
If wishes were horses, though, beggars would ride.*
    There are sentries on guard
and the keys of the gates are held by my father. He is
    my only   70
reason, alas, for fear, the only bar to my hopes.
I would to God that I had no father! Yet God helps
    those
who help themselves, remember, and fortune favours
    the brave.
Another woman whose passion was blazing as strongly
    as mine
would now be already destroying whatever opposed her
    love –   75
and delight in destroying it. Why should another be
    braver than I?
I'd venture to go through fire and sword. Yet fire and
    sword

are not what I need. What I need is my father's magical
      lock.
That crimson lock is far more precious than much fine
      gold.
With the lock I am happy and mistress of all the joy that I
80   pray for!'
   While Scylla was speaking, Nature's most potent
      feeder of heartache,
night, came on, and our heroine's boldness increased
      with the darkness.
During that first quiet time when hearts that are weary
      with cares
of the day are enshrouded in sleep, she silently entered
      Nisus'
bedroom and cut the fateful lock from his head – that a
85   daughter
should do such a thing to her father! Clutching her
      impious prize,
she made her way through the midst of the foe,
      self-righteously confident,
into the royal presence and spoke to the horrified
      Minos:
'Driven to crime by love, I, Princess Scylla, the
90   daughter
of Nisus, surrender to you the gods of my country and
      household.
I ask no reward but yourself. As the pledge of my
      passion, receive
this crimson lock. This is no mere ringlet of hair,
      believe me.
My father's life is now in your power!' With hand
      outstretched
she tendered her damnable gift. King Minos recoiled
95   from her offer
and, deeply troubled to witness an act so unparalleled,
      answered,
'You blot on our age! I pray that the gods will banish
      you far

from their own bright sphere and that space is denied you on
      land and ocean.
Certainly *I* shall never allow my own sphere, Crete,
the cradle of Jove, to be made unclean by so evil a
      monster!'   100
   He spoke, and after he'd settled affairs with his captured
      foes
as a just lawgiver, he ordered his crews to untie the hawsers
loose from their moorings and row their bronze-prowed
      warships to sea.
When Scylla saw that the keels were launched and afloat on
      the water
and Minos had given her no reward for her wicked
      surrender,   105
now that her prayers were exhausted, she shifted to violent
      anger.
With streaming hair and her arms outstretched, she shouted
      in fury:
'Where are you fleeing, you traitor, who owe your successes
      to *me*?
I put you before my country, I put you before my father.
Where are you fleeing, pitiless man, whose victory is due   110
to my kindness no less than my crime? Can you not be
      moved by the present
I brought you, moved by my love or moved by the hopes
      that I built
so wholly on you? You've abandoned me, Minos! Where
      can I turn?
To my native land? But it lies defeated. Suppose it were
      standing:
my own betrayal has barred it to me. Turn to my father,   115
the man I presented to you? My countrymen rightly
      detest me,
the neighbouring peoples fear my example. I banished
      myself
from the rest of the world, that Crete alone should be open
      to me.
If you exclude me also from Crete and abandon me here,

120 you ungrateful man, it was not Europa who gave you life
but an African quicksand, Armenian tigress or swirling
         Charýbdis.*
Jupiter wasn't your father. He didn't seduce your
         mother
disguised as a bull. That story's a lie. A genuine bull
was your true begetter. Take your revenge now, Nisus,
125   my father!
Rejoice in my misery, walls of my city that I have so
         lately
betrayed! I confess that I brought it upon myself and
         deserve
to die; but still I could wish my destruction to come
         from someone
I hurt by my treachery. Why should *you* punish me,
         Minos, seeing
you triumphed because of my guilt? Let my crime
130   against father and country
be thought of as service to you! She truly deserved to
         have you
as mate, your adulterous queen* who cheated the
         fierce-eyed bull
with a cow of wood and the fruit of her womb was a
         hybrid monster.
Do you hear what I'm saying? Or are the winds that
         follow your navy
sweeping away my words, you ungrateful creature, to
135   nothing?
Now no wonder at all that Pasíphaë worshipped her
         bull-mate
more than she worshipped you, as you were the
         beastlier creature.
Heavens! He's telling his men to row faster. I hear the
         splash
of their dipping oars. The shore and I are receding
         together.
Your haste is in vain! You shan't be allowed to forget
140   what you owe me.

Like it or not, I'll follow you, holding tight to your curving
stern, to be dragged through the length of the sea!' She had
         hardly spoken,
when into the waves she leapt and, strong in the strength of
         her passion,
she clung, an unwelcome appendage, behind the Cnossian
         warship.
There she was spotted by Nisus (her father had lately been
         changed   145
to a falcon with tawny wings and was hovering now in the
         air).
He swooped as she clung to the vessel, to tear at his child
         with his hooked beak.
Scylla in terror let go of the stern and, as she was falling,
a light breeze seemed to sustain her and save her from
         touching the water.
Feathers grew over her arms. Transformed to the shape of
         a bird,   150
she is known as Ciris the Shearer,* and takes this name
         from the shorn lock.

THE MINOTAUR AND ARIADNE

When Minos had disembarked and stood once again on
         Cretan
soil, he offered the sacrifice, promised to Jove, of a hundred
bulls and adorned the walls of his palace with trophies of
         victory.
The family's guilty secret had grown; Pasiphaë's bestial   155
adultery* now was exposed in her monstrous offspring, the
         Minotaur.
Minos determined to hide this disgrace to his marriage-bed
inside the twistings and turns of a dark, inextricable maze.
The labyrinth then was built by an eminent
         master-craftsman,
Daédalus, who had obscured all guiding marks and
         designed it   160

to cheat the eye with bewildering patterns of tortuous
        alleys.
Just as the Phrygian river Maeánder sports and plays
in his running stream with the ebb and flow of his teasing
        course –
as he bends right back on himself, he can see his water
        advancing,
and keeps his wavering currents in motion, back to their
165   headspring
or out to the open sea – so Daedalus' warren of
        passages
wandered this way and that. In such a treacherous
        maze
its very designer could scarcely retrace his steps to the
        entrance.
    Here Minos confined his monster son, half man, half
        bull,
and fed him twice on the blood of Athenian youths and
170   maidens,
chosen by lot as tribute exacted* at nine-year intervals.
But the third repast destroyed the Minotaur. One of
        the youths,
Prince Théseus,* was aided by fair Ariádne, the
        daughter of Minos.
Rewinding the thread that she gave him, he found the
        elusive entrance
which none had regained before him. He carried the
        princess off
and sailed to Naxos, but there on the shore he cruelly
175   abandoned
his loving companion. She wept and wailed in her
        lonely plight,
till Bacchus swept her up in his arms and came to her
        rescue.
'My star,' he declared, 'you must shine for ever!'
        Removing the crown
from her forehead, he launched it skyward. It whirled
        and spun through the air,

and during its flight the gems were changed into brilliant
    fires,   180
coming to rest once more in the shape of a jewelled circlet*
between the Kneeler and bright Ophiúcus, who holds the
    Snake.*

DAEDALUS AND ICARUS

Daedalus now had come to detest his protracted exile*
in Crete and was longing to visit his native country again,
but his way was barred by the sea. 'King Minos can block
    my escape,   185
by land or water,' he sighed. 'The air, at least, is still open;
my path lies there. He is lord of the world, but not lord of
    the sky.'
So saying, he put his mind to techniques unexplored before
and altered the laws of nature. He carefully layered some
    feathers,
the smallest to start with, the shorter positioned next to the
    longer –   190
you'd think they had *grown* like that – as sometimes rustic
    panpipes
rise in a gradual slope with their reeds of unequal length;
and then he bound them with twine in the middle and wax
    at the bottom.
This neatly compacted plumage he curved in a gentle
    camber
to imitate real birds' wings. His young son Icarus, standing   195
beside him and little aware of the threat to himself he was
    touching,
smiled as he caught at the feathers fluttering in the breeze;
and now and again he would carelessly soften the yellow
    wax
with his thumb, enjoying his game as he meddled and
    interfered
with his father's wonderful work. But soon the finishing
    touches   200

were deftly laid, and Daedalus balanced his aged body

on both of his wings, then beat at the air and hovered
        suspended.

Next he instructed his son: 'Now, Icarus, listen carefully!

Keep to the middle way. If you fly too low, the water

will clog your wings; if you fly too high, they'll be

205   scorched by fire.

Fly between sea and sun. No need to determine your
        course

by Boötes, the Bear, or Orion's naked sword, like a
        sailor.

Simply follow my lead.' As he gave his pupil his flying

orders, he fitted the wings on the boy's inexperienced
        shoulders;

and while he did it the old man's cheeks were wet with

210   his tears

and his hands were trembling in fatherly fear. Then
        kissing the lips

of his darling son for the very last time, he rose on his
        wings

and flew in front, as afraid for the lad as a bird
        escorting

her fledgeling out of her mountain nest to float on the
        breezes.

'Follow!' he cried, as he taught him the skills that

215   would prove his downfall.

Moving his own two wings, he kept looking back at
        his son's.

They were spied by a fisherman dangling his catch on
        his quivering rod,

a shepherd at rest on his crook and a ploughman*
        steering his ploughshare.

All watched in amazement, thinking, 'They certainly
        must be gods

to fly through the air!' Now Juno's island, Samos, was

220   coming

up on the left (Delos and Paros were far behind them);

Lebínthos lay to the right with the honey-rich island,
        Calýmne –
when all this adventurous flying went to Icarus' head.
He ceased to follow his leader; he'd fallen in love with
        the sky,
and soared up higher and higher. The scorching rays of
        the sun   225
grew closer and softened the fragrant wax which fastened
        his plumage.
The wax dissolved; and as Icarus flapped his naked arms,
deprived of the wings which had caught the air that was
        buoying them upwards,
'Father!' he shouted, again and again. But the boy and his
        shouting
were drowned in the blue-green main which is called the
        Icárian Sea.   230
His unhappy father, no longer a father, called out, 'Icarus!
Where are you, Icarus? Where on earth shall I find you?
        Icarus!'
he kept crying. And then he caught sight of the wings in the
        water.
Daedalus cursed the skill of his hands and buried his dear
        son's
corpse in a grave. The land where he lies is known as
        Icária.   235

DAEDALUS AND PERDIX

As Daedalus laid his poor son's body to rest in an earth-
        mound,
out of a muddy field-drain peeped a chattering partridge,
who loudly clapped with its wings and uttered a cry of
        triumph.
New at the time to the feathered kingdom, unseen before,
it had lately been changed to a bird and was Daedalus'
        standing reproach.   240

The craftsman's sister, unhappily blind to the future, had
        trusted
her precious son to him as a pupil. The child was a boy
of high intelligence, twelve years old, and responsive to
        teaching.
He'd even observed the pattern of bones on the spine of a
        fish
245 and taken that as a model, cutting a series of teeth
in a strip of metal and so devising the common
        handsaw.
He had also invented the compasses, joining two pieces
        of iron
on a single hinge; if the legs remained at a constant
        distance,
one point could be fixed, while the other described a
        perfect circle.
Daedalus, though, was jealous, and threw him
250   headlong down
from the sacred hill of Minerva,* pretending he'd
        slipped; but Pallas,
the goddess who fosters artistic talent, caught him and
        turned him,
still in mid-air, to a bird and covered his body in
        feathers.
Nevertheless, the strength of his quick intelligence
        filtered
into his wings and his feet, and he stayed with his old
255   name – Perdix.
The bird, however, can't lift its body far from the earth
or build its nest in the branches of trees or on
        mountainous crags.
It flutters close to the ground and lays its eggs in the
        hedgerows,
never forgetting that fall long ago and frightened of
        heights.

MELEÄGER AND THE
CALYDONIAN BOAR

Daedalus now was exhausted and found a home in Sicily;   260
Cócalus welcomed the suppliant kindly and armed to
     defend him.
Back to the story of Theseus. Thanks to the glorious hero,
Athens had ceased to pay King Minos her dismal tribute.
Her temples were wreathed with flowers; and the citizens
     called on Minerva,
goddess of war, on Jove and the other gods, whom they
     duly   265
worshipped with animal sacrifice, gifts and caskets of
     incense.
Wandering rumour had published the name of Theseus
     throughout
the cities of Argos, and his was the help that the peoples of
     wealthy
Greece entreated whenever they fell into serious danger.
His was the help that Cálydon humbly and anxiously
     begged for,   270
although she had Meleäger. The reason for her request
was the boar that served and championed the wrath of
     Diana.
King Oéneus,* the story goes, gave thanks for a year of
     plenty
by yielding the grain's first-fruits to Ceres, and pouring
     libations
of oil to fair-haired Minerva and wine to its deity, Bacchus. 275
After the rural powers, the gods of the sky were given
the honour they all desired. Diana alone was forgotten;
her altars, they say, were neglected and languished without
     any incense.
The gods can feel anger too. 'This slight shall not go
     unpunished,'

she cried. To gain her vengeance, the injured goddess
280   dispatched
a boar through the fields of Aetólia, huge as the bulls
        that graze on
grassy Epírus and even more huge than the bulls of
        Sicily.
Blood and fire were aglow in his eyes; his neck was
        stiff
with bristles as firm as serried spears or the stakes on a
285   rampart.
His massive flanks were flecked with a spray of
        seething foam
from his grunting snorts; his tusks were as long as an
        Indian elephant's.
Lightning flashed from his mouth and his breath-blasts
        shrivelled the grassland.
He'd either trample the young corn down while still in
290   the blade,
or reap the crop which the farmer had prayed for and
        soon would mourn,
by destroying the full-grown grain in the ear; so the
        promised harvests
never arrived at the threshing-floor or the waiting
        granary.
Bunches of grapes were strewn on the ground with
        their trailing vine-shoots;
so were the berries and branches that fell from the
295   evergreen olives.
The flocks had also to suffer his fury: dogs and
        shepherds
failed to protect them, nor could the fierce bulls guard
        the cattle.
The country folk fled from their farms and only felt
        they were safe
behind the walls of their towns – until Meleäger
        assembled
his band of fighters, inspired like him with the longing
300   for glory.

Such were Castor and Pollux, the twins whom Leda the
      wife
of Týndareus mothered, the one an outstanding boxer, the
      other
a brilliant rider; Jason who built the first ship, *Argo*;
Theseus along with his bosom friend, Piríthoüs; Théstius'
sons, Plexíppus and Tóxeus;* Lýnceus and fleet-footed
      Idas,
the sons of Áphareus; Caéneus, now no longer a woman;   305
fierce Leucíppus; Acástus, a splendid javelin-thrower;
Hippóthoüs, Dryas and Phoenix the son of Amýntor;
      Actor's
two sons, Eúrytus and Ctéatus; Phýleus, who hailed from
      Elis;
Télamon too and Péleus, the father of mighty Achílles;
Admétus, the son of Pheres; Boeótian Ioláüs;   310
tireless Eurýtion joined by Echíon, invincible runner;
Lelex from Lócrian Nárycum; Pánopeus, Hýleus and
      bloodthirsty
Híppasus; Nestor of Pylos, still in the prime of his life;
and Spartan Hippócoön's sons, whom he sent from ancient
      Amýclae;
Ulýsses' father, Laértes; Ancaéus born in Arcadia;   315
Mopsus the prophet and Amphiaráüs,* not yet betrayed
by his wife; Atalánta, the pride of the forests on Mount
      Lycaéus,
whose robe was clasped at the neck by a buckle of polished
      metal,
her hair very simply gathered up in a single knot.
Rattling on her left shoulder, there hung the ivory quiver 320
that guarded her arrows, above the bow that she held in her
      left hand.
So much for her garb; and as for her face, you could
      truthfully call it
a girlish face for a boy or a boyish face for a girl.
The moment he saw Atalanta, the young Calydónian hero
longed to possess her, though heaven opposed it. The flames
      of his passion
                                                          325

stole through his heart, and he cried, 'How happy the
    man *that* maiden
chooses to wed!' The occasion and natural shyness
    forbade him
to speak any further. The mighty contest ahead was more
    pressing.
  The scene is a dense primeval forest, untouched by the
    axe;
330 it starts on a level plateau and looks out over the sloping
country below. When the hunters arrived, some spread
    their nets,
another group slipped their hounds from the leash,
    while others followed
the well-marked spoor, all keen to unearth their
    dangerous quarry.
Then picture a valley basin, where streams of
    rainwater trickle
down from the hills to a marshy dell, well filled at the
335   bottom
with pliant osiers, light sedge-grass and dense
    swamp-rushes,
withies and tall bulrushes with short reeds growing
    below.
It was here that the boar was roused from his covert
    and violently hurled himself
straight at his foes, like lightning struck from the
    clashing clouds.
The trees were flattened beneath his onslaught, the
340   trunks crashed down
as he butted against them. Loudly hallooing, the heroes
    bravely
brandished their glittering broad-tipped spears in front
    of their bodies.
The boar charged forward, scattering the various
    hounds which obstructed
his fury, dispersing the baying pack with his thrusts at
    their flanks.

The first long spear to be thrown was launched from
    Echion's shoulder,   345
but all to no purpose; it merely grazed the trunk of a maple.
The next one flew from the sturdy hand of Thessalian
    Jason.
This looked as if it would firmly lodge in the back of its
    target,
but too much force was behind the throw and it overshot.
Then Mopsus cried to Apollo: 'Hear me, Phoebus! I honour
    you   350
now as I ever did. So guide my spear where I aim it!'
The god complied as far as he could. The boar was struck,
but without being wounded. Diana lifted the tip of the
    javelin
off in its flight; the weapon arrived, but the point had gone
    missing.
The wild beast's anger was stirred and blazed like terrible
    lightning.   355
Fire flashed forth from his eyes and the breath of his nostrils
    was flame.
As a massive rock that is forcefully flung from the sling of a
    catapult
flies through the air to demolish a wall or a tower full of
    soldiers,
so were the blows of the hog, whose charge on the
    huntsmen was no less
deadly. He flattened Hippálmus and Pélagon, there on the
    right   360
to protect the wing. Immediately others moved forward to
    rescue
their fallen friends. But Hippocoön's son, Enaésimus, failed
to escape those death-dealing tusks. As he started to run in
    a panic,
the animal slashed at his knee and the strength of his
    tendons deserted him.
Even Nestor might well have perished before he went   365
to the Trojan War; but, using his spear as a pole, he vaulted

powerfully up, to land on a branch of the nearest tree
and there, with his safety assured, look down on the foe
          he had fled from.
The boar then savagely whetted his tusks on the trunk of
          an oak tree,
threatening death; then putting his trust in his sharpened
370   weapons,
he ripped with his turned-up snout at the thigh of the
          mighty Hippasus.

Now Castor and Pollux, the heavenly twins before
          they were stars,*
came forward, both magnificent sights, both riding on
          horses
whiter than gleaming snow, both proudly brandishing
          spears
which quivered within their grasp as the metal tips
375   flashed in the sunlight.
Those spears would surely have wounded the boar, but
          the bristly creature
had slunk off into the thickets where horses and spears
          could not reach him.
Telamon went in pursuit. His excitement made him
          unwary;
his foot was caught in the roots of a tree and he fell on
          his face.
While Peleus was trying to lift him up, Atalanta was
380   ready
to notch a swift arrow, bend her bow and send her
          shaft flying.
It lodged underneath the animal's ear after narrowly
          grazing
the top of his back; so his bristles were stained with a
          trickle of blood.
The success of her shot gave joy to the girl, but even
          more so
to young Meleäger; he saw the blood first, as the story
385   goes,

and he was the first to point it out to his comrades and
          greet
Atalanta: 'A glorious deed! You deserve a reward and shall
          have it!'
The men were blushing with shame. They boosted morale by
          shouting
and urging the next man on, then hurling their weapons at
          random,
so obstructing each other's efforts and making them
          useless.   390
    There now was Ancaeus, wielding his two-headed axe.
          Furiously
tempting fortune, he cried: 'My friends, let me show you
          how far
the arms of a man outclass a mere woman's. Leave this to
          me!
Latona's daughter herself can protect the boar with her
          arrows;
my own right hand shall destroy him, despite the will of
          Diana!'   395
The words had sprung from his boastful lips in the swell of
          his pride.
Then lifting the double-headed axe in both of his hands,
he rose high up on his toes, all poised for the downward
          stroke.
He was bold, but the boar was before him and drove with
          his two sharp tusks
at the upper part of the groin, where the pathway to death
          is the shortest.   400
Ancaeus collapsed; his bowels burst out in a seething
          mixture
of gore and gut, and the earth beneath him was soaked with
          his blood.
    Pirithoüs,* son of Ixíon, now ventured to enter the battle
against the monster. His strong right hand was shaking his
          boar-spear,
when Theseus cried out, 'Keep back! Your life is dearer to
          me   405

than my own; you are half of my soul. Brave heroes may
      fight at a prudent
distance. Ancaeus was brave, but his rashness destroyed
      him.'
With that he himself discharged his weighty
      bronze-tipped javelin.
Beautifully poised, the weapon seemed likely to reach its
      mark,
but its flight through the air was blocked by a leafy
410   branch on an oak tree.
Jason also sent his spear flying, and this was diverted
by chance from the boar to an innocent dog who was
      pierced in the flank;
the weapon ran through the poor yelper and pinned
      him fast to the ground.
Meleäger's throwing was more successful. He launched
      two spears:
the first hit the ground, but the second struck home in
415   the back of his quarry.
At once, as the boar struggled wildly, spinning around
      in a circle,
bubbling with foam at the mouth and streaming with
      blood from his new wound,
the man who had dealt it advanced, to provoke his
      prey to fresh fury
and, as it attacked, to bury his gleaming boar-spear
      deep
in its shoulders. His friends cheered loudly, to signal
420   their joy in his triumph,
eager to clasp the victorious hero's hand in their own.
They gazed in awe at the size of the great brute,
      sprawling over
so vast an expanse of earth. They still believed it was
      dangerous
to touch it, but each of them separately dipped his
      spear in the blood.
   Meleäger himself then planted his foot on that
425   merciless head

and hailed Atalanta: 'Now take the prize which is mine by
      right,
Nonácrian maid! My glory must surely be shared with you.'
At once he presented the girl with his spoils, the spiky hide
of the bristled boar and its head in the pride of its huge
      white tusks.
Atalanta's joy in the gift was matched by her joy in the
      giver;   430
but others were jealous and angry murmurs ran through the
      crowd.
Meleäger's uncles, Plexippus and Toxeus, stretching their
      arms out,
shouted, 'Down with those spoils! You're a woman; don't
      try to usurp
the honours due to us men. You'd better not trust to your
      beauty
too far. Your generous lover may not be there to defend
      you!'   435
At once they seized the spoils from the girl and removed
      Meleäger's
right to award them. This was too much for a son of
      Mars.*
Grinding his teeth in rising fury, he tackled them boldly:
'You filchers of others' prizes, you seem unaware of the vital
difference that lies between threats and actions.' Then
      taking Plexippus
quite by surprise, he plunged his sword through his uncle's
      heart.   440
What was Toxeus to do? He wavered, hoping to take
      revenge
for his brother but also afraid of sharing his brother's fate.
He was not permitted to waver for long. Meleäger's sword,
still warm with the blood of one kinsman, was heated again
      by the other's.

Queen Althaéa was bearing gifts to the temples in thanks   445
for her son's great feat, when she saw men bearing her
      brothers' corpses.

Wildly beating her breast, she filled the streets of the city
with cries of lament and changed her garments from gold
    to black.
But as soon as the name of the killer was published, her
    sorrow was totally
banished. Her tears dried up and yielded to passion for
450   vengeance.
  At the time when Althaea was giving birth to her son
    Meleäger,
a fragment of wood had been cast in the fire on the
    hearth by the Three Fates.
Spinning with thumb and finger at destiny's threads,
    the Sisters
uttered these words: 'We assign the same life-span to
    this wooden
455 log as we do to this new-born child.' The spell was cast
and the goddesses made their departure. At once the
    mother extracted
the burning branch from the flames and doused it in
    running water.
For years that log had been hidden away in the depths
    of an inner
store-room and, thus preserved, had preserved the life
    of the young prince.
His mother now brought it out. She ordered her
460   servants to lay
some pinewood and kindling, and then she applied the
    fatal taper.
Four times she withdrew it. A conflict raged between
    mother and sister;
the two names pulled at a single heart in a tug of war.
Often her cheeks grew pale in dread of the crime she
465   was plotting;
her eyes would as often be red with the burning anger
    that glowed there.
One moment her face would assume an expression
    suggestive of cruel

menace; the next you might well suppose she was moved by
      compassion.
Once her tears had been dried by the heat of her violent
      anger,
they gushed once more from her sorrowful eyes. As a vessel
      at sea   470
which is caught between wind and tide and pulled in
      different directions,
subject to two strong forces, uncertainly wavers between
      them,
so Théstius' daughter wavered between her warring
      emotions,
quenching her anger again and again, at once to
      rekindle it.
But now the sister began to overpower the mother.   475
To appease the ghosts of her blood by bloodshed, family
      duty
was intermingled with family guilt. When the flames of
      devouring
fire grew strong, she prayed that the funeral pyre might
      consume
her own flesh also. Grimly clutching the fateful log,
she took her stand, poor lady, before that altar of death,   480
and cried: 'Euménides, three dread sisters, powers of
      punishment,
turn your gaze on these sacred rites of retributive fury!
Vengeance is mine by sin, and death is atoned for by death;
crime must needs be added to crime, and a body to bodies.
Perish the guilt-cursed house in sorrow heaped upon
      sorrow!   485
Is Oeneus blithely to take delight in his son's fine victory,
while Thestius grieves for his loss? Better that both should
      mourn.
I pray to the shades and the newly departed souls of my
      brethren:
take regard of the honour I show you; accept my sacrifice,
offered at such dear cost, the evil fruit of my own womb! – 490

Stop, Althaea! You brothers of mine, pray pardon a
      mother.
I cannot go on; my hands are too weak. I freely admit
he deserves to die; but I cannot become my own son's
      murderer. –
And so must he go unpunished, to live victorious and
      mount
the throne of Calydon, puffed with the pride of his
495   impious triumph,
while you lie dead in a handful of ash, poor shivering
      ghosts?
I cannot allow it. The wretch must die. Let him carry
      off with him
his father's hopes and his kingdom, and lay his country
      in ruins! –
Oh, where is my mother's heart, the love that I owe to
      my own child?
What of the pains I endured as those nine long months
500   went by?
How dearly I wish you had burnt in that earlier fire,
      and I
had suffered the loss of my baby. You owed your life
      to my giving;
now owe your death to your own deserts; now take
      your reward;
now return the life that was doubly given you, once
      when I bore you,
once when I rescued the log, or lay me next to my
505   brothers.
I wish for his death, but am powerless, confused! One
      moment I picture
my brothers' wounds and that scene of murderous
      carnage; but then
my spirit is broken by love and the name that I own as
      a mother.
Oh, I am lost! Though your triumph is evil, you win,
      my brothers,

so long as I'm granted a share in the comfort I bring you
    and follow you   510
down to the shades.' When she'd spoken these words, she
    averted her face
as with trembling hand she tossed the death brand into the
    blaze.
The log itself gave a moan of pain, or so it appeared,
when the fire reluctantly caught at the wood and it burst
    into flames.
   Meleäger, away from the house, knew nothing of this,
    but the flames   515
began to burn at him too; he could feel his vitals scorching
with hidden fire. He bravely mastered the terrible pain,
but still it was hard to be facing a bloodless death like a
    coward.
'Lucky Ancaeus!' he thought; 'he died of his wounds.'
    Pathetically
moaning, he called on his aged father, his brother and
    loving   520
sisters and now, with his dying breath, on the wife he had
    slept with,
perhaps on his mother too. The fire and his pain flared up
and then subsided again, till both were extinguished
    together.
His spirit gradually filtered into the insubstantial
air, as the ashes gradually shrouded the glowing embers.   525

Calydon's heights brought low! All sorrowed, both young
    and old;
nobles and common folk wailed alike. By the river Evénus
the mothers of Calydon tore at their tresses and smote on
    their bosoms.
Sprawled on the ground, Meleäger's old father begrimed his
    face
and his hoary hairs in the dust, cursing the length of his
    days.   530
Aware of her frightful deed, his mother had used her guilty

hand to punish herself by thrusting a sword in her vitals.
As for the dismal plaints of his wretched sisters, I could
        not
rehearse them, had I been granted by heaven a hundred
        tongues,
535   unlimited wit and the inspiration of all the Muses.
Reckless of all decorum, they bruised their breasts with
        their fist-blows;
and, while the body was there, they stroked it over and
        over,
kissing their brother and kissing the bier now laid on
        the pyre.
When he'd burnt to ashes, they gathered them up and
        pressed the urn
to their hearts; then prostrate over his tomb, they clung
540   to the gravestone,
weeping until their tears poured into the name that was
        carved there.
Sated at last with the havoc she'd wreaked on the
        house of Partháön,
Diana made feathers sprout from their bodies – from
        all except Gorge
and Deïaníra.* She stretched long wings on the arms of
        the rest,
she turned their lips into horny beaks; and thus
545   transformed
into guinea-fowl,* up the sisters were lifted and
        launched on the breezes.

ACHELOÜS, THE NAIADS AND PERIMELE

Theseus having discharged his role in the communal
        boar hunt,
was now on his journey home to Eréchtheus' city of
        Athens.
His way was barred by a river in flood, the god
        Achelóüs,*

who forced him to wait: 'Pray enter my house, illustrious
    hero   550
of Cecrops' line. Do not trust yourself to these greedy
    waters.
Beware of the thick tree-trunks and zigzagging boulders,
    rolling
and crashing down. I have seen the flood-tide sweeping
    away
the lofty stables, cattle and all, that adjoin my margins;
the ox's strength and the horse's speed have availed them
    nothing.   555
After the snows on the mountains have melted, this torrent
    has also
claimed the lives of many young men in its eddying
    currents.
Safer to rest for a while, till my swollen stream is confined
to its wonted limits and narrowed down to its natural
    channel.'
'Yes, Acheloüs,' replied the hero, 'I'll gladly avail   560
myself of your house and advice.' And he made good use of
    them both.
  Theseus entered a grotto of porous pumice and
    rough-grained
tufa; the soft earth floor beneath him was watery moss,
while the ceiling was panelled with rows of mussel and
    murex shells.
Now that the sun god had run two thirds of his course to
    the evening,   565
Theseus and his companions reclined on their several
    couches.
On one side sat Pirithoüs, son of Ixion; there sat
Lelex of Troézen, starting now to go grey round the
    temples,
and other guests whom the Acarnánian river had honoured
no less, in his pleasure at welcoming so distinguished a
    visitor.   570
At once barefooted nymphs set tables beside them and
    loaded

these with a lavish banquet. Then, when the food was
    removed,
unwatered wine was offered in jewelled cups. At this
    point
Theseus, looking over the sea below them and pointing,
enquired, 'What place is that? And tell me the name of
575   the island
facing us there, which hardly looks like a single island.'
The river-god answered: 'The land you see doesn't
    form one whole.
Five islands are there, but the distance obscures the
    gaps that divide them.
Diana's resentment in sending the boar was nothing to
    wonder at.
These islands used to be naiads, who put ten bullocks
580   to slaughter
and then invited the rural gods to share in the feasting;
but when they started the ritual dance, they forgot
    about me.
I swelled in my rage and swept along in as mighty a
    spate
as I ever achieve, the power of my waters matching the
    power
of my wrath. I sundered forest from forest and field
585   from field,
and rolled the place where the nymphs were standing
    into the waves –
they remembered me then. My waters next combined
    with the sea
to split the continuous land mass and break it up into
    five,
to form the Echínades, Hedgehog Isles, that you see in
    mid-ocean.
But look! You can spot it yourself, far off in the
590   distance, my favourite,
a single island beyond the rest. Periméle the sailors
call it. I loved that girl and stole her virginity from her.

Her father Hippódamas took it unkindly and forcibly
    pushed
his erring daughter over a cliff to be drowned in the waves.
I caught her up and, supporting her while she swam, cried
    out: 595
"Neptune, lord of the trident, whose realm is the wandering
    ocean,*   596
second alone to the heavens, I pray for your help! Grant
    space   601
to an innocent drowned by a cruel father, or let her
    become   602
a space in herself." As I spoke, new land enfolded her
    floating   609
limbs, and an island of substance grew from her
    transformed body.'   610

PHILEMON AND BAUCIS

The river-god held his peace. His amazing story had
    moved
the whole of the company. One poured scorn on their
    credulous wonder,
Pirithoüs, a young tearaway, who had no use for the gods.
'Pure fiction!' he said. 'Acheloüs, you credit the gods with
    too much
power, if you think they create and then alter the shapes in
    Nature.'   615
All were aghast at these blasphemous words and voiced
    disapproval,
especially Lelex, whose mind reflected his riper years.
'The power of heaven cannot be measured,' he answered
    firmly.
'It knows no bounds. Whatever the gods decree is
    accomplished.
To ease your impious doubts, you should visit the Phrygian
    hills   620

to look at an oak tree and linden nearby, both ringed by
    a low wall.
I've been to the place myself, when Píttheus sent me from
    Troezen
to Phrygia's lands, where his father Pelops had once been
    king.
Not far from the spot is a fen which used to be habitable
    land
but is now under water and haunted merely by coots and
625   divers.
Jupiter once came here, disguised as a mortal, and with
    him
his son, the messenger Mercury, wand and wings set
    aside.
Looking for shelter and rest, they called at a thousand
    homesteads;
a thousand doors were bolted against them. One
    house, however,
did make them welcome, a humble abode with a roof
630   of straw
and marsh reed, one that knew its duty to gods and men.
Here good Philémon and Baucis had happily passed
    their youth
and here they had reached old age, enduring their
    poverty lightly
by owning it freely and being content with the little
    they had.
If you came, it made no difference to ask for the
635   masters or servants;
the household consisted of two, each giving and taking
    the orders.
  'So when the gods had found their way to this
    humble dwelling
(the door was so low, they could only cross the
    threshold by stooping),
Philemon moved forward a bench and asked them to
    rest their limbs,

while Baucis bustled around to spread a rough covering
        over it,   640
then crossed to the hearth to brush the wood-ash away
        from the embers
of yesterday's fire and bring it to life by feeding it leaves
and dry tree bark, with only her feeble puffing for bellows;
then fetching some splits of kindling and pieces of dry
        branch down
from the roof, she broke them up further and set them
        under her bronze pot.   645
Next she stripped the outer leaves of the cabbage her
        husband
had picked from his watered garden, while he, with the help
        of a forked stick,
lifted a chine of bacon off from the blackened beam,
and chopped a piece from the back they had carefully saved
        for so long,
then dropped the cut in the pot to cook in the boiling
        water.   650
While all were waiting, they passed the time in agreeable
        talk
and the hours went by in a flash. On a hook there was
        hanging a sturdy-
handled bucket of beechwood, and this was filled with
        warm water
so that the guests could wash their limbs. A sedge-stuffed
        cushion   655
was laid on top of a couch with a frame and legs of
        willow-wood;
then it was covered with drapes which were only brought
        out on special
occasions – still tawdry and worn, if they didn't disgrace the
        couch.
    'The gods reclined. With her skirts tucked up and with
        shaking hands,   660
old Baucis positioned a three-legged table beside them; but
        one

of the legs was too short and she had to level it up with a
    potsherd.
Once the table was steady, she wiped its surface with
    green mint,
then laid a spread of unsalted olives, both green and
    black,
665 endive and radish, pickle of autumn cornel-cherries,
cream cheese and eggs very lightly cooked on a
    moderate ash-heat,
served in earthenware dishes. When that was finished,
    a moulded
wine-bowl of similar "silver" was set on the table with
    goblets
carved out of beech and coated with golden wax on the
670   inside.
After that it did not take long for the hot main course
to be brought from the hearth. The young wine next
    was returned to the table,*
but soon removed for a while to clear the space for
    dessert,
consisting of nuts with a mixture of figs and wrinkled
    palm-dates,
plums and sweet-smelling apples arranged in broad flat
675   baskets,
grapes new-picked from the purple vine, with a
    honeycomb placed
in the table's centre. To crown this humble fare, the
    smiles
on the old folk's faces betokened a wealth of unfailing
    kindness.
   'Meanwhile, whenever the mixing-bowl got empty,
    it seemed
to refill of its own accord, with the wine welling up by
680   itself.
Stunned and scared by this wonder, Philemon,
    trembling, and Baucis
lifted their upturned hands to heaven and fervently
    prayed

for forgiveness after serving so poorly prepared a repast.
They then set out to placate their mysterious guests by
        killing
the goose, their only one, which guarded the tiny farm;   685
but the bird kept fluttering around, exhausting the elderly
        couple
and long eluding their grasp, till at last it appeared to have
        flown
to the gods themselves for refuge. "You must not kill it,"
        they said.
"We are gods. Your neighbours shall pay the price they
        deserve for their wicked
impiety. You alone shall be spared from the coming
        disaster.   690
We simply ask you to leave your home and walk in our
        footsteps
up to the mountains." The couple obeyed and, using their
        sticks
to support them, they wearily climbed the long steep slope.
        They were just
a bowshot away from the top, when they turned and saw
        that the other   695
houses were under water, with only their own still
        standing.
And while they gazed in amazement, lamenting the fate of
        their neighbours,
their little old cottage, a small home even for two to
        inhabit,
was changed to a temple. The fork-shaped props were
        replaced by columns,   700
the thatch turned yellow, and now it appeared that the roof
        was gilded,
the doors engraved with reliefs and the ground paved over
        with marble.
   'At last King Jupiter gently addressed them: "You good
        old man,
and you the wife that his goodness deserves, now name
        whatever

boon you desire." Philemon conferred for a moment
705   with Baucis,
before advising the gods of their joint decision: "We
      ask
to be priests and to guard your temple; and since we
      have passed our years
together in peace, let the same hour carry us off, so I
      need not
look on my dear wife's grave, nor she have to bury my
710   body."
Their wish was granted; as long as life was allowed
      them, they served
as the temple's guardians. When time had taken its
      final toll,
and while they were casually standing in front of the
      steps of the building,
telling the sanctuary's history, both Philemon and
      Baucis
witnessed their partner sprouting leaves on their worn
715   old limbs.
As the tops of the trees spread over their faces, they
      spoke to each other
once more while they could. "Farewell, my beloved!"
      they said in a single
breath, as the bark closed over their lips and concealed
      them for ever.
Still to this day the peasants of Phrygia point to the oak
and the linden nearby which once were the forms of
720   Philemon and Baucis.
The story was told me by trustworthy elders who had
      no reason
to lie or deceive. I saw for myself the wreaths that were
      hanging
upon the branches and, placing a fresh wreath,
      murmured, "Let those
who are loved by the gods be gods, and those who
      have worshipped be worshipped."'

ERYSICHTHON

Lelex fell silent. All had been moved by the tale and its
        teller,   725
Theseus especially. 'Tell me more of the wonders
        performed
by the gods!' he cried. Then leaning upon his elbow, the
        river
of Calydon said to him: 'Bravest of heroes, we know of a
        number
whose form has changed only once and never again been
        altered.
Others have had the power to assume a whole range of
        shapes,   730
like Próteus, a god who dwells in the earth-encompassing
        ocean.
Men saw him both as a handsome youth and a ravening
        lion;
at other times he became a savage boar, or a bull
with a pair of menacing horns, or a serpent, dangerous to
        handle.
He could often appear like the stones and often again like
        the trees;   735
sometimes he'd turn into flowing water and take the form
of a river; sometimes he'd change to the contrary element,
        fire.
   'Erysíchthon's daughter, Mestra,* the wife of Autólycus,
        also
possessed such a power. Her father was one who despised
        the gods,
and the savour of burning sacrifice never rose up from his
        altars.   740
He, as the story goes, audaciously took an axe
to the grove of Ceres and desecrated her ancient woodland.
Standing there was a mighty oak of great antiquity,
a wood on its own. It was hung all round with suppliant
        wool-bands,

745 votive tablets and garlands offered for prayers fulfilled.
     In its shade the dryads often conducted their festal
           dances;
     hand in hand they would trip and circle around the
           trunk,
     whose girth was more than twenty-two feet, while its
           height exceeded
     the rest of the trees by as much as they topped the grass
750   beneath them.
     But that was no cause for the wild Thessalian brute
           Erysichthon
     to hold his axe at a distance. He ordered his slaves to
           get cutting
     the sacred oak at its base; then, seeing them shrink
           from the task,
     the infidel seized an axe from one of them, savagely
           shouting:
     "This needn't be merely the goddess' tree, but the
755   goddess herself,
     for all I care, but its leafy top must be brought to the
           ground!"
     With that, as he raised his threatening weapon to strike
           from the side,
     the oak of Ceres gave a great shudder and uttered a
           groan;
     a pallor crept over the acorns, the leaves and the length
760   of the branches.
     As soon as that impious hand had inflicted a wound on
           the trunk,
     blood poured from the shattered bark as it streams
           from the severed neck
     of a huge sacrificial bull when it falls in front of the
           altar.
     All were appalled, but one who was bolder than all the
765   others
     endeavoured to halt this evil and counter the axe's
           cruelty.

Seeing him, "Here's the reward for your piety!" cried
    Erysichthon,
and switched the axe from the tree to his servant to lop the
    man's head,
before returning to hack away at the oak's great side.
Suddenly then, from the heart of the tree, a voice rang out: 770
"I am the nymph, beloved of Ceres, who dwells in this
    oak!
I prophesy now as I die. Vengeance will come! You shall
    pay
the price for your impious deed and make amends for my
    death!"
But the monster pursued his crime to the end. Reeling under
his numberless blows, heaved down by ropes, the oak tree
    finally 775
crashed to the ground and toppled a mass of the forest
    beneath it.
   'Horrified by this loss to the woods and of one of their
    sisters,
the dryads all vested themselves in garments of mourning
    black
and hastened to Ceres, to beg her to punish the vile
    Erysichthon.
The goddess agreed and, as she nodded her beautiful
    head, 780
she shook the fields, now heavily laden with ripening corn,
and contrived a revenge which might have excited pity –
    except
that no one could possibly pity a man who had acted so
    shamefully.
"Let pestilent Hunger torture his body!" was her grim
    sentence.
And since she could not approach that demon herself (for
    the Fates 785
will never let Ceres and Hunger meet), she called to a rural
óreäd, one of the mountain spirits, and gave her
    instructions:

"Go to a place on the farthest borders of icy Scythia,
gloomy terrain, where the earth is barren of crops and of
         trees.
Sluggish Cold has its home in that land, with Pallor and
790   Trembling,
ravenous Hunger too. Tell Hunger to fasten herself
in the cursed maw of that impious man, and never to
         yield
to abundance of food. Let her vie with my nourishing
         power – and defeat it!
Do not be dismayed by the length of your journey.
         Take my chariot,
harness my serpents and guide their course through the
795   heavens on high!"
   'The oreäd took the dragon-chariot and drove
         through the air
till she landed in Scythia. There on the heights of the
         rugged Caucasus
mountains, she freed her snakes from the yoke and
         quickly departed
in search of Hunger. She tracked her down in a stony
         wasteland.
The spirit was plucking with nail and tooth at the
800   scanty herbage.
Her hair was tangled, her eyes like hollows,
         complexion pallid,
her lips grimy and grey, her throat scabrous and scurfy.
Her skin was so hard and fleshless, the entrails were
         visible through it;
her shrunken bones protruded under her sagging loins;
her belly was merely an empty space; her pendulous
805   breasts
appeared to be strung on nothing except the cage of
         her backbone;
her leanness had swollen all of her joints; the rounds of
         her knees
were bulbous; her ankles were grossly enlarged to a
         puffy excrescence.

The oreäd spied her but, lacking the courage to move any
    closer,
carefully kept her distance to give her the goddess's
    message.   810
Instantly, though she remained far off and despite her
    recent
arrival, she felt a sensation of hunger and turned the chariot
round to pilot the serpents back through the sky to
    Thessaly.
  'Hunger acted on Ceres' bidding, although their functions
are always opposed. She directed her flight on the wind to
    the palace   815
as ordered, and rapidly made her way to the reprobate's
    chamber.
It was night and she found him buried in sleep. Then
    twining her arms
around him, she poured herself deep inside as she breathed
    on his throat,
on his breast, on his mouth, and dispersed starvation
    throughout his veins.   820
Her mission accomplished, she left the world of plenty
    behind her
and took herself back to the caves she knew in the mansions
    of want.
  'Gentle sleep on her peaceful wings still held Erysichthon
fast in her soothing embrace. In his dreams he craved for a
    meal,
as he munched away on a void and ground his teeth to no
    purpose,   825
gulping down imaginary food in his cheated oesophagus,
vainly devouring a banquet of air without any substance.
But when he awoke, a passion for eating was raging inside
    him,
reigning supreme in his ravenous gullet and burning belly.
At once he demands to be filled with the produce of earth,
    sea and sky.   830
When tables loaded with food are provided, he moans, "I
    am starving!"

A banquet is laid for him; "Food!" he demands. What
    could satisfy cities
or even a nation will not be enough for his single
    appetite.
The fuller he crammed his insatiable maw, his hunger
    grew stronger,
just as the ocean absorbs the streams that flow from a
835   whole land,
yet still unsatisfied drains the waters of far-off rivers;
or just as a raging fire will never refuse any fuel
but burns an infinite number of logs (the more it is fed,
the more it requires, abundance merely augmenting its
    greed),
840 so a feast had only to touch Erysichthon's impious lips,
and he asked for more. His food had simply become a
    reason
for food. His eating always led on to an empty
    stomach.

'Appetite now had diminished his father's wealth, as he
    swallowed it
down in his belly's abyss; but the pangs of his
    desperate hunger
remained undiminished. The flames of his still
845   unsatisfied gluttony
rose to new heights. At last, with his capital wasted
    inside him,
his daughter was all he had left. Though she little
    deserved such a father,
he sold her off with the rest. Too noble to tolerate
    slavery,
Mestra ran to the edge of the sea and, stretching her
    arms out,
shouted to Neptune: "You snatched the prize of my
850   maidenly virtue;
now snatch me away from life as a drudge!" The god
    who had raped her

did not say no to her prayer. Though her owner was in
    pursuit
and had just caught sight of her, Neptune altered her form
    and gave her
the face of a man and a fisherman's garb. When her master
    set eyes
on this stranger, he said: "Hey, you there, casting your line
    and hook   855
with a tiny morsel to hide it, I wish you a clear calm sea
and a gullible fish which will rise to your bait till it's caught
    and landed.
Tell me, where is the woman I saw just now? She was
    standing
here on the shore in shabby clothes, with her hair
    dishevelled.   860
I saw her, I tell you. You must know, surely. Her tracks
    stop here!"
Mestra saw that the god's protection was working.
    Delighted
at being questioned about herself, she quickly responded:
"Excuse me, sir, whoever you are. My eyes have been fixed
on the water here. In my concentration on fishing, they've
    never   865
wandered. I swear by Neptune, the god of the sea, who I
    pray
will assist my skill, throughout this time no man has stood
on this part of the shore, except for myself, and no woman
    either."
Her owner believed her, turned on his heels and trudged
    through the sand
as he went off, duped. And Mestra recovered her normal
    shape.   870
  'When her father saw that his daughter's body could be
    transformed,
he sold her a number of times to different owners; but then
she would change to a bird or a mare or a cow or a deer and
    escape from them,

so providing her gluttonous sire with his fraudulent
     fodder.
875 But after his violent affliction had wasted away the whole
of his substance and nothing was left to fuel his
     virulent malady,
he finally started to bite his own limbs and tear them
     apart
with his jaws; the poor wretch nourished his body by
     making it smaller.

'Why should I dwell on the stories of others? I,
     Acheloüs,
possess the power to alter my shape in a limited
880   number
of ways, young Theseus. Sometimes I am as you see me
     now;
sometimes I change to a serpent or lead the herd as a
     strong-horned
bull – or did when I could. But now one side of my
     forehead
has lost its defence* – you can see for yourself.' And he
     sighed as he ended.

BOOK 9

Hercules is the key figure in the next group of stories. *Acheloüs and Hercules* (1–97) is a lively account of how the river-god fought with the hero for the hand of Deïanira and acquired his broken horn. The next two episodes, *Hercules and Nessus* (98–133) and *The Death of Hercules* (134–272), are so obviously based on Sophocles' play *The Women of Trachis* that we may think of Ovid here as doing his 'Sophocles turn'. The poet's narrative displays his usual vividness, but he concentrates more on the gorier details than on the tragic situation of Hercules' betrayed wife, Deïanira (he had to some extent explored this previously in *Heroides* 9). Furthermore, he uses the hero's immolation and apotheosis as the occasion for a satirically pompous speech from Jupiter, which some may find the most enjoyable passage in the whole of this section.

The humorous tone continues in *Alcmena and Galanthis* (273–323), which tells the story of Hercules' birth. *Dryope* (324–93) is similarly lightweight: there is a kind of schmaltzy pathos in the tale of the girl who picks a water plant to amuse her baby and is turned to a lotus tree herself. In *Iolaus and Callirhoe's Sons* (394–417) we have two metamorphoses involving human age, one of rejuvenation, the other of acceleration. The passage is (for us) rather tiresomely allusive and only intelligible with explanatory notes; but it does enable Ovid to work in some more of the standard Theban legend. *Miletus* (418–52) gives us the pleasure of another pompous speech from Jupiter and takes us on, by an artificial transition, to one of Jupiter's sons, our old friend Minos, who is now *very* old and in fear of a young rival Miletus – who flees from Crete to found a new city in Asia Minor and begets the twins, Byblis and Caunus, who are the subject of the next story.

The rest of the book is superb, with Ovid exploring and entering sympathetically into two cases of what might be considered 'abnormal' passions. In *Byblis* (454–665) he takes a popular Hellenistic Greek story and makes it very much his own. His heroine falls desperately in love with her twin brother, and her feelings are chiefly expressed in three major passages: first a long monologue in which she attempts to justify incest, then in a letter of confession which she pens to Caunus, and finally in a second monologue after her advances have been rejected with horror. Drawn-out and rhetorical as all this may appear, it makes for extremely compelling reading and recitation, and Byblis' eventual metamorphosis comes across as a naturally contrived and almost consoling conclusion.

Iphis (666–797) is in some ways a parallel story but also a contrast. This explores the predicament of a girl brought up as a boy (to save her from being killed at birth) and later betrothed to a girl with whom she is genuinely in love. Iphis in her monologue is made to perceive her feelings as monstrous and unnatural, 'a new kind of passion', a view which may have been shared by some of Ovid's audience. However that may be, we are evidently intended to identify with Iphis as we did with Byblis. If we do feel embarrassed, we may be reassured by the story's happy ending. Where Byblis had to fade away in her tears to a stream, Iphis is divinely awarded the necessary sex-change in the nick of time. He and Ianthe can be married and presumably live happily ever after.

ACHELOÜS AND HERCULES

'Why are you sighing and why is the horn on your forehead
        broken?'
Théseus asked Acheloüs. The god of the river, whose
        unkempt
hair was crowned with a garland of reeds, thus made his
        reply:
'What a dismal gift* to demand! Who'd willingly give an
        account
of his own defeats? But I'll tell you the story from start to
        finish;   5
the shame of losing the battle was less than the glory of
        fighting it –
falling to such a distinguished man is a great consolation.
Perhaps you have heard the name of the beautiful Deïaníra,
whose hand in marriage was jealously sought by an army of
        suitors,   10
including myself. As soon as I'd entered her father's palace,
"Son of Parth* áon," I said, "I ask to marry your daughter."
Hercules said the same, and the others withdrew in our
        favour.
My rival pleaded that Jove was his father* and mentioned
        his glorious
labours, the dangerous tasks he'd been set by his
        stepmother Juno.   15
I urged in reply: "What disgrace for a god to give way to a
        mortal!"
(The hero was not yet a god.) "Here am I, the lord of the
        river
which winds its way through your lands, not urging my suit
        as a stranger
dispatched from alien shores, but as one of your fellow
        countrymen,
part of your kingdom. I say that it shouldn't be held against
        me   20

that royal Juno does not detest me and I'm not sentenced
to endless labours at her command. Now, son of
     Alcména,
as for your boast that Jupiter happens to be your father,
you're either a liar or else you must be a bastard. The
     truth
of your claim depends on your mother's adultery. Make
25   up your mind, then:
either the story's a fiction, or else your birth was a
     scandal."

   'Hercules watched me, as I was making my case, with
     a glowering
look in his eyes. His anger was blazing, he couldn't
     control it;
and then he retorted, "My hand has more power to
     persuade than my tongue.
I'll allow you to win the debate, so long as I win in the
30   fighting,"
and forward he stalked looking fierce. As I had been
     speaking so boldly,
I hadn't the face to retreat. My garments of green were
     discarded;
I put up my arms and, holding my hands crooked round
     at the ready
in front of my chest, I was all prepared to wrestle with
     Hercules.
First he gathered some dust in his hollowed palms and
35   sprinkled it
over me; next I covered his body with yellow-gold sand.
Then he lunged at my neck and my nimble legs in
     succession –
or else he pretended to do so – and went for each part of
     my body.
My defence was my solid weight, so all his attempts
     came to nothing.
I stood like a massive rock, assailed by the roaring
40   waves

in a storm but never dislodged, secure in its own great bulk.
For one brief moment we moved apart, then returned to the
         battle,
standing fast in our tracks, determined not to give ground.
My foot was now touching his, my body was thrust well
         forward,
his fingers were gripped in mine and our foreheads were
         forced together.   45
I tell you, we could have been two strong bulls ferociously
         butting
to win the prize of the sleekest cow in the whole of the
         pasture,
with all of the herd looking on in a flurry of terror,
         uncertain
which one of the two will win the victory of such great
         lordship.
Three times the magnificent Hercules unsuccessfully tried   50
to thrust me back as I pressed against him; at last, at the
         fourth
attempt, he managed to break my hold and to shake me
         off.
I was thrown off balance, and then – I'm determined to tell
         you the truth –
he rapidly turned me round and clung to my back with his
         full weight.
Believe me, Theseus – I'm not inventing the details to win
         myself   55
glory – I felt I was being crushed by the weight of a
         mountain.
But still, with a mighty effort, I slipped my arms, all
         dripping
with sweat, under his and wrenched my limbs from his
         bearlike hug.
While I panted for breath, before I recovered my strength,
         he was on me
again, with his hands at my throat. And that was the end of
         the battle.   60

He forced me down to my knees, and I felt the sand in my
      teeth.
  'Since I was weaker in manly strength, I turned to my
      own arts,
slithering out of the hero's grasp in the form of a long
      snake.
My body was looped into sinuous coils and I flickered my
      forked tongue,
hissing like fury. But Hercules laughed and made fun of
65   my magic:
"Dealing with snakes is a task I used to perform in my
      cradle!*
You may surpass other snakes, Acheloüs, but really, a
      single
serpent is hardly a threat when compared with the
      Hydra of Lerna.
That monster blossomed and throve on its wounds;
70   when one of its numerous
heads was cut off, it always recovered by sprouting
      another
two heads in its place. Destruction caused it to grow, as
      it put forth
branches of vipers sprung from the carnage. But I, great
      Hercules,
mastered the creature and cauterized each neck as I
      lopped it.
What do you think will happen to you, who are merely
75   disguised
as a snake, in dubious form, with weapons not yours by
      nature?"
He then proceeded to shackle the top of my neck in his
      fingers.
Helplessly choking, as if my throat had been gripped by
      pincers,
I struggled to tear my jaws away from his strangling
      thumbs;
80 but once again I was beaten. I still had a third shape left,

so I changed once more to a savage bull and returned to the
    fray.
He attacked from the left and clasped my muscular neck in
    his arms;
I then dashed forward, but Hercules followed and pulled
    against me;
soon he had forced my hard horns down till they caught in
    the soil,
and had laid me flat on top of the sand. But he still wasn't
    satisfied.
Grasping one of my horns in his brutal hand, he broke it,   85
tough as it was, and tore it away from my forehead, leaving
    me
maimed. The horn was filled by the naiads with fruit and
    with fragrant
flowers and, thus made holy, enriches the Spirit of Plenty.'*
  The river-god ended his tale and one of his servants, a
    nymph
attired as Diana, with hair spread over her shoulders, came
    forward,   90
displaying the Horn of Plenty and carrying all the choicest
fruits of the autumn to serve to the guests for the second
    course.
Dawn broke; as the sun's first rays were striking the
    mountain peaks,
the young men went on their way. They'd decided no longer
    to wait
till the river was calmly flowing in peace and the flood had
    completely   95
subsided. The country-god Acheloüs then hid his face,
and plunged his head with its wrenched-off horn in the
    midst of his own waves.

HERCULES AND NESSUS

Although the river-god grieved for the loss of his
      beautiful horn,
he was otherwise safe and sound. He could easily cover
      his damaged
head with a garland of willow foliage or reeds from the
100   stream.
But Nessus, the brutal centaur, was wholly destroyed
      by his passion
for Deïanira and shot in the back by a flying arrow.
Hercules, with his newly-wed bride, was travelling
      home
to the city of Tiryns and came to the fast-flowing river
      Evénus.
The stream was swollen and higher than usual because
105   of the winter
rains, and the swirl of the eddying currents made it
      impassable.
Hercules held no fears for himself but was somewhat
      concerned
for his wife, when the sturdy Nessus, who knew the
      shallows, approached him.
'Hercules, listen!' he said. 'Do accept my help. I'll
      deposit
Your wife on the farther bank, while you swim across
110   on your own.'
Deïanira was pale with terror and frightened of Nessus
no less than the stream; but her husband trustingly
      handed her over.
At once, then, just as he was, weighed down by his
      quiver and lion skin
(he'd tossed his club and his bow across to the other
      bank),
he plunged in, crying, 'I've beaten one river, and this is
115   the second!'

Too proud to depend on the waters obligingly taking him
      over,
he didn't wait to explore where the current was most in his
      favour.
Soon he had swum to the bank and was lifting his bow off
      the ground
when he heard a scream. It came from his wife, and Nessus
      was starting
to breach his trust. 'Hey, where are you hurrying?' Hercules
      shouted.   120
'Don't think you can make it, you violent savage! Nessus,
      you monster,
I'm talking to you! Now listen and don't interfere with my
      bride.
If you feel no respect for *me*, at least your father Ixíon's
wheel* should warn you against the rape of another man's
      woman.
You shan't get away and had better not trust in those
      horse's hooves.   125
It's my shafts, not my feet, that will catch you up!' And he
      put his words
to the proof by shooting an arrow, which pierced the
      fugitive's back
right through to the chest, where the point with its
      venomous barb protruded.
As soon as the centaur extracted the weapon, his blood
      leapt out
in a double spurt, commingled with gore from the
      venomous Hydra.*   130
Nessus caught some of the mixture and whispered, 'You'll
      pay for my death!'
And then presented his blood-soaked tunic to Deïanira,
a gift which he told her could serve to excite the love of her
      husband.

THE DEATH OF HERCULES

A number of years went by, and the fame of Hercules'
    deeds
had spread through the world and imbued his
135   stepmother Juno with hatred.
Oechália conquered, he now was about to fulfil his
    vows
at Jupiter's temple on Cape Cenaéum, when chattering
    Rumour
hurried ahead and reached the ears of Deïanira,
Rumour whose joy it is to embroider the truth with
    falsehood
and grows by her lies to gigantic proportions from tiny
    beginnings:
'Amphítryon's son is burning with love for Princess
140   Íole!*'
Hercules' wife believed what she heard; the thought of
    a rival
filled her with dread. At first the poor woman indulged
    her distress
in a deluge of weeping; but later she asked herself,
    'What is the point?
These tears will only give Iole pleasure. What's more,
    she will shortly
be here. I must therefore make haste and think of a
145   plan while I may,
before my place in my husband's bed has been fully
    usurped.
Should I say how I feel, or be silent? Stay here, or
    return to Cálydon?
Leave my own house, or at least put up some show of
    resistance?
Perhaps I had best remember my brother, the brave
    Meleäger,
and strike out boldly. Why shouldn't I show how
150   deadly an injured

woman's resentment can be, by cutting this concubine's
    throat?'
She considered a number of different plans; but the one she
    preferred
was to send her husband the shirt which was stained with
    the blood of the centaur
Nessus, in hope of regaining Hercules' faltering love.
Unaware what sorrow the tunic would bring her, she gave
    it to Lichas,   155
a servant who knew as little as she did, with honeyed
    instructions
to offer this gift to her husband. Her husband in innocence
    took it,
and vested himself in the shirt which the Hydra's venom
    had poisoned.
  The fires had been lit, and now he was offering incense,
    uttering
prayers and pouring libations of wine on the marble altar.   160
The poisoned shirt was exposed to the heat, and its power
    was released
by the flames to creep on its cancerous way through
    Hercules' body.
So long as he could, he suppressed his groans like the hero
    he was.
But after endurance was conquered by pain, he pushed the
    whole altar
over and filled Mount Oeta's* forests with terrible cries.   165
He struggled at once to tear the lethal robe from his
    shoulders;
but where it yielded, it tore at his skin. Revolting to detail,
it either stuck to his limbs as he tried in vain to remove it,
or else it exposed the bleeding flesh and the massive bones.
Even his blood gave a hiss, like the sound of a plate of hot
    metal   170
plunged into icy water, and boiled in the fire of the poison.
The greedy flames relentlessly sucked deep into his vitals.
Black droplets of sweat exuded and trickled all over his
    body.

The charring tendons crackled and snapped. The
     invisible canker
melted the marrow inside his bones. Then he raised his
175   hands
to the stars and cried: 'Now feast on my ruin,
     Saturnian Juno!
Feast, cruel goddess! Look down from above on this
     scene of destruction
and glut the desires of your brutal heart! Or else, if my
     plight
cries out to be pitied even by you, my inveterate enemy,
racked as I am by harrowing torture, relieve me of life,
the life that I hate, the life that was destined for
180   nothing but labours.
Death will now be a boon and a worthy gift from my
     stepmother.
  'Was it for this* that I mastered Busíris who fouled
     his temples
with strangers' blood? That I stole from the violent
     giant Antaéus
the strength that his mother, the Earth, supplied? That
     three-bodied Géryon,
three-headed Cérberus failed to unnerve me? And was
185   it for this
that my hands were able to break the horns of the
     Cretan bull,
that I cleansed the Augéan stables and shot the
     Stymphálian birds,
that I caught the deer of Diana in Mount Parthénius'
     forests;
stole Hippólyta's golden belt by the river Thermódon,
and captured the apples so closely watched by the
190   sleepless dragon?
Was it for this that I conquered the centaurs, and
     overpowered
the boar which was wasting Arcádia's fields? That even
     the Hydra

gained nothing by growing two heads to replace each one
      she had lost?
Remember too that, as soon as I saw Diomédes' horses
fattened on human blood with their mangers cluttered
      with mangled   195
corpses, I slaughtered them all and destroyed their master
      beside them.
Mine are the hands which crushed the life from the lion of
      Neméa;
mine is the head which supported the sky.* Yes, Jove's cruel
      wife
must be weary of setting me tasks, while I am not weary of
      doing them.
   'Now I am faced with a new affliction, which cannot be
      conquered   200
by courage or all of the weapons I own. A devouring fire
is roaming the depths of my lungs and consuming the whole
      of my body.
Eurýstheus, though, is alive and well! Can anyone still
believe that the gods exist?' So speaking, Hercules
      stumbled
in agony over Mount Oeta's heights, like a wounded bull   205
with a hunting spear in its back when the frightened
      assailant has fled.
Imagine the hero, constantly groaning and constantly
      roaring,
constantly trying in vain to tear every stitch of his garments
away from his body, uprooting the tree-trunks or venting
      his anger
against the mountains or stretching his arms to his father's
      domain.   210
   There was Lichas, cowering down in the niche of a rock!
When Hercules saw him, he shouted with all the fury his
      torment
could muster, 'Lichas! Did *you* deliver this present of death?
Will *you* be my killer?' The servant was trembling and
      white with fear,

and said a few nervous words in excuse. But while he
215   was speaking
and on the point of throwing his arms round Hercules'
        knees,
the hero grabbed hold of him, whirled him round
        several times, and tossed him
into the sea of Euboéa with greater force than a
        catapult.
As Lichas fell through the air, his body started to
        harden.
They say that the rain when condensed by the icy
220   blasts of the wind
is turned into snow, and the soft light substance of
        swirling flakes
is later congealed and frozen hard into pellets of hail.
That is what happened to Lichas, according to ancient
        tradition:
when tossed through the void by those powerful arms,
        he was bloodless with terror
and drained of all moisture; so thus he was changed
225   into solid stone.
Even today, in the sea of Euboea, a low rock rises
out of the waves with an outline that hints at the form
        of a man.
Sailors are frightened to step on this rock, as though it
        could feel,
and the name they give it is 'Lichas'.
                             But what then
        happened to Hercules?
Felling some of the trees on the heights of Oeta, he
230   built them
into a pyre; and to set it alight he employed Philoctétes.
To him he entrusted his famous bow and the quiver
        containing
the arrows destined one day to revisit the kingdom of
        Troy.*
And while the flames were licking the sides of the
        funeral pyre,

Hercules covered the piled-up wood with the skin of the
    lion   235
of Nemea, then laid himself down on the pyre with his club
    for a pillow,
smiling as if he were gently reclining, a guest at a banquet,
crowned with a garland and quaffing the unmixed juice of
    the vineyard.

The flames were rising, spreading all round and crackling
    loudly,
licking away at the limbs of the hero, who calmly awaited   240
a foe he despised. The gods were afraid for the Earth's great
    champion;
but Jupiter, sensing their fear and beaming with pure
    satisfaction,
grandly addressed them: 'You gods, this anxiety of yours is
    a pleasure
to me. I offer myself wholehearted congratulations
that I should be called the father and king of a people that
    cares,   245
that a son of mine should be also supported by *your* good
    wishes.
This support is a tribute, I'm sure, to his own magnificent
    exploits,
but I am myself in your debt. Now truly, my faithful
    subjects,
you mustn't be needlessly frightened. Ignore those flames on
    Mount Oeta.
The hero who conquered all will conquer the fire you are
    watching.   250
Vulcan's power will only affect the part he derives
from his mother's side. The part he derives from me is
    eternal,
it cannot be touched by death and is fully resistant to fire.
This part, when its time on earth is complete, will be
    welcomed by me
to the realms of the sky, and I trust this action of mine will
    give pleasure   255

to *all* of the gods. But if any among you by chance is
        against
the admission of Hercules here as a god, he may grudge
        the reward,
but will know it was richly deserved and grant his
        reluctant approval.'
    The gods were all in agreement. Even his royal consort
appeared to be happy, except for her one black look of
260   annoyance
on Jupiter's final words, when he'd singled her out for
        a black mark.
Meanwhile, all that the flames could ravage had been
        disposed of
by Vulcan. Hercules' body no longer survived in a form
which others could recognize. Every feature he owed to
        his mother
had gone, and he only preserved the marks of his
265   father Jupiter.
Just as a snake which has shed old age with its
        sloughed-off skin
will frolic in youthful freshness, its new scales
        brilliantly glinting,
so when the hero of Tiryns discarded his mortal frame,
he gathered strength in his better endowment, he grew
        in stature,
and now was invested with majesty, weight and an
270   awesome authority.*
Jove, his almighty father, swept him up through the
        hollow
clouds in his four-horsed chariot, home to the
        glittering stars.

ALCMENA AND GALANTHIS

Atlas felt the additional weight.* But Eurystheus' anger
was far from exhausted. He savagely vented his hate for
        their father

on Hercules' children. The hero's aged mother, Alcmena,   275
who'd fretted so long, at least could weep on Iole's
        shoulder
and tell her about the labours her son had performed all
        over
the world, as well as her own misfortunes. On Hercules'
        orders,
Hyllus his son had taken the girl to his heart and his bed,
and she was expecting a child of his noble blood. Alcmena   280
then said to Iole: 'Now, let's hope that the gods will be
        kind
to *you* and shorten the length of your pain when your time
        arrives
and you call in your fear on Ilithýia, the goddess of
        childbirth.
That goddess, on Juno's prompting, was most unhelpful to
        me.
When my nine months' waiting was over and Hercules,
        great performer   285
of labours, was due to be born, my womb was stretched to
        its limit;
the child that I carried was huge – so huge you could easily
        tell
it was fathered by Jove. When I went into labour, the strain
        was too great
to endure for long. Even now, as I tell you, an icy shiver   290
runs down my spine and some of the pangs return with the
        memory.
Seven whole days and seven whole nights I was racked with
        torture,
exhausted by pain. I stretched my arms to the heavens and
        shrieked
as I praycd to Lucína* and all the Kneelers, the gods of
        confinement.
Lucina arrived, I can tell you, but Juno had bribed her
        beforehand   295
and she was willing to sacrifice me to the spite of the
        goddess.

As soon as she heard my groans, Lucina sat on the altar
in front of the doors, with her right knee crossed hard
        over her left
and her hands with interlocked fingers firmly pressing on
        top,
while she silently muttered her spells to inhibit the labour
300   I'd started.
I kept on pushing and pushing as, crazy with pain, I
        called down
futile curses on Jove for his failure to help me. I simply
wanted to die; my complaints would have softened the
        hardest of rocks.
As I moaned, the married women of Thebes who were
        there to support me
offered their vows to the gods for my safety and tried
305   to encourage me.
One of my servants, Galánthis, a fair-haired girl from a
        humble
home, who always performed her tasks with a will and
        whose loyal
support had endeared her to me, now realized that
        cruel Juno
was up to some mischief; and while this lass kept
        coming and going
310 in and out of the doors, she noticed Lucina enthroned
on the altar, clasping her knees with her arms and
        interlocked fingers.
"Whoever you are," she said, "do go and congratulate
        Mistress.
Alcmena of Argos is safely delivered; she's now a
        mother,
and all her prayers have been answered." At once the
        goddess of childbirth
leapt to her feet and unlocked her hands in a panic. My
315   bonds
were released and the baby arrived. They say that after
        she'd cheated

Lucina, Galanthis burst into laughter. At this she was
      savagely
grabbed by the goddess and dragged by her hair to the
      ground. As she struggled
to lift herself up, she was held till her arms were transformed
      into forefeet.
She stayed as busy as ever. Her back lost none of its
      human   320
colour, although she had now acquired the form of a
      weasel.
Because by her lying lips she'd assisted Alcmena in labour,
she breeds her young through her mouth* and haunts my
      house as she used to.'

DRYOPE

Alcmena sighed as she ended, distressed to remember the
      servant
who'd served her so well. Then her grandson's wife, fair
      Iole, spoke to her: 325
'Mother, you grieve for the change to Galanthis' form, but
      she never
was one of our family. Now let me tell you the curious fate
of my very own sister – although my tears of sorrow
      constrain me
and almost prevent my speaking. She was an only child
(as I had a different mother) and known as the loveliest
      girl   330
in Oechalia – Drýope. Long in the past she'd been raped by
      Apollo,
the god of Delos and Delphi. Although she wasn't a virgin,
Andraémon made her his wife and the match was
      considered a good one.
Picture a lake with sloping banks like the shore of the
      ocean,
ringed by a circle of myrtle trees. Here Dryope came,   335

unaware of her destined fate and hoping – this makes the
    story
even more dreadful – to gather some flowers for a wreath
    to the nymphs.
In her arms she was holding her special treasure, a baby
    boy,
not yet a year old, and feeding him milk from her soft,
    warm breast.
Not far from the watery pool was growing the plant of a
340   lotus,*
bedecked with blossom of Tyrian purple in promise of
    berries.
Dryope plucked a few flowers to show to her baby and
    give him
pleasure. I thought (as I was there too) that I'd do the
    same,
when I suddenly saw that blood was dripping down
    from the stems
of the flowers and the branches were all astir with a
345   tremulous shudder.
It is only now that the story is told, too late, by the
    peasants,
how Lotis the nymph, when fleeing Priápus' disgusting
    attentions,
altered her features, while keeping her name, to those
    of a lotus.
My sister, to whom this tale was unknown, was
    thoroughly startled;
she tried to step back and, after invoking the nymphs,
350   to depart.
But her feet were rooted fast to the ground. She
    struggled to get free,
but found she could only move from her waist, as a
    coating of pliant
bark crept up from below and gradually sheathed her
    loins.
She at once attempted to tear her hair in a ritual
    gesture;

but the hand that she raised was filled with the leaves which
      had grown on her head.   355
The baby Amphíssus (the name he'd received from his
      grandfather Eúrytus)
felt the teat on his mother's breast going hard and stiff,
and the milk wouldn't come when he sucked. I stood there,
      watching my sister's
desperate plight, but unable to help – though I did my best 360
to delay the growth of the trunk and branches by clasping
      her tight
in my arms and wishing, I own, that the bark would
      envelop me too.
   'Enter her husband Andraemon and poor old father
      Eurytus,
searching for Dryope. "Where is your sister?" they asked. I
      directed
their eyes to the lotus tree. Its wood was still warm and
      they fell   365
to their knees to kiss it and clung to the roots of their
      darling tree.
Already my dearest sister was nothing but tree, except
for her face. Her tears rained down on the leaves
      new-formed from her body,
and while her lips were there to allow her voice any outlet,
the words of her sad lament were wafted into the air: 370
'If the oaths of the cursed can ever be trusted, I swear by
      the gods
that I never deserved this wrong. How cruel to be punished
      for nothing!
My life has been guiltless. If that is not true, I pray I may
      wither
and lose every leaf that I have and be chopped by the axe
      for the bonfire.
Now take my tiny baby out of his mother's branches   375
to rest in the arms of a nurse. Please see that this place here,
      under
my tree, is where he enjoys his milk and comes for his
      playtime.

Then, when he's able to talk, please see that he greets his
    mother
and wistfully says, 'My mother is hiding inside this
    tree-trunk.'
And please make sure that he's frightened of pools, that
380   he never picks blossom,
and thinks any shrub that he sees is the precious abode
    of a goddess.
Farewell, my beloved husband, my father, and you,
    dear sister.
If I have any claim on your love, look after me
    carefully;
defend my leaves from the slashing billhook and
    nibbling sheep.
And since I am able no longer to lower my body
385   towards you,
reach up to me here, come close to my lips while they
    still can be touched;
and lift my darling baby again for a kiss from his
    mother.
Now I can say no more. The bark's soft growth is
    already
stealing over my milk-white neck and my head's
    disappearing
inside the top of the tree. You may keep your hands
390   from my eyes;
the coating of bark will cover and close them without
    your help."*
She breathed her last in her final words. Though
    Dryope's body
was changed, its warmth persisted for long in the
    fresh-grown branches.'

IOLAÜS AND CALLIRHOË'S SONS

This curious story was hardly ended, its teller still weeping;
Alcmena was tenderly wiping the tears from Iolc's cheeks   395
and weeping no less herself, when the sadness they felt was
        completely
dispelled by a strange arrival. For there in the lofty doorway
a young man stood, who was hardly more than a
        smooth-cheeked boy –
Ioláüs, with all his features restored to their youthful prime.
This gift had been granted by Hebe, the goddess of youth,
        in response   400
to her husband Hercules' prayers.* She had been on the
        point of swearing
she'd never accord such a boon to anyone else in the
        future,
when Themis prevented her, saying: 'Thebes is embroiled at
        this moment
in civil strife.* Bold Cápaneus cannot be beaten, except
by Jupiter's lightning. Two brothers will settle their quarrel
        by killing   405
each other. A prophet, still living, shall see his own ghost,
        as he's swallowed
up by the earth into Hades. His son,* in a crime that is also
a duty, shall dare to avenge his father by killing his
        mother.
Alcmaeon, shocked by his sin into madness and forced into
        exile,
will then be pursued by his mother's ghost and the
        dog-faced Furies,   410
until his new wife insists he obtain her the curse-ridden
        golden
necklace and Phégeus' sword has drained the blood of his
        kinsman.
So then Callírhoë, falling at mighty Jupiter's feet,
will ask him to add the years Iolaüs has lost to the age

of her infant sons, so that they can avenge the death of
415   their father.
Hebe's gift of the prime of life shall thus be advanced
through Jove's intervention, and children be turned
       into full-grown men.'

MILETUS

When Themis who knows the future had uttered this
       stream of prophetic
wisdom, the gods indulged in a series of noisy protests.
'Why can't a similar boon be granted to others?' they
420   grumbled.
Auróra complained that the years of her husband
       Tithónus were sadly
prolonged, while beautiful Céres bewailed her Iásion's
       white hairs.
Vulcan maintained that his son Erichthónius ought to
       be fully
rejuvenated, while Venus, with half an eye to the
       future,*
was ready to offer a deal for renewal of youth in
425   Anchíses.
Each of the gods had their favoured candidate. Rowdy
       dissension
grew amid all the competing claims, till Jupiter finally
opened his mouth. 'Have you any respect for *me*?' he
       thundered.
'Where will this end? Does anyone think they can
       really defy
the decrees of Fate? It was Fate that allowed Iolaüs'
430   return
to the years of his youth. It is only by Fate that
       Callirhoë's children
will shoot to their prime, not a matter for canvassing
       votes or for fighting.

You all are subject to Fate, and – if this makes your
      subjection
more easy to bear – so am I. If I had the power to change
      things,
I'd favour my own sons: Aéacus' back would not be so
      bent   435
in his years of decline; Rhadamánthus would cull the flower
      of perpetual
youth; and so would Minos,* who now is despised for the
      bitter
weight of his crabbed old age and has lost his kingly
      authority.'
   Jupiter's speech won over the gods; and none of them,
      seeing
Aeacus, Minos and old Rhadamanthus weak and
      exhausted,   440
felt justified in complaining. When Minos was still in his
      prime,
his very name was enough to strike terror in mighty
      nations;
but now enfeebled, he lived in fear of Deïone's son,
the proud Milétus, a sturdy young man whom Apollo had
      fathered.
Though Minos believed that the youth was plotting an
      insurrection,   445
he hadn't the face to drive him out of his house and home.
Miletus fled of his own accord, got hold of a fast-sailing
vessel and crossed the Aegean, until he landed in Asia
and built the walls of the famous town* named after its
      founder.
Here he encountered Cyáneë, child of the winding
      Maeánder,   450
wandering round the bends of her father's stream. The
      result
of their union was Byblis and Caunus, twins of astonishing
      beauty.

BYBLIS

Byblis' fate is a warning against prohibited love.
Byblis was seized by desire for Apollo's grandson, her
₄₅₅   brother;
she loved him not as she ought to have done, with a
        sister's affection.
At first she did not understand the growing passion
        inside her.
She saw nothing wrong in kissing him on the lips
        rather often,
or tenderly throwing her arms round Caunus' neck to
        caress it.
For long she deluded herself this feeling was perfectly
₄₆₀   natural;
but natural affection was slowly subverted. To visit her
        brother
she'd dress herself up and was over-keen to display her
        charms;
she was jealous of anyone else who was more attractive
        than she was.
The truth hadn't dawned on her yet, however. Her
        passion inspired
no prayers to the gods – but the fire was raging inside
₄₆₅   her heart.
No longer was Caunus her brother – she hated the
        name – but 'my master';*
she wished he'd address her as Byblis and not keep
        calling her 'sister'.
   Still, in her waking moments, she wouldn't allow
        incestuous
thoughts to invade her mind. But when she was
        peacefully resting,
a vision of love would appear. She even dreamed that
₄₇₀   her brother
and she were one flesh; although she was lying asleep,
        she blushed.

When she woke, she lay quiet for a while, as she tried to
      recapture the picture
she'd seen in her dream; then, torn by conflicting emotions,
      she cried out:
'How wretched I am! What on earth can it mean, this dream
      in the night?
No, no, it mustn't come true! – But why am I having these
      dreams?   475
He's beautiful! Even his worst detractors would have to say
      so.
I like him, and I could love him, if only he weren't my
      brother;
and he would be worthy to have me. But sadly, I am his
      sister. –
So long as I never attempt to commit such a sin in the
      daytime,
it doesn't matter how often it happens at night in my
      dreams.   480
No one can witness a dream, and dreams give a kind of
      mock pleasure.
O Venus, O Cupid, winged god who attends on your
      mother so tender,
what great joy you have brought me! How vivid the passion
      that thrilled
my body! What pure satisfaction I felt in the depths of my
      being!
The memory brings it back! But the pleasure was all too
      brief;   485
the night hurried past so quickly and grudged me the rest of
      my joy.
  'Oh Caunus, if I were permitted to change my name as
      your sister
and be your wife, how good a daughter I'd be to your
      father!
What's more, dear Caunus, how good a son you would be
      to mine!
If the gods would allow it, there's nothing we shouldn't be
      sharing in common,   490

except for our blood – though I'd wish you were nobler
     born than myself!
Well, beautiful youth, some woman or other will bear
     you a child,
while I who've been cruelly allotted the selfsame parents
     as you
am merely your sister, and all that we share is the bar
     that divides us.
So what is the meaning behind my dreams? But what's in
495   a dream!
Can it have any substance? – Yet even a dream can
     come true, perhaps.
May the gods forbid it! – But gods have certainly slept
     with their sisters.
Saturn was married to Ops, whose blood was the same
     as his own;
Ocean and Tethys are husband and wife, like Juno and
     Jove. –
But the gods have rules of their own. It is idle to
500   measure our human
codes and customs against the different conventions of
     heaven.
No, I must either expel this forbidden desire from my
     heart,
or else, if I cannot, I pray for death before I give way,
and so to be laid on my funeral pyre, where my brother
     can finally
505 kiss my lips. Yet kisses require two lovers' agreement:
I may be willing, but *he* will judge it a hideous crime.
   'But Aéolus' sons weren't frightened of going to bed
     with their sisters* –
but how do I know about them? And why do I quote
     this example?
Where am I rushing? Away, away, you incestuous
     longings!
Don't force me to love my brother, except as a sister
510   should! –

If Caunus himself, however, had fallen in love with me first,
if *he* were burning with passion, perhaps I could gladly
    surrender.
In that case, Byblis, if you would never reject his advances,
woo him yourself! Will I manage to speak and confess that I
    love him?
Yes, your love will compel you to do it! If shame makes you
    tongue-tied,   515
your hidden feelings can be revealed in a secret letter.'
   Thus she decided and thus she resolved her conflicting
    emotions.
Leaning up on her side and resting her arm on her elbow,
'Now I'll show him!' she said. 'I'll confess that I love him to
    madness. –
Heavens! Where am I drifting? The fire is consuming my
    heart!'   520
With trembling fingers she scratched the words she had
    formed in her mind,
her right hand guiding the pen and her left controlling the
    tablet.
She'd start and she'd stop; she'd write on the wax, then
    curse what she'd written;
inscribing and then deleting, emending, rejecting,
    approving;
alternately putting the tablets down and picking them up.   525
She just didn't know what she wanted. Whatever she
    thought she would do,
she at once was averse to. Her face was a mixture of shame
    and defiance.
She started her message, 'Your sister . . .', but quickly
    decided against it.
Smoothing it out, she scored the following words on the
    tablet:
'Your lover wishes you well; and unless you respond to her
    greeting,   530
she'll never be well in herself. She's ashamed, so ashamed to
    give you

her name; but if you would know my desire, I wish I
          could argue
my cause without disclosing my name till my prayers are
          answered,
my hopes are fulfilled, and you acknowledge and call me
          – your Byblis.
     'You might indeed have guessed for yourself how
535   wounded my heart is.
My pale, lean cheeks and my sad expression, the eyes
          that so often
are filled with tears, the sighs that I utter for no clear
          reason –
they all could have told you. Perhaps you remember
          my frequent embraces
and noticed the kisses I gave you were scarcely those of
          a sister.
But all I could do I did. Though grievously wounded
540   by love,
though the fire of passion was raging inside me, I tried
          so hard –
the gods will bear witness – I tried at last to come to
          my senses.
I fought so long, poor girl that I was, to escape from
          the deadly
arrows of Cupid. The pain I bore was greater than any
you'd think that a girl could endure. But now I'm
545   defeated and forced
to confess that I love you. In fear and trembling I beg
          you to help me.
You have the power to save or destroy the one who
          adores you.
Decide which choice you will make. This isn't the
          prayer of a foe,
but of one, though she couldn't be closer, who asks to
          be closer yet,
who asks to be bonded to you by chains which will
550   fully unite us.

Rules are for prudish old men. Leave *them* to explore what's
    permitted,
to define what's right and what's wrong, and observe nice
    legal distinctions.
Young people in love can afford to be flexible, even foolish.
We still don't know what acts are allowed. We take it that
    nothing
is barred, and in this we follow the heavenly gods' example. 555
We are not to be stopped by a stern old father, by solemn
regard for our name or by fear; if we have any reason to
    fear,
we can hide our dalliance under our cover as brother and
    sister.
There's nothing to stop my holding a conversation in
    private
with *you*. We already embrace and kiss each other in
    public.   560
What more do we need? Oh, pity the one who confesses
    her passion
and wouldn't confess it unless she were forced by a love so
    extreme.
Don't let your name be carved on my grave as the cause of
    my death!'
  The tablet was full when she'd traced these futile words
    in the wax,
so full indeed that the final line was scrawled in the
    margin.   565
At once she sealed the proof of her guilt with a precious
    stone,
which she dampened with tears as her tongue was too dry
    to provide any moisture.
Finally, blushing with shame, she called to one of her
    servants
and nervously flattered him, saying: 'My friend, I know I
    can trust you.
Please carry this letter to' – after a pause she added, 'my
    brother.'   570

Just as she gave him the tablets to take, they slipped from
    her hands
to the ground. Though the omen perturbed her, the letter
    was sent; and the servant
found a suitable time to deliver the secret inside it.

Young Caunus was simply appalled and had only read
    part of the message
before he suddenly flushed with anger and threw the
575   thing down.
Then scarcely refraining from striking the terrified
    servant's face,
he shouted, 'Get out while you can, you vile incestuous
    pander!
You'd pay with your life, if your murder wouldn't
    disgrace my name.'
The poor wretch took to his heels and reported this
580   savage reply
to his mistress. Byblis paled when she learned of her
    cruel rejection
and trembled in fear as an icy chill swept over her
    body.
But once her senses returned, her passion was kindled
    anew,
and soon the air was echoing round with her furious
    outburst:
585 'I've brought it upon myself! Oh, why was I such a fool
as to show how deeply I loved him? Why, when I
    ought to have hidden
my wicked desires, did I make such haste to commit
    them to writing?
I ought to have sounded his feelings out beforehand, by
    carefully
dropping mysterious hints. I ought to have taken note
of the wind by reefing my sails, and made sure it was
590   blowing behind me.
My voyage would then have been perfectly safe and
    have brought me home,

when now I have spread my canvas to winds that I left
    untested.
The storm is sweeping me on to the rocks! My ship has
    capsized!
I am sinking into the ocean depths and there's no way back!
  'What is more, clear omens warned me against indulging
    my love   595
at the time when I ordered my servant to take the letter. The
    tablets
were dashed to the ground and showed that my hopes
    would also be dashed.
I surely ought to have changed the day or the whole of my
    plan –
or rather merely the day. The god himself was at work;
his signs were only too plain, if I'd not been utterly crazy.   600
No, my mistake was to write that letter. I ought to have
    spoken
to Caunus in person, declared to his face how much I
    adored him.
He then would have seen my love in my tears and my
    pleading eyes.
I might have expressed much more than those wretched
    tablets had room for.
I might have thrown my arms round his neck as he backed
    away;   605
and if he had sent me packing, I might have pretended to be
at death's door and begged for my life on my knees, hands
    clasping his feet.
If any appeals could have softened his heart, they would
    have been tried;
and if each entreaty had failed, they might have succeeded
    together.
It may be the case that the servant I sent was in some way at
    fault.   610
He can't have approached him correctly or chosen a
    suitable moment;
he failed to wait for a time when Caunus was free to take
    notice.

'These errors have harmed me. But Caunus isn't the
      son of a tigress;

his heart isn't made of unyielding rock or intractable
      iron,

compounded of adamant; nor did he suck at a lioness'
615   teats.

He'll yield! I must woo him again. So long as I've
      breath in my body,

I'll keep on trying to bring my pursuit to a happy
      conclusion.

If what I have done could be cancelled, best not to have
      spoken to start with;

but failing that, I must go on fighting until I have won.

Supposing I now abandon the struggle, my Caunus will
620   never

be able to put my audacious attempt quite out of his
      mind.

He'll imagine, because I have given up, that I never was
      serious,

or else I was testing him out and doing my best to
      entrap him.

He'll certainly think me the victim of common desire,
      and not

of the god who is burning and breaking my heart with
625   the power of his full strength.

Finally, I have committed a wrong which I cannot
      undo.

I've written my letter and asked for his love; my
      intention's exposed.

If I venture no more, my reputation's already
      tarnished;

there's little to lose by further appeals, but much to be
      gained.'

Thus she reasoned; and such was the war in her
630   wavering heart

that she wanted and hated to make the approach. But
      reason lost out

in the end, and the poor girl suffered the pain of repeated
        rejections.
When Byblis' pursuit was ended, her Caunus fled from the
        country,
as well as from incest, and built a new city* on foreign
        soil.

It was then, they say, that Miletus' daughter was driven by
        sorrow   635
completely out of her mind. It was then that she tore her
        garments
away from her breast and pummelled her arms in her
        frenzied grief.
Her madness was now for the world to see, as she freely
        admitted
her criminal passion by leaving her native land and the
        family
home she detested, to follow after her fugitive brother.   640
Just as the Thracian maenads, aroused by the thyrsus of
        Bacchus,
return again to their third-year rites when the time comes
        round,
so Byblis was seen by the brides of Bubássus, raving and
        screaming
through all the breadth of their country. Her travels took
        her through Caria,
home of the warrior Léleges, thence into Lycia's pastures.   645
Soon she had passed by Cragus* and Límyre, crossed the
        waters
of Xanthus and come to the ridge of Chimaéra,* the
        monster with fire
in its belly, the breast and head of a lion and the tail of a
        serpent.
When Byblis emerged at the edge of the forest, too tired to
        pursue
any more, she at last collapsed on the hard earth, hair
        dishevelled,   650

and lay with her face pressed down on a pillow of fallen
          leaves.
The Carian nymphs* repeatedly tried to support her
          limbs
in their gentle arms and suggest how her lovesick heart
          could be cured.
But her ears were deaf to all consolation. She lay
655   unspeaking,
her nails digging into the grass as she watered the earth
          with her tears.
They say that the naiads supplied these tears with an
          underground stream
which could never dry up – the greatest tribute they
          could have accorded.
At once, like resin-drops dotting the bark of a new-cut
          pine,
660 or bitumen stickily oozing out of the oil-rich earth,
or ice which melts in the sun when the spring returns
          with the balmy
breath of the mild west wind; so Byblis, Apollo's
          grandchild,
melted away in her weeping and changed to a
          mountain spring,
which even today is known in the valley as Byblis'
          spring
and steadily trickles out by the foot of a dark-leaved
665   ilex.

IPHIS

The story of Byblis' miraculous change would perhaps
          have spread
through the hundred cities of Crete,* if the island had
          not been faced
with a recent surprise near home in the transformation
          of Iphis.

Long ages ago, in the region of Phaestos, not far from the
    kingdom
of Cnossos, there lived a little-known man with the name
    of Ligdus,   670
a free-born person though one of the people, with wealth
    no greater
than might be presumed from his humble birth, but
    thoroughly honest
and well respected by all. When his wife was expecting a
    baby
and coming close to the time of the birth, he gave her a
    warning:
'My prayers are two: they are first that your labour will
    prove as easy   675
as possible; second, I hope you will bear me a boy, or else
I'll be faced with a burden beyond my means. So if by
    chance
(pray god it won't happen!) your child is a girl – though I
    say it reluctantly,
asking forgiveness for such an unfatherly thought – you
    must kill her.'
After he'd spoken, the tears poured down the cheeks of
    them both,   680
the husband who'd given the order no less than the wife
    who'd received it.
Despite his command, Telethúsa persistently begged her
    husband
not to restrict her hopes to a boy, but her prayers were
    useless.
Ligdus' mind was firmly made up. At last, when the
    woman
could hardly endure the weight of the growing child in her
    body,   685
one night, in the depths of her sleep, she dreamed that Isis*
    (once Io,
Ínachus' daughter) was standing in front of her bed,
    attended

by all of her sacred train. The brow of the goddess was
    decked
with horns like a crescent moon, her garland of golden
    corn-spikes
and royal insignia. Close to her side were dog-headed
690   Anúbis,
divine Bubástis, Apis the bull with his dappled hide,
the child-god* asking for silence with finger pressed to
    his lips;
Osíris,* the search for whom is never abandoned; the
    timbrels
and snake from Egypt* whose neck is puffed with
    sleep-giving venom.
All these were so clear to the dreamer (she might have
695   been fully awake),
when the goddess addressed her thus: 'Telethusa, my
    faithful worshipper,
banish your heavy cares and defy your husband's
    instructions.
After your child is at last delivered, you mustn't be
    frightened
to rear whatever is born. Yes, I am the goddess of Help
and respond to appeals for my aid. You'll never
700   complain that your worship
of Isis was unrewarded.' So speaking, she passed from
    the chamber.
The Cretan woman then rose from her bed and, lifting
    her innocent
hands to the stars, she humbly prayed for her dream to
    come true.
    Telethusa went into labour. Her baby was quickly
    delivered
and entered the world – as a girl, though the truth was
705   withheld from her father.
The mother enjoined her people to take good care of
    her boy;
the pretence was accepted and only the nurse was let
    into the secret.

Ligdus fulfilled his vows to the gods and called the child
      Iphis,
his grandfather's name. This pleased Telethusa because it
      was common
to either sex and meant she could use it without deceit.   710
So the falsehood, inspired by her motherly instinct, went
      undetected.
The child was always dressed as a boy; and whether you'd
      think
of a girl or a boy, her form and features were lovely to
      look at.

Thirteen years had gone by when Iphis' father arranged
a marriage between his 'son' and a fair-haired girl called
      Iánthe.   715
This girl was the daughter of Cretan Teléstus and famed
      for her beautiful
looks – a dowry indeed – among the maidens of Phaestos.
Equal in age as well as in beauty, the two young children
received their earliest lessons in school from the selfsame
      teachers;
hence their falling in love with each other. Their innocent
      hearts   720
were aglow with a similar fire, but their expectations were
      different.
Ianthe looked forward with joy to the wedding night they'd
      agreed on
and thought that the lover she took for a man was her man
      to be;
but Iphis loved without hope of ever enjoying her loved
      one,
which made her passion the stronger – a girl in love with a
      girl!   725
Almost in tears, she sighed: 'Oh, what will become of me
      now?
I'm possessed by a love that no one has heard of, a new
      kind of passion,
a monstrous desire! If heaven had truly wanted to spare me,

it ought to have done so. If not, and the gods were out to
    destroy me,
they might at least have sent me some natural, normal
730   affliction.
Cows never burn with desire for cows, nor mares for
    mares;
ewes are attracted to rams and every stag has his hind;
the same with the mating of birds. Throughout the
    animal kingdom
the female is never smitten with passionate love for a
    female.
I wish I had never been born a woman, I wish I were
735   dead!
But Crete is the land of every perversion. Pasíphaë*
    lusted
after a bull – but her love was a male. My passion is
    wilder
than that, if the truth be told. Pasiphaë, though, could
    hope
for her lust to be satisfied. Daédalus built her the
    wooden cow*
and by this trick she enjoyed her bull. She at least had a
740   lover
to cheat into taking her. Even if all the skill in the
    world
could be mustered here, if Daedalus ever returned to
    Crete
on his waxen wings, what on earth could he do? Could
    he use his arts
to transform a girl like me to a boy? Could he change
    Ianthe?
    'Iphis, you must be brave, now, and take control of
745   your feelings.
Shake off this reckless and foolish passion! Remember
    what sex
you belong to, unless you can cheat yourself with your
    own deception.

Aim to achieve what is right and love as a woman is
    bound to.
Love cannot be born, it cannot be nourished without some
    hope;
but *your* situation is hopeless. You're not kept off from your
    lover's   750
embraces by guards, the watchful eye of a jealous spouse,
or a troublesome father; she doesn't herself reject your
    advances.
But still you can never come to possess her. Whatever may
    happen,
for all the efforts of gods or of men, you cannot be happy.
So far, to be sure, not one of my prayers has been refused;   755
the gods have been kind and have granted me all that they
    possibly could;
my wishes are backed by my father, Ianthe herself, and
    Ianthe's
father. It's Nature alone, more powerful than all, who
    opposes
the match and is out to destroy me. Look, the day that I
    long for,
my wedding-day, is approaching. Ianthe will soon be my
    wife,   760
but not be my own. Surrounded by water, we'll die of
    thirst.
O Juno, goddess of marriage, O Hymen! Why are you
    gracing
a wedding between two brides, where the groom has failed
    to appear?'
    With that, her complainings ceased. Ianthe's emotions
    were also
in violent turmoil. She prayed to Hymen to speed his
    arrival.   765
Her longing was matched by the fear which troubled the
    mother of Iphis,
who kept postponing the marriage and playing for time by
    pretending

illness or pleading omens and dreams. But soon her
        fictitious
excuses were all used up. The moment for lighting the
        torches
770   was almost upon them and only a day remained. So then
Telethusa removed the fillets encircling her own and
        her daughter's
heads, and with hair flowing free she clung to the altar
        of Isis:
'Goddess who haunts Paraetónium, Lake Mareótis and
        Pharos,
who dwells on the Nile which divides itself into seven
        branches.
Help us, we pray you,' she cried, 'and allay the fear in
775   our hearts.
It was you that I saw long ago in my dream, with your
        well-known emblems,
and recognized all – your attendant train and the
        jingling beat
of your tambourines. It was your commands that I
        stored in my memory,
yours the counsel and yours the gift which allowed my
        child
to survive and me to escape from my husband's anger.
780   Oh pity
us both and grant us your help!' Telethusa wept as she
        ended.
The altar of Isis stirred – apparently moved by the
        goddess.
The doors of the temple trembled, the moonlike horns
        of the statue
shimmered with light and the sound was heard of the
        rattling timbrel.
Still anxious, but heartened at least by such a
785   propitious omen,
the mother then left the temple; and Iphis followed
        behind her –

with longer strides than she normally took. Her girlish
    complexion
had lost its whiteness, her limbs grew stronger, and even her
    features
sharpened. Her bandless hair seemed cut to a shorter length.
She felt a new vigour* she'd never enjoyed as the female
    she'd been   790
till a moment before. That female was now transformed to
    a male!
Telethusa and Iphis, bring your gifts* to the temples in
    fearless,
confident joy! So the two of them brought their gifts to the
    temples,
and added a brief inscription, a plaque containing this one
    verse:
OFFERINGS IPHIS PLEDGED AS A GIRL AND PAID AS A
    BOY.
Dawn broke on the following day and the world was
    flooded with sunshine.   795
Venus, Juno and Hymen assembled close to the nuptial
torches, and Iphis the boy then won his beloved Ianthe.

BOOK 10

Iphis' happy wedding contrasts with the ill-omened nuptials of *Orpheus and Eurydice* (1–85). Ovid tells this famous story very much in his own playful way. He clearly wanted to do it differently from Virgil's beautiful treatment in *Georgics* 4, and his naughtier touches are at odds with the pathos of Orpheus' second loss of his wife on his return from the underworld. The last three lines, rather unexpectedly, introduce the theme of male homosexuality, which is developed later in the book.

Orpheus' power to draw trees behind him motivates the catalogue of trees (86–105) and so the story of *Cyparissus* (106–42), the favourite of Apollo, transformed to a cypress tree in grief for the pet stag which the boy has inadvertently killed with his spear. The rest of the book purports to be a song recital by Orpheus on the themes of boys (like Cyparissus) 'whom the gods have loved' and girls (like Byblis) 'inspired to a frenzy of lawless passion'. Some of the stories which follow, but not all, fit into this programme; and we quickly forget about Orpheus himself.

We are first very briefly told of the rape of the Trojan *Ganymede* (155–61) by Jupiter in the form of an eagle, but pass on more substantially to *Hyacinthus* (162–219), a boy from Sparta and another favourite of Apollo, who is killed by the god himself in an accident with a discus. The scene then changes to Cyprus, where Orpheus' themes are abandoned for the next two episodes. The *Cerastae and Propoetides* (220–43a) provide us with two short metamorphoses connected with Cyprus, the second because it suited Ovid to work in some reference to the renowned temple prostitutes. The theme also provides him with a good lead into *Pygmalion* (243b–97), one of the highspots of the whole poem, not to be spoilt for the reader in advance. Suffice it to note that the fate of the Propoetides, whose cold hard hearts turn them to granite, is beautifully reversed in the metamorphosis of the ivory statue into warm soft flesh.

Myrrha (298–502) is the centrepiece of Book 10 and returns us to the incest-motif established by Byblis in Book 9. This time the girl is passionately in love with her father and incest actually takes place. Ovid prefaces the tale with a melodramatic flourish of aversion; but he still persuades us to sympathize with his heroine in the long soliloquy in which she debates her predicament, torn between passion and self-disgust. We identify further with Myrrha in the dramatic scene with the Nurse (inspired, no doubt, by Euripides' *Hippolytus*) and in the atmospheric build-up to the fatal union. As with Byblis, metamorphosis brings a measure of comfort to the tragic conclusion.

The final item in Orpheus' recital is *Venus and Adonis* (503–59, 708–38), with the longer *Atalanta and Hippomenes* (560–707) rather artificially inset. Adonis is Myrrha's baby grown to manhood and followed around by Venus, whose change of life-style mirrors that of Apollo pursuing Hyacinthus earlier in the book and may lead us to anticipate a similarly disastrous conclusion. The story of the chaste Atalanta's race and of how Hippomenes beat her with the help of Venus is very excitingly told, though the aftermath hardly fits the setting. Atalanta has been warned by an oracle to 'avoid all knowledge of men'; but in letting Hippomenes take her she seems more a victim of circumstances than a wicked sinner like Myrrha.

ORPHEUS AND EURYDICE

Hymen, the god of the marriage feast, in his robes of
    saffron,
flew from Crete through the measureless sky to the land
    of the Thracian
Cícones. Órpheus was calling the god to his wedding,
    though all
to no purpose. The god attended, for sure; but the ritual
    words,
the joyful faces and omens of favour were sadly
5   missing.
Even the torch in his hand kept sputtering smoke,
    brought tears
to the eyes but never ignited, however strongly he
    waved it.
The outcome was even worse than foreshadowed: the
    newly-wed bride,
while taking a stroll through the grass with her band of
    attendant naiads,
suddenly fell down dead with the fangs of a snake in
10   her ankle.
When Orpheus, the Thracian bard, had indulged his
    grief to the full
in the air above, he felt he must also appeal to the
    shades,
and dared to descend to the river Styx through the
    Taénaran gateway.*
Making his way through the shadowy tribes and the
    ghosts of the buried,
he came to Prosérpina, throned beside the Lord of the
15   Shadows
who rules that dismal domain; and plucking the strings
    of his lyre,
he began: 'You powers divine of the subterranean
    kingdom,

where all of mortal creation must one day sink to our doom,
if you will give me permission to tell you the truth
        unvarnished
by shifty pretences, I've not come down to explore the
        murky   20
regions of Tártarus, nor to enchain the three-headed
        monster*
Medúsa bore, the dog whose coat is bristling with adders.
I'm here in search of my wife, cut off in the years of her
        youth
when a viper she trampled discharged its venom inside her
        ankle.
I'd hoped to be able to bear my loss and confess that I tried. 25
But Love was too strong. That god is well known in the
        world above,
and I wonder whether you know him here; I divine that you
        do.
If rumour has not invented the tale of that old abduction,*
you too are united by Love. In the name of these confines of
        fear,
in the name of this vast abyss and your realm of infinite
        silence,   30
I, Orpheus, implore you, unravel the web of my dear
        Eurýdice's
early passing. We all are destined for you. We may tarry
a little but, sooner or later, we speed to our one habitation.
This is the place that we all are bound for, our final
        dwelling,
and yours is the longest reign that the human race must
        endure.   35
Eurydice too, when her due of years has been ripely
        completed,
shall own your sway. Till then, I beg you to let me enjoy
        her.
If fate forbids you to show my wife any mercy, I'll never
return from Hades myself. You may joy in the deaths of us
        both.'

As Orpheus pleaded his cause, enhancing his words
40   with his music,
he moved the bloodless spirits to tears. For a moment*
          Tántalus
ceased to clutch at the fleeting pool, Ixíon's wheel
was spellbound, the vultures halted their pecking at
          Títyos' liver,
the Dánaids dropped their urns and Sísyphus sat on his
          boulder.
The Furies' hearts were assuaged by the song, and the
45   story goes
that they wept real tears for the very first time. The king
          and queen
of the world below forbore to refuse such a moving
          appeal,
and they summoned Eurydice. Leaving the rest of the
          ghosts who had newly
arrived, she slowly trailed along on her wounded
          ankle.
Orpheus was told he could lead her away, on one
50   condition:
to walk in front and never look back until he had left
the Vale of Avérnus, or else the concession would count
          for nothing.
In deadly silence the two of them followed the upward
          slope;
the track was steep, it was dark and shrouded in thick
          black mist.
Not far to go now; the exit to earth and the light was
55   ahead!
But Orpheus was frightened his love was falling behind;
          he was desperate
to see her. He turned, and at once she sank back into
          the dark.
She stretched out her arms to him, struggled to feel his
          hands on her own,
but all she was able to catch, poor soul, was the
          yielding air.

And now, as she died for the second time, she never
    complained   60
that her husband had failed her – what could she complain
    of, except that he'd loved her?
She only uttered her last 'farewell', so faintly he hardly
could hear it, and then she was swept once more to the land
    of the shadows.
   Robbed of his wife all over again, poor Orpheus was
    stunned
like the terrified person* who once caught sight of the
    three-headed hell-hound,   65
Cerberus, chained by the middle neck, and whose fear never
    left him
until his nature had changed and the stone crept over his
    body;
or poor Lethaéa,* transformed to stone for her pride in her
    beauty,
whose husband Ólenus took her offence on himself and
    hoped
to be changed in her place – two hearts that once were
    united in love   70
and now are separate rocks on the snowy heights of
    Mount Ida.
Orpheus wanted to cross the Styx for a second time,
but his pleas were in vain and the ferryman pushed him
    away from the bank.
So he sat there in rags for a week, without eating a morsel
    of food;
his anguish, his grief and his tears were all that kept him
    alive.   75
Cursing the gods of the dark for their cruel unkindness, he
    finally
took himself back to Rhódope's heights and to windswept
    Haemus.*
   Three years went by, with the sun god traversing watery
    Pisces*
to mark their ending. Orpheus now would have nothing
    to do

with the love of women, perhaps because of his fortune
80   in love,
or he may have plighted his troth for ever. But scores
       of women
were burning to sleep with the bard and suffered the
       pain of rejection.
Orpheus even started the practice among the Thracian
tribes of turning for love to immature males and of
       plucking
the flower of a boy's brief spring before he has come to
85   his manhood.

CYPARISSUS

Picture a hill and above the hill an expanse of plateau,
green with a carpet of grass, but totally lacking in
       shade.
Shade was provided when Orpheus, the heaven-born
       bard, sat down
and started to play on his lyre. Trees suddenly came on
       the scene:*
the oak of Dodóna,* a copse of poplars, the high-leaved
90   durmast,*
lindens, the beech and the virgin laurel; the brittle hazel,
the ash that is made into spears, the knot-free fir and
       the ilex
bending under the weight of its acorns; the genial plane
       tree,
the maple of many colours, the willow that weeps by
95   the river;
the waterside lotus, the evergreen box and the slender
       tamarisk;
myrtle with black and green berries and laurustinus*
       with blue.
Some of these trees were covered in creeping spirals of
       ivy;
100 vines came, either in tendrils or else supported on elms.

Then rowan, spruce and the arbutus laden with berries of
      red;
the flexible palm which serves for the victor's crown, and
      also
the pine with its long bare trunk and luxuriant top, the
      beloved
of Cýbele, mother of gods, since her favourite Attis*
      discarded
his masculine parts for this tree and hardened into its
      trunk.   105

Amongst this arboreal throng was, lastly, the cone-shaped
      cypress,
now a tree, but a boy in the past, and the darling of
      Phoebus
Apollo, the god who pulls on the bow-string and plays on
      the lyre-string.
This is the story. The boy Cyparíssus adored a stag
which was sacred to all the nymphs who haunt the
      Carthaéan plains,
a magnificent creature with spreading antlers that cast a
      shadow   110
above its head. The horns were brilliantly tipped in gold;
and over the shoulder, around the smooth round neck, they
      had hung
a collar studded with jewels. On its forehead there dangled
      a silver
amulet held by the lightest of thongs; while – no less
      fetchingly –   115
pendants of pearls gleamed down from its two ears next to
      the temples.
This fearless animal, utterly lacking in natural timidity,
visited people's houses, and even strangers were welcome
to stroke its neck. But the one who cherished it most of all
was young Cyparissus, the best-looking boy on the island
      of Ceos.   120
This lad would take the animal out to browse in new
      pastures

or drink from the clear, refreshing springs. He'd garland
    those antlers
with bright-coloured flowers, ride to and fro on its back
    like the proudest
125 horseman, and bridle the gentle muzzle with purple reins.
    Sweltering heat at noon in the month of Cancer the
    Crab,*
whose claws were aglow on the shore in the burning
    rays of the sun.
Resting his weary limbs on the grassy earth, the stag
was quietly enjoying the cool beneath the shade of a
    tree,
when a sharp spear pierced him, unthinkingly thrown
130   by the young Cyparissus.
Seeing the creature he loved was cruelly wounded and
    dying,
the boy was determined to die himself. Though Apollo
    consoled him
as far as he possibly could and implored him not to
    distress himself
overmuch, Cyparissus kept sobbing away and asked,
as a final gift from the gods, to mourn till the end of
135   time.
He wept and he wailed till his blood drained out and
    the whole of his body
started to turn the colour of green. The hair that was
    hanging
over his creamy forehead was changed to a shaggy
    profusion,
which stiffened and rose to the starry sky in a slender
140   point.
The god sighed deeply and sadly exclaimed: 'You'll be
    mourned by me,
you will mourn for others and always be there when
    they mourn for their loved ones.'*

ORPHEUS' SONG: INTRODUCTION

Such was the shady cluster of trees which Orpheus attracted,
sitting amidst a crowded assembly of birds and of beasts.
When he'd tested his strings with the touch of his thumb to
      his own satisfaction,   145
and judged that the notes at their different pitches were
      tuned to produce
harmonious chords, he burst into song in the following
      strain:
'Let Jove be the start* of my song, Callíope – Muse and my
      mother!
Jove holds sway over all. Jove's might I have often
      proclaimed
of old, when in weightier vein I sang of the Títans' defeat   150
and the crash of victorious thunderbolts over the plain of
      Phlegraéa.
Now there is call for a lighter note. Let my song be of boys
whom the gods have loved and of girls who have been
      inspired to a frenzy
of lawless passion and paid the price for their lustful
      desires.

ORPHEUS' SONG: GANYMEDE

'The king of the gods once fell in love with a Phrygian
      youth
                         155
whose name was Gánymede. Jupiter found a form he
      preferred
to his usual guise, the form of a bird – but no mere
      fledgeling
would do for him! It must be able to carry his lightning.
He quickly beat the air on the borrowed wings of his eagle
and thus abducted the Trojan, who still, to Juno's
      annoyance,   160
mixes Jupiter's nectar and serves the cup at his table.

ORPHEUS' SONG: HYACINTHUS

'Phoebus adored Hyacínthus, the son of Amýclas, and
        wanted
to raise him too to the skies; but sadly, fate intervened
too soon. In a way, however, the boy is immortal: when
        winter
is banished by spring and the Ram replaces the watery
165   Fish,
the hyacinth flower appears and blooms in the fresh
        green grass.
My father Apollo admired Hyacinthus above all
        others.
Forsaking his shrine at Delphi, the navel of earth, he
        haunted
the unwalled city of Sparta, close to the river Eurótas.
His arrows and lyre were abandoned; his normal
170   pursuits were forgotten.
He'd willingly carry his favourite's nets, hold on to his
        hounds,
or follow him over the rugged ridges of dangerous
        mountains.
His passion was fuelled by all the hours that they spent
        together.
One day, when the sun was about at its zenith, halfway
        between
the twilight of dawn and of dusk, the two of them
175   stripped off their clothes
and anointed their bodies with gleaming oil, to
        compete with each other
in throwing the discus. Apollo went first; he poised the
        plate
and launched it into the sky, where it severed the
        clouds in its path.
180 A long time later the disc descended to solid earth,
     revealing the skill no less than the physical strength of
        the thrower.

At once, unthinkingly,* carried away by his sporting zeal,
the Lacónian boy dashed forward to pick the plate up, but
        it landed
hard on the soil with tremendous force and then
        rebounded
straight in his beautiful face. The god went as deathly pale   185
as the lad himself and caught his arms as he fell to the
        ground.
To save the life of his friend, he desperately rubbed the
        body,
dabbed at the wound and applied his herbs; but all his
        medical
arts were in vain. His lover's injury couldn't be healed.
In a watered garden, if somebody breaks the stem of a
        violet,   190
poppy or lily with yellow stamens thick in its cup,
the flower will droop and suddenly lower its shrivelling
        head;
it can't stand up any more; it is gazing down on the earth:
so with the head of the dying youth. His disabled neck,
too weak to bear the weight it was carrying, sank to his
        shoulder.   195
   ' "Fading away, Hyacinthus! Cheated of youth's sweet
        bloom!"'
lamented Apollo. "I see your wound, and I see my guilt.
You are my sorrow and you are my shame. You died by my
        hand,
and so shall your epitaph say. I, I am the cause of your
        death.
Yet how can it be my fault, unless to have played a game   200
or have fondly loved can be called a fault? How I wish I
        could die
in your place or beside you! But since we are subject to
        destiny's laws,
you can only survive in my heart, be recalled in the words
        of my lips.
Your name will resound in the music I play, in the songs
        that I sing.   205

My sighs shall be imaged in you and scored in the marks
    on a new flower.*
Later, the time will come when Aias,* bravest of
    heroes,
shall link his fate to this flower and his name be read on
    your petals."
  'And while Apollo was speaking these words with
    prophetic lips,
the blood which had spilled from the wound to the
210   ground and darkened the green grass
suddenly ceased to be blood; and a flower brighter
    than Tyrian
purple rose from the earth and took the form of a
    lily –
except that its colour was deepest red,* where the lily
    is silver.
That wasn't enough for the god who had wrought this
    miraculous tribute:
the cries that had welled from his heart were engraved
215   on the flower, and AIAI,
those four letters of mourning and grief, could be read
    in the petals.
Sparta was not ashamed of her son Hyacinthus. His
    honour
endures to the present time; each year, by ancient
    tradition,
the people process in the solemn festival called
    Hyacinthia.

ORPHEUS' SONG: THE CERASTAE
AND PROPOETIDES

'But if you happened to ask the people of metal-rich
220   Amathus
whether they took any pride in the women they called
    Propoétides,

"No!" they would answer. They'd say the same of the men
    whose foreheads
were once disfigured by horns, and hence their name of
    Cerástae.
Before the doors of these people there stood an altar of
    Jupiter,
guardian of guests. If an innocent stranger observed this
    altar   225
covered in blood, he might have supposed that the sacrificed
    victims
were suckling calves or sheep which had grazed in the local
    meadows.
In fact, the victims were human guests. These horrible rites
affronted Venus, the mother of life and the goddess of
    Cyprus.
She thought of deserting her cities and island. But then she
    questioned: 230
"How have my cities offended? What's wrong with this
    beautiful island?
No, it's the fault of one impious family. *They* should be
    punished
by exile or death, or something between the two. What
    punishment
could this be – but metamorphósis?" And while she
    wondered
what new appearance to give them, she cast her eyes on
    their horns   235
and had an idea. "Good!" she said. "I can leave them
    those."
And so she reshaped their ogre-like frames into fierce young
    bulls.*
  'But the lewd Propoetides went as far as asserting that
    Venus
wasn't a goddess at all. Because of the deity's anger,
it's said that they were the first to offer their bodies and
    beauty   240
for sale.* Then after these harlots had lost all shame, and
    the blood

no longer ran to their cheeks but congealed as hard as
     their natures,
it didn't take much of a change to transform them to
     solid granite.

ORPHEUS' SONG: PYGMALION

'These women's scandalous way of life was observed by
     a sculptor,
Pygmálion. Sick of the vices with which the female sex
has been so richly endowed, he chose for a number of
245   years
to remain unmarried, without a partner to share his
     bed.
In the course of time he successfully carved an
     amazingly skilful
statue in ivory, white as snow, an image of perfect
feminine beauty – and fell in love with his own
     creation.
This heavenly woman appeared to be real; you'd surely
250   suppose her
alive and ready to move, if modesty didn't preclude it;*
art was concealed by art to a rare degree. Pygmalion's
marvelling soul was inflamed with desire for a
     semblance of body.
Again and again his hands moved over his work to
     explore it.
255 Flesh or ivory? No, it couldn't be ivory now!
He kissed it and thought it was kissing him too. He
     talked to it, held it,
imagined his fingers sinking into the limbs he was
     touching,
frightened of bruising those pure white arms as he
     gripped them tight.
He'd whisper sweet nothings or bring his idol the gifts
     which give pleasure

to girls, such as shells from the shore, smooth pebbles or
    tiny birds,   260
flowers of a thousand colours, lilies and painted balls,
or tears of amber dropped from the trees. He even dressed it
in clothes, put rings on the fingers and necklaces round the
    throat,
hung jewels from the ears and girdled the breasts with
    elegant bands.   265
All these looked well – though the naked body was equally
    lovely.
He laid this down on a couch, well strewn with covers of
    Tyrian
purple, and called it his darling mistress; then lifted the
    resting
head on the soft white pillows, as though it could relish
    their comfort.
   'Venus' festival now had arrived, and the whole of
    Cyprus   270
was making holiday. Heifers with gold on their spreading
    horns
had fallen, struck by the axe on their snow-white necks, and
    incense
was smoking. His offering laid, Pygmalion stood by the
    altar
and nervously asked: "You gods, all gifts are within your
    power.
Grant me to wed . . ." – not daring to say "my ivory
    maiden",   275
he used the words "a woman resembling my ivory maiden".
Golden Venus was present herself for her own celebration.
She understood what Pygmalion meant and she signalled
    her favour:
the fire on her altar, with shooting tongues, flared up three
    times.
As soon as the sculptor returned, he made for his loved
    one's statue,   280
and bending over the couch, he gave her a kiss. Was she
    warm?

He pressed his lips to hers once again; and then he
          started
to stroke her breasts. The ivory gradually lost its
          hardness,
softening, sinking, yielding beneath his sensitive fingers.
Imagine beeswax from Mount Hyméttus, softening
285   under
the rays of the sun; imagine it moulded by human
          thumbs
into hundreds of different shapes, each touch
          contributing value.
Astonished, in doubtful joy, afraid that he might be
          deluded,
Pygmalion fondled that longed-for body again and
          again.
Yes, she was living flesh! He could feel the throb of her
290   veins
as he gently stroked and explored. At last the hero of
          Paphos
opened his heart in a paean of thanks to Venus, and
          pressed
his lips to the lips of a woman. She felt his kisses, and
          blushed;
then timidly raised her eyes to the light and saw her
          lover
against the sky. The goddess graced the union she'd
295   granted;
and soon, when the horns of the moon had grown nine
          times to their fullness,
a daughter was born called Paphos, who gives her
          name to the island.

ORPHEUS' SONG: MYRRHA

'Paphos gave birth to a son called Cínyras. If he'd been
    childless,
Cinyras might have been counted among the most blessèd of
    men.
It's a shocking story. Daughters and fathers, I strongly
    advise you   300
to shut your ears! Or, if you cannot resist my poems,
at least you mustn't believe this story or take it for fact.
If you do believe it, then also believe that the crime was
    punished.
If nature, however, allows such a crime to be perpetrated,
I have to congratulate this domain* on her distance from
    countries   305
where horrors as foul as this have been witnessed. The land
    of Panchaéa
may boast of her fabulous riches in balsam, cinnamon,
    spices,
frankincense sweated from trees, and her various scented
    flora,
so long as she keeps her myrrh to herself. That new-formed
    tree
was a worthless addition. Cupid himself denies that his
    arrows   310
were Myrrha's downfall and clears his torches of such an
    indictment.
One of the three dread Furies applied a Stygian firebrand
or filled her with viper's venom. To hate one's father is
    wickedly
wrong; but incestuous love is even more wicked than
    hatred.   315
  'The maiden was courted on every side. From over the
    East
her suitors flocked to compete for her hand. Now, Myrrha,
    choose one,

choose one from them all for your husband, though *one*
    must not be among them!
The girl was fully aware of her guilty passion and battled
against it. She said to herself: "Oh, where are these foul
320   thoughts leading me?
What am I trying to do? I pray to you, gods, by the
    bonds
of family love and the sacred laws of parents and
    children,
avert this terrible evil; resist the crime in my heart –
if this is indeed a crime. I wonder, for daughterly duty
325 cannot condemn this love. All other creatures can mate
as they choose for themselves. It isn't considered a
    scandal for bulls
to mount the heifers they've sired or for stallions to
    serve their own fillies;
goats may cover the young that they've spawned, and
    even a bird
can conceive her chicks by a mate who happens to be
    her father.
How lucky they are to do as they please! How
    spitefully human
morality governs our lives! What nature freely allows
330 us,
the jealous law will refuse. And yet there are said to be
    countries
where mothers can sleep with their sons and daughters
    can sleep with their fathers,
and natural love is intensified by the double
    attachment.
How sad that it wasn't my lot to be born in one of
    those places!
I'm merely the victim of chance. – But why am I talking
335 like *this*?
Such thoughts are forbidden, I must dispel them! Of
    course it's my duty
to love him, but just as a father. – And so, if I weren't
    the daughter

of royal Cinyras, I should be able to share his bed.
But since he's already my own, he cannot be mine, and his
    very
closeness to me is my loss. I could hope for more as a
    stranger.   340
I'd willingly move away and abandon my homeland, if I
    could
escape from the taint of guilt. But my evil passion
    prevents me.
I need to be here to see his face, to touch him, to talk
    to him,
kiss his lips, if I'm not permitted to go any further. –
Further, undaughterly girl? Can you contemplate anything
    further?   345
Don't you see you're confusing all names and natural ties?
Will *you* play the role of your mother's supplanter and
    father's mistress?
Will *you* be known as your own son's sister and brother's
    mother?
Will you feel no fear of the Furies, those sisters with black
    snakes writhing
on top of their heads, who flourish their flaming brands in
    the eyes   350
and faces of guilty souls? No, Myrrha, so far your body
is free from the taint of sin. Do not sin in your mind; you
    must not
defile great Nature's unbreakable bonds with incestuous
    union.
Although you may wish it, it cannot be done. Your father is
    good
and knows what is right – how I wish that he felt a passion
    like mine!"   355
  'So Myrrha debated. But Cinyras, wondering how he
    should deal
with such an abundance of qualified suitors, went to his
    daughter,
ran over their names and asked her whom she would
    choose for her husband.

At first she said nothing and merely gazed on her father's
    face,
her eyes suffused with her warm salt tears in her mental
360   turmoil.
Interpreting these as a token of maidenly modesty,
    Cinyras
said, "Don't cry!" as he dried her cheeks and tenderly
    kissed her.
Ecstatic with joy at the kiss, the girl replied to his
    question
about the husband she wanted by saying, "A man like
    you."
Misunderstanding her meaning, her father warmly
365   commended her,
"Dutiful child! Be always as good!" That mention of
    duty
awakened her guilty conscience and caused her to
    lower her eyes.
   'It was deep midnight, when bodies and anxious
    minds are at rest.
But Cinyras' daughter was lying awake, tormented by
    passion
she couldn't control and the frantic longings that
370   constantly haunted her.
Desperate now, then ready to dare, her shame in
    conflict
with wild desire, she could form no plan; and like an
    enormous
tree which is almost felled and awaiting the final
    stroke
of the axe (none knows which way it will fall, fear
    reigns all round it),
so Myrrha, assaulted and shaken by warring emotions,
375   swayed
uncertainly this way and that, inclining in either
    direction,
unable to see any end or relief from her passion but
    death.

Death seemed to her best. She rose from her bed, determined
　　　to strangle
herself in a halter and tied her girdle around a crossbeam.
Then crying, "Farewell, dear Cinyras, now you can
　　　understand   380
why your daughter died!" she attached the noose to her
　　　pale white neck.

'The story continues that Myrrha's words were confusedly
　　　caught
by the loyal old nurse who still kept watch on her charge's
　　　threshold.
The woman got up, flung open the doors, caught sight of
　　　the girdle,
and screamed the moment she realized what Myrrha
　　　intended to do.   385
Then beating her breast and tearing her garments, she
　　　snatched the noose
from the suicide's neck and tore it apart. At last there was
　　　time
to burst into tears, to clasp the girl in her arms and to ask
　　　her,
"What does this halter mean?" But Myrrha said nothing
　　　and stood there
still as a statue, her eyes turned down to the ground in
　　　shame,
angry at being forestalled in her vain suicidal attempt.   390
The old woman insisted; unveiling her white hair, baring
　　　her flaccid
breasts, she implored the girl, by her crib and the milk she
　　　had sucked
as a baby, to share whatever was causing her pain. But
　　　Myrrha
turned away with a sigh. The nurse was firmly determined
to know the answer and promised her more than a
　　　trustworthy ear.   395
"Tell me," she said, "let me help you. I've still some energy
　　　left.

If it's passion, I know a woman who'll cure you by spells
        and herbs;
if you're under a curse, we can purify you with magical
        rites;
if the gods are angry, a sacrifice will appease their anger.
What else can I think is the trouble? Your family
400   fortunes, at least,
are safely assured for the future. You still have your
        mother and father."
That last word, "father", provoked the girl to a deep,
        deep sigh;
but the nurse still hadn't the slightest inkling that
        Myrrha was fighting
unnatural desire, though she did suspect that she might
        be in love.
She refused to give up and implored the poor girl to
405   confide her secret,
whatever it might be. Drawing her close to her aged
        bosom
and hugging her tight as she sobbed away in those frail
        old arms,
"I know what's the matter," she said, "you're in love.
        Your busy old Nursie
will help you once more, my darling. Don't worry, I
        shan't breathe a word
to your father." Myrrha broke free from her nurse's
410   embrace in a fury,
buried her face in her pillows and shouted, "Just leave
        me alone
and spare my feelings of shame!" When the nurse
        persisted, she pleaded,
"Please leave me, or else stop asking me why I'm
        unhappy. The trouble
you're trying so keenly to probe is a crime!" The old
        nurse shuddered;
her hands were trembling as much with fear as with
        age, as she stretched out

her arms like a beggar and threw herself down at her
      darling's feet.   415
First she wheedled, then tried to scare her. "Come out with
      the truth,"
she said, "or I'll tell your father you tried to strangle
      yourself.
If you'll only admit to your love, I faithfully promise to help
      you."
Myrrha lifted her head and pressed her cheek, all streaming
with tears, to her nurse's breast. She tried several times to
      confess,   420
but couldn't come out with the words. In her shame she
      covered her eyes
with her dress and exclaimed, "Oh mother, how lucky you
      are in your husband!"
Nothing but that, then a sigh. The nurse's body went cold;
a shudder ran through her bones as she tumbled at last to
      the truth;
and stiffly, roughly, her white hairs rose up over her scalp.   425
"Banish this hideous love, if you can!" she protested, and
      said
much more in the same vein. Myrrha knew the advice was
      right,
but remained determined to die, if she couldn't obtain what
      she wanted.
"All right," said the nurse, "you must live and shall have
      your . . ." – she stopped as she couldn't
say "father", although she called on the gods to witness her
      promise.   430

'Just then the married women were holding the annual rites
of dutiful Ceres, when dressed in garments as white as snow
they dedicate wreaths of golden corn, first-fruits of the
      harvest.
For nine nights, also, all acts of love and sexual contact
with men are counted taboo. King Cinyras' wife,
      Cenchréïs,   435

was one of the throng of women engaged in these holy
        mysteries.
So when the king was deprived for a time of his rightful
        partner,
that busybody, the nurse, got hold of him when he'd
        been drinking,
and told him about a beautiful girl who truly adored
        him,
though lying about her name. When asked the age of the
440   girl,
"The same as Myrrha's," she answered, and then was
        ordered to fetch her.
As soon as she came back home, she announced, "My
        darling child,
you can now be happy, we've won!" Poor Myrrha's
        delight was not wholly
unmingled; her mind was too much troubled by
        gloomy forebodings.
But still she could feel some joy; her emotions were all
445   in confusion.
    'Midnight, the hour when silence reigns and Boötes
        the Ploughman
has tilted the shaft of the Wagon between the Bears at
        their zenith.
Myrrha set out on her guilty mission. The golden
        moon*
had fled from the sky, the stars were hiding and
        shrouded in black clouds.
Night was missing her fires: first, Ícarus covered his
450   face,
then his daughter Erígone,* sanctified for her filial
        piety.
Three evil-omened stumbles warned the girl back,
        three hoots
of the deathly screech-owl chanting its sinister,
        mournful music.
She still went forward (the darkness of black night
        tempered her shame),

holding on to the nurse with her left hand, groping her way 455
through the gloom with her right. And now she stood on
    the chamber threshold;
now she opened the door and was led inside. Her knees
were trembling and giving way, the blood had gone from
    her cheeks
and all her courage had failed. The closer she came to her
    criminal
goal, the more she shivered, the more she regretted her
    boldness,   460
the more she wished she could turn and run before she was
    recognized.
While she faltered, the crone took hold of her hand and
    conducted her
up to the king's high bed; then letting her go with the
    words,
"Cinyras, take her, she's yours," she united their two
    doomed bodies.
The father welcomed his flesh and blood to that bed of
    uncleanness,   465
gently calming her virginal fears with words of assurance.
Perhaps, because of her age, he even called her "my
    daughter"
and she said "father", to put the finishing touch to their
    incest.
  'Filled with her father's unhallowed seed, she withdrew
    from the chamber,
bearing the fruit of her monstrous crime in her impious
    womb.   470
The act was repeated the following night and other nights
    after.
Finally Cinyras, eager to know the mistress he'd taken
so many times in his arms, came in with a torch, which
    allowed him
to see his daughter and what he had done. Speechless with
    rage,
he reached for his gleaming sword in the scabbard that
    hung close by him.   475

Myrrha took to her heels. The shadows of night and the
    darkness
mercifully saved her from death. Then roaming over the
    country,
she left Arabia, land of palms, and the fields of Panchaea.
Thence she wandered for nine long months, until she
    eventually
480 rested in Saba,* exhausted and scarcely able to carry
the weight in her womb. Unsure what to pray for,
    divided between
her terror of death and disgust for life, she united her
    thoughts
in the following plea: "You heavenly powers, if any
    there be,
whose ears are open to those who confess their vile
    wrong-doings,
I cannot deny that I richly deserve to be cruelly
    punished,
but hate to pollute the living by staying on earth, or the
485   dead
by passing below. Debar me, I pray you, from either
    kingdom.
Refuse me life and refuse me death by changing my
    form."
  'There *is* a power that responds to confession. At
    least, her final
prayer found gods of its own to fulfil it. While she was
    speaking,
the earth closed over her feet, and roots spread out to
490   the sides
through the broken nails of her toes, to provide the
    base of a slender
trunk. Her bones became wood, and the marrow inside
    them survived
as her blood was turned into sap. Her arms were
    converted to branches,
her fingers to twigs, and her skin was hardened to form
    new bark.

By now the developing tree had encompassed her pregnant
      belly,   495
had sheathed her breasts and was on the point of hiding her
      neck.
But Myrrha could wait no longer and moved to meet the
      advancing
growth by sinking down and plunging her head in the
      bark.
Although the emotions she once had felt were lost with her
      body,
she still continues to weep and her warm tears drip from
      the new tree.   500
Even tears can have honour. The resin distilled from the
      bark
is given the name and fame of myrrh in lasting
      remembrance.

ORPHEUS' SONG:
VENUS AND ADONIS (1)

'The baby, however, so wrongly conceived, had grown in
      the tree-trunk
and now was trying to find a way of leaving its mother
and issuing forth. Inside its prison the pregnant belly   505
swelled and stretched with its load. No cries attended the
      birth-pangs;
no voice was left to invoke Lucína in time of travail.
But still the tree resembled a woman in labour; bent double,
it groaned again and again and was drenched in a
      downpour of tears.
Gentle Lucina then took her place by the pain-wracked
      branches   510
and, laying her hands on them, chanted the spells that
      assist delivery.
Cracks appeared on the tree; the bark split open, and out
came a living baby, a wailing boy, whom the naiads at once

laid down on the soft green grass and anointed with
    myrrh from his mother.
A beautiful child! Even Envy would say so. He looked
515   exactly
like one of the naked cupids you see in a picture,
    provided
you gave him a quiver or took theirs out to remove any
    difference.

'Time glides stealthily past in its fleeting passage,
    unnoticed;
nothing has greater speed than the years. The child,
520   who was born
of his sister and sired by his grandfather, not long since
    had been hidden
inside a tree and had just emerged as a beautiful baby.
He soon was a youth, then a man, and now more
    handsome than ever,
enough to attract even Venus and so to avenge the
    passionate
love which had ruined Myrrha. What happened was
    this. While Cupid,
wearing his quiver over his shoulder, was giving his
525   mother
a kiss, he unwittingly grazed her breast with the tip of
    an arrow.
The wounded goddess thrust him away; but the scratch
    went deeper
than showed on the surface and Venus herself didn't
    feel it to start with.
Later, entranced by our young man's beauty, she cared
    no more
for her usual haunts: the shore of Cythéra or sea-girt
530   Paphos,
Cnidos, teeming with fish, and Amathus, wealthy in
    metals.
She even absented herself from the sky for the love of
    Adónis.

Him she clung to and constantly shadowed. The goddess
        who always
liked to pamper herself in the shade and who took great
        pains
to enhance her beauty, was roaming the mountain ridges
        and forests,   535
jumping the brambly rocks, with her dress drawn up to her
        knees
like Diana's, hallooing the hounds and chasing more
        harmless quarry:
the quick-footed hare, tall-antlered stag and the gentle deer.
But she kept her distance from fearless boars and avoided
        the ravening   540
wolf, the sharp-clawed bear and the lion that slaughters the
        cattle.
She counselled Adonis too – if counsel can make any
        difference –
to steer very clear of the wilder game: "Be brave when your
        quarry
is timid," she said. "It's dangerous to counter boldness with
        boldness.
Take no risks, dear lover, at my expense, or allow   545
yourself to provoke what is well provided with weapons
        by nature.
I would not wish your glory to cost me dear. Your youth,
your beauty and all that Venus adores will never
        discourage
the lions, the bristly boars or beasts with threatening eyes.
Boars carry the power of the lightning flash in their
        sharp-hooked tusks,   550
and tawny lions are hugely aggressive and angry creatures;
I hate and detest the whole breed!" When Adonis asked her
        the cause
of her hatred, she answered: "I'll tell you how I was deeply
        insulted
long years ago; the strange conclusion will surely amaze
        you.
But all this unwonted hunting has tired me out. Now look,

how convenient! Here's a delightful poplar to give us
555   some shade,
with a couch of grass underneath. I'd like to rest with
          you here . . ."
and she lay on the ground to recline on the grass and
          recline on Adonis,
pressing her burning cheek to the naked breast of her
          lover;
then, interspersing her words with kisses, she started
          her story:

VENUS' STORY:
ATALANTA AND HIPPOMENES

' "Perhaps you have heard of a girl who outstripped the
560   fastest of men
in running. The rumour isn't a fiction; she really could
          beat them.
Moreover, you couldn't have said if her speed of foot
          or her beauty
was more prodigious. One day, when she went to
          consult the god
regarding a husband, the oracle answered: 'No need of
          a husband
for you, Atalánta.* Avoid all knowledge of men if you
565   can.
But you shall not escape. You will lose yourself,
          without losing your life.'
Alarmed by the oracle's warning, she lived in the
          depths of the forest
unmarried, and fiercely repulsed the pressing throng of
          her suitors
by setting them terms. 'I cannot be won,' she
          explained, 'unless
I am first defeated in running. Compete with me in a
570   foot-race.

The winner's reward shall be my hand and body in
      marriage;
the loser's forfeit is death. These must be the rules of our
      contest.'
Young Atalanta was ruthless; but such was the power of her
      beauty
that all her impetuous suitors accepted her terms and
      competed.
One of the crowd who came to watch this unequal race   575
was a youth, Hippómenes. While he was taking his seat, he
      was thinking,
'How could anyone take such a risk in pursuit of a wife?'
And thus he dismissed the extravagant passion of all the
      contenders.
But once he had seen Atalanta's face and her unclothed
      body –
as lovely as mine or as yours, Adonis, if you were a
      woman –
he gasped in wonder and, raising his arms, said, 'Kindly
      forgive me,   580
all whom I blamed just now. The worth of the prize you
      were seeking
had not yet entered my mind.' His heart caught fire as he
      praised her.
In hoping that none of the others should win, his jealousy
      made him
afraid that they might. Then he asked, 'Why shouldn't I try
      my luck   585
in the contest? Fortune favours the brave!' As Hippomenes
      carcfully
weighed his chances, the girl passed by on her flying feet.
To the youth from Boeótia she seemed to be running as fast
      as an arrow
fired from a Scythian archer's bow, but her beauty
      astonished
Hippomenes even more; indeed her running enhanced it.   590
He saw the bright-coloured ribbons attached to her knees
      and her ankles

fluttering gaily behind her, while over her ivory shoulders
her hair streamed back in the wind. The white of her
          girlish skin
595 was all suffused with a rosy glow, as a marble hall
will be steeped by the sun in counterfeit shade through
          a purple awning.
As Hippomenes watched her, the final lap was run to
          the finish,
and soon Atalanta was crowned with the laurel wreath
          of the victor.
The losers groaned in despair and paid their forfeit as
          promised.
   ' "Undeterred by the suitors' fate, Hippomenes
600   boldly
marched to the front with his eyes firm-set on the
          young girl's face.
'Why cultivate easy glory,' he said, 'by trouncing these
          laggards?
You'd better compete with me. If fortune allows me
          the victory,
you'll not be angry at losing to such a hero as I am:
my father is Mégareus, king of Onchéstus, and his
605   grandfather
was Neptune; so I am the great-grandson of the Lord
          of the Seas.
Moreover, my birth is matched by my courage; and if I
          am beaten,
what glory, great and abiding, must come from
          defeating Hippomenes!'
While he was making this speech, Atalanta observed
          him with tender
looks, uncertain whether she'd rather be winner or
610   loser.
'Who is the god,' she reflected, 'who hates all beauty
          and wants
to destroy this man, by bidding him venture his own
          dear life

in order to gain my hand? I cannot be worth such a price.
It isn't his beauty that moves me – though that could also
    affect me;
he's only a boy! I am touched much more by his age than
    himself.   615
And yet he's a man of courage, undaunted by fear of death.
He's descended from Neptune, the god of the sea, in the
    fourth generation.
What's more, he loves me and longs so much to make me
    his wife
that he's ready to die if an unkind fortune refuses me to
    him.
Go while you may, fair stranger. My bed is polluted by
    bloodshed;   620
marriage to me is a cruel goal. No other woman
will spurn your suit and a sensible girl would be eager to
    win you. –
Yet why should I worry for *him*, when I've killed so many
    already?
It's his decision. Why shouldn't he die, since he isn't
    deterred
by the deaths of so many rivals and seems to be weary of
    living? –   625
So must he die because he wanted to live at my side?
Must he pay the price for his love in a death he doesn't
    deserve?
The violent hatred my victory will cost me could never be
    borne! –
But who will be guilty? Not I! – If only you'd give me up!
Or else, if you must be so crazy, if only you'd win the race! 630
How lovely he is with his boyish face, as fresh as a girl's!
Poor Hippomenes, no! I wish you had never seen me.
You truly deserved to live. If I had been blessed with a
    happier
lot and a churlish fate had not denied me a husband,
you were the one with whom I should gladly have shared
    my bed.'   635

She spoke like a girl who has never fallen in love before,
not knowing what she is doing, not understanding her
          feelings.
   ' "Atalanta's father and all the people were now
          demanding
the usual race, when Neptune's scion, Hippomenes,
          anxiously
640   called upon me: 'O Venus, I humbly pray, watch over
this daring attempt of mine and foster the love you
          have kindled!'
This touching prayer was wafted to me on a kindly
          breeze.
My heart was moved, I admit, and I didn't delay my
          assistance.
In Cyprus one of the richest parts of the land is
          Támasus
645   (so the inhabitants call it); the council in olden times
once consecrated the region to me as a special gift
to enrich my temples. Right in its centre there gleams a
          tree
with foliage of yellow and branches rustling with
          yellow gold.
I chanced to be coming from there with three gold
          apples I'd plucked
650   in my hand. I then went up to Hippomenes – nobody else
could see me – and gave him instructions on how he
          should use the apples.
The trumpets sounded the signal and both competitors
          sprang
like a flash from the starting line, heads forward, at full
          speed grazing
the top of the sandy track. You'd think they could
          skim the ocean
dry-footed or brush the standing ears in a white
655   cornfield.
The young man's spirits were lifted by all the cries of
          support

which rang in his ears: 'Get a move on! Go for it, go for it
        now!
Faster, Hippomenes, faster! Now give it all you have got!
Don't dawdle, you're winning!' I couldn't be sure whether
        Megareus' son
or Schoéneus' daughter was more delighted by all this
        shouting.   660
Again and again Atalanta held back when she could have
        gone forward,
and after a long gaze into his eyes would reluctantly pass
        him.
Hippomenes' mouth was dry with exhaustion, he panted
        for breath,
and the finishing post was still in the distance. That was the
        moment.
He dropped the first of the three gold apples I'd plucked
        from the tree.   665
The girl was dazzled. Possessed by a wish for the gleaming
        fruit,
she swerved from the track to pick up the rolling golden
        temptation.
Hippomenes hurtled past and the stands resounded with
        cheers.
Atalanta soon made up for the time she had lost as she
        gathered
speed and advanced, till she'd left the youth behind her
        again.   670
Hippomenes threw her the second apple; she stopped, then
        followed
and overtook him once more. The end of the course was in
        sight.
'O goddess who showed me the way,' said Hippomenes, 'be
        with me now!'
Then out to the edge of the course, to slow Atalanta's
        return,
he tossed the glittering gold with all the power of his
        youthful   675

strength. Would she stop? Atalanta appeared to waver. I
         forced her
to fetch it, then made the apple more heavy, and so she
         was hindered
as much by the extra weight as the further delay that it
         cost.
My story must not outlast the time of the race itself.
Atalanta was beaten; the victor took his reward by the
680   hand.

' "Surely, Adonis, I should have been thanked for my
         help and honoured
with incense. Hippomenes never remembered and
         failed to offer
incense or thanks. My goodwill suddenly turned to
         anger.
Smarting under this insult, I wasn't prepared to
         allow it
to happen again and I roused myself to make an
685   example
of both. They were passing near to a temple, deep in
         the forest,
which once the hero Echíon, fulfilling a vow, had built
to Cýbele, mother of gods. Their journey had made
         them tired
and they needed to rest for a while. It was here that,
         excited by me,
Hippomenes felt an untimely urge to make love to his
690   wife.
Quite close to the temple they managed to find a
         cavernous shelter,
dimly lit and covered above with natural limestone.
The place was hallowed by ancient worship and filled
         with the numerous
wooden statues of primitive gods that the priests had
         left there.
Hippomenes ventured inside and profaned the shrine
695   with his lust.

The statues averted their eyes and tower-crowned* Cybele
    pondered
whether to plunge the guilty lovers beneath the Styx.
But the punishment seemed too light.* So their smooth
    white necks were thickly
covered in tawny manes, their fingers were bent into claws,
their shoulders became forequarters, their weight was
    centred inside   700
their massive chests and they swept the top of the sand
    with their tails.
Their faces were mirrors of anger, their conversation was
    growls.
Their marriage-bed was the forest floor. They were lions,
    and frightened
all but the Mighty Mother who tamed them to draw her
    chariot.
Dearest Adonis, avoid the lions,* avoid all kinds   705
of creatures that won't turn tail but bare their teeth for a
    fight.
Avoid them, I beg you. Don't let your courage destroy us
    both!"

ORPHEUS' SONG: VENUS AND ADONIS (2)

'So Venus warned and travelled away through the sky in her
    swan-drawn
chariot. Warnings, however, are never heeded by courage.
It chanced that Adonis' hounds had followed a well-marked
    trail   710
and roused a boar from its lair. As it tried to escape from
    the woodland,
Cinyras' youthful grandson pierced its flank with his
    weapon.
The creature at once dislodged the bloodstained point of the
    spear
with the crook of his snout. As Adonis backed for safety in
    panic,

the animal savagely charged and buried its tusks* deep
715   into
his groin, so bringing him down on the gold sand,
      fatally wounded.
  'Venus was driving across the sky in her light-built
      chariot,
borne on the wings of her swans, and still on her
      journey to Cyprus,
when far in the distance she heard the groans of her
      dying lover.
She pulled at the reins of her white-plumed birds till
720   she faced his direction;
from high in the ether she saw him dead, in a pool of
      his own blood.
Leaping down to the earth, she tore her dress from her
      bosom,
she tore her hair and violently, bitterly, beat on her
      breast.
  'Reviling the Fates for their harshness, "You shan't
      hold absolute sway!"
she cried. "My grief, Adonis, shall have an enduring
725   memorial.
Every year your untimely death shall be re-enacted,*
and so the tale of my sad lamentation shall last for
      ever.
For now, your blood shall be changed to a flower.
      Proserpina* once
was allowed to change a beloved nymph into fragrant
      mint.
Shall I be grudged the transformation of Cinyras'
730   grandson?"
So speaking, she sprinkled the blood of Adonis with
      scented nectar.
Touched by the droplets, the blood swelled up, like
      gleaming, transparent
bubbles rising in yellow mud. No more than a single
hour had passed when a deep red flower rose out of the
      blood,

like the flower of that fruit which hides its seeds in its
     leathery rind,
the pomegranate fruit.* But this new flower has only a
     short life:
flimsy and loose on its stem, it is easily shaken and blown
away by the winds which give it the name of anemone –
     wind-flower.'*

BOOK 11

In *The Death of Orpheus* (1–66) we return to the famous minstrel. The description, in the style of a messenger-speech in Greek tragedy, of his violent death at the hands of the maenads must remind us of the death of Pentheus in 3.708–31. Orpheus' head floating downstream (taken from Virgil) and then crossing the sea allows Ovid to contrive a short metamorphosis of the snake which attacks it. In *The Punishment of the Maenads* (67–84) Bacchus changes the Thracian women to trees in a longer, more detailed transformation.

Bacchus is the link with the popular story of the Phrygian king, *Midas* (85–193), whose kindness the god rewarded by allowing him to choose whatever he wanted – in his case, the power to turn everything he touched to gold. The consequences of this foolish choice are memorably described, as is the further consequence of Midas' renewed stupidity in backing Pan against Apollo in a music contest.

Apollo transfers the scene a little way to Troy, where the poem's continuity will be based until 13.622. *Laömedon's Treachery* (194–220) tells of the city's first destruction by Hercules, aided by Telamon and his brother Peleus. This leads on to *Peleus and Thetis* (221–65), in which the mortal hero succeeds in dominating the sea-goddess, despite her power of self-metamorphosis. Peleus then falls on less happy times. After murdering his half-brother Phocus, he takes refuge at the *Court of Ceÿx*, king of Trachis (266–90, 346–409), where he learns how Ceÿx's brother *Daedalion* (291–345) was changed to a hawk in his anger and frustration at the callous lust or spite meted out to his daughter Chione by three of the gods – the old theme persists. Peleus next learns from one of his own people, once again in exciting 'Greek messenger' mode, how all his cattle have been destroyed by a monster wolf, which turns out to have been sent by the Nereïd Psamathe in revenge for her murdered son Phocus. Psamathe has to be persuaded by her sister Thetis to dispose of the wolf by metamorphosis.

The various stories in this book so far, while ingeniously interconnected, may seem to have followed one another in slightly bewildering succession. For the next 339 lines Ovid asks his audience to concentrate on one long magnificent tale, *Ceÿx and Alcyone* (410–748). Although parts of this are composed in a grand epic manner, it is more than anything a romance, in which a devoted husband and wife, through no fault of their own, are parted and reunited by the power of the sea and the winds. The reunion is only partial, as one of the couple is dead, but metamorphosis makes it complete. The centrepiece is the tremendous description of the storm at sea, framed by Ceÿx' ship's gradual disappearance over the waves as he leaves his wife, and (after the interlude of Alcyone's dream) by the gradual reappearance of Ceÿx' drowned body as it is tossed towards the shore. The dream sequence has its own, typically Ovidian, character and includes a wonderful *ecphrasis* on the cave of Sleep. The closing lines, when the new-formed kingfishers breed their young at sea in the 'halcyon days', bring the romance to a tranquil and moving conclusion. This story differs from others in the poem in showing human beings as the victims of the elements in nature rather than of the gods, each other or their own desires.

The story of *Aesacus* (749–95), the son of Priam and brother of Hector, serves chiefly as a bridge to the Trojan War material which follows in Books 12 and 13. It also picks up themes from earlier stories in Book 11: metamorphosis to a bird is associated (as for Daedalion) with frustrated passion; and the death of Hesperia as a result of a snake bite recalls that of Eurydice and so the image of Orpheus at the very beginning of the book.

THE DEATH OF ORPHEUS

With songs such as these the Thracian minstrel*
      bewitched the forests,
entranced the beasts and compelled the rocks to follow
      behind him.
The wild Cicónian women, attired in their dappled
      fawnskins,
suddenly saw him from where they stood on a hilltop –
      Órpheus,
chanting his lays in gentle accord with the strings of his
5   lyre.
One of the bacchanals, tossing her flowing hair in the
      breeze,
cried, 'Look! Look there! The man who rejects us!' and
      launched her thyrsus
straight at the head of the great musician who served
      Apollo.
The ivy-tipped spear inflicted a bruise without drawing
      blood.
Another maenad picked up a stone; it flew through the
10   air,
but lyre and voice united to break its force, and it fell
in front of the poet's feet, as though it were begging
      forgiveness
for such a frenzied assault. Yet the women continued
      their reckless
aggression, restraint had fled and the spirit of madness
      reigned.
Orpheus' singing could well have weakened their shots,
15   but cacophony
won. The hideous screech of the Phrygian pipe with its
      curved bell,
the banging of drums, the clapping of hands and the
      bacchanals' shrieking
drowned the sound of the lyre, and the voice of the bard
      could no longer

be heard. So the women's stones were at long last stained
          with his blood.
First the maenads pounced on the innocent creatures that
          still   20
lay under the spell of his music: the numberless birds and
          the snakes,
the line of beasts which had followed in Orpheus' triumphal
          procession.
Then, with their hands well bloodied, they turned on
          Orpheus in person,
massing together like birds who have spied the nocturnal
          screech-owl
flitting around in the daytime, or dogs at the morning fight   25
in the amphitheatre* who prey on a mortally wounded stag.
Each woman attacked the bard by flinging her leafy
          thyrsus,
a weapon not made for such violent use. They then threw
          clods
of earth, sharp-pointed rocks or branches ripped from the
          trees.
Their madness had further weapons on which to draw. As it
          happened,   30
some oxen were ploughing a nearby field, and the brawny
          peasants
were sweating away as they dug the soil for the fruits of the
          earth.
On sight of the maenad horde, the workmen took to their
          heels
and abandoned their tools, the hoes, the heavy rakes and
          the mattocks
lying dispersed on the empty fields. These tools were seized   35
by the savage women, who ripped the fierce-horned oxen to
          pieces
and then rushed back to complete the murder of Orpheus.
          The poet
extended his helpless arms. He spoke, but now for the first
          time
spoke to no purpose; his voice had lost all power to move.   40

Those impious women destroyed him, and through those
          lips, whose wonderful
songs had attracted the rocks and touched the hearts of
          the beasts,
his soul passed forth with his breath and melted into the
          winds.
     All his companions wept for Orpheus: the sorrowing
          birds,
the beasts of the wild, the stubborn rocks and the trees
45   which so often
had followed his singing. The trees, indeed, dropped all
          of their leaves
and mourned shorn-headed. It's also said that the rivers
          were swollen
with tears they had shed themselves; while the nymphs
          of the streams and woodlands
edged their garments with black and allowed their hair
          to flow loose.
Orpheus' limbs lay scattered around; but his lyre and
50   his head
were thrown in the river Hebrus. Afloat mid-stream –
          oh wonder! –
the instrument uttered a plaintive moan, the lifeless
          tongue
emitted a feeble dirge and the banks re-echoed in
          sorrow.
The river carried them both to the sea, where the poet
          took leave
of his homeland and found his way to Methýmna on
55   Lesbos' coast.
Here, as his head lay exposed on an alien shore, the hair
still dripping with salt sea-spray, a fierce snake made to
          attack it.
Apollo at last intervened. The snake had opened its
          fangs,
but its gaping jaws were hardened to stone and frozen
60   in motion.

Orpheus' shade passed under the earth. He recognized
    all
the places he'd seen before. As he searched the Elýsian
    Fields,
he found the wife he had lost and held her close in his arms.
At last the lovers could stroll together, side by side –
or she went ahead and he followed; then Orpheus ventured
    in front   65
and knew he could now look back on his own Eurýdice
    safely.

THE PUNISHMENT OF
THE MAENADS

Bacchus, however, was angry at losing the priest of his
    mysteries*
and would not allow the crime of his murder to go
    unpunished.
There in the forest were all the Thracian women who'd
    taken
part in the outrage. At once he tied them in twisted
    tree-roots.   70
Attacking each one at the point where she'd stopped her
    pursuit, he extended
her toes and forced the extremities down into solid earth.
Imagine a bird which has caught her leg in a crafty
    bird-catcher's
hidden snare and knows that she's trapped; imagine her
    flapping
her wings in terror and drawing the cord of the noose ever
    tighter.   75
So, when a woman was stuck on her own with her feet
    embedded,
she tried in a panic to pull herself free; but the supple roots
had her tight in their clutches and held her down as she
    struggled to jump out.

Desperately searching to find her feet, her toes and her
        toenails,
she saw that the bark was creeping over her slender
80   calves.
As she tried to beat on her thigh to express her grief and
        frustration,
her fist's power struck upon wood; her breasts then
        turned into wood,
and soon her shoulders were wood. You'd suppose that
        her outstretched arms
were genuine branches – indeed you'd be perfectly right
        in supposing it.

MIDAS

Bacchus still was displeased. He abandoned Thrace
85   altogether
and, taking a worthier band of dancers, he made for
        Tmolus'
vines and the river Pactólus, although its waters were
        not yet
golden and men hadn't started to covet its precious
        sand.*
Surrounding the god was the usual throng of bacchants
        and satyrs.
Only Silénus* was not in attendance. The Phrygian
90   peasants
had found the old drunkard reeling, bedecked in his
        garland of flowers,
and brought him to Midas, the king whom Orpheus
        from Thrace had instructed
in Dionýsiac rites when he taught Eumólpus* of Athens.
As soon as the king understood that his guest was a
        fellow initiate,
95 to honour Silenus' arrival, in genial spirit he ordered
    a feast which lasted for ten continuous days and nights.

At the end of that time, when the morning star had brought
        up the rear
of the other stars in the sky, King Midas blithely went out
to the Lydian fields and restored the old man to his
        foster-child, Bacchus.

   Delighted to see his father again, Dionýsus gave Midas   100
the welcome but dangerous right to choose any boon he
        desired.
The king, not one to employ such a gift very sensibly,
        answered,
'Grant that whatever I touch with my body may turn to
        gold.'
Bacchus agreed to this wish and gave its asker the power
which would prove his downfall, sad that the king hadn't
        chosen more wisely.   105
Midas departed in high delight with his bane of a present,
and put the gift to the test at once by touching some
        objects.
Passing an oak with low green boughs, he uncertainly
        pulled
at a leafy twig; the twig and its foliage turned to gold.
He lifted a stone from the ground; that also became pure
        gold.   110
He touched a clod; the power in his fingers converted the
        soft earth
into a hard nugget. Plucking the ears in a ripe cornfield,
he reaped a harvest of gold. He picked an apple and
        held it –
a present from the Hespérides' garden? He rested his
        hands
on the doors of his lofty palace: the doors appeared to be
        glowing.   115
Again, if he washed his hands in running water, the shower
he shook from his fingers might well have seduced fair
        Dánaë's virtue.*
'Gold! A world full of gold!' he exclaimed; his mind could
        barely

contain his hopes. As he gloated, his servants laid him a
     table
piled with the choicest of meats and loaves of bread in
120   abundance.
That was the moment of truth. When Midas hungrily
     touched
the bread with his fingers, Ceres' gifts grew rigidly
     hard.
Or if he attempted to tear some meat in his greedy
     teeth,
he found he was uselessly crunching on wafers of
     yellowish metal.
He mixed fresh water with wine, the god who had
125   granted his wish;
but all that entered his throat was a trickle of molten
     gold.
   Stunned by this turn of events, now wealthy but
     desolate, Midas
longed to escape from his riches and loathed the thing
     that he'd prayed for.
Platefuls to eat, but perpetually hungry! His throat was
     parched
with a burning thirst. By his own act, gold had become
130   his detested
torturer. Raising his hands and his radiant arms to the
     sky,
'O father Bacchus,' he cried, 'forgive me! I know I have
     sinned,
But pity my plight and rescue me now from the curse
     that seduced me!'
The gods can be kind. So Bacchus, when Midas
     admitted his error,
cancelled the gift he had faithfully yielded and cured
135   the affliction.
'So that you needn't remain,' he said, 'encased in the
     gold
you desired so unwisely, proceed to the river that flows
     by the mighty

city of Sardis. Follow the ridge of the bank upstream
and travel along it until you come to Pactolus' source.
Then plunge your head in the foaming spring where it
        gushes most strongly,   140
and purge your guilt as you cleanse your body.' The king
        went up
to the water as bidden. The power of the Midas touch
        imbued it
with gold and passed from his human body into the river.
The vein is now old, but the particles still flood over the
        fields
to harden the soil with gold and to dye the earth-clods
        yellow.   145

Disgusted by wealth, King Midas haunted the fields and the
        forests,
worshipping Pan, who always inhabits the mountain caves.
But his wits remained as obtuse as ever. Moreover, his utter
stupidity, once again, was destined to prove his downfall.
You've heard of Tmolus, the rocky mountain which steeply
        ascends   150
to a wide view over the straits, with a range extending as far
as Sardis up to the north, in the south to tiny Hypaépa.
Here Pan was boasting about his piping skills to the lissom
nymphs. As he practised an easy tune on his wax-bound
        reeds,
he dared to disparage Apollo's playing compared with his
        own   155
and entered an ill-matched competition, with Tmolus as
        judge.*
    The venerable judge assumed his seat on the mountain he
        ruled
and brushed the trees away from his ears. His dark green
        ringlets
were only wreathed in the foliage of oak, with acorns
        dangling
around his temples. Then, with a glance at the god of the
        flocks,   160

he said, 'I am ready.' So Pan performed on his rustic
     pipes,
and his barbarous strains entranced the ears of Midas,
     who chanced
to be there when he played. When the piece was finished,
     Tmolus solemnly
turned his head in Apollo's direction, and so did his
     forest.
Phoebus was crowned with a wreath of Parnássian bay
165   on his golden
hair, and he swept the ground with his mantle of
     Tyrian purple.
His lyre was richly inlaid with jewels and Indian ivory.
Holding the instrument firm in his left hand, plectrum
     in right,
he struck the pose of a maestro; and then he plucked at
     the strings
with his practised thumb, till Tmolus, enthralled by the
170   beautiful music,
notified Pan that his pipes must yield the palm to the
     lyre.
    All agreed with the judgment pronounced by the
     sacred mountain;
only Midas challenged the verdict and called it unfair.
Apollo couldn't allow such insensitive ears to preserve
their human appearance. He lengthened them out; he
175   filled them with shaggy
grey hairs; he made them floppy and able to waggle
     their tips.
The rest of King Midas belonged to a man: his other
     members
remained intact, but he wore the ears of a lumbering
     donkey.
Needless to say, he was anxious to hide them and tried
180   to undo
the effect of his shameful appendage by wearing a
     purple tiara.*

But, sadly, the servant who cut his hair was bound to
        notice
the shocking additions. Although the barber was itching to
        broadcast
what he had seen, he hadn't the nerve to betray his master.
Unable, however, to keep the secret all to himself,   185
he slipped away, dug a hole in the ground and whispered
        inside it,
'King Midas has ass's ears!' He then re-shovelled the soil
in the empty hole, to bury all trace of his words, and quietly
vanished. But soon a close-packed cluster of quivering
        reeds   190
began to grow on the spot and, after a year of ripening,
gave the planter away. In the breeze from the south they
        would rustle
and whistle the buried words, 'King Midas has ass's ears!'

LAÖMEDON'S TREACHERY

His vengeance completed, divine Apollo took off from
        Tmolus.
He flew through the sky towards the straits of Néphele's
        daughter,   195
Helle,* and landed on Trojan soil, Laömedon's country.
Close to the sea, to the right of Sigéum, the left of
        Rhoetéum,
there stands an old altar of Jove the oracular, god of the
        thunder.
Here Apollo could see Laömedon starting to build
the walls of recently founded Troy. The great undertaking   200
was only progressing slowly and help was certainly needed.
So he and Neptune, the god of the trident and lord of the
        swelling
ocean, took on the appearance of mortals and struck a
        bargain
with Phrygia's king to construct his walls for a sum of gold.

When the work was finished, the king refused to pay up
205   and crowned
his broken promise by swearing he'd never agreed to
        reward them.
'You shan't get away with this!' cried Neptune, and
        promptly diverted
the mass of his waters to swamp the shores of the
        miserly Trojan.
He flooded the land till it looked like sea, depriving the
        farmers
of all their crops and submerging the fields in the rush
210   of the tide.
That wasn't enough: Laömedon's daughter, Hesíone,
        had to be
offered up to a fierce sea-monster. Hercules rescued
the girl from the rock where they'd chained her, but
        when he demanded the horses
agreed as his prize for the exploit, his promised reward
        was denied him;
and so he subdued twice-perjured Troy and captured
215   her walls.
Young Télamon joined the campaign and achieved the
        distinction of winning
Hesione's hand. His brother Péleus, who also took
        part,
had a goddess for wife and was famous already – as
        glad to be wedded
to Néreus' daughter as proud of his grandfather.*
        Plenty of mortals
are grandsons of Jove, but only Peleus married a
220   goddess.

PELEUS AND THETIS

How was this marriage arranged? Old Próteus* had said to
        Thetis,
'You need to conceive a child, wave-goddess; you're destined
        to bear
a hero who, grown to his prime, shall challenge the deeds of
        his father
and merit a mightier name.' Now Jupiter hotly desired
fair Thetis, but could he allow the world to contain a being 225
more mighty than him? He couldn't; and so, to avoid a
        union
with Nereus' daughter, he ordered his grandson Peleus to
        woo her
in place of himself and take the maid of the sea to his
        bosom.
    Picture a sickle-shaped bay on Thessaly's coast, with its
        arms
jutting out like the ends of a bow. If the water inside it were
        deeper,   230
there'd be a harbour; but only a film of sea spreads over
the top of the sand. The shore is so firm that it shows no
        footprints,
it's easy to walk on and isn't bestrewn with squelching
        seaweed.
Nearby is a coppice of myrtles, laden with black and green
        berries.
There, in its heart, imagine a grotto, which could be
        natural   235
or artificial, more likely the latter; and this is where Thetis,
riding her bridled dolphin, would often arrive quite naked.
One day she was lying there fast asleep, when Peleus
        surprised her
as ordered, and then, since she wouldn't respond to his
        wooing entreaties,
he clasped her neck in his amorous arms and attempted to
        rape her.   240

His boldness would have succeeded if Thetis hadn't
      made use
of the magical skills she possessed and kept on changing
      her shape.
She took the form of a bird, but he still held on to the
      bird.
She changed to a sturdy tree, and he clung to the trunk
      like ivy.
She next adopted the shape of a black-striped tigress; at
245   last
her assailant, in terror, relaxed the hold of his arms on
      her body.
   Peleus next appealed to the sea-gods, pouring wine
on the waves and offering entrails of sheep with
      smoking incense,
until the Carpathian prophet, Proteus, rose from the
      depths
and said to him, 'Aeacus' son, you shall win the bride
250   you are seeking.
All you must do is to catch her asleep in the rocky cave
and trap her unconscious limbs in the tangling snare of
      a rope.
Don't let her elude you by falsely assuming a hundred
      disguises.
Just squeeze her firmly until she returns to her normal
      shape.'
When Proteus had given this counsel, he plunged his
255   face in the sea,
and his native waves closed over his head on his final
      words.
   Titan the sun god was sinking and guiding his
      chariot downwards
into the western waves as the beautiful Néreïd, Thetis,
left her home in the water and went to her usual
      bedroom.
Peleus hardly had time to entrap the nymph in his
260   noose

when she started to take new shapes, until she saw she was
    tightly
gripped, with her arms stretched out on either side of her
    body.
At last she gave in, as she sighed, 'You win! Some god must
    be helping you.'
Now she was Thetis for real! The hero fondly embraced her;
he had his desire and planted the seed of the mighty
    Achílles.   265

PELEUS AT THE COURT OF CEŸX (1)

Peleus was lucky, lucky both in his wife and his son,
and all went well for the hero, except for the guilt he
    incurred
in the murder of Phocus, his half-brother.* Banished from
    home with the blood
still fresh on his hands, he finally found a welcome in
    Trachis,
a land that was free of bloodshed and violence under its
    ruler   270
Céÿx, Lucifer's son, whose face most often reflected
his father's brightness; but then it was overcast with
    untypical
gloom, because he was mourning the sudden loss of his
    brother.*
When Peleus arrived in this country, depressed and tired
    from his travels,
he passed through the gates of the city with only a handful
    of followers,   275
leaving the flocks of sheep and the herds he had driven
    along
in a shady valley not far from the walls. As soon as he
    gained
the chance of a royal audience, he entered the hall as a
    suppliant,

holding an olive-branch wreathed in wool, and declared
    his name
and the name of his father. The only thing he concealed
280   was his blood-guilt;
his exile was falsely explained away. When he asked
    permission
to earn his bread in the city of Trachis or out in the
    country,
Ceÿx gently replied: 'This kingdom welcomes all
    strangers.
Our comforts are open for even the humblest of folk to
    enjoy.
Kindness apart, you're a famous man and Jove is your
285   grandfather –
powerful points in your favour. You need not ask for
    assistance.
All that you seek shall be yours, and whatever your
    eyes can see
you may call your own, for what it is worth – though I
    wish it were better!'
Ceÿx was weeping. When Peleus, backed by his
    followers, asked him
what was causing him such distress, he told them his
290   story:

CEÿX'S STORY: DAEDALION

'Look at that bird of prey in the sky, upsetting all
of the other birds. Perhaps you suppose that he always
    had wings.
He used to be human, already a sharp-eyed, violent and
    warlike
creature – character seems to survive any
    transformation.
295 His name was Daedálion. He and I were sons of the star
who summons the dawn in the morning and vanishes
    after the others.

Mine was a peace-loving nature. I cherished peace as I
   cherished
my wedded life, but my brother's delight was in brutal
   warfare.
His manly courage was shown in the conquest of kings and
   their peoples,
where now in his altered shape he pursues the doves of
   Beoótia.   300
He had a daughter, a girl of exceptional loveliness, Chíone,
wooed by a thousand suitors and ready for marriage at
   fourteen.
One day, when Apollo and Mercury, Maia's son, were
   returning,
the one from his temple at Delphi, the other from Mount
   Cylléne,
both at once set eyes on the girl and were fired with
   passion.   305
Apollo deferred his hopes of enjoyment until it was night,
but Mercury couldn't endure to wait and touched young
   Chione's
face with his wand of sleep. She yielded at once to his
   magic,
and so he was able to rape her. The sky was dotted with
   stars
when Phoebus disguised himself as a crone and stole the
   pleasure   310
his brother had taken before him. Nine months went by
   and Chione,
pregnant by wing-footed Mercury, bore him a son, the
   knavish
Autólycus, wily and skilful in every kind of deception,
a rogue who was thoroughly versed in his father's arts and
   perfectly
happy to turn pure white into black, jet black into white.   315
Chione's son by Apollo (she actually brought forth twins)
was called Philámmon, famed for his singing and skill on
   the lyre.
But what is the use of producing twins, of having attracted

two of the gods, of being descended from such a brave
    father
320 and starry grandfather? Glory, perhaps, is often a snare.
It certainly was so for one, since Chione ventured to
    claim
she surpassed Diana and moved the goddess to violent
    anger
by finding fault with her face. "No doubt she'll be
    happy with *facts*!"
Diana retorted in fury, and instantly drew her bow
to release an arrow which pierced the tongue of her
325   wicked traducer.
The tongue went silent, the voice was lost and the
    words wouldn't follow;
as Chione struggled to speak, her life flowed out with
    her blood.
I, her poor uncle Ceÿx, wretchedly cradled her body
and grieved as a father might. How sadly I broke the
    news
to my brother who loved his daughter so dearly, and
    tried to console him!
Daedalion seemed to respond like a rock unmoved by
330   the crash
of the waves; he was utterly sunk in grief for the loss of
    his daughter.
But when he set eyes on the pyre with her burning
    body, he tried
four times to throw himself into the flames. Four times
    he was beaten
back. Then he took to his heels in a frenzy and rushed
    all over
the fields, like a bullock stung on the neck by a swarm
335   of hornets.
Already I fancied his running was superhumanly fast,
and you might quite well have supposed that wings
    had grown on his feet.
Daedalion managed to dodge us all; in his longing for
    death,

he ran right up to the top of Parnássus and jumped from a
    precipice.
Phoebus in pity transformed him into a bird and suddenly   340
raised him, suspended on wings in the air. He gave him a
    hooked beak,
talons to claw at his prey, the courage he'd owned from his
    birth,
and a strength more powerful than you would expect in so
    small a body.
Now he's a hawk, a mischievous creature who vents his
    rage
on the kingdom of birds and inflicts his pain and distress on
    his neighbours.'   345

PELEUS AT THE COURT
OF CEŸX (2)

While Ceÿx, Lucifer's son, was telling this curious story
about the change to his brother, a man burst into the
    palace,
gasping for breath. It was Peleus' herdsman, Phócian
    Onétor.
'Peleus! Peleus!' he shouted, 'I bring you news of a dreadful
disaster!' Peleus told him at once to come out with his
    message,   350
and even Ceÿx, with quivering cheeks, was filled with
    suspense.
The herdsman went on: 'I had driven my weary cattle down
to the curving shore when the sun had just arrived at its
    zenith,
one half of its daily course now run, with the other ahead.
Some of the herd had sunk to their knees on the yellow
    sand   355
and were lying there, gazing across the broad expanse of the
    ocean.
Some were slowly and aimlessly wandering over the beach,

while others were swimming with only their heads and
    necks above water.
Close by is a shrine, not a splendid temple of marble and
    gold,
but a timber structure, set in the shade of an ancient
360   wood.
Nereus and his daughters are worshipped here – a
    fisherman drying
his nets on the shore explained that they are the local
    sea-gods.
Next to the shrine is a swamp, surrounded by thickets
    of willow
and caused by the wash of the nearby waves. From
    here a succession
of crashes and howls could be heard, to the terror of
365   neighbouring farms,
when a huge and sinister monster, a wolf, emerged
    from the marsh reeds.
His snapping jaws were horribly smeared with foam
    and with clotted
blood, while his glaring eyes were ablaze with a fiery
    glow.
Crazed as the creature was with rage and hunger alike,
his rage was the stronger. He wasn't concerned to avert
370   starvation
or ease his hunger by slaughtering only a few of the
    cattle.
He had to destroy the whole of the herd and to get his
    teeth
into every animal. Some of my fellow servants also
were savaged and mauled to death while trying to fend
    him off.
Blood streamed on the beach, in the shallow waves, in
375   the swamp where the bellows
of pain still echoed. But no hesitation, delay will be
    fatal!
While anything's left to be saved, we must pull
    together. To arms,

to arms, my friends! Let us all join forces to fight the
    monster!'
  The herdsman's story was ended. Peleus calmly
    accepted
his losses; he guessed they must be a funeral gift from the
    Nereïd   380
Psámathe, paid to Phocus her son, the brother he'd killed.
But his host, King Ceÿx, ordered his men to put on their
    armour
and grab their spears for the fray. He was making ready to
    join them
himself, but his wife Alcýone, roused by the general uproar,
rushed from her chamber. Her hair was not yet properly
    dressed   385
and fell into disarray as she clung to her husband's neck
and implored him with tears in her eyes to send the
    necessary help,
without going in person, and so to preserve two lives in one.
Peleus said to the queen, 'Though your wifely fears do you
    credit,
please lay them aside. I thank you both for the help you
    have promised,   390
but would not wish you to fight this monster on my
    account.
First I must pray to the Nereïd.' All climbed up to a tower
on the top of the fortress, a lighthouse used as a welcome
    landmark
for battered vessels; and here they groaned in horror to
    view
the cattle strewn on the shore and the killer wolf with his
    fangs   395
still dripping, his shaggy coat all stained and matted with
    blood.
Then Peleus stretched his arms to the shore of the open sea
and called on the green nymph, Psamathe. 'Now put an end
    to your anger
and grant me your help!' he prayed. These words of
    entreaty failed

to persuade the goddess, so Thetis* added her prayers to
400   her husband's
and won forgiveness. But though the wolf had been
        ordered away
from his murderous feast, he was rabid with blood's
        sweet taste and continued
until, when his jaws had closed on the neck of a heifer
        he'd mangled,
Psamathe turned him to marble. His body retained its
        shape
and all but its colour; the colour of marble sufficed to
405   show
that this was a wolf no longer and none need fear it in
        future.
Fate, however, would not permit the fugitive Peleus
to settle in Trachis. His wanderings took him as far as
        Magnésia,
and there Acástus, the king of Thessaly, purged him of
        blood-guilt.

CEŸX AND ALCYONE

Meanwhile, King Ceÿx, deeply disturbed by his
410   brother's miraculous
transformation, as well as the strange events that had
        followed,
decided he ought to consult the oracle, mankind's
        comfort,
and made arrangements to visit Apollo's temple at
        Claros*
(Delphi was blocked by brigands led by the impious
        Phorbas).
Before he sailed, he unfolded his plan to his faithful
415   wife,
Alcyone. Chilled to the bone, she immediately turned
        as pale

as the wood of a boxtree; and floods of tears streamed down
    her cheeks.
Three times she attempted to speak, but words were stifled
    by weeping.
Her tender reproaches were constantly interrupted by sobs, 420
as she said: 'My dearest husband, what have I done? Have
    your feelings
towards me changed? Your first concern was always for me.
Can you now abandon your wife without some qualm of
    misgiving?
Do you have to travel so far? Will you love me more if
    we're parted?
Just tell me you're journeying overland; then I'll only miss
    you   425
and won't be also afraid. I'll fret without being frightened.
But no, you are going by sea, and that is the ugly picture
which fills me with terror. I recently noticed a wrecked
    ship's boards
on the shore, and I've often read names on graves
    containing no bodies.
Don't be tricked into thinking that you'll be safer because 430
your wife is the daughter of Aéolus, god of the winds, who
    confines
their powerful blasts in his prison and calms the seas as he
    wishes.
As soon as those winds are released and have taken control
    of the waves,
they can do whatever they please; both land and sea are
    defenceless
from end to end of the world; the clouds are thrown into
    chaos,   435
wildly colliding and sparking with bright red flashes of
    lightning.
The more I have come to know the winds (as I did as a
    child
in my father's house), the more I believe that they ought to
    be feared.

But if, my beloved husband, no prayers can ever
          persuade you
to change your decision, and if you are so determined to
440   go,
please take me with you. At least we shall ride the
          storm together.
With you I shall only fear what I'm facing. Whatever
          that is,
we shall share the danger and brave the waves in each
          other's company.'
     The son of the morning star was moved by Aeolus'
          daughter's
445 tearful words. He adored his wife as fondly as ever,
but Ceÿx wasn't prepared to abandon his purposed
          voyage
or to grant Alcyone's wish to sail into danger beside
          him.
He tried again and again to allay her fears, but failed
entirely to gain her support. Then he offered one
          further sop,
which changed the mind of his loving wife and settled
450   the matter:
'For us any parting is bound to be long, but I solemnly
          swear
by my father's rays that, provided destiny brings me
          home,
you shall see me return before two moons have grown
          to their fullness.'
This promise induced her at last to hope that he might
          come back.
At once he ordered a ship to be brought out of dock
455   and launched
with all its proper equipment. As soon as Alcyone
          saw it,
she shuddered again, as though she divined what was
          going to happen.
The tears welled up as she clasped her husband's neck
          in her arms

for her last pathetic farewell, before she collapsed on the
     ground.   460
Though Ceÿx looked for excuses to dally, his crew in their
     two ranks
started to pull their oars to their sturdy chests and to cut
the waves with their evenly balanced strokes. Eyes
     streaming, Alcyone
raised her head and watched her husband standing aloft
on the stern and waving goodbye. Then she waved back. As
     the ship   465
pulled further away from land and the faces on board grew
     blurred,
her eyes continued to follow the craft as it swiftly receded
towards the horizon. The hull disappeared, but the sails
     were still visible,
fluttering high on the mast. When those had vanished as
     well,   470
Alcyone trudged back home to her empty chamber and
     sank
on her bed. As her head hit the pillow, she burst once more
     into tears;
lying there made her remember the part of her life she was
     missing.

The ship was clear of the port and the rigging had started to
     rattle.
The crew stopped rowing and turned their oars alongside
     the vessel;   475
they braced the yard to the top of the mast and unfurled the
     sails
to their fullest extent, in order to catch the favouring
     breeze.
Half of the voyage was still to be run – it could have been
     more
than half – and land was a long way off, both ahead and
     behind,
when, as night was falling, the sea began to grow choppy
     and white;   480

a driving wind sprang up with greater force from the
    east.
'Lower the yard,' the captain shouted, 'and take in sail!'
But his orders were drowned by the shrieking gale; not a
    single word
of command could be heard for the crash of the waves.
485   But orders weren't needed.
The sailors jumped to the different tasks of shipping
    the oars,
plugging the oar-holes, furling the sail and grabbing
    the yard
to fasten it down; or baling out water and pouring the
    sea
back into the sea. Throughout this scurry of hectic
    activity
the storm grew wilder and wilder; the winds engaged
490   from all quarters
in violent conflict and roused the waves to an angry
    turmoil.
The captain panicked and had to admit that the whole
    situation
was out of control; he had no idea what orders to give.
Disaster had struck with a force too great for his skill
    to contend with.
The sounds were deafening: yells of the sailors,
495   creaking of cables,
the roar of the rushing waves, with the claps and rolls
    of the thunder.
The sea was lifted towards the sky and appeared to
    touch it,
drenching the layers of lowering cloud in showers of
    spray.
Its colour kept changing: now it was yellow with sand
    churned up
from the bottommost depths, and then it was black as
500   the streams of the Styx,
and sometimes white when it flattened out into hissing
    foam.

The Trachínian vessel herself was subjected to similar
      changes:
now high up in the air, as though on top of a mountain,
she appeared to look down on the valleys below, with hell at
      the bottom;
then, after she'd plunged to the depths, ringed round by a
      circle of sea,   505
you'd think she was gazing up to the sky from a whirling
      abyss.
Often you'd hear an enormous crash as her sides were
      pounded,
a crash as loud as the noise of an iron battering-ram
or a catapult forcing a breach in the crumbling walls of a
      fortress.
Imagine a savage lion, who gains new strength as he
      charges   510
and boldly confronts the weapons and spears held out by
      the hunters;
so, when the winds sprang up and lashed the waves to a
      fury,
the waters attacked the ship's defences and towered above
      them.
Soon the wedges which tightened the boards worked loose,
      and cracks
appeared as the caulking failed, admitting the deadly flood. 515
  The clouds then suddenly burst and the rain poured
      down in torrents.
You'd think that the whole of the sky was falling into the
      sea,
or else that the sea had swollen and risen as far as the sky.
The sails of the ship were drenched as the waters of heaven
      and ocean
were intermingled completely. The stars had all
      disappeared,   520
and the darkness of night was intensified by the black of the
      storm.
The impenetrable gloom was only broken by brilliant
      flashes

of lightning, which made the waves resemble a blazing
          inferno.
The sea now started to leap right into the hollow frame
of the vessel. Imagine a soldier, braver than all his
525   comrades,
repeatedly trying to scale a beleaguered city's walls
and at last succeeding as, fired with heroic ambition, he
          holds
his position single-handed against a thousand
          defenders.
So after the waves had pounded the ship's steep sides
          nine times,
a tenth wave, rising with more gigantic strength than
530   the others,
never abandoned its tireless assault on the battered
          hull,
until it had landed between the walls of the captured
          vessel.
Thus part of the sea was still attempting to force an
          entry,
while part was already inside. The crew were all in
          confusion,
535 like men in a city with some of the enemy undermining
the walls from outside and others firmly established
          within.
     Seamanship failed and morale had collapsed. Such
          an onrush of waves,
such an onrush of death was breaking over the sailors'
          heads.
They burst into tears, or gaped dumbfounded, or
          blessed their friends
who could hope to be buried. Perhaps they appealed to
540   the gods in prayer,
uselessly raising their arms towards the invisible
          heavens
and begging for help. Perhaps they thought of their
          brothers and parents,

their homes with their wives and children, and all they had
    left behind them.
Ceÿx remembered his dear Alcyone. Hers was the only
name on his lips. His wife was all he regretted and longed
    for,   545
although he was glad that she wasn't beside him. He wished
    he could look
once more in his country's direction and face his home for
    the last time,
but didn't know where to turn. The sea was churning and
    swirling
so wildly, the whole of the sky was hidden behind those
    murky
layers of pitch-black clouds, and the night was darker than
    ever.   550
   In a spinning gust of tempestuous rain the mast was
    shattered,
and so was the helm. Then one huge wave in a soaring
    curve,
like a victor triumphantly straddling his spoils, looked
    down on the others
and dropped with a crash on the ship with a force like the
    Athos and Pindus
mountains, should they be wrenched from their own
    foundations and bodily   555
thrown in the open sea. The blow was as powerful as heavy,
and plunged the boat to the bottom. Most of the sailors
    were also
thrust below in the swirl; they never returned to gasp air
and the ocean took them. The rest grabbed hold of planks
    from the keel
and fragments of wreckage. Ceÿx himself clung on with the
    hand   560
that once had wielded a sceptre, invoking the names of his
    father,
the morning star, and his wife's great father, the god of the
    winds –

to no purpose, alas! As he struggled to stay afloat, he
        chiefly
called on Alcyone; she was the one he remembered and
        thought of.
He prayed that the waves might carry his body where *she*
        might find it,
and loving hands should be able to bury his lifeless
565   remains.
Whenever the waves permitted the swimmer to open
        his lips,
he shouted the name of the wife from whom he was
        parted, or murmured it
into the billows. But then the waves on which he was
        tossing
were suddenly overwhelmed by a single arch of black
        water,
which broke on top of his head and finally forced him
        under.
The morning star on the following day was completely
570   obscured
and no one could have observed it. Since Lucifer
        wasn't permitted
to leave the sky, he covered his face in a mantle of
        clouds.

Meanwhile, Alcyone, still unaware of this dreadful
        disaster,
was counting each night that passed and eagerly
        working on garments
for Ceÿx to wear, or weaving clothes for herself to
575   greet
his return, as she fondly promised herself he would
        come back home.
She worshipped all of the gods with the pious tribute
        of incense,
but visited Juno's temple* more than the shrines of the
        others.

She came to the goddess's altar to offer prayers for the
        husband
who was no more – for his safety at sea and return to her
        own arms,   580
not to the arms of another woman. This final petition,
of all her requests, was the only one which could ever be
        granted.
    But Juno was not prepared to continue receiving prayers
for a lifeless corpse; her altars could not be polluted by
        unclean
hands.* So she said to Iris, her trusty conveyor of orders: 585
'Quick, now! I want you to visit the palace of drowsy
        Sleep.
Instruct him to send a dream to Alcyone. Say it must take
the form of Ceÿx and tell the truth of his sad demise.'
Juno had spoken. Then Iris dressed herself in her cloak
of a thousand colours, she painted the sky with the arch of
        the rainbow,   590
and made as she had been told for the cloud-wrapped
        palace of Somnus.
    Picture a long, deep cave, not far from Cimmérian
        country,*
bored in a mountain, where indolent Sleep has his hearth
        and his home.
The sun never filters into this place with its light in the
        morning,
at noon or at close of day. Here vapour and murky fog   595
are exhaled from the lungs of the earth in a strange,
        mysterious twilight.
No crested cockerels are wide awake and ready to
        summon
the dawn with their crowing. The silence is undisturbed by
        the barking
of jittery dogs or the squawking of even more watchful
        geese.*
Not a sound can be heard; no howling of beasts, no lowing
        of cattle,   600

no rustling of branches, nor human voices raised in a
      quarrel.
This is the dwelling of noiseless repose, except that a
      trickling
stream of water from Lethe,* down at the cave's very
      bottom,
babbles along and induces sleep with the tinkle of
      pebbles.
In front of the cavern's mouth luxuriant poppies are
605   blooming,
with numberless herbs from whose juices sleep is
      distilled by the dewy
night and sprinkled over the darkened lands of the
      earth.
To avoid any creaking of doors as they turn on their
      hinges, there isn't
a single door to the house nor a single guard on the
      threshold.
But deep in the heart of the cave, raised high, there's a
610   couch made of ebony,
covered in feathery cushions, black, with a dusky
      bedspread.
Here Somnus himself is resting his body, relaxed and
      lethargic;
and round their master, in various forms of disguise,
      are lying
the phantom dreams, as many to count as the leaves in
      the forest,
the ears in a harvest field or the grains of sand on the
615   seashore.
   As soon as Iris had entered the cave and brushed
      aside
the dreams that were blocking her path, the house of
      Sleep was aglow
with the sheen from her dress. But the god was hardly
      able to open
his sluggish, weighed-down eyelids. He kept repeatedly
      sinking

back on the couch and nodding his drooping head on his
  chest.   620
He finally shook himself out of himself, to rise on his elbow
and question Iris (he knew who she was) on the cause of her
  visit.
'Sleep,' she replied, 'who quietens the world, most gentle of
  gods,
O Sleep, who gives peace to the mind, who banishes care,
  who refreshes
bodies exhausted by painful tasks and renews them for
  fresh toil,   625
order your dreams, who mimic the likeness of genuine
  forms,
to go to Trachis, Hercules' home, in the guise of King Ceÿx,
and enter Alcyone's mind to fashion the wraith of a
  shipwreck.
These are Juno's commands.' Her mission duly
  accomplished,
Iris departed. She couldn't endure the power of slumber 630
a moment longer. She felt it stealing over her body
and made her escape to return, as she came, by way of the
  rainbow.
  Somnus, out of the horde of his thousand children,
  awakened
Mórpheus, the master mimic, the quickest of all to
  capture   635
a person's walk, his facial expression and tone of voice;
he'll also adopt his original's clothing and typical language.
Morpheus, however, can only imitate human beings.
Another, called Ícelos by the gods, Phobétor* by ordinary
mortals, can turn into birds or beasts or long-tailed
  reptiles.   640
A third in the family, Phántasos, practises different skills:
his deception involves transforming himself into earth or
  water,
mountainous rocks or trees, and other inanimate objects.
Some of the dreams will appear at night to kings or to
  prominent

figures, while others will visit the general mass of the
645   people.
Old Sleep passed all of them by, till he picked out one
       of the brethren,
Morpheus, the dream whom he specially wanted to
       execute Iris'
commission. Then overcome once again by languid
       exhaustion,
he climbed back on to his couch and his head sank
       down on the pillow.

Morpheus floated on noiseless wings through the
650   murky darkness,
and soon he arrived in the city of Trachis, where,
       doffing his wings,
he assumed the form and likeness of Ceÿx. Sickly pale
as a lifeless corpse, and wearing no clothes, he stood at
       the foot
of the wretched Alcyone's bed. His beard appeared to
655   be dripping,
and sea-water might have been flowing in streams from
       his sodden locks.
Then leaning over the bed and weeping profusely, he
       poured
these words in the sleeper's ears: 'My unhappy wife, do
       you recognize
Ceÿx, or am I so altered by death? One look, and
       you'll know me.
In place of your husband, your husband's ghost is
660   standing before you.
None of your prayers for my safety, Alcyone, helped
       me at all.
I am dead, and you mustn't pretend to yourself that I'll
       ever come back.
As I sailed across the Aegean, my ship was caught in a
       violent
gale from the south and tossed by its stormy blasts to
       destruction.

My voice was vainly shouting your name when the waves
    washed over   665
my head and silenced all speech. This isn't a message of
    doubtful
meaning or substance. It isn't a wandering rumour. No!
It is I, your shipwrecked Ceÿx in person, reporting my own
    death.
Rise, then, and weep! Put on garments of black! Do not
    send me down
to the shadowy ghosts of Hades without the rituals of
    mourning!'   670
Morpheus mimicked the voice of Ceÿx, to make Alcyone
think that Ceÿx was there. Moreover, the tears he was
    shedding
appeared to be real, and his gestures exactly resembled her
    husband's.
   Sobbing and weeping, the queen kept flailing about in her
    sleep,
as she felt with her arms for a body, but only captured the
    air.   675
'Wait!' she shouted. 'Don't hurry away, you must take me
    with you!'
The sound of her voice with the sight of her 'husband' then
    startled and shook her
awake. She first looked round to establish if what she had
    seen
was physically there (the servants, aroused by her cries, had
    entered
the chamber with torches). When Ceÿx was not to be
    found in the room,   680
she struck on her cheeks and ripped her dress away from
    her bosom
to beat her breasts. She didn't trouble to loosen her hair,
but tore it out as it was. When her nurse asked why she was
    grieving,
Alcyone answered, 'I'm finished, I'm finished! My Ceÿx is
    dead,

and I am dead too. Don't try to console me, your words
685   will be wasted.
Ceÿx is shipwrecked and drowned. I saw him, I knew
      who he was.
As he started to leave me, I wanted to stop him and
      held out my arms.
It was only his ghost, but even his ghost was so clear, it
      was truly
my husband. I'll freely admit that his face was not as it
      usually
looks; it lacked the starry brightness he owes to his
690   father.
Oh pity me, nurse! I saw his body all naked and pale,
his hair still dripping with water. Look over here to the
      place
where the poor wretch stood!' Then turning to see if
      he'd left any footprints,
'Oh Ceÿx,' she sighed; 'your fate was what I foreboded
      and feared
when I begged you not to desert me and risk such a
695   dangerous voyage.
But since you were going away to your death, I wish at
      least
you had taken me with you too. Far better for me to
      have joined you.
We then should have lived the whole of our lives and
      have died together.
Now I am dead, I am tossed on the waves, at the cruel
700   sea's mercy,
without being properly there. My will would be even
      more cruel
to me than the cruel sea, if I strove to prolong my life
and struggled to master my grief. That struggle shall
      never be fought.
I'll never forsake you, my poor dear Ceÿx. At least I
      can join you
705 now. We shall be united, if not in an urn, in the letters

engraved on our tomb – not dust touching dust, but name
    touching name.'
Sorrow prevented her speaking further. Words were
    succeeded
by gesturcs of mourning and anguished cries from her
    broken heart.

Next morning Alcyone left the palace and went to the
    seashore.   710
Sadly she looked for the place from where she had watched
    his departure,
and lingered, saying: 'Here he released the ship from its
    moorings,
there he gave me his parting kiss.' And while she was
    linking
places with actions and gazing over the sea, she sighted
out in the water, away in the distance, an object which
    faintly   715
resembled a body. At first she couldn't be sure what it
    was;
but after the waves had washed it a little closer, although
it still was a fair way off, she could see it was clearly a body.
'Some shipwrecked sailor,' she thought to herself – a
    disturbing omen.
And then she murmured, as if a stranger were prompting
    her tears,   720
'Poor man, whoever you are! How I pity your wife, if you
    have one!'
The waves advanced and the body came nearer. The more
    she kept looking,
the more distraught Alcyone grew. It was steadily bobbing
closer and closer to land. It was close enough to be
    recognized.
Yes, it was Ceÿx! 'My husband, my husband!' Alcyone
    shouted,   725
tearing her face, her hair and her clothes. Extending her
    trembling

hands to the corpse, 'Beloved Ceÿx,' she cried, 'poor
    soul,
did you need to return to your wife like this?' On the
    water's edge
was a mole, constructed to break the ocean's initial fury
and weaken the force of the tide before it arrived on the
730   beach.
Alcyone leapt on the groyne – an astonishing feat! She
    was suddenly
flying on new-found wings through the air and
    skimming the ocean,
turned to a sorrowing bird. In the course of her flight,
    she emitted
a querulous, dirge-like croaking noise from her slender
735   beak.
As soon as she reached the silent and bloodless body,
    she folded
her new wings round the limbs of her loved one and
    vainly attempted
to kiss his lips; the bill was too hard and the kisses
    were cold.
People wondered if Ceÿx felt them or merely appeared
to raise his head as it tossed on the waves – but he
740   certainly felt them.
At last the gods took pity and both were changed into
    birds.
Now that they'd suffered the selfsame fate, their love
    could continue.
Even today, in their life as birds, their marriage is never
dissolved. They are free to mate and produce their
    young. Each winter
745 a week of calmer weather occurs, the halcyon days,
when Alcyone broods on her floating nest on top of the
    billows.
The waves are perfectly smooth and still; and Aeolus
    firmly
confines the winds in his cave, to leave the sea to his
    grandsons.

AESACUS

As the two kingfishers were flying over the sea together,
an old man watched them and praised the love they had
    kept to the end.   750
A friend who was standing nearby – though it might have
    been the same person* –
remarked, 'Do you see that other bird skimming the sea,
    with his legs
tucked under his wings?' (he was pointing towards a
    long-necked diver).
'That bird is of royal descent. If you want to trace the
    continuous
line of its pedigree back, its noble forebears included   755
Ilus, Assáracus, Gánymede stolen away by Jupiter,
old Laömedon, Priam the king whose famous reign
coincided with Troy's last days. Our diver's brother was
    Hector.
He himself met a curious fate in his early manhood,
and but for that, his fame might well have equalled his
    brother's –   760
though Hector's mother was Hécuba, Dymas' daughter,
while Aésacus, so they say, was born in secret on shady
Mount Ida to horned Granícus the river-god's child,
    Alexírhoë.
  Aesacus hated the towns and shunned the glittering
    palace
to lead a secluded and unpretentious life in the mountains 765
and fields. He seldom went into Troy for a public gathering.
Still, he wasn't a country bumpkin. His heart was not
impervious to love. He had often pursued Hespéria,
    daughter
of Cebren, another river-god, through the woods of the
    region.
One day he sighted her drying her flowing hair in the sun   770
on her father's banks. As soon as she saw him, the nymph
    ran away

like a terrified hind with a tawny wolf on its heels, or a
    wild duck
fleeing a hawk who's surprised it away from its usual
    pool.
Aesacus swiftly gave chase, impelled by love as his
    quarry
was driven by fear. But an adder was lurking there in the
775   grass;
it bit the fugitive's foot* with its fangs and injected its
    venom.
That was the end of Hesperia's flight and the end of
    her life.
Aesacus frantically took his beloved's corpse in his
    arms
as he cried, 'I'm sorry, I'm sorry! I shouldn't have
    chased you. I never
foresaw such an end. I'd never have paid such a price
    to outrun you.
Two killers have caused your unhappy death; the
780   snake dealt the wound,
but I was really your murderer. I am the guiltier party.
I have to console you for dying so young by dying
    myself.'
    So speaking, he jumped from a crag which the
    roaring waves had eroded
below, down into the sea. As he fell, he was gently
    caught
by pitying Tethys. She covered his body with wings as
785   it floated
over the sea, and didn't allow him the death that he
    longed for.
The lover was deeply angry at being forced to live on,
and that obstacles had to be thrown in his way when
    he simply wanted
to die. As soon as his new-given wings had grown on
    his shoulders,
he dived and flung his body again to the water's
790   surface.

His plumage lightened his fall. Then Aesacus furiously
    lowered
his head and plunged to the depths. He repeatedly tried to
    discover
a pathway to death and never stopped trying. His love made
    him thin,
and all of him lengthened out: his legs on their knotted
    joints,
his neck with the head so far from the body. He loves the
    sea,
and because he is constantly diving down it, we call him the
    diver.   795

BOOK 12

We have reached the Trojan War (from which the mythology of Rome was ultimately derived) in the poem's 'chronological' framework. A brief reference to the abduction of Helen introduces *The Greeks at Aulis* (1–38), in which Ovid makes more of the metamorphosis of an ominous snake than he does of Iphigenia's sacrifice. In anticipation of the Greeks' arrival at Troy, he seizes the opportunity to rival Virgil (*Aeneid* 4.173 ff.) in a brilliant, if gratuitous, description of *Rumour* (39–62). The earliest days of the war at Troy are typified by the unwarlike fight between Achilles and *Cycnus* (64–145), Neptune's son, who cannot be wounded. The great hero's initial lack of success is reminiscent of the similar fiascos in the Calydonian Boar sequence (Book 8, especially 345–79). When Achilles finally does kill Cycnus, his stripping of the body for spoils is apparently aborted by its metamorphosis.

Cycnus' inviolability to wounding is the main topic of conversation in *Achilles' Victory Celebration* (146–88). This leads the aged Nestor on to relate the story of Caeneus, who possessed a similar impregnability and had originally been a woman called *Caenis* (189–209). The sex-change, following on another rape by Neptune, is fairly briefly narrated, before Nestor continues with the book's centrepiece, *The Battle of the Lapiths and Centaurs* (210–535), at the wedding-feast of Pirithoüs and Hippodamia. Ovid now treats us to another mock-epic fight in a banqueting hall, similar to the one at Perseus' wedding (5.1–249), except that fresh scope was doubtless afforded by the half-animal centaurs and their use of the furniture and other unorthodox implements as weapons. As in the earlier fight, violent incidents follow each other in rapid and vivid succession, only relieved by the little idyll of the young centaur sweethearts, Cyllarus and Hylonome, who are swept up in the brawl. Gory details abound and the tone of the entertainment seems to be pitched at a lower level, perhaps in anticipation of the more sophisticated and subtle fare to follow in the first half of Book 13 (though another view of the burlesque is suggested in the Introduction, p. xxv). The intelligentsia might have been intrigued by the plethora of Greek proper names (twenty-three Lapiths and allies, fifty-five centaurs), many of them made up by Ovid himself (compare Actaeon's dogs in 3.206 ff.) and some with feral or other aggressive resonances. The translation does its best to make clear who are Lapiths and who are centaurs. Metamorphosis is only introduced at the very end when the unwoundable Caeneus (whom we had quite forgotten) returns to the picture to be eventually choked, like Cycnus at 140–45, and also changed to a bird. Nestor ends his lengthy narrative with the story of his brother *Periclymenus* (536–79), whom the power of self-metamorphosis failed to rescue from Hercules' bow.

Back to Cycnus. Neptune engages the help of Apollo, and through him, of Paris, in avenging his son by *The Death of Achilles* (580–628). The book moves rapidly to a conclusion emphasizing the great hero's posthumous fame and setting the scene for *The Judgment of Arms*, with which Ovid is to engage our attention over (very nearly) the next 400 lines.

THE GREEKS AT AULIS

Priam* had no idea that his son had been changed to a
    bird
and was still alive, so he went into mourning. Aésacus'
    name
was inscribed on a tomb where Hector offered his
    funeral gifts –
to no good purpose – along with his brothers. Only Paris
was missing, the prince who later involved his country in
5   war,
long years of war, along with Helen, his stolen bride.*
A confederate fleet of a thousand ships from the whole
    of Greece
was formed to pursue them; and vengeance would not
    have been long delayed
if stormy winds hadn't barred the seas and frustratingly
    stranded
the vessels at Aulis, famous for fish, in the bay of
10   Boeótia.
Here the host of the Greeks had prepared to offer the
    customary
sacrifices to Jove; the fires on an ancient altar
had duly been lit and the glowing coals were awaiting a
    victim,
when all of a sudden the people noticed a blue-green
    serpent
spiralling up a plane tree, close to the sacred precinct.
Right at the top of the tree was a nest which contained
15   eight fledgelings.
These were seized in the serpent's fangs and greedily
    gulped down,
before it devoured the mother bird as she fluttered
    around
the chicks she was losing. The crowd was
    dumbfounded, but Calchas the prophet

unfolded his vision: 'Rejoice, you Greeks! We surely will
      triumph.
Troy must fall, but our toil shall be long. These nine dead
      birds   20
presage nine years of war!' The snake, still coiled in the
      tree's green
branches, turned into stone in the form of a serpentine
      sculpture.
   The storm continued to rage on the sea in the straits of
      Euboéa.
The fleet couldn't sail to war. There were some who
      believed that Neptune   25
was sparing Troy because he had built the walls of the city.
But not so Calchas the prophet, who knew full well and
      loudly
proclaimed that the wrath of a virgin goddess* must be
      appeased
by a virgin's blood. When a father's love for his daughter
      had yielded
to kingly thought for the public good, and Iphigenía,   30
surrounded by weeping attendants, was standing in front of
      the altar
to offer her innocent blood, the goddess was moved to pity
and shrouded the scene in a blanket of mist. As the business
      proceeded,
amidst the confusion of ritual and voices uplifted in prayer,
the story goes that she substituted a hind for the maiden.
And so Diana was soothed, as required, by a victim's death,   35
and along with the wrath of the goddess, the wrath of the
      sea subsided.
The Greeks in their thousand ships set sail with a following
      wind,
and after all they had suffered arrived on the Trojan
      beaches.

RUMOUR

Picture a space at the heart of the world, between the
      earth,
the sea and the sky, on the frontiers of all three parts of
40   the universe.
Here there are eyes for whatever goes on, no matter
      how distant;
and here there are ears whose hollows no voice can fail
      to penetrate.
This is the kingdom of Rumour, who chose to live on a
      mountain,
with numberless entrances into her house and a
      thousand additional
holes, though none of her thresholds are barred with a
45   gate or a door.
Open by night and by day, constructed entirely of
      sounding
brass, the whole place hums and echoes, repeating
      whatever
it hears. Not one of the rooms is silent or quiet, but
      none
is disturbed by shouting. The noise is merely a
      murmuring babble,
low like the waves of the sea which you hear from afar,
50   or the last faint
rumble of thunder, when storm-black clouds have
      clashed in the sky.
The hall is filled by a crowd which is constantly coming
      and going,
a flimsy throng of a thousand rumours, true and
      fictitious,
wandering far and wide in a turbulent tangle of
55   language.
They chatter in empty ears or pass on stories to others;
the fiction grows and detail is added by each new teller.
This is the haunt of credulity, irresponsible error,

groundless joy, unreasoning panic, impulsive sedition   60
and whispering gossip. Rumour herself spies every
    occurrence
on earth, at sea, in the sky; and her scrutiny ranges the
    universe.

CYCNUS

Rumour had spread the report in Troy that a fleet was
    approaching
from Greece with an army on board. So when the expected
    invaders   65
arrived, the Trojans were watching the shore to prevent the
    landing.
The first Greek destined to fall to the spear of the valiant
    Hector
was Protesiláüs. Battles were fought which cost the Dánaäns
dear, and Hector's courage was known in the deaths he
    inflicted;
Achaéan might was also attested by Phrygian* losses.   70
  By now the shores of Sigéum were red with blood. By
    now
the Trojan offspring of Neptune, Cycnus,* had taken a
    thousand
lives; while Achílles the Greek charged round in his chariot,
    laying
whole ranks of his enemies low with his spear of ash from
    Mount Pélion.
Searching the battle lines for either Cycnus or Hector,   75
he lighted on Cycnus (his duel with Hector was not to take
    place
for another nine years). At once, with a shout to his
    white-maned horses,
he steered his chariot straight at his foe and cried, as he
    powerfully
brandished his weapons, 'Whoever you are, young man,
    you will have this   80

consolation in death: you were slain by the mighty
          Achilles!'
He spoke, and followed his words with a cast of his
          mighty spear.
The weapon was perfectly aimed, but the aim was
          perfectly useless.
The point was blunted and merely succeeded in bruising
85   its target's
chest. 'Son of Thetis,' Cycnus replied, 'yes, rumour has
          told me
all about you. Why be so surprised that I haven't been
          wounded?'
(Achilles was certainly looking surprised.) 'This helmet
          with chestnut
horsehair plumes and the shield you can see on my left
          arm offer me
90 no protection at all. I wear them purely for show –
just as Mars the war god is dressed for show. You can
          take every piece
of my armour away, but I'll leave without the slightest
          of scratches.
I'm not the son of a Nereïd. No, I'm the son of the god
who is lord of the sea and of Néreus and all the
          daughters of Nereus!'
So speaking, he flung his spear, but it only lodged in
95   Achilles'
shield, where it pierced the cover of bronze and the
          layers of oxhide,
nine of them, lying behind, to be finally stopped by the
          tenth.
It was shaken off by the hero, who hurled a second
          quivering
weapon with all the strength of his arm; but his target
          remained
unwounded and whole. A third attempt was no more
100   successful;
though Cycnus presented his body unguarded, it bore
          not a scratch.

Achilles exploded with rage, like a bull in an open arena,
which savagely charges the scarlet cloak held up to provoke
          him
but finds he has dealt no wound and his dangerous horns
          have been thwarted.
He wondered whether the tip of his weapon had fallen off,   105
but no, it was fixed to the shaft. Then he asked, 'Has my
          arm gone feeble
and wasted all of its earlier strength on a single opponent?
It must have been strong when I led the attack on
          Lyrnéssus' walls,
when I washed Eëtion's city of Thebae and Ténedos island   110
in blood, when the Mýsian river Caïcus was red with the
          slaughter
of all its people, when Télephus twice was touched by my
          spear.*
Here also in Troy, when I look at the piles of corpses I've
          scattered
along the shore, I can see that my hand has been strong and
          remains so.'
Such were his thoughts when, as though he mistrusted his
          former achievements,   115
he flung his spear at a Lycian, Menoétes, advancing towards
          him,
and pierced the warrior's corselet through to the breast it
          protected.
As soon as his dying victim struck the ground with his
          head,
Achilles extracted the spear, still warm, from the wound
          and he cried out,
'This is the hand and this is the spear which have won me
          my victory;   120
now I shall use them on *him*, and I pray for a victory as
          certain!'
So speaking, he aimed at Cycnus again. The ash spear
          travelled
straight to its mark and struck with a clang on the man's
          left shoulder,

then bounced right off, as it might from a wall or a
    mountain cliff.
Yet Achilles observed that the place where Cycnus had
125   taken the impact
was stained in blood, and he crowed in delight. But his
    joy was unfounded,
he hadn't inflicted a wound; the blood had come from
    Menoetes.
   Yelling with rage and frustration, he bounded down
    from his chariot,
drawing his glittering sword to attack his
    imperturbable
foe at close quarters. He found that his weapon was
130   easily denting
the helmet and shield, but was damaged itself when
    struck on the body.
This was the limit. He lowered his shield to his side to
    come closer,
and used his sword-hilt to hammer his enemy full in
    the face
and the forehead, again and again. As Cycnus
    retreated, Achilles
followed, maintaining the pressure: he hassled and
    rushed him; he left
his bewildered opponent no peace. The Trojan started
135   to panic;
dark shadows were floating in front of his eyes. Then
    while he was moving
backwards across the plain, his steps were checked by
    a rock.
Achilles thrust him down on his back right over the
    boulder,
violently twisted him round and dashed him on to the
    earth.
Then pressing his shield with his knees hard down on
140   his victim's ribs,
he pulled on the thongs of his helmet and tightened
    them under his chin

till the man was throttled and beaten at last. As Achilles got
 ready
to strip the corpse, he saw that the armour was empty.
 Neptune
had changed his son to the white-plumed bird called cycnus,
 the swan.   145

ACHILLES' VICTORY CELEBRATION

This strenuous fight led on to a truce which lasted for several
days, when weapons were laid aside and the war was
 suspended;
the Trojans patrolled their walls, while the Greeks kept
 watch on their earthworks.
There came a festival day when the duel's victor, Achilles, 150
was wooing Athena's* favour by sacrificing a heifer.
After the victim's entrails were laid on the altar flames
and the smell so welcome to heaven had wafted upwards,
 the gods
received their share of the meat and the rest was assigned to
 the banquet.
The chiefs reclined on their couches and gorged themselves
 on the roasted   155
flesh, with wine to relieve their cares no less than their
 thirst.
They didn't rely for their entertainment on singing and
 music
performed on the lyre or the multiple stops of the boxwood
 pipe.
The night was spun out in serious talk, and the principal
 topic
was manly courage. They described their battles, their own
 and the enemy's,   160
taking turns to recite the dangers they'd faced and
 surmounted,
many times over. What else would Achilles choose to
 expand on,

and what would others prefer to discuss in his glorious
        presence?
The conversation centred, of course, on Achilles' recent
success in vanquishing Cycnus. Everyone found it
165   amazing
that someone should have a body that spears could
        never transfix,
that made swords blunt and couldn't be overpowered
        by wounding.
None of the Greeks, not Achilles himself, could solve
        the mystery,
when Nestor commented: 'Yes,' he said, 'in your
        generation
Cycnus was surely unique in despising swords and
170   possessing
a body no spear could wound. But I, long ago, saw a
        person
who suffered a thousand cuts unscathed. His name was
        Caéneus,
Perrhaébian Caeneus, whose early home was
        Thessálian Óthrys.
His exploits won him renown, the more surprisingly so
as he started life as a woman.'* Nestor's novel
175   pronouncement
prompted a call from the company, voiced by Achilles,
        for details:
'Out with the story, old Nestor! We're all of us eager
        to hear it;
and you are the wisest man of our time, with a talent
        for speaking.
Now tell us who Caeneus was. And why did he change
        his sex?
On what campaign did you get to know him? Whom
180   was he fighting?
And who in the world, if anyone, finally proved his
        undoing?'
Nestor replied: 'Old age has slowed my memory down,

and there's much that I saw in my youngest days that I've
    now forgotten.
But still I remember more, and there's nothing engraved on
    my mind
more strongly than this particular story. I've done many
    things,   185
both in war and in peace; and if anyone had the good
    fortune to witness
plenty of gallant action because of prolonged old age –
well, I've lived a couple of centuries and now am into my
    third.

CAENIS

'Caenis, Élatus' daughter, was highly renowned for her
    beauty.
Of all the maidens in Thessaly she was the fairest, and
    courted   190
in vain by a wealth of suitors from all the neighbouring
    cities,
and yours, Achilles, as well (her home was likewise in
    Phthia).
Even your father, Péleus, might well have offered his hand
if he hadn't already been married – or firmly engaged,
    perhaps –
to Thetis, your mother. But Caenis accepted none of her
    suitors.   195
One day she was strolling along a secluded beach on her
    own,
when, according to rumour's report, she was raped by the
    god of the sea.
As Neptune savoured the joy of his latest conquest, he said,
'I'll allow you to ask for a gift which I promise not to refuse
    you.
Now choose what you want to ask me!' (so the rumour
    continued).   200

Caenis replied, 'The wrong you have done me is great, so
    I'll ask you
the greatest of favours I can: let me never be able to
    suffer
such wrong again. If you will make me a woman no
    more,
your promise will be fulfilled.' She delivered those final
    words
in a lower voice, and they might have appeared to come
    from a man –
205 as they surely did. The god of the sea had already granted
Caenis' request and had also bestowed an additional
    power:
the new male body could never be wounded or fall at a
    sword's point.
Caeneus departed, well pleased with the gift, and
    devoted his life
to manly pursuits as he roamed the fields by the river
    Penéüs.

THE BATTLE OF THE
LAPITHS AND CENTAURS

210 'Piríthoüs, son of Ixíon and king of the Lapiths,
had married Hippodamía. He invited the cloud-born
    centaurs*
to join the banquet at tables arranged in a leafy glen.
The chieftains of Thessaly came; I, Nestor, also
    attended.
The palace was filled with the festive hubbub of
    thronging guests.
Now hark to the wedding-hymn! Torches and rising
215   smoke in the great hall!
Enter the bride, escorted by matrons and younger
    women,

and looking a picture. We all declared how blessed Pirithoüs
was in his beautiful wife. But our praise's effect as a lucky
omen was almost undone, when the wildest of all the wild
    centaurs,
Eúrytus, drunk already, was further inflamed by the sight   220
of the bride, and the power of wine reinforced by desire
    took over.
Tables were upside down in a flash, the feast was reduced
to a shambles, as Eurytus seized Pirithoüs' newly-wed bride
by the hair and forced her away, while each of the other
    centaurs
grabbed any woman he fancied or found. The chaos
    resembled   225
a captured city, and women were screaming all over the
    palace.
We quickly rose from our couches. 'Eurytus!' shouted
    Théseus,
taking the lead, 'you must be crazy! How dare you provoke
Pirithoüs while *I* live and foolishly injure us both?'*
The centaur said nothing – he couldn't defend his
    outrageous behaviour   232
by words – but used his unruly fists to punch the prince
on the jaw and to pummel his chest. On a table nearby
    there chanced
to be lying an antique wine-bowl, richly embossed with
    figures   235
in high relief. The bowl was huge, but Theseus was huger;
he lifted it up and hurled it directly in Eurytus' face.
As globules of blood and fragments of brain poured out of
    the wound,
the centaur, vomiting wine from his mouth, fell backwards
    and drummed
with his heels on the sodden sand. His brothers, enraged by
    the carnage,   240
vied with each other in shouting as one, 'To arms, to arms!'
Inspired by the wine with courage, they started the battle by
    sending

their goblets flying, then breakable jars and round-lipped
    vessels,
objects intended for feasts, now used for war and for
    slaughter.
   'Ámycus, son of Ophíon, was first among the
245   rampaging
centaurs to raid the inner rooms of the palace and
    plunder
an iron stand which supported a cluster of burning
    candles.
He lifted the whole thing high, like a priest at a
    sacrifice straining
to raise the axe which will cleave the neck of a pure
    white bull,
then dashed it down on the forehead of Céladon, one
250   of the Lapiths.
This fractured his skull and mangled his face past all
    recognition.
His eyes burst out of their sockets, the bones of his
    cheeks were shattered,
the nose smashed inwards and jammed beneath the
    roof of his mouth.
But another Lapith called Pélates wrenched the leg
    from a maplewood
table and used it to hammer Amycus down to the
255   ground,
with his chin forced into his chest. As the centaur
    sputtered his teeth out
mingled with gore, a second blow dispatched him to
    Hades.
   'Next to the fore came Grýneus, who'd stood there,
    grimly inspecting
the smoking altar and said, "Why don't we make use
    of this?"
With a frightening glare in his eyes, he lifted the hefty
260   structure,
fires and all, and hurled it into a group of the Lapiths.

Two were crushed by the mountainous weight, Bróteas and
        Oríos
(Orios' mother was Mýcale, said to have often succeeded
in drawing down the horns of the moon with her
        incantations).
"You won't get away with this, if I can get hold of a
        weapon!"   265
Exádius said, and then caught sight of some antlers nailed
to a tall pine tree as a votive offering. There was his
        weapon!
Armed with the horns of a stag, Exadius aimed for the
        centaur's
eyeballs and gouged them out. One eye stuck fast on the
        antlers,
and one rolled down on to Gryneus' beard, blood-coated,
        and clung there.   270
    'There was Rhoétus, another centaur, snatching a
        blazing
plum-wood brand from the altar and next attacking
        Charáxus
to fracture his brow from the right. It was covered with
        golden curls,
and the hair caught fire in an instant, like crops in a dry
        cornfield.
The blood which flowed from the scorching wound made
        a terrible sizzling   275
noise like the sound of a red-hot bar of iron, when a
        blacksmith
draws it with tongs from the furnace and plunges it into his
        trough:
the metal sizzles and hisses when dipped in the cooling
        water.
The wounded Lapith shook out the greedy fire from his
        curly   280
hair and, tearing a slab from the threshold floor, he lifted it
on to his shoulders. The mass was too heavy to reach the
        centaur

(it weighed enough to be drawn by a cart); it landed
         instead
on Cométes, a friend who was standing closer at hand,
         and it crushed him.
Rhoetus couldn't contain his joy, and shouting, "May
285   all
the rest of your crew be as brave!" he returned with his
         half-burnt torch
to the wound he had started. With heavy, repeated
         blows, he battered
Charaxus' skull, till bone and brains were reduced to a
         pulp.
         'The victorious Rhoetus next attacked Euágrus,
290   Dryas
and Córythus, only a youth with the first fine hairs on
         his chin.
When Corythus fell to the ground, Euagrus cried to the
         centaur,
"What glory is there in killing a boy?" The great brute
         wouldn't
allow him to speak any further and savagely thrust his
         flaming
295 torch in Euagrus' open mouth and forced it right down
into his gullet. He then went after the furious Dryas,
whirling the brand round his head. This time he was
         less successful.
There he was, gloating over all the Lapiths he'd
         slaughtered,
when Dryas pierced him where shoulder meets neck,
         with the point of a charred stake.
Roaring, the centaur painfully wrenched the
300   implement out
from where it was lodged in the bone, and fled, now
         soaked in his own blood.
Ornéüs and Lýcabas followed him; Medon, gashed in
         his strong right
shoulder, Pisénor and Thaumas; Mérmerus too, who
         had lately

outstripped his brothers in running but, since he'd been
    wounded, was only
able to limp. Pholus and Mélaneus joined in the rout,   305
with Abas, the hunter of bears, and Ásbolus, a prophet
    who'd vainly
tried to dissuade the others from fighting. When Nessus was
    also
fleeing in terror, Asbolus shouted out to him, saying,
"*You* needn't run! You are being reserved for Hercules'
    bow."*
However, Eurýnomus, Lýcidas, Ímbreus along with Aréüs   310
failed to escape from death. They were all confronted by
    Dryas
and felled to the ground. Crenaéus was also struck in the
    face,
although he had turned in flight. As he glanced behind him,
    a javelin
caught him between the eyes where the nose grows out of
    the forehead.   315
  'In the midst of all this confusion Aphídas, a centaur, was
    lying
completely befuddled with wine, flat out, with his sleep
    unbroken,
still holding his cup in his drooping hand and sprawled on
    the shaggy
skin of a mountain bear. When Phorbas, a Lapith, observed
    him
across the hall, immobile and taking no part in the battle,   320
he slipped his fingers inside the thong of his ash spear,
    crying,
"Now you must mix your wine with Stygian water!" then
    instantly
hurled his javelin towards the youth; and the iron-tipped
    weapon
transfixed his neck as he happened to lie with his head
    thrown back.
Aphidas died feeling nothing. The dark blood welled from
    his throat   325

and spilled all over the couch and even into his goblet.
   'I, Nestor, noticed Petraéus, another centaur, trying
to lift an oak from the earth. While his arms were
      clasping it tightly,
shaking it this way and that, and the roots were
      beginning to loosen,
330 Pirithoüs cast his spear, which entered Petraeus' ribcage,
passed through his straining chest and nailed him fast
      to the hard trunk.
They say it was due to Pirithoüs' courage that Lycus
      and Chromis
fell to the earth. But neither brought their conqueror
      greater
glory than Dictys and Helops. The latter was killed by
335   a javelin
thrown from the right, which pierced his temples
      through to the left ear.
Dictys was fleeing the son of Ixion's pursuit in a panic
and slipped from a mountain ridge, to tumble
      headlong and shatter
a massive ash tree below, where his groin was impaled
340   on the splinters.
   'Áphareus rushed to avenge him and, tearing a rock
      from the mountain,
attempted to throw it. But Theseus forestalled him in
      the attempt
by wielding an oak-wood cudgel to break the bones of
      his massive
forearm. This put Aphareus out of action, and Theseus
345 lacked the time or the inclination to finish him off.
Instead he leapt on the back of the towering centaur
      Biënor,
who'd never accepted a rider before but himself. Then
      digging
his knees in the flanks of his mount, he gripped the
      curls of Biënor's
hair with his left hand, forced the head back, lifted his
      knotted

club, and battered the centaur's face on the bony temples
and slaughter-threatening lips. Brave Theseus also
    succeeded   350
in knocking over Nedýmnus, the javelin-thrower Lycópes,
and Híppasus, whose broad torso was veiled by his long
    beard; Rípheus,
taller than all the trees, and Théreus, trapper of bears,
who transported them home from Thessaly's mountains,
    alive and angry.
  'Theseus' successes in fighting could not be further
    endured   355
by the centaur Demóleon. Racing across to an age-old
    pine,
he strained very hard to uproot it with trunk intact, but he
    failed;
so he broke it off near the roots and flung it against his foe.
As it hurtled towards him, Theseus retreated well out of
    range –
on Pallas Athena's prompting, or so he would have us
    believe.   360
But the pine didn't fall before it had done some damage; it
    severed
the breast and his strong left shoulder away from the neck
    of the tall
Dolópian Crantor, your father's armour-bearer, Achilles;
(his king Amýntor, defeated in war, had handed him over
to Aéacus' son as a token and pledge of the peace between
    them).   365
When Peleus saw from a distance that Crantor was foully
    dismembered,
he cried out, "Dearest of henchmen, at least I can pay you a
    funeral
tribute." His muscular arm then launched his javelin of
    ashwood
straight at the centaur with all the strength of his body
    behind it.
The weapon ruptured its target's ribcage and quivered,
    lodged   370

in the bones. Demoleon managed to draw the shaft from
      his body –
though that came slowly enough – but the tip was
      trapped in his lung.
The pain inspired him with courage. Despite his
      faintness, he straightened
his body and kicked right out at his foe with his horse's
      hooves.
Peleus took the clattering blows on his shield and
      helmet;
375
then, guarding his shoulders by holding his weapons
      well forward, he pierced
the brute's double torso, horse's and man's, with a
      single thrust.
  'Peleus had earlier killed Phlegraéus and Hyles at
      long range;
Iphínoüs perished in hand-to-hand combat, and
      likewise Clanis.
Dórylas made one more, who was wearing a wolfskin
      cap
380
on his head and whose hand wasn't armed with a
      pointed spear but a splendid
bracket of crooked-in bull's horns, richly reddened
      with blood.
Here *I* was involved as I plucked up courage to shout
      to the centaur,
"Here now, see what your horns can do to counter my
      steel!"
and I threw my javelin. He couldn't avoid it and lifted
385
      his right hand
up to his brow for protection. His hand was pinned to
      his forehead.
A roar went up from the crowd and, as Dorylas
      helplessly stood there,
stunned by the pain of his injury, Peleus, who was
      standing
nearby, came forward and thrust his sword right under
      the belly.

The centaur then bounded forward, trailing his guts on the
    ground;   390
as he trailed them, he trampled them under his hooves;
    what he trampled he burst,
till he caught his legs in the sludge and fell with his
    abdomen emptied.
  'How about Cýllarus? He was a beauty, if centaurs can
    ever
be called good-looking. But Cyllarus' looks couldn't save
    him in battle.
His beard was just starting to grow, in a golden colour,
    gold   395
as the golden mane which streamed from his shoulders
    down to his withers.
His face was handsome and strong. His neck and his
    shoulders, his hands
and his torso – all indeed of his human features – were like
the work of a famous sculptor. His horse's parts lower
    down
were no less perfect, unblemished. A mount for Castor, if
    given   400
a head and a neck! Such a ridable back, such a muscular
    chest!
He was blacker than pitch all over, except for his legs and
    his tail
which were white. Many female centaurs pursued him, but
    only Hylónome,
fairest of all her kind to inhabit the forest, succeeded.   405
Cyllarus hers alone! She held him by sweet endearments,
by loving and saying she loved him, by making herself look
    attractive
as far as a centaur can. She'd smooth her hair with a comb
and entwine it with garlands of rosemary, violets or roses,
    and sometimes   410
with pure white lilies. Twice every day she would wash her
    face
in a spring which cascaded down from the heights of
    Págasae's woods

and twice a day she would bathe in the river. She'd only drape
her shoulder and side with animal fleeces which specially
415   suited her.
The lovers adored each other alike. They'd roam the mountains
or rest in caves together. On this occasion they'd entered
the hall of the Lapiths and joined in the fight at each other's side.
Cast by a person unknown, a spear flew in from the left,
420 and wounded Cyllarus just below the top of his chest.
The heart had only been slightly injured, but after the weapon
was pulled from his body, both heart and body went totally cold.
Hylonome hurried to catch her expiring love as he fell;
resting her hand on the wound, she soothed it; and pressing her lips
on his, she tried to prevent the escape of his fleeting
425   breath.
When she saw he was dead, she spoke a few words which the noise of battle
prevented my hearing, before she fell on the spear that had wounded
her partner, and died as she held him close in her arms for the last time.
   'Another centaur I see in my mind had his horse's and human
parts protected alike by a blanket fashioned of lion
430   skins,
six of them, fastened together by knots. His name was Phaeócomes.
Hurling a log which a pair of ox-teams could barely have shifted,
he cracked the head of Téctaphus, Ólenus' son, on the crown.

Then, while he was trying to strip the arms from his
      prostrate victim,
I, Nestor – as Peleus your father, Achilles, will surely
      confirm –   440
I plunged my blade in the spoiler's side. Old Chthónius too
and Teléboäs fell to my sword. The former was wielding a
      forked branch,
the other a spear, with which he actually gave me a wound.
You can see the mark of it here, in the scar still showing
      from that time –
the time in my life when I ought to have come to the siege
      of Troy!*   445
That was the time when I might have checked, if I couldn't
      have beaten,
the mighty Hector in battle. But Hector hadn't been born
      yet,
or else he was only a boy; and now I'm too ancient to fight
      him.
   'No need to mention how Périphas mastered the centaur
      Pyraéthus,
or tell the story of Ampyx, who managed to drive his
      unpointed   450
cornel spear right into the face of four-footed Echéclus.
Mácareus killed Erigdúpus, who came from the vale of
      Peláthron,
by ramming a crowbar into his chest. I also remember
a hunting-spear flung by Nessus which lodged in the groin
      of Cymélus.
You'd never suppose from what happened that Mopsus,*
      Ámpycus' son,   455
was merely a prophet. When Mopsus speared the centaur
      Hodítes,
his victim fell to the ground and vainly attempted to utter
some words, but his tongue had been pinned to his chin and
      his chin to his throat.

   'How about Caeneus? He killed five centaurs: Antímachus,
      Stýphelus,

Élymus, Bromus and lastly Pyrácmus, who fought with
460   an axe.
(I can't remember their wounds, but only their names
      and the number.)
Then Látreus, a centaur of massive physique, rushed
      forward to face him,
armed with the spoils of Halésus, a Macedonian he'd
      slaughtered.
In age he was past his youth and his temples were
      flecked with grey,
but his strength was still a young man's. His helmet,
465   shield and exotic
pike attracted all eyes as he proudly turned to each
      army,
brandished his weapons and pranced around in a
      well-traced circle,
flinging a torrent of insolent taunts in the empty air:
"Caenis, you bitch! Must I tolerate *you*? You will
470   always be female
and Caenis to *me*. Perhaps you forget your original
      sex.
Do you ever recall what you did to deserve your
      reward? Do you think
of the price which you paid to achieve this specious
      masculine body?
Look at the girl you were born and the shame that she
      suffered. Then go,
return to your distaff and basket of wool. Go back to
475   your spinning,
and leave the fighting to *men*!" As Latreus was
      galloping past him,
shouting these insults, Caeneus let fly with his spear,
      which made a great
gash in the mocker's side where man and horse are
      united.
Maddened by pain, the centaur cast at the hero's
      uncovered

head with his pike. The weapon rebounded like hail off a
    rooftop   480
or pebbles dropped on a drum. Then Latreus attacked at
    close quarters
and struggled to bury his sword in the young man's side,
    but the side
was too hard; there was no way in. "You won't escape me,"
    he shouted.
"You'll die on the edge of my sword, since the point's been
    blunted!" So turning   485
his weapon sideways, he reached to slash him around his
    thighs,
but the blow produced no more than a thud – the flesh
    might well have been
marble. The metal was broken to splinters on striking such
    tough skin.
Caeneus was tired of exposing his still unwounded limbs
to the stupefied centaur. "Come on!" he said to him, "now
    let's see   490
how your body responds to *my* steel"; and he plunged his
    death-dealing sword
right up to the hilt in his enemy's trunk and compounded
    the damage
by turning and twisting the sunken blade right into his
    vitals.
On came the centaurs, shouting and yelling, rushing in
    frenzy,
everyone hurling or thrusting their weapons against one
    foe.   495
Those weapons were blunted and fell to the ground, while
    Caeneus remained
unscathed by all of their blows; not a drop of his blood had
    been spilt.
  'This turn of events left the centaurs dumbfounded.
    "Shameful, disgraceful!"
Mónychus cried. "Our whole tribe worsted by one man,
    hardly

500 a man at that! No, *he* is a man and we are behaving
     as feebly as women. What use is this massive girth of
        our bodies?
     What of our double strength? Has nature combined in
        ourselves
     the courage and force of the world's two mightiest
        creatures for nothing?
     Our mother a goddess? I don't believe it. Our father
        cannot
505 have been Ixion, a mortal with pride enough to aspire
     to sleep with Juno on high, when *we* are defeated by
        someone
     whose sex is in doubt! Let us roll the boulders, the
        trees, whole mountains
     on top of this upstart. Let's hurl the forests and crush
        the life
     from his living body. His throat will be choked by the
        bulk of it all,
     and the weight will prove as good as a wound." So
510   saying, he seized
     a trunk knocked down, as it chanced, by the south
        wind's fury, and threw it
     against his unwoundable foe. The rest did the same; in
        a short while
     Othrys was stripped of its trees and Pelion empty of
        shade.
     Crushed beneath that enormous layer, the hero
        sweltered
     under the weight of the trees, and heaved with his
515   sturdy shoulders
     to raise the pile, but after the load grew greater and
        greater
     over his head and he couldn't breathe through his
        mouth any longer,
     consciousness left him. But then he recovered and
        vainly attempted
     to roll the trees off his body and lift himself up to
        obtain

some air. For a while he succeeded in moving the surface,
    as if   520
Mount Ida,* which look! we can see over there, was
    disturbed by an earthquake.
No one is certain what happened next. Some said that his
    body
was thrust right down by the mass of the trees to the
    shadows of Hades.
Mopsus the seer said no. He'd noticed a rust-winged bird*
emerging out of the pile and soaring into the air.   525
I also sighted the bird that day for the first and the last
    time.
Mopsus watched it gently circling the camp and he heard it
loudly clapping its wings. As he thoughtfully followed it
    round
with his eyes, he exclaimed, 'All hail! Hail Caeneus, pride
    of the Lapiths,   530
once unique among men, and now sole bird of your kind!"
The prophet said it and we believed it. Grief made our
    anger
all the more bitter. That one man's life should be crushed by
    so many!
To vent our sorrow, we turned on the centaurs and didn't
    cease fighting
till most had been killed and the rest were in rout or were
    rescued by night.'   535

PERICLYMENUS

As Nestor described the battle between the Lapiths and
    centaurs,
Tlepólemus, Hercules' son, was deeply distressed that his
    father
had not been mentioned* and couldn't contain his
    resentment in silence.
'Sir Nestor,' he cried, 'I'm amazed that you have forgotten
    Hercules'

glorious exploits. I'm sure that my father frequently told
540   me
the centaurs were conquered by *him*.' Old Nestor
        ruefully answered him:
'Why must you force me now to remember wrongs and
        reopen
sorrows that time has healed? Do I need to explain the
        reasons
which led me to hate your father? His deeds, heaven
        knows, surpassed
belief and the world must acknowledge the good that
545   he did – though I'd rather
be able myself to deny it. My praises haven't included
Deíphobus or Pulýdamas, even Hector, for nobody
praises his foes. Your illustrious father had razed the
        walls
of Messéne, and next he destroyed the innocent cities
550   of Elis
and Pylos, where my palace was ravaged by fire and
        sword.
Of the many he slaughtered I'll only refer to the sons of
        Néleus,
twelve of us then, and we made a splendid group of
        young warriors.
Hercules killed all twelve, with the sole exception of
        me.
I had to accept the death of my other brothers, but one
555   strange
death stands out, Periclýmenus'. Neptune, the founder
        of Neleus'
line, had invested this youth with the power of
        adopting whatever
shape he desired and of changing back to his normal
        form.
At Hercules' coming, he'd run the gamut of
        metamorphosis
without the slightest effect, till he changed to the form
560   of the bird,

so dear to the king of the gods, which transports his bolts in
    its talons.
Using his eagle's strength, Periclymenus tore at Hercules'
face with his flapping wings, hooked beak and his sharp
    curved claws.
The hero from Tiryns then bent his all-too-unerring bow
against the creature and, while it was hovering high in the
    clouds,   565
an arrow entered its breast quite close to one of its wings.
The wound was not very deep, but the sinews torn on that
    side
could serve it no longer, all movement and flying power
    were lost.
The eagle fell to the earth, as its weakened wings could no
    longer
catch the air to support them; and where the arrow had
    lightly   570
lodged in the wing, it was forced by the weight of the
    crashing body
through to the top of the breast and out by the neck on the
    left side.
Now, Tlepolemus, handsome chief of the Rhodian fleet,
do you really believe that I owe your father a public
    eulogy?
Nevertheless, my silence about his exploits completes   575
the vengeance I owe my brothers; my friendship with *you*
    is unbroken.'
So Nélean Nestor charmingly answered Hercules' son.
When the old man's story was finished, the wine went
    round once again,
and everyone rose from their couches to sleep for the rest of
    the night.

THE DEATH OF ACHILLES

But the god who rules the waves with his trident grieved
580   as a father
for Cycnus, the son whose body he'd changed to a
       swan like Pháëthon's
friend.* He detested the cruel Achilles so much that he
       crossed
the bounds of civilized conduct to vent his implacable
       anger.
The war against Troy had now dragged on for about
       ten years,
when Neptune strongly appealed to his long-haired
585   Sminthian* nephew:
'Apollo, the one of my brother Jupiter's sons whom I
       love
the best, who joined me in building the walls of Troy
       unrewarded,*
do you heave a sigh when you look at these towers, so
       soon to fall?
Do you rue the slaughter of so many thousands
       defending the city?
Not to mention each one, are you haunted at least by
590   the ghost
of Hector, whose body was dragged* all round the
       stronghold he fought for?
Meanwhile that monster Achilles, a man more
       blood-polluted
than war itself, lives on to ravage the work of our
       hands.
Let him come my way: I'll ensure that he feels the
       power of my trident.
But since I may not engage with my foe directly,* I ask
595   you
to shoot an invisible arrow to catch the brute
       unawares.'

Apollo agreed; his wishes exactly accorded with Neptune's.*
Hiding his presence in cloud, he came to the Trojan lines,
and there in the midst of the general carnage he noticed
          Paris
shooting away in desultory fashion at common Greek
          soldiers.   600
The god revealed who he was and said to him, 'Why are
          you wasting
your shafts on the rank and file? If you care at all for your
          family,
target Achilles and take revenge for your slaughtered
          brethren.'
So saying, he pointed the hero out, still hacking the
          Trojans
down; then turning Paris' bow in the same direction   605
he guided an arrow with deadly aim at Achilles' heel.
If Priam, after the death of Hector, had cause for rejoicing,
this surely was it. So Achilles who'd vanquished the
          mightiest heroes
was vanquished himself by a coward who'd stolen the wife
          of his Greek host.
If he was destined to die at the hands of a woman in war,   610
he'd rather have been cut down by the axe of Penthesilea.*

Now the terror of all the Trojans, the pride and bulwark
of Greece's name, Achilles the hero unequalled in battle,
had ended in flames.* Vulcan, the god who had forged his
          armour,
had fired his body to ashes; all that remained of Achilles   615
the great was a small amount of material, barely sufficient
to fill an urn. But his fame lives on to fill the expanse
of the whole wide world. His glory measures up to the man;
it matches his noble self, untouched by shadowy Hades.
     Even the shield of Achilles proclaimed the hero who'd
          owned it.   620
It prompted a conflict, and arms were taken up for his
          arms.

None of the others ventured to claim them – not
    Diomédes,
Ajax, the son of Oéleus, not Meneláüs, not even
his elder and far more valiant brother, King
    Agamémnon.
Only Ulýsses and Ajax, the son of Télamon, reckoned
their prowess was such as to merit a prize so very
625   prestigious.
To avoid the invidious task of deciding between them
    himself,
Agamemnon summoned the Argive chiefs to a court in
    the heart
of the camp, and referred the dispute to the judgment
    of all in the session.

BOOK 13

This is the longest book in *The Metamorphoses* – striking, as always, for its internal variety and for its wide range of literary associations with the different genres of epic, tragic and pastoral poetry. Those who enjoy the game will find thematic links between some of the stories. Long speeches, mostly of persuasion or appeal, are a unifying feature.

The Judgment of Arms (1–381) is a formal debate between the heroes Ajax and Ulysses, each of whom is claiming the divinely-made arms of the dead Achilles. The two speakers – the brave but stolid-minded warrior, Ajax, and the wily tactician, Ulysses – are skilfully characterized and contrasted. Note that Ajax unwisely addresses himself to the crowd of onlookers, while Ulysses argues his case directly to the chieftains who have been asked to decide the issue. Although the speeches contain a strong flavour of the rhetorical exercises set to young Romans in their educational curriculum, both will strike the modern reader as vital and entertaining. In the subject-matter Ovid traverses much of the ground covered in Homer's *Iliad*, and in post-Homeric poems of the seventh and sixth centuries BC, known as the Epic Cycle, about the fall of Troy. His audience would have appreciated the way in which he makes each of his two contestants distort some of the familiar detail in his own favour. After Ulysses has won, we have *Ajax's Suicide* (382–98), where Ovid refrains from alluding to the terrible madness which lies at the core of Sophocles' tragedy *Ajax*. The hero's suicide is contrived to lead up to a metamorphosis linking his death, not very appropriately, with that of Apollo's boy-friend, Hyacinthus (10.162–219).

The substance and tone of Euripides' tragedies, however, are strongly recalled in *The Fall of Troy* (398b–428) and *The Sufferings of Hecuba* (429–575). In the former we will find no reference to the famous Wooden Horse – Virgil had done that too well in *Aeneid* 2. The latter is based remarkably closely on Euripides' *Hecuba*, with its double plot which shows the Trojan queen facing and responding to the deaths of her daughter Polyxena and her youngest son Polydorus. The episode includes some fine speeches for the princess Polyxena confronting sacrifice to Achilles' ghost and for the old queen herself as she laments her daughter's and her own fate. In its conclusion, Ovid inevitably draws on the strange tradition that the grief-stricken Hecuba was ultimately transformed to a howling dog.

The tone grows less intense in the last Trojan story, of the dawn goddess Aurora's dead son, *Memnon* (576–622), whose ashes take the form of two bird armies as they rise from his funeral pyre. We pass on quickly to *The Wanderings of Aeneas* (1) (623a–31, 705–39), where Ovid does move into Virgilian territory. His 'little *Aeneid*' provides a framework for the metamorphoses which follow, as for the death of Aeneas in 14.581–607; and it leads after that into the mythology of Rome itself. When the Trojans reach Delos, Ovid works in the change-stories of *The Daughters of Anius* (632–74) and *The Daughters of Orion* (675–704), both fairly low-key episodes; but the book achieves a superb lift when the wanderers' voyage brings them to Sicily. There the myth of Scylla (in her pre-monster days) incorporates *Acis, Galatea and Polyphemus* (740–897), a favourite story chiefly familiar from the Greek pastoral poet Theocritus (third century BC). The song of the wild and hairy Cyclops wooing the nymph Galatea is another high-spot of the poem. In conclusion, we have the first part of *Glaucus and Scylla* (898–967), in which another girl is unsuccessfully appealed to at length by the merman who was formerly a mortal youth.

THE JUDGMENT OF ARMS

The chieftains had taken their seats. A crowd gathered
    round in a ring,
and they were the audience that Ajax, lord of the sevenfold
    shield,*
stood up to address. Unable, as usual, to govern his temper,
he grimly surveyed the ships along the shore of Sigéum,
then with a gesture towards them, he said: 'In the name of
    Jupiter,   5
here are the two of us putting our case in front of those
    vessels,*
and I, great Ajax, am asked to compare myself with
    Ulýsses!
He beat a hasty retreat* when Hector attacked with his
    torches,
while I stood my ground and saved the fleet by routing the
    foe.
It's safer, it seems, to fight with lies and ingenious talk
than engage in arms like a man. But speaking isn't my chief
    strength,   10
as action is not my opponent's. My power in the fury of
    battle
is matched by his skill in debate. No need, I think, to recite
my actions to you, my Argive friends, as you saw them
    yourselves.
Ulysses may tell you his own, the actions for which he
    cannot
produce one witness, the actions which only the night is
    aware of.   15
The prize that I seek is a great one, I freely admit. But my
    rival
detracts from its value. It isn't an honour for Ajax to win
whatever Ulysses has hoped to achieve, no matter how
    splendid.
Ulysses has won a prize as it is: when he loses this match,

he'll be sure of the glory of having competed with Ajax,
20   with me!
      'What's more, if anyone chose to question the valour
            of Ajax,
my noble birth would give me the edge. My father was
      Télamon,
hero who captured the walls of Troy when the valiant
      Hercules
led the attack, and joined the Argonauts sailing to
      Colchis.
His father was Aéacus, now a judge of the spirits in
25   Hades,
where shifty Sísyphus strains against the weight of his
      rock.
King Jupiter frankly acknowledges Aeacus' place as a
      son
of his own; so Ajax is third in line of descent from
      Jove.
However, my ancestry shouldn't be used as a point in
      my favour,
30 unless I share it with great Achilles. He was my cousin,
and I am demanding my cousin's arms. As Sisyphus'
      scion,*
Ulysses, and equal in fraud and deceit, are you trying to
      graft
the name of an alien line on Aeacus' family tree?
      'Must the arms be denied to me because I entered the
      war
before my opponent and wasn't enrolled by a sneaking
35   informer?*
Should *he* be accorded the prior claim when he joined
      up last,
when he tried to escape from military service by feigning
      madness,
until another more crafty fellow – although he was
      doing
himself no good – Palamédes, exposed his cowardly
      fiction

and dragged him along to the expedition he'd sought to
    avoid?
Is he to take the best arms, because he refused to take up   40
any? Am I to be slighted, deprived of the prize which
    belonged
to my cousin, since I was first to throw myself into danger?
   'I wish, indeed, that Ulysses' madness had either been real
or believed to be real. I wish that this instigator of crime
had never accompanied us to the fortress of Troy. If so,   45
Philoctétes* would not be marooned on Lemnos to our
    discredit,
hidden, they say, in tree-covered caves, disturbing the
    rocks
with his groans and raining curses on vile Ulysses, curses
richly deserved, which must be fulfilled if the gods exist.
And now that hero, who took the same oath of alliance as
    we did,   50
one of our captains, to whom the dying Hercules handed
his bow, is broken by sickness, starving, clothed and fed
by the birds which he kills with arrows that ought to be
    killing the Trojans.
But still, Philoctetes lives, since he did not go with Ulysses   55
to Troy, while poor Palamedes would rather have been
    abandoned.
He was the man who'd exposed my opponent's pretended
    madness
and had to pay. Ulysses remembered it all too well.
He falsely accused Palamedes of treason against the Greeks.
What evidence did he produce? It was gold he had buried
    beforehand.   60
This shows how Ulysses has sapped our strength by exile
    or murder.
That's how he fights and that is the kind of fear he inspires.
   'Ulysses' eloquence may surpass even trusty Nestor's,
but that will never induce me to think his desertion of
    Nestor*
was other than shamefully wrong. The tired old man was in
    trouble   65

because his horse had been wounded. He cried to Ulysses
    for help,
but his comrade betrayed him. Ulysses' friend Diomédes
    can vouch
that I'm not making this up, as he shouted Ulysses' name
again and again and castigated his cowardly flight.
But the gods survey the actions of mortals with eyes of
70   justice.
Ulysses was later in need of the help* which he'd failed
    to supply;
in abandoning Nestor, he'd shown how he himself
    should be treated.
He yelled for his friends. I, Ajax, arrived and could see
    him quaking,
pale and trembling with fear at the thought of the death
    confronting him.
75 Setting my massive shield in front of his prostrate body,
I saved his life – small credit in saving so feeble a
    sluggard!
(Listen to me! If you want to persist in this contest, let's
    go
once more to the spot; you can bring the enemy back,
    with your wound
and your typical fear. Hide under my shield and
    compete with me there!)
But then – what happened? The man whose wounds
80   had prevented him standing,
after I'd rescued him, ran, and there wasn't a wound on
    his body.

  'Hector arrived* and entered the fray with the gods
    on his side.
Wherever he charged on the field, he struck astonishing
    terror
not only in cowards like you, Ulysses, but brave men
    too.
As he revelled in all the havoc he'd wreaked and the
85   blood he had shed,

I threw an enormous stone from a distance and laid him flat.
Earlier on, when he challenged a Greek to engage in a duel,
I took him on by myself. When the lots were cast, you
      Greeks
all prayed that I should be chosen to fight, and your prayers
      were answered.
How did the duel turn out? I wasn't defeated by Hector.   90
Later the Trojans attacked our ships with fire and sword
and Jupiter's help. Where now was the brilliant speaker,
      Ulysses?
I, with my manly body, protected the thousand ships,
your hopes of return. So give me those arms for my own
      protection.
But allow me to tell you the truth of the matter: those arms
      are owed   95
a greater tribute than I am; their glory and mine are
      united.
Ajax isn't claiming the arms; the arms claim Ajax.
   'Ulysses may set his own deeds against mine: the deaths
      of King Rhesus*
and Dolon* the craven spy, the capture of Príam's son
      Hélenus,
the theft of Pallas Athena's statue.* None of those actions
took place in the daytime; what's more, Diomedes was
      always beside him.   100
If you were disposed to award these arms for such trivial
      exploits,
you ought to divide them and give Diomedes the larger
      share.
   'But *why* should Ulysses receive them? He always
      operates under
cover and carries no arms when he steals on the foe with his
      ruses.
The glint which shines from Achilles' golden helmet by
      moonlight   105
will give him away and show him up as he lurks in ambush.
The Íthacan's head will never be able to carry the weight

of that great plumed helmet; the spear of Pélian ash will
          be far too
massive and heavy for feeble arms such as his to throw;
and the shield,* embossed with its picture displaying the
          whole wide world,
110   can hardly look well on that soft left hand with its
          talent for stealing.
How can you claim a reward which will sap your
          strength? You are shameless!
Even supposing the Greeks were foolish enough to
          agree,
you won't give the Trojans a reason to fear you, but
          only to rob you.
Retreat, the single art in which you excel, you
115   cowardly
weakling, will grind to a halt, if you're trailing that
          great heavy object
behind you in flight. Moreover, the shield that you
          have so rarely
employed in battle is perfectly sound, while mine,
          which is riddled
with countless holes from the spears it has stopped, is
          in need of replacement.
In short, is argument needed? Much better to judge us
120   in action.
Cast the brave hero's arms, Greeks, into the ranks of
          the foe.
Then call for those arms to be fetched, and let the
          recoverer keep them!'

The high-born Ajax ended his speech, and his final
          words
drew a buzz from the crowd, which continued until the
          noble Ulysses
rose to his feet. For a while he fixed his gaze on the
125   ground;
then he looked straight up at the chiefs who were
          eagerly waiting in silence

and opened his speech in words as engaging as they were
    persuasive:
  'Princes of Greece, if only my prayers along with your
    own
had prevailed, the victor in this grand contest would not be
    in doubt.
Achilles would still have his arms, and we should still have
    Achilles.   130
Since fate has so unkindly denied him to all of you
and to me,' (he spoke with a gesture of wiping the tears
    away
from his eyes) 'what better person to follow the great
    Achilles
than I, who enabled the great Achilles to follow the Greek
    cause?
You shouldn't let Ajax' dullness of intellect count in his
    favour   135
or hold my quickness against myself; it has always been
    used
in your service, my lords. Don't grudge me my eloquence,
    such as it is;
it has often pleaded for you in the past, and now it is bound
to plead for its master. We cannot ignore the gifts that we
    have.
  'Ancestry, forebears, titles we haven't achieved for
    ourselves,   140
are scarcely points we can urge. But Ajax has argued that
    he is
Jupiter's great-grandson. My extraction also goes back
to Jupiter; I, like Ajax, am third in the line of descent.
I am the son of Laértes, son of Arcésius, fathered
by Jove; and my pedigree doesn't include a convict in
    exile.*   145
I also enjoy high birth through my mother, as she is
    descended
from Mercury. Traces of god can be found in both of my
    parents.
However, my claim to the arms of Achilles is not dependent

either on being more nobly born on my mother's side
or on having a father untouched by the guilt of killing his
      brother.
Judge this case on our personal merits – provided that
150   Ajax
receives no credit for being Achilles' cousin as Péleus
was Telamon's brother. No, let the judgment of arms
      be a tribute
to valour. Or else, if the next of kin must be first to
      inherit
and that is the test, then Achilles' weapons should
      surely be given
to Peleus his father or Pyrrhus his son – no room there
155   for Ajax.
Arrange for those weapons to be dispatched to Phthia
      or Scyros!*
And Teucer,* no less than Ajax, has rights as a cousin.
      Is *he*
pursuing a claim? And supposing he did, would he be
      successful?
  'In short, this contest depends on actions, purely and
      simply,
and I have performed more deeds than I have the skill
160   to encompass
in words. But still, let me tell them in order, as each
      occurred.
  'The sea-goddess Thetis knew that her son was fated
      to die
if he went to Troy, so she dressed Achilles up as a girl;
and everyone, Ajax included, was taken in by the
      female
165 disguise. But I, to excite his masculine interest, inserted
some arms amongst our feminine wares. He still was
      dressed
in the clothes of a girl when I caught him holding a
      spear and shield,
and said to him, "Son of a goddess, Pérgamum,
      doomed to perish,

is waiting for *you*. Why shrink from destroying magnificent
    Troy?''
Then I gripped his shoulder and sent him forth to a warrior's
    glory.   170
Therefore Achilles' deeds are my own. It was I whose spear
disabled our enemy Télephus,* I who later applied
that spear to the conquered king, when he begged to be
    healed of his wounds.
The fall of Thebae is my achievement; attribute to me
the capture of Lesbos, Scyros, Apollo's cities of Ténedos,
Chryse and Cilla; my hand it was that battered Lyrnéssus'   175
walls and laid them in ruins. Indeed, it was I who
    provided
the man who was able to kill fierce Hector, to mention no
    others.
I floored the notorious Hector! So then, in return for the
    weapons
through which I discovered Achilles, I claim these weapons
    before us.
I gave him arms while he lived, and demand arms back
    from him dead.   180
  'When one man's grievance came to involve the whole
    of Greece,
and the thousand ships were assembled at Aulis to back
    Meneláüs,
they waited for many months, but the winds were always
    against them
or failed entirely to blow. Then a harsh announcement
    required
Agamémnon to slaughter his innocent daughter* to cruel
    Diana.   185
This he refused to do. He resented the gods' decree,
and the king still harboured a father's love. But my
    persuasions*
induced him to harden his heart for the sake of the common
    good.
It was I (I have to confess, and I hope that royal
    Agamemnon

will pardon me for it) who argued that difficult case in
190   front of
a partial judge. In the end, he was swayed by the
          people's interest,
his brother's wrongs and his role as commander to
          balance his honour
against the blood of his daughter. I then was
          dispatched to the mother,*
who needed deceiving more than persuading to send
          her child.
If Ajax had gone, the fleet would still be stranded at
195   Aulis.
     'Next I was sent on a dangerous mission to Troy as
          an envoy.*
I saw and entered the council-chamber on Ílium's
          heights,
when the city was still well crowded with men. I
          fearlessly argued
the case on behalf of the Greek coalition as I'd been
          instructed,
200 accusing Paris and firmly demanding Helen's return
with all the possessions she'd taken. Priam was moved
          to agree,
and so was Anténor. But Paris, his brothers and
          fellow-abductors
could hardly restrain their iniquitous hands – as you
          know full well,
Menelaüs. That day was the first when I backed you at
          risk to my own life.
     'There isn't the time to recount the contribution I
205   made
to planning and action throughout the length of that
          tedious war.
After the early battles the Trojans confined themselves
inside the walls of their city. A long while passed when
          there wasn't
the chance of an open engagement (we finally fought in
          the tenth year).

What were you doing, Ajax, in all that time? You only   210
knew about fighting, and otherwise weren't any use;
    while I
was busily occupied, laying traps for the enemy, ringing
our lines with trenches, raising the troops' morale to enable
    them
better to cope with the boredom, making supply
    arrangements
for food and arms, and going on missions as need
    demanded.   215
  'Then lo and behold! Deceived by a dream which Jupiter
    sends him,
King Agamemnon commands the chiefs to abort
    operations,*
justifying this order by claiming that Jupiter wills it.
Would Ajax oppose this change and demand the
    destruction of Troy?
Would he fight – which is all he can do? Why didn't he stop
    the withdrawal?   220
Why didn't he seize his arms to offer some lead to the
    wavering
rabble? It wasn't too much to expect of a person whose
    every
word is a brag. What actually happened? He joined in the rout!
I saw you, Ajax, to my great shame, when you ran for your
    life
and issued those shameful orders to spread the sails of your
    ship.
I instantly shouted, "What are you up to? You must be
    crazy,   225
my friends, stampeding to give up Troy when it's virtually
    taken.
Ten years have gone by and all you are taking home is
    dishonour!"
With words such as these, and others inspired by my
    indignation,
I made the runaways turn and brought them back from the
    ships.

Agamemnon summoned the troops, still quaking with
230   fear, to a meeting.
But even then the heroic Ajax hadn't the courage
to open his mouth (Thersítes* actually ventured to
          challenge
the kings – and was punished by *me* for his rudeness). I
          rose to my feet
and exhorted my frightened countrymen to confront
          the Trojans,
thus restoring the courage they'd lost. And ever since
235   then,
whatever valiant deeds my rival may seem to have
          done
can be counted my own, as I dragged him back when
          he tried to retreat.
          'Finally, who on our side ever praises or seeks you
          out?
Diomedes shares his adventures with me, and I am the
          man
whom he wants for his comrade; he always feels safe
240   when Ulysses is with him.
It's no mean thing to be specially picked by *him* out of
          all those
thousands of Greeks. I wasn't chosen by lot for the
          venture,
but all the same I defied the risks of a night patrol
and disposed of a foe who was out, like us, on a
          dangerous mission,
Dolon the Phrygian. I killed him, but not before I had
245   forced him
to talk and betray the plans which the treacherous
          Trojans were laying.
Now in possession of all the information I needed,
I could have returned to base and won the acclaim I'd
          been promised.
But not content with so little, I made for Rhesus'
          encampment,

and there I slaughtered the king and his staff in their very
    own tents.   250
So thus victorious, my hopes accomplished, I captured and
    mounted
the royal chariot; I might have been riding in glorious
    triumph!*
My lords, if you now deny me the arms of Achilles, whose
    horses
Dolon demanded as *his* reward for the work of that night,
you'll be meaner than Ajax, who said Diomedes and I
    should divide them.
  'No point in recalling the havoc I wreaked with my
    sword in the ranks   255
of Lycian Sarpédon; neither the blood that flowed when I
    slaughtered
Coéranus, Íphitus' son, with Alástor, Alcánder, Noémon,
Chrómius, Hálius, Prýtanis; cut down Thoön and
    Charops,
Chersídamas, Énnomus, forced to his death by a merciless
    fate,   260
and others less famous who fell by my hand close up to the
    walls.
I also have wounds to display, my friends. They were nobly
    won,
on the front of my body. Don't trust in my empty words.
    Look here!'
(And he opened his tunic.) 'This heart has been always
    engaged in your service!   265
But what about Ajax? In all these years he has shed not a
    single
drop of blood for his friends, and his body remains
    unmarked!
  'What does it really matter if Ajax claims he defended
the fleet of the Greeks against the Trojans when Jupiter
    backed them?
I admit that he did so, of course – it's not my way to be
    spiteful   270

or denigrate what's well done; but he shouldn't reserve
    for himself
what belongs to all. He should give some credit to you,
    my lords.
Patróclus,* safely disguised in Achilles' armour, repulsed
the Trojans before they could burn the ships with Ajax
    inside them.
My rival reckons that none but he had the courage to
275   duel
with Hector – forgetting the king and the chiefs, and
    forgetting myself.
In fact, he was ninth to come forward and only
    selected by lot.
But what was the final result of your fight with Hector,
    you bravest
of warriors? Hector went off without one wound on
    his body!
   'My lords, I find it exceedingly painful to be
280   reminded
of that black hour when Achilles, the bulwark of all
    the Greeks,
laid down his life. But my tears, my sorrow, my fear of
    the enemy
never prevented my lifting his body to carry it home.
These, these, I say, were the shoulders on which the
    corpse of Achilles
was borne from the field with the weapons I now am
285   striving to win.
I have the physical strength that is needed to bear such
    a weight,
and I have the mind which will surely value this tribute
    from you.
Why was Achilles' Néreïd mother so deeply concerned
to obtain fresh arms* for her son? Did she really intend
    that present
from Vulcan, that work of consummate art, to be worn
290   by a brainless

and uncouth soldier? He couldn't describe the features
     engraved
on the shield: the ocean, the earth and the sky with its
     constellations,
the Pleiads and Hyads, the Bear that never sinks in the sea,
the circles of sun and moon and the gleaming sword of
     Oríon.
He's asking you to award him arms which he cannot
     appreciate.   295
   'Ajax attacks me for shirking the hardships of war and
     arriving
late on the scene when the expedition was under way.
Has he no idea that he's also maligning the valiant
     Achilles?
If you call dissembling a crime, then we both dissembled,
     Achilles
and I. If delay is a fault, then I arrived before he did.   300
I was detained by my wife's devotion, and he by his
     mother's.*
We gave our youth to our loved ones, the rest of our lives to
     Greece.
If I couldn't refute the charge, I should still be proud to
     have shared
my guilt with a hero such as Achilles – though he was
     detected
by *my* intelligence; I was not detected by Ajax.   305
   'My lords, we mustn't be too surprised that Ajax is
     flinging
his stupid slanders at me. You also are being accused
of disgraceful behaviour. Or was it a shocking scandal for
     me
to have falsely accused Palamedes, but splendid for *you* to
     convict him?
In fact, Palamedes could not rebut the indictment of
     treason   310
or challenge the evidence levelled against him. You didn't
     just hear it;

you *saw* what he'd done. The case was proved by the
        bribes he had taken.*
    'I don't deserve to be blamed because Philoctetes is
        stranded
on Vulcan's island of Lemnos. Defend *your* part in the
        action,
my lords, since you approved it. I grant that I offered my
315   view
that he'd better withdraw himself from the war and the
        arduous journey,
and try, by resting, to ease the terrible pain of his
        wound.
Philoctetes agreed – and survives to this day. My
        advice was not only
well meant, though that would have been enough; it
        was also effective.
Now the seers declare he is needed for Troy's
320   destruction.
Don't send *me* to escort him! He's crazed by his pain
        and resentment.
Far better for Ajax to go and use *his* powers of
        persuasion
to soften his fury and bring him to Troy by some crafty
        stratagem!
Seriously, though, the Símoïs river will flow upstream,
Mount Ida stand leafless and Greece will promise her
325   aid to Troy,
before I tire in my thoughtful efforts on your behalf
and you have to call on the cunning wits of the witless
        Ajax.
No matter how much self-willed Philoctetes may hate
        his old allies,
detest Agamemnon, abominate me and endlessly rain
        down
curses upon my head; or pray that fortune will place
330   me
within his pain-stricken reach and allow him to drain
        my blood;

I shall go for him all the same and endeavour to bring him to
    Troy.
With luck I shall seize his arrows, as surely as I took
    Helenus
prisoner, the prophet through whom I revealed the oracle's
    word   335
how Troy could be captured; then ventured into the heart
    of the foe
to seize the statue of Pallas which stood in her innermost
    shrine.
In the light of this, can Ajax compare himself to Ulysses?
  'The Fates, indeed, had declared that Troy could never be
    captured
without that image. But where, my lords, was the valiant
    Ajax?   340
Where were the strong man's boasts? And why should he
    then be frightened?
Why did Ulysses dare to make his way through the watch,
entrust himself to the night and brave the swords of the foe,
not merely to enter the walls of the Trojans but mount
    right up
to the top of the citadel, thence to steal the goddess away
from her sacred temple and carry her back through the
    enemy lines?   345
Without this achievement of mine, Telamonian Ajax' arm
would have wielded the sevenfold layers of his oxhide shield
    to no purpose.
That night, by my doing, the victory was won and Troy was
    defeated.
Pergamum fell at the instant I made it no longer invincible.
  'Ajax, stop pointing out with your mutters and sullen
    looks   350
that I always could use Diomedes. Far be it from me to
    deny it.
You weren't alone when you bore your shield in defence of
    the allied
fleet; a crowd was behind you, while only one person
    accompanied

me. If he wasn't aware that fighters come lower than
     thinkers
and prizes aren't owed to a strong right arm, however
355   unflinching,
he'd claim those weapons himself, and so would Ajax
     the lesser,
warlike Eurýpylus, Thoäs the son of the famous
     Andraémon;
so would Idómeneus, Mériones his companion from
     Crete,
and royal Agamemnon's younger brother, the brave
     Menelaüs.
Of course they are sturdy warriors, fully my equals in
360   battle –
but not in the *tactics* of warfare. Your physical might
     serves well
on the field, but your limited powers of thinking need
     my direction.
Your strength is mindless, where my concern is to plan
     ahead.
You surely can fight, but it's I who advises the king
     when he's choosing
the critical moment for action. Your simple brawn
365   must be measured
against my brains. In a ship the helmsman takes
     precedence over
the rower; in war the commander has more respect
     than the soldier;
so I must rank above you. In the make-up of human
     beings,
intelligence counts for more than our hands, and that is
     our true strength.
     'Princes of Greece, I call on you now to reward your
370   watchman.
Reward me for all those years of anxious and careful
     devotion.
I ask you to give me the prize which I'm owed for my
     dutiful service.

My work is complete: by removing the obstacle fate had
    imposed,
by enabling the capture of Ilium's towers, I achieved their
    capture.
By all the hopes that we share, by the toppling defences of
    Troy,   375
in the name of the gods whose aid I recently stole from the
    foe,
by anything yet to be done where intelligent action is
    needed,
remember Ulysses! Or else, if it cannot be mine, let this
    armour   380
be *hers*!' – and he pointed towards the fateful image of
    Pallas.

AJAX'S SUICIDE

The chieftains were swayed by Ulysses, and oratory's power
    was proved
when the valiant warrior's arms were won by the skilful
    speaker.
The loser, who'd fought with Hector in single combat,
    who'd often
withstood the assaults of fire and sword and of Jupiter, only
failed to withstand his own anger. The hero whom no one
    had beaten   385
was beaten at last by resentment. Grasping his sword he
    cried,
'This at least is mine! Or is this also claimed by Ulysses?
It must be wielded against myself. The weapon so often
stained with the blood of the Trojans must now be stained
    with its master's.
No one shall have the power to conquer Ajax, but Ajax!'   390
He spoke, and into the breast which had never been
    wounded before*
he drove his murderous sword till he buried it up to the
    hilt.

His hands were too weak to draw out the deeply
    embedded weapon;
it was only expelled by the force of his blood, which
    reddened the earth
and there gave rise to a purple flower from the soft green
395   turf,
a flower which had once been born from the wound of
    the young Hyacinthus.
Both boy and man were recalled in the letters inscribed
    on the petals,
AIAI* for a cry of lament, AIAI for the name of a
    hero.

THE FALL OF TROY

The victor Ulysses then sailed on a quest to the island of
    Lemnos,
a land that once had been ruled by Hypsípyle, daughter
    of Thoäs,
notorious too as a place where the women had
400   murdered their husbands;*
he went to procure the arrows which Hercules gave
    Philoctetes.
After these had been brought, with their master, back
    to the Greeks,
an unduly protracted struggle at long last reached a
    conclusion.
Ilium blazed, and before the flames had fully subsided,
Jupiter's altar was stained by the murder of aged,
    thin-blooded
Priam; Cassándra, Apollo's priestess, was dragged
410   away
by the hair, extending her arms to the sky in a useless
    appeal.
The Dardánian women clung to the statues of Troy's
    old gods

for as long as they could, but were ruthlessly torn from the
      burning shrines
by the conquering Greeks – a prize which excited the wrath
      divine.
Astýanax, Hector's son, was cast from the towers,* from
      where   415
his eyes so often had followed his mother's finger and
      watched
his father fighting to guard both him and their forefathers'
      kingdom.
   Soon a wind from the north was inviting the Greeks to
      depart;
the sails flapped loud in the breeze and the sailors shouted
      'Away!'
'Farewell, dear city!' the women of Troy cried out as they
      knelt   420
to kiss the soil of their land and abandoned the smoking
      ruins.
The last of the women to go on board, and a pitiful sight,
was Hécuba.* Soldiers had found her wandering round the
      graves
of her sons; as she clung to the mounds and was kissing the
      bones, she was forcibly
dragged away by Ulysses. Still, she had managed to rescue   425
the ashes of Hector and bear them off in the folds of her
      garments.
On Hector's tomb she had left a lock of her silvery hair;
that lock and her tears were the only funeral gifts she could
      offer.

THE SUFFERINGS OF HECUBA

Across the water from Phrygia, the region where Troy once
      stood,
you will find the land of the Thracians; and there was the
      splendid palace   430

of rich Polyméstor, to whom King Priam had secretly
    sent
his youngest son, Polydórus. His father had wanted the
    lad
to be brought up safely and kept away from the Trojan
    War –
a sensible plan, if a hoard of wealth hadn't gone with the
    boy
to provoke his guardian's greed and prove a temptation
    to murder.
When Ilium's fortunes fell, the treacherous king of the
435   Thracians
picked up his sword and plunged it into his charge's
    throat;
and then, as though all trace of the crime could be
    killed with the victim,
he tossed Polydorus' corpse from a cliff to be lost in the
    billows.
    Nearby, on the Thracian coast, Agamemnon had
        anchored his fleet;
he needed a sea that was perfectly calm and a friendlier
440   wind.
Here, all of a sudden, a crack appeared in the earth,
    and Achilles
emerged, in presence as tall and strong as he'd been in
    his lifetime;
the dangerous gleam in his threatening eyes recalled
    the day
when he'd drawn his sword on King Agamemnon in
    murderous anger.*
'Greeks!' he exclaimed. 'Can you sail away without
445   remembering
me? Have your thanks for my valour been buried along
    with my ashes?
Do not commit such a sin! My grave must not go
    unhonoured.
Appease the ghost of Achilles, by sacrificing Polýxena!'

So he spoke, and his comrades obeyed the pitiless phantom.
Torn from Hecuba's arms – she was almost the only
    comfort   450
her mother had left – the ill-starred maiden displayed a
    courage
transcending a woman's, as guards led her up to the hero's
    mound
to be laid on his grave as a victim. Once in front of the fatal
altar, she realized the cruel rite was intended for her,
but she never forgot who she was. When she saw
    Neoptólemus waiting,   455
sword in hand, with his eyes intently fixed on her own,
she said to him: 'Take my noble blood and delay no longer.
I am prepared. All *you* need do is to bury your sword
in my throat or my breast' – and she bared her throat and
    her bosom together.
'Polyxena surely would never consent to be any man's
    slave.   460
I only wish that the news of my death could be kept from
    my mother;
the thought of her sorrow detracts from the joy that my
    sacrifice brings me –
although it's her own life, hardly my death, which should
    cause her to tremble.'
Next she turned to her guards and said: 'May I ask one
    thing?
Please leave me, I beg you, and stand far off. My wish is to
    pass   465
to the Stygian ghosts as free as I've lived. Do not sully a
    maiden's
body with your male hands. The spirit, whoever he is,
whose anger you seek to appease, will be satisfied better by
    blood
that flows from a willing victim. Yet one boon more, if my
    final
words have the power to move – it is Priam's daughter, no
    captive   470

who asks you: restore my remains to my mother without
demanding
a ransom. Allow her to pay with her tears, not in gold,
for the dismal
right to bury my body. She paid gold too when she
could.'
As she finished speaking, the people could not restrain
the tears
which she had avoided. Even the priest, Neoptolemus,
wept
and plunged his sword through her offered breast with
a heavy heart.
Polyxena's knees gave way and she sank to the ground,
still keeping
the fearless look on her face till the final moment of
death.
And even then, as she fell, she preserved her maidenly
virtue,
arranging her garments to cover the parts men's eyes
should not see.
    The women of Troy then lifted her body. They
counted the children
Priam had lost and reckoned the blood that had flowed
from a single
house. They lamented the maiden, lamented the queen,
so recently
known as the consort and mother of kings, the mirror
of Asia's
glory, and now no more than a meagre share of the
loot,
whom the victor Ulysses would scorn if she weren't
after all the mother
of Hector – yes, Hector secured his captive mother a
master!
Embracing the brave Polyxena's lifeless body, Hecuba
shed for her daughter the tears she so often had shed
for her country,

475

480

485

her sons and her husband. She washed her dear child's
    wounds with those tears;   490
she covered her lips with kisses and rained fresh blows on
    her own poor
breasts; then sweeping her white hair over the clotted
    blood
and tearing her bosom, she cried in the course of a long
    lamentation:
  'My daughter, the last of your mother's sorrows – what
    else can befall me? –
my child, you are dead and I see your wound, *my* wound
    no less.   495
Yes, you too have a wound; I wasn't allowed to lose
one child without blood being spilt. I thought, since you
    were a girl,
you'd be safe from the sword; but girl though you were, the
    sword has destroyed you.
The selfsame butcher who murdered your brothers has
    murdered you –
Achilles, who ruined Troy and has left me bereft of my
    children.   500
And yet, when he fell to the arrows of Paris and Phoebus
    Apollo,
I reckoned, "At least Achilles is not to be feared any
    more."
But I needed to fear him still; for even his buried ashes
are angry with our great house; his spite can be felt from the
    tomb.
I carried all those children for *him*! Great Ilium's flattened; 505
the people's affliction has come to an end in the fall of their
    city,
but still it has *ended*. It's only for me that Pergamum's
    standing;
my tale of sorrow goes on. I was once the most powerful
    woman
in all the world; I was strong in my husband, my sons and
    my daughters.

Now I've been torn from my loved ones' graves and am
510   helplessly dragged
into exile, to serve as Penélope's prize. As I spin my
           daily
portion of wool, she'll point me out to the Ithacan
           women
and proudly say to them, "There is the famous mother
           of Hector,
there is the wife of King Priam!" Then after so many
           losses,
you, my daughter, the only companion surviving to
           comfort
a mother's griefs, have been slaughtered to soothe an
515   enemy's ghost.
I bore my enemy's funeral gift! Oh, why should my
           heart
of iron endure any longer? Why wait for death to
           arrive?
What good can come in these weary years? Why keep
           an old woman
alive, you unfeeling gods, if I'm only to see more
           corpses?
Who would have thought that Priam could ever be
520   talked of as happy
after the fall of Troy? He is happy because of his own
           death.
He cannot see your lifeless remains before his eyes,
my beloved daughter. He lost his life when he lost his
           kingdom.
Well, no doubt, as a royal princess you'll be dowered
           with funeral
rites, and your body will find a home in the family
           vault!
Alas, that isn't the luck of our house. The only
525   offerings
you will receive are your mother's tears and a handful
           of alien
dust. Yes, all is lost . . . But there *is* one reason to cling

to life for a short while longer: one specially favourite child,
the only son who remains to me now and once was my
      youngest,
the boy whom we sent to the Thracian king on these shores
      – Polydorus.   530
But why, meanwhile, am I still delaying to wash my
      Polyxena's
cruel wounds and the face so ruthlessly spattered with
      blood?'

So, saying, the luckless Hecuba hobbled down to the shore,
tearing her hoary locks. As she called to her Trojan women
to hand her a pitcher for drawing water out of the waves,   535
she saw, cast up on the beach, the corpse of her son
      Polydorus,
mangled with gaping wounds from the sword of the
      Thracian king.
Her attendants screamed, but the queen was totally dumb
      in her anguish.
Her voice was stifled; the tears which were welling behind
      her eyes
never came. She stood there frozen in grief, as rigid as
      granite.   540
She stared at the ground directly before her, or else, with a
      grim look,
lifted her eyes to the sky, then gazed on her son as he lay
      there,
gazed on his face and gazed on his wounds, his wounds
      above all,
while she armed herself with smouldering fury and
      marshalled her wrath.
As her anger burst into flames, she resolved to punish the
      killer –   545
Queen Hecuba still! – and her mind was filled with her
      picture of vengeance.
As a lioness out on the warpath, newly deprived of her
      suckling
cub, discovers and follows the trail of her unseen foe,

so Hecuba, after her grief was mingled with anger,
      forgetting
her age, but not forgetting her rage, made straight for the
      vile
550 Polymestor, the man who had foully contrived to
      murder her boy.
She requested a meeting, and told the king that she
      wanted to show him
a hoard of gold that she'd hidden, to be returned to her
      son.
The Thracian tyrant believed her and, scenting the
      whiff of yet further
555 booty, he came to the lonely spot. Then craftily smiling
he said to the queen, 'Come on, now, Hecuba; give me
      the gold
for your son. I swear by the gods in heaven that all you
      give now
and gave in the past shall be his.' As he perjured
      himself by these lies,
she ferociously watched, till her temper mounted and
      boiled right over.
And then she grabbed hold of him tight, with a shout
560   to her posse of female
captives, and dug her fingers into his treacherous eyes,
to gouge the balls from their sockets – the power was
      lent by her anger.
Next she defiled her hands in his guilty blood, by
      plunging them
into his face and clawing, not at his eyes (they were
      gone),
but the holes where his eyes had been. The people of
565   Thrace were enraged
by this savage assault on their king, and started to pelt
      the Trojan
woman with weapons and stones. But she just snapped
      with a snarling
growl at the rocks which they threw. As she opened
      her jaws in a vain

attempt to give tongue, she barked. (The place where this
     miracle happened
exists to this day and is suitably called Cynosséma, the
     Dog's Tomb.)
Even after this change, old Hecuba long remembered   570
her ancient wrongs, and the plains of Thrace were filled
     with her doleful
howling. Her Trojan friends and her Grecian foes were
     distressed
alike by the fate of the queen; and all of the gods were
     affected –
every one of them. Even Jupiter's sister and consort
declared that Hecuba hadn't deserved such an ending as
     that!   575

MEMNON

Only Auróra felt no pain at Troy's and Hecuba's
ruinous fall, although she had backed their cause in the war.
She hadn't the time; she was touched by a closer, personal
     grief
in the loss of Memnon, the son whom the goddess with
     robes of saffron
had watched being killed on the Phrygian plains by the
     spear of Achilles.   580
That moment, the rosy red which tinges the sky in the
     morning
turned to a deadly pallor and heaven was hidden in cloud.
When Memnon's body was laid on the funeral pyre, his
     mother
was too heart-broken to watch. With her hair still loosened
     in token
of mourning, she humbly prostrated herself at the knees of
     almighty   585
Jove and addressed him in tears: 'I know that I am the
     lowest
of all the gods in the golden heavens (my temples are few

and widely scattered across the world), but I still am a
          goddess.
I've not come here to obtain more shrines or festival days
or altars to blaze with sacrificed victims. If you would
590   consider
what useful service I render, although I am only a
          woman,
each dawn when I check the night from encroaching on
          day's domain,
you'd judge I should have some reward. But I'm not
          concerned in my present
state of distress to claim the worship I'm justly owed.
I am here because I have lost my Memnon, who
595   doughtily fought,
though in vain, for his uncle Priam and then was
          condemned by you gods
to be killed in the prime of his life at the hands of the
          doughty Achilles.
Supreme ruler of heaven, I pray you to comfort his
          spirit
by paying some tribute, and so to soothe the wounds
          of his mother.'
     Jupiter nodded assent. Young Memnon's high-built
600   pyre
collapsed, the flames leapt up, and rolling columns of
          black smoke
darkened the light of day, as vapour rises like breath
from the rivers and forms a fog which the sun's bright
          rays cannot penetrate.
Cinders of charcoal flew to the sky, then massed and
          thickened
605 into a single body, assuming an outline and drawing
heat and life from the fire. The ash's lightness provided
its wings. Could it be a winged creature? At first no
          more than a phantom,
but soon a rustle of feathers – a bird! Then a flock of
          her sisters

was beating their wings beside her, and all derived from the
    same source.
They circled the pyre three times; three times their unison
    wailing   610
rang through the air. The fourth time round, they divided
    their forces;
two armies, marshalled on different sides, engaged in a
    savage
battle, angrily using their beaks and the hooks of their
    talons
to tear the breasts and to tire the wings of the enemy facing
    them.
Bodies created from dead man's ash fell down from the air 615
to be funeral gifts in remembrance of Memnon, the hero
    from whom
they were sprung, and who also gave these miraculous
    fledglings their name
of Memnónides.* Each year, when the sun has completed
    its zodiac
round, they go to war once again and die like their
    parents.*
And so, while others lamented the change of Hecuba into 620
a barking dog, Aurora was wholly absorbed in her own
    grief.
She weeps to this day, and the morning dew is her dutiful
    mourning.*

THE WANDERINGS OF AENEAS (1)

Yet destiny wouldn't allow Troy's hopes to be overturned
along with her walls. Aenéas, the hero whose mother was
    Venus,
rescued his household gods and, through the flames, on his
    shoulders
he carried a burden as sacred, his venerable father
    Anchíses.   625

These, with his own dear son Ascánius, formed the spoil
which Aeneas the dutiful* chose to salvage from all his
      possessions.
Fleeing across the sea with his people in ships from
      Antándros,
he came to the infamous coast of Thrace, where the
      young Polydorus
had stained the earth with his blood; but he quickly
      abandoned the visit.
Next, with the backing of wind and tide, he arrived at
      Apollo's
630 island of Delos and entered the city with all his
      companions.

THE DAUGHTERS OF ANIUS

Ánius, king of the people, who also served as the priest
of Apollo, welcomed Aeneas into the palace and
      temple.
He showed him the town with its famous shrines and
      the stumps of the two trees
gripped long ago by Leto's arms in the pangs of her
635   labour.*
Incense was cast in the flames, and wine was poured on
      the incense;
entrails of sacrificed oxen were burnt in traditional
      manner.
That done, all made for the palace hall, where they
      rested on high-raised
couches and freely partook of the gifts of Ceres and
      Bacchus.
640 Then said pious Anchises: 'Chosen priest of Apollo,
I could be mistaken, but when I entered these walls for
      the first time,
I seem to remember your family boasting a son and
      four daughters.'

Anius shook his head, encircled in snow-white bands,
and sadly replied: 'You are perfectly right, most mighty
        Anchises.
You saw a man who was blessed with five magnificent
        offspring;   645
but now, so fickle in human fortune, I'm almost bereft
of my children. What help can my son afford, when he lives
        as my regent
far away on the island of Andros which bears his name?
Apollo gave him prophetic powers, while Bacchus
        endowed   650
my daughters with other talents surpassing hope or belief.
All that they touched was transformed into corn or wine or
        the juice
of the grey-green olive – which made them a source of
        exceptional profit.
This came to the ears, on his voyage to Troy, of King
        Agamemnon   655
(we also were hit to a certain degree by the storm
        advancing
on you), and he used armed force to tear my daughters
        away
from their loving father against their will; then he told them
        to use
their miraculous powers to supply the Argive fleet with
        provisions.
They all escaped where they could: two found a home in
        Euboéa,   660
the other pair got away to their brother's island of Andros.
An army arrived with an ultimatum, demanding the
        women's
surrender. Fear prevailed over brotherly love, and Andros
handed his sisters over to pay the price for their flight –
forgivable weakness, perhaps; no Aeneas was there to
        defend him,   665
no Hector whose courage enabled you all to survive ten
        years.

The prisoners' arms were awaiting their shackles; but
      while they were still free,
both of them raised their hands to the sky and called
      upon Bacchus
to come to their aid – which he did, if strangely losing
670   one's shape
is aid of a sort, though how they lost it I never have
      known
and couldn't say now. But the final disaster was all too
      plain:
my daughters were covered with feathers and changed
      into snow-white doves,
the birds that are sacred to Venus, your own dear
      consort, Anchises.'

THE DAUGHTERS OF ORION

The banquet passed in the telling of these and similar
675   stories.
The tables were taken away, and all retired to their
      beds.
Rising at dawn, the Trojan wanderers visited Phoebus'
oracular shrine. The god enjoined them to 'search for
      their ancient
mother and kindred shores'.* As they left, the king
      escorted them
down to the ships and gave them presents to speed
      their departure.
Anchises received a staff, his grandson a cloak and a
680   quiver,
Aeneas a mixing-bowl which his host had been
      brought as a gift
in the past by one of his guest-friends, Therses of
      Thebes in Boeotia.
The bowl had been crafted by Alcon of Rhodes and
      told a long story

embossed on the metal. It showed a city with seven gates
(you could easily point them out), which stood for the
    name of the city*   685
and said what it was. Outside a funeral scene was depicted,
with burial mounds and funeral pyres; there were women
    with naked
breasts and wildly dishevelled hair in token of mourning.
Nymphs could also be seen in tears, bemoaning their
    dried-up
springs; the leafless trees were standing all stiff and bare,   690
while goats were nibbling at rocks and grazing on
    withered lichen.
There, in the middle of Thebes, the artist had pictured
    Oríon's
daughters, who died for their people.* Their bodies were
    being carried   695
along the streets to the square in a lovely cortège, for
    cremation;
and then, to continue the family line, from out of the
    maidens'
ashes there rose two youths, whom legend knows as
    Coróni,
and these were portrayed as leading a second solemn
    procession
to carry the ashes from which they had sprung from pyre to
    tomb.
So much for the gleaming figures embossed on the ancient
    bronzework;   700
the rim of the bowl was adorned in relief with gilded
    acanthus.
The Trojans reciprocated these presents with others as
    handsome.
The priest of Apollo was given a casket for storing his
    incense,
a splendid libation-bowl and a gold crown studded with
    jewels.

THE WANDERINGS OF AENEAS (2)

From Delos they sailed to Crete, the homeland of
705   Teucer, to whom
the Trojans remembered they owed their descent;* but
        they couldn't endure
the climate for long. So they left the isle of a hundred
        cities
and eagerly set their course for their promised Italian
        land.
But a storm blew up which battered their ships and
        drove them into
the Stróphades' port. This proved a treacherous
        shelter, as hope
was turned to dismay by Aëllo the Harpy's*
710   frightening prophecies.
Soon they had passed Dulíchium's harbour, Íthaca,
        Samos
and Néritos' town, which was part of the kingdom of
        crafty Ulysses.
Then they sighted Ambrácia, the city three gods had
        competed
to have for their own, with the rock in the shape of the
        shepherd judge*
who had been transformed. (Ambracia is now well
715   known for Apollo's
temple at Áctium,* crowning the cape.) They called at
        Dodóna,
grove of the talking oaks, and entered Chaónia's bay,
where good King Múnichus'* sons escaped from the
        flames, when impious
robbers set fire to their house, by being changed into
        birds.
    Next they made for Corcýra, an island of fruitful
        orchards,
but came to port in Epírus, where Helenus reigned in
720   Buthrótum,

the city he called New Troy.* When the prophet had
        faithfully warned them
of all the dangers ahead, they put to sea once again
and landed on Sicily's soil. This island can boast three
        capes:
Pachýnus facing the south with its rainy winds, Lilybaéum   725
the gentler breezes that blow from the west, and Pelórus the
        Bears
and the freezing blasts of the north. The Trojans arrived at
        Pelorus.
Rowing ashore on a favouring tide as the night came on,
they discovered a sandy cove for their ships on the coast of
        Messána.
The straits on the left are unsafe because of the restless
        Charýbdis,   730
who catches the passing ships to gulp them down in her
        whirlpool
and then to vomit them forth. The right is infested by
        Scylla,
a monster whose foul black belly is girdled with ravening
        dogs.
Her face is a girl's and, assuming the stories that poets have
        left us
are not completely untrue, she *had* been a girl who was
        courted
by numerous wooers – though Scylla rejected them all and
        often   735
went down to the ocean-nymphs, who were always
        delighted to see her,
to gossip about the various lovers whose suit she'd evaded.
One day she was combing the hair of one of the nymphs,
        Galatéa,
who heaved a series of sighs and then protested with
        feeling:

ACIS, GALATEA AND POLYPHEMUS

740 'O Scylla, a civilized class of wooer is trying to win
your hand, and you aren't at risk in refusing them all
        as you're doing.
But I, whose father is Néreus, whose mother is
        sea-green Doris,
I who am also blessed with a throng of sisters to guard
        me,
have only escaped from the Cyclops' love at a grievous
        price!'
Her voice, as she spoke, was choked with tears. When
745   Scylla had wiped
Galatea's eyes with her smooth white fingers and given
        her comfort,
she said to the goddess, 'My dearest friend, please tell
        me your trouble.
Why are you sad? Don't keep it a secret; you know you
        can trust me.'
The Nereïd thus responded to Scylla's compassionate
        questions:
    'Faunus, a god of the countryside, had a son called
750   Acis.
The child had been born to a nymph who was sprung
        from the river Symaéthus,
and gave the greatest of joy to both his father and
        mother,
but joy even greater to me, as he was my only lover –
a beautiful boy of sixteen, with the first smooth down
        on his cheeks!
While I kept sighing for *him*, I was chased night and
755   day by the Cyclops.
If you asked me whether I hated the Cyclops more than
        I worshipped
Acis, I couldn't give you an answer. My love and my
        loathing

were equally balanced. O Venus, our mother, with what
    strong power
you govern our hearts! The Cyclops was such a barbaric
    creature.
Even the woods were appalled by his presence; no stranger
    could safely   760
encounter the giant who scorned the gods and the heights
    of Olympus.
And yet he discovered the meaning of love, and neglected
    his flocks
and his cave when the flames of his violent passion were
    raging inside him.
Now, in his longing to please me, he bothered about his
    appearance.
The wild Polyphémus was combing his prickly locks with
    a mattock,   765
attempting to trim his shaggy beard with a pruning-hook,
and trying to look less fierce when he gazed at his face in a
    pool.
His passion for slaughter, his brutal ways and his boundless
    bloodlust
were all in abeyance; the ships could arrive and depart
    without danger.
One day a visitor put into Sicily close to Mount Etna,   770
Télemus, Eúrymus' son, an infallible augur of omens.
He came to the grim Polyphemus and said, "You are
    doomed to be robbed
of that single eye on the front of your brow by a man called
    Ulysses."
The Cyclops replied with a laugh, "You are wrong, most
    stupid of prophets.
My eye has already been robbed by another!" And so he
    rejected   775
that truthful but useless warning, and pompously trampled
    the shore
with his giant's steps, or withdrew tired out to the depths of
    his cave.

Picture a wedge-like promontory jutting over the sea
in a long sharp point, while the waves swirl round each
     side at the bottom.
Here the fierce Polyphemus climbed and eased himself
780   down
where the view was the best, with his leaderless sheep
     all trailing behind him.
He dropped the pine trunk, tall as a mast, which served
     for his staff,
by his feet, and produced an enormous pipe of a
     hundred reeds.
His shepherd's whistling was heard by the waves and
785   across the whole range
of surrounding mountains. I also drank it in from a
     distance,
hiding close to the cliff and reclined in the arms of my
     Acis.
These are the words which I heard him sing and fixed
     in my memory:
   ' "Whiter than snowy petals of privet, my fair
     Galatea,
richer in bloom than the meadows, more slender and
790   tall than the alder,
sparkling as crystal glass, more sprightly and free than
     a young kid,
smoother than all the shells that are worn away by the
     ocean,
welcome as sun in the winter or shade in the heat of
     the summer,
you nimble gazelle, you lovelier sight than the tallest of
     plane trees,
gleaming more brightly than ice and sweeter than
795   grapes in the harvest,
softer than curdled milk or the feathery wings of a
     swan,
more lush than a beautiful garden – if only you
     wouldn't avoid me.

' "Wilder too than an untamed heifer, my fair Galatea,
harder than ancient oak, more wayward than shifting
          waves,
tougher than shoots of the pliant willow or bryony bine,   800
more stubborn than this stone crag, more rough than a river
          in full spate,
proud as a peacock in grand display, more fiery than fire,
more prickly than thorns, more fierce than the she-bear
          nursing her young,
more deaf than the sea, more vicious and cruel than a
          trampled snake;
with the power that I wish above all I could take away
          from your nature,   805
the fleetness of foot to outpace not only the stag when he's
          chased
by the baying pack, but even the winds and the wing-swift
          breezes.
   ' "Oh, if you only knew, you'd regret having shunned me,
          you'd even
curse your own coyness and do your utmost to hold my
          affections.
I own a cave on the mountain side; it is vaulted over   810
in living rock, and it never lets in the heat of the midday
sun or the winter's cold. My orchards are groaning with
          apples,
my trailing vines are swollen with grapes, both golden
          yellow
and purply red; I am storing each harvest for your delight.
With your own fair hands you will pick the most delicious
          of strawberries   815
growing under the trees, the cornel berries in autumn,
and juicy plums, not only the dark blue kind, but also
the choicer sort with the golden colour of fresh-made wax.
With me as your lover, you'll have sweet chestnuts and
          arbutus fruits
in the richest abundance; so every tree shall be at your
          service.   820

' "All these sheep are my own; many others are
        roaming the valleys,
browsing apart in the woods or safely penned in my
        cave.
If you asked me, I shouldn't be able to tell you how many
        there are;
only a poor man counts his sheep. But you needn't
        believe
what I say in their praise. If you come to the fold, you
825   will see for yourself
that their legs can hardly straddle the udders, they're so
        distended.
You'll see my lambs in their snug warm pens and my
        baby goats.
I always have pailfuls of rich white milk, and I keep
        one part
to be drunk as it is, while the rest is hardened by rennet
830   to cheeses.
    ' "The pets that I lay in your lap won't only be
        ordinary presents,
the easy ones to obtain, like a doe or a hare or a goat,
a pair of doves or a nest of birds removed from a
        treetop.
I've found a couple of twins whom you'll be able to
        play with,
so like each other, you'll hardly be able to tell them
835   apart,
some cubs that I took on the mountain peak – from a
        shaggy bear!
When I found them, I said to myself, 'I'll keep those
        cubs for my mistress!'
Now, Galatea, do raise your glistening head from the
        deep blue
sea and come to my arms. Don't scorn the gifts that I
        offer.
840   ' "Truly, I know myself, I recently saw my reflection
in pure clear water and liked the image that met my
        gaze.

Look at my massive size! Great Jupiter, high in the
        heavens,
hasn't a larger frame (in the tale you people keep telling
some Jove or other* is reigning up there). A forest of hair
towers over my strong stern features and shades my
        magnificent shoulders.   845
Don't think me ugly because my body's a bristling thicket
of prickly hair. A tree is ugly without any foliage;
so is a horse, if a mane doesn't cover his tawny neck;
birds are bedecked in plumage, and sheep are clothed in
        their own wool.
Men look well with a beard and a carpet of hair on their
        chests.   850
I've only one eye on my brow, in the middle, but that is as
        big
as a fair-sized shield. Does it matter? The Sun looks down
        from the sky
on the whole wide world, and he watches it all with a single
        eye.
    '"Remember, my father* is king in your own abode of
        the sea;
I'm giving you *him* for a father-in-law! Have pity, I beg
        you,   855
and hear your suppliant's pleas. You're the only being I
        bow to;
I scorn proud Jove and his sky and the piercing bolt of his
        lightning.
It's *you* that I fear, Galatea; your anger is fiercer than
        lightning.
To tell you the truth, I could better endure this cruel
        contempt,
if *all* your suitors were shunned. But why reject
        Polyphemus   860
and turn to Acis for love? What are Acis' embraces to mine?
Very well, let him fancy himself; and you have my reluctant
        permission
to fancy him too, Galatea. But let chance bring him my
        way,

and he'll soon discover the giant's strength in my giant's
     frame.
I'll draw his guts from his living body, then tear it to
865   pieces
and scatter his limbs all over the fields and the waves
     where your home is –
yes, he can mate with you there like that! Oh see, I am
     burning,
the fire of the terrible wrong you have done me is
     blazing more fiercely!
Mount Etna has moved! I can feel it erupting inside my
     heart
with all its volcanic power – and it leaves you cold,
     Galatea!"
   'The Cyclops finished his futile lament. I was
870   watching and saw him
rise and keep on the move as he stumped away through
     the well-known
pastures and woods, like a frantic bull deprived of his
     cow.
Acis and I were entirely unready for what happened
     next:
the wild brute suddenly saw us and cried aloud, "I can
     see you,
and I'll make certain that this is the last of your loving
875   encounters!"
The tone of his voice was as loud as you might expect
     in a furious
Cyclops; his shouting created a quake in the whole of
     Mount Etna.
My own response was to dive straight into the sea in a
     panic,
while Acis, my hero, turned and took to his heels as he
     yelled out,
"Help me! Help, Galatea, I beg you! Oh help me, my
880   parents!
I'm going to die. You must let me into your watery
     kingdom!"

The Cyclops followed him close, then wrenched a part of the
       mountain
away from its side, and hurled it at Acis. Although his rival
was only struck by the edge of the rock, it crushed him
       completely.
   'I then did the only thing which the fates would allow: I
       gave   885
my lover the powers of his mother's father, the river
       Symaethus.
A trickle of crimson blood was flowing from under the
       boulder,
but after a little while the redness started to vanish.
First it turned to the muddy brown of a swollen torrent,
then slowly it cleared completely. That moment, I touched
       the rock   890
and it gaped wide open. A tall green seed shot up from the
       crack;
the hollow mouth of the opening rang with the roar of
       cascading
water; and wonder of wonders, there suddenly rose
       waist-high
a youth with horns on his brow, which were wreathed in a
       garland of rushes.
The youth was Acis, except he was taller and all of his face 895
was the colour of dark sea-green. But even so it was Acis,
transformed to a river* whose course has retained his
       original name.'

GLAUCUS AND SCYLLA (1)

Galatea's story was ended, and all her Nereïd sisters
around her dispersed as they swam to their homes through
       the peaceful waves.
But Scylla returned to the shore, for she dared not trust
       herself   900
to the open sea; and she either roamed unclothed on the
       thirsty

sand or, when she was tired, she would look for a
      land-locked cove
and take a refreshing bathe in the swirl of a sea-water
      pool.
Suddenly, skimming the waves, there arrived a new
      sea-dweller, Glaucus,
who'd recently suffered a change of shape in Boeótian

905   Anthédon.
As soon as he sighted the fair young girl, he was snared
      by her beauty
and said whatever he hoped might prevent her running
      away.
But his words went for nothing; she fled as fast as she
      could in her terror
and climbed right up to the top of the mountain
      adjoining the shore.
Now picture a huge crag,* facing the strait; it peaks in

910   a single
point and slopes, well covered with trees, far into the
      sea.
Here Scylla was safe and she came to a halt. Unsure
      whether Glaucus
was monster or god, she gazed in awe at his blue-green
      body,
the hair which covered his shoulders and back, and the
      flexible fishtail
mounting as far as his loins. The sea-god realized that

915   Scylla
was struck with amazement and, leaning up on a
      nearby rock,
'Fair maiden,' he said, 'I am not some monster or
      dangerous beast,
but a god of the sea. My sway in the ocean is no less
      mighty
than Próteus or Triton wields, or Áthamas' offspring,
      Palaémon.*
I once was mortal, but even then I was destined for

920   life

in the depths of the sea and passed my days in the joys of the
    ocean,
drawing the nets which were drawing the fish, or busily
    plying
my rod as I sat on the rocks. Right next to the shore lies a
    meadow;
one side of the beach you have waves, and the other is
    bordered by grass.   925
This grass has never been cropped by the sharp-horned
    heifers, or browsed
by peaceful sheep or the hairy goats. The pollen's not
    gathered
by busy bees, and the flowers aren't plucked for festival
    garlands.
The field has never been mown with a sickle; and I was the
    first   930
to sit on the ground there, drying my meshes and
    spreading the fish
on the grass, to count the catch brought into my nets by
    chance,
or lured by the bait to the hook on my line. You may not
    believe
what I'm going to tell you now, but why should I want to
    deceive you?   935
As soon as the fish were placed on the grass, they started
    to move,
to flop right over and travel across the ground as they'd
    used
to glide in the sea. And while I was waiting in wonder, they
    all jumped
into the waves to abandon the shore and the master who'd
    caught them.
I was dumbfounded and long perplexed as I searched for a
    cause: 940
had a god produced this effect, or was it some juice in the
    grass?
"No grass in the world has a power like this!" I said to
    myself,

as I casually plucked a couple of blades and started to
    chew them.
I'd barely swallowed the unfamiliar juices down,
945   when I suddenly felt a powerful flutter inside my heart
and was seized with an overwhelming desire to belong
    to the sea.
I couldn't remain where I was, and I cried out, "Earth,
    I shall never
tread you again, farewell!" Then I instantly dived
    under water.
The sea-gods received me and judged me worthy of
    joining their number.
Ocean and Tethys were asked to purge me of all my
950   mortal
features, and quickly they both took charge of my
    ritual cleansing.
After they'd chanted a spell nine times for my
    purification,
I next was told to immerse myself in a hundred
    streams.
At once the rivers discharged their waters from every
    direction
and swirled in a deluge over my head. So much I
955   remember
and thus can tell you what ought to be told; of the rest
    I know nothing.
As soon as my senses returned, my body was totally
    different
from what it had been before; and I wasn't the same in
    my mind.
It was then that I first set eyes on this beard encrusted
    with green,
on the hair which sweeps in my wake as I swim far
960   over the sea,
my colossal shoulders, my blue-coloured arms and my
    curving legs
which vanish away to a fish with fins. But what is this
    form worth?

What is the point of the sea-gods' approval, of being a god,
if it all means nothing to you?' The god was still speaking
    and would have   965
said more,* but Scylla had fled. Enraged by this cruel
    rejection,
he made for the halls of the sun god's daughter, the
    sorceress Círce.

BOOK 14

In this book we move, via Ovid's 'little *Aeneid*', from the mythology of Greece and Troy to that of Italy and Rome itself, though we are treated on the way to two fine episodes based on Homer's *Odyssey*. A pivotal character in the sequence is the Titaness Circe, a familiar figure in Greek poetry, whose fabulous island was later identified with the promontory of Circeii on the coast of Latium in western Italy. After the death of Aeneas, the kings of Alba Longa down to Romulus provide a framework for the last erotic story. As a whole, the book is the most broken-up in the poem and accommodates no fewer than sixteen metamorphoses – something of a rag-bag, but still with many extremely enjoyable passages.

The story of *Glaucus and Scylla* (1–74) continues with Glaucus' appeal to the sorceress Circe for a charm to win Scylla for him. But Circe wants Glaucus for herself and spitefully turns Scylla into the well-known monster with dogs' heads round her waist.

The Wanderings of Aeneas (3) (75–100) incorporates an account of the metamorphosis of the inhabitants of Pithecusae to apes and also prompts the story of *The Sibyl of Cumae* (101–52). At the place later to be called Caieta, Ovid contrives a meeting between two of Ulysses' former companions, Achaemenides and Macareus. This motivates the former's account of the ordeal of *Ulysses' Men in Polyphemus' Cave* (154–222) – no metamorphosis here, but with plenty of scope for bloodthirsty detail. Macareus responds with Ovid's version of *Ulysses'* encounter with *Circe* (223–307), in which he dwells with relish on the details of the sailors' metamorphosis to pigs and on the reverse transformation. Macareus also relates an old Italian story (308–440), learned from one of Circe's attendants, about an early Italian king *Picus* whom *Circe* turned into a woodpecker because he preferred the charms of his wife *Canens* to her own – we are reminded of her spiteful treatment of Glaucus.

The Wanderings of Aeneas (4) (441–53b) brings the Trojans up the Tiber; and the war with the Rutulians under Turnus, which occupies most of *Aeneid* 7–12, is rapidly started. This occasions an unsuccessful appeal for military aid by the Rutulian Venulus to the former Greek hero Diomedes, who has now settled in Apulia. Diomedes explains that he cannot help as he has lost a number of his *Mutinous Companions* (454–512) by metamorphosis on his voyage from Greece to Italy. Venulus' return from his mission includes another transformation in the brief story of *The Apulian Shepherd* (513–26). Ovid continues with an episode, taken from Virgil *Aeneid* 9, when Turnus fires the *The Ships of Aeneas* (527–65), and they are only saved through the agency of Cybele, who transforms them into nymphs. After the death of Turnus, the fall of the chief Rutulian city of *Ardea* (566–80) allows the mysterious appearance of a heron (Latin *ardea*) out of the ruins. The final metamorphosis in this section is *The Apotheosis of Aeneas* himself (581–607), when Venus persuades Jupiter to admit her son to heaven.

A brief catalogue of *Aeneas' Descendants* (the mythical kings of Alba Longa) follows (608–21). The reign of Proca occasions the last love story in the poem (622–771), which links *Pomona*, the Roman goddess of fruits, with the Etruscan god *Vertumnus*. Inset in this appealing narrative is the Cypriot tale of *Iphis and Anaxarete* (698–761), which Vertumnus, disguised as a crone, uses to warn Pomona against hardheartedness.

The reign of *Romulus* (772–804) marks the foundation of Rome. The war following the rape of the Sabine women leads to the Sabines' attack on Rome being obstructed by the metamorphosis of an icy spring to an impassable geyser. The book concludes with *The Apotheosis of Romulus* (805–51), at his father Mars' request, followed by the translation to the sky of his wife Hersilië.

GLAUCUS AND SCYLLA (2)

Glaucus, who'd left Euboéa for life in the swell of the
          ocean,
had now passed Etna, the mountain piled on the throat
          of the giant
Typhon. He'd passed the fields of the Cyclops, which
          never had known
the working of harrow or plough and owed no debt to
          yoked oxen.
He'd passed Messána and also the walls of Rhégium
5   opposite,
finding his way through the dangerous strait, where the
          waters are bounded
by Italy's soil on the one side and Sicily's coast on the
          other.
Thence powerfully swimming across the Etruscan Sea,*
          he arrived
at the herb-green hills and the halls of Circe, the sun
          god's daughter,
halls that were crowded with various beasts. Once he
          had seen her
10
and greetings had been exchanged, the guest appealed
          to his hostess:
'Goddess, I pray you, pity a god! You alone can lighten
this longing of mine, if you will but judge me worth
          your compassion.
Titaness, no one knows the power of herbs and grasses
better than I, for my transformation was due to their
15   magic.
But let me tell you the cause of the passion raging inside
          me:
on Italy's coast, where it faces the walls of Messana, I
          saw her,
I saw my Scylla. Shame forbids me to tell you the
          promises,

prayers and wheedling words I employed – to be cruelly
        rejected.
Oh Circe, if spells can hold any sway, now open those holy   20
lips to utter a spell; or if herbs will be more effectual,
use the proven power of a herb which will do what is
        needed.
I do not ask to be cured myself, or my wound to be healed,
or an end to my love, but for Scylla to share the heat of my
        passion!'
    Circe, however, possessed a heart more open than others   25
to love's strong flames (it might have been her own nature,
        or caused
by Venus, who'd never forgotten that Circe's father, the sun
        god,
betrayed her affair with Mars*), and so she responded to
        Glaucus:
'You'd do far better to follow a woman whose wishes and
        prayers
are at one with your own, whose heart is fired by an equal
        passion.
You deserved to be actively wooed for yourself – you could
        have been, surely.   30
Offer some hope and, believe me, you *shall* be wooed
        without wooing.
To banish all doubt and distrust you may have in your
        power to attract,
look into my eyes. I may be a goddess, the daughter born
to the gleaming Sun; the power of my spells and my herbs
        may be great;
but I pray that I may be yours. Reject the one who rejects
        you,   35
respond to her who pursues you, and give two women at
        once
the payment you owe them.' To these advances Glaucus
        replied,
'While Scylla is living, my love for her will not alter, till
        foliage

grows in the ocean and seaweed sprouts on the peaks of
  the mountains!'
  The goddess was deeply offended. She couldn't do
40   mischief to Glaucus
(moreover, she loved him too well), but she vented her
  spleen on the girl
he preferred to herself. Enraged because he had scorned
  her attentions,
she promptly pounded together some plants which were
  noxious with sinister
juices, and chanted the spells of her witchcraft over the
  mixture.
Then donning a sea-blue cloak, she grandly advanced
45   through the throng
of her fawning beasts as she went on her way from the
  heart of the palace.
She made for Rhegium, over the strait from the rocks of
  Messana,
and there she walked on the seething waves of a stormy
  sea,
as though it were solid land, and skimmed the surface
50   with dry feet.
  Picture a little pool, with its margin curved like a
  bow,
where Scylla delighted to rest. It was here she would
  find a retreat
from the fury of sea and the sky when the noonday
  sunbeams were burning
most fiercely and shadows were shortest. This pool was
  polluted by Circe
beforehand; she fouled it with monster-producing
55   poisons, by sprinkling
the juice from a baleful root, as she darkly muttered her
  magical
spell thrice nine times over in mazy, mysterious
  language.
Scylla arrived at the pool and had stepped in up to the
  waist

when she saw that her loins were disfigured by horrible
    barking creatures.   60
At first she had no idea that these formed part of her body
and shrank to the side in fear as she tried to repel the
    importunate
snapping intruders, but merely dragged at what she was
    fleeing.
She frantically felt for the flesh of her thighs, her legs and
    her feet,
but all that she found was a cluster of gaping hell-hounds.
    She'd nothing   65
to stand on but rabid dogs, whose bestial backs she was
    holding
in check beneath her truncated loins and protuberant belly.
  Glaucus, her lover, wept. Fair Circe had been so
    malicious
in using the magical power of her herbs, and he spurned her
    embraces.
Scylla remained where she was and took the first chance she
    was given   70
to show her hatred for Circe by grabbing Ulýsses'
    companions.
Later on she would also have drowned the ships of the
    Trojans,
had she not first been changed to a headland of rock,*
    which still stands
there to this day and is shunned by sailors as carefully as
    ever.

THE WANDERINGS OF AENEAS (3)

The Trojans had deftly manoeuvred their ships past Scylla's
    rock   75
and Charýbdis' whirlpool and now were almost
    approaching Italian
shores, when a storm diverted them south to the coast of
    Africa.

There they were taken to hearth and heart by Sidónian
    Dido,*
who found Aenéas' sudden departure a cruel
    separation.
80   She built a funeral pyre on false religious pretences,
and fell on her sword, so cheating the world as she had
    been cheated.
    In backward flight from the new city walls on the
        sandy coast,
Aeneas returned to his friend Acéstes at Eryx, to offer
sacrifice where his father had died and to honour the
    grave.
When the fleet had almost been burnt by Iris at Juno's
85   bidding,*
the Trojans set sail once more. They passed the Aeólian
    islands,
where sulphurous smoke pours out of the earth, then
    the rocks of the Sirens.
Aeneas' ship was deprived of his helmsman, the
    drowned Palinúrus,
but soon it was skirting Inárime, Próchyte, past
    Pithecúsae,
placed on a barren hill and called Apetown from the
90   people
who live there. They'd once been known as Cercópians;
    later, however,
Jupiter changed them to misshaped creatures, because
    he detested
their lying, deceitful ways and the treacherous crimes
    they'd committed.
He wanted them both to be different from men and
    resemble them too.
So he shortened their limbs and flattened their noses; he
95   furrowed their faces
with elderly wrinkles; he covered their bodies
    completely in tawny
hair; then he set them to live on this island. But first he
    denied them

the use of their tongues and words to utter their dreadful
    perjuries;
all that remained was their power of complaining – in
    raucous screeches.   100

THE SIBYL OF CUMAE

When he'd passed this place to the right and Parthénope's
    city of Naples,
Aeneas arrived on the shores of the marshy region of
    Cumae,
and entered the cave of the long-lived Sybil. His prayer was
    to traverse
the underworld kingdom in order to visit the shade of his
    father.   105
The prophetess held her gaze long fixed on the earth, till
    she raised
her head as her soul was possessed by the god, and finally
    uttered
in frenzy: 'You ask great things, you greatest of heroes,
    whose valour
was proved by your sword in the fray and whose love as a
    son and a father
was tested by fire. But, noble Trojan, you need not be
    troubled.   110
Your prayer shall be granted and I shall guide you to
    Pluto's realm,*
where you'll see the Elysian Fields and meet your father's
    dear spirit.
No path is closed to the virtuous man.' So speaking, she
    showed him
a golden bough which gleamed on a tree in Prosérpina's
    forest
and told him to break it off from the trunk. Aeneas obeyed
    her   115
and so was allowed to descend and set eyes on the wealth
    of the awesome

god of the dead, on his own forefathers and lastly the
    ghost
of aged Anchíses, the great of heart, who taught him the
    laws
which govern Avérnus and also the dangers facing his
    people
in wars to come. Thence wearily climbing the uphill
120   track
to the earth, he lightened the tiring journey in talk with
    the Sibyl;
and while he was plodding his fearful way through the
    murky twilight,
he said to his guide from Cumae, 'You may be truly a
    goddess,
or merely beloved of the gods; but by me you shall
    always be counted
125 a spirit divine, and I shall owe it to your consent
that I came to the land of the dead and returned thence
    after I'd seen it.
For these great mercies, when I am restored to the air
    above,
I shall build you a sacred temple and pay you the
    tribute of incense.'
   The Sibyl turned to Aeneas and, heaving a deep sigh,
    said to him:
'Goddess I never have been; and a mortal creature may
130   not
be accorded the tribute of holy incense. Yet ignorance
    must not
lead you astray. Eternal life was there for the taking,
if only I'd offered my maidenhood up to the love of
    Apollo;
but while he hoped that I'd yield and desired to seduce
    me with gifts,
he said to me, "Maiden of Cumae, now choose what
135   you wish to be yours,
and your wish shall be granted." I showed him a pile of
    dust that I'd gathered

and foolishly asked for my birthdays to equal the number of
    sand-grains,
failing also to ask that those years should always be
    youthful.
Yet Phoebus agreed and offered perpetual youth as well,   140
if I'd let him enjoy my body. I spurned his gift and remain
forever a virgin unwedded. But now the joy of my
    springtime
is past, and weak old age with its trembling gait is
    upon me,
age to be long endured. I have lived seven hundred years,
but still have to see three hundred harvests and seasons of
    vintage   145
to equal the number of grains in the pile. The time will
    arrive
when the length of days shall shrink my body from all it has
    been
to a tiny frame, and my age-worn limbs be reduced to the
    weight
of a feather. Then no one will ever believe that I once was
    adored
and desired by a god. Yes, even Phoebus may fail to recall
    me,   150
or else he'll deny that he loved me. So changed, so invisible!
    Yet,
the fates will leave me my voice, the voice by which men
    will know me.'*

ACHAEMENIDES' STORY:
ULYSSES' MEN IN POLYPHEMUS' CAVE

Mounting the slope to the earth, the Sibyl recounted her
    history,
until they emerged from the Stygian world in the township
    of Cumae,   155
where Trojan Aeneas offered the sacrifice due to the gods.

Next he put into shore at the place which was not yet
  called
by the name of his faithful nurse.* Another person who'd
  stopped there
after many exhausting adventures was Íthacan
  Mácareus,
once a seasoned companion of much-enduring Ulysses.
Macareus spotted a friend, Achaeménides,* there with
160 the Trojans,
someone abandoned long since by the Greeks on the
  rocks of Mount Etna
but rescued and taken on board by Aeneas. Astonished
  at suddenly
finding his former companion alive, 'What chance or
  what god
has preserved you?' he said to his old friend. 'How can
  a Greek be permitted
to sail in a Trojan vessel? What land are you heading
  for now?'
So Macareus asked; Achaemenides answered, no
165 longer apparelled
in hairy clothing fastened by thorns, once more his
  own master:
'Listen, I'd rather remain on this ship than return to
  my home
in Ithaca. Force me to see Polyphémus* again, with his
  jaws
all dripping with human blood, if I'm telling a lie. I
  swear
that I hold Aeneas in greater respect than I hold my
170 father.
I'll never be able to thank him enough, whatever I give
  him.
I speak and I breathe; I can see the sky and the sun's
  bright rays.
Could I fail to be grateful for that or ever forget what I
  owe him?

It's due to him that my life didn't vanish inside the mouth
of the Cyclops. If death overtakes me now, I shall still be
  properly   175
buried, at least not swallowed inside the maw of that
  monster.
  'What were my feelings (except that fear had deprived me
    entirely
of feeling and sense), when I saw you heading out to the
  deep –
and was left behind? I wanted to shout for your help, but I
  dared not
give my position away. The shouts of Ulysses had almost   180
destroyed your vessel. I watched Polyphemus tear an
  enormous
piece of rock from the mountain and cast it into the waves.
I watched him hurling a second boulder; his giant's arm
had a catapult's power. I was desperately frightened the
  ship would be sunk
by the wind gust caused by the rock or the backward wash
  of a wave,   185
and forgot that I wasn't on board. But when your rowing
  had saved you
from certain death, the Cyclops stumbled over Mount
  Etna
groaning, groping his way through the woods and blindly
  bumping
against the boulders. Stretching his gore-fouled arms in
  the ocean's   190
direction, he cursed the whole Grecian race as he wildly
  exclaimed:
"How I wish some chance would return me Ulysses or one
  of his comrades
on whom my anger could rage, whose guts I'd devour and
  whose living
body I'd tear apart, whose blood could flood the path   195
to my gullet, whose limbs would quiver beneath my teeth
  as I crunched them!

With that the loss of my sight would count for little or
    nothing."
  'All that and more in his fury; while I turned pale in a
    seizure
of horror, my gaze transfixed by the face still dripping
    with gore,
the violent hands and the sightless eye, the gargantuan
200   limbs
and the beard all matted with human blood. Yes, death
    was before me;
but that was the least of my terrors. I thought he was
    going to seize me,
going at once to down my vitals inside his own;
and the picture stuck in my mind of the awful time
205   when I'd seen him
grabbing my comrades, two at a time, and repeatedly
    dashing
their heads on the floor, then crouching lion-like over
    their bodies
to swallow the flesh and the guts, the bones full of
    succulent marrow,
the limbs still pulsing with life, down into that
    ravening belly.
I quivered like them and stood there, bloodless in grief,
210   as I watched him
chewing and spewing his bloody feast and vomiting
    gobbets
of flesh in a splutter of neat wine. That was the fate I
    imagined
awaited me during those many days when I lurked in
    my hide-out,
trembling at every noise, both frightened and longing
215   to die.
With acorns, grasses and leaves I kept starvation at
    bay,
helpless, hopeless and lonely, abandoned to death and
    to hardship.

Then after a long, long time I sighted this ship in the
    distance.
I waved my arms in a plea to be rescued, I ran to the shore,
and I moved their pity. A Greek was taken on board by
    Trojans!   220
Macareus, dearest of friends, now tell me your own
    adventures.
What of our leader, Ulysses? And what of the crew who
    were with you?'

MACAREUS' STORY:
ULYSSES AND CIRCE

Macareus first explained how Ulysses had visited Aéolus,*
lord of the Tuscan Sea, who confines the winds in their
    prison.
To hasten his homeward voyage, the king had made him a
    special   225
present of all the winds tied firmly up in an ox-skin.
For nine whole days they had sailed with a favouring breeze
    behind them,
and Ithaca now was in sight. But on the following morning,
Ulysses' companions were overcome by rapacious envy;
thinking the skin carried gold, they untied the strings and
    released   230
the winds, which immediately swept their ship back over
    the sea
they had recently crossed and drove them again into Aeolus'
    harbour.
'From there,' Macareus continued, 'we sailed to the ancient
    city
of Laestrygónian Lamus, where King Antíphates ruled.
I, with two others, was sent to see him; but out of the three
    of us,   235
one companion and I succeeded in fleeing to safety.

The other was caught in Antiphates' cannibal jaws and
      coloured them
red with his blood. We were chased by the king and a
      crowd of excited
people behind him, who gathered and pelted the ships of
      Ulysses
with rocks and with branches, sinking the vessels and
240   drowning the crews.
One ship, however, escaped, the one which was
      carrying me
and Ulysses himself. In distress at losing the bulk of
      our comrades
and sadly lamenting our lot, we finally came to the
      island
you see in the distance from here – I've been there
      myself and, believe me,
it's better observed from a distance. I warn you, most
245   righteous of Trojans,
son of a goddess (the war is over, Aeneas, I cannot
call you a foe), stay firmly away from the island of
      Circe.
  'We too, after mooring our ship on the shore of that
      dangerous island,
remembered Antiphates, not to mention the brutal
      Cyclops,
and so we refused to go on or to enter the house of a
250   stranger.
But lots were cast, and a party consisting of me and the
      faithful
Polítes, Eurýlochus, boozy Elpénor,* with eighteen
      others,
was chosen to venture away from the shore to the
      palace of Circe.
As soon as we reached it and stood on the threshold,
      we cowered in terror
from hundreds of wolves, lionesses and she-bears
255   rushing to greet us,

though none, in fact, gave cause for alarm or was likely to
    hurt us.
Far from it; they all were wagging their tails in the friendliest
    fashion
and licking our hands as we moved indoors, until we were
    welcomed
by female attendants, who guided us through a magnificent
    marble   260
hall to their mistress' presence. The goddess was throned
    on a splendid
chair in a beautiful apse and wearing a dazzling robe
wrapped round with a golden cloak. The nymphs and
    Néreïds by her
weren't carding the wool of a fleece or spinning thread in
    their fingers,   265
but sorting out grasses or neatly arranging a jumble of
    scattered
flowers, or herbs of various colours, in separate baskets.
Circe herself was directing the work, as she well understood
the use of the different leaves and how they ought to be
    blended,
keeping an eye on her women and checking the weight of
    each substance.   270
  'As soon as she saw us and formal greetings had been
    exchanged,
she graciously smiled and reciprocated our kind good
    wishes,
then promptly ordered her nymphs to concoct a potion,
    consisting
of barley-grains, honey, a powerful wine and milk that had
    curdled.
To this she added some juices which wouldn't be noticed
    in so much   275
sweetness. We gladly accepted the cup from the goddess's
    hand
as our lips were parched. But as soon as we'd swallowed the
    potion down,

the sorceress touched the tops of our heads with her
        wand. In a moment
(I tell the tale to my shame) I started to prickle all over
with bristles.* My voice had deserted me; all the words I
280   could utter
were snorting grunts. I was falling down to the earth,
        head first.
I could feel my nose and my mouth going hard in a
        long round snout;
my neck was swelling in folds of muscle; the hands
        which had lifted
the cup just now to my lips were marking the soil with
        hoof prints.
Others had suffered the same (those charms are so
285   strong!) and I joined them,
penned in a sty. We saw that we all had been turned
        into swine –
except for Eurylochus. He alone had rejected the
        potion
and, had he not done so, I'd still be one of a herd of
        bristly
porkers today. Ulysses would never have learned from
        the man
of this dreadful disaster and come to save us from
290   Circe's enchantment.
    'Luckily, Mercury, god of peace, had given our
        leader
a flower which the gods call moly, a pure white flower
        with a black root.
Armed with that and the god's instructions, Ulysses
        entered
the palace of Circe and, when she offered her
        treacherous potion
and tried to caress his hair with her wand, to her
295   startled amazement
he violently pushed her away and frightened her off
        with his drawn sword.

Solemn pledges were then exchanged: Ulysses was happy
to join fair Circe in bed, but insisted that she must restore
his friends to their normal shape to fulfil her part of the
      bargain.
And so we were sprinkled with juice from a strange but
      rather more wholesome
herb and firmly struck on the head with a blow from the
      other   300
end of her wand, while a spell commuted her curse to a
      blessing.
And while her chanting continued, our bodies gradually
      rose
till we stood on our feet, our bristles fell off, the cracks in
      our cloven
trotters were gone, our shoulders returned, and we found
      we had upper arms,
elbows and forearms. Ulysses was weeping; we wept
      ourselves   305
as we fondly embraced him and clung to his neck. The first
      of the new-found
words that we uttered expressed our heartfelt thanks to our
      leader.

MACAREUS' STORY:

PICUS, CANENS AND CIRCE

'We stayed in Circe's house for a year, and during that long
      time
I was a witness to many sights and heard many stories.
These included a tale which was told me in private by one   310
of the four attendants whom Circe employed in her
      magical rites.
One day, while her mistress was idly dawdling alone with
      Ulysses,
this nice nymph showed me a statue, carved in the whitest
      of marble,

portraying a man with a woodpecker perched on top of
      his head.
The statue was set in a shrine and festooned with
315   garlands. Curious
to know, I enquired who the young man was and why
      he was worshipped
there in the shrine and why he carried that bird on his
      head.
"I'll tell you, Macareus," answered the girl; "it's
      another example
of Circe's magic. So please attend while I try to
      explain.
  '"Picus,* the offspring of Saturn, was once the king
320   in the land
of Ausónia. Horses for battle in war were his
      passionate interest.
This statue shows how he looked as a man. You can
      see for yourself
how handsome he was and admire his mien on the
      strength of his portrait.
His person was matched by his fineness of nature. He
      wasn't yet twenty
and couldn't have watched the Olympics in Elis as
325   many as four times.
His wonderful looks attracted the dryads born in the
      mountains
of Látium; the nymphs of the fountains sighed for him
      too; and the naiads
who dwell in the Alban Tiber, the streams of Numícius
      or Ánio,
Almo whose course is the shortest, cascading Nar, or
330   the shady
waters of Farfa; and others whose haunts are Tauric
      Diana's
woodland pool* or the lakes nearby. But Picus rejected
      them
all and courted a nymph whom Venília bore, so they
      say,

long ages ago on the Pálatine hill to two-headed Janus.
As soon as this beautiful girl was old enough to be
     married,   335
they gave her away to the favoured suitor, Lauréntian
     Picus.
Though rare in beauty, in singing's arts she was rarer yet,
so her name was Cánens, the singer.* She'd move the trees
     and the rocks,
she'd calm the fiercest of beasts, she would slow the course
     of the longest
rivers and halt the birds on the wing with her musical
     singing.   340
  '"One day, when Canens was trilling at home in her
     lovely soprano,
Picus went out to the fields of Lauréntum to chase the boar.
He was riding his mettled steed, two hunting-spears in his
     left hand,
wearing a scarlet cloak with a golden brooch on his
     shoulder.   345
It chanced that Circe had also entered the woods at the
     same time,
leaving the fields called after her name in order to gather
new herbs on the fertile hills. As soon as she saw young
     Picus
from where she was hidden inside a thicket, her breath was
     completely
taken away. She dropped the herbs she had carefully
     gathered   350
and felt the flames of passion pervading the whole of her
     being.
Once the heat had subsided a little and she had recovered
her senses, she longed to confess her desire but couldn't
     approach him
because of his galloping horse and all of his thronging
     attendants.
'The wind may snatch you away,' she said, 'but you shan't
     escape me,   355
if only I know myself, if the magical power of my herbs

hasn't vanished entirely, if all the spells I can chant don't
     fail me.'
So saying, she conjured up an illusion, a phantom boar,
which she ordered to scamper across the trail in the
     king's full view
and appear to enter the wood where the trees were
360   thickest, the ground
was cluttered with fallen trunks and a horse couldn't
     possibly pass through.
Picus was fooled and at once went after this ghost of a
     quarry.
He quickly leapt to the ground from his foaming steed
     and wandered
on foot through the depths of the wood in pursuit of
     an empty hope.
  '"Meanwhile, fair Circe was framing her prayers in
365   sorcery's language,
worshipping unknown gods in outlandish charms
     which she commonly
used to obscure the face of a silvery moon or to weave
a curtain of rain-sodden clouds beneath her father, the
     sun god.
So it was then as she chanted her spell: the heavens
     were darkened,
mist steamed up from the earth, and all the king's
370   followers blindly
wandered and trailed through the wood, so that none
     was left to protect him.
Circe now had contrived the time and the place for her
     ambush.
'I appeal to you, Picus,' she said, 'by your eyes which
     have captured my own,
by your beauty, most handsome of men, which
     compels me, though I am a goddess,
to kneel at your feet, be kind to my passion. Accept the
375   all-seeing
Sun as your father, don't cruelly scorn the Titaness
     Circe!'

' "But Picus firmly rejected both Circe herself and her
　　　prayers.
'Whoever you are,' he replied, 'I cannot be yours, as
　　　another
has captured and holds my heart in her keeping. I pray she
　　　retains it
for ever and ever. I cannot be false to the vows of my
　　　marriage,   380
so long as the fates preserve me the daughter of Janus, my
　　　Canens.'
Circe appealed to Picus again many times to no purpose.
'Your hardness will cost you dear,' she exclaimed. 'Your
　　　Canens shall never
see you again. You'll learn what a woman in love who is
　　　injured
can do; and Circe is surely an injured woman in love!'
The sorceress then turned twice to the west and twice to
　　　the east;   386
she struck the young king with her wand three times, and
　　　she spoke three spells.
Picus took to his heels but soon was surprised to discover
himself running faster than usual. Wings had sprung from
　　　his body!
A new type of bird had suddenly joined the forests of
　　　Latium.   390
Furious to find it was he, he pecked at the wild tree-trunks
with his hard beak, angrily dealing wounds in the length of
　　　the branches.
His wings had taken the hue of his scarlet cloak, and the
　　　golden
brooch with the pin which had gripped his garments was
　　　turned into plumage.
His neck was ringed with a circle of golden yellow, and
　　　nothing   395
remained of his former self but the name of the
　　　woodpecker, *picus*.
' "Meanwhile, the attendants of Picus who'd frequently
　　　shouted in vain

for their master over the countryside and had found him
        nowhere,
came upon Circe, who'd cleared the sky by this time and
        permitted
the mists to disperse in the sun and the wind. They plied
400   her with questions,
accused her of what she had actually done and
        demanded their king back.
Force was threatened; their pointed swords were ready
        for action,
when Circe sprinkled a noxious substance and
        poisonous juices
upon them, summoning Night and the powers of
        darkness from Chaos
and Érebus, praying to Hécate, goddess of witchcraft,
405   in drawn-out
wailing and shrieks. Then, wonder of wonders, the
        woods all jumped,
the earth gave a rumbling groan, and the trees in the
        glade turned yellow.
The poison-bespattered grass was running with
        droplets of blood.
It appeared that the rocks were hoarsely bellowing,
        dogs were barking,
the earth was crawling with rough-scaled serpents as
410   black as the night,
and the air was filled with the flitting ghosts of the
        silent departed.
The party of men was appalled by these hideous
        marvels. Then Circe
touched their wondering faces of fear with her
        poisoned wand.
They succumbed to her magic; the poor young men
        were transformed to a medley
of monstrous beasts, and none of them kept his normal
415   appearance.
    ' "The fiery sun had set in the west on the shores of
        Tartéssus.

Canens was anxiously waiting and watching out for her
        husband
the king, but he hadn't returned. Search parties of servants
        and townsfolk
scoured the forest in all directions with torches to find him.
It wasn't enough for the nymph to be weeping or tearing
        her tresses   420
or beating her breasts (though she did every one of those
        things), but she rushed
right out of the palace and roamed distractedly over
        Latium.
For six long days and for six long nights she travelled at
        random,
without any food and without any sleep, through the hills
        and the valleys.   425
She finally came to the Tiber, who saw her, exhausted by
        sorrow
and all her travels, prostrating her limbs on the bank of his
        long stream.
There, as she wept, she vented even her grief in an aria*
sung in a soft, faint voice to express her despair, as we
        sometimes
listen ourselves to the funeral dirge of the dying swan.   430
In conclusion, her tender marrow was turned to water by
        mourning;
she wasted and, little by little, she vanished away into
        nothing.
Her fame, however, is marked by the spot which the ancient
        Muses
fitly called Canens, after the name of the musical nymph."
    'Such were the many stories I heard and the sights that I
        saw   435
in that tedious year. Doing nothing had made us sluggish
        and slow,
when they told us to launch our vessels and spread our sails
        once again.
Circe had warned that our purposed voyage would be long
        and uncertain,

and detailed the dangers still to be faced on the cruel sea.
I was scared, I admit; and once I arrived in this country, I
440   stayed.'

THE WANDERINGS OF AENEAS (4)

Macareus' story was ended. An urn with Aeneas'
        nurse's
ashes was laid in a marble tomb, with this brief
        inscription:
        HERE LIES CAIÉTA. SHE NURSED A HERO
        RENOWNED FOR HIS GOODNESS.
        HE SAVED HER FROM TROY'S GREAT FIRE AND
        GAVE HER THE FIRE THAT HE OWED HER.

The cable which moored Aeneas' ship to a grassy
445   embankment
was now cast off. The sailors kept well away from the
        treacherous
island and palace of infamous Circe and made for the
        woods
where the yellow sands of the shady Tiber invade the
        ocean.
And here Aeneas was given a home and pledged a
        daughter
in marriage by Faunus' offspring Latínus* – but not
450   without conflict.
A war broke out with a savage people, whose
        champion Turnus
struggled with reckless fury to win the bride he'd been
        promised.
Latium clashed with the whole of Etrúria; many an
        anxious
day was spent in the heat of battle for hard-won
        victory.

THE MUTINOUS COMPANIONS
OF DIOMEDES

Each side was supported by help from abroad. The clans
    were gathered
to back the Rutúlians; many defended the Trojan camp.   455
Aeneas appealed with success to Evánder,* the king of
    Pallánteum;
Vénulus fared less well when he entered the walls of the
    exiled
King Diomédes, who'd actually founded a spacious city
and occupied land as a dowry from Iapýgian Daunus.
However, when Venulus boldly delivered his message
    from Turnus   460
and asked for his aid, Diomedes flatly refused it and
    pleaded
his weakness: he couldn't commit himself or the subjects of
    Daunus,
his father-in-law, to a fight, and he had no men of his own
    Greek
people to arm for a war. 'These aren't false pretexts,' he
    added.
'I'll bring myself to explain, although my sadness and
    sorrow   465
are reawakened when I recall them. Ilium's towers
had been burnt to the ground and Troy devoured by the
    Grecian flames;
Narýcian Ajax* had brutally forced the virgin Cassándra
away from the shrine of the virgin Athena and raped her,
    bringing
on all of the Greeks the punishment owed to none but
    himself.
So our fleet was scattered and forced by winds on the
    hostile ocean   470

to face the lightning, the dark and the rain, to endure the
            full fury
of sea and of sky and be finally wrecked on the rocks of
            Caphéreus.
I won't delay you by telling the whole sad story in detail,
but Greece at that time might even have moved King
            Priam to tears.
Though I was rescued and snatched from the waves
475   through the care of the warrior
goddess Athena, yet once again, I was forced to
            abandon
my father's estate in Argos, as kindly Venus
            remembered
the wound I dealt her at Troy long ago* and made me
            atone
for her injury now. I have lived through such great
            trials on the deep
and in battles on land, that I've often declared those
480   others were lucky
who perished beneath the waves by Caphereus'
            merciless cape
in the storm which attacked us all, and wished I had
            gone down too.
    'My companions had suffered all they could take on
            sea or in battle;
morale had collapsed and they now demanded an end
            to their wanderings.
But Acmon, whose hot-headed nature was chafed even
485   more by disaster,
protested. "Sailors!" he said, "what's left to encounter
            that lies
beyond your endurance to bear? What further damage
            can Venus
inflict, supposing she wanted to? Prayers can avail, if
            worse
is *yet* to be feared; but when the worst has already
            occurred,

fear lies at our feet and the crown of misfortune is freedom
    from care.   490
No matter if Venus can hear my words; never mind if she
    loathes
Diomedes' crew to a man; we can treat her loathing with
    scorn
to a man. Her power may be great, but it counts for little
    with *us*!"
Such were the taunting words with which the insolent
    Acmon
goaded the goddess and quickly revived her inveterate
    anger.   495
More of his friends reproved him for what he had said
    than the few
who agreed. When he tried to respond to our strictures, his
    voice grew thin
as his throat grew thin. His hair was turned into feathers;
    his breast,
his back and his new-shaped neck were also covered with
    plumage.
His arms expanded and bent at the elbows to form light
    wings;   500
his toes disappeared in the rest of his large webbed feet;
    and his mouth
went stiff as it hardened to horn and tapered into a sharp
    point.
Lycus stared at Acmon in wonder and so did Idas;
so did Rhexénor, Nýcteus and Abas; and while they were
    staring,   505
they all took on the same likeness. Most of my crew
    flew up
from the ship and circled around the oars as they flapped
    their wings.
If you ask what these strange new birds were like, I can only
    tell you
that, while they were different from swans, they resembled
    the swan very closely.

The story explains why, although I can call King Daunus
510   my father
by marriage, this settlement takes some trouble to rule,
    and I plough
these drought-stricken fields with a tiny remnant of
    people to help me.'

THE APULIAN SHEPHERD

Thus far Diomedes; so Venulus left the Apúlian
    kingdom
and passed the Peucétian gulf and Messápian fields. On
    his journey
he sighted a cave, well shaded by woods and dripping
515   with water,
which now is the home of the half-goat Pan and once
    had belonged
to the nymphs. One day these spirits were chased from
    their cave in a fright
by a local shepherd, who scared them at first with his
    sudden arrival;
but soon, when their courage returned and they saw
    that their doltish pursuer
could well be ignored, they joined once more in their
520   rhythmical dancing.
The shepherd then jeered and jumped about in a crude
    imitation;
what's more, he clownishly scoffed at their rites with
    obscene abuse.
He never stopped shouting his insults, until his mouth
    was obstructed
by what he is now – by a tree; and the fruit will tell you
    its nature.
The mark of his tongue survives in the bitter tang of
525   wild olive
berries; his roughness of language passed into tartness
    of flavour.

THE SHIPS OF AENEAS

After the envoys returned to Turnus and brought Diomedes'
refusal to help, the Rutulians pressed ahead with their
     purposed
war without his support. Much bloodshed followed on both
     sides.
Suddenly Turnus attacked the pinewood ships of the
     Trojans   530
with ravening torches, and timbers previously spared on
     the water
now were threatened with fire. The flames were already at
     work
on the pitch, the wax and the other combustible matter on
     board;
they were mounting the lofty masts to the sails, and the
     benches crossing
the rounded hulls were starting to smoke, when the thought
     occurred   535
to Cýbele, known as the holy mother of all the gods,
that the pine composing these ships had been felled on the
     peaks of Mount Ida.*
She filled the air with the clashing of cymbals and skirling of
     boxwood
pipes, then riding across the sky in her lion-drawn chariot,
'Turnus,' she shouted, 'you impious man, you are throwing
     those torches
in vain! I will rescue those ships, as I cannot allow the
     consuming   540
flames to devour any root or branch of my sacred forest.'
A clap of thunder as Cybele spoke! Its rolling subsided,
then torrents of rain and of bouncing hailstones burst from
     the clouds.
The storm winds suddenly clashed; great chaos reigned in
     the sky
and over the swollen sea as the brothers engaged in their
     battle.   545

The earth-mother goddess employed the strength of one
    of the gales
to snap the hempen cables which moored the Phrygian
    vessels,
to force the ships forward and plunge them all in the
    midst of the waves.
As the wood in them gradually softened, the boats were
    changed into bodies,
the rounded sterns were transformed into heads, and the
550   oars vanished into
the legs and toes of a swimmer. The sides continued as
    sides,
and the keel down the middle below was altered to
    serve as a backbone.
Rigging became soft hair, and arms appeared on the
    sail-yards.
The colour was still sea-green. The ships were nymphs
555   of the ocean,
girlishly playing among the waves which had formerly
    scared them.
Although they had started their lives as trees on the
    rock-hard mountains,
they haunted the yielding waves without any thought
    of their birthplace.
But none of them ever forgot the many dangers they'd
    faced
and endured on the cruel sea; so their hands would
560   often support
any vessels caught in a storm, except those carrying
    Greeks.
They still remembered the sack of Troy and detested
    the Argives.
Their faces lit up with delight when they sighted the
    fragments of wreckage
which came from Ulysses' ship, and were equally glad
    when they saw
Alcínoüs' bark* grow hard with the rock encrusting its
565   timbers.

ARDEA

Now that the fleet was transformed into living sea-nymphs,
    the Trojans
hoped that Turnus, in fear of this portent, might halt the
    fighting.
But Turnus went on. There were gods on both sides and, no
    less important,
the men had their courage to help them. They weren't any
    longer pursuing
Lavinia's hand, with the kingdom and throne of her father
    for dowry;   570
they simply wanted to win and continued the fight as they
    felt
too ashamed to abandon it now. Eventually Venus saw
Aeneas' victory assured, while Turnus fell in the battle.
Árdea fell, a powerful city in Turnus' lifetime.
After the Trojan torches had razed her walls to the ground
and her ruined buildings were smothered in piles of
    smouldering ashes,   575
a bird never seen before flew up from the midst of the
    rubble,
lashing the embers with flapping wings. The cries of sorrow,
the lean, pale faces and all that betokens a captured city
survived in that bird; yes, even the name, as the heron called
    ardea
beats her wings in her grief for the city from which she
    arose.   580

THE APOTHEOSIS OF AENEAS

Aeneas' courage by now had compelled the gods, including
Juno herself, to end the anger they'd nursed so long.
Iúlus was reaching his prime and his fortunes were firmly
    established.
So Venus' heroic son was ripe for translation to heaven.

Venus had canvassed the body of gods and, throwing her
585   arms
round Jupiter's neck, had said to him: 'Dearest father,
     you've never
been harsh or unyielding to *me*; now be at your
     kindest, I beg you.
Please help my Aeneas, your grandson born of our
     blood divine,
and make him a god, no matter how humble, O
     highest of gods,
so long as he joins our ranks. He already has seen the
590   unlovely
kingdom of Hades and crossed the Styx. Is once not
     enough?'
The gods all agreed, and even Queen Juno's reaction to
     Venus
was far from impassive; she gave her consent with a
     gracious smile.
Then Jupiter answered his daughter: 'This grant of
     heavenly status
is due to Aeneas and you who apply for it. Take what
595   you ask for!'
   Venus was simply delighted and thanked her father
     profusely.
Then riding her chariot, drawn by doves, through the
     gentle breezes,
she duly arrived on the Laúrentine coast, where the
     river Numicius
snakes on its course with its mantle of reeds to the
     neighbouring sea.
600 She asked it to wash away whatever parts of Aeneas
were subject to death and silently carry them down to
     the ocean.
The horned god did as Venus commanded, and used
     his own waters
to sprinkle Aeneas and cleanse his nature of all that
     was mortal,

while leaving him all that was best. His mother anointed his
    purified
body with fragrance divine and touched his lips with
    ambrosia   605
mingled with nectar. She made him a god, whom Romulus'
    people
titled Índiges, Native, and honoured with temple and altars.

AENEAS' DESCENDANTS

So Alba and Latium thereafter were under the rule of Iulus,
also known as Ascánius. He was succeeded by Sílvius,
whose son Latinus also came to the throne of the ancient   610
king of the same name. After Latinus, illustrious Alba.
Épytus next; and he was followed by Cápetus, Capys
(though Capys came first) and then Tiberínus, who ruled
    for a while
but was drowned in a Tuscan stream and gave his name to
    the river.   615
He had two sons: first Rémulus, second the warlike Ácrota.
The elder, Remulus, tried to mimic the thunder and
    lightning
and died when struck by a lightning bolt. The more
    temperate brother,
Acrota, handed the kingdom over to brave Aventínus,   620
who reigned on the hill which is called by his name and is
    where he was buried.

POMONA AND VERTUMNUS

At the time of this story, Proca was ruling the Palatine
    people.*
Pomóna, the goddess of fruits, was one of the dryads of
    Latium
during the reign of this king; and none was more skilful a
    gardener

625 or more devoted to cultivating the various fruit trees.
Hence her name of Pomona. She showed no love for
          the forests
or rivers, but only for orchards and trees with fruit on
          their branches.
She never wielded a hunting-spear but a pruning-hook,
with which she would check luxuriant growth and
          prevent any branches
from spreading too wildly; or else she would use it for
630   splitting the bark
to engraft a cutting and offer the sap to an alien shoot.
She'd never allow her plants to be thirsty but watered
          the greedy
Roots with trickling channels to feed their flexible
          fibres.
This was her love and her passion; she had no interest
          in Venus.
Indeed in her fear of assault by some peasant, she
635   fenced her orchard
And stayed inside it to shun and forestall all contact
          with men.
What didn't they do to possess her – those lecherous
          dancers, the satyrs,
The Pans with their horns encircled by wreaths of pine,
          pot-bellied
Silénus who always acted too young for his old man's
          years,
And Priápus,* the god who terrifies thieves with his
640   knife or his phallus!

One spirit was more in love with Pomona than all of
          these others,
but didn't succeed any better. Vertúmnus, 'the
          Turner',* was always
appearing in different disguises. He'd come in the garb
          of a rugged
reaper, with ears of corn in a trug, and was very
          convincing!

Or else, if you saw the fresh-cut hay in a band on his
         forehead,   645
you'd think he'd been tossing the new-mown grass like a
         genuine haymaker.
Often he'd carry a goad in his hard rough hand; you could
         honestly
call him a ploughman who'd just unyoked his exhausted
         oxen.
Give him a hook and he might be a pruner or stripper of
         vines;
a ladder to carry, and off he'd be going to harvest the
         apples.   650
All these forms he adopted again and again to get close
to Pomona and so to enjoy the sight of her beautiful
         person.
   One day he even put on a grey wig with a bright-coloured
         headscarf,
crouched down over a stick and pretended to be an old
         woman.   655
He entered the orchard, admired the apples and said to
         Pomona,
'They make you all the more tempting!'; then followed this
         compliment up
by kissing her once or twice on the lips as a real old woman
would never have done. Next, resting her tired, bowed back
         on the earth,
the hag looked up at the branches, bowed with the fruits
         of the autumn.   660
'You see that elm tree,' she said, 'supporting the beautiful
         clusters
of shiny grapes? How lovely it looks with the vine it belongs
         to!
Supposing that trunk were a bachelor, without the shoots
         which entwine it,
there'd be no reason, apart from its leaves, to look for its
         company.
So with the vine which happily rests in the arms of the elm
         tree: 665

unmarried, it simply would trail on the ground with the
    earth for its pillow.
You, my dear, don't seem to respond to the vine's
    example.
You need to mate, to belong to a man, but you show no
    interest.
If only you *would* desire it! You'd have more suitors then
    Helen,
or Hippodamía, who caused the fight of the Lapiths and
670   centaurs.
Even now, though you shrink and turn from your
    wooers in loathing,
a thousand men are longing to have you, gods and
    demigods,
all the spirits that make their homes in the Alban
    hills.*
Pomona, won't you be sensible? Take an old woman's
675   advice
and make a good match! I love you more than all of
    the others,
more indeed than you think. Have nothing to do with
    those common
admirers, but choose Vertumnus to share your bed.
    You can take
my word for his honour. I know him as well as he
    knows himself.
He doesn't wander all over the world in search of new
680   women;
he sticks to his own patch. Nor does he fall in love
    with the latest
girl he has seen, like most of your suitors. *You*'ll be his
    passion,
his first and his last; he'll devote his life entirely to *you*.
    'What's more, he is young and he's blessed by nature
    with wonderful looks;
he can change into any form that he likes to suit the
685   occasion.

He'll be whatever you tell him to be, no matter how strange.
You like the same things; he's the first to get hold of the
            apples you grow,
and adores to feel them inside his hand. But neither the fruit
which is plucked from your trees, nor the succulent grass
            which grows in your garden,
nothing at all is the slightest interest to him but you.   690
Pity his passion. Imagine your lover is standing before you
in person and speaking through me to implore your
            bountiful favour.
Remember, the gods are vindictive; unyielding hearts are
            detested
by Venus; Némesis never forgets and her wrath is relentless.
And now, to add to your fear, since my age has allowed
            me to know   695
many things, I shall tell you a story familiar all over Cyprus.
I hope it will soften your heart and make you more easy to
            win.

IPHIS AND ANAXARETE

'Iphis, a youth of inferior birth, had seen Anaxárete,
who was a proud princess in the line of Teucer's
            descendants,
and fallen deeply in love. For long he struggled against it,   700
but found he was quite unable to conquer his passion by
            reason.
He therefore went to the lady's house to plead for her pity.
He tried to open his bleeding heart to her nurse, whom he
            earnestly
begged, by her hopes for the child she had reared, to show
            him some kindness.
He also attempted to charm each one of the numerous
            servants   705
and asked them in anxious tones to lend their weight to
            his wooing.

He'd often present them with sweet love-letters to take to
      their mistress;
or else he'd festoon the posts at the palace entrance with
      garlands
bedewed with his tears and impetuously throw himself
      down on the threshold,
soft against hard, where he gloomily rained abuse on the
710   door-bolts.
But she was more harsh than the rising waves in the
      stormy season,
tougher than iron that is smelted by fire in Nóricum's*
      forges,
harder than living rock still firmly embedded in
      earth.
She scorned her lover and savagely mocked him. Her
      merciless deeds
were backed by her arrogant words, till even his hopes
715   were extinguished.
Iphis could take no more of this cruel, protracted
      torture,
and these were the final words that he spoke on his
      mistress' doorstep:
  ' "You win, Anaxarete! No need now to be vexed
      any more
by my wearisome wooing. I'm finished. Enjoy your
      glorious triumph,
invoke Apollo and wreathe your head in glistening
720   laurel.
You win, and I gladly die. Be happy, then, heart of
      iron!
At least you'll have something to praise in my love,
      some small satisfaction,
something to make you acknowledge my service. Yet
      always remember,
my fondness for you never ended until I had ended my
      life.
In the sun and your eyes I shall lose two lights at a
725   single moment.

It won't be a rumour that brings you the news of my death.
        To remove
all doubt of it, *I* shall be there. You will see me in person
        before you.
I want your unfeeling eyes to feast on my lifeless body.
O gods, if you look on the actions of mortals, remember
        poor Iphis
(there's nothing else that my feeble tongue has the strength
        to implore),   730
and ensure that my story is told right down the length of
        the ages.
Restore the years you have taken away from my life to my
        fame!"
  'So speaking, he lifted his streaming eyes and his pale
        white arms
to the parts of the palace doors he had often adorned with
        his garlands,
and said, as he tied a noose to the beam surmounting the
        entrance,   735
"This garland will give you pleasure, you cruel and
        faithless girl!"
He thrust his head, still facing towards her, inside the noose,
and at once he was strangled, his luckless body suspended
        in air.
The drum of his quivering feet on the door made a knock,
        as of someone
demanding to enter the house. When the servants answered
        the summons,   740
they were able to see what had happened and cried aloud in
        dismay.
They lifted the body out of the halter – but all to no
        purpose –
and carried it back to his mother's threshold (his father was
        dead).
The woman enfolded her son's cold limbs in a loving
        embrace;
then after she'd uttered her cries and performed her ritual
        gestures   745

of mourning, she led the gloomy cortège through the
    heart of the city,
bearing the death-pale corpse on a bier to the funeral
    pyre.
  'By chance, Anaxarete's house was close to the street
    where the woeful
procession was passing. The sounds of lament came
    through to the ears
of the hard princess, whom a vengeful god was already
750   pursuing.
Moved, in spite of her nature, she said, "Let us take a
    look
at the funeral train," and climbed aloft to watch
    through a window.
She'd hardly caught sight of Iphis' corpse laid out on
    the bier,
when her eyes glazed over and froze, the warm blood
    fled from her body,
her skin turned horribly pale. She attempted to step
755   right back,
but her feet were stuck where they were. Then she tried
    to avert her gaze
and failed once again. Little by little, the stone which
    had always
been there in her hard, cold heart took over the whole
    of her body.
To prove this isn't an idle fiction, Sálamis still
preserves Anaxarete's statue. It also possesses a
760   shrine
dedicated to Venus the Watcher.* My dear Pomona, I
    beg you,
remember this story. Abandon your proud,
    slow-yielding resistance,
and give yourself to your lover. If you will take my
    advice,
I shall pray that the frosts in the spring won't nip the
    buds on your trees,

nor the blasts of the wind shake off the fruit when it ripens
    in autumn.'

Thus the god disguised as a crone appealed to Pomona,   765
but all in vain. He returned to his young man's guise and
    discarded
the old woman's trappings. The vision that now confronted
    the maid
was like the brilliant face of the Sun, when he clears the
    obstructing
clouds and shines once again with his glory fully revealed.
Vertumnus was ready to force his will, but force wasn't
    needed;   770
the nymph was entranced by his radiant form and
    responded with passion.

ROMULUS

Proca was followed as king by Amúlius.* He had unjustly
seized the Ausónian state by force of arms from his brother.
Númitor later recovered the throne with the aid of his
    grandson,
Rómulus. So, on the feast of Pales, the god of the shepherds,
the walls of the city of Rome were founded. A war was
    then started   775
by Tátius the Sabine, leading the fathers of women
    abducted
by Romulus' men. Tarpeía,* who'd opened a path to the
    fortress,
deservedly lost her life as the shields of the enemy crushed
    her.
From there the Sabines, hushed and silent as wolves on the
    prowl,
came down on the Romans while they were dead to the
    world, and made for   780
the gates of the city, which Ília's son had firmly secured.

But one had been noiselessly turned on its hinges and
        opened by Juno,
and only Venus had noticed the fall of the bars. She'd
        have closed it,
but gods are never allowed to undo the work of each
        other.
Now close to this gate and to Janus' shrine* the
785   Ausonian naiads
lived by an icy spring. When Venus requested their aid,
her plea was too just for the nymphs to refuse, and
        they willingly called
on their spring to pour through all of its channels.
        However, the water
had not yet cut off the route which led to the open
790   gateway
of two-headed Janus. So yellow sulphur was placed in
        the gushing
spring and the underground courses were fired with
        smoking pitch.
The heat generated by these and other materials found
its way to the depths of the spring, so that waters
        which once had competed
795 with Alpine cold were now as hot as a fire can burn.
The posts at the temple doors were steaming with
        flaming spray;
and the open gate, where the rugged Sabines had vainly
        been promised
entry by Juno, was blocked by this strange new spring,
        till the Roman
soldiers had time to arm. Then Romulus took the
        offensive
and soon the bodies of Sabines and Romans were
800   strewn on the ground,
while fathers whose daughters our people had raped
        were godlessly shedding
the blood of their sons, and sons were shedding the
        blood of their fathers.

But peace was eventually made. They decided not to
    continue
the fight to the end, and the royal power was divided with
    Tatius.

THE APOTHEOSIS OF ROMULUS

After the death of Tatius, Romulus reigned on his own   805
over Roman and Sabine alike. Then Mars respectfully
    doffed
his helmet and thus addressed the father of gods and of
    men:
'My father, since Rome is firmly established on grand
    foundations
and ruled again by a single leader, the time has arrived
to pay the reward already promised to me and your
    worthy   810
grandson, by raising him up from the earth to a place in
    the heavens.
May I remind you of words that you spoke long ago in the
    presence
of all the gods in council, those fatherly words that I
have faithfully treasured: "One man there shall be whom
    thou wilt uplift
to the azure blue of the sky." Now let those words be
    fulfilled!'   815
The omnipotent father nodded assent. The heavens were
    veiled
in a mantle of clouds, and the world was confounded by
    thunder and lightning.
Mars knew that these signs foreboded his own son's
    promised translation.
He leant on his spear and fearlessly mounted his chariot,
    drawn
by steeds pressed under his blood-stained yoke; then he
    gave them a lash   820

of his cracking whip, and glided headlong down through
            the air,
till he came to a halt on the top of the wooded Palatine
            Hill,
where Ilia's son was humanely dispensing justice
            amongst
his citizen people, and carried him off. The hero's mortal
825 body dissolved on his upward path, as a leaden pellet
shot from a broad sling melts away in the midst of the
            sky.
A glorious form took its place, more worthy of gods on
            their high-placed
couches,* the form of Quirínus* arrayed in his toga of
            honour.

Hersílië, Romulus' wife, was bewailing her husband as
            lost,
when queenly Juno commanded Iris to follow her
830   rainbow
path right down to the earth and to bear the widow
            these orders:
'Lady, chief glory of all the Latian and Sabine peoples,
most worthy once to have been the wife of so mighty a
            hero
and now the wife of Quirinus, I bid you cease your
            lamenting.
And if you are still desirous of seeing your late lord,
835   follow me
up to the grave on Quirinus' hill, where his temple is
            shaded
by verdant trees.'* So Iris obeyed and, gliding down
to the earth on her rainbow, she brought Hersílië
            Juno's message.
The woman was bashful and scarcely could raise her
840   eyes, but responded,
'Goddess (I cannot say who you are, but you must be a
            goddess),

lead, oh lead me, I pray you, and show me the face of my
    husband.
If fate will allow me only to see him once, I shall boast
that I have been lifted to heaven!' Post-haste, with Iris
    beside her,   845
she came to Romulus' hill. And there, from above them, a
    shooting
star swooped down to the earth. Her hair ablaze with its
    fire,
Hersilië, joining the star, rose up to the sky, to be welcomed
into the long-familiar arms of the founder of Rome.
He changed her bodily form and also gave her a new
    name,   850
Hora. So now she's a goddess and one with Quirinus for
    ever.

BOOK 15

Though not the most immediately accessible book in the *Meta-morphoses*, Book 15 is certainly one of the most interesting. In the second part (from 479) Ovid uses a skilful foreshadowing technique to build towards his climactic Roman episode (see notes on 534 and 589). For the political dimension see the Introduction, p. xviii.

In *Myscelus* (1–59), we learn how Romulus' successor, King Numa, extended his mind as a younger man by travelling to Croton in southern Italy, a Greek city whose foundation from Argos is explained by a local elder in the story of Myscelus. The speaker goes on to tell Numa about the famous Greek philosopher *Pythagoras* (60–478), who settled at Croton but is presumed by Ovid, quite unhistorically, to have done so before the time of Numa's visit. We are then treated to a discourse, purporting to come from the lips of Pythagoras, which offers a structural counterpart to Ovid's account of the Creation in Book 1 and marks a return to the didactic mode of Lucretius and of Virgil's *Georgics*. Pythagoras is essentially the mouthpiece for a discussion by Ovid on change as a fundamental principle in nature. However, it starts and ends with a plea for vegetarianism, based on the famous Pythagorean doctrine of Metempsychosis or Reincarnation, which implies that animal slaughter may mean dispossessing the soul of some relative. The idea of the soul moving from one body to another introduces a long series of examples of change, including the annual seasons, the ageing human body and various other phenomena, of a factual or miraculous kind, which Ovid has derived from Hellenistic scholarship. The list culminates in the rise and fall of civilizations, leading inevitably to Rome as a growing power. The arrangement of Ovid's examples is not always clearly defined; but this section makes compelling reading, because the detail, even if somewhat recondite, is always vividly imagined. Ovid is not a philosopher in his own right, but he makes fascinating use of this opportunity to carry his theme of metamorphosis back into the genre of didactic, as distinct from narrative, poetry.

Egeria and Hippolytus (479–551) returns us once more to the world of Greek tragedy. After Numa's death, an attempt is made to comfort his grieving widow by Hippolytus, the revived hero of Euripides' play, on the grounds that his sufferings were far worse than hers. In this we are bound to enjoy Ovid's version of the messenger-speech which narrates Hippolytus' destruction by the bull that comes in from the sea.

Two mini-metamorphoses from Etruscan and Roman legend, *Tages* (552–9) and *Romulus' Spear* (560–64), are followed by the story of *Cipus* (565–621), who was designated by an omen for kingship but rejected the opportunity as he abominated the thought of tyranny. *Aesculapius* (622–744) tells how the god of healing abandoned his shrine at Epidaurus, in the form of a huge snake, for a new home in the heart of Rome. Ovid's narrative is now moving closer to his 'own lifetime' (1.4), as the plague, which led the Romans to fetch the god, was a historical event of the early third century BC; but the story-telling preserves a mythical quality and the religious atmosphere provides an appropriately grand lead into the final episode.

The Apotheosis of Julius Caesar (745–870), whose murder occurred only a year before Ovid was born, is not easy to evaluate. The description of the sinister omens which preceded the assassination is deeply impressive. But how should we interpret the poet's extravagant praise of the emperor Augustus and the odd touch of irreverent humour which continues to mark his characterization of the gods? Readers who have found their way to the end of this monumental work may wish to explore this question in further reading. At all events, they will admit the claim in Ovid's *Epilogue* (871–9) that his achievement in the *Metamorphoses* is indestructible and lives 'throughout all ages'.

MYSCELUS

Meanwhile, an enquiry:* who could sustain the
    awesome burden
of power and come to Rómulus' throne as a worthy
    successor?*
The excellent man marked out by prescient rumour for
    kingship
was Núma, a capable thinker, who wasn't content with
    having
researched the religious rites of the Sabines. His restless,
5   ambitious
mind led him on to explore the mysteries of nature*
    itself.
This passionate interest made him forsake his birthplace
    at Cúres
and find his way to the city of Croton, whose walls were
    erected
close to where Hercules long in the past had stayed as a
    guest.
On arrival, Numa enquired who had founded a new
10   Greek town
on Italian soil, and received this answer from one of the
    elders
born and bred in the place and thus well versed in its
    history:
'The story goes that when Hercules left the Ocean, with
    Géryon's
cattle from Spain as his prize, he was safely brought to
    the coast
of Lacínium. There, while his herd was grazing the soft
    green pasture,
he entered great Croton's house to receive a hospitable
15   welcome
and so was able to rest at the end of his arduous labour.
He said to his host as he took his leave, "One day in the
    future

this place will be home to a city." That promise was
    faithfully kept.
  'In Argos there once was a man called Mýscelus, son of
    Alémon.
No one of his generation was better esteemed by the gods.   20
One night, as he lay asleep, the Club-Bearer* came to his
    bedside
and, leaning over him, said, "Rise, leave the home of your
    fathers.
Go and travel afar to the stony stream of the Aesar.*
Many terrible things will ensue if you fail to obey me."
Hercules then departed and Myscelus woke. He instantly   25
rose from his bed and silently brooded over the dream
he had just been sent. A long debate took place in his
    mind:
a god was bidding him go, but the laws of his country
    forbade it,
and death was prescribed for a person who wished to
    abandon his homeland.
After the sun had hidden his shining head in the ocean   30
and darkest night was crowned once more by the stars in
    the heavens,
the god appeared in a second dream and repeated his order,
with threats of further disaster and worse if he wasn't
    obeyed.
  'So Myscelus, deeply frightened, made ready to move his
    ancestral
shrine to a new abode; but a rumour went round, and the
    townsfolk
put him on trial for contempt of the law. When the case   35
    against him
was fully made and the charge was proved without a
    requirement
to call any witness, the poor defendant, in suppliant rags,
uplifted his hands and his face to the sky and appealed to
    Hercules:
"Hero whose twelve great labours secured your title to
    heaven,

help me, I pray you, now. My crime was prompted by

40   you!"

Now the custom in ancient times was for jurors to vote
      for a verdict

with black and white pebbles, black for conviction and
      white for acquittal.

This procedure was followed at Myscelus' trial, when
      every

one of the pebbles cast in the urn was black for
      conviction.

But after the pot was turned and the votes fell out to be

45   counted,

all of the pebbles were found to have changed from
      black to white.

Thus Hercules' intervention ensured that the son of
      Alemon

was duly acquitted. Myscelus thanked the god for his
      goodness

and then, with the wind behind him, he sailed across the
      Ionian

Sea. His route* took him past Nerétum, the Sállentine

50   city,

Spartan Taréntum, the bay of Siris, Sýbaris, Crímese,

Íapyx' country too; and finally, while he was skirting

the coastline, he found his destiny close to the mouth of
      the Aesar.

Not far from there was a mound where Croton's

55   hallowed remains

lay buried in earth; and on that site, as the god had
      commanded,

Myscelus founded a town called after the man who was
      buried there.

That, according to ancient tradition, explains this city's

beginnings and how it came to be built on Italian soil.

PYTHAGORAS

'Here in Croton there lived a man* who was born on
    Samos.   60
He'd fled from the island because he detested the tyrants*
    who ruled there,
and gone into voluntary exile. His mind came close to the
    gods,*
remote as they are in the heavens above; what nature
    debarred
to human vision he saw with the eyes of the spirit within
    him.
All that this insight, backed by untiring effort, discovered,   65
he wanted to share with others. His audiences listened in
    wondering
silence while he explained how the universe first began,*
discoursed at length upon causes, defined what Nature and
    God were,
showed how the snow was formed and what was the source
    of the lightning;
whether the winds or Jupiter thundered from clouds in
    collision;   70
the reason for earthquakes, the laws which govern the stars
    in their courses,
and all the secrets of nature. This sage was the first to
    condemn
the consumption of animal food and the first to express
    such a doctrine,
informed as it was but not given credit, in words such as
    these:
  '"Mortals, do not defile your bodies with sinful eating.   75
You have the crops to sustain you, the fruit which forces the
    branches
to bend down under its weight, the grapes that swell on the
    vine,
scented herbs and vegetables that fire can soften;

milk's sweet flow cannot fail you, nor honey fragrant with
80   thyme.
The earth supplies her riches and nourishing food in
        lavish
abundance; she offers you feasts that demand no
        slaughter or bloodshed.
Meat assuages the hunger of animals – not every
        species,
since horses, cattle and sheep all happily flourish on
        grass.
Only the beasts whose natural instincts are savage and
85   untamed –
angry lions, Armenian tigers, or bears and wolves –
delight in the taste of blood. What a heinous crime is
        committed
when guts disappear inside a fellow-creature's
        intestines,
when greedy bodies grow fat on the flesh of the bodies
        they've eaten,
and one living thing depends for its life on the death of
90   its neighbour!
Here is this wondrous wealth which the earth, the
        kindest of mothers,
produces; and yet you are happy to bite cruel wounds in
        your victims,
chomping them up with your teeth in the grisly style of
        a cyclops.
You have no way of relieving the hunger-pangs of your
        greedy,
uncivilized bellies except by destroying the life of
95   another.
    ' "That famous age to which we have given the title of
        'Golden'*
was blessed in the fruit of the trees and the plants
        produced by the earth.
Man never polluted his lips with blood. The birds could
        safely

fly on their way through the air; the hare never feared to
    cross over   100
a field; and the fish didn't rise to the bait to be caught on a
    hook.
In a world of peace no traps or snares were there to alarm.
But someone, whoever he was, must have envied the lions
    their food
and set a fatal example by filling his greedy stomach   105
with meat. He opened the gate to crime. The killing of
    beasts
might first explain the staining of iron with steaming blood,
and that would have been enough. We may kill any animal
    seeking
to kill ourselves, we admit, without any scruple of
    conscience.
But while we may kill it, we don't have to make it a course
    in a banquet.   110
  '"The rot continued: the sow, it is commonly thought,
    was the first
to be picked as a victim for sacrifice. Why? Because she'd
    uprooted
the planted seeds with her snout and interfered with the
    harvest.
The goat who had nibbled away at a vine was led to the
    altar
of Bacchus, there to be offered up to the god he'd offended.
These two were punished for damage they'd caused. But
    how have the sheep   115
done wrong – those peaceful grazers, intended by nature to
    help us,
whose udders are filled with delicious milk, whose fleeces
    provide us
with soft warm clothes, and who serve us better by living
    than dying?
What have the oxen done, those totally guileless creatures,   120
those simple, innocuous beasts who were born to a life of
    labour?

How could a man have the heart to remove the yoke of
    the plough
from his faithful worker and almost at once to make him
    a victim,
wielding his axe on that toil-worn neck, whose strength
    had allowed him
to break and renew the soil each year that had yielded a
125   harvest?
A man so ungrateful hardly deserves the crops he is
    reaping.
   '"But not content with such wicked behaviour, men
    choose to involve
the gods themselves in their guilt. They reckon the
    powers of heaven
are filled with delight when a loyal, hard-working
    bullock is slaughtered.
A victim unblemished and perfectly formed (its beauty
130   its downfall),
adorned with ribbons and gold on its horns, is set by
    the altar.
It listens to prayers which it can't understand and can
    feel the sprinkling,
between the horns of its forehead, of barley it helped to
    produce.
Its throat is cut and the blood runs on to the knife,
    whose reflection
135 the animal may already have seen in the lustral water.
The priests move quickly to snatch and inspect the
    lungs from the throbbing
breast of the victim, in order to scan the purpose
    divine.
And then, O race of mortals, so great is man's lust for
    prohibited
food – you dare to gorge on your victim's flesh. Now
    stop,
I implore you, and mark my words. When you cram
140   your mouths with the members

of slaughtered oxen, remember you're eating your own
      farm-workers!

' "Now, since a god is moving my lips, I shall duly obey
that god who inspires me. I'll vent the spirit of Delphi
      within me,
unveil the heavens, unlock the decrees of the mind sublime. 145
I'll utter great mysteries, never explored by our fathers'
      intelligence,
mysteries long concealed in the dark. My will is to traverse
the stars on high, to abandon this clogging abode on earth,
to ride the clouds and to stand on the shoulders of mighty
      Atlas,
gaze down from afar on men who are helplessly straying at
      random,   150
empty of reason, trembling and troubled by fear of their
      ending,
and so to embolden their hearts by unrolling the scroll of
      fate!
  ' "Oh why does the human race, paralysed by the terror
      of chill death,
why does it fear the Styx and its darkness, the meaningless
      names
that are bandied by poets, the bogeys of life in imaginary
      worlds?*   155
Our bodies, you know, can suffer no further ills, whether
      flames
on the funeral pyre or rotting time in the grave has
      destroyed them.
Our souls, however, are free from death. They simply
      depart
from their former homes and continue their lives in new
      habitations.*
I myself, I recall, at the time of the Trojan War   160
was called Euphórbus, Pánthoüs' son, and I once was
      wounded
close to the heart by the powerful spear of King Meneláüs.

Not long ago, in the temple of Juno at Argos, I noticed
a shield and knew that I once had borne it myself on my
      left arm!
165   All is subject to change and nothing to death. The spirit
in each of us wanders from place to place; it enters
      whatever
body it pleases, crossing over from beast to man,
and back again to a beast. It never perishes wholly.
As pliable wax is easily stamped with a new impression
and never remains as it was nor preserves one single
170   shape,
but still is the selfsame wax, so I say that our souls are
      always
the same, though they move from home to home in
      different bodies.
Therefore, hark to my voice! Let love and family duty
never be overpowered by the lusts of the belly. Beware
the impious slaughter which dispossesses the soul of a
      kinsman,
and never be tempted to feed your blood with the
175   blood of another!

'"My vessel is launched on the boundless main and my
      sails are spread
to the wind! In the whole of the world there is nothing
      that stays unchanged.
All is in flux.* Any shape that is formed is constantly
      shifting.
Time itself flows steadily by in perpetual motion.
180   Think of a river: no river can ever arrest its current,
nor can the fleeting hour. But as water is forced
      downstream
by the water behind it and presses no less on the water
      ahead,
so time is in constant flight and pursuit, continually new.
The present turns into the past and the future replaces
      the present;

every moment that passes is new and eternally changing.   185
   ' "You see how the night that has measured its course
         moves on to the day,
and the radiant beams of the sun then follow the blackness
         of night.
The sky has a different colour when weary creatures are
         sleeping
at dead of night and later when Lucifer brightly emerges
out of the sea on his pearl-white steed; then again when
         Auróra,   190
the herald of dawn, emblazons the world for surrender to
         Phoebus.
The sun's round shield when it's lifted up from below the
         horizon
is red in the morning and red once more when it sinks to its
         rest;
it is brilliant white at its zenith, for then the ether is purer
and earth's contagion is farthest removed. The moon is
         constantly   195
changing in size and in shape. If waxing, she's always
         smaller
today than she will be tomorrow and always larger when
         waning.
   ' "Again, you can see that the year has four new forms in
         succession.
Her phases copy the total course of our human lives.   200
In early springtime, the year is tender and milky,
         resembling
the age of our childhood: the grass is fresh and swelling to
         fullness
but wanting in firmness and strength; the farmer delights in
         its promise.
Everything then is in bloom, and the nurturing fields are a
         riot
of bright-coloured flowers, though the leaves on the trees
         still lack any vigour.   205
When spring is over, a sturdier year moves on into summer

and now is a strong young man. No season or time of life
is more hardy or fertile, no age when the heat is burning
   more fiercely.
Then follows the autumn, when youth's excitements and
   passions are over,
ripe and mellow, the bridge which leads from youth to
210   old age,
when the climate is milder and streaks of grey appear
   on the temples.
Finally, winter arrives, which totters along like an old
   man,
shivering, bald as a coot, or white if he has any hair
   left.
 ' "Our bodies also are constantly changing and never
   at rest;
what we were once and we are today, we shall not be
215   tomorrow.
Time was, we were hidden away in the dark of our
   mothers' wombs,
no more than seeds and the early hopes of a human
   being.
Then nature conspired with a midwife's art in a firm
   refusal
to let us be strangled inside our mothers' distended
   bellies,
and thrust us out of the house to survive in the open
220   air.
So thus brought forth to the light, we helplessly lay in
   our cradles;
but soon we were starting to move like animals,
   crawling on all fours.
Little by little, with wobbly knees, we shakily rose
to our feet and supported our frames with some firm
   prop to hold on to.
After that we are strong and swift; and we traverse the
225   span
of our active lives, till we've served the time in between
   and can follow

the downward path of declining years like the setting sun,
when the strength of our earlier years is undermined and
     demolished.
Milo the wrestler* weeps when he's old and examines the
     arms
which once had the power of Hercules' limbs and were
     bulging with muscles,   230
but now hang down by his sides, limp, flaccid and useless.
Helen weeps too when she looks in her mirror to see her old
     woman's
wrinkles, and wonders how she came to be twice
     abducted.*
Time, the universal devourer, and spiteful decay,
there is nothing you cannot destroy. You close your
     envenomed jaws   235
and little by little consume all things in a lingering death!
  '"This law of impermanence also applies to what we call
     elements.*
Pay attention, and I shall explain the changes they pass
     through.
The world eternal contains four bodies which generate
     matter.
Two of them, earth and water, are heavy and gravitate
     downwards;   240
the other two, air and fire, which is even purer, are
     weightless
and tend to make their way up, if nothing is pressing them
     down.
Although these elements occupy different positions in
     space,
they form the source and the end of all matter. When
     earth breaks up,   245
it is rarefied into water; the moisture is thinned still further
and changes to wind and to air; which in time, relieved of
     its weight
and now as thin as can be, darts up to the fire in the ether.
The process is then unravelled, and all the elements change
     back:

250 fire is thickened and crosses again into denser air,
air forms into water, and water's compressed into firm,
hard earth.
  ' "Nothing retains its original form, but Nature, the
goddess
of all renewal, keeps altering one shape into another.
Nothing at all in the world can perish, you have to
believe me;
things merely vary and change their appearance. What
255 we call birth
is merely becoming a different entity; what we call
death
is ceasing to be the same. Though the parts may
possibly shift
their position from here to there, the wholeness in
nature is constant.

  ' "I, for one, would believe that nothing continues the
same
for long. The Golden Age eventually changed to the
260 Iron;
and places also have often been subject to
transformation.
I've seen myself what was once the solidest stretch of
earth
replaced by water and land formations supplanting the
ocean.
Shells can be seen on the ground some distance away
from a shore,
and ancient anchors have been discovered on mountain
265 summits.
Plains have been turned into valleys by rushing torrents
in full spate;
flooding can likewise flatten a mountain to level
ground.
Marshes can dry into sand and arid deserts be watered
to form great pools. New springs can gush at the
270 bidding of Nature,

while others will trickle to nothing. When earthquakes cause
 an upheaval,
rivers have gushed from the ground or else dried up and
 subsided.
So, when a chasm swallows the Lycus up, it emerges
again some distance away, reborn from a different mouth.
So also a river which starts in Arcadia glides on its way   275
underground, and appears once more as the grand Erasínus
 in Argos.
They say that the Mysus was so ashamed of its source and
 its earlier
banks that today it flows elsewhere as the river Caïcus.
In Sicily's hills Amenánus may now be rolling the sand
downstream; if its source runs dry, the bed will be parched
 and empty.   280
Once you could drink the water which flows in the river
 Anígrus,
but now it is foul, since the centaurs used it to wash the
 wounds
inflicted by club-bearing Hercules' arrows – unless the
 stories
of poets are worth no credence at all. We also know
that the water of Hýpanis' stream is fresh and drinkable
 close   285
to its source in the Scythian mountains, but then grows
 brackish and nasty.
 '"Antíssa, Pharos and Tyre, that famous Phoenician city,
were once surrounded by waves, but none is an island
 today.
In the time of its early inhabitants Leucas was part of the
 mainland,
where now it is ringed by the sea. They also say that
 Messána   290
was joined to Italian soil, till the sea abolished the
 common
boundary and formed the strait which divides the isle from
 the mainland.
The Achaéan cities of Buris and Hélice are to be found,

if you look for them, under water. The sailors will still
    point out
the toppled buildings and walls beneath the floods that
295   submerged them.
Close to Troézen, the kingdom of Píttheus, a lofty and
    treeless
bulge has appeared in the form of a mound, where
    once the plain
was completely level. The story's a frightening one to
    relate:
the winds had been trapped inside their underground
    cave and were trying
to breathe their furious violence out, but had struggled
300   in vain
to find any outlet. There wasn't a crack in the whole of
    their prison
through which their blasts could have possibly
    travelled. Their puffing and blowing
caused the ceiling of earth to stretch and to swell, like a
    bladder
or goatskin when they are inflated. The ground stayed
305   swollen, and hardened
in time to the shape of the hill which now towers over
    Methóne.
   ' "Though many more instances come to mind that
    I've found or have heard of,
I'll only mention a few. Even water both causes and also
is subject to change. The spring at the temple of horn-
    crowned Ammon
is cold at noon but agreeably warm at sunrise and
310   sunset.
They say that at Jupiter's shrine in Dodóna the torches
    are kindled
by bringing them up to the spring when the moon has
    shrunk to its smallest.
The Cícones live by a river whose water petrifies
    entrails

when people have drunk it and turns whatever it touches to
    marble.
Crathis and Sýbaris, two adjoining rivers in these parts,   315
cause one's hair to be tinted in colours of gold and amber.
And more astonishing still, there are waters with power to
    change
not only our bodies but even our minds. You must have
    heard
of Sálmacis' pool,* whose waves emasculate men who have
    bathed there;
the Ethiopian lake, where anyone drinking the water   320
either goes mad or passes out in a stupefied coma.
Whoever relieves his thirst at the spring in Arcadian Clitor
becomes an abstainer, avoids all wine and enjoys pure
    water.
That spring may possess a power which stops wine's
    heating effect;
or perhaps, as the locals explain, when the prophet
    Melámpus had used   325
his herbs with a spell to cure the frenzied daughters of
    Proetus
of madness, he threw the dregs of his medicines into the
    water,
and so the detestation of wine survived in the spring.
Lyncéstis' river produces a different effect on its drinkers;
even a moderate sip will cause them to stagger around   330
as if they'd imbibed neat wine. There's also a place in
    Arcadia,
known as Phéneos once, where the water is dangerously
    suspect:
drink it during the day, but never at night when it's
    harmful.
Such are the new and various powers which rivers and
    lakes   335
can acquire. Long ages ago Ortýgia* floated in sea,
but today she sits firm. The Argonauts feared the
    Symplégades, clashing

rocks that were splashed by the spray from the waves in
      the shock of collision;
the same rocks now stand still and the winds are
      powerless to shift them.
  ' "Take the sulphurous furnaces raging in Etna's
340   volcano;
the fire won't always be active and was not so in the
      past.
Volcanoes' possible explanations support this
      statement.
One is that the earth is an animate creature with
      breathing-holes
through which she discharges flame in a number of
      different places;
this means that, whenever she quakes, she is able to
      alter her breathing
channels and open new craters while rendering others
345   inactive.
Another theory: craters confine light winds in their
      depths;
suppose that these winds toss rocks against rocks,
      material holding
the seeds of flame, and it's that which generates fire by
      friction;
the craters will then grow cold as soon as the winds
      have abated.
Or else the fire may be caused by bitumen quickly
350   igniting
or yellow sulphur which burns in wispy spirals of
      smoke;
but, of course, when the earth no longer supplies any
      food or richness
to nourish the flames (as time has exhausted all her
      resources),
and when devouring nature is thus deprived of the fuel
it needs, unable to bear starvation, she'll starve her
355   volcanoes.

‘ "The story goes that the men in hyperboréan Palléne
frequently grow light feathers which cover the whole of their
      bodies,
after they've bathed nine times in the waters of Lake
      Tritónis.
I cannot believe it myself, but the Scythian witches are
      also
reported to put on feathers by sprinkling themselves with
      their poisons.   360
  ‘ "But if one can speak of 'believing' facts that are fully
      established,
you see that bodies which time or heat has rotted to liquid
are turned into tiny animals. Dig me a ditch and then
      bury
a sacrificed bull. Experience shows that bees will be born
all over the mouldering carcass.* The bees will follow the
      parents   365
they sprung from in busily cropping the flowers in the
      fields they inhabit,
never shirking their task, as they always have plenty to
      work for.
A war-horse buried in soil will become the source of a
      hornet;
or if you remove the branching claws of a crab on the
      seashore
and bury the rest in the earth, a scorpion will shortly
      emerge   370
from the part you have carefully covered, and threaten
      your feet with its hooked tail.
Farmers have often observed the larvae weaving the
      threads
of their white cocoons on the leaves of the trees and finally
      changing
into the form of a butterfly, such as we see on a
      tombstone.*
  ‘ "Mud has seeds which produce green frogs; they are
      legless to start with,   375

but soon they acquire the limbs which allow them to
          swim and to take great
leaps with hind-legs longer than those they're endowed
          with in front.
When a bear reproduces, she doesn't give birth to a
          full-formed cub
but a half-living lump of flesh, which she carefully licks
380   into shape
and eventually moulds to the kind of form she exhibits
          herself.
You see how the larvae, created by bees who make
          honey inside
the hexagonal cells of the comb, are memberless bodies
          at birth
and only later assume the feet and the wings for their
          business.
The bird of Juno, the peacock who carries the stars in
385   her tail,
the eagle that bears Jove's bolts and the doves of
          beautiful Venus,
the whole of the avian family – who would suppose
          they could grow
from the yolk of an egg, if one didn't know for a fact
          that they did?
When a human backbone has decomposed in a
          well-sealed tomb,
some think that the spinal marrow is then transformed
390   to a snake.
     ' "All these creatures can trace their beginnings to
          alien forms.
There's one, however, which seeds and produces itself
          – the bird
the Assyrians call the phoenix.* He doesn't depend on
          the grass
or the grain, but lives on teardrops of incense and juice
          of amomum.*
Once his allotted span, five hundred years, is
395   completed,

he promptly uses his talons and unsoiled beak to
    construct
a nest in the branches high at the top of a quivering palm-
    tree.
As soon as this nest has been lined with spikes of the mildest
    nard,
with grated cinnamon, red-gold myrrh and cassia bark,
he rests his body upon them and ends his life in their
    fragrance.   400
And so, they say, from out of his father's body, a baby
phoenix is born, which is due to live for the next five
    centuries.
When time has given him strength and he's able to carry a
    load,
removing the weight of the nest from the heights of the
    palm-tree's branches,
he faithfully carries his cradle, the grave of his father before
    him,   405
into the breezes; and when he arrives at the sun god's
    city,*
he lays it in front of the sacred doors of Hypérion's
    temple.
    '"But if these curious facts and stories inspire us with
    wonder,
we may be surprised by the change of sex, when the female
    hyena
who once was served by a male appears to have grown male
    organs.   410
Chameleons too, which obtain their food from the winds
    and the air,
at once take on the colour of anything else they are
    touching.
Vanquished India gave to Bacchus, the god of the
    grapevine,
all of her lynxes, whose urine, they say, is converted to
    pebbles
and hardens in contact with air. The same with coral,* a
    soft plant   415

under the water, which hardens at once when exposed to
     the air.

' "The day will come to an end and Phoebus will plunge
          his panting
steeds in the ocean deep before I complete my recital
of change to new forms. We see times change and
420   civilizations
rise and fall. Yes, Troy was great in her riches and
          people;
for ten long years she was able to spend the blood of so
          many
sons in her cause; but now she is humbled and all she
          can show
for her glorious wealth is ancestral barrows and
425   ancient ruins.
Sparta was highly renowned and so was powerful
          Mycénae;
so flourished the cities of Cecrops at Athens and
          Theban Amphíon.
Sparta is bare, flat earth and the towers of Mycenae
          were toppled;
nothing remains of Oedipus' Thebes or Pandíon's
          Athens,
except for their names. And now word goes that
430   Dardánian Rome
is rising; close to the river that's born in the Ápennines,
          Tiber,
foundations are being laid of a mighty city and empire.
Rome is changing her shape as she grows. Some time in
          the future
she'll form the head of the boundless world. So
435   prophets, they tell us,
and soothsaying oracles loudly proclaim. When Troy
          was collapsing,
Hélenus,* son of Priam, declared to the weeping
          Aenéas –

as far as I can recall – when the hero despaired of his safety:
'Son of a goddess, you know my mind has the power of
    clairvoyance.
Troy shall not fall entirely, if you are alive and in safety.   440
Fire and sword shall give way before you. You'll go on
    your mission,
bearing with you the gods that you've snatched from the
    flames, until
you come to a strange new land which is kinder to you and
    to Troy
than the country you left. I can see a city of Phrygian
    grandsons,
greater than any that is or has been or shall rise hereafter.   445
Other leaders, over the centuries, will render her powerful;
but one man born of Iúlus' blood will make her the
    mistress
of all the world. When the earth has enjoyed his presence,
    the realms
of the sky will enjoy him too; he is finally destined for
    heaven.'*
So I remember that Helenus said to the pious Aeneas   450
bearing his household gods. I rejoice that the walls of my
    kinsmen*
are rising so fast, that the Greeks won a war for the good of
    the Trojans.

' "But not to stray too far from the track (have my horses
    forgotten
to run to their goal?): the sky and all that exists beneath it
can change its form, and so can the earth with all it
    contains.   455
We too are part of the world and are more than physical
    bodies;
we also possess winged souls. We are able to make our
    abodes
inside wild beasts and to hide away in the hearts of the
    cattle.

The creatures we see may well embody the souls of our
  parents
or brothers or people to whom we've been bonded – of
460 human beings
at least. So let us allow them their safety and proper
  respect,
and refrain from gorging on feasts of our own flesh
  and blood, like Thyéstes.*
How evil a habit is formed, what an impious shedding
  of human
blood is contrived, when the throat of a calf is slit with
  a knife,
and the ears of the butcher are deaf to its mother's
465 pitiful lowing!
How could anyone slaughter a goat as it cries in
  distress
like a baby, or eat a bird that he's fed with his own
  hand? Downright
murder I'd venture to call it! And where does it all lead
  on to?
The ox should remain at his plough and blame old age
470 for his death.
Let the sheep provide our defence against the blasts of
  the north wind.
Goats should continue to offer their swollen udders for
  milking.
All of these nets and traps and snares and crafty
  devices –
have done with them! Cease to deceive the birds with
  your treacherous limed twigs,
duping the deer by stringing feathers on ropes to
475 unnerve them,
luring the fish with bait on the hidden hooks of your
  lines.
If an animal harms you, destroy it; but do no more
  than destroy it.
Cleave to a diet that sheds no blood and is kind to all
  creatures."'

EGERIA AND HIPPOLYTUS

Such, and much else besides, was the learning they say that
        Numa
imbibed before he returned to his native land and accepted   480
the invitation to guide and govern the Latian people.
Blessed with a nymph for his wife and the Muses to show
        him the way,
he instructed the Romans in priestly rites and converted a
        nation
practised in brutal war to follow the arts of peace.
When old King Numa had ended his life, the senate and
        people   485
and women of Látium bemoaned his death. His wife Egéria
left the city to hide in the woods of the Áricine valley,
and there with her wailing dirges disturbed the worship of
        Tauric
Diana.* The nymphs of the forest and neighbouring lake
        repeatedly   490
warned her to stop and tried to console her with words of
        comfort.
Often Theseus' heroic son would discover her weeping
and say: 'Put an end to your tears. You aren't alone in your
        sad
misfortune. Consider the trials of others, and then you will
        find
your own more easy to bear. Let me tell you a story to
        lighten   495
your grief. I wish it were not my own, but it may prove
        helpful.
   'You must have heard of Hippólytus,* sent to his death
        by a wicked
stepmother's cruel deceit and his father Theseus' credulity.
What I am going to say will surprise you and cannot be
        proved;
but I am Hippolytus. Once Pasíphaë's daughter, Phaedra,   500

failed to make me betray my father by sharing her bed,
and then denounced me for wanting what she herself had
　　　been guilty
of wanting. Perhaps she feared I would give her away, or
　　　was angry
because I rejected her love. At any rate, I was convicted;
although I had done no wrong, my father expelled me
　　　from Athens
and laid a deadly curse on my head as I went into
505　　exile.
　　'My chariot and horses were making for Pittheus'
　　　city of Troezen,
and soon I was driving along the coast of the isthmus
　　　of Corinth,
when half of the sea rose up. A gargantuan tidal wave,
as tall as a mountain, appeared to swell in a monstrous
　　　crescent,
bellowing loudly, and then to divide at its highest
510　　point.
At once, as the waves burst open, a bull* sprang out of
　　　the ocean,
a bull with menacing horns, breast-high in the yielding
　　　air,
spouting masses of sea from his gaping mouth and his
　　　nostrils.
My friends were terrified; I was absorbed in the
　　　prospect of exile
and stayed unafraid – when my horses suddenly bolted
515　　and wheeled
across the shore to the sea, long ears pricked up in their
　　　panic.
Wild with fear of the bull, they were going to hurtle my
　　　chariot
on to the towering rocks. I vainly struggled to
　　　manage
the foam-flecked bridles; I leant right back on my heels
　　　and pulled

on the supple reins as hard as I could. The furious
    horses   520
would still have been under control, if one of the wheels,
    at the very
point where it turned on the axle, had not crashed into a
    tree-stump.
Crack, and the wheel was broken to pieces! My body was
    flung
from the chariot, twined in the reins; and you might have
    observed my living
flesh being trailed on the ground, my sinews caught on the
    tree-stump,   525
some of my limbs being dragged along, with others
    obstructed
and left behind, as my bones were noisily snapped and
    splintered.
My weary spirit at last gave out, and there wasn't a part
of my body which could have been known as mine. It was
    all one wound.
   'Now can you, Egeria, dare you compare your misfortune
    with mine?   530
I then had to visit the kingdom of darkness, to bathe my
    mangled
body in Phlégethon's waters. Only the healing gifts
of Apollo's son allowed me the chance to return from
    Hades.
Aesculápius'* powerful herbs and his medical skill,
to Pluto's annoyance, restored me to life. Diana was
    frightened   535
my visible presence would add to the envy inspired by this
    privileged
treatment, and so she concealed me behind a blanket of
    cloud.
But then, to allow me to show my face without any
    danger
in public, she added some years to my age and altered my
    features.

She wondered for quite some time whether Crete or
540   Delos would suit me
best for a home; in the end she decided on neither and
        settled me
here. She also told me to change my name, as it might
have served to remind me of horses,* and said:
        "Hippolytus now can be
Virbius, twice a man!" Since then I have lived in this
        forest
545 as one of the minor gods and no one knows who I am,
as I'm under Diana's protection and count as one of
        her household.'
    Egeria's sorrow, however, could not be relieved by
        stories
of others' misfortunes. She laid herself down at the
        foot of the mountains
and melted away into tears, till the goddess Diana was
        moved
by the widow's dutiful grief and thinned her limbs into
550   water
for ever. Egeria now had been changed to a cooling
        spring.

TAGES, ROMULUS' SPEAR, CIPUS

The nymphs were impressed by this strange occurrence.
        Hippolytus also
was no less amazed than the Tuscan ploughman who
        sighted the fateful
555 lump of earth in his fields, first moving freely in air,
then losing the shape of a clod to assume the form of a
        man,
who finally opened his new-found lips to reveal the
        future:
the natives know him as Tages, the earthborn man and
        the first

to teach the Etruscans the skill of predicting events to
    come.

Rómulus too was astonished, the time when he saw the
    spear   560
he had cast one day and planted deep in the Palatine
    suddenly
burst into leaf, no longer fixed on its point of iron
but grounded in new-grown roots. It had changed from a
    spear to a tree,
whose pliant branches surprisingly offered some welcome
    shade.

Cipus* was just as surprised, when he looked in the river
    and actually   565
saw there were horns on his head. Supposing it must be
    illusion,
he raised his fingers a number of times to his brow and
    found
he could touch what he'd seen; so he ceased to put the
    blame on his eyes.
At the time he was journeying home in triumph after a
    victory;
he halted and, raising his arms and eyes to heaven, he
    cried out: 570
'Gods, whatever this omen signifies, if it be good,
let it be for the good of my country and Romulus' people;
    if adverse,
adverse for me alone.' So he made an altar of green turf,
worshipped its gods with burning incense and poured
    libations,
then duly consulted the quivering entrails of sacrificed
    victims,   575
to learn what they might portend. The Etruscan augurer
    took
one look and observed the signs of a mighty crisis
    impending,

though none too clearly at first; but after he'd lifted his
     sharp gaze
up from the guts of the sheep to the horns of Cipus, he
580   shouted:
'Hail, O King!* It is you, great Cipus, you with your
     horns
whom fate determines shall rule this place and the
     fortress of Latium.
Only cut short delay. Make haste to pass through the
     open
gates! It is destiny's will. When once you have entered
     our city,
you'll be our king and wield the sceptre in safety for
585   ever!'
Cipus at once stepped back and, grimly turning his
     eyes
away from the walls, he exclaimed: 'Oh drive such evil
     omens
away, you gods, far away! Much better that I should
     pass
my life in exile than reign as king* on the Capitol Hill!'
  When he'd spoken these words, he immediately
590   summoned the Senate and people.
First he concealed his horns in a wreath of triumphal
     laurel,
then mounted a platform of earth which his valiant
     soldiers had built him.
After he'd made the traditional prayers to the gods, he
     addressed
his audience thus: 'There is one man here who shall be
     your king,
unless you drive him out of the city. I'll not reveal
that person by name but by means of a sign: he has
595   horns on his forehead.
The augur declares, if he enters Rome, he will make
     you his slaves.
He might, I can tell you, have forced his way through
     the open gates;

but I withstood him, though none is closer to me than
    he is.
Roman citizens, bar that man from your city for ever;   600
or, if he deserves it, bind him fast in the heaviest chains,
or else put an end to your fear by the death of a deadly
    tyrant!'
  A murmur ran through the crowd, just like the boisterous
    east wind
whistling in bush-topped pines, or the waves of the sea in
    the distance.   605
Amid the confusion of babbling sounds, one cry rang over
the others. 'Who is he?' it asked. And everyone carefully
    examined
his neighbours' foreheads to find the horns that the speaker
    had mentioned.
Then Cipus addressed them again, 'Look, here is the man
    you are seeking!'   610
He took the wreath from his brow, though the crowd
    tried hard to prevent him;
and there were the two conspicuous horns surmounting his
    temples.
The people lowered their eyes and groaned, till in puzzled
    reluctance
they looked at the warrior's glorious head. But they
    wouldn't permit him
to stay unhonoured for long and replaced the wreath on
    his forehead.   615
Since Cipus was now forbidden to enter the walls of the
    city,
the elders gave him a parcel of land as a mark of honour,
large as the space that a man could enclose with the blade
    of his ploughshare,
driving his oxen throughout one day from sunrise to
    sunset;
and horns which recalled his miraculous form were
    engraved on the brazen   620
gateposts, there to preserve his memory down through the
    ages.

AESCULAPIUS

Reveal to me now, O Muses,* you guardian spirits of
    poets
(you know the truth, and your memory cannot be
    dulled by time),
how Aesculapius, son of Corónis, was brought to the
    island
625 ringed by the Tiber to join the gods of Romulus' city.
    A terrible plague* had once polluted the air of
        Latium;
the sufferers' bodies were pallid as ghosts and foully
    neglected.
Weary of funeral rites, the people decided that human
efforts were useless and medical arts could do nothing
    to help.
So they looked for heavenly aid and sent a mission to
630   Delphi,
Apollo's oracular shrine which is set at the earth's very
    centre.
The envoys humbly implored the god for a
    health-giving answer,
to help them in trouble and end their mighty city's
    afflictions.
The temple floor and the laurel tree shook, and so did
    the quiver
635 worn by Apollo himself. The listeners quaked in terror
as out of the innermost shrine these words came forth
    from the cauldron:
'Romans, the aid which you seek from here had better
    be looked for
nearer to home. Now search for it nearer to home.
    Your need
is not for Apollo to lighten your woes, but the son of
    Apollo.
Go on your way with my blessing and summon my
640   offspring to heal you.'

   After the thoughtful senate received the oracle's answer,
they managed to trace the city where Phoebus' son had his
      precinct,
and sent a party by ship to the port which serves
      Epidaúrus. *
As soon as the curved ship's prow was beached on the
      shingle, the envoys
approached the council of Grecian elders and begged
      them to part   645
with the god, whose presence would cure the plague
      destroying the people
of Italy; that was the oracle's promise which must be
      fulfilled.
Opinion was badly divided: according to some of the
      elders,
help should not be refused; but many believed they'd be
      wiser
to keep the aid of the god to themselves and not to release
      him.   650
The matter was still in suspense as dusk excluded the
      daylight.
Darkness had fully enveloped the world in the shadow of
      earth,
when the god of healing appeared in a dream to one of the
      envoys,
standing in front of the Roman's bed in the form of the
      statue
we see in his temple, holding a countryman's staff in his
      left hand,   655
stroking his flowing beard with his right. Then quietly and
      calmly
he said: 'Fear not. I shall come to your aid and forsake my
      images.
Now take a careful look at this snake entwining my staff,
and fix it well in your memory, so that you know it is I
when you see it again. I shall change to its likeness but seem
      to be greater,   660

great as a god should appear when the form of his body
    is changed.'
The divine voice faded, the god went away and so did the
    Roman's
sleep, on whose heels there followed the kindly,
    life-giving day.
  Now that the dawn had banished the fiery stars from
665   the heavens,
the elders, still undecided, came to the elegant temple
of Aesculapius and prayed that the god might show by
    a clear sign
whether he wished to be taken to Rome or remain
    where he was.
They had barely ended their prayer when the god, in
    the form of a snake
with a towering golden crest, announced his advent by
670   hissing.
His statue, the altar, the doors, the marble floor and
    the golden
gables trembled. Then raised breast-high in the heart of
    the temple,
he stood there, gazing round on the crowd with his
    fire-flashing eyes.
The people were stricken with fear, but the priest,
675   whose locks were bound
in the woollen headband of holiness, knew the
    divinity's presence.
'The god is amongst us!' he cried. 'All hearts and
    tongues be auspicious,
ye that are here! Most glorious deity, grant that this
    vision
of thee be a blessing. Assist the peoples before thine
    altar!'
All who were present worshipped the god as the priest
680   commanded,
repeating the words of his prayers as he spoke them.
    Devout as Aeneas,

the Roman visitors too showed reverent hearts and
        tongues.
    The god made clear his assent by nodding his crest, and
        thrice
emitted a hiss from his darting tongue to confirm his
        approval;
then, gliding down the shimmering steps and turning his
        head,   685
he looked once more at the ancient altar he now was
        deserting
and bade farewell to the temple and home he had known so
        long.
From there the enormous serpent slithered along a carpet
of flowers spread over the ground, and went on his way
        through the city
down to the port, which was fortified by a curving
        embankment.   690
Here he halted and, turning round with a kindly
        expression,
appeared to dismiss the escort of worshippers thronging
        behind him.
Quickly he boarded and lay in the Roman ship, which felt
the weight of the god and settled deeper into the water.
The Romans joyfully offered a slaughtered bull on the
        shore,   695
set garlands of flowers on the prow and unfastened the
        mooring cables.

The ship was wafted along by a gentle wind. The snake-god
lifted his body aloft and rested his neck on the curved prow,
gazing down on the blue below. On the mildest of breezes
he crossed the Ionian Sea and, five dawns on, he arrived   700
off Italy. There his voyage continued* past Lacinium,
famed for its splendid temple of Juno, and past Scylacéum.
He put Iapýgia behind him, avoiding Amphrýsia's rocks
to the left and Celénnia's crags on the right. Then skirting
        Rométhium,

Caulon and Locri, he braved the narrow straits of
705   Pelórus'
headland in Sicily. Next he made for Aéolus' islands,
Témese's mines, Leucósia's isle and the gardens of
      sunny
Paestum, where roses abound. Thence, passing the
      Cape of Minerva and Cápri,
Surréntum's hills with their noble vineyards, he came
710   to Stábiae,
Herculáneum, Parthenopéan Naples, perfect
for lazy living, on to the shrine of the Sibyl at Cumae.
Next to the medicinal springs* of the region,
      Litérnum's forest
of mastic trees, the river Voltúrnus with all the sand
swirling along on its bed, and the haunt of the doves,
715   Sinuéssa.
On from there to unhealthy, swamp-infested
      Mintúrnae,
to Fórmiae, once Antíphates'* awful domain, Caiéta
where pious Aeneas buried his old nurse, Trachas,
      surrounded
by marshes, Circe's country and Ántium's beach with
      its firm sand.
   Here the crew directed the sailing ship to the shore
as the sea had turned rough. On landing the god
720   unfolded his coils
and, gliding along in voluminous folds with his sinuous
      spiral,
he came to his father Apollo's temple adjoining the
      sands.
When the spirit most close to himself had given him
      shelter until
the sea had calmed down, the serpent left the altar of
      Phoebus
and furrowed the sand to the ship with the track of his
725   rustling scales.
He mounted the rudder and rested his head once more
      on the prow.

Shortly he passed by Castrum, Ínuüs' camp, sailed on
to Lavínium's sacred town and entered the mouth of the
        Tiber.
Here on the banks he could see a crowd of commoners,
        matrons,
elders, the virgins who watch the fires in the temple of
        Vesta,   730
rushing to meet him and greet his arrival with cheers of
        rejoicing.
The ship moved swiftly upstream. On a row of improvised
        altars
incense was smoking and crackling, perfuming the air on
        the two banks;
knives were dripping with blood, still warm, from sacrificed
        victims.   735
And now he had entered the city of Rome, the world's
        great capital.
Raising his serpent's body aloft and supporting his neck
on the top of the mast, the god looked round for a home
        that would suit him.
He'd come to a point where the Tiber divides and its waters
        encircle
a plot which is known as the Island; the river extends its
        arms   740
in an equal embrace to either side of the land it's
        surrounding.
Here the serpent-son of Apollo abandoned the Latian
pine ship and landed. Resuming his heavenly form, he
        brought
the plague to an end and answered the prayers of the city
        for healing.

THE APOTHEOSIS OF JULIUS CAESAR

745 Aesculapius came from abroad to dwell in our shrines,
     but Caesar is god in his native city. He showed his
          genius
     in war and in peace; but all his campaigns that ended
          in triumphs,
     all his achievements at home and his rapid promotion
          to glory
     did less to secure his change to a constellation or comet
     than what was decreed by his son. Of the deeds of
750   Julius Caesar
     none can be greater than standing father to Caesar
          Augustus.
     Julius surely could boast that he conquered the islander
          Britons;
     he led a victorious fleet up the Nile with its
          seven-mouthed delta
     and banks so rich in papyrus; he brought the
          Numídian rebels,
     Cinýphian Juba, the realm of Pontus, which swells
755   with pride
     in the name Mithridátes, beneath the sway of the
          Roman people;
     he rode in triumphs and merited more. But how can
          the glory
     of all these exploits amount to the glory of having
          begotten*
     so glorious a son – a leader, with whom at the head of
          our empire,
     the gods have showered the richest of blessings on all
          mankind?
          Yet Julius' son could not have been born from seed
760   that was mortal,
     so Julius had to be made a god. When Aeneas' golden
     mother perceived this and also saw that a tragic death

awaited her priest* at the hands of traitors sworn to his
     murder,
her cheeks grew pale and she said to each of the gods she
     encountered,
'Look at the massive power of the treachery marshalled
     against me,   765
look at the dangerous plot which threatens a life that I
     dearly
cherish, the only surviving descendant of Trojan Iúlus.
Must I be the only god to be wracked by justified anguish?
One day I receive a wound from the spear of the Greek
     Diomédes;*
next I grieve for the walls of Troy so poorly defended;   770
then I must watch my son through endless wanderings –
     hounded,
tossed on the ocean, forced to enter the ghostly kingdom,
fighting his wars with Turnus, or rather with Juno's hate,
if the truth be told. But why recite the trials of my family
long in the past? My present alarm excludes remembrance   775
of earlier fears. Look there! You can see them, sharpening
     their daggers,
the traitors! Stop them, I beg you. Avert this iniquity.
     Vesta's
fires must never be quenched by the brutal death of her high
     priest!'
  Such were the anxious complaints that Venus
     unsuccessfully
aired all over Olympus. The gods were certainly moved;   780
although they couldn't defy the iron decrees of the Fates,
they still were able to give clear signs* of looming disaster.
Men say that the crime was foreshadowed by clashing arms
     in the black clouds;
trumpets and horns were awesomely blaring and braying in
     heaven.
The sun's face also was gloomy and steeped the uneasy
     earth   785
in a ghostly pallor, shooting stars were constantly streaking

across the sky, and drops of blood were discharged from
    the rainclouds.
The face of the morning star was dimmed and bespeckled
    with dirty
rust-coloured spots; blood spattered the chariot bearing
790   the moon.
All over the city the Stygian owl was hooting its
    sinister
omens, ivory statues wept, and voices chanting
dirges of doom could be heard, they say, in the sacred
    groves.
Every sacrificed victim presented signs of bad omen;
the lobe of a liver had been cut off by the priest, to be
795   found
in the entrails and so give token of mighty upheavals
    impending.
Out in the forum, around men's houses and close to
    the temples,
the night was disturbed by the howling of dogs; the
    streets were haunted
by roaming ghosts of the dead; and the city was shaken
    by tremors.
But warnings from heaven were powerless to halt the
    plot or forestall
what fate had decreed. The conspirators entered the
800   hall of the Senate,*
naked swords in their hands. No other building in
    Rome
but that sacred place would serve for their crime, for
    the infamous murder.
    That was the moment when Venus beat her breast
    with both
of her hands and attempted to hide Aeneas' descendant
805   in cloud,
as once she had stolen Paris away from his foe
    Menelaüs
and helped Aeneas himself to escape Diomedes' sword.

Then Jupiter said to her: 'Daughter, must you be the only
     goddess
to fight invincible fate? You may go yourself to the hall
of the Sisters Three, and there you will visit the Records of
     Fortune,*
a massive structure of tablets inscribed in brass and the
     solidest   810
iron. These tablets fear no clashing of clouds, nor the
     thunderbolt's
wrath, nor destruction, however it come; they are safe and
     abiding.
There you will find your family's destinies cast in
     enduring
adamant. I myself have perused and noted their contents.
Pay heed to the truth; you must not be left in the dark
     any longer.   815
  'The man for whom you are labouring, Venus, has
     come to the end
of his time; the years he has owed to the earth are duly
     completed.
Now he will rise to the sky as a god and be worshipped in
     temples.
You will ensure it – you with the son who is heir to his
     name
and will shoulder the lonely burden of state. With us for
     his allies   820
in war, this bravest of men shall avenge the death of his
     father.
He shall be lord of the day when beleaguered Mútina's*
     captured
and sues for peace. His might shall be felt on Phársalus'
     plain,
when it's drenched with blood for a second time on the field
     of Philíppi.*
Sextus Pompeíus* shall suffer defeat in Sicilian waters.   825
A Roman general's Egyptian mistress,* who trusted the
     marriage

torch to her cost, shall fall; and her threat will be given
        the lie,
that Rome's strong Capitol Hill should bow to her isle of
        Canópus.
But why should I list barbarian lands and the nations
        that lie
to the east and the west? Where men can live and be fed
830   by the soil,
that land shall be his. The sea shall follow and know
        him as master.
    'When peace has come to the earth, he will turn his
        mind to the duties
and rights of his people at home. Most just as a giver
        of laws,
he will guide men's ways by his own example. His eye
        for the future,
for all his descendants to come, will lead him to order
835   the holy
Livia's son* to adopt his name with the cares of his
        office.
Only when he has come to Pýlian Nestor's years
shall he rise to our home in the heavens and join the
        star of his kinsman.
Meanwhile you must rescue his father's soul from his
840   cut-ridden body
and make him a comet,* that deified Julius' image may
        always
gaze on my Capitol Hill from the height of his shrine in
        the Forum.'*
    Scarcely had Jupiter ended his speech, when
        life-giving Venus
set herself down in the heart of the Senate, though no
        one could see her,
and caught the soul of her Caesar up as it passed from
845   his body.
She did not allow its component atoms* to be
        dispersed

into air, but carried it straight as it was to the stars in the
    heavens.
During her journey, she felt it glowing and catching fire,
so she let it escape from out of her bosom and fly right
    upwards.
Higher far than the moon it soared, displaying a
    sweeping
trail of flame in its wake, till it finally took the form
of a gleaming star. Now Julius watches his son's
    achievements   850
and proudly admits they surpass his own. Though
    Augustus will never
let it be said that his deeds are greater than those of his
    father,
speech that is free and unfettered, in spite of the emperor's
    wishes,
declares him supreme, and ventures only in this to oppose
    him.
Átreus gives way to his son Agamémnon's title to glory,   855
Aégeus to Theseus' greatness and Péleus to godlike
    Achílles.
Lastly, to take an example which matches the case of our
    Caesars,
Saturn is likewise lower than Jupiter. Jupiter governs
the heavenly heights and all the realms of the three-formed
    universe;
earth is under Augustus; and each is ruler and father.*   860
  I call on you, gods who attended Aeneas through fire
    and sword
and compelled them to yield; you native Italian gods and
    Quirínus
who founded our city; on Mars who fathered unconquered
    Quirinus;
Vesta whom Caesar reveres amongst the gods of his
    household;
Apollo, an honoured neighbour of Caesar* as surely as
    Vesta;   865

Jupiter, throned in his temple surmounting the heights of
      Tarpeía;*
and all of the other gods whom a righteous poet may
      worship –
slow to dawn be that day, long after my time, when
      Augustus
leaves the world that he rules and rises up to the heavens.
So may he lend a favouring ear to our prayers from his
870   new home.

EPILOGUE

Now I have finished my work, which nothing can ever
      destroy –
not Jupiter's wrath,* nor fire or sword, nor devouring
      time.
That day which has power over nothing except this
      body of mine
may come when it will and end the uncertain span of
      my life.
875 But the finer part of myself shall sweep me into eternity,
higher than all the stars. My name shall be never
      forgotten.
Wherever the might of Rome extends in the lands she
      has conquered,
the people shall read and recite my words. Throughout
      all ages,
if poets have vision to prophesy truth, I shall live in my
      fame.

Notes

References are to lines of the translation, which follows the numbering of the original as closely as possible. In cases where five lines of Latin are represented by six of English, the referencing follows the pattern 1, 2, 3a, 3b, 4, 5 or 6, 7, 8a, 8b, 9, 10; if by only four, it excludes lines ending in 3 or 8. A cross-reference to a line or lines in the *same* book omits the number of the book. Glosses on personal names are usually from Greek.

BOOK 1

Prologue: This sub-heading and all the succeeding story-titles in the translation have been introduced to help the reader. They do not appear in Ovid's original.

3   *transformed my art*: The translation is based on a widely accepted emendation to the received text. At the end of line 2, Ovid is probably alluding to the (for him revolutionary) change in his verse from self-contained elegiac couplets to the flowing hexameters associated with epic in both Greek and Latin. Ovid's poetry has itself undergone a metamorphosis, which he attributes to the gods whose inspiration he is praying for. See Introduction, pp. xxiii–xxiv.

21   *The god who is nature*: Ovid here reflects the Stoic view that God and nature are synonymous. A nameless creator is also implied in 32, 47, 78.

24   *the elements*: The theory of the four elements – earth, air, fire and water – is ascribed to Empedocles of Agrigentum (*c.* 493–*c.* 433 BC).

48   *five separate zones*: This notion, like that of the world as a sphere (35), is associated with the followers of Pythagoras (late fifth century BC).

56   *lightning that burns ... flashes*: Forked lightning and sheet

lightning, both thought to be caused by the collision of clouds in the wind.

62   *the mountains*: Perhaps the Himalayas or the Hindu Kush.

113   *Saturn*: The god was particularly associated with the Golden Age. He was deposed from the rule of Olympus by his son Jupiter and banished to the underworld.

149   *Justice the Maiden*: Justice had lingered among the countryfolk who had still clung to the virtues of the Golden Age. She occupied a place in heaven as the constellation Virgo.

152   *giants*: Said by the Greek poet Hesiod (*c.* 700 BC) to be the offspring of Earth and the blood of Uranus, Saturn's father. Their war with the Olympians, the Gigantomachy, was a frequent theme in Greek and Roman poetry and art.

164   *gruesome banquet*: The story of this 'banquet' is told in 226–30.

176   *Palatine Hill*: Where the grand imperial residences stood at Rome in the time of Augustus and after. Modern equivalents would be Whitehall in London or Capitol Hill in Washington. There is an element of contemporary satire in the whole 'gods' assembly' passage.

201   *murdering Caesar*: This possible reference in a simile to the assassination of Julius Caesar in 44 BC would have its counterpart in the actual event described in Book 15. It could also refer to one of several conspiracies against the reigning Caesar, Augustus.

205   *Augustus*: A flattering reference, elaborated in Book 15, to the Roman emperor who was eventually to banish Ovid.

232   *household gods*: In a surprising anachronism Ovid here introduces the *penates* who feature so prominently in Roman religion.

255   *ether*: The upper air, closest to the gods, with a fiery nature (26–8).

256   *a time would arrive*: Ovid anticipates the conflagration of the world caused by Phaëthon in Book 2.

333   *murex*: The shellfish which yields the dye for 'Tyrian' purple.

369   *Cephisus*: The river flows twelve miles to the north of Delphi, where the oracle of Themis (later Apollo, see 322) was situated. Ovid was probably thinking of the Castalian spring on Mount Parnassus, which was closely associated with the oracle.

390   *Epimetheus*: 'Afterthought', the brother of Prometheus, 'Forethought', who had created man out of clay (82–8).

430–33   *When heat and moisture are blended . . . enmity*: This theory, with the view that the world is a warring concourse of opposites, goes back to the Greek philosopher Anaximander (sixth century BC). It recurs in Lucretius, *De Rerum Natura* 5. 797–8.

447 *Pythian Games*: An ancient Greek festival, second only to the Olympics, held at Delphi every four years after 582 BC and involving competitions in music and athletics.

562–3 *Augustus' gates . . . oak-leaves*: Two laurels grew outside the entrance to the emperor's palace on the Palatine. The door was surmounted by an oak-wreath, awarded for saving the life of a comrade in battle and voted to Augustus as saviour of the Roman people – another flattering reference.

583 *Inachus*: Here Ovid shifts the geographical focus from Thessaly to Argos (601), through which the river Inachus flows.

648 *Two letters*: IO for Io's name, but also one of the Greek exclamations of grief, taken up in Inachus' 'Woe and alas!'.

747 *a goddess*: Io was identified with Isis, the great goddess of the Egyptians, who had a cult in Rome during Ovid's time; her son Epaphus (748) was identified with Apis, the bull-god of Memphis.

775 *your spirit impels you*: These words used of Phaëthon near the end of the book deliberately echo those that Ovid uses of himself at the very beginning in line 1. See Translator's Note, p. xxxviii.

BOOK 2

8 *sea-gods*: The learned members of Ovid's audiences would recognize the list as based on the procession of marine deities attending the abduction of Europa in the poem by the late Greek poet Moschus (second century BC). These lines near the start of the book thus link with the picture of Europa herself in the closing story (833–75).

23 *Phoebus*: Here identified with the sun-god known in Greek as Helios or Titan. In this capacity his character is very different from the Phoebus Apollo who is Daphne's amorous pursuer in Book 1 or Coronis' jealous lover later in Book 2.

78 *beasts*: The signs of the zodiac.

138–9 *Serpent . . . Altar*: Constellations, respectively high and low in the sky.

156 *Tethys*: The wife of Ocean, the sea encircling the earth (1.13–4) which the sun rises out of and sets into. She is pictured here as Ocean's doorkeeper. She is also the mother of Clymene, so Phaëthon is her grandson.

173 *barred to them*: The Great Bear never sinks below the horizon (in the northern hemisphere).

197 *two whole signs*: The Scorpion's claws also form Libra, the Balance.

245 *when it fought with Achilles*: As narrated in Homer, *Iliad* 21.328 ff.

255 *lies hidden*: The source of the Nile was a mystery in the ancient world.

258–9 *Padus . . . Tiber*: The first Italian names in the poem.

454 *heat of her brother*: Diana, the moon goddess, and Apollo, the sun god, were the twin children of Latona (6.185 ff.).

495 *her father Lycaön*: Lycaön was transformed into a wolf (1.232–9) before the Flood, which he and Callisto now appear to have survived. Ovid does not seem worried by such inconsistencies.

507 *neighbouring constellations*: Ursa Major and Ursa Minor.

517 *farthest point of the axis*: Juno's rhetoric appears to undermine itself by mentioning the *remoteness* of the Bears as well as their height which she finds so insulting.

527 *foster-parents*: Ocean and Tethys bore and reared many of the gods.

528 *debar those Bears*: See 173a. Another inconsistency. The Great Bear has already existed and been excluded from the waves at the time of Phaëthon's ride.

537–8 *watchful geese . . . Capitol*: A reference to the famous occasion about 390 BC when the Gauls made a night attack on Rome and the city was saved when the geese in Juno's temple gave the alarm.

553 *born of the soil*: Vulcan, when trying to rape Minerva, discharged his semen on her thigh. The goddess wiped it off on to the ground and so gave rise to Erichthonius, 'Earth-born'.

555 *two-formed Cecrops*: A mythical king of Athens with the body of a man and the tail of a snake.

564 *the owl*: Traditionally sacred to Minerva/Athena and portrayed on Athenian coins. Her story follows at 591–5.

570 *Coroneus*: Nothing to do with Apollo's love, Coronis. Ovid seems, rather confusingly, to have chosen this name as *korone* is Greek for 'crow'.

592 *corrupted her father*: Probably the crow's malicious invention. The tradition went that Nyctimene was forced into incest.

629 *his son*: Aesculapius, the god of medicine, who comes to Rome in 15.622–5. See also note on 648.

630 *Chiron the centaur*: Chiron, half man and half horse, educated many of the famous Greek heroes.

638 *Ocyrhoë*: 'Swift-flowing'.

648 *two changes*: Aesculapius was given divine powers of healing, but incurred Jupiter's displeasure by bringing Hippolytus back to life (15.534–5). He was therefore blasted by lightning and so a

'lifeless body' (647), until Apollo secured his deification and his cult as a god of healing was established.

652 *blood of the Hydra*: Chiron was accidentally shot by Hercules with an arrow tipped with the venom of the Hydra of Lerna, a snake with seven heads, which the hero had killed on the second of his famous labours.

654 *Sisters Three*: The Greek Moirai or Fates, who allotted each mortal his destiny at birth.

675 *Hippe*: 'Mare'.

688 *Battus*: 'Chatterer'.

707 *touchstone*: The stone used to test base metal pretending to be gold.

712 *temple of Pallas*: The Parthenon on the Acropolis. Ovid sets his story at the time of the Great Panathenaea, a festival held at Athens every three years.

728 *Balearic sling*: The inhabitants of the Balearic Islands were renowned for their use of the sling or catapult.

840 *your mother's star*: Maia was one of the seven Pleiades.

845 *Tyrian*: Ovid equates the old Phoenician cities of Tyre and Sidon (840).

873 *frightened prize*: The picture derives from Moschus' *Europa*. See note on 8.

BOOK 3

5 *iniquitous . . . devotion*: The ambivalent description of Agenor's behaviour is reflected at the end of the book (727–8) in the image of Agave's iniquity in displaying her son Pentheus' severed head as an act inspired by her devotion to Bacchus.

13 *Boeotia*: The name is derived from the Greek for 'cow.'

14 *Castalia's cave*: The recess or 'cave' from which the Delphic oracle spoke was often associated with the Castalian spring on Mount Parnassus some way away.

45 *Snake*: The constellation Draco.

53 *skin of a lion*: Ovid is here associating Cadmus with Hercules, who was commonly portrayed as wearing the weapon-proof skin of the Nemean Lion, killed on the first of his labours.

111 *tapestry frontcloth*: This engaging simile is drawn from the Roman stage, where a curtain with embroidered figures was drawn up from the floor at the end of a play to close off what lay behind.

126 *Echion*: 'Viper'. He married Cadmus' daughter Agave and was

the father of Pentheus, who features in the last story of this book.

142 *No crime . . . a pure mistake*: The language is identical with words
eventually used by Ovid to describe the offence for which he was
exiled to Tomis. Moreover, in *Tristia* 2.103 ff. the poet actually
compares himself to Actaeon. It is therefore possible that 141–2
are a later addition; or Ovid may subsequently have been quoting
from himself.

198 *Autonoë*: Another daughter of Cadmus who, like Agave, is one
of the bacchanals in the Pentheus story.

207 *Blackfoot . . . Tracker*: Ovid uses made-up Greek names (here
given English equivalents) for his catalogue of Actaeon's hounds,
which many in his audience would have understood and enjoyed.

271 *to bear him a child*: In Greek mythology, Hera (Juno) is credited
with the birth of Ares (Mars), Hephaestus (Vulcan), Hebe (god-
dess of youth) and Ilithyia (Lucina, goddess of childbirth).

310 *baby*: He will become the god known in Greek as Dionysus or
Bacchus, among other names. His return to Thebes as a 'new god'
is predicted at 520.

342 *Liriope*: 'Lily-like'. For reasons of euphony and metre, this proper
name is stressed on the first and not the second syllable, in breach
of the traditional pronunciation convention in English.

348 *he never knows himself*: Ovid is playing ironically with the
famous Greek religious injunction, 'Know yourself', which was
inscribed in the temple of Apollo at Delphi. The story which
follows shows Narcissus coming to know himself in an unexpec-
ted way and dying in consequence.

463 *I know myself*: See note on 348.

513 *Pentheus*: Cadmus' grandson, now the young king of Thebes.

520 *Liber*: 'Free', originally the name of an Italian vegetation god,
later identified with the Greek god Bacchus. The name reflects
the liberating effect of the god of wine and ecstatic joy.

539 *to found a new Tyre*: A wild misrepresentation. Cadmus did *not*
come, like the Trojan Aeneas to Rome, bearing his household
gods; and the Theban elders owe their ancestry to the rump of
the armed men sprung from the dragon's teeth (126–30, 531–2).

542 *thyrsus*: The bacchic 'wand', consisting of a staff topped with a
bunch of ivy leaves.

559 *King Acrisius*: Normally a character in the Perseus story. His
opposition to Bacchus only occurs in Ovid and is mentioned again
in 4.607–14.

568 *as . . . I have seen*: The intrusion of the poet himself in the first
person is very rare in epic and would have jarred, particularly in

an 'epic' simile – but Ovid seems to have enjoyed this kind of naughty incongruity.

664 *tangled with ivy*: The ivy, grape clusters (667) and animals mentioned (669) are all associated with Bacchus in his full manifestation.

675 *scaly*: A curious detail. Ovid seems to have ignored the fact that dolphins have no scales.

720 *Actaeon's ghost*: A poignant link with the Actaeon story, though Pentheus is much to blame where his cousin was not.

727 *Displaying it high*: See note on 5.

BOOK 4

11 *different titles*: Gods would be invoked by all their various names, guises, functions, etc., with a saving clause at the end (16) to guard against possible omissions.

13a *child of two mothers*: See 3.310–13.

13b *Thyone*: Another name for Semele; but the title Thyoneus is derived from the Greek for 'to rave'.

15 *Iacchus*: From one of the bacchanals' ecstatic cries, *iacche*.

19 *hornless epiphany*: Bacchus could appear as a horned bull, a snake or lion, as well as in the form of an androgynous human male.

23b *Lydian sailors*: The story was told in 3.597–686.

38 *Minerva*: Here in her role as the goddess who presides over women's indoor activities and so over the sisters' 'untoward housecraft' (33). Although she is over-ridden by Bacchus in the first part of this book, her authority is reasserted at the end.

43 *many tales*: Ovid, by a common rhetorical device, shows his learning by mentioning three mini-metamorphoses, only to reject them.

47 *Dercetis' daughter*: The queen Semiramis, who built the famous walls (58) of Babylon.

88 *Ninus' tomb*: Semiramis was the widow of Ninus, king of Nineveh, where his tomb, a well-known monument in antiquity, was probably sited, rather than in Babylon.

122 *a spurt from a waterpipe*: The simile takes us to the streets of Ovid's Rome and can only strike modern readers as bizarre. But Pyramus' blood has somehow to reach the fruit of the mulberry tree!

170 *'Loves of the Sun God'*: Here again the Sun of the Phaëthon story. See 245–6.

172 *Mars and Venus*: This famous story first appears in Homer's
     Odyssey (8.266 ff.) and had previously been told by Ovid in his
     Ars Amatoria (2.561 ff.). Here he works it in to motivate the
     stories of Leucothoë and Clytië which follow.

204 *Rhodos*: The mother, by the Sun, of Phaëthon's sisters, the
     Heliades (2.340–66.).

209 *land of incense*: Here Persia rather than Arabia.

213 *Belus*: The name is a Greek form of the Old Testament 'Baal'.

270 *in its new form*: The heliotrope takes its name from the Greek
     words for 'sun' and 'turn'.

276 *No more of the loves*: Another list of stories mentioned only to
     be rejected. See note on 43.

282 *Curetes*: A Cretan tribe, said to have drowned the cries of the
     infant Zeus by dancing and clashing their weapons to prevent his
     father Cronos finding his son to devour him. Their birth from a
     rain-shower is presumably suggested by this association with the
     sky god.

291 *Hermaphroditus*: The name is derived from the Greek names for
     Mercury (Hermes) and Venus (Aphrodite).

320 *she spoke*: Salmacis' speech is a parody of the much more modest
     appeal made by the shipwrecked (and naked) Odysseus to
     Nausicaä, the princess of Phaeacia, in the *Odyssey* (6.149 ff.).

333 *cymbals are clashed*: Eclipses were considered ill-omened and
     loud noises were thought to avert their effects.

362 *like a huge snake*: In the traditional simile of the snake and the
     eagle, the former is usually the victim, but here it has the upper
     hand.

392 *Phrygian pipes*: Exotic instruments with curving bells.

395 *curtains of ivy*: The ivy and vines on the women's looms symbolize
     the triumph of Bacchus over Minerva.

415 *Latin name from the evening*: Bats in Latin are *vespertiliones*.

421 *nursed in his cradle*: See 3.313–15.

456 *House of the Damned*: The place in which the great sinners whose
     names follow received their famous punishments for crimes com-
     mitted on earth. The giant *Tityos* (457) had tried to rape Latona,
     the mother of Apollo and Diana. *Tantalus* (458), according to
     one story, tested the gods' omniscience by feasting them on the
     flesh of his dismembered son Pelops. *Sisyphus* (460) was a notori-
     ous trickster who betrayed one of Jupiter's love-affairs. *Ixion*
     (461) had tried to rape Juno and was crucified on an eternally
     revolving wheel of fire. The offence of the fifty daughters of
     Danaus (462) is given by Ovid as well as their punishment.

466   *Aeolus*: Not (here) the god of the winds, but Hellen's son who became the first ruler of Thessaly.

474   *Tisiphone*: 'Avenger of murder', the senior Fury.

533   *granddaughter*: Venus was the mother of Harmonia, Cadmus' wife.

538   *my Greek name*: Aphrodite, from *aphros*, 'foam'.

568   *Illyrian frontier*: Cadmus and Harmonia seem to have travelled a long way north-west, as far as modern Albania.

575   *long-bellied serpent*: Cadmus' prayer recalls Minerva's prophecy in 3.98–9.

607   *Acrisius*: See 3.559–60. His opposition to Bacchus is not recorded elsewhere and must be an invention of Ovid's to provide a link between the Theban legend (which he has now largely finished with) and the story of Perseus.

611   *Danaë*: An oracle had said she would bear a son who would kill her father. Acrisius therefore put her in prison, where she was visited by Jupiter in the form of a shower of gold. The result was Perseus, who eventually killed his grandfather accidentally with a discus while competing in some funeral games.

615   *whirring wings*: The winged sandals given to Perseus by Mercury.

616   *snake-headed Gorgon*: Medusa, of whom we hear more later (779 ff.). Her glance turned all who looked on her to stone.

669   *Cepheus*: The boasts of his wife Cassiopeia had provoked the anger of the Nereïds and also of Neptune, who had afflicted the country with a great flood and a terrible sea-monster. The oracle of Jupiter Ammon had declared that deliverance could only be obtained if the princess Andromeda were chained to a rock as an offering to the monster.

753   *three of the gods*: Mercury and Minerva had helped Perseus to kill the Gorgon, and Jupiter was his father.

774   *daughters of Phorcys*: The two (or in some accounts three) Graiae (777) were sisters of Medusa and the other two Gorgons (779).

785   *Pegasus*: The famous winged horse. His brother Chrysaor was human.

799   *her aegis*: This must refer here to Minerva's shield, since she is covering her eyes with it. The term is also applied (as at 2.754) to her 'breastplate', a betasselled goatskin tabard, fringed with snakes and decorated centrally with the Gorgon's head.

802–3 *That explains why . . . on the front of her bosom*: In an authorial addition to Perseus' story, Ovid gives the origin of Minerva's common representation in her 'breastplate' aegis. The final image of the book is of the goddess, after her defeat by Bacchus earlier in the poetic sequence (9–10, 394–8), asserting her authority at its most terrifying.

BOOK 5

11 *bride*: Andromeda had previously been betrothed to Phineus.

12 *counterfeit gold*: See note on 4.611.

47 *aegis*: This must be Minerva's shield. See note on 4.799. Minerva comes to help Perseus, as Athena supports Odysseus in his fight with the suitors (*Odyssey* 22).

155 *goddess of war*: Ovid calls her Bellona, but he is presumably thinking of Minerva, who is present (46–7, 250–51).

215 *sideways*: Phineus dares not look at Perseus face to face.

238 *by challenging Proetus*: A detail only found in Ovid. In other versions, Perseus accidentally kills his grandfather with a discus at this stage and fulfils the prophecy Acrisius sought to avert. See notes on 242 below and 4.611.

242 *Polydectes*: King of Seriphos (pronounced here with the first syllable stressed), who had rescued Danaë and the infant Perseus after they had been set adrift in a boat by Acrisius. He sent Perseus on the quest for the Gorgon's head, so he could be free to seduce Danaë.

257 *winged horse*: Pegasus (4.785–6). The fountain was called Hippocrene, 'horse spring', and regarded as a source of poetic inspiration.

274 *Pyreneus*: A tyrannical king, not otherwise known of.

283 *humbler abodes*: This looks forward to the story of *Philemon and Baucis* (8.629–724).

288 *taking wing*: Ovid finds it convenient here to give the Muses wings, which they do not normally possess.

319 *war in the sky*: A new account of the Gigantomachy (1.151–62), blasphemously attributing defeat to the gods.

327 *became a ram*: In several cases, the Pierid singer is equating the Olympians with the animal manifestations of their Egyptian counterparts.

338 *Calliope*: 'Beautiful-voiced', often regarded as the Muse of epic poetry.

347 *Typhon*: Now represented not as a victor (323) but a prisoner inside the earth from which he sprang.

359 *monarch of Hades*: In Greek Hades was originally the name of the god of the dead, later of the whole underworld (as here). The Roman name for its king was Pluto or Dis.

368 *world's three kingdoms*: When the universe was divided up between the three sons of Saturn, Jupiter drew the first lot (the sky), Neptune the second (the sea) and Pluto the last (the underworld).

379 *her uncle's wife*: Proserpina is the daughter of Jupiter and so Neptune's niece.

406 *Bacchiadae*: The founders of Corinth. The Corinthian Archias had founded a Greek colony at Syracuse.

499 *in a timelier hour*: The story of Alpheüs' pursuit of Arethusa is told at 572–642.

528b *different kingdoms*: See note on 368.

541 *Acheron*: 'Wailing', a river in Hades, here personified.

543 *Erebus*: 'Gloom', another river in Hades.

544 *Phlegethon*: 'Fiery', one more underworld river.

552 *Sirens*: Half women, half birds, best known from Homer's *Odyssey* 12.39 ff., 166 ff. Their metamorphosis is very artificially woven in here.

567 *six months*: The Proserpina story is the famous myth which accounts for the seasons.

585 *Stymphalus*: About forty miles away from the Alpheüs.

607–8 *Orchomenus . . . Elis*: Arethusa's wild and exhausting journey makes rough geographical sense, though Ovid must also be playing with the sound of the names.

640 *Ortygia*: 'Quail-island', where the so-called Fountain of Arethusa at Syracuse can still be seen today. Diana was called the Ortygian goddess as Ortygia was an early name for Delos, where she was born.

646 *Triptolemus*: The cult-hero and mythical inventor of agriculture, who established the worship of Ceres (Demeter) and the famous Mysteries of Eleusis near Athens.

678 *raucous, chattering birds*: The book ends, as it began (2–7), in aggressive noise.

BOOK 6

5 *Lydian*: The scene has now shifted from mainland Greece to Lydia in central Ionia (Asia Minor).

6 *Arachne*: 'Spider'.

9–10 *Phocaean / purple*: The purple dye came from a shellfish found off the Ionian coast at a town called Phocaea.

26 *as a hag*: We may be reminded of Juno visiting Semele in a similar disguise (3.273–86).

70   *rock of Mars*: The Areopagus to the west of the Acropolis at
      Athens. The contest between Minerva/Athena and Neptune/
      Poseidon, as to which of the two gods should own the land and
      determine its name, traditionally took place on the Acropolis
      itself.

87   *Haemus and Rhodope*: A young couple so passionately in love
      that they called each other Jupiter and Juno and were transformed
      into mountain ranges for their presumption.

90   *queen of the Pygmies*: A woman who had been turned into a
      crane for challenging Juno's majesty and claiming the worship of
      her people. The result was a permanent state of war between
      cranes and Pygmies.

93   *Antigone*: Not the heroine of Sophocles' tragedy but a Trojan
      princess changed to a stork because she had rashly vied with
      Juno.

98   *Cinyras*: Otherwise unknown. Presumably his daughters had
      boasted of their beauty and been transformed to the stone which
      formed the temple steps of the deity they had offended.

103 *Arachne's picture*: The mortal woman's tapestry challenges
      Minerva's warnings and the gods generally by its depictions of
      twenty-one 'misdemeanours' (131) committed by five of the
      gods.

116 *daughter of Aeolus*: Canace.

161 *her two children*: Apollo and Diana (205).

174 *feast with the gods*: See note on 4.456. An ironical touch, as
      Tantalus had been punished for abusing his privilege.

190–91 *Delos, who said ... shifting island*: The island of Delos is
      personified in its welcome to Latona. It was originally a floating
      island (see also 334), until it was fixed to the seabed as a reward
      for its kindness to the goddess.

213 *as her father's*: Ovid may be referring to one version of the
      Tantalus story which said he was punished for divulging the gods'
      secrets to men.

311 *mountain summit*: Mount Sipylus in Phrygia, where a certain
      crag with a stream dripping down its face was identified by the
      ancients with Niobe, because (from a distance) it resembled a
      weeping woman bowed with grief. It still does.

407 *dismembered the boy*: See note on 4.456.

410 *empty space*: The shoulder had been irretrievably consumed by
      Ceres in her distraction for the loss of Proserpina.

416 *wrath of Diana*: The story will be told in Book 8.

668–9 *nightingale ... swallow*: In Greek literature Procne is changed to the nightingale and Philomela to the swallow; but in the Roman poets it is usually the other way round. Ovid does not specify which sister becomes which bird and may thus be cleverly exploiting the mythological confusion. For the Greek tragedians, Procne, perpetually grieving for Itys, had been (like Niobe) a paradigm of mourning, but that is not so here.

680 *Procris*: The story of her and Cephalus is told in 7.694–862.

681 *Orithyia*: 'Mountain-raver'.

721 *first of all ships*: Traditionally so, but Tereus and others have crossed the sea earlier in this book (422–3, 445–6, 511–19).
Golden Fleece: The fleece at the end of the book echoes the fleece from which Arachne was spinning wool close to the beginning (20–21).

BOOK 7

7–8 *Golden Fleece*: Originally of a ram born to Theophane after she was raped by Neptune in a ram's form (6.118a). Jason had been sent by his evil uncle Pelias, king of Iolcus in Thessaly, to bring it back from Colchis to Greece – a dangerous task as the fleece was guarded by an unsleeping dragon.

11 *reason was powerless . . . passion*: Here follows the first of several long soliloquies in the poem, delivered by characters torn and wavering between conflicting forces.

62 *mountainous rocks*: The Symplegades, 'clashers', which like Scylla (64) and Charybdis (63) are dangers encountered at sea by Odysseus in Homer (who calls them the Wandering Rocks) and are all mentioned again in the *Metamorphoses*.

94–5 *threefold / goddess*: Hecate was the underworld counterpart of Diana on earth and the Moon in the sky.

96 *sun god*: The father of Aeëtes and so Medea's grandfather.

121 *teeth of the Theban dragon*: The dragon killed by Cadmus in Book 3. The teeth were divided by Athena between Cadmus and Acëtes, who must have supplied them to Jason for this second dangerous task.

145–6 *exulted in silence . . . magical powers*: There is some corruption of the Latin text of these lines and the general sense is reproduced here.

182–3 *Her robes hung loosely . . . shoulders*: Medea's attire avoids all knots, which are resistant to magic.

207 *cymbals may clash*: See note on 4.333.

233 *transformation of Glaucus*: The story is told at 13.904–67.

295 *his nurses*: Obscure, as they cannot be Bacchus' nurses of 3.313–15. 294–6 seems to be a filler, to mark off the two contrasting Medea stories involving Aeson and Pelias.

298 *Pelias' house*: See note on 7–8.

324 *Ebro*: Close to the western ocean where the sun sank.

351 *flight through the air*: Medea's tour round the Aegean and back to the Greek mainland may be followed in a classical atlas (with the help of the Glossary Index) by those with the interest to do so. Her route seems to be dictated by Ovid's wish to work in about fifteen minor metamorphoses and a few other mythological references, which need hardly detain the reader any more than they detained Medea.

358 *petrified snake*: The story is told at 11.56–60.

372 *Cycnus*: Not Phaëthon's friend, also changed to a swan at 2.367–77.

393 *rain-fed mushroom*: The tradition is unique to this passage.

394 *Jason's new bride*: Here Ovid comes very briefly to the content of Euripides' tragedy *Medea*, in which Medea, in outraged pride, murders Jason's newly-wedded bride with a poisoned robe and then kills the two children she herself had borne Jason, to spite their treacherous father.

405 *heroic deeds*: Theseus, on his coastal journey from Troezen to Athens, disinfested the road of various robbers and beasts, as later recounted in the eulogy accorded him by the Athenian people at 433–50.

434 *dangerous Cretan bull*: Theseus killed a bull that was destroying crops and killing farmers in the plain of Marathon. It is not to be confused with the Minotaur, also killed by Theseus, but was identified with the Cretan bull which Hercules captured and brought to Argos on his seventh labour (see 9.186).

438 *Procrustes*: His visitors were lopped or stretched to fit his famous bed.

439 *Cercyon*: He challenged travellers to a wrestling bout and killed them when they lost.

442 *victim's fragments*: Sinis would tie the arms of someone he had captured to one pine-top and his legs to another before letting the trees go.

443 *Sciron*: Who robbed his victims and made them wash his feet, then kicked them on to the rocks below.

457 *Androgeos*: Minos' son, who (according to one account) had been murdered by his fellow-competitors after winning the Panathenaic games.

460 *scouring the sea*: Here Ovid takes the opportunity for a catalogue of the Aegean islands.

470 *Peparethos*: All the other islands mentioned in 469–70 are in the Cyclades group. In 471 Minos turns westward for Aegina; but Peparethos is about 90 miles almost due north of Aegina, and it was noted for its production of wine, not of olive oil. Might Ovid have been thinking of the metrically identical Prepesinthos, a smaller island in the Cyclades and (like the others) south-west of Aegina?

524 *her rival*: Aegina, a girl originally called Oenone (cf. Oenopia 472), whom Jupiter had abducted to the island and there fathered Aeacus on her. Hence Juno's hatred.

654 *Myrmidons after the ants*: The Greek for 'ant' is *myrmex*.

660 *east wind*: As Athens is north-north-east of Aegina, an *east* wind is hardly precise, but it fits metrically in Latin. By mentioning it twice, perhaps Ovid is making a joke of his navigational inaccuracy.

688–9 *the price / he had paid*: This is thought to refer to a detail in Ovid's sources for this story: Procris, to prove to Cephalus that he could be tempted into worse things than he was accusing her of, disguised herself as a boy and offered her husband the spear in return for a homosexual act. If this is right, Ovid is presumably giving his sophisticated audience notice early on that *his* treatment will be excluding (as it does) this particular incident.

690 *son of a goddess*: Phocus' mother was the Nereïd Psamathe, who returns later in the story of Peleus (11.379–406).

759 *riddle*: 'What walks on four legs in the morning, two at noon and three in the evening?' The Sphinx killed any who failed to solve her riddle by throwing them over a cliff. When Oedipus arrived and gave the correct answer ('Man'), the Sphinx threw herself over and he became king of Thebes. Ovid's audience would certainly know this story, as many do today.

864 *pair of his sons*: Peleus and Telamon (669). Ovid began the book by referring to 'Boreas' twins' (3), Zetes and Calaïs. Another couple of brothers balances them in the penultimate line.

BOOK 8

58–9 *the son / who was murdered*: See note on 7.457.

69 *If wishes were horses ... beggars would ride*: Here, as in 72–3 and 79, Ovid introduces sententious clichés into Scylla's rhetoric.

How sympathetically is he treating this heroine in her internal conflict?

121 *swirling Charybdis*: The famous whirlpool off the coast of Sicily, usually associated (as in 7.63–5) with the monster Scylla – but a different Scylla from the subject of this episode and therefore not mentioned now. (Her story is told later on in Books 13 and 14.)

132 *adulterous queen*: Pasiphaë, who fell in love with a bull and achieved intercourse with it by placing herself inside a wooden cow contrived by Daedalus. The 'hybrid monster' (133) she produced was the Minotaur, half man and half bull.

151 *Ciris the Shearer*: Probably just a mythological bird, not otherwise identified.

155–6 *bestial / adultery*: See note on 132.

171 *tribute exacted*: Eventually achieved by Minos for the murder of Androgeos. See note on 7.457.

173a *Prince Theseus*: He had volunteered to be one of the seven youths and maidens and to kill the Minotaur.

181 *jewelled circlet*: The constellation known as Corona, the Crown.

182 *Kneeler . . . Snake*: The first is a constellation commonly identified with Hercules, the second the constellation Draco.

183 *protracted exile*: Daedalus had been expelled from Athens for murdering his nephew Perdix (241–51).

218 *ploughman*: This and the other details in 217–18 are famously captured in Pieter Brueghel the Elder's painting *Landscape with the Fall of Icarus* (*c.* 1558), itself recalled by W. H. Auden in *Museé des Beaux Arts* (1940).

251 *sacred hill of Minerva*: The Acropolis at Athens.

273 *King Oeneus*: The legal father of Meleäger, who is later (437) referred to as a son of Mars.

304 *Plexippus and Toxeus*: The brothers of Meleäger's mother, Althaea.

316 *Amphiaraüs*: A prophet tricked by his wife Eriphyle into becoming one of the Argive champions who backed Polynices against his brother for the disputed sovereignty of Thebes. See notes on 9.404 and 9.407–17.

372 *before they were stars*: The constellation Gemini.

403 *Pirithoüs*: The son of Ixion (see note on 4.456) and a close friend of Theseus, with whom he later attempted to abduct Proserpina from Hades.

437 *son of Mars*: See note on 273. The description asserts Meleäger's heroic status at a dramatic moment.

544 *Deïanira*: (pronounced in five syllables) Later the wife of Hercules. Her story is told in Book 9.

546 *guinea-fowl*: Ovid's audience would know that the bird described was known in Greek as *meleagris*, a female relative of Meleäger.

549 *god Acheloüs*: West of Calydon and not really on Theseus' route back to Athens.

596–610 The received Latin text at this point appears to incorporate two alternative versions, both possibly written by Ovid himself. I have translated the shorter version, as I thought it the better one in the context.

672 *returned to the table*: There was only one wine and it was young – all that the humble hosts could afford.

738 *Mestra*: Ovid does not actually give her name, but his audience would know it from earlier versions of the story.

884 *has lost its defence*: River-gods were often represented with horns. In Book 9 Acheloüs goes on to explain how one of his horns was damaged. The detail of such a potent feature balances and recalls Nisus' crimson lock at the very start of the book (8–10).

BOOK 9

4   *gift*: Acheloüs' narrative is a kind of hospitality-gift to his guest Theseus.

14   *Jove was his father*: For the story of Hercules' birth see 285–323.

66   *in my cradle*: The infant Hercules strangled two snakes which Juno sent to destroy him.

88   *Spirit of Plenty*: The Cornucopia, the traditional horn of plenty.

123–4 *Ixion's / wheel*: See 4.461 and note on 4.456.

130 *gore from the venomous Hydra*: Hercules' arrows were tipped with the Hydra's venom. See 69–74.

140 *Princess Iole*: The captive daughter of Eurytus, king of Oechalia, a city which Hercules sacked (136).

165 *Mount Oeta*: Another geographical licence. Oeta is not on Euboea but in Trachis, on the Greek mainland.

182 *Was it for this*: Here Ovid lists a variety of Hercules' exploits, including all of the twelve labours (set him by King Eurystheus of Argos at Juno's behest) and several other feats. For the details, see the Glossary Index or a classical dictionary.

198 *supported the sky*: Hercules held up the sky for Atlas, while the giant (according to one version of the story) went to fetch the golden apples of the Hesperides (190).

233 *kingdom of Troy*: Hercules used his bow in the first destruction

of Troy, provoked by King Laömedon's broken promise (the story is told at 11.199–210).

270 *awesome authority*: Ovid uses the adjective *augustus*. The emperor was often identified with Hercules by the poets of the period.

273 *additional weight*: Hercules' apotheosis increases the weight of the sky!

294 *Lucina*: The Roman name for Ilithyia (283).

323 *through her mouth*: There was an ancient belief, referred to by Aristotle, that weasels gave birth through the mouth.

340 *lotus*: Certainly not the water-lily as we know it, although it grows near water. Dryope is later turned into a tree called the lotus (365), which the *Oxford Latin Dictionary* identifies as the nettle-tree or *Celtis australis*. It turns up again in the catalogue of trees which follow Orpheus in 10.90–105.

390–91 *eyes . . . without your help*: Dryope refers to the ritual custom of closing a dead person's eyes.

401 *her husband Hercules' prayers*: Hebe was given as wife to the deified Hercules. Iolaüs was Hercules' nephew and squire-charioteer. His youth was restored so that he could help the children of Hercules when they were being persecuted by Eurystheus (273–5).

404 *civil strife*: The dispute over the sovereignty of Thebes between the two sons of Oedipus (405), who had agreed to reign for a year in turn. When Eteocles refused to hand over after his year, his brother Polynices attacked the city with the help of six other champions from Argos (the Seven against Thebes). These included Capaneus (404), a boaster who was struck down by Zeus' lightning, and Amphiaraüs, a prophet who foresaw his own death and was swallowed up in the earth (see note on 8.316).

407–17 *his son . . . full-grown men*: Alcmaeon. A long story, obscurely compressed into a few lines. Alcmaeon killed his mother Eriphyle in revenge for his father, because she had been bribed by Polynices with the gift of a golden necklace to send Amphiaraüs off among the Seven to his death at Thebes. Driven by remorseful madness into exile, he found refuge in Arcadia at the house of Phegeus (412), whose daughter Alphesiboea he married and presented with the same necklace with which his mother had been bribed. When madness descended on him again, he wandered as far as the Acheloüs and there married the river-god's daughter Callirhoë (413). When his new wife asked him for the 'curse-ridden . . . necklace' (411–12), he returned to Phegeus, his former father-in-law, and obtained it on a false pretext. Phegeus later discovered the truth and had Alcmaeon murdered (412). Thus Callirhoë came to ask Jupiter to accelerate her own children's coming to manhood, so that they could avenge their father's death.

424 *eye to the future*: Venus is thinking of the foundation of Rome by the descendants of Aeneas, her son by Anchises. Ovid here looks forward to the later books which cover the mythology of Rome.

435–7 *Aeacus ... Rhadamanthus ... Minos*: Aeacus was king (and son) of Aegina; we first met him at 7.474. Rhadamanthus and Minos (the latter also met before) were the sons of Europa. After their deaths, these three sons of Jupiter composed a trinity of judges in the underworld.

449 *famous town*: Miletus, in Caria, on the south-west coast of modern Turkey.

466 *'my master'*: Dominus, used as a term of affection in Latin.

507 *Aeolus' sons ... their sisters*: Referred to in the *Odyssey* (10.1–7). In *Heroides* 11, Ovid makes one of Aeolus' daughters, Canace, write a pre-suicide letter to her brother Macareus by whom she had a child. In Byblis' questions (508) the poet could be slyly referring to his own work.

634 *new city*: Caunus in Caria.

646–7 *Cragus ... Limyre ... Xanthus*: Cragus is a mountain in Lycia, to the east of Caria, Limyre and Xanthus are rivers. All are well past Caunus, if Byblis is still pursuing her brother.

647 *ridge of Chimaera*: The three-formed mythical creature with the torso of a goat, as Ovid's audience would have known.

652 *Carian nymphs*: Byblis has evidently returned westward.

667 *Crete*: Byblis' father was Miletus, who had originally come from Crete (447–9) to escape from Minos. The fact provides the transition to the next story.

686 *Isis*: Last met at 1.747. The goddess is attended by other Egyptian deities and their trappings (690–94). It is interesting to ask why Ovid chose an Egyptian god (with a cult at Rome) as the presiding deity in this story rather than the Graeco-Roman Leto (Latona) in his source. Crete is, of course, in the southern Mediterranean, not too far north-west of Egypt. Perhaps the poet felt that this context called for an indubitably benign figure, untarnished by the meaner qualities with which he has vested his Olympians. Isis was known particularly as a protectress of children.

692 *child-god*: Harpocrates, the Greek name for an Egyptian god whose name meant 'Horus-child'. Statues showed him with his

finger in his mouth to suggest childhood, though the Greeks and Romans thought this denoted a call to silence.

693 *Osiris*: The husband of Isis, who was killed by his brother Seph and torn to pieces, then searched for by Isis until she secured his revival. The 'search for whom is never abandoned' refers to the annual ritual commemorating this myth.

694 *snake from Egypt*: Snakes were part of Isis-worship and associated with the life-giving properties of the Nile.

736 *Pasiphaë*: Her story was told at 8.131–7.

739 *wooden cow*: See note on 8.132.

790 *new vigour*: The name Iph*is* is derived from a Greek word for masculine strength.

792 *gifts*: The verbal link between the beginning and end of this book. In asking Acheloüs to explain his broken horn in line 1, Theseus is demanding what the river calls 'a dismal gift' (4). Here Telethusa and Iphis are called on to bring their gifts to the temple in joy. The gift motif is also used poignantly with the tunic of Nessus (133, 157, 213).

BOOK 10

13 *Taenaran gateway*: Taenarus, at the tip of the middle peninsula at the south of the Peloponnese, was a conventional entrance to the underworld.

21 *three-headed monster*: Cerberus. Orpheus is making it clear that he is not another Hercules, whose removal of the dog from Hades is referred to at 7.410–15 and 9.185.

28 *that old abduction*: The story of Proserpina's kidnap by Pluto, told by Orpheus' mother, Calliope, at 5.385–571.

41–4 *For a moment . . . boulder*: Activity in the House of the Damned (4.456) is suspended by Ovid to entertaining effect.

65 *terrified person*: Otherwise unknown. Ovid is working in a mini-metamorphosis.

68 *Lethaea*: Another obscure reference involving a mini-metamorphosis. The images of unity and separation in 70–71 fit the Orpheus story, but Eurydice was not guilty like Lethaea.

77 *Rhodope . . . Haemus*: Mountains in Thrace, referred to as metamorphosed lovers at 6.87–9. Haemus is also linked with Orpheus at 2.219–20.

78 *Pisces*: The twelfth sign of the zodiac, indicating the end of the winter. Ovid also connects the seasons with the zodiac at 126 and 165.

89   *Trees suddenly came on the scene*: Orpheus was renowned for
       his power to draw trees and rocks behind him with his music.

90   *oak of Dodona*: The large Eurasian oak, here associated with
       Jupiter's famous oracle at Dodona in Epirus. Responses were
       given through the rustling of the sacred oaks.
       high-leaved durmast: The Italian oak, the tallest oak species.

97   *laurustinus*: An evergreen winter-flowering shrub.

104   *Attis*: The young male escort of the Phrygian mother-goddess
       Cybele, whose worship was fostered at Rome. His self-castration
       formed part of the ritual associated with the cult. The pine tree
       also featured, but Attis' actual metamorphosis into a pine seems
       to be an invention of Ovid's.

126   *Cancer the Crab*: This stands for the beginning of summer, though
       in 127 Ovid imagines the Crab as literally alive on the seashore.

142   *always be there . . . loved ones*: The cypress was traditionally the
       tree of death and funerals.

148   *Let Jove be the start*: The grand invocation of Jupiter, and a fresh
       reference to the Gigantomachy (see 1.152-62, 5.319) on the
       plains of Phlegraea (150-51), are in mock contrast with Orpheus'
       subject-matter as projected in 152-4.

182   *unthinkingly*: Just like Cyparissus (130).

206   *My sighs . . . in the marks of a new flower*: The letters AIAI, a
       Greek word of lamentation. See 215-16.

207   *Aias*: The Greek form of Ajax, whose death and production of a
       hyacinth from his blood are described at 13.383b-96. Sophocles
       in his tragedy *Ajax* played on the pun between his hero's name
       and the Greek word for 'Alas!' (206). The point recurs at
       13.396-8.

213   *deepest red*: The Roman hyacinth is evidently not the species we
       should recognize.

237   *fierce young bulls*: So now very suitable for sacrifice themselves.

240-41 *offer their bodies . . . for sale*: Ovid is making his own
       intriguing use of the historical fact that temple prostitutes prac-
       tised their trade in the shrine of Venus at Paphos.

251   *if modesty didn't preclude it*: The old idea that nudity is 'art' in
       stillness, but indecent in motion.

305   *congratulate this domain*: Orpheus is speaking and so made,
       ironically, to ignore the Thracian predilection for sex noted at
       6.458-60 and also the practices introduced by himself in 83-5.
       Since, however, we may well have forgotten about Orpheus, the
       minstrel's voice in Thrace may here be subtly merged with the
       voice of Ovid at Rome.

448 *golden moon*: A symbol of chastity, which has appropriately fled in horror.

450–51 *Icarus . . . Erigone*: An ideal father–daughter pair to contrast with Cinyras and Myrrha. When Icarus (not Daedalus' son and better known as Icarius) was killed, Erigone hanged herself and they both joined the constellations as Boötes (446) and Virgo.

480 *Saba*: Myrrha is now back in Arabia.

565 *Atalanta*: A different Atalanta from the Arcadian girl admired by Meleäger in Book 8.

696 *tower-crowned*: Cybele, the 'Mighty Mother' (704), was commonly represented with a 'battlemented' crown.

698 *too light*: The actual punishment of metamorphosis into tamed lions hardly seems more severe than consignment to the underworld.

705 *avoid the lions*: Venus' story may have explained why she detests lions (552) but is hardly a forceful warning against the hunting of more dangerous animals. Anyway, Adonis ignores it (709).

715 *its tusks*: The Latin echoes the word used for the 'fang' of the viper which bit the foot of Eurydice (10). The book ends as it began with the image of the corpse of a young person whose death has been caused by an animal 'tooth' or 'teeth'.

726 *shall be re-enacted*: Adonis' death was ritually commemorated in a summer festival, like the Hyacinthia at Sparta (219), called the Adonia.

728 *Proserpina*: This balances the mention of the goddess as the power whom Orpheus first appeals to when he visits the underworld at the beginning of the book (15). There is little other reason for her to appear at this point.

736 *pomegranate fruit*: Another reminder of Proserpina. See 5.536–8.

738 *anemone – wind-flower*: *Anemos* is the Greek word for 'wind'.

BOOK 11

1 *Thracian minstrel*: Orpheus here returns to the foreground.

25–6 *morning fight / in the amphitheatre*: The simile, as at 3.111, is drawn from the contemporary Roman world of popular entertainment. Gladiatorial contests were preceded in the morning by shows of animal hunting.

67 *priest of his mysteries*: Orpheus was prominent in the cult of Dionysus. See 92–3.

88 *precious sand*: See 142–5.

90 *Silenus*: See 4.26–8.

93   *Eumolpus*: The founder of the Mysteries at Eleusis near Athens,
       which historically included a 'descent into Hades' like that of
       Orpheus.

117   *Danaë's virtue*: See note on 4.611.

156   *Tmolus as judge*: The mountain here becomes a god in human
       form, like the river Acheloüs (8.549–610 and 9.1–88).

181   *tiara*: A kind of turban which fastened under the chin.

195–6 *straits of . . . Helle*: The Hellespont or the modern Dardanelles.

219   *grandfather*: Jupiter was Peleus' grandfather through Aeacus, the
       king of Aegina encountered in Book 7.

221   *Proteus*: See 8.731–7. Here the old man of the sea is a sort of
       prophet.

268   *Phocus, his half-brother*: The son of the Nereïd Psamathe. Peleus
       and Telamon were supposed to have killed him because he
       excelled in athletic sports.

273   *his brother*: Daedalion, whose story is told at 291–300.

400   *Thetis*: Returned now, evidently, to the sea.

413   *Claros*: Apollo's oracle here was second only to that of Delphi.

578   *Juno's temple*: Juno as the goddess of marriage.

584–5 *polluted by unclean / hands*: Until a dead man had been properly
       buried, his family was regarded as unclean.

592   *Cimmerian country*: The Cimmerians were a mythical people
       who were said to dwell by Ocean in mist and cloud, close to the
       country of dreams.

599   *watchful geese*: See note on 2.538.

603   *Lethe*: Here located, by poetic licence, in Cimmerian territory.

639   *Icelos . . . Phobetor*: 'Like' . . . 'Scarer'.

751   *same person*: Ovid is making a joke of his own vagueness regard-
       ing the identity of his narrator.

776   *fugitive's foot*: Here, near the end of the book, we are inevitably
       reminded of Eurydice, and so of Orpheus, with whose image the
       book began.

BOOK 12

1   *Priam*: Aesacus' metamorphosis to the diver at the end of Book
       11 leads on at once to his royal father. For the relationship of
       lines 1–4 with the end of the book, see note on 614.

5–6   *prince . . . stolen bride*: The traditional cause of the Trojan War.
       Paris breached the laws of hospitality by eloping with Helen, the
       wife of Menelaüs, king of Sparta. The Greek fleet of a thousand
       ships, raised to rescue Helen and punish the Trojans, was

assembled under the command of Agamemnon, king of Mycenae
and Menelaüs' brother.

28   *virgin goddess*: Diana, whom Agamemnon had offended by (in
some versions) shooting one of her deer. The sacrifice of Iphigenia
was a favourite theme in Greek and Roman tragedy.

68–70   *Danaäns ... Achaean ... Phrygian*: Variant names, the first
two for the Greeks, the last for the Trojans.

72   *Cycnus*: The third Cycnus in the poem, yet another to be meta-
morphosed to a swan.

109–12   *when I led the attack ... touched by my spear*: In these lines
Achilles is referring to various of his exploits in the early part of
the Trojan War, outside Troy itself. Telephus was the king of
Mysia, wounded by Achilles on his way to Troy and later healed
with the touch of rust from the same spear in accordance with an
oracle.

151   *Athena*: Achilles might have been wiser to placate Neptune,
Cycnus' father. See 580–97.

175   *as a woman*: Called Caenis (189). The names Caeneus and Caenis
derive from a Greek word for 'new', a point picked up by Ovid
in the 'novelty' of Nestor's pronouncement.

211   *cloud-born centaurs*: The cloud was an imitation of Juno, made
by Jupiter and impregnated by Ixion (see note on 4.456), who
was also the father of Pirithoüs.

229   *injure us both*: Theseus and Pirithoüs were well known as bosom
friends. The following two lines (230–31) are omitted in this
translation as spurious.

309   *reserved for Hercules' bow*: The story has already been told at
9.101–30, but Nestor's narration refers to the more distant past.

445   *I ought to have come to ... Troy*: Nestor here deplores the old
age he took some pride in at 185–8.

455   *Mopsus*: Here commended for his fighting qualities. His prophetic
powers are deployed at 530–32.

521   *Mount Ida*: A reminder that the story is being narrated by Nestor
at Troy.

524   *rust-winged bird*: Apparently unique (526, 531) and not other-
wise identified.

537–8   *his father ... not been mentioned*: At 9.191 Hercules includes
his fight with the centaurs in the list of his achievements. He was
certainly involved on the Lapith side in one traditional account
of the battle.

581–2   *Phaëthon's / friend*: See 2.367–9.

585   *Sminthian*: A title Apollo is given once in Homer's *Iliad* (1.39),

referring to Sminthe, a place near Troy, or meaning 'protector against mice' (*sminthos* is Greek for 'mouse')

587   *unrewarded*: See 11.199–206.

591   *Hector, whose body was dragged*: After Achilles had killed Hector, he dragged the dead hero's body behind his chariot wheels three times a day around the walls of Troy (*Iliad* 22).

595   *I may not engage . . . directly*: The tradition was clear that Achilles was shot in the heel by Paris, with Apollo's help.

597   *accorded with Neptune's*: Apollo always sides with the Trojans in Homer.

611   *Penthesilea*: The queen of the Amazons, who came to help the Trojans after the death of Hector.

614   *ended in flames*: The obsequies of Achilles balance those of Aesacus in the first four lines of the book. Where Aesacus' body is not present to occupy a 'tomb', Achilles' ashes are 'barely sufficient / to fill an urn' (616–17). There are two verbal links: as 'the pride and bulwark / of Greece's *name*' (612–13), Achilles may recall the 'name' (2) inscribed on Priam's son's empty tomb; and the Latin adjective used to describe Hector's funeral-gifts offered 'to no good purpose' (4) is the same as that used for 'shadowy' (619) Hades. Shifts in the meaning of words are another kind of metamorphosis.

BOOK 13

2   *sevenfold shield*: Ajax's famous tower-like shield, made of seven layers of oxhide. See 347.

6   *in front of these vessels*: Ajax uses the debate's setting to remind his audience of his great defence of the Greek fleet as described by Homer in *Iliad* 15.674 ff.

8a   *He beat a hasty retreat*: There is no mention of this in Homer!

31   *Sisyphus' scion*: Ajax follows a tradition that the trickster Sisyphus, not Laertes, was Ulysses' natural father.

35   *sneaking informer*: Ajax alludes to a post-Homeric story in which Ulysses pretended to be mad in order to avoid service at Troy but was caught out by Palamedes, on whom Ulysses later took revenge by getting him put to death on a false charge (56–60).

46   *Philoctetes*: A Greek who inherited Hercules' unerring bow and arrows. On the voyage to Troy he was bitten on the foot by a snake on the island of Lemnos and marooned there because the stench of his wound made him unbearable to live with. In the tenth year of the war, after an oracle declared that Troy could

not be captured without Hercules' weapons, Ulysses was dispatched to Lemnos to fetch them, along with Philoctetes himself. The story was dramatized in an extant play by Sophocles.

64 *desertion of Nestor*: An incident occurring in *Iliad* 8.80 ff., though there it is Diomedes and not Nestor himself who shouts for Ulysses' help.

71 *Ulysses . . . in need of the help*: Another incident in the *Iliad* (11.456 ff.), when Ulysses, who has been bravely fighting against impossible odds, is rescued by Ajax and Menelaüs. In Homer there is no question of his cowardice and he is in fact wounded (contrast 81).

82–94 *Hector arrived . . . return*: Ajax once again presses the details of Homer's story unfairly to his own advantage. Ulysses answers him at 268–369.

98a *Rhesus*: The king of Thrace and one of Troy's allies. In *Iliad* 10 Ulysses makes a night raid on his camp and captures his horses. The incident is described by Ulysses at 249–52.

98b *Dolon*: A Trojan spy whom Ulysses and Diomedes capture on their night raid and so obtain information about the enemy.

98b–99 *Helenus . . . Athena's statue*: Helenus was a son of Priam and a prophet who was said by the Greek seer Calchas to know how Troy could be taken. In one of the Epic Cycle poems Ulysses and Diomedes (after the death of Ajax, though) entered Troy and forced Helenus to reveal that the city would fall if the Trojans were deprived of the Palladium, a wooden image of Athena/ Minerva. This the two Greeks later returned to capture, an achievement which Ulysses makes much of at 334–49 and 373–6.

110 *the shield*: Achilles' famous shield, made for him by Hephaestus/ Vulcan and engraved with a wealth of scenes from everyday life (*Iliad* 18.478 ff.). Ulysses later (286–95) uses the shield to make a point against Ajax.

145 *convict in exile*: Peleus, Achilles' father and Ajax's uncle, had murdered his half-brother Phocus (11.267–9). Ulysses forbears to include his knavish grandfather Autolycus (11.312–15) in his own pedigree.

156 *Phthia or Scyros*: The homes, respectively, of Peleus and Pyrrhus.

157 *Teucer*: Ajax's half-brother by his father Telamon and so equally Achilles' cousin.

172 *Telephus*: See note on 12.109–12.

185 *his innocent daughter*: Iphigenia (12.28–34).

187 *my persuasions*: An invention of Ovid's Ulysses, introduced to

win over Agamemnon to his side by aligning himself with the king over the sacrifice.

193   *the mother*: Clytemnestra, who was tricked into sending her daughter to Aulis in the belief that she was to marry Achilles.

196   *as an envoy*: Ulysses' and Menelaüs' embassy to Troy is referred to twice in the *Iliad* (3.205 ff., 11.138 ff.).

217   *abort operations*: In *Iliad* 2 Agamemnon gives an order for flight to test the loyalty of his troops, in the hope that they will all refuse. Unfortunately they start to obey. Though Ulysses plays a part in halting the retreat, what he says here about Ajax is not in Homer.

232   *Thersites*: A noisy trouble-maker who abuses Agamemnon in the assembly, *Iliad* 2.212 ff., and is thrashed by Ulysses for his insolence.

252   *in glorious triumph*: Ulysses does not include Diomedes in his celebrations.

273   *Patroclus*: Achilles' friend, who fought in his armour and whose killing by Hector brought Achilles back into battle.

289   *fresh arms*: The new arms made for Achilles by Vulcan at his mother's request, since the old ones had been lost with Patroclus.

301   *he by his mother's*: See 162–70.

312   *bribes he had taken*: In fact the gold which Ulysses had himself contrived to 'plant' under Palamedes' tent.

391   *never been wounded before*: Ovid is probably alluding to a post-Homeric tradition that Ajax was vulnerable only to himself.

398   *AIAI*: See notes on 10.206 and 10.207.

400   *murdered their husbands*: The women of Lemnos were punished for neglecting the worship of Aphrodite/Venus by being inflicted with an unpleasant smell. Their husbands resorted to other women and were consequently murdered.

415   *cast from the towers*: The death of Astyanax plays a major part in Euripides' *Trojan Women* (see introduction to this book).

423   *Hecuba*: The widow of Priam and traditionally a paradigm of human suffering, in Renaissance as well as classical literature.

444   *in murderous anger*: Ovid recalls the initial quarrel between Achilles and Agamemnon in *Iliad* 1.

618   *Memnonides*: Daughters of Memnon, usually identified with ruffs on the basis of the birds' fighting habits.

618–19   *Each year ... die like their parents*: The reference is to the annual Roman festival of the Parentalia, when sacrifices were offered to the dead and gladiatorial contests also were held.

622   *morning dew ... mourning*: The translation attempts to produce

an equivalent for Ovid's pun, which links the dawn goddess Au*rora* with *rorare*, 'to bedew'. The use of 'dutiful' at the end of this story is also a link with the 'dutiful' Aeneas near the start of the next (see note on 627).

627 *Aeneas the dutiful*: Virgil (followed here by Ovid) famously characterizes his hero with the Latin epithet *pius*. *Pietas* denotes a sense of duty, a quality of commitment to the claims of religion, country and family.

635 *pangs of her labour*: See 6.332–6.

678a–b *search for . . . kindred shores*: The oracle comes directly from Virgil's *Aeneid* 3.94–8 and refers to Italy, since Dardanus, the ancestor of the Trojans, was supposed to have come from Latium.

685 *stood for the name of the city*: Thebes was renowned for its seven gates.

695 *died for their people*: Orion's daughters sacrificed themselves to save their country from a plague. Lines 693–4 in the original have been omitted.

706 *owed their descent*: The Trojans were known as Teucrians as well as Dardanians (see note on 678a–b). The landing in Crete is a false start on the voyage to found a new Troy.

710 *Aëllo the Harpy*: She cryptically warned the Trojans that hunger would force them to 'eat their tables' when they arrived in Italy (*Aeneid* 3.255–7).

713–14 *three gods . . . shepherd judge*: The rival gods were Apollo, Diana and Hercules, who chose a wise old shepherd, Cragaleus, as arbiter. When the judge awarded Ambracia to Hercules, Apollo turned the shepherd to stone.

715–16 *Apollo's / temple at Actium*: The temple on the promontory near which Octavian (later Augustus) won his celebrated victory over Antony and Cleopatra. Apollo's patronage was an important feature of the Augustan legend.

718a *Munichus*: Jupiter changed him and his sons into birds as a reward for their piety.

720–21 *Helenus . . . New Troy*: The son of Priam, referred to earlier in the book (see note on 98b–99), who like Aeneas had escaped after the fall of Troy and founded a new city in north-west Greece.

844 *some Jove or other*: Contempt of the gods is a feature of the Homeric Cyclops.

854 *my father*: Neptune.

897 *river*: The Acis rose at the foot of Mount Etna and reached the sea on the east coast of Sicily.

910 *huge crag*: The feature foreshadows the monster Scylla's future lair (14.72–4)

919 *Palaemon*: See 4.542.

965–6 *still speaking . . . said more*: The book began with a speech by Ajax. Its pervasive theme of speech is reiterated once more at the very end.

BOOK 14

8   *Etruscan Sea*: Off south-west Italy.

28a *betrayed her affair with Mars*: See 4.171–89.

73   *changed to a headland of rock*: The timing of Scylla's second metamorphosis is inconsistent with 13.732–3, where Aeneas' ship is evidently in danger of Scylla the monster.

78   *Sidonian Dido*: The queen who founded Carthage in north Africa came from the Phoenician city of Sidon. Her tragic love-affair with Aeneas is the subject of Virgil *Aeneid* 4. Aeneas abandoned her when ordered by Jupiter to pursue his higher destiny of founding a new Troy in Italy. Ovid explored Dido's predicament in *Heroides* 7.

85   *the fleet . . . at Juno's bidding*: An incident treated by Virgil in *Aeneid* 5.

111 *Pluto's realm*: Aeneas' visit to the underworld is the subject of *Aeneid* 6, arguably the finest book in Virgil's epic.

152 *voice by which men will know me*: This suggests disembodied voices proceeding from the prophetess's cave, as in *Aeneid* 6.43.

158a *faithful nurse*: Caieta, whose death and burial are mentioned at 441–4.

160 *Achaemenides*: His rescue by Aeneas comes in Virgil, but his meeting with Macareus is a convenient invention of Ovid's.

168 *Polyphemus*: The Cyclops is an even wilder creature here than in 13.759–69. The story is based on Homer *Odyssey* 9.

223 *had visited Aeolus*: The story now is based on *Odyssey* 10.

252 *boozy Elpenor*: So called because later on in the Homeric story he goes to sleep drunk on Circe's roof and topples over the edge to his death.

279–80 *to prickle . . . with bristles*: Ovid's typical enjoyment of all the details of this metamorphosis is worth contrasting with the economy (and pathos) of the change as described by Homer in *Odyssey* 10.239–41.

320 *Picus*: Here we leave Homer and move on to Italian mythology.

331–2 *Tauric Diana's . . . pool*: Lake Aricia. Diana is the Artemis of

Euripides' *Iphigenia among the Taurians*. See note on 15.489–90.

338 *Canens, the singer*: From Latin *cano*, 'I sing'.

428 *an aria*: Canens is imagined here as the ideal singer who, even in grief, sings a proper melody as distinct from the indeterminate musical quality of normal mourning sounds.

450 *Latinus*: King of the Latins, whose daughter Lavinia had previously been betrothed to Turnus, king of the Rutuli. Hence the ensuing war.

456 *Evander*: Formerly a king in Arcadia, who emigrated to Latium, where he founded his new city of Pallanteum on the site where Rome eventually stood.

468a *Narycian Ajax*: The lesser Ajax, from Narycum in Locris.

478 *the wound I dealt her . . . long ago*: The story is told in *Iliad* 5.329 ff.

537 *Mount Ida*: Cybele had a sacred grove there.

565 *Alcinoüs' bark*: Alcinoüs was the king of the Phaeacians, who sent Ulysses back to Ithaca on one of his ships. On its return the vessel was petrified by Neptune, who hated Ulysses (*Odyssey* 13.159 ff.).

622 *Palatine people*: An anachronistic description, since the Palatine Hill at Rome had no special significance as yet.

640 *Priapus*: A deity whose obscene wooden image was often placed in Roman gardens and orchards.

642 *Vertumnus, 'the Turner'*: An Etruscan god, who was generally associated with changes in the seasons.

674 *Alban hills*: About ten miles south-east of Rome.

712 *Noricum*: Famous for its iron products.

761 *Venus the Watcher*: Ovid is here suggesting an explanation for a particular cult (or statue?) of Venus in Anaxarete's 'watching' (752).

772 *Amulius*: According to the historian Livy, he ousted his elder brother Numitor and murdered Numitor's children except for Rhea Silvia/Ilia, whom he made a vestal virgin. She nevertheless gave birth to twins, Romulus and Remus, claiming Mars as their father. Romulus helped to restore Numitor and then left Alba Longa to found Rome.

777 *Tarpeia*: The daughter of the commander of the Roman citadel on the Capitol, who was bribed by the Sabine king Tatius to admit a party of his soldiers into the fortress (here imagined as outside the city gates). Once inside, however, the men crushed her to death with their shields.

785 *Janus' shrine*: Not the temple of Janus in the later Forum, which

was closed in time of peace, but some other building close to the unbarred gate, wherever that was.

827–8   *high-placed/couches*: Effigies of the gods were displayed on raised couches at feasts of supplication.

828   *Quirinus*: Originally a Sabine god, later identified with the deified Romulus. The toga of honour was a short ceremonial robe associated with the early Roman kings. Ovid may be thinking of a known statue here.

836–7   *Quirinus' hill ... verdant trees*: The setting provided for Hersilië's departure at the end of the book recalls the 'herb-green hills and the halls of Circe' at which Glaucus arrives near the beginning (9).

BOOK 15

1   *an enquiry*: A new 'scientific' note is struck at the outset.

1–2   *awesome burden ... worthy successor*: Ovid is using the language of imperial responsibility, and the theme of monarchical succession is a vital element in the final episode of the poem, in which Julius Caesar is seen as being followed by the emperor Augustus (751, 850–58) and Augustus' own succession by Tiberius is also foretold (834–6).

6   *mysteries of nature*: The Latin recalls Lucretius' *De Rerum Natura* ('On the nature of the universe'), a work which Ovid later draws on heavily in Pythagoras' speech.

21   *Club-Bearer*: Hercules. His club, like the lion skin, was an identifying feature of the hero.

23   *Aesar*: The river which reaches the sea just north of Croton.

50   *route*: Myscelus' approach to his destination can be roughly followed on the map, though Ovid juggles the order of some place-names to fit his metre.

60   *there lived a man*: Pythagoras, who came to Croton from Samos about 531 BC – a wild anachronism as Numa traditionally succeeded Romulus in 715 BC.

61   *tyrants*: Polycrates and his brothers.

62   *close to the gods*: The language recalls what Lucretius said of the atomic philosopher Epicurus (fourth–third century BC), who inspired his work.

67   *how the universe first began*: This and the following list of topics down to 72 fit Epicurus and Lucretius rather than what is known about Pythagoras' teaching.

96   *the title of 'Golden'*: See 1.89–112.

153–5 *terror of chill death . . . worlds*: Ovid is still putting Epicurean/Lucretian thinking into Pythagoras' mouth.

158–9 *Our souls . . . in new habitations*: Here at last Ovid introduces the Pythagorean doctrine of Reincarnation, on which the argument for vegetarianism chiefly depends (173a–5, 457–62).

179 *All is in flux*: The famous saying attributed to the early Greek philosopher Heraclitus (about 500 BC), who is also credited with the original observation about the ever-changing river.

229 *Milo the wrestler*: A famous contemporary and disciple of Pythagoras.

233 *twice abducted*: Helen was carried off by Theseus before she eloped with Paris.

237 *elements*: The doctrine of Empedocles. See note on 1.24.

319 *Salmacis' pool*: See 4.285–388.

336 *Ortygia*: Delos. See note on 5.640.

364–5 *bees will be born . . . mouldering carcass*: The same strange process is described by Virgil in *Georgics* 4.281 ff. Like Ovid's other examples in 368–71, it is more folklore than fact.

374 *on a tombstone*: The human soul was often represented on tombs as a butterfly.

393 *phoenix*: A symbol of resurrection and immortality even today.

394 *amomum*: An unidentified eastern spice plant.

406 *sun god's city*: Heliopolis in Egypt.

415 *coral*: See 4.744–52.

437 *Helenus*: See 13.720–22. In Virgil (*Aeneid* 3.374 ff.) the prophecy of 439–49 is made to Aeneas *after* Troy's fall and in Buthrotum, where Pythagoras (as Euphorbus) could not have been present.

449 *destined for heaven*: At the middle of this final book, Ovid anticipates the apotheosis of Augustus envisaged at the end (868–70).

451 *my kinsmen*: Pythagoras imagines himself once more as the reincarnated Trojan Euphorbus.

462 *Thyestes*: His brother Atreus, with whom he had quarrelled, served him with the flesh of his two sons – the so-called 'Thyestean banquet'.

489–90 *Tauric / Diana*: The story went that, when Orestes rescued his sister Iphigenia from the Taurians in the Crimea (dramatized in Euripides' play *Iphigenia among the Taurians*), he removed the cult-image of Diana and set it up in Aricia.

497 *Hippolytus*: Another Euripidean hero, identified with the local deity Virbius, who shared the sanctuary at Aricia. 500–505 summarizes the main action of the tragedy *Hippolytus* and 506–29 is Ovid's version of the messenger-speech. The predicament

of Hippolytus' stepmother, Phaedra, had been explored in *Heroides* 4.

511   *bull*: Sent by Neptune in response to his son Theseus' curse (505).

534   *Aesculapius*: See notes on 2.629 and 2.648. His mention here foreshadows the penultimate story of the poem at 622–744.

543   *remind me of horses*: The etymology of the name Hippolytus is 'horse-loosed'.

565   *Cipus*: A praetor (high executive) in the early republican period.

581   O *King!*: 'King' was a word of evil omen after the expulsion of the Roman kings and the institution of the Republic.

589   *than reign as king*: Cipus' rejection of kingship will have echoed actions of Julius Caesar and Augustus who, while in effect monarchs, rejected the outward forms of kingship to placate their republican-minded opponents. Ovid seems here to be subtly foreshadowing the personalities of his final episode. See Introduction, p. xviii.

622   O *Muses*: This grand invocation gives weight and solemnity to the story which follows.

626   *terrible plague*: An actual event dated to 293 BC. Aesculapius' cult was introduced to Rome in the following year.

643   *Epidaurus*: Where the Greek sanctuary of Asclepius was established and sick people attended for cures.

701   *his voyage continued*: There are obscurities in the geography, but the sound of the place-names has an effect in itself which lends dignity to the god's arrival in Italy.

713   *medicinal springs*: Perhaps a reference to the famous resort at Baiae.

717   *Antiphates*: See 14.233–40.

758a   *having begotten*: Augustus was in fact Julius Caesar's great-nephew, adopted and appointed his heir under Julius' will. We may suspect a touch of Ovidian irony here and in 760–61.

763   *priest*: Caesar was the Pontifex Maximus in charge of the state religion.

769   *Greek Diomedes*: An incident in *Iliad* 5.335 ff.

782   *clear signs*: The passage which follows rivals Virgil's description of the portents in *Georgics* 1. 464 ff.

800   *hall of the Senate*: The Curia Pompeia, a consecrated building outside the city boundary.

809   *Records of Fortune*: Ovid amusingly makes Jupiter use the term for Rome's public record office.

822   *Mutina*: The site of a siege and a battle in 43 BC, when Mark Antony's forces were defeated by an army led by the consuls (who

both were killed), with the young Octavian (later Augustus) present.

823–4 *Pharsalus' plain . . . field of Philippi*: Julius Caesar defeated Pompey in 48 BC at the battle of Pharsalia in Thessaly; while Octavian and Mark Antony defeated Brutus and Cassius in 42 BC at Philippi in Macedonia. The two fields were about 150 miles apart, but Ovid followed Virgil in treating them as if they were the same place.

825 *Sextus Pompeius*: The youngest son of Pompey the Great, defeated by Agrippa in 36 BC.

826 *Egyptian mistress*: Queen Cleopatra, who allied herself to Mark Antony and fled ahead of him from Octavian at the battle of Actium in 31 BC.

836 *Livia's son*: Livia was Augustus' empress and her son was Tiberius, by her previous husband.

840–41 *cut-ridden body . . . comet*: Ovid here is punning on Caesar's name. See Introduction, p. xxxi.

842 *height of his shrine in the Forum*: The image of a comet was placed on the head of the deified Julius' statue in his temple in the Forum; and a coin of 36 BC shows a star in the same temple's pediment or 'height'.

846 *component atoms*: Lucretian language, here rather bizarrely employed.

860 *each is ruler and father*: Jupiter is the father of gods: Augustus bears the title *Pater Patriae*, father of the fatherland. The equation between Jupiter and Augustus at 858–60 seems flattering, but would Augustus have appreciated it in the light of Ovid's irreverent and satirical presentation of Jupiter in so many stories of the poem?

865 *neighbour of Caesar*: The temple of Apollo and a shrine of Vesta formed part of the complex of imperial buildings on the Palatine.

866 *heights of Tarpeia*: The Capitol, where Jupiter had his great temple.

872 *Jupiter's wrath*: Ostensibly the lightning, but the image could also refer to Augustus and Ovid's punishment. If so, the words must be a late addition of Ovid's (see note on 3.142).

Glossary Index

This Glossary Index is not exhaustive, but all the names of any importance in the poem have been included. The list of references for each individual entry is complete, but see the next paragraph; references are to lines of the translation.

Where a character or place is referred to by more than one name, a cross-reference is given. Where, however, a name X occurs in the text in a phrase such as 'son *or* daughter of X', the reference will be found only under the character actually referred to as the son/daughter of X.

Further information is given against all but the most obvious headwords, and some context is given against each reference in the entries for people and gods; the reader is advised also to consult any notes on individual passages cited, since this Glossary Index does not include direct references to those notes and overlaps with them have been avoided.

Conventional English forms of classical names are used where they exist (e.g. Jupiter, Priam, Athens). Otherwise, Latin spellings are preferred to Greek, except in the case of very familiar Greek place-names (e.g. Delos, Samos).

The assumed stressing of classical names for the purposes of rhythmical delivery is by an acute accent on the headword (though obviously not on monosyllables). The translation follows the traditional conventions for pronouncing Greek and Latin names in English. In words of two syllables the stress falls on the first (which is then often lengthened in English). In words of more than two syllables, the stress falls on the penultimate syllable when that is quantitatively *heavy* in the ancient languages (e.g. Achílles, Agamémnon, Ulýsses), but on the previous syllable if the penultimate is *light* (e.g. Aéolus, Autólycus, Prosérpina). The latter sometimes results in a short antepenultimate being artificially lengthened in English (e.g. Alcýone and Callíope, both with the second syllable pronounced like 'eye').

The following may also help with pronouncing unfamiliar names:

Vowels

ae and oe   'ee'   as in Aeneas, Caesar, Phoebus
au   'or'   as in Augustus
eu   'yoo'   as in Perseus, Theseus (each as two syllables,
                           rhyming with 'deuce')

A diaeresis shows that two adjoining vowels which could represent a diphthong are to be pronounced separately; it is written over the second sound (e.g. Alpheüs, Autonoë, Ceÿx, Danaë, Pirithoüs). A vowel at the end of a name is to be pronounced (as in Penelope); the only exceptions to this are Crete, Jove, Neptune, Peloponnese and Rome.

Consonants

c is soft (like *s*) before *e, ae, oe, i* and *y*; hard (like *k*) before *a, o* and *u*.
ch is equivalent to a hard *c*.
g is soft (as in 'giant') before *e* and *i*.

RA

Ábas (1) *a companion of Diomedes (2)* turned into a swan-like bird 14.505–6.

Ábas (2) *a centaur* 12.306.

Acástus *king of Thessaly, son of Pelias* at the Calydonian boar hunt 8.306; cleanses Peleus 11.409.

Acéstes *a king of Sicily* visited by Aeneas 14.83.

Achaéa (1) (adj. Achaean) *a country in the northern Peloponnese, here (as often in epic verse) representing Greece as a whole* 5.578, 15.293.

Achaéa (2) *a region in northern Greece to the south of Thessaly* 5.306.

Achaeménides *a companion of Ulysses, rescued by Aeneas from the Cyclops* reunited with Macareus (3), tells of Ulysses' men in Polyphemus' cave 14.160–222.

Achelóüs *a river in northern Greece separating Acarnania and Aetolia; its god* entertains Theseus 8.549–76, 727–8; anger at naiads 8.577–89; loves Perimele 8.590–610; ability to change his shape 8.879–83; battle with Hercules 9.2–100.

Ácheron *a river in the underworld; its god, the lover of Orphne and supposed father of Ascalaphus* 5.541.

Achílles *the bravest and most famous warrior among the Greeks in the Trojan War, son of Peleus and Thetis* his conception 11.265; fights Cycnus (3) 12.73–144; victory celebration 12.146–72; his family 12.191–5; at his victory celebration 12.363; his death 12.582–620; his arms competed for after his death 13.1–383; cousin of Ajax

Amúlius *younger son of Proca, brother of Numitor* dethroned by Romulus after dethroning his own brother 14.772–3.

Amýclae *a town in Laconia, centre of the cult of Hyacinthus* 8.314.

Amýclas *founder of Amyclae, father of Hyacinthus* 10.162.

Ámycus *a centaur* in the battle with the Lapiths 12.245–57.

Amýmone *a spring at Argos* 2.240.

Amýntor *a king in Thessaly, father of Phoenix* hands over Crantor to Peleus as a token of peace 12.364.

Ánaphe *an island in the Cyclades, an ally of Minos* 7.461.

Anápis *a river in Sicily; its god* lover of Cyane 5.417.

Anaxárete *a beautiful Cypriot girl* loved in vain by Iphis (2) 14.698–760; changed into a statue 14.754–8.

Ancaéus *an Arcadian* at the Calydonian boar hunt 8.315; gored to death 8.391–402; his death 8.407, 519.

Anchíses *son of Capys, father of Aeneas* favoured by Venus 9.425; rescued from Troy by Aeneas 13.625–7; on Delos 13.640; given a staff by Anius 13.680; his grave 14.84; visited in Hades by Aeneas 14.105–20.

Andraémon (1) *husband of Dryope, father of Amphissus* his marriage 9.333; finds his wife changed 9.363–91.

Andraémon (2) *an Aetolian king* 13.357.

Andrógeos *son of Minos, murdered at Athens* 7.457–9, 8.58–9.

Andrómeda *daughter of Cepheus and Cassiopeia* rescued and married by Perseus 4.671–761, 5.15; supports her husband 5.152–4.

Ándros (1) *an island in the Cyclades, named after Andros (2)* 7.469; 13.648, 661.

Ándros (2) *ruler of Andros (1), son of Anius* rules as Anius' regent 13.646–7; given prophetic powers by Apollo 13.650; surrenders his sisters to Agamemnon 13.661–4.

anémone *the flower which sprang up from the blood of Adonis* 10.734–8.

Anígrus *a river in Elis* 15.281–4.

Ánio *a river in Latium* 14.329.

Ánius *king and priest of Apollo on Delos, father of Andros* welcomes Aeneas 13.632–79; tells of his daughters pursued by Agamemnon on account of the powers given to them by Bacchus 13.651–74; his daughters changed into doves 13.673.

Antaéus *a giant in Libya who challenged passing strangers to wrestle with him and was invincible while he remained in contact with Mother Earth* killed by Hercules 9.183–4.

Antándros *a town on the coast of the Troad* 13.628.

Anténor *one of the Trojan elders* moved to return Helen 13.202.

Bálearic Islands *islands east of Spain, famous for their slingsmen* 2.727–9, 7.710.

Báttus *an old herdsman in Pylos* sees Apollo's cattle stolen 2.687–707; shown to be a liar, changed into flint by Mercury 2.705–7.

Baúcis *wife of Philemon* entertains Jupiter and Mercury 8.632–724; changed into a tree 8.714–20.

Béroë *Semele's nurse* Juno adopts her form 3.277–86.

Biënor *a centaur* killed by Theseus 12.346–50.

Boeótia (adj. Boeotian) *a country in central Greece* 1.313; 2.239; 3.13, 339; 7.763; 10.588; 11.300; 12.10; 13.682, 905.

Boötes *a constellation* 2.176–7, 8.207, 10.447.

Bóreas *the north wind* 1.64, 6.682–713, 7.3; abducts Orithyia, sister of Procris 7.694–5, 15.471.

Britons *the people of the British Isles, visited by Julius Caesar in 55/54 BC* 15.752.

Bubássus *a town in Caria, on the south-western corner of modern Turkey* 9.643.

Bubástis *an Egyptian god* 9.691.

Busíris *an Egyptian king who killed and ate strangers* killed by Hercules during one of his twelve labours 9.182–3.

Bútes *one of the Athenian envoys to Aegina (2)* 7.500, 665–71, 681–4.

Buthrótum *a town on the coast of Epirus, opposite Corcyra* 13.720–21.

Býblis *daughter of Miletus and Cyaneë, grandchild of Apollo and twin sister of Caunus* incestuous passion for her brother 9.452–666; changed into a mountain spring 9.663–4.

Cádmus *husband of Harmonia, son of Agenor, father of Agave and Autonoë* slays the dragon and founds Thebes 3.3–130; remonstrates with Pentheus 3.564; wanders in exile with Harmonia 4.563–603; changed into a snake 4.576–89.

Caéneus *a young man from Thessaly, born as a girl (Caenis)* at the Calydonian boar hunt 8.305; his fame 12.172–81; raped by Neptune, then changed from female to male and given invulnerability 12.189–209; at the battle between the centaurs and the Lapiths, eventually killed by being choked under the weight of the forest 12.459–531; changed into a bird 12.524–5.

Caénis *see* Caeneus.

Caésar *see* Julius Caesar, Augustus.

Caïcus *a river in Mysia* 2.243, 12.111–12, 15.278.

Caiéta *Aeneas' nurse; a place in Italy, her burial site, which took her name* 14.158, 441–3; 15.717–18.

Crímese *a town in Lucania in southern Italy* 15.51.

Crócus *a young man* changed into a flower after falling in love with Smilax 4.283.

Crómyon *a village near Corinth* home of a boar killed by Theseus 7.435–6.

Cróton (1) *a man from southern Italy who entertained Hercules* 15.9, 15–17.

Cróton (2) *a city in the extreme south of Italy, founded by Myscelus, where Croton (1) was buried* 15.8–18, 55–60.

crow warns the raven to keep his own counsel 2.547–52; punished by Minerva 2.557–65; Corone's transformation into the crow 2.569–90.

Ctéatus *son of Actor* 8.308.

Ctesýlla *daughter of Alcidamas* changed into a dove 7.369–70.

Cúmae *a city on the coast of Italy, home of the Sibyl* 14.102–56, 15.712.

Cupid *god of love, son of Venus* causes Apollo to fall in love with Daphne 1.453–73; Hermaphroditus compared with 4.321; sent by Venus to cause Pluto to fall in love with Proserpina 5.364–84; praised by Byblis 9.482–3, 543–4; denies responsibility for Myrrha's passion 10.310–11; Adonis compared with 10.515–17; scratches his mother with one of his arrows 10.524–6.

Cúres *a Sabine city* 15.7.

Cýane *a Sicilian nymph* protests at Pluto's abduction of Proserpina 5.409–37; changed into the spring that bears her name 5.429–37; unable to tell Ceres verbally of Proserpina's abduction 5.464–70.

Cyáneë *daughter of Maeander, mother of Byblis and Caunus* 9.450.

Cýbele *mother of the gods* the pine her sacred tree 10.104; her temple profaned by Hippomenes 10.686–704; rescues Aeneas' ships in anger at Turnus' impiety 14.535–56.

Cýclades *an archipelago in the Aegean Sea* 2.264.

Cýclop(e)s *a race of giants dwelling on the coast of Sicily, each having only one eye; they forge Jupiter's thunderbolts* 1.259, 3.305; Polyphemus and Galatea 13.744; 14.2, 175, 187; 15.93; *see also* Polyphemus.

Cýcnus (1) *a king of Liguria, son of Sthenelus, friend of Phaëthon* laments Phaëthon 2.367–80; changed into a swan 2.373–7, 12.581–2.

Cýcnus (2) *a hunter, son of Apollo and Hyrië* changed into a swan 7.372–81.

Cýcnus (3) *a Trojan hero, son of Neptune* duels with Achilles 12.71–145; changed into a swan by Neptune 12.145; lamented by Neptune 12.580–82.

Euíppe *wife of Pierus* 5.303–5.

Eumélus *father of Botres, whom he killed after he showed disrespect for Apollo* grieves for his son, who was changed into a bird, the bee-eater, by Apollo 7.390.

Euménides, the *see* Furies.

Eumólpus *a bard who brought the mysteries of Ceres to Eleusis* 11.94.

Euphórbus *son of Panthoüs* reincarnated as Pythagoras 15.161–4.

Európa *daughter of Agenor* loved by Jupiter 2.844–75, 6.103–7; mother of Minos by Jupiter 8.120–23; her beauty 8.49–50.

Eurótas *a river in Laconia* 2.247, 10.169.

Eúrus *the east wind* 1.61, 7.659, 8.2, 11.481.

Eurýdice *wife of Orpheus* dies when bitten by an adder, trapped in Hades because Orpheus looked back when rescuing her 10.1–64; reunited with Orpheus 11.63–6.

Eurýlochus *one of Ulysses' companions* chosen by lot to visit Circe's palace 14.252; alone of Ulysses' companions escapes Circe's magic 14.287–90.

Eurýnome *mother of Leucothoë (1)* 4.210–19.

Eurýpylus (1) *king of Cos* 7.363–4.

Eurýpylus (2) *a Thessalian hero* 13.357.

Eurýstheus *king of Mycenae, son of Sthenelus* Hercules' hatred for him 9.203; his hatred for Hercules' children 9.273–5.

Eúrytus (1) *son of Actor* 8.308.

Eúrytus (2) *a centaur* his behaviour the cause of the battle between the Lapiths and centaurs 12.220–40.

Evánder *king of Pallanteum* offers help to Aeneas 14.456.

Evénus *an Aetolian river, near Calydon* 8.527, 9.104.

Exádius *a Lapith* at the battle with the centaurs 12.265–9.

Fárfa a tributary of the Tiber 14.330–31.

Fates, the *the three goddesses who allot each person an unalterable fate* 1.256, 5.534; curse Meleäger at his birth 8.452–6, 14.152, 15.781–809.

fauns *rustic semi-gods with horns* 1.193, 6.392.

Faúnus (1) *an Italian god identified with Pan, father of Acis* 6.330, 13.750–52.

Faúnus (2) *king of Latium, father of Latinus (1)* 14.450.

Fórmiae *a town on the coast of Latium* 15.717.

Fórum *the market-place which formed the civic, economic and religious heart of Rome* 15.842.

Furies, the [also known as **the Eumenides** (a euphemism meaning 'kindly ones')] *goddesses of vengeance, three sisters (Allecto,*

13.409–10; entreated by Aurora for Memnon 13.586–600; compared to Polyphemus 13.842–4; scorned by Polyphemus 13.857; entreated by Venus for Aeneas' deification, assents 14.585–95; entreated by Mars for Romulus' deification, assents 14.807–16; the thunderer 15.70; his oracle at Dodona 15.311; the eagle that bears his thunderbolts 15.386; grants divine status to Julius Caesar 15.808–43; enthroned as ruler in heaven 15.858–9; prayed to for Augustus' long life before deification 15.866.

Kneeler *a constellation* 1.182.

Kneelers, the *three goddesses, guardians of women in labour* 9.294.

lábyrinth *a secure maze designed by Daedalus, built at Minos' command to house his monster son, the Minotaur* 8.158–74.

Lacínium *a promontory in Bruttium (southern Italy) near Croton* 15.14, 701–2.

Lacónia *see* **Sparta**.

Laërtes *son of Arcesius, father of Ulysses* at the Calydonian boar hunt 8.315; his lineage 13.144.

Láïus *father of Oedipus* 7.759.

Lampátië *sister of Phaëthon, one of the Heliades* 2.348.

Laömedon *king of Troy, father of Priam* helped by Apollo and Neptune to build the walls of Troy but refuses them payment 11.196–210; his lineage 11.755–7.

Lápiths *a people in Thessaly* 12.210–536, 14.670.

Latínus (1) *king of Laurentium, son of Faunus (2), father of Lavinia* 14.450.

Latínus (2) *king of Alba* 14.610–11.

Látium *the region of central Italy in which Rome is located* 14.390, 422, 453, 608, 623, 832; 15.480–86, 582, 626, 742.

Latóna [Greek Leto] *daughter of the Titan Coeus, mother of Apollo and Diana* Manto her prophet 6.161–4; envied and insulted by Niobe 6.185–214, 274–99; anger against Lycians 6.313–70; Calaurea dear to her 7.384; gives birth on Delos 13.634–5.

Látreus *a centaur* in the battle with the Lapiths 12.462–93.

Lauréntum (adj. Lauréntian, Laúrentine) *a district in Latium* 14.336–42, 598.

Lavínia *daughter of Latinus (1)* pledged to Aeneas as wife 14.569–70.

Lavínium *a city in Latium built by Aeneas* 15.728.

Leärchus *son of Athamas and Ino* killed by his father 4.516–19.

Léda *wife of Tyndareus, raped by Jupiter in the form of a swan, mother to Castor and Pollux* depicted on Arachne's weaving 6.109.

Memory *see* **Mnemosyne.**

Meneláüs *a Greek hero at Troy, king of Sparta, husband of Helen, younger son of Atreus, brother of Agamemnon* dares not claim Achilles' shield 12.623; the Greek fleet gathers to back him at Aulis 13.181–95; present at the contest for Achilles' arms 13.204; Ajax's equal in battle 13.359; kills Euphorbus 15.162; Paris stolen from his grasp 15.806.

Menéphron *an Arcadian man* commits incest 7.386–7.

Menoétes *a Lycian* killed by Achilles 11.116–27.

Ménthe *a nymph* changed into mint 10.729.

Mércury *messenger god (particularly for Jupiter), son of Jupiter and Maia* ordered to kill Argus 1.669–89; kills Argus 1.713–19; discovers and punishes Battus' lies 2.685–751; visits Athens, attempts to seduce Herse, obstructed by Aglauros 2.708–52, 815–35; drives cattle to shore of Sidon at Jupiter's request 2.836–45; affair with Venus 4.288; worshipped by Perseus 4.754–6; his sword used to kill Echemmon 5.176; worshipped as an ibis 5.331; made welcome by Baucis and Philemon 8.627–38; rapes Chione 11.303–12; as ancestor of Ulysses 13.146; aids Ulysses against Circe 14.291–3.

Mérmerus *a centaur* wounded in the battle with the Lapiths 12.303–5.

Mérops *king of Ethiopia, husband of Clymene* putative father of Phaëthon 1.763–4, 2.184.

Messána *a town on the coast of Sicily opposite the Italian mainland* 13.729; 14.5, 17, 47; 15.290–92.

Messápian fields *part of Calabria (southern Italy)* 14.514.

Messéne *a city in the Peloponnese* 6.417, 12.549.

Méstra *daughter of Erysichthon, wife of Autolycus* given power by Neptune to change her shape 8.738, 847–78.

Methóne *a hill near Troezen said to have been formed when the winds tried to escape from underground and caused a bubble* 15.305–6.

Methýmna *a city on Lesbos* 11.55.

Mídas *son of Cybele* rewarded by Bacchus with the 'Midas touch' for reuniting him with Silenus 11.93–145; supports Pan in the music contest with Apollo 11.146–93; given donkey's ears 11.175–9.

Milétus (1) *son of Apollo and Deïone, father of Caunus and Byblis* flees from Minos 9.443–50.

Milétus (2) *a city on the coast of Caria, founded by Miletus (1)* 9.449.

Minérva [also known as **Pallas Athena**] *goddess of wisdom and skill, also goddess of war, daughter of Jupiter, from whose head she sprang fully formed* hides Erichthonius 2.553–63; protectress of Athens 2.709–14, 835; 5.645; takes revenge on Aglauros, visits cave of Envy 2.749–88; patron of Cadmus 3.101–3; rescues Echion and four other companions of Cadmus 3.127; worshipped by the daughters of Minyas 4.38; worshipped by Perseus 4.754–6; her shrine and aegis 4.798–803; protects Perseus 5.46–7; at work in the riot at Perseus' wedding-feast 5.155; visits the Muses 5.250–336; rejection of Venus 5.375; engages in a weaving contest with Arachne 6.1–140; the olive tree sacred to her 6.335; changes Perdix into a partridge 8.251–2; worshipped at Athens 8.264–6; worshipped by Oeneus 8.275; worshipped by Achilles 12.150–51; her image stolen by Ulysses 13.99, 337, 345, 381; her shrine 14.468; rescues Diomedes (2) 14.475–6; her promontory off the coast of Campania (central Italy) 15.709.

Mínos *husband of Pasiphaë, son of Europa and Jupiter, father of Androgeos and Ariadne* threatens war against Athens 7.455–504; rejects Scylla's love 8.6–151; confines the Minotaur in the labyrinth 8.152–71; no longer paid tribute by Athens 8.263; Jupiter cannot grant him immortality 9.437–46.

Mínotaur *half-man half-bull monster son of Minos and Pasiphaë* hybrid son of a bestial relationship 8.133, 155–6; confined in the labyrinth, killed by Theseus 8.157–74.

Mintúrnae *a city on the southern border of Latium* 15.716.

Mínyae *the* **Argonauts**, *so-called because some claimed descent from Minyas.*

Mínyas, daughters of *(Minyas was the king and founder of Orchomenus in Boeotia) Leuconoë, Arsippe and Alcithoë, followers of Minerva* reject Bacchus 4.1–4, 32–54, 388–415; changed into bats by Bacchus 4.407–13, 425.

Mithridátes *a king of Pontus, conquered by the Romans in 63 BC* 15.755–6.

Mnemósyne [also known as **Memory**] *mother of the Muses* raped by Jupiter in the form of a shepherd 6.114.

móly *a magic herb* 14.291–3.

Mónychus *a centaur* in the battle with the Lapiths 12.498–511.

Moon *sometimes identified with Diana as the sister of Apollo (in his guise as the Sun)* 1.11; 2.205–208, 723; 7.206.

Mopsópia *see* **Athens.**

Mópsus *a Lapith prophet, son of Ampyx (2)* at the Calydonian boar hunt 8.316–17, 350–53; in the battle with the centaurs 12.455–8; recognizes Caeneus as a bird 12.524–32.

Mórpheus *son of Somnus* imitates Ceÿx 11.635–73.

Múnichus, sons of *(Munichus was the king of the Molossians in Epirus)* changed into birds together with their father 13.718–19.

Múses, the *patrons of the arts, the nine daughters of Jupiter and*

Mnemosyne 2.219; visited by Minerva 5.254–340; victors in the contest with the daughters of Pierus 5.662–70; 10.148; 14.433; 15.482, 622.

Mútina *a city in Cisalpine Gaul (northern Italy), now Modena* 15.822–3.

Mýcale *a Thessalian witch, mother of Orios* said to have charmed the moon with incantations 12.263–4.

Mycénae *a city in Argolis of which Agamemnon was king* 6.414; 15.426, 428.

Mýconos *an island in the Cyclades* 7.463.

Mýrmidons repopulate Aegina (2) 7.623–58; ants changed into Aeacus' new subjects 7.635–42.

Mýrrha *daughter of Cinyras (2), mother of Adonis* her incestuous desire for her father 10.309–502; changed into the myrrh tree 10.490–500; her love to be avenged 10.524.

Mýscelus *an Argive, founder of Croton (2), son of Alemon* 15.19–57.

Mýsia *a country in Asia Minor* 15.277–8.

naíads *water-nymphs* 1.641, 690; 2.325; 3.505; 4.49, 289, 304; 6.330, 452; some changed by Diana into the Hedgehog Isles 8.580–89; 9.87; grant Byblis a stream for her tears 9.657–8; 10.9, 514; mourn Orpheus 11.48–9; 14.328; help to obstruct Sabine attack on Rome 14.785.

Naples *a town on the coast of Campania (central Italy)* 14.101, 15.711.

Nar *a river in Umbria (to the north of Latium)* 14.330.

Narcíssus *son of Liriope and Cephisus* his birth and Teiresias' prophecy 3.345–50; his rejection of Echo and others 3.351–406; falls in love with his own reflection, dies 3.407–509; changed into a flower 3.510.

Nárycum (adj. Narýcian) *a town in Locris* 8.312, 14.468.

Nature *personified* 8.81, 615; 9.757–8; 10.330; 15.252–3, 270.

Náxos *the largest island in the Cyclades* 3.636–49, 690; 8.175.

Néleus *king of Pylos, son of Neptune and Tyro, father of Nestor* Battus his servant 2.690; all but one of his twelve sons killed by Hercules 12.552–77.

Neméa (adj. Nemean) *a town in Argolis, home to a famous lion killed by Hercules as one of his twelve labours* 9.197, 235–6.

Némesis *goddess of retribution, punisher of pride and arrogance among mortals* retribution against Narcissus 3.406; to be feared 14.694.

Neoptólemus [also known as **Pyrrhus**] *son of Achilles* proposed recipient of his father's arms 13.155; deputed to sacrifice Polyxena 13.455–6; sacrifices Polyxena 13.475–6.

Phócus *son of Aeacus and Psamathe, half-brother of Peleus* 7.477; welcomes Cephalus 7.668–90; asks about Cephalus' spear 7.794–8; murdered by Peleus 11.267–9.

Phoébe *see* **Diana.**

Phoébus *see* **Apollo.**

Phoenícia (adj. Phoenician) *a country on the Syrian coast, whose chief towns were Tyre and Sidon* 3.46.

Phoénix *companion of Achilles, son of Amyntor* at the Calydonian boar hunt 8.307.

phoénix *a mythical bird* 15.392–407.

Phórbas *a Lapith* kills Aphidas 12.319–26.

Phórcys, daughters of (1) *see* **Gorgons.**

Phórcys, daughters of (2) [also known as **Graiae**] *two sisters, guardians of the Gorgons* 4.774.

Phrýgia (adj. Phrygian) *a country in Asia Minor, often used to refer indirectly to Troy and its people* 6.147, 177, 400; 8.162, 620–23, 719; 10.155; 11.16; 12.70; 13.429, 580; 14.79, 547; 15.444.

Phthía *a city in Thessaly* 13.156.

Phýleus at the Calydonian boar hunt 8.308.

Phýlius *lover of Cycnus (2)* 7.373–7.

Pícus *king of Latium, son of Saturn (a king of Latium)* loves Canens, rejects Circe 14.320–98; changed into a woodpecker by Circe 14.387–96.

Piérus, daughters of [also known as **Pierides**] *named after the Muses by their father* challenge the Muses to a song contest 5.302–32; losers in their contest with the Muses 5.664–78, 6.1–2; changed into magpies 5.671–4.

Píndus *a mountain in Thessaly* 1.570, 2.225, 7.225, 11.554.

Piréne *a spring at Corinth* 2.240, 7.391–2.

Piríthoüs *a Lapith, son of Ixion* at the Calydonian boar hunt 8.304, 403–4; at Acheloüs' banquet 8.567, 612–16; his marriage to Hippodamia 12.210–29; at the battle with the centaurs 12.332.

Pítane *a city on the coast of Aetolia* 7.357.

Pithecúsae [also known as **Apetown**] *an island off the bay of Naples* 14.89–100.

Píttheus *king of Troezen, son of Pelops, father of Aethra (mother of Theseus)* his city 6.419; 15.296, 506; Lelex sent to his land 8.622.

Pleíad *one of the seven daughters of Atlas and Pleione (known together as the Pleiads or Pleiades); a constellation* 1.670, 3.595, 6.174; depicted on Achilles' shield 13.293.

Pleúron *a town in Aetolia* 7.382.

raven informs Apollo of Coronis' unfaithfulness, against the warning of the crow 2.534–632; changed from white to black 2.632.

Rémulus *a king of Alba* 14.616–19.

Rhadamánthus *son of Jupiter and Europa* old and exhausted 9.436–7, 440.

Rhégium *a town in Bruttium on the straits of Sicily* 14.5, 47.

Rhésus *a king of Thrace and ally of Troy* killed by Ulysses in a night-time raid 13.98, 249–52.

Rhexénor *one of Diomedes' companions* changed into a bird 14.505.

Rhodes (adj. Rhodian) *an island to the south-west of the coast of Asia Minor, in the Aegean Sea* 7.365, 12.573.

Rhódope *a mountain range in Thrace; its goddess, sister of Haemus* 2.222; changed into a mountain for calling herself Juno 6.86, 589; 10.77.

Rhoétum *a promontory to the north of Troy* 11.197.

Rhoétus *a centaur* at the battle with the Lapiths 12.271–301.

Romans 15.483, 600, 682, 693–6, 756.

Rome *a city in Latium* 1.201; 14.775–849; 15.430–31, 596, 637, 668, 736, 744, 801, 828.

Rométhium *a place in southern Italy* 15.704.

Rómulus *son of Mars and Ilia (Rhea Silvia)* the Romans his people 14.606; regains Numitor's kingdom, founds Rome, war against the Sabines 14.773–806; carried off to become a god by Mars, receives the name Quirinus 14.806–28; his successor 15.2; his spear changed into a tree 15.560–64.

Rumour *personified* 9.137–9; described 12.43–63.

Rutúlians *a people of Latium* clash with Aeneas over Lavinia 14.451–5, 528–9.

Sába *a place in south-western Arabia, proverbial for its riches* 10.480.

Sábines *a people of central Italy* 14.775–832, 15.5.

Sálamis *a city on Cyprus* 14.759.

Sállentines *a people in Calabria* 15.50.

Sálmacis *a spring in Caria; its nymph* pursues Hermaphroditus 4.285–388, 15.319.

Sáme *an island in the Ionian Sea* 13.711.

Sámos (adj. Samian) *an island off the coast of Asia Minor, sacred to Juno* 8.220; original home of Pythagoras 15.60.

Sárdis *the capital city of Lydia* 11.138, 152.

Sáturn *an ancient Italian god, identified with the Greek Cronos, husband and brother of Ops, father of Jupiter, Juno, Neptune and Pluto*

Témese *a town in Bruttium (in southern Italy) famed for its mines* 15.707.

Témpe *a valley of the river Peneüs* 1.568–9, 7.222.

Ténedos *an island in the Aegean near Troy* 1.516, 12.110–11, 13.174.

Ténos *an island in the Cyclades* 7.469.

Téreus *king of Thrace* marries Procne, subsequently rapes her sister Philomela 6.424–570; subjected to revenge at the hands of Philomela and Procne 6.614–74; changed into a hoopoe 6.671–4.

Téthys *a sea-goddess, wife of Ocean, mother of Clymene* receives the Sun's chariot at sunset 2.68–9, 156–7; visited by Juno 2.509–31; 9.499; changes Aesacus into a bird 11.784–6; purifies Glaucus 13.950–65.

Teúcer (1) *a Cretan who became an early king of Troy* 13.705.

Teúcer (2) *son of Telamon and Hesione, cousin of Achilles, founder of Salamis on Cyprus* possible recipient of Achilles' arms 13.157–8; ancestor of Anaxarete 14.699.

Thébae *a city in the Troad* 12.110, 13.174.

Thebes *a city in Boeotia* 3.131, 549–61; 4.417; women changed into stones or gulls 4.543–62; 5.254; 6.148–313, 413; 7.764; women present at Alcmena's labour 9.304, 403; 13.682–700; 15.427, 429.

Thémis *goddess of justice, daughter of Uranus (Heaven) and Gaia (Earth), associated with oracles* 1.321–2, 367–81; 4.643; 9.403–19.

Theóphane *daughter of Bisaltes, raped by Neptune in the form of a ram, gave birth to the ram with the Golden Fleece* 6.118.

Thermódon *a river in Pontus, home of the Amazons* 2.249, 9.189.

Thersítes *a loud-mouthed Greek at Troy* 13.232–3.

Théseus *son of Aegeus and Aethra, he spent his childhood with his mother in Troezen and, when grown up, set off for Athens, overcoming a number of challenges on the way* at the court of Aegeus 7.404–52; defeats the Minotaur 8.172–6; called on to help at the Calydonian boar hunt 8.262–71; aims his spear at the boar 8.405–10; at Acheloüs' banquet 8.547–66, 726–7, 881; 9.1–2, 55; at the wedding-banquet of Pirithoüs 12.227–37; at the battle between the Lapiths and centaurs 12.342–60; father of Hippolytus 15.497; succeeds his father 15.856.

Théssaly (adj. Thessálian) [also known as **Haemonia**] *a country in the north of Greece* 1.568; 2.543, 599; 5.306; 7.159, 222, 264, 314; 8.347, 751, 813; 11.230, 409, 652; 12.173, 190, 213, 354.

Théstius *father of Althaea, Toxeus and Plexippus* 8.304, 473.

Thétis *a sea-nymph, wife of Peleus, daughter of Nereus and Doris, mother of Achilles* her conquest by Peleus 11.218–64; supports

Peleus' plea to Psamathe 11.400; mother of Achilles 12.86; tries to save Achilles from his fate 13.162; her ambition for Achilles 13.288.

Thísbe *a young Babylonian girl* in love with Pyramus 4.56–166; kills herself in grief at Pyramus' death 4.162–3.

Thóäs *a Greek at Troy, son of Andraemon (2)* 13.357.

Thrace (adj. Thracian) *a country in the north-east of Macedonia* 2.257; 5.277; 6.86, 425–35, 459–60, 590, 661, 683; 9.641–2; 10.11, 83–5; 11.1, 69, 85; 13.430–39, 565–72, 629.

Thyéstes *son of Pelops, brother of Atreus* 15.462.

Tíber *the river flowing through Rome* 2.259; 14.328, 426–7, 448; 15.431, 625, 728–43.

Tiberínus *a king of Alba, his name given to the Tiber* 14.614.

Tíryns *a city in Argolis, associated with Hercules* 7.410, 9.104, 12.564.

Tisíphone *one of the Furies* 4.474–511.

Títan *usually referring to the* Sun, *who was the son of the Titan, Hyperion.*

Títaness *see* Circe.

Títans *the children of Uranus (Heaven) and Gaia (Earth) defeated by* Jupiter 10.150–51.

Tithónus *husband of Aurora granted eternal life but not eternal youth* 9.421.

Títyos *son of Jupiter, punished in Hades for insulting Latona* 4.457–8, 10.43.

Tlepólemus *leader of the Rhodians, son of Hercules* asks Nestor about his father 12.537–41, 573–7.

Tmólus *a mountain in Lydia; its god* 2.217; 6.15; 11.86–7; judges the contest between Apollo and Pan 11.156–72.

Tóxeus *son of Thestius, uncle of Meleäger* at the Calydonian boar hunt 8.304; insults Atalanta (1), killed by Meleäger 8.432–46.

Tráchas *a town in Latium* 15.718–19.

Tráchis *a city in Thessaly* 11.269–77, 282, 408, 502, 627, 651.

Triptólemus *the inventor of agriculture, son of Celeus (king of Eleusis)* scatters Ceres' seed across Europe and Asia, attacked by Lyncus in Scythia 5.646–61; changed into a lynx by Ceres 5.660.

Tríton *sea-god, son of Neptune* 1.331–40, 2.8, 13.919.

Tritónis *a lake in Africa near where Minerva supposedly first appeared* 15.358.

Tróad *the area around Troy* 7.364.

Troézen *a town in Argolis* 6.418; 8.568; 15.296, 506.

Trójans [also known as **Dardanians**] *the people of Troy* 14.72, 86, 160, 220, 455, 566–74; 15.452.

Troy (adj. Trojan) [also known as **Pergamum**, **Ilium**, its citizens also as **Dardanians**] *a city in Asia Minor, besieged for ten years and finally captured by the Greeks* 8.366; 9.233, 268; 10.160; 11.26, 38, 64–72, 196–215, 758, 767; 12.113–14, 135, 445, 584–614; 13.23–381, 408–505, 520, 623; 14.444, 458, 466, 562; 15.160, 421–5, 436, 442–3, 770.

Túrnus *a king of the Rutulians, engaged to Lavinia* 14.451–7, 526–39; *his death* 14.566–74, 15.773.

Tuscan Sea *see* **Etruscan Sea.**

Túscany *a region in Italy* 14.615, 15.554.

Týndareus *a Spartan king, husband of Leda, sometimes presented as the real father of Castor and Pollux* 8.302.

Týphon *a hundred-headed giant* cast down by Jupiter 3.302–3; 5.321–4, 348–55.

Tyre (adj. Tyrian) *a city in Phoenicia* 2.845; 3.35, 259, 539; 5.51, 391; 6.61, 223; 9.341; 10.211, 267–8; 11.166; 15.287.

Ulýsses [the Homeric **Odysseus**] *king of Ithaca, husband of Penelope, son of Laërtes, father of Telemachus, a Greek hero in the Trojan War renowned for his wily nature; on his return voyage he drifted lost at sea for ten years* seeks Achilles' shield after his death 12.624–5; wins Achilles' shield in the contest with Ajax, many of his deeds in the war recounted 13.7–387; rescues Philoctetes, his role in the fall of Troy 13.398–425; does not scorn Hecuba 13.486; his kingdom of Ithaca 13.712; fated to blind Polyphemus 13.773; his companions caught by Scylla 14.71; Macareus his companion 14.159; fleeing the Cyclops 14.180; cursed by Polyphemus 14.192–7; his wanderings, comes to Circe's island 14.222–312; his ship hated by the sea-nymphs (formerly Trojan vessels) 14.564.

Uránia *one of the Muses* welcomes Minerva 5.260–68.

Venília *wife of Janus, mother of Canens* 14.333–4.

Vénulus *a Rutulian* seeks Diomedes' (2) aid for Turnus 14.457–61, 513.

Vénus *goddess of love, wife of Vulcan, mother of Cupid* personification of sexual love 3.295, 321–3; 6.460; 13.758; affair with Mars 4.172–86, 14.27; revenge on the Sun 4.190; mother of Hermaphroditus 4.288; intercedes for Ino and her child with Neptune 4.531–42; worshipped as a fish 5.331; sends Cupid to engender love between Pluto and Proserpina 5.364–79; Procris compared with her 7.803; argues for rejuvenation of Anchises 9.424–5; invoked by Byblis 9.482; at the marriage of Iphis (1) 9.796; anger at the Cerastae 10.229–37; anger at the Propoetides 10.238–43; her festival on

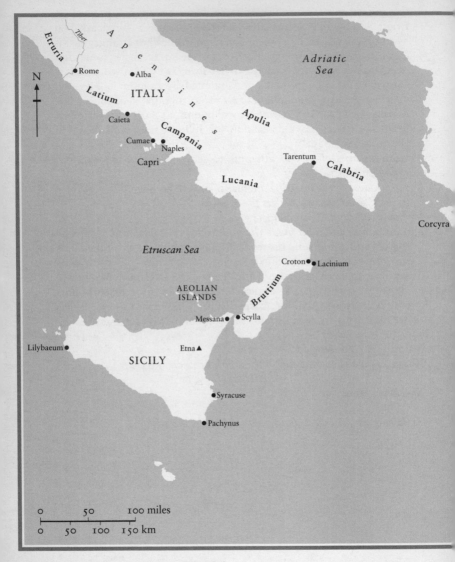

Ovid's Mediterranean World

▲Rhodope

Thrace

Black Sea

Macedonia

Philippi●

Phrygia

▲Athos

Sigeüm● ●Troy

Troad

▲Ida **Mysia**

ASIA MINOR

▲Olympus

Lemnos

Tenedos

Thessaly ▲Ossa

Peneüs

●Dodona

Enipeus

Pagasae ●▲Pelion

Aegean Sea

Lesbos

Aeolia

Caïcus

Pactolus

Lydia

pirus

Acheloüs

●Pindus

▲

Spercheüs

▲Othrys

●Trachis

Scyros

Sipylus▲

●Sardis

▲Tmolus

●Hypaepa

ium

Acarnania

Euboea

Chios

Ionia

Caÿster

Maeander

Aetolia

Oeta▲**Phocis**

Cephisus

Delphi●

Boeotia ●Aulis

Attica

●Caphereus

Samos

Caria

Calydon●

Helicon▲ Thebes●

Evenus

Ithaca

Achaea

Megara● Eleusis

Andros

Icarian Sea

●Miletus

Erymanthus●

Corinth●

●Athens

▲Cyllene▲

Epidaurus●

Gyaros

Elis

●Pylos

Mycenae●

Delos

Inachus

Argolis

Aegina

Ceos

Alpheüs

Argos● Troezen●

PELOPONNESE

Tiryns●

Cythnos

CYCLADES

onian

Arcadia

Eurotas

Seriphos

Paros

Naxos

Sea

●Sparta

Cos

●Messene

Laconia

Anaphe

Anaphe

Rhodes

Cythera

Crete

Cnossos●

Phaestos●

THE STORY OF PENGUIN CLASSICS

Before 1946 ...'Classics' are mainly the domain of academics and students, without readable editions for everyone else. This all changes when a little-known classicist, E. V. Rieu, presents Penguin founder Allen Lane with the translation of Homer's *Odyssey* that he has been working on and reading to his wife Nelly in his spare time.

1946 *The Odyssey* becomes the first Penguin Classic published, and promptly sells three million copies. Suddenly, classic books are no longer for the privileged few.

1950s Rieu, now series editor, turns to professional writers for the best modern, readable translations, including Dorothy L. Sayers's *Inferno* and Robert Graves's *The Twelve Caesars*, which revives the salacious original.

1960s The Classics are given the distinctive black jackets that have remained a constant throughout the series's various looks. Rieu retires in 1964, hailing the Penguin Classics list as 'the greatest educative force of the 20th century'.

1970s A new generation of translators arrives to swell the Penguin Classics ranks, and the list grows to encompass more philosophy, religion, science, history and politics.

1980s The Penguin American Library joins the Classics stable, with titles such as *The Last of the Mohicans* safeguarded. Penguin Classics now offers the most comprehensive library of world literature available.

1990s The launch of Penguin Audiobooks brings the classics to a listening audience for the first time, and in 1999 the launch of the Penguin Classics website takes them online to a larger global readership than ever before.

The 21st Century Penguin Classics are rejacketed for the first time in nearly twenty years. This world famous series now consists of more than 1300 titles, making the widest range of the best books ever written available to millions – and constantly redefining the meaning of what makes a 'classic'.

The Odyssey continues ...

The best books ever written

PENGUIN 🐧 CLASSICS

SINCE 1946

Find out more at www.penguinclassics.com